GW00732690

NIGHT

Praise for The Mirror Chronicles series:

...came totally immersed in an amazing world of painted
... breathtaking and an absolute joy to read. A book that
... reflect on for the rest of your life. Just like when you
The Hobbit or took your first stroll along the story
... of Terry Pratchett... An epic masterpiece."
Mr Ripley's Enchanted Books

...he effortlessly conjures up elaborate worlds rich in both
... fantasy. *The Bell Between Worlds* has an enchanting
... shoulder to shoulder with the
... *Materials...*

"This is a beautifully written book featuring a vividly imagined alternative world. The author does a great job of bringing the fantasy world to life and creating a new vision of magic and wonder… A must-read for fans of jaw-dropping fantasy."
From the Writer's Nest

"Dramatic, with perils that are both real and colourfully described. Highly recommended."
The Bookbag

"Not since *Harry Potter* have I devoured a fantasy world as much as this. I can tell Ian Johnstone will sit high up on the fantasy author list."
Readaraptor

Books by Ian Johnstone

The Mirror Chronicles: The Bell Between Worlds
The Mirror Chronicles: Circles of Stone
The Mirror Chronicles

IAN JOHNSTONE

THE MIRROR CHRONICLES

THE LAST NIGHT

HarperCollins *Children's Books*

First published in the United Kingdom by
HarperCollins *Children's Books* in 2022
HarperCollins *Children's Books* is a division of HarperCollins*Publishers* Ltd
1 London Bridge Street
London SE1 9GF

www.harpercollins.co.uk

HarperCollins*Publishers*
1st Floor, Watermarque Building, Ringsend Road
Dublin 4, Ireland

1

Text copyright © Ian Johnstone 2022
Cover design copyright © HarperCollins*Publishers* Ltd 2022
All rights reserved

ISBN 978–0–00–749114–8

Ian Johnstone asserts the moral right to be
identified as the author of the work respectively.

A CIP catalogue record for this title is available from the British Library.

Typeset in Caslon Classico by
Palimpsest Book Production Ltd, Falkirk, Stirlingshire

Printed and bound in the UK using 100% renewable electricity
at CPI Group (UK) Ltd

Conditions of Sale
This book is sold subject to the condition that it shall not, by way of trade
or otherwise, be lent, re-sold, hired out or otherwise circulated without the
publisher's prior consent in any form, binding or cover other than that in which
it is published and without a similar condition including this condition being
imposed on the subsequent purchaser.
No part of this publication may be reproduced, stored in a retrieval system or
transmitted in any form or by any means, electronic, mechanical, photocopying,
recording or otherwise, without the prior permission of HarperCollins*Publishers* Ltd.

MIX
Paper from
responsible sources
FSC™ C007454

This book is produced from independently certified FSC™ paper
to ensure responsible forest management.

For more information visit: www.harpercollins.co.uk/green

For Ella Neo

PART ONE

Quintessence

1

Rise

"Now rise, fear not where none have gone,
For then, at last, we may be one."

THEY RAN LIKE A desert squall, a chaos of dust, legless and sprawling. They howled like a sandstorm because now they were close. They sensed it in their sands. They saw it in the trails of the fleeing Suhl.

The ground was different here: no longer the crazed, hard-packed dirt of the plains, but lowland grit. A shallow slope climbed ever upwards towards the promise of hills, the ghost of a forest, the beginning of fully formed things.

They surged on, snouts down, scenting a chance to change.

And then, finally, it came.

The gale of dust halted. The howls quieted. The ash fell. The palls of filth hovered, formless but for gigantic, half-made shoulders and black clouds between, in which blazed the fiery coals of eyes. Hungrily they surveyed the hills, the earth, the trees, and finally they saw some nearby rocks, sandblast-smooth, glistening in the morning light.

There was a hiss of approval and they began to sway expectantly. One of them drifted forward and extended a streak of dust to touch the nearest stone.

It was not an instant change, but it was swift. Swirls of dust turned in upon themselves, gaining form and texture, until a hand appeared, as large as a boulder, with fingers like spears of stone. Then there was an arm, thick and massive, like a bulging plinth of rock. And next, a chest like a looming cliff.

The creature filled that chest, heaving a gale through its cavernous mouth, and for a moment it was silent, its blistering eyes turned up to the skies. Then it let out a triumphal howl: a roar like rock cleaving from rock; like a mountain crumbling to dust.

S

"Are you ready?" asked Sylas, rubbing his palms together.

Simia winced. "Not... sure."

"It's just a tree, Simsi."

Her eyelids flickered with irritation. "But it's not, Sylas, is it? It's not just *any* tree. It's *this* tree. It's the Tree of the Feather."

Sylas shrugged and flashed her a grin. "Still a tree. Don't worry. Paiscion showed me how."

Before she could reply, he bowed his head, closed his eyes and lost himself in his imagination.

Imagining felt different to him now because he knew its power. He knew that it was just the beginning of something: something that reached far, far beyond himself. It was the beginning of Essenfayle. And so his imagination had carried him and his companions safely away from the Meander Mill, and from the attack of the Ghor and the Slithen. His imagination had guided him across the wastes of the Barrens to Gheroth, and Paiscion, and the *Windrush*, and the Dirgheon, where he had found Naeo, his second self. His Glimmer. And ultimately it was imagination and Essenfayle that had taken them on two mirrored journeys across two worlds: his to find Isia; hers to find Mr Zhi.

So now, as he imagined the spreading roots beneath the earth, and the colossal trunk swelling with sap, and the hundreds of limbs and branches above, his skin tingled and his breath quickened. Because he felt the stirrings of Essenfayle and he knew what was to come.

The forest fell silent. Gone were the birdcalls, the rustles in the undergrowth, the murmurings of a chill winter wind. There was only quiet expectation. Pools of light warped as though seen through a lens, and somewhere above a bird took flight, sending down a shower of bronze leaves.

Then Simia gasped.

A giant bough flew at her from above, sweeping over the forest floor until its forked limbs straddled her slim body, scooping her up beneath the arms.

There was a shriek and then she was gone.

She sailed upwards, kicking and flailing as she went. "Stop!" she cried. "Sylas! Make it STOP!"

Sylas craned his neck to watch her go. "Relax!" he called. "Just relax and you'll be fine!"

An instant later two more branches caught him under the shoulders and flicked him skywards. In a trice, he was among the boughs of the great tree, rising through veils of leaves. Then he was at Simia's side, watching her struggling like a cat caught by the collar.

"I wouldn't do that if I were you!" he warned, pointing. "It's a long way down!"

Simia dropped her eyes and instantly slapped her arms round the branches, clinging on for all she was worth.

"Get — me — DOWN!" she yelled.

"Really, Simsi, it's *all right*," said Sylas, more softly now. "Remember, the tree's trying to help you... you just have to let it!"

He gave another grin, and with that he shot up in the air, borne aloft in a mighty wooden fist. When the branch reached its full height, it opened wide and he was passed on. Up and up he went, weaving through the tangle of limbs.

"*Just let it*," Simia grumbled reproachfully. But then she pressed her eyes closed and tried to relax. As the moments passed, the touch of the tree began to feel gentler than she had first thought, and the motion of the branch that held her was no longer jarring but a soothing sway.

She took a long, deep breath and let herself go.

Almost at once she was caught in a cradle of limbs and hoisted up. Timber fingers opened and closed round her, lofting her through clouds of green and orange leaves. She hurtled upwards, faster and faster, and in no time at all she found herself back at Sylas's side.

She beamed at him and cried out, but before Sylas could respond they were both dropped summarily on the span of a colossal bough. They staggered, teetering on its rounded top until they had regained their footing. Then even this mighty limb trembled into life and, with a low creak, began to climb.

"What did I tell you?" panted Sylas excitedly.

Simia stared at her feet, as though her gaze alone might pin them to the branch. "This is what Paiscion showed you?" she gasped.

Sylas nodded. "Come on! Race you to the top!"

Suddenly two branches swept down and caught them up. These were slighter limbs, supple and whiplash-fast, and Sylas and Simia were less passed between them than thrown. Soon they were crying out with delight as they were juggled through the tangle of branches, darting this way and that towards the emerald roof.

In no time at all, they were there, passing up through the last leaves to the brighter world beyond. Simia saw her chance and kicked against Sylas's branch, sending it swaying high and wide, while her own carried her smoothly to a broad bough. She threw her weight forward and stepped on to it.

"Winner!" she declared, throwing up her hands in triumph. But something about this sudden gesture set her off balance, and her arms began to windmill. The look of glee fell from her face.

"Sylas!" she gasped, toppling backwards. "Help!"

Sylas lunged, but before he reached her the tree itself responded. In a flash, a narrow branch whipped about and thwacked Simia across the backside, knocking her forward and correcting her balance.

"OW!" she yelled, rubbing her rear and staring accusingly at the branch. "It did that deliberately!"

Sylas stepped on to the bough beside her. "You kicked it, Simsi. What do you expect?"

She pursed her lips for a moment, then a grin spread across her face and they both laughed in the easy, companionable way that had become their custom.

"It's so beautiful up here," said Simia, finally noticing her surroundings. "I didn't really *see* it last time."

Sylas gazed at the breathtaking view of the Valley of Outs: the plumes of green and bronze leaves rolling down the hillsides; the long lake, implausibly clear and blue, sparkling even beneath a cloudy sky; the flocks of birds dancing and playing in the air above.

"It really is," he said wistfully.

The sight warmed him, even in the chill winter wind. Looking at this, it was hard to believe all that had happened in the past days. He and Simia had been attacked and chased and hunted. They had braved the dark, bedevilled streets of Gheroth, and even the sewers beneath them. They had met the great Isia herself, and with her confronted the unthinkable — that it was she, as an innocent girl, who had riven the world in two. That it was she and the Priests of Souls who had split each of us from ourselves.

And then there had been the Place of Tongues, teeming with Thoth's hordes. And there had been Thoth himself.

At times in those few days, it had felt that the world was coming to an end. And yet here remained the Valley of Outs, enticing, mysterious and beautiful, like a promise. A promise of what might be.

His mother should see this view, Sylas thought. This was the kind of wonder she had discovered in her work and told him about as he was growing up. Mountaintops floating like dreams above the clouds. Rainforests like singing blankets of green. Caves like vaulted cathedrals beneath the earth. Places so marvellous to her that, when she had spoken of them, she had seemed to glow with a magical light.

Yes, he thought, if anywhere might persuade her that there was good in this world, this was it.

But even getting her up here would be a problem. The tree would be far too '*impossible*' for her taste: as '*impossible*' as the storm he had commanded on the *Windrush* after their escape from Gheroth, and the strange journey the ship had taken over the forest floor, when it had finally arrived at the Valley of Outs. It was an '*impossible*' that she simply could not accept because it overturned everything she knew as a scientist and as a mother.

This '*impossible*' stood between them now, despite all their time together over the past few days. It was as though she was still in the Other, on the opposite side of the divide, unwilling to believe all that was in front of her. It was as if she was still behind that sheet of glass – the one that had covered the framed photo of her hanging in Sylas's garret room at the top of Gabblety Row.

And, if she found those things impossible, he mused, how could she ever accept the whole truth? Could she ever understand all that he had seen in the Temple of Isia, when he had eaten the Fruit of the Knowing Tree? The silver trails that passed between

8

the worlds? The strange beauty of them, the dreadful truth of them? And how could she ever accept the truth of the blood that ran in their veins — hers and his.

The blood of Isia.

"Come on, come on!" came a voice, urgent and sharp. "What are you waiting for?"

Sylas and Simia turned towards the crown of the tree and saw Paiscion's pale face in the doorway of a peculiar nest-like structure — a great weave of arching limbs that formed an entirely enclosed, perfectly hidden sanctuary at the very pinnacle of the tree. Merimaat's Retreat.

The Magruman pulled up the lapels of his smoking jacket against the cold and stepped out, beckoning to them impatiently.

"Quickly! QUICKLY!" he commanded. "There's little time, and there is something you must see!"

2

Merimaat's Retreat

"No one knows how long Merimaat's Retreat
has stood sentinel over the valley, only that it seems
always to have been here, as much a part of this
magical place as the lake or the forests."

SYLAS AND SIMIA MADE their way as quickly as they dared along
the twisting bough, and stepped into the half-dark of Merimaat's
Retreat. The Magruman was standing at one of the two windows,
looking out towards the distant Barrens, and something about his
stance immediately set Sylas on edge. Paiscion was normally so
poised, so straight-backed, but now he was leaning heavily against
the window frame, his head resting on his forearm as he stared
out of the opening.

He grunted as they drew up beside him. "Look," he said.

They gazed out, over the fringes of the valley and the nearest
meanders of the river to the great swathes of forest beyond.
Everything outside the Valley of Outs was now under a heavy
frost, which made even that bleak and desolate place look almost
beautiful. Nothing seemed out of the ordinary at first but, as they
peered into the distance, their eyes grew wide.

The forest was moving.

The frost-capped trees were shifting to and fro, not in any wind but haphazardly, as though waving in distress. And then, between the winter-bare limbs, shapes flitted through the shadows.

People. Hundreds, perhaps thousands of them. Some ran, others limped and stumbled, and others still dragged their companions along, crashing through the undergrowth towards the valley.

"It's them!" exclaimed Simia, her eyes darting about with excitement. A smile began to curl her lips. "They've made it! They've actually made—"

She stopped short because now she had seen another movement behind them, in the trees on the fringes of the Barrens. This was not the erratic sway of a forest jostled by the fleeing Suhl, this was different. This was decisive and devastating. The trees behind the Suhl were being felled, toppling before some unseen, crushing force. And it too was heading for the Valley of Outs.

"What *is* that?" murmured Sylas.

"Something from the stinking depths of Thoth's birthing chambers," said Paiscion grimly.

"But what?" asked Simia, her eyes still trained on the falling trees. "Ragers?"

Paiscion shook his head. "Something larger. Something longer in the making, which is why we haven't seen them before."

Sylas turned sharply. "Shouldn't we be doing something?"

"Sylas, my boy, I am not sure there's anything to be done," said the Magruman. He removed his glasses and began rubbing them with an embroidered handkerchief. "I don't fear for those poor souls you can see; they are already at the borders of the valley and, once they pass inside, they'll be safe." He placed his glasses back on his nose and gazed out at the furthest parts of the forest. "It's those still out there in the wilderness that weigh heavily upon me. They are much too far away for us to help them. We must hope that they're still strong enough to run, and that Espasian is there to defend them."

Sylas couldn't help thinking of his last memory of Espasian staggering down the steps of the Dirgheon, supported by Bayleon. How different he had seemed from that imposing giant of a man who had first led Sylas to the Passing Bell and journeyed with him across the Barrens. How long ago that seemed now.

"But he looked so weak when we left him," said Sylas. "He could barely walk."

"And yet do not underestimate him," Paiscion shot back. "Espasian is a great Magruman — perhaps the greatest for this time. For a time of war. It was Espasian who led the Suhl at the Reckoning, and he who made Thoth pay so dearly for all he took from us. Our brothers and sisters could wish for no more powerful ally at their side, even if he does have that cursed Black in his veins."

Sylas gazed at the line of falling trees and the crushed wasteland behind. It was as though the grey Barrens were spreading like a contagion towards the valley, consuming all in their path. "But I don't know how anyone could stop *that*," he said.

"Well, we must trust in Espasian," said the Magruman, "because I'm afraid that the plight of our sisters and brothers from Gheroth is far from all we have to worry about." He turned away and began walking towards the other window. "Come," he said, glancing back. "See for yourselves."

For a moment Sylas and Simia hesitated, then with mounting dread they joined Paiscion by the wide opening on the western side of the retreat.

Before them lay the now familiar view of the Valley of Outs, and nothing seemed amiss. Sylas glanced questioningly at the Magruman, but Paiscion simply lifted his chin to the far distance.

Merimaat's Retreat was so high that it surveyed far beyond the bounds of the valley, out to the plains beyond and further still, to the heart of the Westercleft Hills, and it took Sylas some moments to take in the whole scene. He swept his eyes across the entire landscape without seeing anything out of place. But then he noticed something peculiar. The furthest hills were not shrouded in white frosts, as were the others. They were black.

At first he had thought that perhaps this was the shadow of some colossal cloud, but the sky was grey and there was no sun to cast any shade. With a shiver, he realised that this was no trick of the light. Something dark had engulfed the hills; something that, even now, was spreading, consuming more and more of the countryside, leaving not a glimpse of turf or tree. And, as he watched it creeping up another hillside, he realised what it was. It was a sea of figures — thousands, tens of thousands of them — a great tide of people and beasts surging on towards the Valley of Outs. Now he could see among them tiny pinpricks of colour: the bright red of what appeared to be fluttering standards, and the silver glint of bare metal catching the morning light.

"They're... they're all around us," murmured Simia, as if lost in a bad dream.

"It seems so," said Paiscion. "Just as your friend Triste predicted, they've come across the Narrow Sea and the Darkmoor. An entire division of them, by the looks of it. The young Scryer has done us all a great service — had he not warned us, we'd have been surprised by an attack from the west. Now, at least, we have had some time to prepare."

"How long before they get to the valley?" asked Sylas.

"Less than a day. Perhaps no more than a few hours."

"So it's too late!" exclaimed Simia. "There's no way out!"

Paiscion regarded her thoughtfully for a moment, and then he looked at Sylas, his eyes dropping slowly to the Merisi Band. "It will be difficult, but there is... *one* possibility."

Simia followed his gaze to the band. "Which is?"

Paiscion regarded them both, seeming to consider what to do

13

next. "Which is hard to explain," he said. "Come, I'll need to show you." He turned to the window, then — seeming to remember something — he glanced back at them. "We should take the quick way down. Just do as I do."

With that, he took a step forward and launched himself into empty space. He seemed to hang there for a moment, supported by nothing but air, then he fell quickly out of sight.

Sylas stared at Simia and Simia stared back. They both leaned out of the window and looked down.

They saw Paiscion's fluttering jacket, already a third of the way down the tree. The tree was alive once again, but this time its limbs were working more quickly, reaching out, catching and dropping its most precious cargo, so that, in another instant, he had disappeared altogether.

Sylas looked warily at Simia. Her cheeks had blanched to a sickly white.

"After you," she said without looking at him.

"Are you sure?" he asked. Then added hopefully: "Ladies first?"

She gave him a withering look. "The tree's trying to help you, Sylas. You just have to let it."

3

Companions

*"...and so I ask myself what new wonders will
we discover, what new* companions *will we find
when next we pull back the veil of the Other."*

SILENCE CAME TO THE broad clearing. The wind dropped away, the
ferns and bracken fell still and the animals sat up, sniffing the air.

Then, from the darkness between the trees, scores of pale figures
emerged, making their way so quickly and quietly over the tangled
undergrowth that their feet seemed barely to touch the ground.
There were men and women, boys and girls, all of them pale and
sunken-cheeked, adding to the impression that they were spectres.
Wave after wave of them darted across the clearing, their filthy
white rags flying up behind them, none of them making a sound,
their tread passing lightly over leaves and twigs and leaving no
sign of their passing.

But, as the stragglers stole across the clearing, the silence was
broken. A rumble echoed between the trees, startling birds and
sending them fluttering and chirruping into the blank skies.
Rodents and foxes bolted, following the fleeing Suhl. The
undergrowth began to ripple and leap and, as the rumble became
a terrifying thunder, the frozen ground buckled.

Suddenly two figures burst from a thicket. One was broader and more muscular, with a great mane of hair about his head and face. He supported the second dark-skinned man, who moved awkwardly and stiffly, stumbling every few steps. They made ground steadily rather than quickly, but when they reached the centre of the clearing they slowed and turned, eyeing the line of trees behind.

"Come!" panted the larger man. "Let's keep on!"

He wavered on his feet, then mumbled something and dropped to the ground, sitting in the long grass.

"Espasian! What are you doing?" protested his companion. "They'll be upon us in moments!"

"We — I — I must make a stand here," said the Magruman, still watching the trees, which had now shed all their frost, trembling as though in terror at what lay beyond. "Even if we can outrun them, which I doubt, many of our sisters and brothers cannot." He looked up, revealing a dark, handsome face bisected by a livid scar. "And I can't lose any more today." He did his best to smile reassuringly. "You go, Bayleon. Help the others to reach the valley."

Bayleon stared at him incredulously, then he shook his great head of hair and slumped down on to the ground. "You stay," he grunted, "I stay."

Espasian rapped him sharply on the breastplate. "Don't be a fool, man! Go!"

Bayleon crossed his arms. "I go when you go," he grunted. "Just be ready to hang on to this big old beard of mine."

Espasian regarded him closely, then smiled and nodded. He turned back to the quaking trees and drew a deep breath. He was quiet for a moment, seeming to turn into himself, steadying his breathing, gathering his thoughts. Finally he raised his arms but they faltered, seeming weak and uncoordinated, and his face crumpled with the effort. He growled and squeezed his fists tight.

Gradually his arms became still and, as they did so, he opened his fingers wide.

At once the long line of spruce trees steadied, as though waiting for his command. He took another deep breath, brought his hands together in front of his chest, and meshed his fingers.

All at once the trees came alive. The trunks creaked and cracked, bending to the left and right. By the time they slowed, they had bent almost double so that their uppermost branches swept the ground, twisting and snaking between one another until the limbs of each tree were indistinguishable from those of its neighbours.

Bayleon breathed a low chuckle into his beard. "Bravo," he murmured.

The knitted trees had formed a thick, impenetrable wall, the height of four or five people. As Espasian swept his hands wide, so this wall grew, stretching beyond the clearing and deep into the quaking forest.

It was just in time because in that instant there was a deafening crash as something struck the barrier. Timber shards were sent flying and tumbling into the clearing before the two seated men. Then came another collision, and another. Soon the forest echoed to the sound of scores of shuddering crunches and thuds all along the length of the wall. A hail of shattered wood flew up into the air and then peppered the ground. There followed a chorus of timber squeals, explosive cracks and rasping gurgles of sap. And then, with an almighty crash, the entire barrier buckled and swayed as though it was about to fall.

In one motion, Bayleon leapt up, seized his companion by the shoulders and heaved the Magruman to his feet.

"Come, Espasian," he growled, swinging a huge arm about Espasian's waist. "Time to let the Spoorrunner run!"

§

Two days had passed since the peculiar and disturbing events at the circles of stone, and people had started to believe that it might

17

all be over. After all, who had ever heard of an apocalypse pausing for the weekend? And so cautiously at first, but with increasing appetite, people were going shopping. They stocked up on all the essentials, like bottled water, bread, candles, matches and chocolate. In fact, chocolate sales had never been so buoyant, and factories whirred around the clock to meet the demand for something comforting, sweet and, above all, ordinary.

Perhaps because of this sudden rush, the two roads that met at the corner of Gabblety Row were in a particularly irascible mood. They growled and snarled with the voice of many impatient throttles, and both seemed determined to claim the junction as its own. Each sent cars probing and jostling into the path of the other, and the result was foul-tempered deadlock into which everyone threw themselves with enthusiasm.

So it was that nobody noticed the black ooze bubbling up from a grille at the end of the terrace, and no one took any interest as it snaked over the pavement and glooped into the gutter. Passers-by stepped over it and hurried on their way, assuming that it was something to do with that most peculiar of buildings, Gabblety Row. So the Black continued its journey, pooling in the potholes and dribbling down drains. Once underground, it began a long journey through tunnels and sewers until, across town, it gushed from an outlet in the shadow of the Hailing Bridge. There it plunged deep into the passing river and was swept southwards on its journey through a world changed forever.

For a homeless person, Duke, or 'the Duke' as he preferred to be known, was very particular. He always, for instance, wore a waistcoat and highly polished brogues, despite the facts that he slept in a cardboard box beneath a bridge, he ate little but baked beans and jelly cubes, and his hair was so filthy that it stood on end. But he believed that, in this slapdash world, there were certain standards that one must never let slip, and a polished shoe and a decent waistcoat were two among them. So the Duke had been quite put out when things had stopped conforming to any sort of standard whatsoever.

First, there had been that howling in the middle of the night, which sounded like some kind of mountain wolf right here in town. And then there was the strange midnight meeting he had overheard on the bridge — between the boy and that wild-looking fellow called Espen — talking about bells and beasts and things that weren't quite... *decent*. Just a week or so later there had been all those sirens, and helicopters, and people running about and making a terrible fuss. And now there was this strange black stuff coming from his personal water feature, the drain outlet.

He had noticed the slick of blackness first thing that morning and, notwithstanding his own shortcomings with respect to personal hygiene, had wrinkled his nose in distaste. As a defensive measure, he had splashed on some salvaged cologne and put on his hat and gloves, but that had done nothing to stem the flow of the black substance. Later that morning he had peered at it through his monocle and, satisfied at its horridness, shifted his camp upstream.

But what the Duke could not know was that this effort was futile because another outlet just a little further up the river — and another after that — were also disgorging the strange black substance. Neither could he know that, at that very moment, the Black was emerging all across the town, and the country, and indeed the world. It was seeping into sewers, swelling beneath paving slabs, dribbling from disused fountains. It was trickling into empty swimming pools, swilling along underground tunnels and bubbling into basements.

And he was certainly unaware that just a short distance away, on Salisbury Plain, it was welling from Stonehenge as from a mountain spring.

4

The Hollow

*"...but these are the hollow words of the blinkered
and the lost. My eye is clear and my mind is true.
It is for us Bringers to strive ever onwards: to record,
to understand, to bring our worlds to the union
that has been promised to us."*

AMELIE TATE WANDERED THROUGH the forest, her eyes wide, like a child in a world of wonders. One moment she was peering up into the branches of the giant trees, trying to make out the shape of the leaves, or the plumage of some brightly coloured bird that surely could not be there; the next she was gazing, open-mouthed, at the span of a fern, astonished by its height and breadth. And as much as she marvelled, the scientist in her was filled with frustrations. What she would not do for just some of her instruments? And how *could* she be here without a camera, or her reference books, or her computer?

But she was always quickly distracted by some new discovery. This time it was a plant with many yellow flowers dancing in the cool wind. She set down her basket and pulled a notepad from her pocket, turning quickly to a page she had headed *No Right To Be Here – Extinct!* She found a space and wrote *Stinking*

Hawksbeard (Crepis Foetida) immediately below her other scrawled entries:

Summer Lady's Tresses (Spiranthes Aestivalis)

Downy Hemp Nettle (Galeopsis Segetum)

Narrow-leaved Cudweed (Filago Gallica)

Each entry was underlined at least once and some were followed by an exclamation mark. Amelie pocketed the pad, closed her eyes and drew a long breath of fresh, fragrant air. "Impossible," she murmured.

"Mrs Tate?"

She started and looked round to see a pug-nosed boy hopping nervously from foot to foot.

She got to her feet and smiled. "Please, I prefer Amelie."

The boy winced and bit his lip. "S-sorry, Amelie, ma'am."

She laughed and held out her hand. "No need for the ma'am either!"

The boy stared at it, extended his own and gripped her fingers in a frenzied shake. "Filimaya sent me," he mumbled to the forest floor. "They need you to come back to the Hollow. Right now, she said. Sorry, ma'am... Amelie... I mean, sorry."

Amelie retrieved her hand and smiled, picking up her basket of cuttings. "You'd better lead the way. I'm not *quite* sure where I am!"

The boy bowed and hurried gratefully away so that Amelie had to rush to keep up as they wove between the mighty trunks and traversed glades and clearings. Still she gazed about her, wondering at the trees that grew too tall, flowers that bloomed too bright, plants that should not exist at all.

At last the boy led her up a bank of flowers and drew to a halt.

"Here!" he announced, pointing to a particularly gigantic giant redwood tree.

Amelie had already been in the Hollow more than once, but she still found the entrance difficult to see, even when it was pointed out. It was a dark opening beneath the massive root, partly covered by a curtain of ivy and vines. But, as the boy rushed forward and pulled back the green veil, it revealed itself at once: a large opening at least the height of a person, with a dim glow emanating from within.

"Ma'am," he said, waving her inside with a deep bow.

Amelie opened her mouth to correct him again, but then thought better of it, and walked inside. It was clear that, as Sylas's mother, she would have to accept a certain amount of deference from her new companions.

She stepped carefully down the earthen tunnel, feeling her way along its twists and turns until it finally levelled out. Here it opened into a cavernous hall lit by light beams that criss-crossed between mirrors on the walls of hard-packed earth. The ceiling was a complex weave of dark brown roots, most of which flowed from the very centre, like the vaulting of a cathedral. However, at regular intervals more slender roots dangled into the chamber, and from their very tips a clutch of glow-worms cast a warm light. Together these lights formed a Milky Way of glowing stars, but individually each had a purpose of its own, casting a halo of light over a bed of moss below. There were scores of such mossy beds in the chamber, glowing greenly beneath their very own light, and on some, patients reclined, receiving the attentions of helpers, who hurried to and fro. The Hollow may have had the appearance of some mystical sanctuary for tree elves, but it thrummed with all the efficiency of a hospital.

There was no sign of Filimaya, but Amelie made her way purposefully towards three beds that were set a little apart from the rest. As she approached, one of the patients pushed himself up.

"Morning, Amelie," said the young man, running his hand quickly through his hair.

"Tasker!" she beamed. "You look so much better!" She peered at the dressing on his shoulder. "Truly it's remarkable!"

"I can't quite believe it," said Tasker, patting the bandage. "Two doses of that Salve concoction and it's almost completely healed. There isn't even much pain!"

"Incredible!" exclaimed Amelie. "I've never seen anything like it!" She smiled again, but for a moment there was something troubled in her expression. Then she laughed dismissively. "But then here incredible seems to be quite the norm!"

"Yes, but nothing prepares you for it," said Tasker, looking about him. "When I first came to, I thought I was hallucinating. If I will get myself shot, I told myself. But here it is, every time I wake up!"

"Well, if it's a dream," laughed Amelie, "I'm in it with you!" She glanced across at the other beds. "And how are they doing?"

Tasker shifted his attention to his neighbour, who was lying on his back, his bald head glistening beneath the swinging light. "I don't think the Salve works so well on the Black, if at all, but your poultices seem to have helped. They're both definitely much perkier – when they're awake."

Amelie looked closely at the sleeping figure, wincing a little as she saw the black streaks running beneath the skin of his neck, reaching up to the wide-eyed tattoos on his scalp – the marks of a Scryer.

"In any case, Bowe is an ox of a man," continued Tasker. "I'm sure he'll beat the Black – whatever it is. And Naeo's no pushover either. I call her Princess, you know, though she doesn't really..."

He chatted on amiably, but Amelie's attention drifted as she stepped past Bowe to the next bed. There Naeo was sleeping on her side. Her blonde hair had fallen forward over her face so that her features could not be seen. Her slender limbs were curled beneath a blanket but for one arm, which she had stretched out towards her father. Bowe had reached out too, and their fingers were entwined.

Quietly Amelie sat at the end of the bed. She reached out and gently drew back Naeo's hair, her eyes tracing the face that seemed so young considering everything it had seen. It was a face that was at once a mystery and also wonderfully familiar, because something about it was undeniably Sylas. Amelie extended a finger and, with the tenderness of a mother, stroked Naeo's cheek.

She was so engrossed that she did not notice Filimaya as she approached.

"They're doing much better, I think," said Filimaya softly as she stepped into the halo of light. Her long silver hair was gathered in the customary plait, and she was wearing the richly embroidered robes of a Suhl elder, but as ever it was her radiant features that immediately drew the eye.

Amelie quickly collected herself, then stood. "Yes — yes, I think they are," she said quietly. "They're still exhausted, but that's hardly surprising given all they've been through."

Filimaya offered Tasker a kind smile by way of greeting, then motioned for Amelie to follow, and together they headed back down the aisle.

"Thank you for coming so quickly, Amelie," said Filimaya, still speaking quietly to avoid disturbing the other patients. "I think we're about to get very busy, and so we will need much more of your poultice preparation — did you manage to find the ingredients you require?"

"Yes, and more besides," Amelie said, walking swiftly to keep up. "You seem to have a little of everything in this valley!"

"Good. And you must use those resources while you can. Make enough for fifty or so treatments for us to keep, and some for Naeo to take with her. She'll not long be in the valley, I'm afraid, and she'll continue to need your poultice to ease the effects of the Black."

"Of course," said Amelie. "So... what's happening?"

Filimaya nodded and gestured to the end of the hall. "You've noticed that the Hollow has grown since yesterday?"

Amelie frowned at her, then turned and gazed along the chamber. Sure enough, in the shadows there appeared to be at least twenty or thirty new beds of moss, and above them new roots growing down from the ceiling, as yet without their complement of glow-worms.

"How — how can that be?" she said.

Filimaya smiled. "You have much to learn about the Suhl, Amelie. You see, we are the valley, and the valley is us. She knows our needs and she provides. When we are hungry, she gives us food; when we are sick or injured —" she gestured to the end of the hall — "she gives us this."

Amelie was still confused. "But you already have so many beds."

Filimaya sighed. "Yes, but it seems even they will not be enough."

Amelie shook her head. "For... what?"

"For what is to come."

5

A Final Push

*"Have no doubt, even if the Glimmer Myth proves true,
it will take* a final push *the like of which
we can barely imagine to bring it to pass."*

ESPASIAN RAN, DESPITE THE fire burning in his limbs and the
Black surging through his veins. He must not falter, not now, but
the pain was becoming unbearable, and the world around him dim
and pale, as though he was already in the realm of the dead.

"Keep going!" yelled Bayleon, barely audible over the exploding
timber and shattering rocks. "It can't be far now!"

They ran on, up a hill, crashing through thicket and bracken,
weaving between trees and boulders. Bayleon was still strong, and
his Spoorrunner's instincts were as keen as ever, helping him to
avoid the roughest terrain and pick out the quickest and clearest
path. But still their pursuers drew ever closer. Glancing back, they
saw something colossal crushing a nearby trunk and, moments
later, two flaming eyes peering through a storm of leaves and
splinters. For the first time they heard a loathsome cry, something
between a gargle and a roar, which shook them to the bone. Then
more fiery eyes appeared in the murk of the forest, left and right,
streaking ahead to cut them off.

"They're on us, Espasian!" bellowed the Spoorrunner. "Can you fight?"

Espasian looked at him with delirious eyes and tried to answer, but nothing came. Bayleon tightened the arm beneath his shoulder.

"Then run!" he growled. "If we must die, then let it be in the chase!"

They plunged on, despite the riot at their heels and the rage of noise in their ears.

Suddenly something slammed into Bayleon's side. He gave a bearlike roar, but did not slow; he stumbled on, holding his flank. The splintered remains of a tree cartwheeled past them and skidded to a halt at their feet, sending them sprawling, but still they pushed themselves up and staggered on. They ran like men possessed, with wild eyes and faces set in steel; they ran until they heard nothing and felt nothing, until there was only the thunder of their hearts and the roar of blood in their ears.

And then, all at once, something changed. They realised that they could hear the thump of their boots on the earth, the crunch of dry leaves, the rustle of the undergrowth as they passed. The clamour of falling trees was dying away, and no longer were they assailed by the enraged cries and snorts of the beasts.

They faltered, glanced at one another and then looked back.

To their astonishment, the forest was in motion. Just as before the trees were leaning this way and that, weaving together to form an impenetrable mesh. Still the two men stumbled on, but now all of the trees they passed sighed, creaked and closed tight behind them, their branches coiling and grasping until one was indistinct from the next. It was as though the entire forest was drawing about them to keep them safe. The crazed cries of their pursuers could still be heard, furious and desperate, but already they were nowhere to be seen.

Bayleon and Espasian fell to their knees, gasping for breath, and looked at one another in bewilderment.

"Is this you?" gasped Bayleon.

Espasian looked back at the woven forest and shook his head, still disorientated and confused. "No," he panted. "Not me."

Bayleon frowned, but then, slowly, his face widened into a grin. He glanced about him as though seeing the forest for the first time. "The valley!" he cried, suddenly laughing for joy. He turned and slapped his companion on the shoulder. "We made it, Espasian! We're in the Valley of Outs! This is *her* doing!"

The Magruman looked blearily at the trees about him and noticed a canopy of green and bronze leaves. A weak smile formed on his lips. "I think perhaps you're right," he said, looking back the way they had come. There was still no sign of their pursuers, but they could be heard raging at the barricade of trees.

"Do you think it's strong enough?" murmured Bayleon.

Espasian nodded. "Those creatures made short work of my efforts, but they're nothing compared to the magic that binds the valley. The more those beasts try to force their way in, the faster they'll find their way out."

"Let's hope you're right," grunted Bayleon. He glanced about. "And let's hope our sisters and brothers made it too."

"No need to worry about that either," said Espasian, nodding at the trees. "Look."

Bayleon turned and squinted into the gloom of the forest. Suddenly he started.

Just visible in the half-light were a thousand bloodless faces peering round trunks and over bushes and boulders. For some moments they simply stared, gazing between the two men and the lattice of trees as though assuring themselves that it was safe. Then, slowly, they came forward, revealing their thin, malnourished bodies clad in filthy rags.

"Help me up!" hissed Espasian, holding out an arm to Bayleon.

Together they staggered to their feet and, as they hurriedly brushed themselves down, a murmur rose from the trees. It came from the gathering of Suhl, whispered at first, but now growing in strength and volume until the forest echoed with their voices.

"Espasian!" they chanted. "Espasian! ... Espasian! ... Espasian!"

6

A Black Tide

"It will be a black tide – ruinous, irresistible –
and there is no shore it will not reach."

THE SILENCE GNAWED AT Sylas and set him on edge. He had
become accustomed to the gales of birdsong that swept back and
forth across the lake, the sounds of animals in the forest, the
chirruping of cicadas. But now the Valley of Outs was quiet, and
a new foreboding hung over its pleasant glades and wooded heights.

He hurried to catch up with Paiscion and Simia, who were
striding ahead along the base of a cliff. He felt better when he was
around Paiscion. Despite everything, the Magruman seemed
bolder and brighter than ever, utterly changed from the mournful,
taciturn man they had first met on the *Windrush* in Gheroth. He
walked quickly and spoke with a new energy, and even his tired
old smoking jacket now glowed resplendently in the early-morning
light.

They walked on together a little further before Paiscion stopped
abruptly, his head in the air, as though sniffing the wind. Then he
turned slowly about, looking up at the peaks of the hills.

"They're close," he said. "Very close. But she'll be ready."

"Who?" asked Simia, looking around. "Who'll be ready?"

The Magruman peered at her over his spectacles. "The valley, Simia!"

"The... *valley*?" she repeated.

"The valley!" declared Paiscion cheerfully. Then he turned and set off up the path that skirted the cliff. "She's quiet now," he called, "but soon she will wake, you'll see! Keep up! We're almost there!"

Sylas and Simia dutifully followed, trudging up the path that they had taken with Triste a few days earlier, on their way to the Garden of Havens. What an age ago that seemed now, Sylas thought. He remembered the meeting of the Suhl, and their confusion and terror as he had come together with Naeo, and the message that had appeared on the Merisi Band, burning with an enchanted fire.

"*In blood it began*," he murmured, turning the silvery-gold bracelet on his wrist. "*In blood it must end*." He shook his head grimly. How very true that seemed now.

"What's that?" asked Paiscion, stopping and looking round.

"Nothing," blurted Sylas, embarrassed that he had spoken aloud. He glanced about. "So — are we going to the gardens?"

Paiscion shook his head. "Not quite. We're going *beneath* the gardens."

Simia's eyes widened. "Into — into the mines?" she asked excitedly.

The Magruman gave a nod and walked on.

Simia dropped back and whispered in Sylas's ear: "Remember? Triste showed us the entrance to the mines on our way into the gardens." Then she added with some relish: "They're *forbidden*!"

"Not to us!" called Paiscion.

Sylas and Simia both started. They had forgotten Paiscion's talent for eavesdropping.

"Aren't they all closed up?" asked Sylas, remembering Triste's warning. "Something to do with the Black?"

"They are rather overrun with the Black, yes, but they're quite

31

accessible," said the Magruman. "We speak about the Black more to deter intruders than anything else. We have good reason for keeping the mines from prying eyes." He lowered his voice. "They contain something priceless. Something more valuable than all the gold in Gheroth."

Simia exchanged a wide-eyed glance with Sylas. "Which is?"

"Which is not liquid nor gas nor solid," said the Magruman. "Which is neither wet nor dry."

She gazed at him blankly. "I don't get it."

"The old name for it is *Quintessence*, but others call it the fifth element. The one that unites the other four."

Simia shook her head. "What *elements*?" she asked shortly.

Paiscion looked over at Sylas and raised his eyebrows. "I think you know the answer to that, Sylas?"

Sylas stared at him in confusion, and then his mind flew back to something Isia had said to him in the Place of Tongues. "*You have mastered the earth, and the fire and the water*," she had told him. "*Now, master the air!*"

His eyes widened. "You mean earth and air, fire and water!"

"Precisely so!" exclaimed Paiscion. "The earth that feeds us, the air that fills our lungs, the fire that warms us and the water that gives us life."

"So what does this *fifth* element do?" asked Sylas.

"My dear Sylas," cried Paiscion, "Quintessence has been helping you all along!" His eyes drifted down to the beautiful bracelet round Sylas's wrist.

Sylas raised it so that it glowed liquidly before their eyes. "The Merisi Band? Isn't it just gold or silver?"

"It may at times *seem* like gold, but at others it looks like silver, does it not?"

Sylas stared at the band, which, even now, seemed to change before his eyes. "I thought that was just a trick of the light."

"No, Sylas. No tricks. Quintessence! Think about it. Think about how the band sometimes changes form — from solid to liquid, liquid to vapour."

Sylas ran his fingers over the smooth surface of the bracelet, thinking about the moment Espasian had first placed it on his wrist: how the band had tightened, as though it was some living thing. Then he remembered his first meeting with Naeo, in the Dirgheon, when the band had divided into twin trails of vapour, one silver and one gold, to form two new bracelets.

"And the Merisi Band isn't your only experience of Quintessence," continued Paiscion. "Cast your mind back, Sylas. Where else have you encountered it? Retrace your journey, right to the very beginning."

Sylas thought back to the start of his adventure, to Gabblety Row, and the Shop of Things, and Mr Zhi. He thought about the Samarok full of Ravel Runes, and the strange hound that had appeared in the churchyard. Then he remembered the deafening chime that had woken him, and the chase through town, and the—

"The bell!" blurted Simia. "The Passing Bell!" She turned to Sylas. "*That* was bright silvery gold, remember? And after it rang, it just melted away into the ground! Like it had turned to liquid or something!"

Paiscion smiled and nodded. "What else?"

Sylas's mind was already racing. "What about the mirrors?" he said, remembering their strange sheen. "The Glimmer Glass that Mr Zhi showed me in the Shop of Things?"

"And the Glimmer Glass you showed us on the *Windrush*!" exclaimed Simia.

Paiscion chuckled. "Yes! Another creation of the Merisi: two perfect sheets of Quintessence, so pure that they reflect all of you — your two parts as one. You and your Glimmer. The Merisi are very fond of Quintessence. Just think of the Glimmertrome."

Sylas's eyes grew wide as he thought of the peculiar object Naeo brought back from Mr Zhi, which allowed her to see through his eyes, and him through hers. "That's right!" he said excitedly. "The needle that sways from side to side — that's silvery gold too!"

"So now you see," said Paiscion. "These Things and many more are forged of Quintessence. And they could be made of nothing else."

"Why? What's so special about it?" asked Simia.

"*What's so special?*" spluttered Paiscion. "My dear Simia, Quintessence is the perfect blend of all natural things — of earth and air, fire and water — of the very fabric of the world! If any substance might mend what is broken, overcome the rift between our worlds, it is Quintessence!"

"Oh," said Simia. "Right."

Paiscion turned to Sylas. "So now do you see how important it is to your journey?"

"I do," murmured Sylas, gazing at the Merisi Band.

The Magruman turned and continued up the slope. "Of course," he said over his shoulder, "the only problem with Quintessence is how to get hold of it."

Sylas frowned and hurried after him. "But you said there's Quintessence in the mines, didn't you?"

Paiscion grunted. "Yes, but sadly there's very little left. Once the mines were full of it. It pooled below the Living Tree, but over the centuries, as we experimented with ways to heal the division between our worlds, we have mined it remorselessly, some for our own purposes, some for the Merisi. Now we're down to the last traces."

"But if there *is* some," said Sylas, "and we can get hold of it, what will we *do* with it?"

Paiscion arched an eyebrow. "Well, I rather think that will be up to you and Naeo. But just consider for a moment the power you have found in each other. If we use a little more Quintessence to make that bond all it can be — to bind two parts of a broken soul — it may just give you the strength you need to—"

"To escape the valley!" interjected Simia. "Yes, I get it!"

Paiscion smiled. "Good. I'm glad."

Before long they came to the top of the slope, where the path came to an abrupt end at the face of the cliff. The Magruman walked over to an overhang of vines and pulled them back to reveal the dark opening that Sylas remembered from his last visit: the tunnel that led to the Garden of Havens.

They were all about to step inside when something made them stop in their tracks. It was a rumble punctuated by sharp cracks and tremulous booms, which echoed across the lake and startled birds into the skies.

"What was *that*?" breathed Simia, her eyes wide with fear.

Paiscion glanced round the valley, then suddenly turned back to the entrance and pushed them ahead, into the darkness. "Go!" he said anxiously. "Go! There's no more time!"

They hurried down the tunnel in silence and almost complete darkness, trailing their hands along the cold, damp walls to keep their footing. Then came another of the clamorous booms. This time they felt it beneath their fingertips, reverberating in the rocky bowels of the hill.

"They've reached the valley!" said the Magruman, hurrying them on. After a few more paces he stepped into another passage leading off to the left. They walked down it a short way until Paiscion halted. Suddenly there was a sharp crack, followed by a blinding flash of light, and a new orange glow filled the passageway. It illuminated Paiscion carrying a flaming torch, his features ghoulish in the flickering light.

"Follow me," he commanded. "And do not — on any account — touch the walls. The Black is everywhere. If you need to hold on to something, use the ropes."

The halo of light before him, he headed off down the passageway. Sylas and Simia glanced doubtfully at the ropes fastened like a handrail to one wall of the passage, then stuffed their hands into their pockets and hurried after him.

They descended a long flight of rough-hewn steps, which snaked left and right, descending deep into the rock. More passages led away on either side, but Paiscion took none of these and rushed on. When they finally reached the bottom, he paused to make sure that Sylas and Simia were keeping up, but as soon as they were down he plunged on into the darkness. A few paces on they began descending another flight of steps, this one so uneven and slippery that Sylas and Simia had to use the guide ropes to steady themselves, hoping all the while that the wetness in their palms was no more than water.

There was a scent of decay in the air, like rotting leaves, but also something more unusual. Something Sylas could not quite place. It was sharp and chemical, a little like the science labs at school.

After all his years in Gabblety Row he had come to believe that tight spaces no longer worried him, but the more he thought about the immensity of rock above him, its surfaces glistening with Black, the more his chest began to tighten.

All at once the Magruman stopped. They could see him standing stock-still, silhouetted against the torchlight. He was staring ahead at something.

The air felt different here, colder and more humid, and the echo of their footsteps had changed too.

Paiscion raised his torch and, by some trick of Essenfayle, extended its circle of light. The walls had disappeared, and Sylas realised that they were no longer standing in a tunnel but on a wide ledge, staring out into a vast black cavern. It was so broad that the light did not reach the other side, and it towered to the height of a house, where a great tangle of roots and stalactites hung from an unseen ceiling. Sylas looked down, but then immediately leapt back in surprise. Tentatively he leaned forward again and saw himself staring back. It was his own reflection captured in an immense, mirror-smooth pool.

"This is the Source, the heart of the mines," said the Magruman, his words setting off a babble of echoes. "Most of the Quintessence was found right here, in this chamber. It was once a bright, magical place. They say the miners could barely work for staring, such was the beauty of it. There was Quintessence everywhere, flowing up the walls, all the way to the roots of the Living Tree, only to drip back down in an endless shower."

Simia studied the dark, dank cave. "So... what happened?"

"The Quintessence was mined and taken away. The Passing Bell alone used up much of what was in this chamber. Now, as you can see, the Black fills every crack and crevice from which we have taken Quintessence. For reasons we don't quite understand wherever the Quintessence has been the Black tends to follow. Or... or perhaps it's the other way round. We really don't know."

Sylas gazed into the darkness. "It doesn't look like there's any Quintessence left at all."

"You're right," said Paiscion. "But there remains one last corner of these mines where the Quintessence was left untouched. We kept it for just such an emergency as this."

He ushered them on and they moved carefully round the ledge. Every surface was coated in the wet, seeping blackness, and they were forced to turn sideways, edging along with the Black oozing behind them and the pool stretching out ominously below. They were making fairly swift progress when Sylas suddenly saw something out in the shadowy centre of the pool. He stopped and narrowed his eyes, and saw to his surprise a small wave spreading across the surface.

"Did you see that?" he said, in a low voice.

A little ahead of him the other two halted and peered into the dark.

"See what?" asked Paiscion.

"I'm not sure," whispered Sylas. "But I think there's something out there."

The Magruman extended his torch and instantly the flames flared, burning brighter and illuminating most of the chamber.

They all drew a sharp breath.

The centre of the pool was no longer smooth and still. It was heaving upwards into a mound of churning, oily Black. It swelled even as they watched, rising higher and higher into the chamber, feeding from the pool.

Suddenly the Magruman turned. "Quick!" he bellowed, beckoning frantically to Sylas. "Run!"

With that, he hurried off along the ledge, dragging Simia behind him. Sylas followed as fast as he dared, struggling to make out the path by Paiscion's dancing light. He quickly forgot about the Black streaming down the walls and after a few paces he collided with an outcrop of rock, almost staggering over the edge. Still he kept on, eyes on the ledge, trying not to be distracted by the shape that loomed ever larger in the corner of his eye.

Up ahead he saw Paiscion and Simia falter and then stop altogether, giving up on their escape. They were staring out over the pool. Sylas followed their eyes, skin crawling, and peered into the darkness.

Something huge was now towering above them, something made of the Black. It was not the featureless mass Sylas had glimpsed before but something with the hunch of shoulders and the bulge of a drooping head, dripping with the oily Black.

7

Such Stuff
as Dreams

"If we know only our side of the divide, are we not sleeping?
Do we not see in half-truths, as in a dream?
I think sometimes of those lines in Shakespeare:
We are such stuff as dreams are made on,
and our little life is rounded with a sleep."

THE BLACK WAS NO secret now. The fountains and ditches, wells and gullies that had hidden its arrival suddenly drew the eyes of nations. Passers-by gaped in horror at the swelling blackness, caught between fascination and the urge to flee. Children stared in wonder from classroom windows, nudging friends to come and see what was happening in the swimming pool, or the playground, or the nearby park.

The Duke retreated into his cardboard home and slowly raised his monocle to his eye, gazing in disbelief at the middle of the river. Even the junction at the corner of Gabblety Row finally fell silent as the occupants of cars stared with mounting terror at the Church of the Holy Trinity, where something monstrous and dark was rising above the ruins.

And then, all over the world, the Black took shape — not one shape but several. First, it took a form with stooped shoulders, a large head and long, pendulous arms. When black tusks grew from its black jaws, it could be seen for what it was: a kind of ape — perhaps a baboon — powerful and lithe, like a king of beasts.

Even as everyone recoiled, it changed. Its shoulders remained hunched, but its black arms folded into its body, its legs wasted away and its head became longer and narrower. Something grew from its snout: a long protrusion that curved and tapered to a cruel point. Soon it was unmistakably a bird, with distinct predatory features, like an ibis of the ancients. Spectators in forecourts, car parks and village greens gaped in astonishment as the great bird turned its head and surveyed the world, its beak dripping Black.

But it had not yet found its final form. Once again it began to change, keeping the hunch in its shoulders and the droop of its head, but its feathers becoming a glistening cloak with an open hood. Its wings grew crooked hands, twisted with age, and these it drew forward, the fingers knitted as though in prayer.

And then, with lips hidden in shadow, it spoke.

"Wake," it said. "For you have been sleeping."

It spoke in a cacophony of thousands of voices, young and old, male and female, monstrous and tender.

"You have wrapped yourselves in dreams," it continued. "Now, wake from your little lives and I will tell you the truth of things." It leaned forward as though imparting a secret. "Our world is made of opposites: day and night, summer and winter, male and female, the face and the reflection. It is time for you to know your reflection."

The figure swelled then, growing to a new height and raising its hands to the hood. Crowds shrank away and small children whimpered with fear as, slowly, it drew back the blackness. Beneath was a dark, endlessly changing visage, with eyes that grew and narrowed and swam across the face; a nose that was at once large and small and pug and fine; cheekbones that sometimes protruded and sometimes supported full, youthful cheeks. Each spectator saw faces in that malaise, but no two saw the same.

"We are the face in the mirror," said the voice of many. "I am Thoth, Priest of Souls and scribe to the gods. Behind me stands a world unknown to you, a people and an empire of which you know nothing. We are your second self."

Across the world, crowds of people turned to one another in bewilderment and terror, but before they could speak Thoth continued.

"Since the beginning, you have lived in a borrowed light. Your world was spawned in the image of our greater realm. We yielded to you an equal measure of Nature's bounty, and with it a chance to forge your own path. But, from the start, you forsook the gods that raised you from the void. You forgot the Empire that gave you life. You cast down the teachings of the ancients. You sought your own power, reaching beyond the Four Ways given to us to find a Fifth. The Way you call *science*."

He uttered the word with tight-lipped contempt, spitting rather than speaking it. He laughed an empty laugh and bellowed: "Science! As if all can be known! As if your truth is greater than that of the gods!" He took a wheezing breath as though to calm his ire. "I have watched this hubris, these heresies, with forbearance, as a teacher watches a child: quietly and closely, with a care for your mistakes. But now you go too far.

"With your science, you have created things of war that threaten the boundary between our worlds, and with it peace. In these past days, I have taken these things from you. I have brought them close, and learned them, to restore the balance between us."

The gathered masses could restrain themselves no longer and

openly spoke among themselves, confused and appalled, but still Thoth continued.

"But you have gone further still. Your world has long harboured an ungodly order that meddles with the rules that keep us safe; an order that plays on doubts and disorder. These *Merisi* have dispatched two children to upset the balance between our worlds — a boy called Sylas Tate and a girl named Naeo, daughter of Bowe."

The gigantic figure turned its head, dripping slick trails of Black. He cast dark eyes over the astonished crowds in plazas and parks and streets. "This is an act of war!" he boomed. "It will not stand! And yet still I have come here in peace, to warn you to step back from the brink, to entreat you to yield and surrender your arms. But if you defy me," he said, looming over those who watched, "I will make you suffer even as the ancients suffered. You will be five times undone. You will know the evils of our world and you will despair."

He raised his arms so that curtains of black slime fell at his sides. "To show you my intent, I have released into your world a pure blackness, darker than death, and you will know it, and it will know you. This is the first undoing. Should you resist me still, I will bring such pestilence upon you that you will be glad of the end when it comes, as surely it will. It will come in a final darkness, in a last night, from which there will be no dawn.

"The ancients divided their world into an Upper and a Lower Kingdom," he declared as he swelled to new and fearsome dimensions. "It is time to teach you which is which. I am Thoth, three times great: Priest of Souls, scribe to the gods and soon, A'an, Lord of Equilibrium. I will bring a different union to our worlds. A union of light and hope, or if you refuse me, a union of endless dark.

"Listen to the great poet of your history. Your world is rounded with a sleep. Now wake, while still there is time."

The giant figure suddenly lost its form. It cascaded down so that the pool of Black heaved and slopped, almost overwhelming the stone ledge. Sylas gazed in horror at the vacant space where Thoth had appeared, and he heard those dreadful words still echoing from the walls of the cavern.

"...while still there is light."

"...while still there is light."

"...while still there is light."

For some moments no one spoke.

Finally, still staring into the darkness, Sylas said: "He can't mean it, can he? A last night, with no dawn?"

Paiscion seemed to think about this, then he let out a sad, almost weary sigh. "I have learned, Sylas, that Thoth means exactly what he says, however unthinkable that may be. We know that the Black has found its way between the worlds — he has used it to deliver this message. We know that his forces have violated the stone circles and entered your world: Naeo saw that for herself. And we have long known of his ambitions to control the divide between the worlds. That is almost certainly what led to the Undoing. And if he is capable of one Undoing..." He took off his glasses and pinched the bridge of his nose. "But on this *scale*... '*five times undone*...'" He shook his head with a look of self-reproach. "I didn't foresee this. I *should* have."

The three of them fell silent and stared down at the pool of Black, which had now returned to its ominous mirror-like stillness.

"This is why we only have one moon left," murmured Simia at last.

Sylas looked up. "What's that?"

"That line in Isia's song," said Simia, meeting his eyes. "You know, the song in the Samarok. How did it go? '*Our hope quickly won will die in one moon.*' Well, *this* is why we have only one moon."

"Because... if we don't find a way to bring the two worlds together," said Sylas, "then it'll happen anyway, before the next new moon!"

"Because Thoth will make it happen," said Simia. "Not in the way we thought, not by bringing the two parts together as one—"

"But by war," said Sylas. "By making my world a slave to this one."

"'*A union of light and hope, or of an endless dark,*'" said Paiscion, looking up at them both, his eyes once again bright behind his glasses. "He talks as though he offers a choice, but in truth he knows only one way. If there is a choice, Sylas, it is between his way and yours. His is the dark and yours is the light."

"Which means we absolutely *have* to keep on," said Simia with a steely look, "and get to Old Kemetis like Isia told us – the centre of the Empire, the place where it all began!"

Sylas nodded, his heart pounding once again. "And all before the new moon..."

They exchanged glances and then gazed back out into the darkness.

"So... hadn't we better find this Quintessence?" said Simia after a moment.

"This way," said Paiscion.

They resumed their precarious journey along the ledge, doing their best to pick up pace. All the while Thoth's words rang in Sylas's ears. So much rested upon him now – him and Naeo – more than he could possibly comprehend. His throat began to close, and he felt a clutch of panic in his gut. He stopped, pressed his eyes shut and forced himself to breathe the cool, dank air, until his hammering heart began to slow. Finally he pressed on after the others.

Soon they were edging round an outcrop of rock and sidestepping carefully along the narrowing ledge. They found themselves entering a deep, hidden recess. By the light of Paiscion's torchlight, they could see a stout wooden door ahead into which had been carved an intricate feather, its white pigment now faded to a dull grey.

"This is the place," said the Magruman.

He held out his torch and, to his companions' surprise, the flames left the oiled cloth and flickered and spluttered towards the door. As they reached the timber, they crept into the grooves of the carving until the feather itself glowed with orange fire. Suddenly there was a loud clunk and the door creaked open.

Paiscion quickly stepped along the last part of the ledge and across the threshold. As Sylas and Simia followed him inside, he raised his torch and filled the chamber beyond with a brilliant light.

Before them, and spilling across almost half of the stone floor, was another pool of Black. But what drew their eyes was a finger of rock that descended from the ceiling, because hanging from its very tip was an exquisitely beautiful teardrop. It glowed in the torchlight, seeming to radiate more light than there was in the room, and at some moments it looked silver, at others gold. Its gleaming sides swelled to a full sphere at its base, at least the size of a football, and it drew so close to the pool of Black below that at first Sylas thought that they touched. But something strange had happened to the surface of the pool. There was a depression exactly the same shape as the base of the teardrop. It was as though the Black was being repelled by the Quintessence.

As he stared, Sylas felt his Merisi Band changing, becoming looser, its edges less distinct, as though it was losing its solid form.

"There it is," said Paiscion, his eyes alive in the golden fire. "The last drop of Quintessence!"

Simia stepped forward, an enchanted light dancing across her face. "It's beautiful!"

"Isn't it?" said Paiscion. "Merimaat used to say that while there was Quintessence there was hope: hope for the valley, for the Suhl, for the world." He joined Simia at the edge of the pool and sighed. "Our last drop of hope — until Sylas came to us, of course. There's not a lot of it, but—"

He stopped mid-sentence, frowned and turned back towards the doorway.

"What is it?" hissed Simia.

Paiscion raised a finger to his lips and walked slowly to the doorway.

"Who's there?" he bellowed, his voice echoing around the cavern beyond.

Sylas and Simia looked at one another in alarm, then walked nervously to the opening and peered round the Magruman.

At once they saw another torch across the cave.

"It's — it's Hebber, sir!" said a rather frightened voice. "I was sent to get you. There's to be an urgent meeting, now, in the Churn. They need all of you!"

Paiscion frowned. "And who has called this meeting?"

"That's just it, sir," called Hebber excitedly. "Espasian called the meeting! He's here! In the valley!"

8

The Churn

"They took me then to a place called the Churn, a place beyond sight and hearing, a place to speak the unspeakable."

WITH HIS MOTHER, THE Garden of Havens had been a whole new wonder. She had clasped his hand so tightly that it almost hurt, and she had walked about and turned on the spot, gazing at silver vines and waterfalls and flower-flecked meadows. And, as she had gaped at the singing cascades and the sunlit heights, Sylas had drunk in her happiness.

Sometimes, over the past days, the fierceness of her happiness had frightened him because he knew that it was about him, about having him at her side at last, after her long years at Winterfern. But *this* part of her happiness, about being here in this beautiful garden – the part that made her wide-eyed like a child – had made everything worthwhile. The whole journey. All of it. Just for this.

When she had noticed the Arbor Vital – the 'Living Tree' as Triste had called it – she had led Sylas to a grassy bank and sat down, and stayed there, wordlessly, for what seemed like forever and no time at all. They had breathed the freshest air their lungs had ever known, and looked out at that majestic old tree, imposing but beautiful, and they had drawn close, just like they used to on the hill behind the cottage.

But, when finally he had turned to her, her eyes had been full of tears.

"I can't make sense of it all, Sylas," she had said. "I'm a *scientist*. I'm used to seeing how a garden is made — knowing the names of things, the purpose of things. But in *this* garden... I don't see species or — or habitats. I can't even think of those things. I just see the beauty of it all. It's like it's —" she had laughed through her tears, seeming embarrassed — "*perfect*. Does that make any sense?"

Sylas had replied without hesitation. "Yes," he had said simply. The gardens made him feel just the same. That everything was as it should be. That nothing was out of place. That this might very well be the most beautiful place in the world.

"The Garden of Havens," she had said, gazing about her. Then she had laughed. "How *they* say it, it could almost be 'Eden', couldn't it?" She had looked at him in that way that undid him, that made him feel like a young boy again, and she had pulled him close and held him tight. "Thank you for bringing me here."

She had meant here to the gardens, of course, not here to the Other. Sylas knew she felt quite differently about the Other. But it hardly mattered, not in that moment, because they had been truly happy and, wrapped in warmth and possibility, he had felt certain they were going to be all right.

But now, as he ran beneath that very same Living Tree, and across that same grassy bank, it felt as though that moment had never happened. Instead his mind was in the cavern with the Black, and Thoth, and his hope was lost in an everlasting night.

He saw Paiscion and Simia slow to a halt and wait on the far side of the garden. He ran up to them, and at once the Magruman led them through a scattering of bushes to the face of the cliff.

There was a dark opening, partly hidden between two mossy plinths of stone, and Paiscion walked forward and stooped inside.

As Sylas entered, the peace of the gardens disappeared. Instead there was darkness, and the rock about him rumbled with the violence of a nearby waterfall, and icy water showered down from the ceiling, drenching his hair and clothes. He felt the familiar ache round the Merisi Band and the shifting of his insides that told him that Naeo was near.

In some strange way, he welcomed this discomfort because it was real. The world was falling in and so how else should he feel but cold, and dark, and broken? He saw a light ahead and against it the silhouettes of Paiscion and Simia passing through a curtain of water, disappearing into a blur of light and shadow. Sylas plunged after them, gasping from the shock of it, but almost at once he was through.

He emerged into a deafening clamour, as though he had stumbled into the heart of the waterfall itself. He wiped the wet hair from his eyes and looked about him. He was in a high cavern, with walls of rock on three sides, smooth and rippling as though they had once been liquid. But it was the fourth side that drew his gaze. It was the back of an immense waterfall tumbling in a frothy torrent from high above and plunging into a pool below. Its thunder was so powerful that it was difficult to think.

He saw Filimaya on the far side of the chamber, strands of her silver hair in sodden trails about her cheeks, her robes drenched. She was looking up towards the ceiling and Sylas followed her eyes. He gasped in surprise. There was no ceiling, only the rolling, churning underside of the river passing above them as though suspended in glass. The waters surged and boiled, letting through a swirling green-blue light that danced in shifting patterns around the cavern. Against this glow Sylas could see the silhouettes of shoals of fish swimming against the current, hanging above

Filimaya as though struggling to be close to her, just like the fish in the Aquium of the Meander Mill.

All at once Filimaya raised her arms and, with a look of concentration, closed her outstretched hands. In that very moment, the thunderous noise was silenced. The river continued to churn, the rock trembled still, but there was no sound: no crash and roar of the waterfall, no rumble of the river. Sylas wondered if he had somehow been deafened at a stroke, but suddenly a voice pierced the quiet.

"What did the Greeks say about rivers, Sylas? Something about fate, and destiny, and a border between worlds?"

Sylas whirled about. Propped against a boulder in the rear of the cave he saw none other but Espasian, his dark face creased in a smile.

"They were on to something, eh?"

Sylas laughed, remembering the Magruman's words when they first met on the Hailing Bridge, and ran over to embrace him. "You made it, Espasian!" he exclaimed.

The Magruman staggered as Sylas ran into him. "Good to see you too, Sylas!" he said, chuckling. "And you, Simia Roskoroy!" he added as Simia hugged him from the other side.

They held each other for some moments, and then Sylas stepped back. Now, he saw two other figures in the dancing light. The first was Naeo, leaning up against a wall, weaving a bootlace into a cat's cradle between her hands. The other was Ash, his mass of golden locks gleaming in a shaft of light. He was dressed as untidily as ever, but now his robes were the rich burgundy of a Magruman, which made him look rather grand, if still unkempt.

"No hug for me?" he protested.

Simia rolled her eyes. "We saw you this morning, Ash!"

Paiscion came forward then and embraced Espasian like a lost brother, bidding him welcome and then sharing some quiet words. They nodded, seeming quickly to come to an agreement.

Espasian turned back to the group.

"Sorry to call you all here in such a hurry," he said, "but it seems we have little time and much to discuss. We must forego a Say-So and talk among ourselves. Our enemy is at the outskirts of the valley, and so Filimaya suggested that we meet here, where the waters of the Churn will keep our deliberations safe from spying eyes and ears." He looked from one person to the next. "Secrecy is everything, for this will be our only council of war."

Sylas felt his heart quicken.

"So here we are," continued Espasian. "Three Magrumen for the Suhl; Filimaya for the valley; Sylas and Naeo for themselves, because all rests upon them; and this gentleman, Jeremy Tasker, for the Merisi."

Sylas looked round and for the first time saw Tasker leaning against a large, smooth rock. The Salve had worked wonders, and he was transformed from the white and feverish figure Sylas had first met on the *Windrush*. Now, he stood straight, with colour in his cheeks and a keenness in his eyes. Even his hair had been restored to its previous splendour, with styled fronds sticking out at angles.

"Honoured," he said with a quick bow. He glanced at Espasian. "And... and the name's Tasker."

Espasian took a deep breath, as though preparing himself for a great effort. "So now we must first—"

"What about me?"

All eyes turned to Simia.

"Well... you said what everyone else was here for," she said, a little defiantly. "But what about me?"

There was a moment's silence. "You're here for yourself, Simsi, as ever," said Ash with a grin. It was not meant unkindly but Simia looked wounded.

"Yes, Simia, you *are* here for yourself," said Filimaya, glaring at Ash. "Because, as much as this is Sylas's and Naeo's journey, it is also yours. Isia herself told you that, remember?"

Simia brightened a little and narrowed her eyes at Ash.

"Good, so now we know who we are and why we're here!" said Espasian briskly. "Next, let us agree what it is that we face because only then may we form our plans. I will tell you what I know, and then others may do the same." He settled himself against the boulder. "We are under attack from the east. Those of us who fled across the Barrens were pursued all the way from the Circle of Salsimaine by something like half a division of Thoth's forces — probably all that were left in the Dirgheon. Ghor, Ghorhund, Hamajaks, Tythish, a few Ragers. We had a head start, and we'd probably have reached the valley unscathed, but by the time we reached the fringes of the Barrens there was something else on our trail. Something new." He shook his head grimly. "I believe now that they were Ogresh."

Filimaya looked stricken. "*Ogresh!*" she exclaimed. "How? They would be *years* in the birthing chambers!"

"Then we must assume that the Dirgh has been preparing for years," said Espasian. "Perhaps since the Reckoning because I am certain that is what they were. When they first came, they were wind and dust. By the time they reached the hills, they were shale and rock. In the forest, they were brush and timber."

Paiscion nodded. "I feared as much when I heard their cries. How many?"

"Twenty, perhaps more."

Paiscion raised his eyebrows. "That will go badly for us," he said quietly.

Filimaya hugged herself, as though against a sudden chill.

"And I'm afraid the east is not our only concern," continued Paiscion. "We are under attack from the west too. By my reckoning, an entire division has already descended from the Westercleft Hills and, judging by their pace, they will already be encircling the valley."

"A *division*?" repeated Ash. "Which division?" He winced in anticipation of the answer.

Paiscion pursed his lips. "The Fifth Imperial."

Ash sighed and dropped his head. "Imperials," he groaned. "This gets better and better."

The cavern fell quiet, and Sylas was once again aware of the weird silence of the waterfall, with just a drip, drip, drip in one corner of the chamber.

Tasker cleared his throat. "Shouldn't we talk about the Other too?" he asked, looking at Paiscion and Espasian. "Things are just as desperate there. The raids from the stone circles, the kidnappings, the attack on Winterfern. And then, of course, we lost Mr Zhi."

"*Mr Zhi?*" interjected Espasian, staring at Tasker as though he had spoken of an outrage. "He's... dead?"

Tasker nodded slowly.

Espasian's head and shoulders drooped, exposing three black trails rising up his neck. "How can such a thing be said so lightly," he murmured.

"Scarpia came," said Naeo, "her and a Ray Reaper — looking for me, I think. She was so powerful, Espasian, and Mr Zhi fought with her and defended us — defended me really. He said something about it being a time of sacrifice —" her eyes filled with tears — "but I didn't know what he meant by that, truly I didn't. If I'd known, I... I..." Her voice cracked and she looked down, fidgeting with the band round her wrist.

"You couldn't have done more, Princess," said Tasker. He fell silent for a moment. "But forgive me. If I'm to speak for the Merisi, can I bring us back to the Other? I didn't see it for myself, but if what I hear is true — about Thoth's appearance in the

Black — then everything has taken a much more sinister turn than we expected. I can tell you for certain that the Merisi simply aren't ready for this. We weren't preparing for war — or at least nothing on this scale. How could we? There are so few of us and we do everything in secret. An out-and-out war between the worlds? Well, that's completely beyond our capabilities. And what are we supposed to do about the Black? We don't even know what it is! We're not even remotely geared up for that! These are the ways of your world, not ours. If we're to have any chance, we're going to need your help." He looked around, a wild glint in his eye. "Well, I for one am going back. I've got to do what I can to help."

The gathering of Suhl was silent.

"There's something else we're not talking about," said Naeo finally. "Isia said that Sylas and I have to go back to Old Kemet, to the place where all this began. She said that that's where we might make sense of everything, perhaps even find a way to bring the worlds together. But, with the valley surrounded, how are we supposed even to get out? And, if we do, how will we get past the army on the Westercleft Plain?"

Her question echoed into the enchanted silence. Naeo looked at Espasian and he at Paiscion. Sylas turned to Simia and she to him. Moments passed, and to Sylas they felt like hours.

Finally Espasian cleared his throat. "Good," he said, rubbing his palms together. "So that is where we stand. Now, let us make a plan."

9

Farewell

"I give myself to the chime of the Passing Bell and bid
farewell *to the ordinary. Tonight, I am bound for the Other."*

THE BATTLE DRUMS FORMED a single noise now: those from the
east and those from the west, those beating out a march and those
thundering the promise of war. It was a dread sound, meant to
ferment fear, and Espasian knew not to think of it. Instead he
stood tall on the lakeside and watched the preparations aboard the
Windrush.

The ancient ship looked almost as grand as she had in the early
days when she had ferried the Suhl across that last stretch of sea
to the southern coast, where they would be taken onwards to the
vibrant plains of Salsimaine and, finally, to Grail. Her brass railings
shone like new beneath the cloudy sky, and her buttressed masts
towered high above the busy decks, sprouting a complexity of
rigging and yards and winches. Even her much-abused hull had
been restored to its former glory, rid of the many marks of tooth
and claw from battles recent and long ago. Altogether, the *Windrush*
looked almost ready for the impossible journey that lay before her.

"Almost," breathed Espasian, shaking his head as he watched
the final passengers climb the gangplank.

"You wish you were going with them, don't you?" came Bayleon's gravelly baritone. He was leaning against a tree, his giant arms crossed over his chest.

"Perhaps," said the Magruman. He turned to Bayleon. "But I don't envy them the journey."

"But you believe they can make it all the way to Old Kemet?"

Espasian considered this carefully. "I believe in those children — in Naeo and Sylas," he said. "There's greatness in them and it grows."

Bayleon squinted at the *Windrush*. "And yet it's much to ask of ones so young. I worry that we expect too much."

"I'm certain we expect too much," said Espasian with a shrug, "but what choice do we have?"

They fell silent for a moment, lost in thought. Bayleon's eyes followed a flash of red hair ducking into the lower decks. "You know there's something about that little one too," he said, nodding in her direction. "Simia Roskoroy."

Espasian's lip curled in a smile. "I know it, and I would rather Sylas and Naeo had her by their side than you or me." He stiffened and winced, then rolled a shoulder. "And what about Ash? Paiscion tells me he'll make a good captain."

Bayleon scratched his beard. "I think he'll do fine as a leader of the crew," he said. "And Fawl will more than make up for what he lacks in seamanship."

"Fawl..." repeated Espasian. "Wasn't he a Spoorrunner many moons ago?"

Bayleon nodded. "One of the best until he was injured in the siege of Jerusalem. You can't spoorrun with one arm, whatever your talents. But they say he's mastered the waves as well as ever he did the trail." He grunted and smiled. "I hear that these days he even talks like a seafarer! Ash will be in good hands, that's for certain. He's already made Fawl his Master of the Ship." He was quiet for a moment. "No," he said finally, "if I have doubts about Ash, they're not about him being a captain. They're about him being a Magruman."

Espasian met his gaze. "You don't think he's ready?"

"He may know all the wiles and ways of Essenfayle, but is he ready up here?" Bayleon tapped the side of his head. "There's an impulsiveness about him – a hastiness – and, beneath it all, a *doubt* that I find worrying."

Espasian peered back at the *Windrush*, his eyes searching the crowded deck until he picked out Ash's distinctive golden head of hair. "I've seen what you speak of," he said. "He thinks too much of impressing others and of the Three Ways for my liking. But he did well on his journey to the Other with Naeo. And I hear that Mr Zhi was impressed, which is quite something. It was he, you know, who first suggested that Ash be a Magruman."

Bayleon grunted and gave a quick nod.

Espasian sighed and shook his head. "But, as I say, I understand why you have your doubts. One thing's for certain: this journey will be almost as great a test of Ash as it is of Sylas and Naeo."

He paused, seeming to wrestle with his thoughts. Finally he cleared his throat and continued. "You know, Bayleon, being ready to be a Magruman – being... *worthy* of it – is not something absolute or enduring. I have often doubted my own worthiness. Indeed at times – many times – I have wished myself anything but a Magruman."

Bayleon eyed him closely, realising that he was no longer talking of Ash but of the past. Despite all the time they had spent together in recent days, the two men had never spoken of their argument out on the Barrens, on the way to Gheroth. Neither had they discussed the reason Bayleon had once so loathed Espasian – that on the final day of the Reckoning it was Espasian's orders he had been following — orders that had taken him away from his family in their hour of greatest need. The hour they lost their lives.

His face darkened. "Yes, it must be much to bear such responsibility," he blurted gruffly and turned away, pretending to be distracted by something on the *Windrush*. But, as he watched the toing and froing aboard the ship, his features filled with self-reproach. "But... I have come to know you well these past days, Espasian, and if someone is worthy to be called Magruman it is you." He turned back to his friend. "If young Ash deports himself half as well as you, then Sylas and Naeo are in good hands."

The Magruman met his eyes for a long moment. "You are kind, Bayleon — too kind, I fear." He bowed his head. "But thank you."

Bayleon regarded him, his features still taut. Then he reached down and picked up his pack. "Shouldn't we be getting started?" he asked.

Espasian smiled and nodded. He took up his own pack and hoisted it to his shoulder. "Come," he said, slapping the Spoorrunner's armoured shoulder. "Let us visit the Hollow and then press on. There's much to do."

§

Sylas stood by the mainmast, shaking his head in astonishment. He was gazing down the crowded deck, past the crew who rushed to stow bags and bales and chests to a hastily constructed timber frame in the forecastle of the ship. Suspended in the centre of that frame was the stalactite from the mines, and hanging from its very tip was the gleaming teardrop of Quintessence.

"How did you get it here?" he asked.

Ash leaned against the mast. "Well, Sylas, as much as I'd like to tell you that it was my formidable powers as a Magruman, we just sawed it off and carried it here." He raised an eyebrow. "It was heavy, mind."

"But how did you get it to... stay *on*?"

Ash laughed. "The question, my friend, is how did we get it to come *off*. That Quintessence stuff may have the look of liquid, but it's harder than rock. It wasn't my first choice to chisel through a column of stone, but that's what we had to do." He cocked his head on one side. "There's something about Quintessence, though. More than once, lugging it here, I thought I saw ripples across its surface, like it wasn't solid at all. Downright peculiar it was."

Just then the wind shifted from the east to blow across the waters of the lake. It brought with it a great thunder of battle drums from the head of the valley, louder and more urgent than any they had heard before.

Ash scratched in his matted curls. "The sooner we're out of here, the better," he said. He glanced at Sylas and then nodded towards the Quintessence. "Do you think it'll help?"

"I really don't know," Sylas said honestly. "I'm not even sure what it's *for*. It's all Paiscion's idea."

Ash stared at him. "Well, do me a favour and *pretend* that you do!" He tucked his thumbs under the lapel of his robe. "I'm the captain, you know. I have to think of morale!"

Sylas smiled faintly and was about to reply when he was distracted by the approach of a pile of papers on a pair of very thin and crooked legs. The heap of parchment staggered a little, then lunged towards him and, just as he thought it would walk straight into him, it suddenly drew back and teetered. Fathray's spectacled face peered round the stack.

"Never have I had to wade through such a derangement of documents! Such a litany of literary irrelevance!" cried the old Scribe. "Nothing is where it should be! It's taken me an unconscionable AGE to find just these few piffling parchments. But," he sighed, "here they are, such as they are." He dropped the lowest of the heap of papers on to the deck. "These are charts to take you back through the Kemetian Sea." He took a scroll from under his arm. "Here... blast!" He shook his head to disentangle it from his long hair. "Here is a detailed chart of the Nile itself, including its delta. From what I've read you'll need it. Then there are a few other maps that you should find useful." He dropped another pile of paper at Ash's feet. "And finally these are all we have on the Academy of Souls. Not a lot but important reading, and some written by Merimaat herself."

Ash looked down at all the documents with distaste. "Thank you, Fathray. I'm sure they'll be... fascinating."

Fathray narrowed his eyes. "Just make sure you use them, young man. They could make far more difference than all your antics and tricks, Magruman or no."

"Don't worry," said Ash with a winning grin. "I'll use them."

Fathray seemed satisfied and turned to Sylas. "I only wish I were well enough – and young enough – to come with you, Sylas."

"I wish it too, Fathray," replied Sylas.

"Well, well, make sure you keep up your scribbles in the Samarok. Yours will be one of the greatest of all chronicles, Sylas. We will make a Scribe of you yet!" He turned to go, then glanced back. "Speaking of the Samarok, don't forget to read it on your journey. I daresay there's much in there yet to be unravelled!"

"I will."

"Well then," said the Scribe, looking from one to the other, "good luck!"

"And to you, Fathray," said Ash. "Looks like you'll be needing it here too."

The whiskers of Fathray's moustache parted in a smile. "Well, I am not one for violence, but a good battle will give me plenty to write about!"

With that, he whirled about and rushed away, mumbling as he went.

§

Naeo looked down at her feet, struggling to control her feelings, but then her chest swelled.

"But I don't want to go!" she sobbed. "I can't leave you. Not again. I don't know what I'd do if something happened to you!"

Her father pulled her into his chest and held her, his face quivering with emotion. "You have to go, Naeo," he said, somehow forcing out the words in that calm, gentle voice she knew so well. "We all need you to go, and I'm not strong enough to come with you."

She sank further into him. "But I don't think I can," she murmured.

Bowe lowered his face to hers. "Do you remember the treehouse? The one near Grail?"

Naeo looked up with a wounded expression. "Of *course* I remember."

"Then meet me there," he said. "At sunset each day."

She frowned. "How?"

"In there," he said, tapping her forehead. "Every night at sunset, I'll be here." He tapped his own temple. "Meet me, in the treehouse. Do you understand?"

Naeo swallowed down another sob and nodded.

"Promise?"

She nodded again.

"Good," he said, brushing her golden hair away from her face. "Now, there isn't an easy way to say goodbye so just go, my Nay-no. Go and do what you were born to do."

Before she could reply he turned her by the shoulders and pushed her up the gangplank.

She walked numbly, on legs that were not her own. More than once she glanced back towards him, but somehow she kept going.

Bowe watched Naeo's faltering steps until she disappeared into the shadows of the lower deck, and then he let out a long, forlorn sigh and turned away.

Slowly, wearily, he walked back up the slope towards the forest. He was just reaching the first of the trees when he collided with someone in the crowd. It was a tall young man whose bald head was also marked with the tattoos of a Scryer, if rather disfigured by burns and scars. He blurted an apology and started to rush on, but Bowe grabbed him by the arm.

"Triste!" he exclaimed. "Don't you know me?"

Triste turned and blinked. "Bowe!" he cried. "Of course! But I wish I'd seen you sooner. I have to get to the ship and—"

"I know, it was I who asked for you to travel on the *Windrush*," said Bowe, still gripping his arm. "I won't keep you long."

A look of dawning realisation passed over Triste's face. "Ah!" he exclaimed. "I wondered why Paiscion was so insistent! I thought perhaps it was because I once studied Old Kemet, but there had to be more to it than that!"

"Much more, Triste. You're a gifted Scryer and just as importantly — perhaps more so — you know Sylas. For that reason Naeo will need you. She does not yet understand him. She thinks she does, but she doesn't. And so you have to help her see." He looked back towards the dark entrance into which his daughter had disappeared. "Do what I cannot. Teach her to know herself. *All* of herself."

The smile had long since fallen from Triste's face. "You honour me, Bowe. But I couldn't hope to do as you ask. Sylas and Naeo are like nothing I've ever seen. I just wouldn't know where to begin!"

"No one knows where to begin!" snapped Bowe, his face

flushing slightly. "Naeo has no idea why any of this is happening and yet there she is, boarding the *Windrush* and leaving everything dear to her!" He dropped his eyes, then patted Triste on the chest. "I'm sorry, Triste. You may doubt your skills, but I do not. You're a Scryer of rare talent. You will have some days on the ship to observe, and understand, and all I ask is that you do what you do best: see and learn. And then, when you're ready, teach."

Triste was about to answer when suddenly there was a cry from high above. It was the lookout in the crow's nest. "Smoke!" she yelled, waving frantically and pointing to a thin trail of grey coming from one of the hills. "That's it! That's the signal!"

Ash ran the length of the ship back to the quarterdeck, then turned and cupped his hands round his mouth. "Raise the gangplank!" he cried, and then rather hesitantly: "Hoist the..." He trailed off and cleared his throat. "Make all preparations!"

A very short, one-armed man with a ruddy face quickly joined Ash on the quarterdeck and whispered something in his ear. Ash gave a grateful nod, and all at once his new companion began bellowing orders in an unexpectedly deep, booming voice. "Cast off there!" he yelled, pointing with his one good arm. Then, "Away aloft!" he called, pointing again, this time up into the rigging. Instantly all of the rope ladders of the ship were thrumming with climbing men and women, making their way swiftly to the bundled sails. "Lay out!" he cried and then, when he was satisfied by what he saw, "Let fall! Hoist away!"

Bowe clapped Triste on the shoulder. "Go before they sail without you!"

Triste hesitated and met Bowe's eyes. "I can only promise to do the best I can, but thank you for your faith."

Bowe nodded. "Your best is all I can ask."

Triste gave a quick nod, then sprinted to the water's edge and leapt on to the gangplank even as it began to close. He darted inside and wheeled about, gazing out at the crowds. Just before the gangplank slammed shut he caught one last glimpse of Bowe standing at the top of the high bank. Their eyes met and Bowe lifted his hand to his heart.

Triste stood in the half-dark. "*Teach her to know herself. All of herself,*" he mumbled, shaking his head. "How am I supposed to—"

He stopped. His Scryer's eyes had detected a glow of emotion in the shadows. It was a vague pale blue of hope and at its heart was the piercing yellow of excitement or anticipation.

"I heard you might be coming," came a familiar voice.

He squinted into a shaft of light from a hatchway, and in the brightness he saw a small, lean figure and a tangle of wild red hair.

"Simsi!" he said, smiling. He cocked his head to one side. "So am I welcome on the adventure this time round?"

There was a glow of white teeth. "Perhaps," she said.

"I'm glad to hear it," said Triste. He walked across to her and lowered his voice. "Because I might just be needing your help."

10

A Thousand Miles

"It is as the great philosopher Lao Zi once said:
A journey of a thousand miles begins with a single step."'

SYLAS STOOD ALONE BEFORE the mainmast, wondering at the speed of the preparations. He had sailed aboard the *Windrush* before, of course, but never with a full seafaring crew; and he had never seen a ship rouse herself at battle pace. Fawl strode the length of the vessel, calling his commands, his broad, ruddy face stretched in a grin that lifted hearts and spurred on his crewmates. Sails seemed to fall from everywhere, and no sooner had they unfurled than they had been hauled taut and held fast. Now, gangs of men and women hurried here and there, heaving at ropes, tying them off and rushing on to their next well-drilled task. In a matter of moments, the grey sky was obscured by layer upon layer of swelling canvas, and already the deck stirred beneath them.

"Now, hold fast!" bellowed Fawl. "Let her run!"

There was a great cheer from the shore, and they surged out on to the lake.

Sylas joined the chorus of goodbyes and waved to Bowe, who stood alone at the edge of the forest. His mother too was at the railing, bidding new friends farewell and watching Sylva drift away.

Sylas was relieved that she was there with him. As perilous as their journey would be, he could not bear to be parted again; something he felt all the more because Naeo and Bowe were not so lucky. Much as the Scryer had wanted to come, he had been far too unwell to travel.

The decks lurched as the grand old vessel caught a gust of wind and veered into the centre of the lake, her rigging trim and her keel carving the glassy surface. There was only a narrow span of water between her and the towering, forested hill that formed one side of the valley. But already she raced ahead as though on an open sea. Fawl and Ash called orders from the quarterdeck, but there was less urgency now. The ship was underway, her sails set and the crew's pressing tasks were done. Instead they turned back to Sylas, their faces filled with expectation.

Ash appeared at his side. "We'll stay under full sail," he said. "We can't stop now, so don't hang about!" He patted Sylas's shoulder and stepped back to the helm.

Sylas did his best to hold firm. This was his moment. It had to be. He felt the eyes of the ship upon him, and he knew that everyone was relying on him. And yet it was his mother's gaze that he felt most keenly. He was not sure which was worse: to stand before her, with everyone's hopes at stake, and to fail, or to do what he must, but in so doing make himself even more different in her eyes — even more a part of her '*impossible*'.

But then, to his relief, he was taken away from his thoughts. He felt a familiar twist in his belly and a shift in his bones, and he welcomed it. It was undeniable. A stirring of something bigger than himself.

Naeo appeared from a hatch and walked purposefully across the deck to take her place next to him. The Merisi Band seared Sylas's wrist, and his body felt as though it might be riven limb from limb. But it was not like before, in the Garden of Havens, when they had first come together. Now, he knew how to use this force that would drive them apart. Now, it had a purpose.

The crew watched, spellbound, as the two children moved as one, looking up to the sails, down at the Quintessence, then out past the bowsprit to the approaching shore. All watched in astonishment as the twin parts of the Merisi Band shimmered as though from some internal fire, and then sent out tendrils of silver and gold, which coiled and entwined their wrists.

Naeo delved into herself for the pain she had felt saying goodbye to her father, and found it already buried deep, in the part of her heart that had grown hard and strong. And she set it loose. She freed her pain and let that raw power come howling forth, out into the world, into the skies, raking the clouds and reaching on, and up, to the highest winds. There it became a gale, mighty and irresistible. And this she brought back to the ship.

For the occupants of the *Windrush* there was no warning. One moment she was sailing steadily towards land, about to run aground. In the next, the ship was struck by a fist of wind so powerful that her ropes sang and her timbers squealed. As she struck the shore, all aboard gasped and clung even tighter to the railings, not because the ship had come to a shuddering halt, but because she surged on. Her bow lifted and she mounted sand, and mud, and grass as though they were the lightest surf.

As Naeo was with the winds, Sylas was with the earth, and grit, and trees. He seized his doubts and fears about his mother and turned them to his ends. He imagined his maze of feelings to be the forest ahead of the ship and, as he sought a way through, the trees became soft and yielding, parting before him as though showing him the way. Trunks leaned apart before the *Windrush*, drawing themselves aside and forming an open avenue all the way up the hillside to its very peak. The ship surged on in the gale, her keel sliding against mossy trunks, rolling over roots, and always smoothly and easily as though the timbers were themselves part of the living forest and it was helping its own. As soon as she had passed, the great trees straightened up, their limbs mingling so that the forest once again looked like any other.

"Now she's running!" cried Fawl, a smile spreading across his leathery face. "Now she's running!"

The crew were spellbound, gaping in wonder, but Simia dashed among them, her eyes sparkling with delight. She followed a grand old redwood from the prow all the way towards the stern, resting her hand on it as it passed. As she came to the rear railing, she patted the tree farewell and looked about to share her excitement. She spotted Sylas's mother resting against the bars, her face fixed in astonishment.

Simia stepped up beside her and touched her hand. "Sylas is doing this!" she shouted above the howling gale. She pointed to the helm. "You can see it! Naeo is with the winds — Sylas is with the forest!"

Amelie turned to look at Sylas for the first time since the ship had begun its climb. She saw how his eyes danced, how his and Naeo's hands were looped about with rings of silvery gold. But it was his face that convinced her of the impossible. She knew that expression from when he was little: his brow furrowed in concentration; his eyes keen and bright; his expression one of barely bridled excitement.

She raised her hand to her mouth. "He is," she breathed. "He really is!"

Sylas was too engrossed in his task to notice. He guided the ship carefully through a copse of giant redwoods and then turned her past a bluff to trace a path below a small ridge. There the hill steepened, rising sharply towards its peak, but instantly Naeo's gale swelled, buffeting the sails until they strained at their fastenings, heaving the hull up the slope.

The crew were still transfixed as the last trees of the valley sailed past, but suddenly they were startled by a shout from the crow's nest. The lookout pointed ahead, to where a wide sweep of open sky now began to spread before them. The *Windrush* forged on through thinning trees, heaving herself over one final outcrop of mossy stone until finally she lunged forward on to the soft grass of a level hilltop. The winds eased and the ship slowed to a halt.

For a long moment she lay utterly still and silent. Sylas, Naeo and their companions stared ahead breathlessly.

Before them, and stretching into the distance, was a shifting sea. Its surface rippled with fur and scale, glistened with blade and pike. Its swell and heave were made of swaying forms and bristling manes, and muscle and steel. What sails there were on this living flood were not white but red, and from their bloody centre each showed a face to the world. Skull-like and formless, its empty eyes moving with the wind and seeing all, it was the face of Thoth.

And then, from somewhere in the seething sea, there came the beat of a single drum — deep and low, its rhythm slow and deliberate.

Boom tah-boom, boom tah-boom...

And then another joined it, this time off to one side among the massed regiments of Ghor and Ghorhund.

Boom tah-boom, boom tah-boom...

Now two drums became five, scattered across the ocean of troops, and soon five were ten. Just when it seemed that they could gain no more volume the rhythm rose to a crescendo of drums thrashing out a deafening thunder.

At once the great sea became a tempest. Armour clashed against shield; pikes and swords scythed the air; Hamajaks leapt, apelike, on the shoulders of others; ranks of Ragers burned red, stamping and snorting with fury; Ghorhund strained at leather leashes and let out crazed howls; formations of Ghor swayed back and forth, back and forth, baring their teeth and ripping at the turf.

Aboard the *Windrush* faces that had been full of hope and wonderment grew pale. Eyes that had been filled with light dulled and dropped to the decks. Unconsciously Simia and Amelie drew close, as if against an unforgiving cold. In the rear of the ship, Ash leaned heavily on the helm and despaired.

11

The Tempest

"But if to unite our worlds we must set loose this unknowable power, what is to stop us falling slave to it, or being consumed by the tempest that must surely follow?"

SYLAS KNEW AT ONCE that it was hopeless. The army before them was no lake or forest open to the touch of Essenfayle. This was a gathering of evil, a collection of men and man-made things that were surely impervious to his powers.

But still his heart would not settle. He felt Naeo at his side making him more than he was and, with her there, some part of him felt that anything was possible. He looked down at their hands pressed tightly together, and he watched the silvery-gold trails shimmering from their wrists. And as he watched, he remembered.

He remembered the Quintessence.

Sylas lifted his eyes slowly to the timber frame, and the finger of rock, and the golden teardrop. And he knew what he had to do.

They both knew.

Naeo was already lifting their entwined hands towards the scaffold. In that moment, the trails of gold about their wrists unfurled, reaching out beyond them, weaving along the deck. They swept between the despondent crew, slid through the lattice of ropes, and finally they passed between the timber struts of the frame.

For the crew of the *Windrush* time itself seemed to stand still. The battle cry of Thoth's army seemed to fall away, and the despair of moments before was almost forgotten. All eyes were trained on Sylas and Naeo and on the probing, shining tendrils snaking over the deck.

"What's... *happening*?" murmured Amelie.

Simia took a step forward. "Something amazing!" she said breathlessly.

And then the tendrils reached the teardrop and touched.

To everyone's astonishment, the swollen drop of Quintessence quivered and began swinging slowly but precariously from the finger of rock, as though it was not solid at all but liquid. Almost at once its bulbous base started to sink downwards, as if no longer able to support its own weight, while its upper part stretched and narrowed until the two halves became so fine and delicate that they could barely be seen.

Then, quite suddenly, it snapped.

When the teardrop hit the deck, it made no splash and no sound. It simply pooled outwards from amidships, flowing forward on to the forecastle and back over the quarterdeck. It flooded beneath the feet of the crew, making them leap in fright, but it continued its journey, leaving them untouched. When it reached the railings, it fell in glistening curtains over the sides, sweeping down the hull like some magical cloak. Fingers of gold sprang up the masts, the rigging and the rope ladders, engulfing everything in their path until from the deck the skies seemed to be criss-crossed with gold.

Amelie gasped, staring with childish wonder. The sails were no longer white but great billowing sheets of gold and silver, flowing and rippling like liquid light. Now, the entire ship blazed, bathing the surrounding trees in a shimmering glow, but still the Quintessence climbed and, as it reached the very pinnacle of the mast, it enveloped the fluttering standard. In a trice, the Suhl feather at its centre was transformed into a blazing gold.

Ash gazed at Sylas and Naeo and grinned. "By my threadbare britches..." he breathed.

Heart pounding, Sylas reached out and ran his finger over a shining rope. It felt warm and wet to the touch but, to his surprise, it left no trace on his fingertip. Neither did the Quintessence shift at his touch. It was as though the entire ship had been plated in silvery gold. He had no idea what it might mean for them, but for the first time since they had arrived at the hilltop he felt a stirring of hope.

But, even as the *Windrush* had been transformed, so had the waiting army. At first its chants and drums had fallen silent, but now the Westercleft Plain resonated with a new sound: the sharp report of a horn calling the imperial regiments to arms. Almost instantly fifteen or twenty smaller horns gave their answer in sharper, higher notes, and then there was a commotion out on the plains. In the near distance, one of the few remaining patches of open ground flooded with troops from the south and east, bearing before them the standards of the Gherothian Imperial Guard. Foremost among them was a company of Tythish who were using their long limbs to scuttle at an unnatural speed, like spiders.

"If we're still going to go, we need to go now!" called Ash, looking between Sylas and Naeo. "Are you ready?"

There was a moment's hesitation, then, as one, they both nodded.

Ash whirled about. "Fawl!" he hollered. "Set sail, if you please!"

"Aye!" shouted the Master of the Ship with another wide grin. He began barking orders in all directions, emphasising them with sweeps of his one powerful arm. And, as before, the crew responded with impressive discipline. This time they did not rush to the ladders and the ropes, for the sails were already set; instead they took up posts along the railings, and in the stern, and on either side of the forecastle. Triste walked smartly up to the bow, stopping next to the bowsprit. At first Sylas watched all this uncomprehendingly, but slowly he realised that these were battle positions and he felt his pulse quicken.

And then his stomach turned and his lungs seemed to twist beneath his ribs. Naeo was once again taking his hand, and now the discomfort was worse than ever, as though it had been heightened by the Quintessence. But even then Sylas did not pull away. He knew that this was right; that this was what had to happen.

He closed his fingers round hers and they began.

Naeo summoned all her strength and reached up into the winds. They came more slowly, gradually filling the sails and drawing the ropes taut but, to her surprise, the hull shifted more sharply than before, sending the *Windrush* off at a lively pace. Now, the ship responded to the mildest gust, as though she was as light as the feather flapping from her masthead.

She left the hilltop and began her descent, charging over the turf as though barely grazing the blades of grass. Sylas was already working fast, picking his way ahead, praying that the trees would respond as quickly as they must. They were fewer now, but they still dotted the hillside, and there was no clear way through. But, to his relief, the first cluster heaved themselves apart, trunks and limbs creaking, and the ship whistled between them. This too was different from before. The timbers of the *Windrush* no longer squealed against the bark, but slipped over it without a sound. The crew stared as the sparse forest whisked past in a blur of greens and oranges and browns, the trunks ahead folding back like the unfurling pages of a book.

Ash mounted the quarterdeck and cupped his hands. "Ready!" he bellowed.

His voice carried above the whistling winds and everyone responded, reaching for the pikes and poles stowed beneath the railings, raising them in preparation. Triste clambered on to the bowsprit and twined one arm through the ropes to hold himself fast. Sylas and Naeo tightened their grip and cleared their minds.

Then all eyes turned to look ahead to the unfolding forest.

The *Windrush* was hurtling down the hillside now, almost taking to the air, so there was no warning when she came to the edge of the forest. In a trice, the last of the trees fell away and a black-and-grey vista opened before her. It was made up of beasts and warriors, muscle and mane, sword and spear. Instantly the war drums struck up, and a great throaty roar rose from the ranks of Tythish, Ghor, Ragers and Hamajaks.

But the *Windrush* was not for slowing. She tore down the final stretch of the hill, skipping across an expanse of bracken and through a gully of shale and shingle. The crew crouched as the keel bucked and yawed, swerving directly towards the waiting army.

At the heart of this something happened to Sylas and Naeo. It began where the Quintessence trailed about their wrists, and now it grew up their arms and into their chests. It was a feeling of oneness — not just with each other, though they felt closer than ever before, but with the *Windrush*. In that moment, the press of wind in her sails was the air in their lungs; the joists of her hull were the ribs in their chests; her rigging was the maze of sinews in their own bodies. It was as though the Quintessence that looped about their wrists and coated the decks had melded to make one living whole.

The *Windrush* charged towards a regiment of Sur: not beasts but men, skirmishers with bristling steel dented and tarnished by a hundred battles. As the gleaming hull tore across the final yards, their battle cries died in their throats. The first ranks panicked, pushing back into those behind, and suddenly the disciplined line broke. Men bellowed as they scrambled for safety, leaving a wide gash in the lines.

Into this rift plunged the *Windrush*, knocking aside those too slow or too panicked to jump clear, swerving this way and that as Sylas and Naeo sought out the clearest path. High on the bowsprit, Triste began to wave with his free hand, pointing left and then right, Scrying the thoughts of the army like a mariner reading a treacherous sea. Sylas and Naeo followed his every signal, leaning into tight turns, propelling the *Windrush* deep into the ocean of weapons. Still she had received barely a blow, and some of the crew cried out in delight, jabbing the air with their poles and pikes.

But now the path of the ship took her beyond the Sur, into the Ghor and Ghorhund. These were unafraid, wild-blooded beasts, and they were not about to run. As the *Windrush* swept into them, some were knocked out of the way, but many more threw themselves at the exposed sides of the ship. They grasped at shining timbers and gnashed at the golden anchor but, as they tried to sink their teeth and claws into the ship, the Quintessence responded. In places, it grew anvil-hard, repelling their biting teeth. In others, it became oily smooth, sending them sliding, slithering and howling back into the ranks.

Still the *Windrush* sped on, and for some happy moments Sylas and Naeo began to believe that perhaps she might yet weather the tempest.

But then came the Tythish, sweeping in from both sides, their long limbs bearing them high over the flow of bodies and within easy reach of the deck. Among them leapt the Hamajaks, acrobatic and lithe like apes, and Ragers flaring their hellish red and charging straight into the hull, knocking it from its course and throwing the crew off their feet.

Suddenly the ship was in chaos. Tythish clung to the railings and reached across the decks, clawing at legs and arms. Three of the crew were flung from the ship, and more were fighting for their lives with poles and pikes. The Hamajaks were on deck too, beating their chests in triumph. Ash was wrestling with one by the helm; Triste was on the bowsprit with another on his back and seemed about to fall.

Sylas glanced back and saw, to his horror, that Simia and his mother too were fighting for their lives. Simia was jabbing a pole at the moonlike eyes of one of the Tythish, which had hold of her tunic, while Amelie was fending off the grasping, arm-long fingers of another.

It was too much for Sylas to bear and, with a thought for nothing but helping them, he let go of Naeo's hand.

Naeo grabbed him in a vicelike grip and yanked him back, but their delicate bond had already faltered. They both felt a sharp pain in their wrists and the familiar, gnawing sickness, and then the ship plunged and shuddered into the earth. All on the deck were thrown forward amid an eruption of soil and shale, flailing about for something to cling to. Sylas and Naeo also began to fall, but felt themselves pulled back by the collar.

"What are you doing?" screamed a voice behind them.

It was Ash, his face white and smeared with sweat, his new robes torn and bloodied. He yelled something else, but his words were drowned out by a horrifying roar of triumph from the beasts around the ship. Ash glanced at the swarming, boiling masses of Hamajaks and Ragers, Tythish and Ghor and, in desperation, he grabbed Sylas's and Naeo's hands and squeezed them tightly together.

Sylas and Naeo fought through the pain and the fear, and tried to find what they had lost. Naeo pressed her eyes shut and allowed that fear to swell within her like an unstoppable force, and she made it her strength. She held these feelings close, powerful and consuming, and she reached for the winds.

Sylas saw his mother scrambling from Tythish fingers and, as his shame and horror surged within him, he seized upon them and made them his own. He poured them into the spars and joists of the *Windrush*, into her mighty masts and sails, and he drove her on. He heaved her clear of the earthen furrow in which she was trapped, and steered onwards, into the enemy. He heard the thump of shields and shoulders against the keel, the screech of claws running down the hull, but still he pressed on faster and faster.

Unsure which way to turn, he looked ahead, to the bowsprit: to where Triste should have been showing him the way. But there was no one there. The ropes that the Scryer had clung to were torn, still swinging where Triste had surely fallen.

A new rage burned in Sylas. He shifted his fingers between Naeo's and took an even tighter hold. The Merisi Band glowed with a fierce light and, in response, so did the *Windrush*. She surged on, her bow lifting and cleaving through the army. Sylas's spirits lifted as he saw that there was not far to go — open meadows shimmered greenly just above the black tempest.

But there were still Hamajaks on deck and Tythish clinging to the ship's sides, and where one fell another always found its way aboard.

Ash ran up, his face still pale and his hair matted with sweat. "Take her down again!" he yelled.

"Down?" repeated Naeo, incredulous.

"Yes! Let her dig in!"

They both looked at him in astonishment.

"But we'll go slower!" shouted Naeo.

Ash gave her a crazed grin. "I know! Just keep the bow high and take her down!"

Sylas and Naeo felt each other's doubts, but they did as they had been commanded. There was a growl and clatter as the keel sank into the ground, throwing up a towering wake of soil and earth that pelted the chasing army behind. As she plunged even deeper, the earth roared up the sides of the ship until it could be seen above the railings. One of the Tythish was sent flying, caught in the churn of soil and stones. As they pulled themselves up the railings, two Hamajaks were pummelled by the mud and shingle, and fell squealing into the morass.

But already the *Windrush* was slowing. Sylas and Naeo glanced anxiously at Ash just as he strode into the centre of the main deck, his head high and his robes billowing. He threw out his arms towards each side of the ship, then closed his hands into fists. One of the Tythish saw this and scrambled towards him, but it was too late.

The young Magruman drew his arms together and, as they closed before his chest, the plumes of earth on either side of the ship turned in the air and swept forward and inward, arching over the ship. They rained down with crushing force, not as a deluge but as fingers of soil and grit, columns of mud and stone. Each swept the deck, lashing down upon the shoulders of the Tythish guard and the backs of the Hamajaks. Amid a chorus of screams and yelps, black bodies were sent sprawling across the decks and spinning over the sides.

For the first time Sylas saw Ash for the Magruman that he was. His fists were open now, and his fingers wide, dancing in the air like a pianist at the keyboard. As each finger lifted and turned, so the great hands of earth turned and leapt, clawing the decks and raking the last desperate Hamajaks over the brass rails and into the rear ranks of the enemy.

As the final stragglers fell clear, Ash closed his hands and swept them wide, and in an instant the trails of earth and shingle joined once again into two great flows down the sides of the ship.

He staggered a little and sank to his knees. He looked at his hands, turning them over as though struggling to believe what they had done.

The *Windrush* carved her way onwards through the scattered lines of the rearguard. These were conscripts drawn from the fringes of the Empire, and they had no stomach to fight this strange enchantment, which had swept like a fiery blade through the rest of the army. They levelled half-hearted glancing blows at the bow, but then leapt clear, watching the ship pass out on to open fields, leaving upturned earth in her wake, her shining sails catching a pool of sunlight so that the pasture around shimmered with gold.

The hull rose now, no longer carving into the soil, but once again skipping lightly over the surface and, as the Suhl standard cracked and blazed, the *Windrush* set sail for the south and the open sea.

12
Where it Counts

*"I see now that for all its sacrifice, secrecy and hardship,
my journey with the Merisi is a gift and a privilege.
Here, in the Other, all the theorising and training makes
a glorious kind of sense. This is* Where it counts*."*

FILIMAYA AND PAISCION SLOWED as they approached the top of
the hill, trying to delay the inevitable and have just a few more
moments together, alone. But, far too soon, they saw Tasker
beckoning to them to join him near the crest. They gave one
another a faint smile, then squeezed together their enfolded fingers
and picked up their pace, choosing to look ahead and not dwell
on what could not be.

They could see from Tasker's beaming smile that the news was
good.

"Whatever they're doing, it's working," he said excitedly as he
led them on through the forest towards the signal fire. "The army
started moving away as soon as the horns sounded." He slowed
and glanced back at them. "What *are* they doing?"

Paiscion and Filimaya exchanged a glance and smiled.

"You wouldn't believe us if we told you," said Paiscion.

They had been below at Filimaya's favoured vantage point as

the drama of the *Windrush* had unfolded. It was a little-known cave mouth — the same entrance in which she and Paiscion had met when they were young, with their lives still ahead of them, and their love for one another fresh and fierce, and growing ever stronger. It had seemed the right place to be in these last moments together, before they had to part yet again.

It had been the perfect place to observe the *Windrush* too. Standing there, before the cave, they had had a wonderful view of her as she climbed the hills and then — inexplicably, wonderfully — doused herself in a blaze of gold. In that moment, Paiscion and Filimaya had held hands just as they had in their youth and, as then, they had felt that anything might be possible.

When they reached the signal fire, a single column of white smoke still climbed through the leaves.

Paiscion turned to Tasker. "Where are the provisions?" he asked.

"Already down at the lookout," said Tasker. "Don't worry, we're ready."

Filimaya drew a long breath. "Well," she sighed, "you had better take us down."

Paiscion glanced at her. "You don't have to come, my love."

She raised a hand. "I want to see you safely out of the valley," she said.

Tasker looked from one to the other, then flashed them his golden-toothed smile. "It's just down here," he said, nodding to a faint path in the undergrowth.

The track led them through thinning trees until they began descending the other side of the hill. Soon they were pushing their way through a tangle of rhododendron bushes and great knots of brambles, and could barely see the path ahead. When they reached the enchanted fringes of the valley, Tasker held out his gloved hand as he had been taught, and at once the foliage warped and resettled, allowing them to pass freely from the Valley of Outs.

They continued until the thicket began to thin a little, and finally Tasker stopped. He put his finger to his lips and slowly parted the screen of leaves.

Before them lay another wide valley, a sluggish river winding along its floor between sloping meadows dotted with oaks. Other than this scattering of trees, the valley and the hills beyond it were bare, covered only with turf and bracken.

Tasker pointed upstream, to the north. "Look," he whispered.

There, just disappearing over a rise, was the rear end of a column of several hundred troops, perhaps as many as a large battalion. Judging by their drab uniforms and long pikes, some of them were Sur, but others sported the writhing tails and red crests of Ragers. Above this Ra'ptah regiment was an ensign, from which glowered the visage of Thoth. His staring face was surrounded by a number of other symbols, including the two concentric circles of the Imperial army.

"They're making their way to the other side of the valley," whispered Tasker excitedly. He turned to Paiscion and tipped his head. "Just as you predicted."

Paiscion's eyes searched the valley floor, and then the folds of the far hillside. "It certainly looks that way," he said cautiously. "But we'll have to be careful. They may have left lookouts."

"Perhaps we should send a scout," suggested Filimaya anxiously.

The Magruman considered this, but shook his head. "No time. They will soon be back, whether or not the *Windrush* finds a way through." He turned to her, and when he did so his expression became tender, and his voice softened. "We need to leave now."

Filimaya smiled at Tasker. "May Paiscion and I... have a second?"

Tasker gazed at her for a moment, then seemed to understand. "Of course!" he blurted. "I'll just... make some final preparations."

He walked over to his backpack, fiddled with it, patted it, then smiled awkwardly and retreated into a thicket.

Filimaya turned to Paiscion and smiled that familiar smile. It was one he had seen many times before: a brave smile, the smile she gave him when they had to part, yet again, so that each could do what they were bound to do. They said their farewell in the same way as ever, so that perhaps it would hurt a little less. Filimaya mouthed those words he loved to hear, and then she took his face in her hands and kissed him, not deeply as when they were young but still full of yearning and tenderness. He held her close, and whispered to her, and then kissed her one last time.

But, however well-practised their goodbye, something was different. As Filimaya made her way back through the thicket and bid Tasker farewell, she was thinking only of Paiscion's whisper, and how it had faltered at the end as he spoke those final words in her ear. And back in the clearing, as Paiscion found his pack and drew it over his shoulder, he was thinking only of Filimaya's hands. Because he was quite certain that when they had held his face they had trembled.

§

Corporal Lucien stepped out of the sanctuary of the military vehicle and into a world of noise. Helicopters chattered overhead, trucks roared their way into the camp and a public-announcement system blared out a harsh, insistent voice.

"*Unit commanders to report to block H16 immediately. Repeat, unit commanders...*"

Lucien winced and pulled up the collar of his khaki coat as though to shelter himself from the din.

He looked across at his young escort. "All right, let's go," he said.

A fidgeting, hassled-looking soldier led him swiftly along an avenue of white tents, all of which hummed with activity. At times the young private was so full of nervous energy that he seemed about to break into a run, and Lucien had to bark at him to slow down. He had seen it many times before. This was how all the youngsters were when they first found themselves in combat, and he knew the importance of a raised voice to remind them of their training.

At the end of the avenue they turned and hurried between two rows of shabby shipping containers, and then emerged before some low, ugly buildings huddling at the edge of the camp. The private led him to the nearest of these, then pulled up sharply. Breathing heavily, he stepped back to make way and gave a salute.

Lucien stared at the nameplate above the door, which read VETERINARY CLINIC. "Are you *sure* this is where you were meant to take me, private?" he asked wearily.

The young soldier cleared his throat nervously. "Yes, sir! I was given specific instructions, sir!"

Lucien sighed. "All right then," he said, patting him on the shoulder and pushing on the door. Then he turned. "Private, try to relax. There's enough tension around here without you charging around like a monkey that's lost its nuts. Get me?"

The young man's eyes widened and he clicked his heels. "Yes, sir! Sorry, sir!"

Lucien rolled his eyes. He produced a small paper bag from his coat pocket. "Here, have a lemon sherbet."

The private stared at him, then at the bag. He extended a hand and snatched up a sweet as though it was an egg in a snake's nest. "Thank you, sir!"

Lucien sighed, popped a lemon sherbet in his mouth, then gave a wilting salute.

He breathed an inward sigh of relief as the door closed behind him, leaving him in the quiet and calm of an entrance hall. It was drab and grey, its walls covered with peeling posters about animal infections and viruses.

He crunched his sherbet. "Weird," he grunted.

He walked into a deserted corridor and headed for a set of double doors through which he could hear a murmur of voices. Just before he reached them a young woman stepped out and nearly dropped her bundle of papers in surprise at seeing him there.

"Can I help you?" she asked, in a slight German accent.

"Corporal Lucien, ma'am," he said, straightening and managing a salute. "I was told to report here and to ask for—"

"For the love of lemons, don't salute me!" snapped the woman. "Do I *look* like an officer?"

Lucien raised his eyebrows and took the opportunity to take note of her white coat, her rather severe but pretty face marked by a recent gash across the forehead, the colourful poppy scarf about her neck and the furry slippers on her feet.

"Er, no, ma'am," he said, trying not to stare at the slippers.

"And drop the ma'am too!" she said, stepping forward and holding out her hand. "Yes, I was told to expect you, Corporal. I'm Dr Martha Drescher, but here they just call me Dresch."

Lucien saw now what made her so pretty: she had eyes that smiled even when she was being a bit of a witch.

He shook her hand. "Good to meet you," he said. "But... we're not really supposed to use first names, are we? Not in camp at least."

The woman gave a theatrical glance up and down the corridor before looking back at him. "I don't think anyone's listening," she said, leaning in conspiratorially. "And don't worry, no one will inform on you. I only allow freethinkers in *my* lab." She narrowed her eyes. "But are *you* a freethinker?"

Lucien smiled. "Call me Lucien. No one uses my first name."

She looked at him doubtfully. "Why not? Are you one of those Gilberts? Don't say you're a Humphrey!"

"I'm a James," he said, laughing. "But people do really call me Lucien."

"I don't know why you'd hide a perfectly good name like James," Dresch said with a shrug. Quite openly she looked him up and down, taking in his muscular build, the slight heaviness round his waist, the handgun on his belt and the cast on his arm, on which were sketched caricatures of several prominent army generals. She arched an eyebrow and smiled. "Well, Lucien, I don't know why you've been assigned to me. I hardly need a bodyguard on an army base, for pity's sake! And I can't be holding your hand, not with all this going on."

Lucien gave her a level look. "I think the idea is that I hold *your* hand, not the other way round."

She sighed and turned back towards the double doors. "Well, let's see who needs to hold whose hand once we're in the lab," she said.

Lucien started after her. "Why? What are you *doing* here exactly?"

"We're working on the stuff everyone's talking about," she said over her shoulder. "The Black."

Lucien's steps faltered. "You have it... here?"

"That's right. Of course, we still have no idea what it really is, but then we've only had a couple of days."

She pushed the doors wide to reveal a room buzzing with activity. There were three long lab benches made up of folding tables, and gathered round them were fifteen or twenty white-coated scientists, some poring over books and microscopes, others working feverishly with pipettes and Petri dishes and glass slides. The walls were lined with bulky, complex machines, their glowing displays alive with scrolling data and graphs.

Such was the industry of the place that no one seemed to notice them enter. Dresch led Lucien to one end of the room where there were three large glass cylinders, each the size of a tree trunk, running floor to ceiling. All of them were almost entirely full of an opaque liquid as black as night.

Lucien walked slowly round the nearest cylinder. "Is this it?"

Dresch nodded. "Uh-huh."

"So what *do* you know about it?"

She shrugged. "Very little. It isn't like anything we've seen before. We don't understand its physical properties, we don't understand its chemistry and we don't know where it came from." She nodded at the lab equipment. "We're doing all the usual analysis: separation, extraction, precipitation, spectrometry, chromatography, electrophoresis — you name it, we're trying it — but it just doesn't make any scientific sense. So far, it really has the better of us."

Lucien looked round the room and saw how feverishly the scientists were working, some of them dashing from station to station, some working so quickly with their instruments that he marvelled at their skill. But he also noticed their expressions of perplexity, and the rings beneath their eyes. On the walls he saw an array of whiteboards marked with writing that had been crossed out and equations that had been struck through.

"All we really know about it is what it does," continued Dresch. "It seems to bubble up everywhere, from places deep below ground, perhaps somewhere very far down in the earth's crust. We think it rises through fissures until it finds its way to the surface or — worse — into groundwater. It's already reached most rivers and reservoirs, and it won't be long before it's in the entire water supply."

"And once it's there?"

"That's the strange thing. It doesn't *do* anything as far as we can see. It drifts and accumulates. And if it comes into contact with people — if someone drinks it or touches it — it seems to do the same inside the human body. Drift and accumulate."

Lucien narrowed his eyes. "Like an infection?"

"We're not sure if it's strictly an infection, but it does build up, and it seems to cause some pain. But another effect we have recorded is in here." She tapped a finger on her temple. "It seems to... *verwirren*... What's that in English...? Fog... no, muddle — it *muddles* the mind. Affects our ability to think clearly."

Lucien turned back to the giant cylinders of Black, his eyes moving from one to the next. "And is what they say true?" he asked, lifting his injured arm and touching the glass of the nearest cylinder. "That it came *alive*?"

Dresch pursed her lips. "Much as the scientist in me is screaming 'no', that's exactly what seemed to happen. Even our test samples started behaving strangely: moving of their own accord, slapping against the glass, spilling out of the equipment. It's bizarre." She gave the cylinders a long, troubled look, then frowned. "You didn't see it for yourself? Where've you been?"

Lucien shook his head. "I was in a weapons facility. It was attacked, and we've been locked down ever since."

Dresch looked at him with new interest. "You saw an attack?"

"I was in the thick of it," said Lucien, pointing at the cast on his arm and then to a wound on the back of his neck.

Dresch pointed to the gash across her forehead. "Me too," she said. "An Infection Research lab, in Germany."

"That place in Brunswick? I heard about it. Sounded... bad."

Dresch did not answer, but her eyes became distant for a moment and she gave a shudder.

Lucien knew that look. He had seen enough of it over the past few days. "And that's what brought you here?" he asked quickly.

She sighed and raked her fingers through her hair, as though to sweep away the memories. "There was nothing to stay for, put it that way. And this place needed an epidemiologist with the right experience. I have the right experience."

Lucien grunted. "I can't help feeling they could make better use of my experience out there, where it counts."

Dresch's eyelids flickered. "'Where it *counts*?'"

Lucien drew himself up nervously, realising he had misspoken. "I mean where the fight is, if there's going to be one."

She stared at him with a look of disbelief, then grabbed the sleeve of his coat and pulled him towards the door. "Come with me."

Scarf flying out behind her, Dresch led him from the room, down the corridor and back to the main entrance. She pushed through the swinging door and out into the warm summer air, which still thrummed with the noise of the camp. She pointed to the nearest of the white tents.

"Do you know what's in there?"

Lucien realised where this was heading. "Hospital beds," he said reluctantly.

"Exactly. One hundred and twenty to be precise. And, in that particular tent, almost every one of them is occupied by someone affected by the Black. Civilian and military." She turned and started to walk away. "But that's not all," she called.

She strode along the side of the building until she reached a rusted ladder leading to the roof. "Come on!"

Lucien sighed and jogged over. He looked up just in time to see Dresch's furry slippers skipping up the upper rungs of the ladder and then disappearing on to the roof. His powerful limbs propelled him swiftly after her, despite his injured arm, and in moments he was stepping on to the flat roof.

Dresch was looking back towards the camp. "Go on, take a look."

Lucien gazed around slowly. Before him was the huge military camp encircled by wire fences and sentry towers. He saw now that it was dominated by a vast regiment of identical white tents, at least twenty rows wide and perhaps fifteen deep, and most of them were emblazoned with a red cross.

"These are all here because of the Black?" he murmured.

"Yes."

He looked at her. "Are they... full?"

"No," said Dresch, still surveying the camp. "Not yet. For now we're only using one or two tents, but if we don't understand the Black soon, and find a way to treat it..." She shook her head. "Well, this is a fraction of what we'll need." She looked at him. "So, if you really do want to go 'where it counts' —" she thumped a slippered foot on the roof — "it's right here."

13

Calm

"But to my great joy, through the raging heart of this storm came the golden spectre of the Passing Bell; and then, as it swept above me, an absolute and profound calm."

ESPASIAN SAT ON THE edge of the bed and leaned forward, resting his elbows on his knees. A weary, sallow-faced nurse sat down behind him and began unpacking a box of bandages and ointments.

"Don't tell me it looks bad," said the Magruman. "I know it does. I don't need reminding."

The nurse glanced up at Bayleon, who was standing next to them. He nodded. The woman reached forward and carefully raised Espasian's undershirt. Bayleon winced. It was not so much the weave of battle scars that shocked him – his own back and chest were little better – it was the streaks of Black. They ran beneath the Magruman's dark skin, up the spine and fanned out across his shoulders, like the span of a tree.

Espasian drew a sharp breath as the nurse applied a poultice. "Hurts, does it?" she murmured.

Espasian shook his head. "Go ahead."

Bayleon leaned down for a closer look. "Is it getting worse?"

The Magruman grunted. "Perhaps a little. It's not the pain that worries me." He touched the side of his head. "Sometimes I feel muddled, as though I'm... thinking through mud."

"Been like that long?" asked the nurse as she bandaged his chest.

"Since this damnable Black found its way into my veins. But worse over the past day or so. Pain is one thing – I can handle pain – but *this* –" he indicated his temples, then rubbed them tenderly – "this takes you away from the world."

"Perhaps you should rest, Espasian," said Bayleon. "Others can make the preparations."

"No," was the firm reply. "I need to be there."

"But we can at least get started without you," reasoned Bayleon.

The Magruman seemed lost for words for a moment, then he turned to the nurse. "Tell him what you told me earlier – about the Hollow."

The nurse grunted. Her hands continued to work the bandages, but she nodded to the far end of the chamber. "I just said we've never known the Hollow grow so much and so quick."

Bayleon followed her gaze and looked into the shadows. "We'll soon be under attack. I suppose it stands to reason that—"

"Tell him how many beds in the last day," interjected Espasian.

The nurse gave Bayleon a long look. There was a resignation in her eyes that he did not like. "Ninety, perhaps a hundred. We stopped counting."

Bayleon lowered himself heavily on to the neighbouring bed. "A *hundred*? In a *day*?"

The nurse shrugged as she tied off the last of Espasian's bandages and pulled down his shirt. "Them beds are growing so fast you can see it happening. The walls of the Hollow too. The roots are sweeping away the earth like it was butter. This time tomorrow the place'll be twice the size it was yesterday."

"More than a hundred in a day," murmured the Spoorrunner,

his eyes moving to Espasian. "And we can number no more than... what? Three thousand Suhl in the entire valley?"

Espasian nodded.

Bayleon filled his great chest so that his leather armour creaked. "So this really is it, isn't it?"

Espasian inclined his head. "This is it," he said solemnly. There was a brief, heavy silence, then the Magruman gave a bold, devil-may-care smile. "This is the moment the valley was made for, Bayleon. This is the moment we were born for. The moment we stop hiding and conspiring, and make a proper stand."

Bayleon's grim expression slowly gave way to a smile. He nodded.

Espasian reached for his tunic. "Which is why, my friend, nothing in this world or that will keep me down here. Not you, and certainly not this accursed Black." The Magruman rolled his shoulders and stood stiffly, straightening to his full height. He put his hand on Bayleon's shoulder. "So, shall we go?"

§

The *Windrush* was silent but for the whistling of the wind, and the clatter of a broken yardarm against the mast, and the rumble and churn of earth against the hull.

Sylas felt stretched thin, pulled between the squalling winds behind the ship, the heights of the rigging and the riven earth, so that there seemed barely any of himself left at all. Naeo was not at his side. As ever, it was a relief in many ways because already the pain in his wrist was easing, and his insides no longer felt as though they had shifted out of place. But he knew that he could not be without her for long. Not now.

All about him the passengers and crew sat or lay where they had been when the ship had finally broken through the enemy lines. They stared at the soil-strewn decks and mangled rails and buckled timbers and wondered how they had survived. And, as their euphoria left them, they began to weep for those they had lost. Even Fawl was sprawled against a bulwark, gazing vacantly over the side, his matted brown hair blowing about his face.

At the very centre of the deck was Ash. He had not yet risen from his knees and his head was bowed.

"Ash?"

The captain stirred, but did not lift his head.

"*Ash?*" came the voice, a little louder.

He looked up slowly, and saw Simia crouching before him.

"Are you all right?" she asked.

Ash blinked, seeming to come to himself. He glanced about self-consciously. "Yes, I – I just needed a moment," he said. He paused, biting his lip. "I really don't know why I didn't think of it *sooner*. If I'd only thought of it sooner, I could have saved some of them. I could have…" He looked away and trailed off. "Triste," he said anxiously. "I can't help thinking that if Paiscion had been here he would have found a way to…"

Their eyes travelled to the bowsprit where they had both last seen Triste in a desperate battle with a Hamajak. Simia shuddered as she remembered the moment he had pitched backwards, taking the Hamajak with him.

She turned and looked Ash in the eye. "Paiscion and Triste would be as proud of you as the rest of us, Ash," she said firmly. "Without you, none of us would have made it, even Sylas and Naeo. We had no idea you could even *do* those things!" She grinned and elbowed him in the side. "You, with *Essenfayle*!"

Ash said nothing.

For a moment Simia seemed at a loss, then she leaned closer. "Look around you, Ash," she whispered. "No one knows what to do."

He regarded her for a moment, then took a longer look at the bewildered faces of the crew, and the decks in disarray, and the rigging slapping against the sides of the ship. Self-reproach passed over his face and he dropped his head once more. Then, quite suddenly, he pushed himself up and set out towards the bow.

Taken rather by surprise, Simia scrambled after him and followed closely as Ash stopped here and there to offer encouragement to those he passed, asking each to take on some small task to bring the ship back to order. As they moved steadily down the ship, a liveliness returned to the decks, and a murmur of voices could once again be heard above the winds.

When they came to the bow, Fawl was back on his feet and was already beginning to organise those around him.

He coughed with a pipe-smoker's wheeze. "Cap'n," he said.

Ash gave a brief nod. "We took quite a battering, eh, Fawl?"

"I'll say, sir," he said. "The rigging's in a sorry state, *and* the decks, but it's the hull I'm most worried about. She's not made for this kind of running." He rubbed the railing tenderly. "She's as game as any, but in the end she's meant for the waves, not the plains."

Ash nodded. "That's as may be, but what a runner she is!" he said with a grin. "Almost a fellow Spoorrunner, I'd say!"

Fawl conceded a crooked smile. "Aye, sir, that she is." He glanced back at Sylas and Naeo, then in a lowered, deferential tone he added: "Thanks to Master Sylas and Miss Naeo."

"Well said," said Ash, smiling back at the pair. Then he grasped Fawl by his muscular shoulder. "What say I take the top deck and you go below and see what we're dealing with? If there's any damage, we'll need to fix it before we reach water."

Fawl gave a quick bow. "Aye, sir," he said and walked swiftly to the nearest hatch, then trotted down into the gloom below.

Ash watched him go, then looked up at the rigging. The topsails still looked splendid, gleaming brightly with their metallic silver-gold sheen, but everything below was a mess, hung about with frayed ropes and torn canvas. He crossed his arms and sighed.

"I don't know much about ships," said Simia in a low voice, "but I don't think it's supposed to look like that."

"Nope, Simsi, it isn't," said Ash, shaking his head. "But then she's—"

He was interrupted by a noise behind them. It sounded like a muted cry. They both looked round sharply, but there was nothing to be seen. They were about to dismiss it as the sound of the hull striking something below when it came again. This time it sounded more like an agonised yell coming from the side of the ship. They glanced at one another, then advanced slowly to the rail and peered over.

Just below, hanging upside down from the stock of the anchor, was a man with his legs locked round the wooden shank. He was swinging precariously with every leap and lurch of the ship, occasionally dashing his bald head against the hull.

"Triste!" cried Simia.

"Hang on!" yelled Ash, climbing over the rail and lowering himself on to the stock of the anchor.

"That's exactly what I've been doing!" called Triste testily. "For quite a while!"

Ash grinned as he leaned down and offered his hand. "You sound just fine!"

Triste used a lurch of the ship to swing up and grasp Ash's wrist. For a moment Ash struggled with the weight, but then Simia seized Triste's tunic and, with a collective groan, the three collapsed in a heap on the deck.

When they had untangled their limbs and righted themselves, Ash and Simia saw that Triste had a cut on his cheek, a torn shirt and a tunic full of dirt, but otherwise he looked unharmed.

"So, does the world Scry the same upside down?" asked Ash with another grin.

Triste looked at him soberly. "Not when your head's knocking on the side of a ship."

A smile grew across his lips and they all laughed. They quickly swapped accounts of the battle and, as they did so, their spirits lifted.

At the first opportunity Ash sprang to his feet and began calling to members of the crew, encouraging and cajoling them to their tasks. Decks were swept, railings were hammered back into shape and sails and rigging were attended to. Meanwhile Simia brought Triste Salve and dressings for his wounds, and tended him for as long as he would let her. Then she began moving among the crew, fetching medicine and water for those who needed them. She saw Amelie sitting with her back against the side railing, hugging her knees, as though feeling a piercing cold, and she went over.

"Are you hurt?" she asked.

Amelie looked up distractedly. "I'm fine," she said with a sudden radiant smile. She patted the deck next to her. "Sit with me for a while?"

Simia sat down, and was about to answer, but stopped short. She saw that Amelie was watching Sylas with a quizzical, mystified expression, and something told her that it was best to be quiet. So they sat together in silence, watching Sylas as he gazed ahead of the ship, swaying with its motion as though he and the ship were one, his outstretched arm burning bright with the glow of the Merisi Band. As he raised his head, so the winds surged; as he tipped his hand, the deck tilted; as he twisted his shoulders, so the *Windrush* turned.

"I've seen him do this," said Amelie, breaking the silence.

"You *have*?"

She nodded, her eyes still on Sylas. "His kites. This is how he flew his kites. He moved just like that, and his expression was the same too: completely lost in what he's doing."

Simia looked from Amelie to Sylas. She remembered him talking about his kites. "Birds of paper and string," she murmured.

Amelie looked at her, surprised. "That's what I used to call them," she said, smiling. "Did he say that?"

Simia nodded. "When I first met him."

They both turned back to him. "I think now that this was... *in* him always," said Amelie thoughtfully. "I knew that he was special – of course I did – long before they told me." She laughed to herself. "Though much of the time I told myself I was just a doting mum." She turned to Simia with shining eyes. "I wrote something for him once – an inscription in the front of a book. '*Learn all that you are, my dear Sylas, learn all that you are able to be.*' As if I knew what that might be."

She looked back at Sylas, his hair flying in the wind, his hands open, as though in them was the storm itself. "But how could I have known? How could I have known he was... *this*?"

She shook her head and sighed, then smiled at Simia self-consciously.

Simia said nothing. In truth, she was quite content just to sit there and listen. She felt warmed in a way she had almost forgotten: as she had felt sitting with her own mother, before the Reckoning. It was an unspoken thing, quiet and primal and absolute. It made her lean a little towards Amelie, and want to be seen by her in the way she saw Sylas. In her heart, Simia knew that could never be, but in that moment at least she let herself believe, and she felt wrapped in that same warmth, and love, and belonging.

Until she saw Naeo.

She was leaning on the rear railing, staring over the stern along the snaking trail of earth left by the *Windrush* to where the dark stain of the Imperial army still stretched across the Westercleft Plain. But she was not looking at the army; she was gazing at the high hills that bordered the Valley of Outs. As Naeo looked out, her shoulders convulsed gently, in a way that was all too familiar to Simia. She was sobbing, quietly and privately, trying not to let anyone see. And Simia knew why: Naeo was saying goodbye to her father.

Simia was familiar with the warmth of closeness, but she also knew the pain of separation. And for her the goodbye had been forever.

Feeling both within her then — the joy of closeness and the anguish of loss — she began truly to understand the bond between Sylas and Naeo: a bond of oneness, and of difference. They were two mirrored parts of a whole, like night and day, summer and winter, joy and despair. And whether or not they knew it, in that very instant, they were sharing a moment of love.

To one it gave comfort; to the other only despair.

14

Black and White

"I see now that there is far, far more that unites our two worlds than divides us. It is not as simple as black and white *or light and dark; we are two parts of a whole: inflections of the same thing."*

THE COUNCIL CHAMBER WAS still and dark. The only illumination was a slant of hazy moonlight from a small window high in one wall. The only sounds were hushed whispers, like water over pebbles, ebbing and flowing, ebbing and flowing. Sometimes the whispers died away altogether, but always they would begin again, and always two words were repeated.

"The Black," murmured the twelve as they pointed green-gloved fingers at maps of city and wilderness.

"The Black," they whispered as they pored over reports from around the globe.

"The Black," they breathed as they faced the impossible.

At the centre of this, at the head of the Merisi circle, one man said nothing. Franz Jacob Veeglum sat cross-legged like the rest, his open hands — one gloved and one not — resting loosely on his knees as though in meditation. He listened and he thought, but he did not speak a word. Instead he waited for the Way to reveal itself because he knew that it would. The Way always became clear, as sure as the rising sun and moon. But it only showed itself to the patient, to those at peace, to those true of heart. For now it was for the others to speak, and for him to listen.

So he heard in hurried reports how the Black was pooling and rising, flowing into the rivers like some biblical flood. He heard how Thoth had been seen by people across the world, even as the Merisi Council themselves had seen him. He heard how panic was spreading through parliaments, palace courts and places of worship and power. He heard that the Merisi's carefully constructed myths were coming tumbling down; that the truth of the Other – the Merisi's most precious charge – was now known to all forever.

Known, he thought, but not understood.

He heard all this impassively. The eyes of the Merisi elders searched his face, looking for some sign that he was ready to speak. But still he said nothing because the Way was not clear.

As Veeglum listened, his eyes drifted round the chamber to the engravings on the walls, allowing the Ravel Runes to unfurl before his eyes. He read and he listened at the same time, gathering all that he could to his aid. Because now he needed the wisdom of the one Great Master.

All of the writings were familiar, of course, but now they seemed more resonant than ever, as though Merisu himself was speaking them:

> "The Glimmer is many things.
> It is the courage to our fear.
> It is the shame to our pride.
> It is the answer to our question."

And then:

> "The division of our souls is an open wound. Our spirit may have healed, but we feel the pain of absence. Absence that breeds doubt. Doubt that fosters false faiths. Doubt that stops us being all we should be."

Below that he read:

> "Do not fear what you do not understand.
> Fear is the foothold of superstition,
> Superstition is the excuse not to think,
> And thus, unthinking, we lose the fight to understand."

His gaze shifted to the opposite wall where he read:

> "All now rests upon the glove and the hand, Merisi and Suhl. Isia is the keeper of our souls. Her blood she entrusts to us."

Finally he turned to the engraving writ large on the outside wall of the chamber:

> "Reach for the silvered glimmer on the lake,
> Turn to the sun-streaked shadow in your wake,
> Now, rise: fear not where none have gone,
> For then, at last, we may be one."

He dwelt upon this last inscription for some moments, all the while listening to the anxious whispers. Finally his eyes left the engraved words, following the path of the moonbeam to where the pale blue light pooled round another engraving on the far wall.

There was no writing here, only a large, stark symbol.

This was the first Yin Yang symbol, painted on the wall by Merisu himself and later carved into the stone for all to remember. Veeglum gazed at it now, searching its exquisite arcs for meaning, for some sign that Merisu may have left for him. Something for this very moment. But all he saw was its poise, its balance between yin and yang, its light and dark, its white and black.

Veeglum frowned, shifting his eyes to the segment of black. For a moment he lost himself in the dark, in the *xuan*, wrapping himself in its profound, mysterious depths. His eyes roved round the inky nothingness, then shifted sharply to the centre of the symbol, to the snaking boundary between black and white. He tilted his head to one side and sniffed.

It was barely audible, but it silenced the chamber. Everyone turned to the Merisi Master. They knew the meaning of that sniff. They knew that he was close.

For some time he was silent. Then he sniffed again.

He straightened and rose effortlessly to his full, imposing height. He walked slowly to the window and blinked into the bright moonlight, drawing the fragrant air deep into his lungs. He looked out over the brooding jungle to the scattered temples of Bagan, the stupas, which glowed palely beneath the moon.

In this light, those peculiar temples looked for all the world like gigantic teardrops. It was as though some colossus of a god had wept here once, in the jungles of Myanmar, and these tears remained as monuments to that ancient sadness, frozen in stone. To the Merisi Master, they were structures of breathtaking beauty, their ribbed flanks arcing upwards to a vanishingly fine point, as though they might touch the heavens themselves. The sight of them filled him with an inner peace, and left him assured of the course he must take. Finally the Way was clear to him.

He turned and addressed the room.

"Thank you, my brothers and sisters, for your counsel, your patience." He spoke slowly, taking pains to overcome his German accent, as was his way since becoming Master. "So. This is the moment. The moment our father Merisu foresaw centuries ago. Ze moment when two worlds become one."

The Merisi elders glanced at one another. A grey-haired woman wearing a flowing silk kimono leaned forward a little.

"But, Master," she said, "it is not the union foreseen by Merisu!"

"Merisu did not tell us how the worlds might come together," replied Veeglum, "only that they might. We have always *hoped* that they would unite in a way that makes the two parts greater, in a way that benefits and nourishes both. But as with all things, there is a mirrored path. A darker path." He walked back to his place in the circle and sat. "The Black is ze beginning of just such a path. If Thoth's threats are to believed, the Black is ze beginning of what will be a descent into darkness. A union bound by darkness." He looked from face to face. "The question is, what are we to do about it?"

There was quite a murmur, then the elders waited for him to continue.

"The answer is simple," he said. "We must do nothing."

There was a collective intake of breath.

"More than that," continued Veeglum, "we must convince others to do nothing."

Now, there was only stunned silence.

Veeglum pointed at the Yin Yang symbol, and those assembled turned to look.

"Merisu taught us that all is in balance: dark and light, night and day, black and white. Like an image in a mirror, one is sustained by the other. It seems to me that the movement of ze Black threatens a balance that preserves us all."

"So how can we do *nothing*?" asked the woman in the kimono.

"Because if our world seeks to destroy this Black, if we use our weapons, and violence, if we fight darkness with darkness, we only further upset the balance." He lowered his eyes from the symbol. "If we do this, then ze Black may consume us all."

For some moments the chamber fell into a new and deeper quiet. Then an elderly man with a pointed silver beard leaned forward.

"So we just... wait?"

"We wait, and we tell ze world to wait."

"For what?"

"For the light to balance the dark," said Veeglum. "For ze Glimmer Myth to come to pass. For Sylas and for Naeo."

§

Paiscion and Tasker had been on the move for more than an hour, and the valley was already far behind, beyond folds of hills and forests of beech and oak. But still they crept along stealthily, bodies low, alert to every movement and sound. Whenever they faced open ground, they took a longer way round and, when they had a choice between a well-worn path and a flooded ditch, they plunged into the mire.

Of course, Paiscion did this with rather more readiness than Tasker, who stared at the mud-splattered remains of his Italian shoes with an expression of heartfelt sorrow, as though this act above all others — above forsaking his world and getting himself shot — would be his surpassing act of sacrifice.

It was not so much that he took pride in them — such vanities had come to matter less over recent days. It was more that they were his last connection to the time before: before the stone circles had opened themselves wide, and creatures had poured through them; before Mr Zhi had died, and everything had come undone.

But Tasker knew that it had to be done and so he winced, jutted his jaw and dropped into the sludge, cringing as he felt the muddy ooze flooding his shoes. He pressed quickly on, trying to turn his mind to other things. He went over the meeting in the Churn and his snatched conversations with Paiscion, and then he tried to imagine what might be happening back home in the Other. And from those thoughts, perhaps inevitably given the sensations about his feet, his mind turned to the Black. Unconsciously at first, and then with increasing nervousness, Tasker began searching the surface for any sign of a stain, any trace of darkness that should not be there. And, as the swill began to rise above his knees, he pushed ahead ever more urgently. He caught up with Paiscion at a junction with a small, sluggish brook.

"Is it safe to talk?" he murmured, glancing into the trees.

Paiscion stopped and raised his head, listening, then he nodded. "Quietly," he whispered. "This slop may hide our scent, but the Ghor can hear voices from one end of a valley to another."

Tasker pointed down into the ditch. "Do you think it could be in here?" he whispered. "The Black?"

Paiscion peered over his glasses into the morass. "That's very unlikely."

"Why?"

Paiscion glanced anxiously back along the ditch. "Let's walk as we talk."

They stepped out into the brook, then began wading downstream, keeping shoulder to shoulder so that they could whisper together.

"I'm not sure how or why the Black is appearing in your world," began the Magruman, "but here it only manifests in one of two places. The most common is a place of war. That is, a place where the Three Ways have been used in all their unnatural power. The other place we encounter the Black is rare indeed, and it is where there's a seam of Quintessence, such as in the mines beneath the Valley of Outs. There is a connection between them — Quintessence and the Black; they seem such mirror opposites and yet something draws them together."

Tasker was still eyeing the muddy waters of the brook. "And all this means there shouldn't be any Black here?"

"I think it unlikely. There's never been a battle here to my knowledge. Certainly the Reckoning never spread to these parts. That was confined to Salsimaine." Paiscion paused to clamber over a sodden tree trunk that barred their path, then helped Tasker. "I'm sure that there's no Quintessence here either," he continued. "Merimaat scoured this area when she was forging the Passing Bell. She would not have missed a seam so nearby."

Tasker filled his lungs. "Well, that's something," he said.

They continued a few paces, then he looked at Paiscion and asked: "So what else do you know about the Black? What is it that you want to tell the Merisi?"

Paiscion sighed. "I wish I had more to share with them," he said ruefully. "I have come to understand that the Black is not for knowing or seeing because it was made by the ignorant and the blind. It cannot be mastered by your science, nor by anything of the light, because it is not of the natural world. If it belongs at all in this world, it belongs in its darkest and most infernal places."

Tasker slowed his step. "But you do know *something*," he said, "or you wouldn't be making this journey."

Paiscion waved him on. "Come, we *must* keep moving. Grey Hill is still far away." Only when Tasker was back at his side did he continue. "It is not so much what I know as what I believe. I have spent most of the past few years on the *Windrush*, moored on the banks of the river in Gheroth. That is where I saw the first traces of the Black, on the surface of the river, two or three moons after our defeat at Salsimaine. At first I thought little of it. There was much unspeakable foulness in those waters, particularly after the Reckoning. But then I became fascinated by it. Even those first trails of Black were so striking – so pure and absolute, untainted by all they swam with. Over the months they became such a common sight that no one seemed to take much notice. But something about the Black unnerved me, and so I decided to travel upstream to find its source."

He stopped for no apparent reason beside a low branch. He peered beneath it, grunted and then, without explanation, walked on. Tasker wondered at this, but was keen for the Magruman to finish his tale. "The source?" he pressed. "You said you found the source?"

"That's right," said Paiscion, finding his stride once more. "It was coming from the Barrens, from the battlegrounds of the Reckoning: the very heart of Thoth's hellfire."

"So... *Thoth* made the Black?"

Paiscion paused to look under another branch. "Not directly, but I think the Black was forged in the crucible of his Three Ways. You see the Three Ways fight with Nature – they twist it and turn it upon itself – and something about that gave rise to the Black."

"You mean he created the Black without intending to?"

Paiscion took out a handkerchief and wiped sweat from his brow. "Thoth, his Magrumen and anyone else who uses the Three Ways. In your world, no one intends to create pollution, do they? But it happens nevertheless. It's a – a *by-product* of your science." He tucked his handkerchief back in his pocket. "You have your pollution; we have the Black. And, just as your pollution is harmful, so too is the Black."

Tasker frowned. Something about all this still made no sense. "But, if Thoth didn't *intend* to make it, how is he able to use it the way he does? Like he is in my world. Like he did this morning?"

Paiscion walked on quietly for some moments, considering this. Then he said: "Thoth is the creator of the Three Ways. He sustains them, and they sustain the Black. So, you see, Thoth, the Three Ways and the Black are bound together in a circle of evil. *That* is how he masters the Black."

Once again he stopped and peered under another overhanging branch, but this time he reached out and lifted it.

"Aha!" he exclaimed. "I knew it was around here somewhere!"

Beneath the branch was the upturned hull of a small canoe. He turned to Tasker and smiled. "I used this to reach the valley after my adventures with Sylas and Simia at the Dirgheon. Not the largest vessel, but strong enough for two, I daresay!"

Tasker grinned, showing his golden tooth. "Then let's get our feet dry!"

Together they heaved the canoe from its hiding place, turned it over and set it down in the brook. Carefully they positioned their packs inside the narrow hull, then themselves, and soon they were paddling downstream.

Aided by a strong current, they began to make swift progress, navigating the wooded channels between the hills smoothly and secretly, leaving the neighbourhood of the valley far behind. When finally they emerged from the woods to cross open water meadows, they saw before them, low on the horizon, a smudge of distant hills.

"There," said Paiscion, nodding towards them. "That's where we'll find Grey Hill."

With that, the two companions dipped their paddles with new relish, surging on towards the dark horizon and their passage to another world.

15

A Whole in
Two Parts

"When you consider all of the opposites that
form our universe — light and dark, male and female,
fire and water, air and earth to name a few —
is it really so hard to believe that we, too,
may be a whole in two parts?"

FOR SYLAS THE WORLD had never been so exhilarating, and wild, and free. Standing on the deck of the *Windrush*, it felt to him as though the rules he had always known — the ones that told him that the land and the sea were separate things, opposite things, and that hills were to be climbed, rivers forded, mountains scaled — all these rules were his to change. Before the bow of the *Windrush* all the world seemed a sea to be sailed. Already he knew that she would enter the approaching dell and ride high on the escarpment ahead; that she would turn even before she reached the top and perform a thrilling pirouette before plunging into the forest beyond. And, after that, Sylas knew she would fly on and on towards the sea.

He allowed himself to delight in the fleeting forests and rolling hills, and marvel at the power and majesty of the ship, so responsive to his every command. He glimpsed his mother and Simia watching him and he stood a little taller, enjoying the expression of wonder on their faces.

But then he made a mistake. Perhaps to share the moment he glanced across to where Naeo should have been at his side. Of course, she wasn't there — Sylas remembered now. He had felt her go. He turned to look for her and saw her at the rear of the ship, standing against the railing, gazing back in the direction of the valley. And, as he watched her hair dancing in the breeze, a new feeling stirred beneath his ribs. It grew swiftly and irresistibly into a tightening fist of emotion. It took him by surprise: in the midst of his joy and excitement, there was sorrow, anguish and grief. These feelings came over him like a wave of sickness, making him stagger where he stood. Sylas turned back to the bow and tried desperately to push the feelings away — to focus instead on the heave and yaw of the ship, but the more he denied them, the more they grew.

His concentration began to fail, and with it his grasp of the winds and the ship. He heard an ominous thump as the hull knocked against something, then a growl as the keel dug deep into the soil and grit.

Suddenly the ship slewed to one side and great sheets of earth erupted either side of the hull. Cries of terror went up from the crew, and Sylas could see Ash bellowing something at him, but he could not hear a word.

"No!" Sylas yelled into the wind. "No! No! No!"

He spread his arms and tried desperately to regain control, but the *Windrush* was already beyond him. Her sway became a dangerous swerve left and right, growing in violence. The crew yelled and screamed, throwing themselves down on to the deck and taking hold of whatever they could. Just in time because now the *Windrush* began to capsize, her cargo sliding across the decks and tumbling over the side.

Triste was sitting by the bowsprit, dressing a wound on his leg, when something made him look over at the helm. He saw Sylas standing by himself in front of the ship's wheel, sailing the ship without Naeo's help. Even alone, Sylas seemed in true command of the *Windrush*. Triste watched with Scryer's eyes, fascinated. Any shades of doubt he had once seen in Sylas were no more, and they had given way to a new brightness. The air about him shone with joy and exhilaration, and a new confidence was written in his face.

But just then, as Sylas glanced about, perhaps looking for Naeo, Triste saw something altogether unexpected, something he had not seen in all his Scrying years. It was an emotion nestled in Sylas's heart that did not belong: an emotion that must surely have come from elsewhere.

"Impossible," Triste murmured. But it was unmistakable.

There, in the midst of Sylas's joy and hope, were the dark blues and greys of grief. Triste set his bandages down and leaned forward, focusing on Sylas ever more intently.

His brow furrowed. The closer he looked, the more certain he became. All about Sylas — not just inside him but around him — were subtle trails of those same dark colours of anguish. They snaked across open space, barely visible, until at last they came to the stern of the ship, and to Naeo at the rear railing, staring into the distance. So consumed was she by palls of the same blue and grey that Triste found her slight form difficult to make out. The Scryer glanced from Naeo, to Sylas, and then back to Naeo, beginning to understand.

Triste shook his head in disbelief. "She's sharing it!" he muttered. "She's sharing her pain!"

Suddenly he saw something else within the darkness that

enclosed Naeo. He frowned, rising to his feet, peering intently at a streak of brightness amid the dark. That was when he heard the thump of the hull striking something and the panicked cries of the crew. The deck lurched beneath his feet, forcing him to seize hold of a rope above his head; but still Triste's eyes were on the darkness and the brightness within it. Because now, to his amazement, he saw shining tendrils of joy and hope knitted among those of despair. These too passed back across the space, connecting Sylas with Naeo. Again his eyes flitted between them: Sylas, looking stricken now, struggling desperately to control the ship, and Naeo, seeming to wake from her daze, turning back towards Sylas. And then, for Triste, it all made sense. Sylas and Naeo were exchanging their emotions, each feeling as the other.

And so, as the earth roared about his ears and the ship began to capsize, Triste staggered back against a railing and gazed in amazement at Naeo emerging from the darkness of her own despair. He watched as she walked among the tendrils of Sylas's joy and hope, taking on their brightness, her expression changing, the life returning to her eyes. He watched as she saw what she must do and took her place at Sylas's side.

His eyes filling with tears of wonder, Triste saw their bond bloom once more into a searing brightness, and the gleaming sails of the *Windrush* fill with a wholesome wind, and her decks lift beneath his feet.

16

The Ungodly

*"O, the ungodly things that have been done
in the name of the gods, and the most heinous
of them all is the Ramesses Shield."*

THE VINEYARDS ROLLED OVER gentle hills, beautiful and fragrant even now in the winter months. The air was sharp and chill, but the sun was bright, and cheerful birdsong recalled warmer times.

All at once the birds fell silent. Rabbits and rodents ducked into burrows. Creatures of all kinds, and the vines, and the fields themselves, seemed to hold their breath.

For long moments all was quiet expectation.

Then, at last, there was movement. A shadow crept across the landscape, noiseless and dark. It was as though a storm cloud was passing overhead, consuming two or three fields at a time, turning brilliant day to midnight darkness. Had one of the creatures in the vineyards dared to look up — and none did — it would have seen a dreadful cloud hanging high above: a black swarm of leathery wings, a seething orb that flapped and turned in endless motion, swirling across the petrified sky towards the sea.

As the shadow passed, the sunshine returned. The animals, birds and insects ventured back between the rows of vines, but there was no song, no scurrying, no play. Instead they turned their fearful eyes after the unnatural shadow that had passed. They watched as it churned and rolled over the last of the hills, and drifted towards the furthest reaches of the headland. They saw it approach the hill that did not belong: that distant, jutting pyramid of stone that all of them had learned to dread. It was a structure so large that it dwarfed the hills around it, its pinnacle reaching high into the sky, but the black orb rose higher still, riding the warm winds that rose up the sides of the pyramid to swirl above its highest point.

Once there the swarm hovered for some moments and then plunged downwards, spilling over the upper parts of the pyramid. As it spread, the things that had given the orb its form were revealed: black and winged, with long limbs, hunched shoulders and pale faces. They settled on the terraces, forming regimented lines, and, at last, they were still.

§

Thoth descended the windy stairwell, his cloak trailing behind him. He paid no attention to the Vyrkans that had brought him and were now bowing as he passed; he did not even raise his hooded head to glance out at the patchwork fields below. He descended swiftly and, when he reached a wide opening, he swept inside without a backward glance, his robes crackling like crimson flames behind him.

The way was barred by a small man, who bent low to the stone floor.

"Great Dirgh, you honour us," grovelled the man at Thoth's feet, his voice thin and accented. "I trust your journey from Gheroth was... swift and — and agreeable?"

Thoth lifted his hooded head. His face remained in shadow, but it was clear that he was inspecting the man before him, taking in the ornate headdress of slicked-back feathers, the elaborately embroidered tunic, the tightly clasped, trembling hands.

When the Dirgh spoke, it was in a chorus of voices that shook the stones of the entrance and filled the lavish chamber beyond. "Is this how you command my Dirgheon, Orskiss? On your knees? Concerning yourself with what is agreeable? With —" he extended a long, bony finger towards the crest of feathers — "trifles such as this?"

Orskiss shrank into his plumage. "No, dread Lord. I — I have been busy with preparations, as you requested."

"Of course you have," boomed the Priest of Souls as he stepped past the commander and strode into the Apex Chamber. "Tell me of them and let me hear no more of what is agreeable!"

Orskiss pulled the headdress from his balding head and tossed it into a corner, then hurried after his master. Thoth strode swiftly over rich carpets and furs, towards the black pool at the centre of the chamber.

"I have replenished the Black as you asked, great Dirgh," said Orskiss ingratiatingly as Thoth looked down at the pool and its surrounding steps of white marble. His own visage, which had been painted on the ceiling above, was reflected on the mirror-smooth surface. For a moment he seemed preoccupied by this.

"Go on," he commanded.

"The fleet is prepared and in port, and awaits your instruction," said Orskiss, his pale features twitching. "The armies are gathered at the stone circles of Khousak, and Hassolt, and Vamkrish. Each of the generals knows your will and they await your command." He paused and leaned forward as though looking for some acknowledgement. When there was none, he blurted: "Great Lord, there is much excitement and expectation now that the Undoing is entering its final phase! I have heard some of the generals say that—"

"The raids?" interjected Thoth, the discord of his voices conveying his irritation. "Have they gone to plan?"

"*Very* well, great Dirgh. Very well indeed!" crowed Orskiss, swelling with pride. His quick eyes darted to the far corner of the chamber where three Imperial guards stood over a small group of men and women huddled on the floor. "I took the liberty of assembling a few of our captives in case you wished to inspect them for yourself."

At this Thoth's attention at last shifted from the pool of Black, and his hooded head swung in the direction of the prisoners. "You took... the liberty?"

Orskiss looked stricken. "Yes... I — I thought you might want..."

He trailed off. Thoth had already walked away, skirting the pool and heading across the chamber towards the group. Orskiss followed.

At the Dirgh's approach, some of those on the floor shuffled further into the corner. There were perhaps twenty men and women, of different ages and dressed in all manner of clothing, but they each shared a dazed look of increasing terror. Their wide eyes took in Thoth's dark, hooded visage and bony figure wrapped in silken crimson folds. A young man in a mud-smeared white coat started mumbling something to himself, rocking backwards and forwards, while others forced their eyes to look down at the floor and waited. Only one of them met the Dirgh's gaze, seemingly without fear. It was an older woman with grey, short-cropped hair and pink-rimmed glasses. To everyone's surprise, she rose to her feet.

"What do you want with us?" she asked in a nasal drawl.

Thoth was silent for a moment, his head tilting a little to one side. "What do you think I want with you?"

The woman wavered amid the clamour of Thoth's many voices, but took a calming breath and replied: "Well, let's see," she said, looking about at her companions. "We're scientists, all of us, and scientists of a certain kind: weapons specialists, nuclear scientists, military engineers, experts in infectious disease and biological warfare. It's like you're assembling some kind of — some kind of counsel of war."

Thoth inclined his head further, then said expectantly: "Yes...?"

The woman waited in vain for him to say more, then she burst out, "So it seems obvious that you want to use our science against us, and you expect us to help you!"

Thoth gazed at her from the darkness of his hood and knitted the bony fingers of his hands together, but said nothing.

The woman shifted nervously. "Well, we won't do it!" she announced, turning her gaze to her companions. "Why would we? Against our own world, our own families and loved ones?" She paused and waited for a reply, but none came. "We're *scientists*!" she cried in exasperation. "Don't you understand? We do what we do to *improve* our world, not to destroy it!"

At this Thoth lifted his head a little so that, for the briefest moment, the group caught a glimpse of something pale and shifting in the shadow of his hood. Then he began to laugh, haltingly and mirthlessly, as though it was something he had almost forgotten how to do. The chamber echoed with grotesque peals of laughter: young and old, male and female.

Orskiss too began to laugh — a kind of chimp-like chatter — but, even as he began, his master fell silent. Orskiss quickly quieted himself, then sneered at the scientists.

Thoth inspected the group. "You talk of improving your world, you talk of principles, and yet look at what you have done," he said. "Look at the cruel and ungodly power you wield, the perils you play with. It is you and your precious science that provokes us. Now, we will defend ourselves!"

He seemed to eye each and every one of them, then turned and began walking away towards two great double doors.

The woman threw out her hands imploringly. "You're really doing all this because of our *science*?" She glanced at her companions as though hoping for their support. "But that's madness! We wish you no harm! We didn't even know you were here!"

This outburst seemed to test the patience of one of the Ghor guards who stepped forward, grasped her shoulder and pushed her down to the ground.

She looked up with defiant tears in her eyes. "We won't help you!" she shouted. "You hear me? We'll never help you!"

At this the Dirgh's step slowed and he half turned. "Oh, but you already *are*!" he breathed. "You may not give me your science, but your masters think you will. And so you surrender something far more powerful."

"I – I don't understand," she blurted. "What?"

Thoth strode on through the double doors. "Fear!" boomed the voices of many.

17

Gather the Damned

"Gather the lost and gather the damned,
Gather the Suhl, for here we will stand."

ESPASIAN LEANED AGAINST A tree and looked through the shadows of the forest to the brighter shoreline beyond. The mustering had been done, and the great assembly was quiet now and expectant. Some of the commanders by the lake glanced up to where the Magruman stood, but he knew that he could not be seen, and he wanted it that way. He needed this last moment to himself.

There was a tightness in his chest, and a fierce pain in his back and shoulders. He cursed the Black for his discomfort, but in truth he knew that the infection was only partly to blame. This was as much about what lay before him: the immense responsibility, the totality of the stakes. It was the thought that this time the command was his alone. It was the knowledge that he must lead this feeble army against an adversary that would give no quarter and leave nothing of this precious place behind.

He took a few steps towards the light and allowed his eyes to trace along the ragtag lines of his troops. Beneath a threadbare standard depicting a faded set of scales, he saw all that remained of Merimaat's regiment: their once-proud livery now reduced to an occasional scratched breastplate, or a tattered cloak. There could have been no more than forty warriors in all, none of them properly arrayed for battle.

Next to them, beneath the faded standard of the Eye of Heru, were the last of the Spoorrunners. Some wore the broad leather belts and leather armour of their forbears, some the imposing shoulder plates, but none had their trademark shield embossed with the Eye of Heru. Not one of them wore their prized boots of supple skin, close-sewn for strength and speed.

Behind the Spoorrunners, and beneath no standard at all, was a motley band of several hundred archers and infantry, some carrying pikes, swords and bows, but most making do with a rough-hewn spear, a crude mace or some such weapon made in haste from whatever the forest had to offer.

The Magruman's gaze drifted on, over the wasted and diminished army, weighing its strength. At the furthest sweep of the lakeshore, almost indistinguishable from the forest, were two full regiments of Leaflikes, the famed defenders of the Valley of Outs, camouflaged by hoods and cloaks that had been grown as much as made. They, at least, looked well provisioned and strong in numbers. But next to them was a motley band of Scryers, some of them young and inexperienced, others so old that surely their eyesight was failing, let alone their craft.

Espasian picked out the long green cloaks of the Weavers, who would lend their gift of Essenfayle to the effort, but they too were fewer than he had hoped. He saw other bands of warriors gathered beneath what was once their regimental flag, but was now a tattered rag: the ensign of a last, desperate few. And among all these he saw the volunteers: the common men and women of Sylva, who stood tallest and proudest of them all, perhaps because they knew least of what lay ahead.

He felt an even greater heaviness settle upon him. All of these together could be no more than a thousand strong.

One thousand broken troops, many of whom had languished for years in the Dirgheon or the slums, to defend against at least one division of Thoth's elite Imperial army: Ghor, Ghorhund, Hamajaks, Ragers, Tythish and Mages. And then there were the Ogresh.

Espasian fixed the last two clasps of his tunic before turning to quickly scan the forest. He spied what he was looking for and walked over to the largest of the nearby trees: a mighty oak whose rumpled trunk had the span of several people. He stepped over its snaking roots to kneel by the trunk. He placed both his hands on the tree and let his forehead rest against the bark. Then he closed his eyes.

"Mother of all things," he murmured. "We need you now."

As he spoke, a new silence descended upon the forest, punctuated only by the distant *thump*, *thump*, *thump* of battle drums. It was as though the trees, the wind and the birds had heard him and waited now to hear more.

But the Magruman had said his piece. Abruptly he stood and walked briskly away towards the light. As he strode, he straightened, pulling his weary, pain-wracked limbs into their rightful form, lifting his head. He set his face in an expression of fiery resolution and, as he stepped into the gloomy afternoon light, he looked almost the man he once had been: noble, bold and formidable — a man accustomed to command.

The army saw him at once and a chorus of muted cheers swept along the shoreline. Standards were waved, feet were stamped, weapons were brandished aloft. But there was little enthusiasm in this, and it was clear to Espasian that his warriors were ruled more by fear than passion.

They knew the odds as well as he.

He opened his mouth to speak but, to his surprise, another heartier cheer lingered in the trees behind him. He turned and saw children — hundreds of them — peering between the leaves. They were everywhere: nestled in the crooks of branches, balancing on boughs, peeping from behind tree trunks — all of them wild with excitement and jostling for position. A chant went up among them, which soon filled the depths of the forest.

"*Espa-sian! Espa-sian! Espa-sian!*"

A smile broke across the Magruman's face and he gave a quick bow of appreciation, then he raised his hands for silence.

He turned back to the army. "Brothers and sisters!" he bellowed. "I know your doubts and they are worthy of you. We dislike violence and we despise war, not because we lack the mettle to fight, but because we are a people of peace. We live within the bounds of Nature. We cherish her gifts and strive to give back all we receive. This is the balance."

There was a murmur of agreement from the troops, and Espasian paused before continuing.

"War upturns that balance. It destroys and gives nothing in return." He paused to look along the full length of the assembly. "But, sisters and brothers, today we must take war into our hearts. Today we must make it our own!"

The army was silent. Many glanced at one another in surprise, but Espasian was undeterred.

"For years Thoth has plundered, and ravaged, and destroyed, and his worst cruelties he has saved for the Suhl. We have been hunted and victimised. We have been forced to run and hide. We have cowered in the dark corners of the Dirgheon, languished in the filth of the slums." He opened his hands. "But we are Nature's own people. Do you think Nature wishes her followers so abused? Do you think she is content to witness these wrongs?

"No, sisters and brothers," continued Espasian, keeping his

momentum. "These dark years must come to an end. This is the rightful way, and Nature's way. Balance must be restored, and the Suhl must once again stand equal with all beneath the sun!"

There were rumblings among the crowd and some downcast eyes lifted.

"This is the moment, sisters and brothers. Today in this place of peace; here in the Valley of Outs. Today you are nobody's slave! You are your own man and woman and child, proud of your Suhl blood, true to your Suhl heart!"

There were some cheers from the gathering and Espasian paused, waiting for quiet.

"But we do not stand alone. Even now, Sylas and Naeo are racing across our world, heading for the centre of Thoth's power. In another world, our friends, the Merisi, have begun their stand against Thoth and his Empire. This is Nature's balance being restored. We think of this valley as a place of tranquillity, but today she will be our sister in arms. She will lay herself before your enemy, and fight at your side, and defend you and all that you love!"

A triumphal roar swept along the shoreline. The Leaflikes started stamping in the mud, beating their long staffs against their shields with a rousing *thump*, *thump*, *thump* to rival the battle drums.

"And, sisters, brothers, just as the valley is our protector we must be hers. We must use every ounce of strength, every trace of spirit, every trick of cunning and conjuring that is left to us. Because this is the balance! The valley gives us life, and we must give it to her in return."

Espasian raised his arms and, summoning all his strength, he bellowed: "Come then, army of the Suhl with Nature at your side, and be thankful that you are here. Because yours is Nature's fight! You are hers, and she is yours, and we are one. If you fall, know that she is there to receive you; if you triumph, know that she will build with you a new world of balance, and truth, and hope!" He turned and swept his arm back towards the faces in the trees. "A world worthy of our children!"

At this the entire army began to stamp in time with the Leaflikes, drowning out the drums altogether. The Spoorrunners thumped their breastplates and the soldiers clashed their weapons, each man and woman adding to the warlike rhythm. The children too joined the cacophony, shouting from the treetops.

Somewhere in the rear ranks someone began to sing, and the melody was quickly taken up by those nearby. Soon the entire army was singing to the *thump, thump, thump* rhythm of the standing march. With full hearts and straining voices, they sang the familiar Song of the Valley:

> "*In far lands of dark and high lands and low,*
> *I hear songs of a place where none ever go;*
> *Locked in the hills, 'midst green velvet folds,*
> *A treasure more precious than gem-furnished gold,*
> *For there dwell the Suhl, the last broken band,*
> *There dwell the lost and there dwell the damned.*
> *'Tis their fortress, their temple, their garden of grace,*
> *Their last earthly haven, their glorious place.*"

Espasian knew that the moment had come, and he signalled to the commanders in their ranks. At once each of them ran forward to take their orders. He spoke quickly, shouting over the din, directing one here and another there in the valley. Each commander gave a low bow and then hurried back to their regiment, issuing swift instructions to their followers.

Bayleon was the last to approach, formidable in the full armour of a Spoorrunner, with a high neck guard, spirals of protective leather down his massive arms and the last surviving leather breastplate, embossed with the Eye of Heru. He bowed and then stepped up to Espasian and leaned into his ear.

"Now you've got them going!" he growled. He took a pace back, his beard parting in a smile. "What would you have me do, my Lord?"

Espasian rested a hand on his friend's shoulder and dispensed his orders quickly, so that Bayleon was running back to his regiment even as the other commanders started to lead theirs away. Still they sang, pounding the earth with boots and sandals. Some set out round the lake, heading for the far end of the valley; others struck out for the trees, preparing to climb.

Espasian stood alone, watching them go. He listened to their song, but did not sing. He was thinking about what they would find when they reached the heights of those hills, and the promise that he had made, and the orders that he had given.

So lost was he in these thoughts that he did not notice Filimaya step up behind him. When she touched his arm, he turned and blinked in surprise. She was wearing her splendid burgundy robes embroidered with gold and silver, and he saw that she once again had a purple braid in her long silver hair: the braid said to be made from the last threads of the Suhl standard. But what struck him the most was that she did not look sad or fearful. She was radiant.

"Don't worry yourself, brave Espasian," she said. "You are a fine and true leader, and that is all we can ask."

Espasian lowered his head graciously.

"And you are right," she added. "The valley is at our side."

He searched her face. "I wish I could be so sure."

Filimaya smiled and pointed across the lake. "Look," she said.

Merimaat's regiment was just passing beneath the boughs at the edge of the forest, still singing as they went. Espasian narrowed his eyes, his gaze moving between the marching figures and the forest. He saw at once that the trees surrounding the troops were swaying as though caught in a powerful gust of wind — not in one direction but in all, making a confusion of leaves and limbs. But, as they bowed and twisted, they did not spring back; if anything, the giant trunks and branches seemed to be bending ever lower until the lowest limbs fell between the passing ranks of the army.

The troops hesitated, and the singing faltered, but the Magruman started to smile. He glanced at Filimaya.

"The valley, is she—"

"Yes," said Filimaya, her eyes still fixed on the treeline.

As she spoke, the trees that had engulfed Merimaat's guard began to straighten, their branches sweeping away to reveal an incredible sight. The ragged troops that had led the march had been transformed into menacing warriors, resplendent in the most magnificent armour. They were girded about with a woven mesh of saplings like chain mail, plates of bark like armour and shoulder pads of moss and bracken. Each soldier now wore a fearsome helmet of woven twigs, topped by a splendid crest of leaves, which fanned and tapered in the manner of a feather.

The watching army raised a triumphal yell, and the march quickly resumed. Rank after rank, regiment after regiment pressed forward into the forest; and, as quickly as they went, the forest responded. Trees and bushes came together in an endless whirl of green, brown and orange, enfolding the army and beginning its transformation.

Through it all, the Song of the Valley struck up again, filling the spaces beneath the canopy, echoing across the lake, spilling over the hilltops. And, as those voices of the Suhl reached the Imperial army, the tireless rhythm of the battle drums fell silent, leaving those haunting words hanging in the air:

"Here is our essence, our home and our all,
Here hope fills the breast with a full-throated call:
Gather the lost and gather the damned,
Gather the Suhl, for here we will stand."

As they watched, Filimaya drew close to Espasian, sliding an arm
about his waist. And together they joined in the chorus.

Epilogue

THE SONG HAD LONG since faded, but Filimaya remained on the lakeshore, listening and watching. A new silence had descended upon the valley, as though a deep winter had fallen, cloaking the hills in thick, sound-snuffing snow and freezing the surface of the lake to a perfect mirror. But Filimaya knew that this calm was something else, something deeper.

It was the valley gathering herself, drawing earth, waters, root and sap to a single purpose. To a final, desperate effort.

Suddenly Filimaya realised that she too was holding her breath. She took several deep lungfuls of air and steadied her breathing.

"Come," she muttered, laughing at herself, "that's no way to carry on."

She smoothed down her robes, tucked the purple braid over her ear and set off towards the Hollow.

In the strange silence, she found herself very aware of the crunch of leaves as she walked, the sound of her breathing, the sharp crack of twigs underfoot. Then, to her surprise, she heard another sound: a voice somewhere among the trees. She stopped and listened, and heard it again behind a dense tangle of thorny thicket. She was about to call out when, all at once, Fathray stumbled into view amid a shower of leaves.

"Blasted hawthorn!" he grumbled, pulling his sleeve free of some thorns. "What is the point of you? Impudent shrub!" He yanked at his ensnared shoulder bag. "A useless weed, that's what you are! More pestilence than plant!" He pulled at his moustache, which had somehow woven itself into the thorns.

Filimaya suppressed a smile. "Oh, Fathray! Calm yourself!" she called, walking over to him. She gave a gentle tug on his beard and the thorns yielded. The old Scribe stumbled back and muttered something even more impolite to the bush.

He turned to Filimaya, his face softening. "I'm sorry, Filimaya, I'm just so — so *anxious*." The heavy lines returned to his face. "So terribly anxious."

Filimaya's smile faded. "How could you not be, Fathray?" she said. "We all are."

They fell silent for a moment, lost in their own thoughts.

"But we have the valley!" offered the old Scribe. "And we have Sylas and Naeo, do we not? Off on their adventure to the heart of it all! They may save us yet!"

Filimaya nodded. "They may," she said guardedly. "But we must not expect miracles, Fathray. They face so much and they know so little."

Fathray grunted and absently ran his fingers through his whiskers. There was another silence.

"I'm sorry, I have to go," said Filimaya brightly. "There is still so much to prepare in the Hollow before it's needed." She patted him affectionately on the arm and turned to leave, but then looked back. "Where are you going anyway?"

Fathray grinned and pointed a bony finger at the hilltop. "To where the fight is!"

Filimaya was astonished. "You're going to *fight*?"

"No!" He pulled a journal from his bag and waved it in the air. "To write! I am a Scribe, Filimaya, and I must write!"

Filimaya nodded slowly. "Of course. But really, Fathray, why not send one of the younger—"

"I am a Scribe," interjected Fathray, "and I am here. What else am I to do?" He took her hand. "I will climb these hills, my dear, hawthorns or no, and I will stand by my brothers and sisters, and I will write as though my life depended on it. I will write because, if this is the end, then something of us must remain. And, if this is not the end, I will write because we must remember." He gripped her hand. "It must never come to this again, do you see? Never again."

Filimaya placed her other hand on his. "Of course," she said, her eyes shining. "Of course. You must go."

He nodded, kissed the back of her hand, then he bid her farewell. With that, he marched off into the forest, muttering at the plants as he fought his way through the undergrowth.

Filimaya watched him affectionately and then she shivered, gathering her robes about her as though winter's chill had finally arrived and was gnawing at her bones. Then she too hurried off, in the direction of the Hollow.

PART TWO

At Sea

18

Far from Shore

"But it was far from shore *that the Suhl suffered their greatest losses. They found themselves lost without their kindred forests, meadows and streams and ill-prepared for naval battle."*

THE IMPACT MADE THE deck quiver like the surface of a drum, and two of the stay ropes snapped with a firecracker bang. A silvery sheet of icy seawater erupted skywards, drenching the feather standard, and then cascaded through the rigging, splashing down upon the crew and soaking them to the bone.

To Sylas, the freezing shower was a relief. It brought him back to the moment, back from the winds and the ship and Naeo. Suddenly he was among his companions, gasping for breath and clinging to the handrail, watching the bloom of foam spreading round the *Windrush*. He felt her roll, correcting herself, and then she settled, rocking gently with the waves. He turned and stared in disbelief at the cliff from which they had fallen and the rocks that might have dashed them to pieces. And only then did he realise that they had made it. They had reached the sea.

Just then Simia rushed up to him, fizzing with excitement.

"You did it!" she cried. She looked pale, but she was beaming with delight. "I thought we were going to crash for sure, but then... we just flew!"

Sylas smiled. "For a moment, Simsi. Then we fell!"

She grinned back. "Well, yes."

He looked down, still struggling to gather his thoughts. Moments before he had been lost in timbers and ropes and sails, guiding the *Windrush* through pastures and valleys and woods. All of a sudden there had been a cry from the crow's nest — "Lo! The sea! The sea!" — and, in what seemed a heartbeat, they had been out on the headland, careering down a pillow of soft gorse towards the cliffs. He had felt Naeo's hand tighten round his. Her fear. Her exhilaration. Her conviction that, together, just about anything was possible.

And then, as Simia had said, the *Windrush* had flown.

But now that they were finally here, on the waves, the thrill and that sense of possibility felt very far away. Now, Sylas was overcome by exhaustion. He clung to the handrail, suddenly so weak that if he had let go he might have fallen.

Simia leaned down and peered into his ashen face. "Are you all right?"

He nodded. "Just tired," he said. "Really tired."

"Not surprised!' she exclaimed breathlessly. "You've been going for ages, two hours, maybe three — I've lost track!" She giggled excitedly. "Time kind of... stopped *mattering*, you know?" She hesitated and looked at him more closely. "Sylas, you really do look terrible. You should get some rest."

"I was just going to say the same thing," said Ash, his face appearing between theirs. He was wet through, and he looked rather comical with his great mop of hair plastered to his face. He glanced from one to the other. "Go on, you two, I can take over from here. You need to keep up your strength."

Sylas looked at him gratefully. "Is that all right?"

"Of course!" said Ash brightly. "If I can sail this tub half as well on water as you did on land, we'll be in Old Kemet before you can say Muddlemorph!"

Sylas smiled. "Thanks, Ash."

He straightened and looked about the ship properly for the first time. Already the *Windrush* was bustling. Crew members rushed here and there, collecting pieces of broken rigging, swabbing the decks and lashing down anything that had come loose, all under the watchful direction of Fawl, who seemed to know exactly what needed to be done. There appeared to be a new cheer and confidence about him, perhaps because the ship was back on water where it belonged, and he conducted everything with bold sweeps of his one arm. He gave Sylas a nod and a grin.

"Come on," said Simia, gesturing to the nearest hatch. "I know the way. We're sharing a cabin."

Sylas was about to follow her when he caught a glimpse of his mother talking to one of the women. She glanced at him, clearly anxious to come over, but the woman seemed intent on showing her a cut on her forearm and telling her the tale of how she had got it, and Amelie was too polite to interrupt.

"Did you hear? Ash has made your mum the ship's doctor," said Simia. "She's going to be in the doctor's cabin." She reached for his arm. "Come on, Sylas, if you don't lie down, you're going to fall down!"

And with that she led him to the forward hatch and then down below, leaving his mother staring after him.

Their cabin was the triangular Bow Room that they had visited with Paiscion. A handful of the Magruman's collection of curiosities remained, including the twin mirrors of the Glimmer Glass that were fixed to the angled walls at the very point of the bow, and Paiscion's treasured gramophone with its gigantic brass horn, held fast to the wall by two leather straps. All of Paiscion's scientific objects had been taken away, deemed too precious to make the journey.

Simia helped Sylas to lay down a simple straw mattress with a sheet and a blanket, and then she started to move two more for her and Ash. She would not hear of Sylas helping and, in a rather motherly tone, she told him to lie down and rest.

Just as she finally settled back on her own newly made bed, the ship gave a lurch and the cabin tilted, making several of Paiscion's objects slide across the floor. Waves dashed against the portholes and then fell away, and before long they could hear the thump and rake of waves on the hull as the *Windrush* surged on.

"Ash has got the hang of it then," said Sylas absently.

Simia glanced across. "Can't sleep?"

Sylas shook his head. "I just keep thinking about it all."

"Well, if you can't sleep," said Simia, propping herself up on an elbow, "how about we talk?"

"What about?" asked Sylas, a little wearily.

"I don't know, there's just so much!" she said excitedly. "Tell me about the Quintessence! Tell me how you knew what to do! How it worked?"

Sylas ran his fingers through his salty hair, trying to think back to the beginning of their journey. He found it difficult to sort through his memories. They seemed to him more like a collection of feelings and sensations than events. "I don't know how we knew what to do. It just seemed — I don't know — natural. To reach for the Quintessence, I mean. And then, when it covered the *Windrush*, everything was just... easier."

He glanced at Simia. "I know that doesn't really tell you much. I suppose we felt more... *connected* with everything in the ship, like we were all one thing. I could feel the *Windrush* as though it was part of me, and also the wind in the sails, the way it pulled on the ropes..." He trailed off for a moment as he remembered.

"I was closer to Naeo than before too. I knew what she was going to do before she did it. And I think she knew what I was about to do." He shrugged and gave an embarrassed smile. "It all sounds weird when I say it out loud."

"But you think it was all about the Quintessence? It made it everything possible?"

Sylas blew out his cheeks. "I think so. It was like the feeling I had from the Merisi Band when Naeo and I were first together, but this was... I don't know, sharper... deeper. I'm not sure I was completely myself, if that makes sense. I was *more* than myself. The Quintessence made us part of each other — me, Naeo *and* the *Windrush*."

He waited for one of Simia's wisecracks, but she said nothing. Instead she was quiet for some moments, and then she started rummaging in her bag. She pulled out an old notebook — her Scribbler as she liked to call it — and an inkpot and quill.

"So this Quintessence is somehow part of everything, isn't it?" she said, flicking through the pages.

Sylas nodded. "I think so. That's what Paiscion said."

"So we need to understand it, don't we?" said Simia, choosing a page and scrawling something on it.

Sylas covered his eyes with his forearm. "Maybe."

"So..." said Simia, continuing to scribble, "perhaps it'll help if we work out *everywhere* we've come across it so far, like we started to do with Paiscion. Maybe there's a pattern or something."

"Uh-huh," grunted Sylas, starting to feel weary all over again.

Simia continued to scribble and finally she declared: "Right, so this is my list so far. The Passing Bell. The Merisi Band. The Glimmertrome." She looked up and pointed her quill at the mirrors in the bow. "The Glimmer Glass..."

Sylas lifted his arm from his eyes. "The Flight of Fancy."

Simia frowned. "The what?"

"You know, I told you about it. The mobile of birds that Mr Zhi showed me — back in the Shop of Things. All the birds were hanging from silvery string. That *had* to be Quintessence."

"Right," said Simia, mouthing the words as she noted them down. "And now there's the Quintessence here, on the *Windrush*." She chewed her quill for a moment and then narrowed her eyes. "What about the staff thing that Isia's priestess had — the one she used to scare the Ragers, remember? *That* was silvery gold. And it was magical. Remember how it opened the door to the temple?"

"Yes, maybe you're right," said Sylas. He propped himself up. "It did look like Quintessence."

He was becoming ever more intrigued by Simia's exercise and found himself thinking back over his whole adventure, from the very beginning. As he recalled his first moments in the gloomy Shop of Things, his eyes widened.

"The glove!" he exclaimed.

"Which glove?"

"Mr Zhi's glove! The one he was wearing when I met him! It was embroidered with silver and gold!" His eyes danced as he pieced together his memories. "Ash said all of the Merisi have one. He said they used their gloves to defend themselves, remember?"

"Uh-huh," said Simia eagerly as she wrote 'Merisi gloves' into her Scribbler. When she had finished, she looked into space, tapping the quill on her cheek, then she glanced at Sylas. "Ash told us something else about the Merisi too. Remember the necklace they put on Scarpia at the Winterfern Hospital? He said it seemed to take away all her power."

"You're right!" said Sylas excitedly. "A silver-gold necklace, he said, like the Merisi Band!" He pointed at the Scribbler. "Write it down!"

Simia scribbled, smiling proudly as she looked at the full list. Then her eyes rose slowly from the page.

"You know what this means, don't you?"

Sylas looked at her questioningly.

"Well, think about it!" she said impatiently. "Quintessence really has been part of everything right from the very beginning! From Mr Zhi, to the Shop of Things, to the Merisi Band, to the Passing Bell, to the Glimmer Glass, right here to our cabin!" She jabbed a finger at the mirrors in the bow. "And, even when you and Naeo split up and went your separate ways, the Quintessence was still with you. Naeo found it with the Merisi at that Winterfern Hospital, and you found it at the temple with the priestess and her staff!"

Sylas leaned forward, elbows on his knees. "And, when we came together again, it was by using the Glimmertrome, which is made of Quintessence too!"

Simia looked back at her list, quivering with excitement. "And if it's part of your whole journey, from the beginning all the way to now —" her eyes returned to Sylas — "it has to be part of the end too!"

"The list isn't finished," said Sylas thoughtfully. "Just like this journey isn't finished."

Simia sat still further forward. "You know what you should be doing? You should be reading about Quintessence in there!" She pointed at the rucksack lying beside him. "In the Samarok! The answers might be in there right now!"

Sylas reached for his bag and rummaged through it until his fingers found the soft, warm bulk of the Samarok. As he brought it out and placed it on his lap, he frowned and said, "It's not just Quintessence I need to learn about. Isn't one of those things on your list much, much more important than all the others?"

Simia's eyes returned to her Scribbler.

"Which one took more Quintessence to make than any of the

others?" probed Sylas. "So much that it drained the mines in the valley?"

Simia's eyes grew wide. "The Passing Bell!"

Sylas nodded. "The bell made by Merimaat herself!" He opened the Samarok and laid it gently in his lap. "The bell between worlds!" He started leafing through the pages.

Suddenly Simia murmured: "Sylas?"

He looked up and saw that she was staring at the Samarok.

"Look at the cover," she said breathlessly.

He closed the ancient tome and inspected the front cover. He took in the beautiful gleaming red stones, the S-shaped groove snaking across the faded leather where the Merisi Band had been. Then he saw the stitching that ran in a zigzag pattern all the way round the four edges, gleaming a bright, shining gold. He fumbled the Samarok over and saw that there, adorning the four edges of the rear cover, was the same zigzag pattern, this time in silver.

Simia looked at him with a widening grin. "It's part of the Samarok too!"

He grinned back. "And I've been carrying it all along!"

He parted the covers, flicking through the dry old pages, letting his eyes adjust to the Ravel Runes.

"Bell... bell... bell," he murmured, his eyes scanning the handwritten pages. "It has to be here..." Then his eyes came to rest on a single word. "*Chime*," he said. "Yes, I can start with that!"

He looked up and saw that Simia had edged closer, her eyes sparkling with excitement. "Go on," she said, nodding to the page. "And tell me everything!"

Sylas crossed his legs, laid the Samarok before him and began.

19

The Importance
of Knowing

*"It is impossible to overstate the importance of
knowing how and why all this began. If we do not
know the source, how can we ever know the cure?"*

NAEO LIKED THE SMALLNESS and darkness of her little cabin,
which felt pleasantly familiar after all her time in the stone cells
of the Dirgheon. But her flimsy hammock was a problem. She
found its swinging motion very unsettling, and more than once it
had almost spilled her out. To make matters worse, the tight press
of the canvas had aggravated the pain in her back, which gathered
at the base of her spine and swept up and out across her shoulders.
But what made sleep utterly impossible was Triste sitting in the
corner of the room, staring at her.

She looked down at the Scryer irritably. She had a perfect view
of his tattooed scalp, with its still-livid burns, as he puffed away
at his pipe, sending plumes of pleasant-smelling orange smoke into
the air.

"Triste, are you still here?" she said.

He pulled the pipe from his lips and frowned at the oddness of the question. "Clearly," he said.

"But *why?*"

"Because you said you needed to rest," he said matter-of-factly. "So I'm waiting until you've rested."

"But I *can't* rest with you here."

Triste grunted. "I see." He shrugged. "So... shall we just talk?"

Naeo put her arm over her eyes and sighed. "All right. Why not?"

"Excellent!" he exclaimed, taking another long draw on his pipe.

A long silence ensued until Naeo started to wonder if she was supposed to say something. She looked out from beneath her arm to discover him gazing at her with his fathomless eyes. He looked fascinated.

He blew out a long stream of smoke. "What do you think happened up there?"

Naeo frowned. "You mean in the battle?"

"Yes, and after."

She sighed. "Well, I think Sylas and I connected better than we ever have before, if that's what you're getting at?"

Triste nodded. "And do you think the Quintessence helped?"

"I know it did."

"How so?"

She thought back, trying to make sense of her feelings. "Well, I could feel how much easier it was to connect. It was like we weren't separate at all — me, Sylas, even the *Windrush*. It was as if we were all part of the same thing." She traced a hand over the timber at her side, then looked back at Triste. "Sounds strange to say it now, but the wind in the sails felt like it was pushing *me* along, not the ship."

"So what happened when you lost control?"

Naeo turned away and looked out of the porthole. "I was thinking about my father. About leaving him behind. That I might not see him again." Her thoughts drifted away for a moment. "We had so little time together after all those years apart. And now he's sick. He needs me and I've left him. It just doesn't seem right." She sighed. "And somehow it doesn't seem fair that Sylas..." She trailed off, then took a sharp breath and blurted: "That Sylas has his mother, right here. I don't begrudge him that — of course I don't — but... so much is the *same* between us. I just wish *that* could be too."

Triste was silent for a long moment. He saw the depth of her emotion and chose his next question with care.

"So you lost control when you felt *different* from Sylas?"

Naeo was about to respond when the ship lurched into motion. The old timbers creaked and shuddered. Then there was a thump against the hull. They felt the *Windrush* rise slowly on the waves and begin skipping between their peaks.

"I think Ash has got the hang of it," said Naeo, peering out at the passing surf. She looked back at Triste. "I didn't think he had it in him, you know?"

Triste's eyes were still fixed on her. "Do you think that's what happened, Naeo?" he pressed. "Do you think the difference... *got in the way* somehow?"

Naeo sighed and ran her fingers through her tangled hair. "I suppose, yes. Why are you so interested?"

"Because I think it's important," said the Scryer. Then he shrugged. "And because your father asked me to help you."

Naeo pushed herself up a little. "*Help* me?"

"Yes, and I didn't think I could. But now... Now, I'm starting to think I can."

"How?"

"I think I might be able to help you to understand Sylas, and your connection. What I saw just now, between you and Sylas, was —" his eyes shone even in the dim cabin — "magnificent, Naeo. Incredible. What I saw shouldn't be possible."

Naeo pushed herself up still further. "What did you see?"

Triste pressed his fingertips together and frowned in concentration. "Your bond is powerful, that much is certain. But there's something about it that I would never have expected." He smiled and shook his head, as if finding his own memory hard to believe. "Naeo, you and Sylas *shared* your emotions! I saw it! Your feelings of grief and loss travelled between you, and so did Sylas's feelings of joy and hope." He paused, for a moment lost in his memories. Then he fixed her with his deep, intelligent eyes. "Normally we Scryers see feelings as an aura — a gathering of colour and form around a single soul. But, in you two, your emotions were like... like a river of feeling flowing in both directions!"

Naeo shifted uncomfortably. "You saw that?"

Triste nodded and leaned forward, pointing at her with the stem of his pipe. "You and Sylas are quite distinct, but the bond between you is greater than your gift with Essenfayle. Your outward powers are just the way it shows itself. Your bond goes right to the heart — it's in the way you feel and think. It's in the way you are. Until you understand it, until you truly *know* it, *believe* in it, it'll surprise you, like it did earlier today. It'll rule you instead of you ruling it."

"What does that even mean?" snapped Naeo defensively, unnerved that Triste thought he understood so much about her.

"I'm not entirely sure, Naeo. But I do know this: you and Sylas are a glimpse of something much, much larger than yourselves. You're part of the Glimmer Myth in all its mystery and power. Your struggle goes to the heart of who we all are. And, if you're to face the challenges to come, if you're to make the Glimmer

Myth come true — heal the rift between worlds and souls — the kind of confusion that arose between you earlier today just *can't* happen. It *mustn't* happen. You and Sylas must know one another as well as you know yourselves."

Naeo let her head fall back on to the hammock. She knew Triste was right. She and Sylas had a connection, but she could not say that she knew him.

She remembered then something Espasian had said to her once when they were together in the Dirgheon. He had been teaching her how to summon the Passing Bell, how she had to reach out for Sylas. "*Know him, and he will find you,*" he had said. And later, when she had visited Sylas in his dreams, she had found herself using those very words. "*Know me, and you will find me,*" she had said.

She looked at Triste. "So... if we know each other like you're saying, you think we'll be stronger?"

Triste took another puff of his pipe. "Immeasurably. Your strength is in your connection, and what connection can be stronger than knowing?"

Naeo sat up, swinging rather precariously in her hammock. "So how should I get to know him? It's not easy even to be near each other."

The Scryer blew out a ring of smoke that began orange and then shimmered red. "That's what I was thinking about while you were resting."

"*Trying* to rest," said Naeo pointedly.

"It has something to do with Quintessence," said the Scryer as though he hadn't heard her. "Quintessence seems to be at the heart of it all. And, of all the things of Quintessence, one of them seems to be best suited."

"Which is...?"

"That which allows you to be together even when you're apart," said Triste, his eyes travelling to the shelf at the end of Naeo's hammock, to where the Glimmertrome gleamed dimly by the light of the porthole.

Naeo stared at it for a moment, then reached for it and turned it over in her hands.

"It may not *seem* like you're far apart," said Triste, "but you are in here." He tapped the side of his head with the stem of his pipe. "The Glimmertrome will bring you together without any discomfort, so that you can see him as he truly is. Even better, you can use it when he isn't expecting it. That way you see him not as he is with others but as he is with himself. *That's* how you'll truly learn about him."

As Triste spoke, Naeo took in the fine features of the Glimmertrome: the tapering housing of ancient wood; the twin panels on its front, one white and one black; the ornate needle of gleaming silvery gold. Her mind flew back to when she had last released that needle, shattering her sense of self, sending her hurtling between worlds, into Sylas's thoughts and emotions. She remembered the back and forth between her own mind and his, leaving her bewildered, disorientated, undone. She had hoped never to do it again.

But perhaps this would be different, she mused. Back then she had been flying for her life between the worlds, and Sylas had been in a battle of his own aboard the *Windrush*. Now, they would be here, safe and surrounded by friends.

She looked at Triste. "You really think it'll help?"

"Yes," he said, rising stiffly to his feet. He walked over and stood next to her hammock, gazing down at the Glimmertrome. "And can we really afford not to try?"

She looked back at the Glimmertrome and ran a finger from the base of the needle to the tip, letting it rest on the ornate clasp that held it in place.

"I'm going to try it," she said. "Now."

Triste nodded and placed a large hand on her shoulder. "And I'm here," he said.

Naeo took a breath, then reached over, flipped the clasp and tipped the needle into the black.

20

The Last Word

*"Young Haoran Zhi shows great promise, but for now at
least, Master Hernández has the first and* the last word."

SYLAS BROUGHT HIS FACE close to the page of the Samarok, letting
his eyes adjust to the peculiar curls and coils of the Ravel Runes.

Slowly they revealed their meaning.

It was a passage describing a Suhl tradition called the Mana
Dao in which common people gather to sing *from the chime of
midnight to the break of dawn*. It happened on the summer
and winter solstices, to *give thanks for the power of the
sun and the moon, and the passage between the worlds*.

To his disappointment, there was no mention of the Passing
Bell.

He took a deep breath and rested his eyes on the word *chime*.
Then he did his best to clear his thoughts, forget the sway of the
ship and Simia's excited breathing at his side, and he turned his
mind back to his first sighting of the Passing Bell. He saw it
suspended high above the forest, at one end of its colossal swing,
gleaming in the night sky.

Almost straight away the runes responded to his imaginings.
He watched the tiny lines and loops of the word begin to

uncurl, and soon the entire passage was coiling and writhing like a nest of snakes. Then, as quickly as it had begun, the page settled and became still, and a new passage lay before Sylas's eyes.

He was about to begin reading when something made him look up. He glanced at the door and, seeing that it was closed, he looked round the room.

Simia followed his eyes. "What?" she asked.

"I just..." He trailed off and frowned. "It felt like someone was watching."

"Where?" asked Simia, looking around. "What do you mean?"

Sylas shook his head. "I don't know. Ever get that feeling that someone's looking over your shoulder?"

Simia directed her eyes pointedly to the page. "Are you going to read or not?" she asked witheringly.

He took one more look round the cabin, then dropped his eyes and started to read out loud:

"My first sighting of the Passing Bell was almost impossible to describe. It was not the thing I had read about in my apprenticeship as a Bringer. It was not simply 'burning bright' or 'perfect' or 'grand'. Its chime was not just 'deafening' or 'overwhelming'. It was all of these things and much, much more. My impression of the Passing Bell is no more and no less than pure, heart-rending, exquisite beauty. Beauty that was borrowed from the splendour of the stars, that was at once a sight, and a sound, and a feeling. Beauty that, even now, makes my heart ache to think of it."

Sylas stopped reading and stared at the page. "That's *exactly* what it was like," he breathed.

Simia's eyes shifted impatiently between Sylas and the Samarok. "Right. So what does it say next?"

He scanned down the passage. "It talks about the way the bell moved, how it seemed to pull the clouds towards it." He looked up. "Like it pulled at the rain when it was ringing for me."

Simia nodded. "But what does it say about Quintessence?"

"Nothing," said Sylas, reading on. "The writer just talks about how only they could hear the chime, even though to them it was deafening. That was the same with me too. And they say they saw runes round the rim of the bell, but they blacked out before they could read them. I saw them as well." Sylas shook his head. "That's all. They don't mention Quintessence at all."

Simia shrugged. "So how does that help us?"

"I'm not sure it does." Sylas thought for a moment and then looked up excitedly. "Maybe I'm doing this all wrong! When you use the Ravel Runes, it matters what you're thinking. Just now I was thinking about when I first saw the bell, so I found a piece about exactly that. What I really want is a passage about what the Passing Bell is made of, so I need to think of that!"

He scanned the page for the word bell, then set the book down and turned his mind back to the teardrop of Quintessence in the mines. He thought about the chambers and tunnels as they would once have looked, streaming with Quintessence, and he imagined miners gathering it, channelling it, harvesting it, ready to be worked into the bell.

Already the Ravel Runes had begun to shift. They turned and twisted before his eyes, quickly settling to a new passage written in a very different hand.

Sylas was about to begin reading when he stopped short. His eyes jumped to the opposite page and he stared.

A shiver traced his spine. It was his *own* handwriting. He read the opening line under his breath: *"My name is Sylas Tate and I am not a Bringer. I am my mother's son, and that seems to be enough."*

Simia leaned in. "What's... *that*?"

"That's me," he said. "The first thing I wrote in the Samarok when we were on the Barrens. Which means that this one —" he pointed to the previous facing page — "is the one just before mine: the very last entry in the Samarok."

"But we're not at the back of the book."

Sylas nodded. "It doesn't matter. The Ravel Runes brought us here. That's how they work."

Simia gave a low whistle. "So go on, what does it say?"

He turned back and looked at the entry properly for the first time. It was written in a very different hand from any he had read before. Here the Ravel Runes were tiny and tightly packed, made up of impossibly intricate strokes. His eye travelled to the bottom of the page, where he was hoping to find a name, but it was signed with a simple, solitary 'M'. 'M' for Merisi perhaps? It had to be, he thought. After all this was the last entry of their great work.

But then he began to read.

"They toiled in the darkest confines of the earth, tunnelling and digging, hoisting and carrying without sight of the sun for days on end. And, when the mines had run dry, these same men and women roved beyond the valley, risking discovery and capture, seeking what other traces of Quintessence there might be.

"They did it all without question. It was enough, it seems, that I asked it, even when their labours yielded so little, even when it was clear that Quintessence was

only to be found in any quantity around the roots of the Living Tree. Still they struggled on without complaint because such are the Suhl: loyal and noble and courageous to the last."

Sylas paused and his eyes shifted back down to the solitary 'M' beneath the passage.

He looked up at Simia. "This isn't the Merisi," he declared. "This is Merimaat!"

"I knew the Samarok would be important!" said Simia. "Go on! What does she say about the bell?"

"I think it's *all* about the bell," he said and then read on.

"Whenever I stood before the glowing pool of Quintessence, I saw in its surface not only my own face, but the faces of the many who had given their only years of freedom to make it. And so, when the time came to forge the Thing that would heal the worlds, I called them all to stand with me and bear witness.

"They asked how it would be done, what it would look like, what it would do, and I explained that I did not know. That it would be crafted by Nature herself. It would be her creation because the rift was a wrong done to Her. I knew only that it must bear the inscription given to me by Isia herself: the words—"

He stopped again and stared at the Ravel Runes, skin prickling.

Simia nudged him. "So?" she said impatiently. "What's the inscription?"

He met her eyes. "*So at last we may be one.*"

Simia blinked at him, a smile growing across her face. "Of course it is! The line in Merisu's poem! The start of the whole Glimmer

154

Myth! Of *course* it's that!" She elbowed him sharply. "And that isn't all! It spells your names too! Yours and Naeo's!"

"Yes," said Sylas thoughtfully. "Everything's tied together. Merimaat and the Merisi, Isia and the bell, Naeo and me, we're all—"

And then, quite suddenly, his face fell slack and his eyes went blank, as though his words and his thoughts had been quite snuffed out. As he sat transfixed, the Samarok slid from his fingers and landed on the floor.

"Sylas?" said Simia anxiously. She leaned forward and stared into his face. "Sylas, stop it! You're scaring me!"

§

Naeo came back to herself with a jolt, swaying in the hammock. She nearly dropped the Glimmertrome and Triste snatched it from her, holding it carefully so that the needle was free to travel on across the white panel.

She blinked, then looked down at her arms, turning them over before her eyes as she struggled to get her bearings.

"You were there with him?" asked Triste.

Naeo was silent for a moment. "More like I... *was* him."

"What was he doing?"

"Reading. Reading the Samarok." She looked up into Triste's animated face. "He read the Ravel Runes. I've — I've never seen anything like it. They actually *moved*, like they were alive!"

Triste's eyes danced over her face. "And did you see his thoughts?"

"No," Naeo said, narrowing her eyes. "I only heard what he said to Simia."

Triste looked a little disappointed. "But you saw everything he did?"

Naeo drew her legs up and wrapped her arms round them. She nodded. "He's learning about the Passing Bell and Quintessence.

155

They're together — he and Simia, I mean. They're reading about Merimaat and how she forged the bell."

Triste nodded, waiting for Naeo to say more.

She rested her chin on her knees. "They seem so close, you know, Sylas and Simia. It's like they've always known each other. It was her idea to look in the Samarok — to learn about Quintessence."

Triste smiled. "Simia is much wiser than she seems," he said.

"You said that I need to see things that are different about him — about Sylas," said Naeo. "Well, I suppose Simia's a difference. I don't make friends. Not good friends like that. I never have." She looked out of the porthole. "I don't even know *how*."

Triste seemed intrigued. "Why do you think that is?"

"Not sure. Perhaps I haven't been around people enough. I just can't imagine *trusting* anyone in that way."

The Scryer cocked his head to one side. "Perhaps you don't need to imagine."

She looked at him. "What do you mean?"

"Perhaps Sylas can show you, the way he showed you the Ravel Runes."

Triste looked down at the Glimmertrome and carefully placed a finger on the needle, stopping its slow, sweeping motion across the white panel. Then he carefully drew it back to the midpoint and fixed it with the clasp.

"We're stopping?" asked Naeo, surprised.

"Yes, for now."

"But I'm not sure I've really *learned* anything."

The Scryer smiled. "Oh, I think this was a very good start," he said. "A very good start indeed."

21

The Bell

"After all, the bell occupies a unique place in our lives.
It calls us to prayer and it marks our final departure.
It proclaims our moments of greatest joy and deepest sorrow.
It's as if it's bound up with our very soul."

"A VERY GOOD START indeed," Sylas heard, then he had the bizarre sense that everything about him — the cabin, Triste, the porthole, the hammock — all of it had collapsed into itself. There was a rush of light and noise and then Simia was shaking him. Her eyes were wide and staring.

"Sylas!" she panted. "Sylas, speak to me!"

He reached up and took her by the arms. "I'm all right," he said.

She gazed into his eyes, then slumped back. "I thought it was all happening again! Like in the temple, when you ate that fruit of the Knowing Tree."

Sylas raised hands that felt strangely alien and rubbed his face. "Well, it was a bit like that," he said. "But this was Naeo. She's using the Glimmertrome."

Simia screwed up her face. "She's *what?*"

He shrugged. "She was using the Glimmertrome, like before,

157

when we were on the *Windrush* and she came through the Circle of Salsimaine."

Simia was indignant. "She just went ahead and used it without warning you?"

Until he saw Simia's reaction, it hadn't occurred to Sylas to be annoyed with Naeo. But he found that he wasn't because he knew exactly why she had done it.

"She was with Triste," he explained. "I think she was trying to see me... as I am. She didn't want me to know so that I just acted normally. Just, you know... me."

Simia took a length of her red hair and coiled it round her finger. "So she was *spying* on us all that time we were talking? And when you were reading the Samarok?"

"I don't think she was really spying, Simsi," laughed Sylas. "But yes, I think she was probably there from when I thought someone was watching us."

"Because she was," said Simia with a shudder. She considered all this for a moment, then rubbed her temples. "And then... you were *with* her, after she was *with* you?"

"Yes," said Sylas, surprised at how well he understood it, and how peculiarly natural it all felt. "And she felt *closer* than when we used the Glimmertrome before. I was focused on her this time, not just what was happening. And she was focused on me too. She was talking about us actually, you and me."

Simia leaned in. "Why? What was she saying?"

"She was talking about us being friends. She said she doesn't have anything like that."

Simia flushed a little. "She said that?"

Sylas nodded.

For a moment Simia seemed genuinely lost for words. "Is — is she... *with* you now? Because perhaps you shouldn't be telling me—"

"No, Simsi. Triste stopped the needle."

"Oh." She glanced at him, more intrigued than ever. "So what else did you see?"

He picked up the Samarok from the floor and leafed through it to the page he had been reading. "Not much. She was mainly talking about what *she'd* seen." He looked up. "But it was strange hearing how she saw me. She was pretty amazed at how I read Ravel Runes."

"Well, that is pretty weird, you know," said Simia.

Sylas grinned, but then his smile faded. He was remembering something else. "I could feel her pain, Simsi, as well. Right across here —" he swept his hand over his shoulder — "and right down below my shoulder blades." He met her eyes. "It's bad, you know. She's much stronger than I'd realised. To put up with *that* without saying anything."

"Well, she's definitely *tough*," said Simia thoughtfully. "I've always known that."

They were quiet for a few moments, then Sylas glanced down at the passage he had been reading. "Shall I carry on?" he asked. "We should read it all, shouldn't we?"

"Definitely," said Simia. She peered over his shoulder. After Naeo's comments, she was keener than ever to see the runes at work.

Sylas let his eyes settle on the page, and he began:

"When the day came to summon forth the Thing of Quintessence, there was much excitement and anticipation. The first we saw was a golden ring an arm-span wide. We thought that this must be the creation: a doorway, perhaps, between the worlds. But then it climbed and climbed above the valley floor, until the Passing Bell was revealed in all its splendour: vast and beautiful, like Nature's own teardrop. And there, at its base, was the inscription so full of promise:

"'So at last we may be one.'

"Since that day, the bell has done so much for us. For both the Suhl, and for our brothers and sisters in the Merisi. It has brought us together and, through the Bringers, enabled us to share our knowledge of our two worlds. More than that, it has helped us to plan, in the hope that the Glimmer Myth will one day come to pass.

"But, in truth, it was not the creation we had hoped for. When it chimes, its knell is heard not, as I hoped, by nations and continents but by one person alone. And so it has not repaired the division of the worlds nor healed the souls of humankind.

"Perhaps if the bell had been greater still. Perhaps if we had discovered more Quintessence beneath the valley. Perhaps if the Black had not risen in its place. Perhaps if I had been better at my task...

"But now time is short. Thoth's forces gather on the plains of Salsimaine, and I fear that a kind of reckoning is upon us. So, if this is to be my last entry in the Samarok, I leave you with this: hope. Hope that all we have done is not done in vain. Hope that it is a beginning. Hope that the bell is yet to do its greatest work.

"Or that whoever brings it forth is to do theirs.
M"

Sylas stared at the M, hoping perhaps that this final rune might unravel. Reveal something more. But it stood starkly on the page, unchanging, dark and final.

These were Merimaat's last words, and their significance fell upon him with the weight of the ages. If the bell offered any hope, it was only that it would one day bring him and Naeo together. And so now everything rested on them.

The Samarok slipped again from his fingers and he stared at the floor. He felt Simia's arm across his shoulders, and some unconscious memory made him wince as though it should hurt. But there was no pain, and he let her draw him close.

22

The Two Armies

"There on the fields of Salsimaine the two armies *met:*
one fighting for dominance, the other for life and freedom.
It became known as the Reckoning, but even that is perhaps
too light a term for all that came to pass."

ESPASIAN CLIMBED THE FINAL few yards of Carrion Rock until
he was just feet from the summit. The granite beneath his feet
quaked with the rumble of battle drums and the air about him
trembled, but he did not falter. He had prepared himself and he
knew that his army was watching.

But, as he reached the crest and saw what lay beyond, he almost
missed his step. Before him was the Westercleft Plain, and it was
transformed. Where once there were wide expanses of purple
heather and golden grass, there was now an ocean of mud. Pastures
marbled with silver streams were now a rutted mire, pummelled
by wheel and foot and claw.

And there, where the plains met the hills of the Valley of Outs,
was Thoth's army. It sprawled over the lower reaches of the hills,
forming an unbroken line that stretched away in both directions.
Countless standards fluttered above the masses, all of them bearing
the glaring, empty visage of Thoth and, below, the two concentric

circles of the Imperial army and, beneath them, the marking of the regiment. Some were from the mercenary armies of Baset and Surek, but most bore the insignia of the Fifth Division of the Imperial Army: regiments from Srasgar, Krak, Perisander, Trisk — the northernmost reaches of the Empire. But there were regiments from the Motherland too, from as far away as Karnak of Old Kemet, and to Espasian their presence was telling. This had been long in the planning.

His eyes flicked between the formations of beasts and men. The Ghorhund were at the front, prowling ahead of the masses, scenting the air and snapping at the distant enemy. The Ghor were a chilling contrast behind, gathered in disciplined formation, resplendent in the black and blood-red armour of the Imperial army. He could just make out their half-human faces turned up to the heights of the hills, surveying and calculating. When the attack began, it would be at the direction of the Ghor; it was always that way.

To their rear were three or four lines of Ra'ptahs — the Ragers — with their reptilian tails lashing the air in expectation, bodies glowing with seams of lava red. Their massive forms held at bay a riot of Hamajaks that pranced and leapt, hungry for battle. Above and between all these creatures were the Tythish, their long limbs sprawling between the lines while their large, unblinking eyes searched the treeline above. Espasian cast his eyes quickly over these, and the strange catlike creatures that stalked and patrolled at the very rear, until he was squinting out into the expanses beyond.

He knew they would be there.

He scanned the mashed and crumpled earth, the bruised, upended vegetation, the quagmire that was once a marsh. And then he saw one hunched over a distant mound of earth. Then another at its side. The Ogresh scooped up mud and silt in great earthen hands and fed. He saw their mighty arms, their giant shoulders, their great, pendulous heads, all formed of the stuff they ate: mud and grit and bracken. Such was their form for the moment. He knew they would change soon enough, once the battle had begun.

He could see ten of them now, colossal and irresistible, some hunched over their meal, others loping across the wasteland to some appointed place behind the ranks. There they would wait, and feed, until they were needed.

Espasian hoped his army could not see them yet. That they might be spared that terror at least.

His eyes drifted back now, past the might of Thoth's army up the long slope to the fringes of the forest. There he saw the Suhl strung out before the trees, no more than one man or woman every ten strides. But they too looked menacing, girded as they were in plates of bark lashed tight with vines. Pale faces were hidden behind fearsome helmets topped with great crests of leaves and ferns. And they had new weapons: long timber pikes – not straight because these were forest-grown but strong and wieldy. There were axes and spears made from stout branches and shards of flint, yielded up by the valley and found scattered across the forest floor.

And there was Essenfayle, he reminded himself – there was always Essenfayle. There were Weavers dotted here and there, and many adepts among the warriors themselves. Essenfayle would be their weapon of choice and, when the time came, it would be a mighty storm, worthy of Nature herself.

But he knew that even this was far from enough. Where the Suhl had Essenfayle, their enemy had Kimiyya, and Urgolvane, and Druindil. Where the defenders of the valley had armour of bark and weapons of wood and flint, their opponents had steel and tooth and claw. And what worried Espasian most were the numbers. There were perhaps thirty Imperial troops to every one of the Suhl, each of them born to fight, strong, well fed and ready for battle.

Just then his attention was drawn to something moving in the trees. He spied a child's face peeping between the leaves, and then he saw that there were many such small faces scattered among the canopy all along the crest of the hill.

The children were still watching.

An unexpected fury swelled within him. He thought of the innocents and all that they would witness. The cruelty and the tragedy of war that would play out before them. But now, it was too late to gather them back into the valley. What must be must be.

His rage swelled at the futility of it all, the waste and the wrong, and finally he threw his fists in the air and bellowed not so much a rallying cry as a roar of anger.

And his army roared back.

Spoorrunners, Leaflikes, Scryers, men and women, young and old bellowed their rage and defiance and, for a moment, they silenced the enemy drums. The Suhl stamped their feet and shook their fists and thumped their timber shields. The stunned army below fell silent, and some of the Ghorhund even retreated a little between the ranks. At the sight of this the Suhl stepped forward, clashing their weapons, heads held high, and as soon as they were clear of the trees the Suhl standards went up on long poles, the white feather gleaming bright in the afternoon sun.

But, even as their spirits lifted, horns sounded across the Westercleft Plain. First one and then a chorus of low, haunting wails echoing between the hills. The battle drums resumed their thunderous beat, and creatures and men raised their voices in a bloodthirsty battle cry that drowned out the yells of the Suhl. Riding this tide of noise, the attackers advanced: Ghorhund streaking ahead, manes bristling, heads low; Ghor striding forward, shoulders down; Ragers pounding the earth, tails sweeping like scythes.

This was their moment. This was what they were bred for.

The Suhl wavered, retreating a little, and this emboldened the enemy. They came on ever faster, breaking into a full charge, gaining speed even as they climbed the hill, devouring the open ground.

Espasian could feel the rock quaking beneath his feet and, as he watched, he sensed the courage of his army begin to fail. Some stepped back while others lowered their weapons, seeming to lose their resolve.

The Magruman cupped his hands. "Hold!" he yelled. "Trust each other! Trust the valley!"

Still they hesitated and in desperation Espasian threw up his arms, closed his eyes and reached out for earth and pasture, trees and thicket, preparing to call them into the fight. But, as he tried to find them, something extraordinary happened. He was met by a power greater than his. A power that resisted and pushed back.

He gasped and opened his eyes.

In just moments, the scene before him had changed. Thoth's army was no longer at full charge. The Ghorhund were faltering, and now they were slowing, their snouts high, as though scenting danger. Espasian looked back up the slope and saw something moving on the ground behind the Suhl, snaking away from the trees, not just one thing, but many, all the way along the line. At first he thought it was something in the grass, but then he realised that whatever it was lay beneath the earth, making the surface buckle.

The Suhl too were looking about in alarm, but then one of them shouted and pointed up towards the forest. The roots of the great trees were twisting beneath the turf, winding like eels down towards the Suhl. There they threaded between the Suhl warriors, forming a complex weave beneath the earth.

Then, quite suddenly, they stopped.

For a few seconds the Suhl gazed about at the rumpled pasture, wondering what it could mean. But then they had their answer. The roots began to grow, throbbing and swelling until they broke the earth and parted the grass. They grew at a staggering speed, becoming a maze of low walls round the Suhl army, and then a defensive labyrinth bristling with gnarls of timber.

Espasian gazed in astonishment. But a moment later his attention was drawn back towards the forest, and there he saw a new marvel. The trees now bowed to one side or the other, knitting themselves together so that the delighted children in the branches had to swing this way and that to avoid being knocked from their perches. Soon the entire treeline had been woven to form an impassable wall as deep as it was high.

The Magruman's chest heaved and he looked back into the valley.

"You heard me," he said, his voice thick with emotion. "You heard me."

23

South

"Throughout the meeting the Suhl used the term 'the south'
with almost universal distaste. It was some time before
I realised that for them, 'the south' is not just a point
on the compass, it is Old Kemet, and the empire
and all that it stands for."

THOTH STOOD BEFORE THE mirror, then took a step closer.

All that the silvered glass revealed was the shadow beneath his hood, and behind him the dim recesses of the chamber. He glanced away, resting his eyes instead on the ornate, gilded swirls of the mirror's frame, plated in gold seized in the plunder of Surget. Gold of such quality was reserved exclusively for the frames of the Dirgh's own mirrors. None of the craftsmen knew why; it was a matter not to be questioned.

He raised his white, bony hands to the rim of his hood and then hesitated. This too was his custom. He never removed his hood without a slight pause: born of a reluctance, perhaps, to reveal his face. But then, as the many thousands of times before, he drew back the folds of silk and let them fall to his shoulders.

He swayed a little before the mirror and took several quick, wheezing breaths. Almost at once his black eyes travelled back to the comfort of the beautiful frame, settling on its graceful coils and intricate mouldings, until his breathing settled. They remained there for some moments, until finally they returned to his image: the visage that gazed across an Empire, emblazoned on flags, shields and buildings.

He gazed at his endlessly shifting face blending and morphing at such a rate that none of its myriad features were clear to see. All that could truly be discerned were the two sunken impressions for eyes, the gash for the mouth, the hollow for the nose.

He blinked, and something about that action revealed a fleeting glimpse of oval eyes, eyelashes, a strong brow. He blinked again and had a momentary vision of narrow cheeks, full lips and eyelids. But these things vanished so quickly that they were dreamlike, more imagined than real. The reality was sunken eyes, a gash for a mouth, a hollow for a nose.

His bony figure shrank a little before the mirror and his shifting features blurred into a pained scowl. His chest heaved with a rising passion and, once again, he looked quickly back at the frame, at its grace and gleam, and again his breathing settled.

A sharp knock echoed round the chamber.

Thoth straightened beneath his robe. "Enter," he said, filling the chamber with his swell of voices.

Two towering doors swung slowly on their hinges and a gigantic figure entered, the wolfish head held high, armour glinting in the lamplight.

"What is it, Anubikan?"

The Ghor commander bowed low, revealing its impressive silvered mane. "My Lord, I have word from the Valley of Outs."

The Dirgh nodded. "Is it done?"

Anubikan bowed even lower so that the tips of its ears touched the cold stone floor. "No, great Dirgh." It paused. "The children have escaped."

For some moments Thoth said nothing, but finally his bony figure swelled, the shadows of his face gathering into a dark frown.

"How?" he bellowed, his voices shaking the Apex Chamber.

Anubikan pressed itself still lower. "Aboard the *Windrush*, my Lord."

"I ordered the river dammed!" boomed Thoth. He started walking towards Anubikan. "And the Ogresh were to fall back to the river and prevent their escape!"

"I believe they did, dread Lord," said Anubikan, seeming to struggle to keep its composure. "But the children did not... they did not escape on the river."

Thoth's stride slowed. "But you said that they were aboard the *Windrush*!"

"They were, my Lord. They used the *Windrush* to... *sail* across the Westercleft Plain."

Thoth stopped just two paces away. He tipped his head as though finding this hard to comprehend, then he spoke quietly, as if he had been robbed of his breath.

"The entire Fifth Division is encamped on the plains," he said menacingly. "The valley is surrounded."

Anubikan's ears fell flat against its skull. "The *Windrush* sailed straight through the army, great Dirgh. There were casualties on both sides, but we believe that the two children were unharmed. There are reports that the vessel *changed*, my Lord, that when it cut through the army it was no longer timber but silver or gold. The sails, the decks, the ropes — everything."

Thoth's great stature seemed to diminish, his shoulders slumping and growing narrow, his head lowering. He clasped his hands before him.

"They... *sailed*?" he murmured. His blank brow was knitted in shadow. "Gold? Or... *Quintessence*?" He turned and looked towards the centre of the chamber, to the large square formation of white steps leading down to the pool of Black.

He glanced back at Anubikan. "And their direction? Were they sailing south?"

Anubikan responded with another bow.

Thoth tapped his fingertips together so that the yellow nails clicked, then he said in a rush of whispers: "They are going to Old Kemet."

Anubikan's ears pricked. It rose a little from its stoop. "Great Lord?"

The Priest of Souls was already walking towards the pool at the centre of the chamber. "They are going to the Motherland. To where it all began," he said, his voices charged with a new urgency. He reached the topmost step and stopped.

"Anubikan, tell the fleet to make ready. Prepare this decree and convey it without delay to the commanders and captains. All three- and four-masted ships are to gather their crews and all necessary provisions and set sail for the Jaws of Kemet, there to form a blockade. Tell them what has passed at the Valley of Outs and all we know of the *Windrush* and those who sail on her."

He raised a long finger for emphasis. "Impress upon them, Anubikan, that nothing must pass their blockade. Nothing. Not the *Windrush*. Not any other vessel. Not man, nor woman, nor child. They must take no prizes, give no quarter. They must not be breached. If they are, I will see to it that they drink deep of the sea they sail on. Tell them that, do you hear?"

Anubikan lowered its head once again. "It is done, great Lord."

"And prepare the *Mesektet*. Have her stocked and fitted. We will sail for the Motherland at daybreak."

Anubikan had begun to retreat towards the doors, but now it hesitated. "My Lord, should I send word ahead so that preparations may be made for your arrival?"

Thoth considered this for a moment. "Only to Rhatcotis where we will take on new supplies, and to Khemenu where I will visit the temple. But tell the scribes that I want none of their ceremony. I will be swift. The war for all things has begun, Anubikan, and I must return to the Academy of Souls."

Anubikan raised its head in astonishment. "Forgive me, my Lord, but why not command at Rhatcotis? It is a great fortress."

Thoth breathed a wheezing sigh. "Because, Anubikan, the Academy of Souls is where the Other was born. It is a place with the power to give, and the power to take away. It is the heart of the Empire, and soon it will be the heart of all things: here and in the Other." He lifted his hooded head. "And that too is why the *Windrush* sails south. Now, do you understand?"

"Of course, great Dirgh!" said Anubikan with another bow. It retreated quickly, lifting its head only to take hold of the two great brass handles and heave the doors shut.

Thoth waited until he was alone, then he gazed out over the pool of Black.

"Theirs is Quintessence," he breathed. "Mine is the Black."

He descended the white marble staircase and knelt on the lowest step. He reached for a golden tray upon which stood two small urns and a candle. Taking up each of the urns, he tipped their contents into the Black: first water, then dust. Next he picked up the candle and touched the surface with its flame. An arc of blue fire spread silently across the pool. Thoth waited until the entire surface was aflame, then he spoke an incantation, lowered himself still further and breathed into the fire.

At once the flames flared, reaching up to the ceiling like bright orange fingers, caressing the dark visage painted above. As the inferno burned, the fire began to change: no longer light but dark; no longer flame but leaping tongues of Black. As soon as they had formed, they began to transform, becoming larger, taking on shapes that looked distinctly animal and human, with broad black shoulders and mighty black limbs. Black snouts grew in black faces; black claws grew from black fingers; black eyes opened beneath black brows. In moments, the pool yielded up a gathering of twenty or more figures: Ghor, human, Ra'ptah, Hamajak and other creatures born of the Three Ways.

As soon as they were fully formed, the assembly bowed, their heads and shoulders dripping trails of Black.

Thoth climbed to his feet, his mouth bent in a smile.

"That's right, my friends, clothe yourselves in darkness! For most the Black is a scourge and a terror, but for us it is a bond." He raised his arms. "Now, let it bind us in a council of war."

§

The Black drifted quickly back into the urn where it settled, ceasing its bubble and churn. General Hakka was motionless, stooped over the oily swill, part of him still lost in its depths. He blinked, raised his arm and wiped away some drool on the groomed fur of his forearm. He grinned, showing his parade of jutting teeth, then he brought two clawed fists down on the table with a bang and a clatter.

"Finally!" he growled.

Already he was on his feet, pulling his cloak over his shoulders. He adjusted his armour, then lifted his formidable helmet from the table and set it carefully on his head. The gleaming steel fitted perfectly over his long canine nose, his broad, muscular jaws, his human brow. The design lent him a deliberate, perpetual frown and a mouth twisted in a snarl, while the crest extended his mane high above his head, making him even more imposing.

He stepped out of the pavilion on to the hillside and was buffeted by a chill wind. His personal guard parted before him, bowing and drawing a claw across their chests in salute and, as the way opened, he sighted his army. A clamorous roar thundered up the hillside, so loud and terrifying that many of the guard retreated, but Hakka strode boldly forward, his movements fluent and athletic, despite his great size. He raised his arms in greeting.

Before him was an army of beasts. Legions shifted and rippled, ebbed and flowed like a tide, enclosed within an immense oblong of giant standing stones. These mighty plinths were as great as the skyscrapers upon which they were modelled, and they cast enormous rectangular shadows over the thousands of creatures that milled between them. Shafts of sunlight glinted on the steel of ten thousand weapons, making the dark surface shimmer.

The general licked his ebony lips with a long tongue and, satisfied that all was ready, he turned and looked expectantly at a pavilion not far from where he stood. Canvas flaps parted and something moved from within. As the apparition stepped forth, the army fell silent. It was something real and living, but it had no definite form. It was a blur more than a figure, made up of muddled and distorted light, which gave the impression of a torso and limbs. The spectre walked on towards the general and, as it drew near, Hakka bowed low to the ground. All under his command followed suit so that a great wave seemed to spread out across the tide.

The Ray Reaper paused and looked down, as though weighing the worth of this tribute, and then it walked far out on to the hillside until it was quite alone. There it lifted its ghostly arms and the semblance of a head up to the heavens. Almost at once some part of the sky morphed in a way that made those watching blink and turn to their companions. Sunbeams twisted and bent in the air, light shifted and gathered, and in moments the vast span of blue became a disorder of light and dark.

But what at first seemed chaotic became a design. Light folded into light, beams poured into beams until a single column of radiance robbed the rest of the sky of its light. This bright pillar began high above the world and fell directly upon the vast rectangle of standing stones so that, as the world grew dark, the cordon of stones, and the army within them, grew brighter and brighter, until one was indistinguishable from the other.

24

The Beasts

"Now come the beasts and the creatures of the dark; now come the devils and demons, the sprites and goblins, marching from the chambers like an army of folklore and legend."

DRESCH ROLLED HER SHOULDERS and arched her spine, trying to relieve some of the stiffness in her back. She picked up another Petri dish and, with a weary sigh, slid it on to the stage of her microscope. She rotated the turret to the maximum magnification, then bent low over the eyepieces.

There it was again: the stain of black, pure and absolute. No texture, no pigment: just the same elemental slick of darkness. And yet, despite the absence of cells or particles, it behaved like a living thing, spreading before her eyes until it had consumed the culture. It was as though it was feeding.

"It *has* to be alive," she murmured.

She had used every scientific technique she knew, every piece of equipment in her arsenal, but still she could find nothing to explain the behaviour of the Black. Neither could she explain the pain that it brought, the markings beneath the skin, the confusion. The Black was as much a mystery to her now as it had been forty-eight hours and sixty-two Petri dishes ago.

She threw herself back in her chair and cursed. She stared at the smear of Black in the Petri dish with an intense loathing, drumming her heel on the linoleum floor.

Slowly her eyes rose to the shelf above her head. Her eyes scanned a row of stoppered bottles.

On impulse, she reached out and grabbed one labelled *OLEUM – Fuming Sulphuric Acid*. Beneath that label was another, emblazoned with a skull and crossbones, and the words *EXTREMELY HAZARDOUS*. Dresch took some thick red gloves from the drawer in her desk and slipped them on.

She looked at the Petri dish. "Let's see how you like a taste of your own medicine," she said quietly.

She glanced about to check that no one was in the lab, then she opened a cabinet on the wall and took out a gas mask. She pulled it expertly over her head and yanked the stopper from the bottle. She took a long breath through the mask and, using a clean pipette, she carefully dripped three drops of oleum into the dish.

Almost instantly it erupted with froth and fumes. A grey vapour pooled across her desk and she watched with some pleasure as the dish fizzed and spluttered. She waited for the reaction to subside, then she placed the Petri dish back on the stage of the microscope and bent down to the eyepieces.

She sat bolt upright.

For a moment she stared blankly at the wall ahead of her, breathing deeply. Then, very slowly, she reached up and pulled off her mask. Wincing at the acrid fumes, she slid the Petri dish off the stage of the microscope and placed it on the bench, watching as the last of the vapour cleared.

As she saw the entire dish clearly for the first time, she began to tremble.

The Black was no longer a streak across the centre of the culture; it almost filled the dish. It had doubled in volume and, even as she looked, it grew before her eyes. She leaned closer, watching in morbid fascination.

Suddenly there was a bang across the lab and she nearly fell out of her seat.

"Dresch!"

She whirled about to see Lucien striding through the double doors. She opened her mouth to shout at him for making her start, but then she saw his face. His features were taut, and she sensed at once that he was frightened.

"You need to see this!" he said, grabbing a remote control from a bench and pointing it at one of the televisions.

He came and stood next to her as the screen bloomed into life. The picture was of a newsreader, which was not surprising – there had been little but news on any of the channels for days. But already Dresch could see that something had happened. The image behind the newsreader was not the usual river, or pond, or swimming pool streaked with Black. It was a picture of a stone circle and it was crowded with figures – so many figures that they had flooded out on to the surrounding plain.

Lucien turned up the sound so that they could hear the newsreader's rushed commentary:

"*...similar reports from across Europe and North America. At present we have no formal statements from the authorities, but we have ourselves received confirmation of many thousands of people or... creatures of some description pouring from the sites of recent disturbances. There have been sightings at stone circles in the south of England and Wales, Scotland, France, Germany. We are hearing that the military is mobilising in parts of...*"

Suddenly the screen was filled with a succession of images. There was an aerial view of Stonehenge, which showed hundreds of creatures fanning out from the standing stones, sending the cordon of light military vehicles into swift retreat. Then there was another aerial image of some buildings near the Houses of Parliament in London — a grand circular courtyard bordered on all sides by austere Edwardian frontages. The caption at the bottom of the picture read *Disturbances at Her Majesty's Treasury, Horse Guards Road*. The entire courtyard was seething with bodies and, as Dresch watched, they swept up the walls, climbing swiftly like apes, spilling out over the rooftops.

She stared, wide-eyed, as the image changed again, this time to an aerial view of a modern city at night, with wide roads lit by streetlamps and gigantic skyscrapers glowing bright against the night sky. At the centre of the image was a sweeping rectangle of darkness: an oblong park bordered on all sides by giant buildings. The caption read: *Central Park, New York City*. Her eyes travelled over the picture for some moments before she understood what she was seeing. The park was criss-crossed by the frantic searchlights of helicopters and by their light she could see that the trees, grassland, bridges and pathways were all in motion. The entire park was teeming with the same dark figures that the pictures had shown in Stonehenge and London. They were jostling to reach the edges of the park where they emptied into the streets, running over abandoned cars, sprinting along deserted roads.

"They're everywhere!" exclaimed Dresch breathlessly.

"It's an invasion," said Lucien, his eyes fixed on the screen. He glanced at her. "It'll be all right," he said unconvincingly. "There has to be a plan for something like this. I'm sure they'll have a plan."

Dresch stared at him in disbelief. "A plan?" she said incredulously. "Just like 'they' had a plan for the Black, I suppose?" She shook her head and turned back to the screen. "How can anyone plan for *this*?"

Lucien opened his mouth to answer, but then chose to say nothing. Together they stared at the television, and perhaps unconsciously, Martha took his hand. As the television droned on, they leaned a little closer together.

After a while Lucien riffled in his pocket and brought out a paper bag. He cleared his throat.

"Lemon sherbet?" he asked.

At first Martha stared at him as though he had lost his senses, then she reached out and took one.

So intent were they on everything happening on screen that they did not notice the Petri dish on the workbench behind them. The acrid fumes had long since died away but, as the television droned on, the Black welled up to the brim of the dish and overflowed.

25

Safe

*"I am far from sure that there is any part of this world
that is safe for the Suhl. But if there is such a place,
it is the Valley of Outs."*

SYLAS LAY ON HIS bed, the Samarok propped on his chest, writing
quickly but carefully with his quill. He finished his sentence,
yawned, then put the quill back in its box.

He traced his finger absently along the S-shaped groove on the
front cover of the Samarok, thinking back to when he had first
seen it, with the Merisi Band still in place. How long had it been
since that meeting with Mr Zhi in the Shop of Things? It seemed
distant and dreamlike, as though years had passed, but it could
have been no more than a couple of weeks. And yet everything
had changed. Everything, for everyone. The whole world had
turned upside down. This world and that.

There was a movement in the corner of his eye. He turned to
see his mother standing at the door of the Bow Room. He was
about to say hello, but she quickly put a finger to her lips and
pointed past him at Simia, who was asleep in a crouch, her head
resting on her arms. She had simply slumped forward where she
sat and drifted off.

How Sylas wished he could do that.

He pushed himself up and silently made his way over to his mum. She smiled and gave him a hug, then they walked quietly along the corridor to the nearest ladder and climbed into the pink light of sunset.

The chill, salt air was bracing, and the drowsiness left Sylas almost at once. The seas were bright and calm, glistening in the evening light, and the shoreline was now a distant smudge, low on the horizon. Ash was keeping the *Windrush* at a good speed, skipping lightly over the gentle waves, but he looked tired, and Sylas knew that he or Naeo would have to take their turn before long.

For now he walked with his mum alongside the railing, looking out at the setting sun. She slid her arm through his like she used to when he was little, and smiled in that way that made her the most beautiful and the safest person in the world. She gave his arm a squeeze.

"How are you doing?"

"I'm fine, I suppose," he said. "Tired. You OK?"

Amelie chuckled gently. "Still trying to get used to all this. But I'm fine."

He pulled back, his eyes tracing her face. "Are you, though?"

She laughed. "Only my Sylas would be worried about *me*, with all this going on!"

He held her gaze. "Well, I wish you didn't have to be here. I mean, it's great to have you here, but—"

"I *want* to be here, Sylas. There's nowhere I'd rather be." Her smile skewed a little. "I want to be near you, and — and I can't pretend I don't worry about you, my love." She sighed and winked. "You worry about me, I worry about you. That's how it is."

They walked on round the ship, passing the many crew members hunched over frayed ropes of silver-gold, hammering at gleaming timbers and reshaping the railings. Amelie asked questions as they went: *How did it feel to be with Naeo? What had it been like steering the ship? What was the Quintessence? How did it work?*

Sylas answered as best he could, which was not always well at all, but his replies led to another question, and another, until at last their conversation turned to Simia's list of Things and Merimaat's writings about the Passing Bell.

"So the bell is important, you think?" asked his mother.

Sylas shrugged. "I don't know. Perhaps. It might just have been meant to bring me and Naeo together. But then Quintessence has been with me right from the start, and it sounds like the bell is the most powerful thing anyone's made out of it. And when you think about what Naeo and I are supposed to do — bring the worlds together — it makes sense that—"

"Are you?" interrupted his mother.

"Am I... what?"

"Well, are you really meant to bring the worlds together?"

Sylas blinked at her in surprise. "What do you mean?"

"I mean are you sure that's what you're supposed to do?"

Sylas was perplexed. "You know all about the Glimmer Myth, about Merisu's message," he said. "And I told you about Isia — everything she told us about our bloodline. The fact that she was there when the world was broken, and that—"

"Yes, yes, I know," said Amelie, putting a hand on his shoulder. She smiled. "But that doesn't mean I *understand* it. I've known about all this for a long time, but it still doesn't make sense to me. I marvel at you, I really do, not just because of these things that you're able to do, but... but how you manage to *accept* it all."

Sylas frowned. "I'm not sure I *have* accepted it," he said, a little defensively. "It's all pretty difficult to accept. But I can't see how anything else makes sense."

"But you have, Sylas! You've had to accept the Glimmer Myth and everything Isia told you just to keep going, to find Naeo —" Amelie gestured about her at the golden ship — "to do all the amazing things you and Naeo do. But it's different for me, Sylas. I struggle to accept any of this. I don't know how to be part of this world, and I'm not sure I want to be. I'm a scientist. I believe in the rules that bind our universe. I believe in what has been carefully reasoned and — and tested and proven. The things I see here..." She sighed. "Well, they go against everything I know to be true."

"But things here are like — like a mirror of things back home," protested Sylas. "I'm not sure they're *supposed* to make sense."

"There are no exceptions in science, Sylas. *Everything* makes sense once you've worked out the rules. You don't pick and choose. Do you remember that book I gave you? The *Book of Science*?"

Sylas's mouth fell open and he stared at her. "Of course I remember!" he snapped. "That book was all I had of you when you went away! I know every page of it!"

He looked down, surprised by his own outburst.

"I'm sorry, Sylas," said Amelie.

He swallowed a wave of emotion and blurted: "It's just — just you don't need to tell me about science. And you definitely don't need to tell me about that book."

She reached for him, but he turned away.

"I wasn't saying you don't understand," Amelie said. "Of course I wasn't."

Sylas kept his face to the dipping sun. Once again he had that gut-wrenching feeling that his mum was behind a sheet of glass, that although she was here with him, she was as far from him as ever. Surely she could see that he had no choice? That this journey was his whether he liked it or not? That *everything* had led him to Naeo, to Essenfayle, to the Glimmer Myth, to the deck of this ship. He hadn't asked for it, but neither could he change it. All this was as real and true to him as anything he had read in that *Book of Science.*

"All I was trying to say, Sylas," said his mum, "really badly is that I don't understand how this world and our world are supposed to come together. They're just so... *different.* And what I have no idea about — not the faintest clue — is how we're supposed to come together with — with another part of ourselves. Because, if the worlds are so different, then our Glimmer must be too. And surely it's... well, *unnatural* to bring two such distinct, different parts together?"

Sylas turned and stared at her with red-rimmed eyes. "Unnatural?" he said. "You mean like me and Naeo?"

For a terrible moment she hesitated. "No, Sylas," she said at last, "that's not what I meant! I just meant that—"

"I know what you meant!" he snapped.

"Sylas!" she exclaimed, reaching for him. "I didn't mean you and Naeo at all! You and Naeo aren't—"

But he was already stalking away, heart thumping, blood roaring in his ears. By the time she called his name again, he had reached the hatchway. He heard her, but he did not look back. He plunged down into the darkness below.

§

Naeo stood alone in the bow, watching the sun slip beneath the waves. The sea breeze chilled her, despite the last warming rays, and she was dimly aware that the pain in her back was growing worse again.

Her thoughts were far away. They were back beyond the trailing wake of the ship, across the plains cleaved by its keel, through Thoth's army and over the hills of the Valley of Outs. Her thoughts reached even beyond the valley — where her father was surely fighting for his life — across the borderlands, to the distant grey of the Barrens.

And that was where she found him. Not in desperate battle, not sickly and weary, but young, bold and strong. That was where her father was now, at sunset: where he had said he would be, back in their treehouse at Grail, before any of this had begun. He was laughing, like he used to. He was helping her up the last rungs of the ladder and lifting her so she could see far out across the bright orange and yellow canopy of Grail forest — out to the wide greens of Salsimaine. And, as she wondered at the beauty of it, she felt his strong arms round her, and his warmth, and his permanence. And then he was looking up at her with that all-seeing, all-knowing face, in the way that made him the most beautiful and the safest person in the world.

So lost was she in these memories that she did not hear Sylas's mother calling out to him, begging him to stop. She did not hear Sylas thundering down the ladder to the deck below. Instead Naeo held on to that moment from her past because now it was her present too. Her father really was there with her. He had promised and so he was there. Somewhere in the Valley of Outs he was watching the same setting sun, and thinking of that same faraway treehouse. He was holding her even now.

So, as the last bright arc of the sun dipped from sight, and the *Windrush* blazed copper in its last dying rays, Naeo drew her father close. She told him that she loved him, and she pleaded with him to stay safe for another day.

26

The Scribbler

"What sets the Suhl scribe aside from the scribbler is not just an elegant hand or a grasp of runes and languages, it is a deep learning cultivated since childhood. Here, scribes do not just record and write, they read and read and read..."

SIMIA SAT WITH HER back against a bulwark, trying to write in her Scribbler, despite the failing light, and the wind that riffled the pages, and the spray that whipped across from the bow, blotting her ink. She was determined not to go below. Sylas was in a foul mood. He had barely spoken to her when he had burst back into the Bow Room. He had grunted a few responses, then flung himself down on his bed, picked up the Samarok and lost himself in its pages. She had never seen him like that before and had quickly judged it best to leave him alone. Besides, it was far more pleasant up here, enjoying the sunset.

She kept writing even as the sky darkened above her and the stars and the moon began to appear. She tilted the notebook to gather what light she could, and she added entry after entry to her list.

She had written eight more now: eight Things that she had seen over the years, many before Sylas had come, that Simia now suspected were made of Quintessence. There was the strange ornamental sun and moon above the doors of the Otherly Guild in Grail; there was the strange, silvery gold blade that Merimaat had carried at the Reckoning, which Simia remembered gleaming bright across the battlefield even when Merimaat herself had disappeared into the distance.

But one such Thing stood out from the others, and Simia was positive that it had been made of Quintessence. It was the golden feather on the statue of Merimaat in Grail. Merimaat's figure had been sculpted from glowing white stone, but the feather in her upturned hand had been a beautiful, shimmering gold. That is until it had been broken in the final days of the Reckoning. And that was what made Simia sure. Because when she had seen that broken feather, in one of her desperate, reckless scavenging sorties to the ruins of Grail, the golden coating had gone. It had not been chipped away — stolen, like so much else, by Thoth's marauders — it was simply gone. It was as though, once the feather was broken, the gold had drained away, leaving only the stone behind. Just like the Passing Bell had slipped away into the forest floor until there was not a trace left behind.

"What's this?"

Simia looked round, startled, and saw Triste looming above her, his bald head shining in the moonlight. He sat down beside her, his large eyes fixed on her notebook.

"This?" said Simia, holding it up. "It's my notebook — my Scribbler. I used to write in it a lot, but it's been a while." She flicked back through the pages. "I started it years ago, when I was out on the Barrens. There was no one to talk to so I wrote everything down."

"Like a journal?"

"Sort of. Just random thoughts really." She hesitated, then said: "You can look, if you like."

Triste nodded enthusiastically and took it. He started leafing through pages scrawled with all manner of scribbles, poems, sketches and doodles. There was a rather good picture of the Circle of Salsimaine on one page, and a rushed line drawing of a lone, leafless tree on the next. He scanned several pages full of writing, and paused on a smudged drawing of a broken helmet. Then he continued until he came to a tangle of drawings that looked like dot-to-dot puzzles.

"What are these?" he asked, poring over them.

"Constellations," said Simia. "I used to draw them whenever I could see them, which wasn't very often. Out on the Barrens you only saw a clear sky once or twice a month so the stars were kind of... precious." She tapped the page. "This was a way of keeping hold of them."

Triste glanced at her appraisingly, as though seeing her in a new light, then looked back at the drawings, his eyes tracing the many intricate lines.

Just then the hull struck the crest of a wave, sending up a shower of icy droplets, and he clasped the notebook protectively to his chest.

"Don't worry," laughed Simia, "my Scribbler's seen much worse!"

Triste wiped the cover on his sleeve. "Still you should keep it safe." He looked at her in that piercing way Bowe used to. "It's important to hold on to your memories. They tell you who you are."

She cocked her head to one side. "Funny, that's kind of how I felt about those constellations." She looked down at the open page. "I would repeat their names, just to show myself that I could still remember them. Remembering felt even more important back then, after the Reckoning, when everything had been swept away. It made me feel that I was still... there somehow."

Triste nodded thoughtfully, but said nothing.

Simia's brow furrowed as she remembered. "There was something else, though. I thought that if I could see those stars then perhaps, just perhaps, there were others out there who could see them too." She looked up at the sparkling grains of light above. "I guess they became kind of..." She chuckled. "I don't know, it sounds silly."

"Go on," he said encouragingly.

Simia closed her notebook. "Well, I suppose they became like... friends." She glanced at him self-consciously. "It does. It sounds stupid."

"Not stupid," said Triste softly. "Not stupid at all."

They sat quietly for a while and Simia was surprised at how comfortable she felt with him. It was a trust that had grown during their journey across the Barrens, and their encounter with the Kraven, and all that had come afterwards. But, after all her time alone on the Barrens, that kind of trust remained unexpected, even now. Even though she had found it with Sylas too.

"Simia, there's a reason I came to find you," said Triste after a while. He turned to her. "Do you remember when I first came aboard I said I might need your help?"

"Yes..." said Simia, a little warily. "But you never said what with."

"With Sylas and Naeo."

Simia glanced back at Naeo, who was taking her shift at the helm. "Why? Is something wrong?"

Triste shook his head. "No, not really. But I do think they need some... guidance if they're going to do all that's asked of them. They *seem* ready, but I don't think they really are."

He quickly told Simia about his conversation with Bowe before they left the valley.

"When Bowe said to teach Naeo to know 'all of herself', I

admit I wasn't sure," he said. "Sylas and Naeo seem so strong when they're together, their powers so miraculous, that I couldn't imagine that anything was missing. But then, when they were guiding the *Windrush* across the plains, they faltered. Do you remember?"

"How could I forget?" said Simia.

"Well, that was when I saw just how... *problematic* their bond can be."

Simia frowned. "What do you mean?"

"As a Scryer, I could see that bond threatening to control them rather than the other way round. Does that make sense?"

She shook her head. "Not... *totally*, no."

Triste described Naeo's grief at leaving her father, and how her feelings had somehow found their way to Sylas and vice versa.

Simia looked doubtful. "So... you're saying Sylas felt *Naeo's* feelings?"

"Yes."

"And Naeo felt Sylas's? Without knowing what they were?"

"Exactly," said Triste. "And so you see I believe Bowe's instincts were very well founded. Sylas and Naeo share a bond, but that bond can take them by surprise, just as it did when we sailed away from the valley. To control it, they need to be able to see one another, predict one another, understand when they are feeling as the other feels. If they don't, this journey may all be for nothing. Unless I am very mistaken, much greater challenges lie ahead. If we are to survive, their bond must only work for them and never against them."

Simia looked across at Naeo once again, who was statuesque, silhouetted against the stars. "But what can *I* do to help?"

"You know Sylas, Simia. You know Naeo too, if not as well. You know their journey. You have been drawn along with it, right from the beginning, since the Passing Bell rang for Sylas. And, if my instincts serve me well, you will know where to take it next."

The hairs prickled on Simia's neck. And then, quite suddenly, she remembered something Isia had said to her when they were in the temple. "*You are caught up in the greatest adventure of a lifetime — of any of our lifetimes*." Simia had found it hard to believe then, and it hardly seemed real now, but here she was again, being asked to help Sylas. And it was certainly true that she had shared almost all of Sylas's journey and much of Naeo's. Perhaps Triste was right. Perhaps there *was* a role for her somehow. But she had no idea where to begin.

"Maybe..." she said after a long silence, "maybe I could talk to Sylas. Persuade him to use the Glimmertrome, like Naeo did. Maybe that would help him to see her — I don't know — more clearly? Wasn't that what you were trying to do when Naeo used it? Help her to see Sylas?"

Triste nodded slowly, his face now hidden in shadow. "Yes, that could help," he said rather doubtfully. "Perhaps that's all that is needed: more time with the Glimmertrome."

"But... you think it needs more, don't you?" probed Simia.

Triste reached into his pocket and pulled out his pipe. "Yes, I do," he said, rummaging for his flint. "I'm sure that the Glimmertrome will work given enough time, but time is something we simply don't have. Now that Thoth knows their strength, we must expect the worst; they may be tested at any moment and in ways we cannot yet imagine."

Simia leaned closer. "You think what's coming might be even worse than what we've already been through?"

Triste's face bloomed with yellow light as he struck his flint. "We're going to the heart of the Empire, to where it all began." He paused to puff at his pipe, then blew out a stream of silvery smoke. "It will only get worse. Much worse."

Simia stared at him for a long moment, hoping that he would

offer a crumb of reassurance, but nothing came. He simply looked up at the night sky and puffed thoughtfully on his pipe. Simia sank back against the bulwark, turning a curl of hair round her finger. She became aware of the deepening pitch of darkness about them, and she listened to the empty howl of the wind through the rigging. She shuddered and gathered her jacket about her, feeling the lack of the comforting folds of her father's coat.

With some effort, she forced her mind back to the task. What could be more powerful than the Glimmertrome? And how were they to find it here, on the *Windrush*? In desperation, she took a mental inventory of the last few curious objects Paiscion had left in the Bow Room. Perhaps one of those might help. But then she didn't even know how they worked. And, if they were important, surely Paiscion would have mentioned them?

She thumped her head against the wooden panel in exasperation and stared up at the stars. She was quiet for some time, listening to the waves and the winds, and then she glanced across at Triste.

"The Glimmertrome shows them what it's like to be the other, right?" she asked.

Triste nodded and grunted as he finished another draw on his pipe.

"And we want them to see what's different about the other one, don't we?"

The Scryer furrowed his brow as he gave this some thought. "Yes, I think that's right."

"So wouldn't it be best if they use the Glimmertrome when they're doing the same thing? Wouldn't that show them *exactly* how they're different?"

Triste's eyes shot to hers and he blew out a blast of smoke. "Yes," he said excitedly. "Yes, that could work. But what do you have in mind?"

Simia grinned at him. "I know just the thing!"

27

The Turning Tide

"What will mark the turning tide, *I wonder? Will it be
a grand proclamation of a victory in some war against
the Empire, or will it be quiet, and secret and subtle?
A child, perhaps, grasping the hand of their Glimmer
and seeing a truth that we can only dream of?"*

THOTH'S ARMY CAME ON in waves, pounding the hills of the
Valley of Outs like a tempest thrashing the shore. Regiments
splashed up the slopes and crashed against the defences before
retreating into the agitated sea. On and on they came, rolling in
from the darkness: an endless tide of claw and blade.

But the Suhl defences were strong. The roots of the forest made
mighty buttresses of living wood, which threw back each assault
with seeming ease. Those of the enemy that managed to climb
over the first walls of timber found themselves scattered in a
labyrinth of twisted pathways, many leading to dead ends, others
into traps. And, with the space to fight and the valley to aid them,
the Suhl were proving themselves a fearsome foe. They jabbed
and parried with their weapons born of the forest, and those that
could took up another more powerful weapon. With Essenfayle,
they turned thinner roots to lashes, flogging the enemy with a

whistle and a crack; they made the earth fall away, catching their foe in steep-sided pits between the twisting ramparts; and they heaved together the mightier roots so that men and beasts had to flee, or be crushed.

Night had now fallen, but the Suhl found their efforts lit by a strange, ethereal light, which spiralled down from the moon above. By some strange design, it pooled only behind the Suhl lines: just enough to see by, but not to reveal their positions. Had any of the Suhl found a moment to glance about, they might have seen the conjuror of this radiance walking quietly along the crests of the hills, his hand cast to the skies.

Since the first charge of the battle, Espasian had never been still. First, he had paced Carrion Rock, issuing his commands to Bayleon's Spoorrunners, the messengers of the battle, who one by one turned and ran like the wind, relaying the Magruman's orders along the length and breadth of the valley. Then Espasian had walked out along the edge of the forest, tracing a path behind his troops, yelling commands and encouragements until he was hoarse. Along the way he had sometimes spied children hiding among the branches, and each time he had commanded them to return to the safety of Sylva. Most had done as they were told, but many pleaded to stay and be near their loved ones, and support them where they could, if only with prayers to Isia. And, more than once, Espasian had let them.

He had been struck in particular by one headstrong girl who had steadfastly refused to leave her branch, saying that her father simply could not be without her. She had explained that they were not just father and daughter, but "partnas", and she had pointed him out with pride: a tall man with an eyepatch hurling rocks down the slopes with great sweeps of his powerful arms. She was Faysa, she had said, daughter of Takk and, if the Magruman thought that children were not suited to battle, perhaps he would like to explain that to her friend Sylas. Because she had travelled once with Sylas Tate on a journey through the labyrinth of sewers beneath Gheroth. And, at this, the Magruman had listened with interest, then smiled quietly and bowed, and left her in peace.

When he had reached the Rift — a deep cleft that scarred one of the hills — he had taken time to talk to those fighting there because he knew that this was a place of weakness. If pressured, it might allow Thoth's forces to surge unseen past the outer ramparts and into the valley beyond. But he saw that his instructions had been followed perfectly, and that the valley had laid her own defences, steepening the slopes to a perilous climb and girding the cleft with stout roots, like battlements.

So he had walked on, circling the entire valley. He had stopped briefly to talk to Fathray, whom he found sitting against a tree, writing feverishly in his journal, recording the events of the day. The old Scribe had been keen to hear what was happening in the furthest reaches of the battle, and Espasian had given him what brief details he could. But he had not dallied for long, and had soon resumed his circuit of the valley, despite the raging pain in his limbs, and the Black burning beneath his skin, and the fog that clogged his mind. Because he knew that it was important for a commander to be seen.

So it was that, as darkness fell, he was still walking the hilltops and, when Thoth's army showed no sign of resting for the night, Espasian had resolved not to rest himself. He had brought down the light of the moon, and continued to pace behind the lines, and offer words of encouragement here and there, and meet his commanders. Filimaya too had caught up with him for a brief while, to tend to his scars and to tell him how they fared in the Hollow. One hundred and twenty beds had so far been taken, she explained, but a good number of the patients could be treated with Salve, and would be fighting fit within a day. This was welcome news and now, as Espasian continued his walk, he even felt the first stirrings of hope.

But he had only walked a short distance when a horn sounded out in the night. It seemed to be a signal because abruptly the waves of attack came to an end. The last surge fell back into the darkness, melting into the sea of men and beasts, and then something strange and unsettling happened. Everything fell quiet. The battle drums quelled their thunder, the shouts and snarls died away, and the clink and clatter of weapons and armour ceased.

Espasian lifted his head, listening and watching. Then suddenly he turned and ran. He forced down the pain and sprinted back along the lines, darting past bewildered commanders, leaving his troops staring after him. And next he was heaving himself up on to Carrion Rock, staggering and gasping. His head swam from the pain, but just as he thought he might fall he felt an arm round his waist. He glanced up to see Bayleon, his broad face straining with the effort of lifting his friend. The two men took the last few staggering strides together, then stood swaying on the summit.

Before them was only blackness. In the dim moonlight, they could just make out a shifting motion on the Westercleft Plain, but they could not see details or formations, or anything to explain the sudden silence.

His chest still heaving, Espasian reached above his head with open hands and lost himself in the night. The light of the moon responded, gathering swiftly at the Magruman's will and streaming down upon the valley. He moved a hand forward and, at once, a pool of silver light drifted out over the Suhl lines and down the slopes. Soon it was passing over the Imperial army: the disarray of mercenaries, Ghorhund, Ghor, Tythish and Hamajaks, muddled and chaotic, their formations broken after a long day of fighting.

Still there was nothing to explain the quiet.

But then Bayleon drew a sharp breath and pointed. In the next moment, Espasian saw it too.

The sea was parting, not in one place but in many, all along the front. Espasian focused on the nearest and saw, at the point of the divide, giant shoulders moulded from mud, a great earthen head swinging low between, and two volcanic red eyes. Beasts and men scrambled out of its path, saving themselves from its colossal arms and crushing fists.

"Ogresh," he murmured, shaking his head. Casting his eyes about, he saw ten, perhaps twelve of them advancing at speed. "They were feeding and now they're ready."

The advancing Ogresh were gathering pace. Now they were at a run, heads low, earthen arms pumping the air, massive feet pounding the earth and sending up a spray of mud and shale. The final ranks ahead of them threw themselves apart and finally the Ogresh burst clear, charging headlong up the slope. As they reached the rutted pastures of the hills, several of them passed directly through a pool of moonlight, revealing broad backs, bulging stomachs and sturdy legs, all of them in the mottled shades of earth. Their heads were surprisingly large, and their facial features were nothing more than a narrow mouth strangely low on the face, a heavy brow and two fierce eyes, like embers.

But, as they reached grass and shrubs, the creatures changed. They gathered about them sinews of green until their limbs and muscles were clutches of grass, twisting and flexing like living flesh. In a few more strides, they were part of the hillside, almost invisible against the broken pasture. Still they did not slow, careering up the steep slope as though it was not there.

"The defences!" exclaimed Bayleon. "They're going to break—"

He was cut short by a cacophony of thuds and cracks as the Ogresh slammed headlong into the root buttresses. Shards of green wood erupted into the air and showered the Suhl defences, sending everyone running for cover. The Ogresh reared and began clawing at the remains before them, tearing with massive claws, ripping away fistfuls of living wood. And, as they laid waste to all before them, they changed again: knuckles no longer clumps of green but gnarls of wood; arms not tight-twisted grass but giant boughs. Now their claws were a tangle of branches and their heads were knots of wood, crowned by a dark mane of leafy green.

Already they were almost through the first line of defences, and some were striding over to attack the next. Suhl defenders hurled their spears and pikes, but the weapons seemed to do little damage, and the Ogresh struck out at their attackers, sending them sprawling. They cut swathes through the Suhl army, catching two or three defenders with every devastating swing, and leaving many crumpled and lifeless in their wake.

"We won't hold long," murmured Espasian, his eyes darting from one skirmish to the next.

Bayleon grasped the Magruman's shoulder. "Tell me what to do! Tell me what the Spoorrunners can do!"

Espasian looked at him for a moment with a pained expression, then shook his head: "There's nothing, Bayleon. I must call upon the valley to—"

"Yes! There *is* something!" cried Bayleon. "I can see it in your eyes! Just tell me!"

Espasian looked away. "No, I can't ask this of you, my friend. The cost would be too high." He seemed to wrestle with himself, then he looked Bayleon in the eyes. "You have suffered enough at my bidding."

Bayleon stared at him. "The Reckoning is long gone, Espasian, and I was wrong to blame you for it. There is no one to blame but the Dirgh. It is he who took my family from me." He placed his huge hands on Espasian's shoulders. "If it's my time to join them, so be it. I welcome it."

Espasian held his gaze, but was still conflicted. "But I don't even know that it will work."

Bayleon smiled. "You forget that now I know you, Espasian. I know that if this scheme has even crossed your mind, it has a chance. That's enough for me and my Spoorrunners."

Espasian said nothing, but he raised a hand and pressed it to Bayleon's breastplate. Then he smiled a sad smile, and looked away to a place far across the valley. He pointed. "There," he said, squinting at something in the darkness. "That is where you need to be."

28

Grey Hill

"Just about all of the stone circles have been used to pass between the worlds at one time or another, and not just the prominent ones like Stonehenge, Avebury, Brodgar or Rujum El-Hiri, but the lesser ones too, like Stanton Drew, Castlerigg or Grey Hill."

TASKER PRESSED HIMSELF FURTHER into the shady crook of the tree and gazed in horror between the branches. The broad column of beasts marched silently along the length of the valley floor, the only sound the clank of armour and shields. When they reached the lowest reaches of Grey Hill, they began their climb. Still in close formation, Ghor, Ghorhund, Tythish, Ragers, Hamajaks and creatures Tasker could not name snaked purposefully up a steep slope of rocks and bracken to the highest reaches. There the stone circle glowed in the moonlight.

As they drew near, their discipline broke. The Ghorhund snapped at bushes and rocks as they passed and Hamajaks gibbered, unable to contain their excitement. This was the moment they had been bred for, the passing to another world they had been promised. They could see it in the rippling light between the stones; they could sniff it in the air: that ozone tang, like a breaking storm. But, as they strayed, their Ghor handlers snapped the reins taut with a crack, yanking them back into line. Soon all of them once again moved as one, disciplined and alert and, within moments, the first of them plunged into the light.

"It's hopeless," whispered Tasker, shaking his head as he looked at the number climbing the slope. "We don't stand a chance!"

Paiscion glanced down from the branch above. "If we wait until the last of this column has passed," he said softly, "we should be able to make the crossing before the next."

"I don't mean hopeless for us," murmured Tasker. "Hopeless for everyone else. The Merisi just aren't prepared. Not for this!"

Paiscion gazed across the valley, his pale features glowing by the light of the stone circle. "Our hope we place in Sylas and Naeo," he said. "Anything we or the Merisi do now will only delay the inevitable. But, if that delay might help Sylas and Naeo in their task, then—"

"*If* it helps them!" hissed Tasker, his voice quavering. "*If* the *Windrush* makes it all the way to Old Kemet. *If* they can work out what to do when they get there!"

"Sylas and Naeo's journey is their own," said Paiscion calmly. "We can do nothing about it. Let us worry about ours."

Tasker looked up at the Magruman, then shook his head. "You're right. I know," he said. "We don't have any choice. I suppose I'm just..."

"You are worried about your kin, and it is to your credit," said Paiscion. "But we must remain focused on our task. Our part of this great effort. That is how we can help."

Tasker was lost in his own thoughts for a moment, then he nodded. "So... we wait."

He turned his attention back to Thoth's army. He watched the towering figures of the Tythish striding over the other creatures, like giants, and beyond a procession of Ragers whose mighty curved horns and pointed tails lashing the air made them seem like the spawn of the Devil himself. Behind them came a troop of Hamajaks, bounding and leaping like crazed demons, weaving among other creatures that slunk, lithe and low, like fiends.

"This is why Mr Zhi was so fascinated by superstitions," Tasker said. "Giants, devils, demons. They were right here all along."

"Indeed they were," said the Magruman ruefully. "Though, of course, even here they began with superstitions and myths."

Tasker glanced up. "How do you mean?"

The Magruman raised a bushy eyebrow. "Did the Merisi not teach you this?" He sighed and took off his spectacles to rub the bridge of his nose. "I was always telling them to spend more time on Old Kemet and the ancients," he grumbled. He replaced his glasses and turned to the moonlit hills. "Well, the Priests of Souls created their creatures in the image of the gods they so adored: Anubis, Bastet, Ptah and many others. A kind of... perverse tribute, I suppose. The Hamajaks there – those apelike creatures – they're a tribute to Thoth or A'an, the baboon-headed god of equilibrium, the one whose name the Dirgh says he will take as his own." He smiled bitterly. "So you see, these creatures are as much myth as muscle and bone. They found their way out of our myths to make this appalling reality, and in your world they became myth once again. New myths, like devils and demons, werewolves and fiends."

Tasker looked back at the tail end of the passing column and then up to the dazzling radiance of the stone circle. "But not myth any more," he said grimly.

"No, not any more."

For some time they watched the column of beasts snaking up the hill and then disappearing into the ethereal light, row after row after row.

"Where do they all come from?" asked Tasker.

Paiscion took a small loaf from his pack, tore it in half and gave a piece to Tasker. "The Dirgh has been rearing such beasts for centuries, mostly in his Dirghea and the birthing chambers of Thebes. Some are not of his own making, of course. The other priests had their own creations, but after the War of Souls Thoth brought them all under the Sekhmeti, the Imperial crown. These days the Imperial forces are quite beyond measure and spread throughout the Four Lands. What you see here are merely a few regiments of a single division of one army. Unless I am mistaken, and I fear I am not, this will be just one of what are probably hundreds of incursions into your world."

Tasker's features turned deathly pale.

The Magruman smiled and took a hip flask from his belt. "Here, have some. You look like you need it."

Tasker accepted it gratefully and took a deep swig of warming wine. He handed it back, and Paiscion had a sip before returning it to his belt. He looked across the valley. "There now," he said, "we seem to have the place to ourselves."

Sure enough, the standing stones appeared deserted. The spiralling shafts of moonlight had vanished, and their radiance had dissolved from the spaces between the stones. The only evidence of the beasts was a trail of rutted earth leading up to the stone circle.

"We should go now, before others come along," said Paiscion, easing himself down from his perch. "It's still close to midnight, which will make the passing easier."

With surprising athleticism for a man of his age, he jumped all the way from above Tasker's head down to the bottom of the tree, his cloak flying up about him. As soon as he had steadied himself, he held out a hand for Tasker, but the younger man proudly brushed it aside and jumped. He landed awkwardly on what remained of his shoes, slipped, tumbled forward and planted his elegant hairstyle in the mud.

"The gravity of another world can be a tricky thing," chuckled Paiscion.

Tasker smiled and took Paiscion's hand. "I think it's the shoes of another world that are the problem," he said, pulling himself to his feet. "Blasted things. I don't know what I was thinking wearing them here."

Paiscion adjusted his glasses and peered closely at his companion. "You know there's a certain smoking jacket that I often wear. A lovely thing once, but old and tired now. But still I put it on. It's a comfort to me, like an old friend. Do you know where that smoking jacket is now?"

Tasker looked at him enquiringly.

Paiscion patted the pack on his shoulder. "In here. I'm rarely without it."

Tasker smiled, his golden tooth gleaming by the light of the moon. "Kindred spirits perhaps."

Paiscion looked at him intently. "Perhaps so," he said. "Do you know what else is in my pack?"

The younger man shook his head.

"A pair of walking boots." The Magruman opened the bag and drew out two worn but sturdy leather boots. He handed them to Tasker. "My own in fact. But now yours."

Tasker stared at them gratefully. "Thank you!" he said, kicking off his ruined shoes.

"Well, I knew you wouldn't get far in those," said Paiscion, watching with pleasure as his companion pulled on the boots. "And that's the thing about these little comforts of ours. They have their time and place. This is neither the time nor the place."

He patted Tasker lightly on the shoulder and headed off between the last trees, towards the valley and Grey Hill.

Tasker stared after him for a moment, then hurriedly stuffed his shoes into his pack and scrambled to catch him up.

29

Hell

*"I begin to wonder how much of scripture comes to us
from the Other. I have even heard it said by the Scribes
that the burning skies and boiling sands of the
Ramesses Shield are the origins of hell itself."*

"WHAT'S THIS ALL ABOUT?" grumbled Sylas, following Simia up
the ladder and out on deck.

Simia spread her arms with a flourish, like a conjuror revealing
a trick. "You can't miss a night like this!" she exclaimed. "Look!"

Sylas rubbed his bleary eyes. He had been sleeping when
she had come for him: a fitful sleep disturbed by a peculiar
dream. His mother had been reading to him from a book that
was sometimes the *Book of Science* she had given him, sometimes
the Samarok. Each time he had begun to understand what she
was reading, her words had become a meaningless babble of
baffling scientific terms and magical incantations. It had been
a disturbing, bewildering dream and it had clung on even as
Simia had dragged him from his bed and hauled him up the
steps.

But now, as he looked about him, it vanished.

A breathtaking sky arched above, glittering with millions of stars that stretched between the black horizons, forming silver swirls, diamond glows and piercing, pinprick glints. Beneath this beautiful display the silver-crested waves clawed the darkness, sending up their own silver sparkles, as though competing with the stars.

Sylas had never seen a sky like this — so dark, clear and bright. But what made his head swim were the stars beneath his feet. The shining decks of the *Windrush* were mirrors to the sky, and now they shone with a glorious carpet of constellations. As the rigging creaked and the decks rolled, the reflections shifted too, panning across solar systems and galaxies, like the sweep of a heavenly mirror.

"What did I tell you?" exclaimed Simia triumphantly. "Isn't it incredible? I just had to come and get you!"

"It is," said Sylas, grinning. "Thanks, Simsi."

"Come on," she said, grabbing his hand. "You have to see it from the bow — the sails don't get in the way there!"

She dragged him along the deck as he stared up at the sky and, when they reached the bow, she sat and pulled him down next to her. "Come on! It's best like this," she said, lying back with her hands behind her head.

Sylas smiled at her familiar bossiness, but did as he was told. As he lay back and crossed his arms behind his head, he was surprised by a great swell of happiness. It wasn't just the exhilaration of being out in the sea breeze, or beneath such a jaw-dropping sky, or the fun of lying there in the bow, with Simia fizzing with excitement beside him. It was the fact that right then — and for the first time he could remember — he couldn't think about anything else. Not Naeo, nor their journey, nor all that was expected of them. Not even his argument with his mother. Suddenly all those things were distant, and all that mattered were the things around him: the heave of the sea, and the thump of the waves against the keel, the chill spray on his skin, and the stars.

And it was the stars that took him now.

§

Naeo was relieved when she saw two figures approaching in the darkness. She had been at the helm for so long that her mind had started to play tricks on her. In her dreamlike daze, she had begun to see as she had through Sylas's eyes, so that she thought she saw the strange designs of Ravel Runes in the stars as they brightened around her. Soon she had begun to hear Merimaat's message about the forging of the bell, spoken not by Sylas this time but by Amelie. And, as Amelie spoke, it had become a weird gibberish of strange words and incantations, as though in a dream.

"You must be exhausted," came a voice from the darkness. "Time I gave you a break."

She blinked and saw Ash's untidy silhouette against the stars. Triste stood a little behind, puffing on his pipe.

"I thought I was on for a while longer?" she said.

"Ah well, I need the practice."

"And… isn't it Sylas's turn next?"

"Yes, but he doesn't need the practice," said Ash, his white teeth glowing in a grin. "But don't worry, I'll make sure he does his share. Ain't no one slackin' on this 'ere ship, not on my watch!" he said in a rather unconvincing seafarer's drawl.

"Well, I *could* do with a rest," said Naeo, thinking of her strange reveries of moments before. "Right now?"

Ash stepped to one side. "Ready when you are," he said, raising his arms and turning his palms upwards.

Slowly Naeo dropped her hands to her sides and let go of the winds. They escaped her like a sigh, leaving her smaller and diminished, and as she breathed them out the ship left her too. She could no longer feel the stout timber frame in her bones, the tautness of the ropes in her muscles, or the cool of the decks against her skin.

As Naeo came to herself, Ash gave himself to the *Windrush*. The old ship dipped a little and bounced heavily on several crests, but he was soon her master, lifting her clear of the swell until she skipped lightly once more.

Naeo was about to head towards the hatch and go below when Triste stepped forward and caught her arm.

"Before you go," he said, "can we sit for a moment and talk?"

Naeo's shoulders sank. "I'm so tired, Triste. Can't this wait until the morning?"

"I'm sorry, but no," he said, taking her gently by the arm and leading her towards the stern. "I need to show you something."

"Can't we at least do this below deck where it's warm?"

"I'm afraid not," said Triste. "What I need to show you is up here."

They quickly came to the very stern of the ship where the views of the night sky were astounding and, to Naeo's surprise, Triste sat down on the deck and patted the spot next to him.

"Come on," he said. "It won't take long."

Naeo sighed and dropped to the floor in protest, slumping back against some folded canvas. "What's so important?"

Triste lifted his hand above their heads and pointed. "That."

Naeo looked up. "The stars? I've been staring at the stars all night!"

"Not how I want you to see them," he said mysteriously. "I want you to see them as Sylas sees them."

Her skin tingled a little. "How am I supposed to do that?"

"Try not to see them as you normally do, with your instincts in the way of Essenfayle," he said as though what he was suggesting was simple. "Try to see them as you would if you came from the Other. Here, this may help."

Triste put something smooth and angular into Naeo's palm. She looked down and saw the Glimmertrome: the tapering, polished sides, the black and white panels and the glint of something delicate and ornate in the centre. Before she could say a word the Scryer reached over and tipped the needle into the black.

§

A sudden radiance blazed through their eyelids and seared their faces, making them stagger backwards. They reached out and steadied themselves against the standing stones.

"Well, this isn't the Grey Hill I remember," panted Paiscion, blinking into the light.

Tasker peered through wincing eyes, trying to make sense of what he was seeing. It was no longer night but a dim, murky day, and great grey and yellow clouds rolled lazily between the stones. There were shafts of light — not moonbeams but sharper and more distinct — like roving fingers of fire. And there was a smell, metallic and sulphurous, which clung to the roof of his mouth. He knew that smell — he wished he didn't but he did. It was the scent of modern battle: that toxic cocktail of gunpowder and burnt metal he remembered from his brief stint in the army.

Paiscion gripped his arm and pushed him on. "Keep moving!"

They stumbled and coughed through a yellow cloud, leaving the stone circle behind them. The ground had been churned into thick, claggy mud, which sucked at their feet and slowed their progress, but they kept on, helping one another through the quagmire. All the while they could hear a distant *thump... thud-thud... thump*, like a mighty, faltering heartbeat deep in the earth. Soon they began to see the faint flashes of distant blasts through the smoke, followed quickly by powerful aftershocks beneath their feet.

The passing clouds of smoke muddled their way, and once they nearly fell into a crater — the result of an earlier devastating explosion. Thereafter they took care to avoid these, but some were so large they could only skirt their very rim, taking great care not to slip. As they trudged round one of these, Paiscion slowed his pace, then groaned. He drew Tasker back.

"Look!" he said, pointing into the pit.

Tasker struggled at first to see through the noxious vapours, but as a breeze drew them away he saw that the crater was half full of a thick black liquid: not water, not mud, but an oily slick.

"The fools!" murmured the Magruman. "They don't know what they're doing!"

Tasker looked confused. "What *are* they doing?"

"They're feeding it!" exclaimed Paiscion. He gestured around. "With all this! The more they fight, the more weapons and chemicals they use, the more devastation they—"

He was silenced by a beam of light that suddenly bathed them in an unbearable glare. They both threw their hands over their eyes.

"HALT!" came a harsh, metallic voice. "DON'T MOVE!"

Both men froze, wincing into the light.

"SLOWLY RAISE YOUR HANDS ABOVE YOUR HEADS!"

They did as they were told and almost at once there was movement either side of the light. Shadows appeared in the gloom that became eight prowling figures, each of them in a half-crouch, a weapon pressed to their shoulder.

Tasker began lowering one of his arms.

"STOP!" barked the voice. "KEEP YOUR HANDS IN THE AIR!"

Tasker paused, but then he continued to drop his hand, sliding it inside his tunic.

Paiscion glanced at him anxiously. "Tasker, don't! You'll—"

"STOP OR WE'LL SHOOT!"

Tasker pulled his hand slowly out. There was something between his fingers, and now those fingers began to move, writhing about as though the thing they held was alive.

"Drop it!" yelled one of the soldiers, running forward and pointing the muzzle of his gun directly at Tasker's heart. "NOW!"

Tasker dropped nothing, but he raised his trembling hand for all to see.

It was clothed in a green velvet glove.

The soldier peered at the glove, then cocked his weapon and lowered his eye to the gunsights.

"Stand down!" called a female voice from behind the soldiers.

At once the soldier's body seemed to relax and he lowered his weapon.

A woman emerged from the smoke behind him. She was short and heavy-set, with hair that rose in a bundle on her head. She was not wearing the military fatigues of her companions but a long green tunic.

Her expression was severe as she came to a halt in front of them. She stared intently at Paiscion, then turned to Tasker, looking him up and down with a deliberate gaze. Finally she scrutinised his glove.

A thin smile appeared on her face. She reached into a hip pocket and took something out. Then, slowly, she pulled on her own green glove.

"Gentlemen," she said, holding out her gloved hand. "Welcome to hell."

30

Stargazing

"The more I learned from the Merisi the more questions I had about the Other. Would the teachings of science still apply? Were even the laws of Nature the same as here? As a girl brought up to love stargazing, I began to wonder if even the cosmos would be the same!"

NAEO STARED UP AT the night sky, dimly aware that the dark silhouettes of the sails were not as she would expect them to be: they were billowing towards her, not away. That was strange enough, but her attention was captured by something else. At first the stars twinkling in the wide dome of darkness had seemed as familiar as ever, but she quickly became certain that they were not the same at all. They were utterly different. Breathtakingly different. And what was most peculiar of all was that she had no idea how.

She considered the stars old friends, or even family. So many times her father had taken her out on to the plain of Salsimaine with warm blankets and a midnight feast of sweet pistachio cakes and goat's milk, and they had gazed at the stars for hours. He had told her their stories and the stories of the constellations: the eight orphans of Ra, god of the sun; the Silver River that bore him off and would one day reunite him with all of his creation; the Glassy Gates, high in the Southern Sky, bidding welcome to those who dared to pass; the Court of the Ten, their flames burning in eternal judgement. He had told Naeo these tales, and many more, until she had known something of each part of the night sky.

But it was as she had grown older that the stars had truly become her kin. That was when she learned the mysterious ways of Essenfayle, and to experience the natural world around her, and sense her place in it. Only then had her father's stories ceased to be so important. Instead she became fascinated by how the stars made her feel.

And that was it, Naeo thought suddenly. *That* was the difference now, on the *Windrush*, looking at the stars as Sylas saw them. She could no longer *feel* them. They were remote and far away. She sensed – no, she was certain – that they were more distant than she could imagine, than she had ever considered possible. They were worlds away, blinking across a vast emptiness, sending light that did not just exist but *travelled*, spanning a great divide.

Her head swam with the immensity of what she saw. She tried to shut her eyes, but realised with a pang of panic that these were not her eyes to shut. They were Sylas's. So, like him, she gazed up at the stars and a universe that felt more remote and strange to her than she had thought possible. And, unable to feel, Naeo found herself trying to understand. What *was* that light in all that darkness?

Almost as soon as she asked herself the question she knew the answer. Because Sylas knew. She saw that these pinpricks of light were not cool and quiet, as she had thought, but wild and fierce and made of fire. She knew that they blazed like the sun, and that all stars were suns, and that they warmed countless undiscovered worlds. Worlds beyond imagining. Worlds in endless motion. Worlds liquid-hot and deathly cold. Worlds alive with perpetual storms, and others dark and dead. Worlds that lived and died in their own unfathomable cycle of life, with its origin in the beginning of everything.

It was overwhelming, terrifying, but also magical and beautiful. Naeo felt connected to all she saw not as she had with Essenfayle — not by feelings and instinct — but by knowing. She wished she could turn to Triste and tell him, share with him the wonder of it all. But, when she did turn, to her surprise she saw Simia's freckled face glowing silver in the moonlight.

"Sylas?" Simia said, fascinated. "Is that still you?"

Sylas tried to reply, but he could not speak because, quite suddenly, his tongue was not his own. Without wishing to, he looked down at his hands, which were also not his — these were delicate and feminine. He saw that they clasped the Glimmertrome, and he watched as its fine needle passed into the white.

He looked up and saw Triste where Simia had been a moment before. The Scryer was peering at him with a look of fascination.

"Now let him see," Triste said. "Let Sylas see as you see."

There was a hesitation and then Naeo's gaze — because surely that was what it was — turned up to the night sky.

It was a relief at first. The skies, at least, were surely the same for her as they were for him. He saw the great sweep of the Milky Way, and instinctively he searched for the constellation he had been looking at before, with Simia, the one he had remembered from his *Book of Science*: Scorpio, a collection of stars in the shape of a scorpion, arranged round a giant red star.

But the longer he searched, the more confused he became. It was nowhere to be seen. In fact, this was not even the sky he had seen moments before when he had looked at it with Simia. With the exception of the Milky Way, nothing about it was familiar.

But how could that be? He knew the stars almost as though

they were family. Even before he went to school, his mother had taken him on clear summer nights up the snaking path behind their old cottage to where they had a favourite place to lie in the long grass. And there, with her finger silhouetted against the cosmos, she had pointed and whispered to him about stars, galaxies, supernovas, nebulas and black holes. Astronomy was a science she loved almost as much as her own, and her excitement and wonder overflowed and became his.

By the time he had gone to school, Sylas had known ten constellations and could find them in the night sky. When he had gone to live with his uncle in Gabblety Row, he had often escaped out of his garret-room window at night, with his *Book of Science* tucked under his arm. And there, on the roof, he had spent long, solitary hours tracing the shapes of constellations in the sky, and discovering the brightest stars and the planets of the solar system. And, when he had done this, he had felt close to his mother again, until soon the stars, like his kites, had become the family he did not have.

But there was nothing there for him now. The stars seemed further from him than ever before. Anonymous and unknowable.

He felt a tremor of panic and attempted to look away. But it was hopeless – his eyes were Naeo's now. He tried to calm himself. This was another world, so of course the sky would be a little different. Perhaps this was just a part of the sky that was less familiar. As his nerves settled, Sylas started to have that peculiar sense he had when he was using Essenfayle: the feeling that the things around him were in some way connected – them to each other and he to them.

But even this was different. This was something immense, grand and unfathomable. It was not a connection to the things around him – the waves and the winds – it was a connection to everything. Everything in the world, and everything beyond it, in that vast, velvet sky.

As the moments passed, his feelings only became stronger. He felt the cold emptiness of space, the pull of the stars, the forces of orbits, the heat of the suns. He felt the dizzying spin of planets and solar systems, how the universe was not many things but one, how it was a story told in light and dark, fire and ice, life and death. It was a story spanning eons, from the furthest future to the beginning of all beginnings.

Had he been himself, he would have gaped like his childhood self lying in the long grass. He would have laughed in delight and squeezed Simia's hand, just as he had his mother's. But he could do none of those things, and so he marvelled, wondering how it was that he had never seen and felt like this before.

It was a clearer way of seeing; not like through a telescope — the seeing of astronomers and scientists, revealing the shape of things, the place of things, their colour and motion. This was a kind of seeing that found no mystery and answered no question, that made him feel one with everything, from the tips of his fingers to the furthest star. It set his heart racing and opened him wide.

In that moment, he wished that he was Naeo. He wished that she was him and that they were one. He wished that they would never be apart again.

§

Somehow Bayleon's crouch did not slow his speed, and neither did his massive frame, which was accustomed to the sprint. He was a Spoorrunner and he was born to run. He traversed slopes, mounted banks and leapt across ditches almost as though they were not there. He passed so softly that he might have been a shadow, breathing through his nose in deep, silent breaths, running lightly on his toes, leaving barely a track behind.

So it was that he passed beneath the noses of an entire regiment of Ghor guards even as they lined up for their next attack. He stole through a loose rabble of men taking a rest round hastily lit campfires. He stalked through a platoon of Hamajaks bivouacked in one large heap, which huffed and steamed in the night. And at last he crept silently between two Tythish sentinels whose moonlike eyes panned expertly across the plain, alert to an attack from the rear, but blind to the shadow at their feet.

Bayleon crawled on into the darkness, and when he reached a place of safety he paused until he spied what he was looking for. He pressed on towards a great upheaval of earth and only came to a halt when he reached its outer edge. It was a gigantic crater gouged from the earth by claw and tooth. Its sodden sides were laid about with broken trees, boulders, piles of heather and all kinds of vegetation: anything that might be eaten. This was an Ogresh nest, carved hungrily from the plain and left ready for their next meal.

Bayleon plunged in, slithering down the side of the crater until he came to a sudden stop against a pile of leaves. The nest reeked of the Ogresh — the smell of earth, cracked timber and brackish water — and he could see all about him the gashes left by their claws and giant teeth. He swung his pack from his shoulder and pulled from it a small glass phial, which he emptied over the leaves. Then he took out a shard of flint and struck it sharply against another stone, which issued a brief flash of fire.

"Come on! Come on!" he murmured.

He struck again, and this time a blue flame pooled over the surface of the leaves. A moment later tongues of yellow and orange sprang up, growing into a smoky fire.

Bayleon grinned and then stuffed his belongings back into his bag. Digging his toes into the mud to gain purchase, he clambered up the side of the Hollow, and vaulted over the ridge of earth at the top. He turned back to check the fire. It was growing swiftly, spreading to the nearby carcass of a tree and from there to a pile of heather. The well of the crater was glowing orange now, and sparks and fingers of flame were starting to show over its sides. He lifted his eyes and scanned the darkness.

Suddenly a fierce screech cut like a blade through the night. He turned to see the outline of the nearest Tythish guard, its back arched, its head high, steam pouring from its mouth. Its scream died away and it lowered its giant eyes, glaring at him through the darkness, its features twisted with malice. Bayleon squared himself and held its gaze, daring it to give chase. But, before the Tythish guard could respond, it was distracted by another fire out in the darkness, behind the army lines. An instant later another identical blaze flickered into life and, even as it gained height and brightness, a handful more leapt up in the dark. Bayleon spied even more fires blooming on the plain like beacons. Each and every one seemed to be growing out of the nests of the Ogresh.

"All right then," murmured Bayleon. "So now it begins!"

Suddenly a roar thundered down the hills like an avalanche of rock. Bayleon looked up to see the massive shapes of the Ogresh heaving themselves from the heart of the battle, their fiery eyes fixed on their burning nests. They staggered as they changed direction, pushing aside the shattered roots of the Valley of Outs, wading through beasts and men. As they broke loose, their colossal forms morphed from knots of timber to great clods of earth, and they came at a furious charge, their great earthen shoulders swinging, their clawed feet ripping up the hillside.

Bayleon was unmoved. Calmly he dropped his bag from his shoulder and pulled out what looked like a fortune-teller's ball. He struck it sharply with his fingertip and instantly a silver glow flared at the centre of the orb, growing quickly into a dazzling white light. He held it aloft so that it cast an arc of light round him.

At this the Ogresh bellowed their fury, several of them turning to charge directly towards him. The ground started to tremble at their approach, but still Bayleon did not flinch. Instead he looked along the line of fires and watched as identical flares of white light blinked into life, each of them illuminating a single figure clad in the leathers of a Spoorrunner.

He turned back to the Ogresh, a smile on his lips.

"Now then," he growled, "come see how the Spoorrunners run!"

31

The Trap

"And isn't that the trap? That we start to believe that all these superstitions — these stories we have told ourselves to explain the inexplicable — that they are the answers to all our doubts? Those, and not the potential within ourselves?"

SIMIA STOOD AS QUIETLY as she could and made her way back along the railing, towards the centre of the main deck where Triste was sitting on a chest, the glow of his pipe illuminating his face.

"I think it's working!" she whispered, her eyes shining with excitement. "I think it's really working!"

Triste gave a rare smile, then blew out a long stream of silver smoke, which was carried away on the wind. "It is," he said. "Thanks to you, Simsi."

Simia flushed with pride and grinned. She looked towards the stern of the ship where Naeo lay. "Is she still watching?"

Triste nodded. "Three times the needle has passed from the black into the white, but Naeo shows no sign of stopping."

Simia's smile faded a little. "Do you think they're OK?"

"If Naeo wanted to stop, she could," said the Scryer. "She's holding the Glimmertrome. She and Sylas are learning, that's all. It's just as we hoped. They are meeting each other, properly and for the first time." He took another draw on his pipe and exhaled in a series of puffs. "I think they may even be learning to like one another," he added thoughtfully. "Which I suppose is no less than coming to like themselves."

"I suppose," said Simia absently. She stared at Naeo for a moment, then turned her eyes up to the stars.

Triste watched her intently, his expression somewhere between interest and amusement. Finally he said: "There's no need, you know."

Simia glanced at him. "No need to... what?"

He tapped the tobacco out of his pipe. "You don't need to envy them."

Simia gasped theatrically. "I do NOT envy them! Why would you even say that?"

Triste started to refill his pipe. "You realise, don't you," he said, "that if Sylas and Naeo do make the most of their connection, if they harness their gift, then it might not be long before you know your own Glimmer, before you're sharing all this —" he pointed the stem of his pipe up at the stars — "with your own second self. Think of that."

Simia frowned. She did not like being told how she felt, even by a Scryer, and so she crossed her arms and gazed moodily up at the stars. Finally she looked at him.

"You will too, you know," she said. "It's not just me. You'll be sharing all this with another part of *you* as well."

Triste nodded slowly. "If Sylas and Naeo are who we think they are, soon we will all be changed quite completely and forever."

Simia was quiet for a moment, then she asked: "What do you think it'll be *like*?"

"I see much as a Scryer," he said, blowing out green, luminous smoke rings. "I've seen the great power of the connection between people, but also the terrible hurt and harm of separation. I've seen how it hollows out the soul, and how we can be left forever yearning. I've seen how it can fill us with unspeakable anguish and doubt. I've seen the loss of hope, and the stories we tell ourselves to ease the pain." He drew again on his pipe. "If that can happen when we lose another person, imagine the doubt and anguish of losing part of ourselves, even if we have never known that those feelings are even there."

He blew out another long stream of smoke and fixed Simia with his penetrating gaze. "Now, imagine what it will be like to find that other part of ourselves again."

Simia swallowed. "So... you're sure that it'll be... a *good* thing?"

Triste raised an eyebrow and blinked. "Simsi, if I am right, it will not be good because that does not even begin to describe it." He leaned forward. "It will be miraculous — a thing of wonder."

§

Bayleon was lost in the sprint: the rhythm of it, the thrill of it. His muscles sang and his body thrummed and his heart beat loud. He found the path as surely as if it was day, tearing through rutted pasture, hurling himself across hollows, leaping over boulders and fallen trees. He was the stag and the falcon; he was blood coursing in veins; he was strength and speed and power. He barely heard the thunder of the Ogresh behind him — its huff and grunt, its fists crushing all in its path. And he did not look back. He was a Spoorrunner and, if he was to die, it would be with his eyes on the path ahead.

When he did glance away, it was to check the position of the others. He saw the silver lights of the Spoorrunners darting from side to side across the dark plain. The movements seemed random, driven more by panic than design. But Bayleon knew better and the sight filled him with pride. He saw how each of the lights moved along the base of the hill, converging in an area not far from where his own chase had begun. He saw how everything was going to plan.

But, each time he allowed himself to look, he also saw that another light had disappeared, and he knew that one of his Spoorrunners had succumbed to an Ogresh. *It would have been over in an instant*, he told himself. *This is how they would have wanted to die.* And yet each extinguished light made the night darker and the winter wind colder.

Run, he told himself. *Run now. It is all about the run.*

He ran even as he felt the blast of Ogresh breath in his hair. He ran along ditches, across fields of mud and banks of shale; he ran between the burning nests and across vast, open stretches of the plain.

"Where's that blasted horn?" he panted. "It has to be soon!"

But there was no horn, and still the Ogresh followed, close and fierce, and Bayleon felt sure he would soon be crushed by a single blow of a flailing fist. When he glanced about again, there were two fewer lights, leaving only seven still burning in the darkness. Another went out even as he looked. Then another.

"Blow the blasted horn!" he cried.

The word was still on his lips when the horn gave answer. A long, mournful note sounded in the night, drifting from high in the hills. It was not the harsh report of one of the Imperial battle horns, but low and melancholy, haunting the plain.

"Yes!" growled Bayleon.

He leapt in the air, slammed both feet into a bank of earth and used it to turn sharply to one side.

Then he headed directly for the Valley of Outs.

§

Espasian lowered the horn from his lips and peered into the darkness. Below him, the last five lights had already changed direction and were heading towards the valley, each of them darting from side to side as the Spoorrunners struggled to evade their pursuers.

His eyes shifted back to the steep sides of the Rift, searching the moonlit chasm for any remaining defenders. He could see none, but still it had taken too long to clear them from their posts. Far too long. He had been forced to watch as light after light, Spoorrunner after Spoorrunner was snuffed out, and had felt an almost physical clench of pain at the thought that another had given their life for this hopeless plan. For *his* plan. And, each time, he thought of Bayleon, and found himself praying to Isia for his friend's safe passage.

A shout across the gully made him turn. In the darkness, he could just make out one of the Leaflikes he had set to work digging the tunnel, waving his arms and gesticulating towards the plain. Espasian looked to where he was pointing and instantly felt a deathly chill.

There were only three lights left.

They were not far out now, but they were frantic, weaving between one another in a desperate last attempt to elude the Ogresh. He knew that the creatures would be pressed in behind the Spoorrunners now, sensing victory, forming a single massive crush of fists and limbs. He knew but could do nothing. And Espasian knew too that this was the anguish of command. He must stand, and watch, and wait. If it all came to nothing, if this had to be the end of the Spoorrunners, then he must witness it, knowing that they did it for him.

And so he squared his shoulders and he watched. Because, if they must suffer, then so must he.

He could hear the charge of the Ogresh now. It was a low rumble like an earthquake, and it came from everywhere. It was as though the hills were tearing themselves loose, or colossal waves were crashing on the dark shore of the Valley of Outs. But Espasian was intent upon the three lights, now so near that he could just make out the figures running beneath them.

Was that Bayleon he saw at the rear? Those broad shoulders, that loping gait? Was that not his beard?

Espasian was about to cry out when he froze. His limbs went slack.

"No!" he exclaimed in a wavering voice.

The light had gone out.

He felt suddenly weak and sick. The pain of the Black surged within him. He wanted to turn away, but he could not.

He must not. Not until the end.

There was a cry from somewhere below, from one of the remaining Spoorrunners, and Espasian pulled himself back to the moment. There were two lights still and now they were coming together right at the entrance to the Rift. The glow of the orbs lit the frothing surface of the mountain stream and, behind, a tumbling, boiling motion with the burning red embers of Ogresh eyes in its midst.

The two white lights shifted from side to side, as in a dance, sometimes drawing so close it seemed they would collide, sometimes dividing sharply, splitting up those that hunted them. And then, as one of them swung sharply about, the light seemed to fall to the ground, bouncing and coming to a halt. Espasian held his breath, but it was snuffed out.

Now there was only one.

It was not for slowing. It danced over rocks and boulders, vaulting from bank to bank of the stream. And suddenly it was there, inside the Rift, blinking as it passed behind the trees.

Espasian raised his arms in readiness, waiting for the Spoorrunner to reach the safety of the cave entrance. From there they would be able to take refuge deep in the hillside. There was no escape tunnel yet, but the Leaflikes were still hard at it, digging in shifts of four, and soon they would break through.

But it was a long run to the entrance. The Spoorrunner was darting ever more frantically between the trees, clearly tiring now, keeping ahead by agility alone rather than speed. But, behind, the Ogresh already spanned the gully, and it would not be long before they were able to cut off the way ahead.

Espasian braced himself, hands held out, knowing that the crisis would come at any moment.

"Run!" he bellowed. "You're nearly there!"

But, even as his voice echoed across the gully, the Spoorrunner turned sharply and headed straight towards the Magruman.

"No!" cried Espasian, jabbing the air. "To the cave!"

But the Spoorrunner came on, leaping across the stream and climbing the slope towards Espasian, the dancing orb casting ghoulish shadows all round the Rift.

Suddenly the figure broke free of the trees and started to sprint up a barren slope, revealing his features for the first time: a massive, bearlike frame clad in leather; a mane of hair matted with sweat; a great tangle of a beard.

"Bayleon!" yelled Espasian.

But, even as his heart leapt, the forest behind Bayleon ceased to exist. It was flattened in an instant, and all that was left was a spray of splinters and a haze of sap. Through this the Ogresh came: at least a dozen of them, their gargantuan bodies forged of earth, rock, timber and shale. And, as the Spoorrunner struggled up the slope, they sensed their triumph. It sent them into a frenzy so that they lashed out at one another in their thirst to claim this prize as their own.

But then Bayleon stopped.

To Espasian's astonishment, his friend came to a sudden halt, still far below, and leapt on to a rock. The Ogresh shuddered to a halt, their fists and limbs thundering into the earth. Their burning eyes glowed as they weighed up the scene, glancing about, sensing a trap.

All the while Espasian gazed at his friend who was covered in mud and grime, chest heaving, body steaming in the light of the orb. He saw Bayleon's wide, swarthy face streaming with sweat, his eyes still bright with the thrill of the chase, and that great beard parting in a smile.

The Spoorrunner lifted the orb. "Espasian!" he yelled. "My friend, send me home. Send me to my family!"

And, as he spoke the last word, he cast the orb down against the rock where it shattered into a thousand pieces. The light was snuffed out in an instant, leaving Espasian blinking into the darkness.

For a brief moment he wondered why Bayleon had given up his light. But then his skin prickled. Of course, he thought, *that* was why. It was Bayleon's final gift, from one friend to another. He had given darkness so that Espasian would not have to watch.

Already the Ogresh had resumed their charge and were bearing down upon Bayleon's rock. With streaming eyes, the Magruman raised his arms, lost himself in the root and rock beneath his feet and called to the valley.

So it was that, as the Ogresh reached Bayleon, the valley met their thunder with its own. The slope suddenly ripped itself loose, surging outwards into the abyss, leaning ever more to the vertical. And, as it tilted, its surface became a fierce torrent of earth, shale and vegetation, roaring as it rolled and tumbled, consuming all in its path. The far slope too seemed to come uncoupled from the hillside, leaning nearer and nearer to the opposing slope until the two sides of the gully closed like the mighty jaws of some beast of the nether world, with teeth of granite and a throat that was a bottomless darkness. And in this great maw the Ogresh were swallowed, their cries lost in the growl of the earth.

And with them went Bayleon, the Spoorrunner.

In the darkness, Espasian did not see his friend fall, but he saw the pale glow of the rock tumbling into the morass. And this, at least, he forced himself to watch as it disappeared into the frenzy of earth and rock. He stared after it long and hard until it was lost. But even then he did not weep. Because in his heart he knew that his friend would not share the fate of the Ogresh. Bayleon would not be swallowed in the cold and dark of the deepest places, far from the light of the sun.

Instead he would go to his family. And to the valley. And to peace.

32

The Mesektet

*"The fleet may be vast and well provisioned, but it is
the Mesektet that casts her shadow across the seas
and that strikes dread into all who cross her path."*

THE *Mesektet* LAY UNDER anchor, dark and silent, its vast black
sails hanging limply in the cool northerly wind. The rigging was
loose, the decks deserted, the standard furled; and yet there was
an undeniable, obscure energy in the mighty hulk, as though its
thick timbers and massive masts were primed for effort, and an
untold power thrummed in the dark of the lower decks.

Thoth reclined on the quarterdeck, his bony figure almost lost
beneath the folds of his rich robes, which spilled from a golden
throne. He had been as motionless as his flagship, but now, at last,
he stirred. His hooded eyes turned to the rising sun in the west
and surveyed the pink shimmer of the Kemetian Sea.

A dry rasp of pleasure sounded in his throat.

The smooth line of the horizon was interrupted by distant
shapes, like black fangs jutting upwards towards the sky. They
were the tapering rigs of battleships, at least a hundred in number,
their sails full, their standards flying high. Already they were many
leagues hence and they were making good time. It would not be

long before they set their blockade and muzzled the Jaws of Kemet.

"So now the Jaws have teeth!" proclaimed the Priest of Souls, in voices that filled the sails, and rumbled in the companion-ways, and whispered in the deepest recesses of the ship. "Guide them, Nu, chaos of the deep, and let them feast upon their prize!"

As the many voices died away, the earliest rays of the morning sun passed over the *Mesektet*, striking the mastheads and then sweeping down the sails in a crimson cascade. Sunbeams pierced the rigging and sent fingers of light sprawling across the decks.

But at the very centre of the ship one large oblong of blackness remained in shadow. It was set deep into the polished timbers, and only as the sun rose did the light penetrate, revealing a dark, glistening surface: a mirror to the sails and rigging above. The sea breeze rippled the surface, showing the contents to be liquid, but, even as the ship yawed and swayed, the pool of Black was still, governed by a physical law of its own.

But then Thoth raised a hand and the Black suddenly surged forward in a wave, as though craving to be near. It rolled towards him until it slapped violently against the side of the pool.

He rose imperiously from his throne, looking from the pool of Black to the decks and the rigging. With a wheeze of satisfaction, he turned his outstretched palm upwards.

The *Mesektet* responded in an instant. The clatter of a doughty chain shattered the silence. The anchor began to rise, ropes snapped taut and wound themselves tightly round spars and cleats, half-furled sails fell swiftly from the yards and, in a moment, filled with the freshening wind. Above, the Imperial standard unravelled from the main masthead, cracking sharply as Thoth's visage glowered across the Kemetian Sea.

The Priest of Souls extended a bony finger and the *Mesektet* did his bidding. With a heave and a groan, the flagship of the Imperial fleet surged from its mooring and set a course due south, towards the nearest shores of the Motherland.

33

Daybreak

"There are daybreaks that come too slowly
and those that come too soon, but that last daybreak
of my time in the Other I wish had never come at all."

SYLAS WOKE TO THE sounds and scents of the sea, the warmth of the sun on his face and the soothing motion of the ship. For the first few sleepy moments he wanted only to bask in the ease of it all and allow his mind to drift into wakefulness. But then he remembered the night before.

His eyes flicked open and he saw before him a magnificent dawn flecked with glowing clouds and wisps of pink. There were still a few fading stars in the furthest cobalt reaches of the sky, but already the sun was above the waves and the day had begun.

He pushed himself up and looked about. Simia had gone, leaving her rumpled blanket next to him, and the rest of the crew were busy up in the rigging or below deck. Sylas wondered how long he had slept — he couldn't even remember drifting off. The last he remembered he had still been staring up at the stars.

He rubbed his eyes and gazed at the rising sun. The memories of all that had happened were still strong, and he found himself carried back to the toing and froing of the Glimmertrome, and the stark beauty of the night sky, and that strange feeling of being at one with the stars.

And then he felt a new electric tingle.

The feeling was still there.

As he stared out to sea, Sylas realised that he was not just *seeing* the sparkling waves, the sunbeams, the blazing sun. He was *feeling* them. The warmth of the sun was no longer skin-deep: it reached far down inside him. He felt the ebb and flow of the sea, and he breathed with its rise and fall. Even the northerly wind was no longer wild, but something close and familiar. The stars may have disappeared, but Sylas felt everything he had the previous night: how all things were connected in a single story. How it was to feel as Naeo. And it was wonderful.

Then he remembered something that he had almost forgotten, something from his first encounter with Mr Zhi in the Shop of Things, before any of this had begun. Mr Zhi had just shown him the Flight of Fancy — the mobile of birds that had seemed to come alive — and the old man had leaned close and said: "*You are able to see the world as it is promised to us!*"

Perhaps this was what he had meant!

He glanced about for Simia, eager to share everything he had discovered, but the deck was still empty. The only person he could see was Ash at the helm, guiding the ship with upturned hands. Sylas stood and walked back along the railing, marvelling as he went at how quickly the crew had repaired the ship and restored her to all her glory. The decks shone and the railings gleamed, straight and true.

As he reached the quarterdeck, he saw at once that Ash was exhausted, his eyes ringed with shadow, his shoulders rounded, his hair even more dishevelled than normal. Sylas felt a twist of guilt. He should have relieved the young Magruman long before dawn. And yet, as Ash saw Sylas approaching, he straightened and gave his customary grin.

"Ah, the dreamer awakes!" he declared. "How are you?"

"Fine," said Sylas. "Listen, Ash, I'm really sorry about last night. I was—"

"Not a jot of it!" interjected Ash. "You did exactly what you were supposed to do! Simia and Triste let me in on everything."

"You knew about it?"

"Yes, but don't be cross. Triste said that you would only be truly open if you were taken by surprise. He said if we told you about it you might see what you expected to see, instead of what Naeo sees." He raised his eyebrows expectantly. "So? Did it work?"

Sylas smiled. "I think it actually *did*," he said.

He told Ash everything he had seen and felt the night before, from the moment he had first joined Simia on deck to when he had woken that morning, and Ash listened intently.

"Clever old Triste," he said when Sylas had finished. "And you think this will help you and Naeo?"

Sylas frowned. He hadn't actually considered what all this might mean for the two of them but, as his thoughts turned to her now, he felt a difference there too. Naeo had always been a little like the image he had seen in the Glimmer Glass: distant and half seen, as though she was eclipsed. But now she felt close, almost as though she was there on the quarterdeck with them. And her nearness was nothing like the feeling from before: that bone-grating, gut-churning sense that she might open him wide. This was warm and familiar. The more Sylas thought of her, the more certain he became that he could feel the warmth and comfort of her hammock, and even, perhaps, glimpse her dreams: dreams of stars in solar systems. Stars of gas and flame. Scientific stars. *His* stars. And then he became sure that just as he was captivated by her vision of the world so she was enthralled by his.

He felt another surge of excitement and looked up at Ash. "I really think it might help," he said, his voice quavering. "I think — I think we're starting to understand each other."

"Well, boil my barnacles, this *is* something to get excited about!" cried Ash. "We have to try it out!" He looked up into the rigging. "I'll send someone to fetch Naeo right away! Hoy there!"

Sylas grabbed his arm. "Not now, Ash. She's sleeping."

Ash turned and looked at him in astonishment. "And I suppose you know that too?"

Sylas just smiled and shrugged.

"Well, aren't you full of surprises?" declared Ash, eyeing him closely. "Fine, but you'd better get to it soon." He turned back to the choppy seas. "We're going even quicker than I'd hoped. According to Fathray's charts, we've already crossed the Bay of Amun, and Fawl tells me that, at this rate, we should reach the Jaws of Kemet by this evening."

"Aye, and by then we'll need to be ready for anything." They both turned to see Fawl himself climbing down the nearest rope ladder. He descended with incredible ease, his one arm wrapped round the full span of the ladder, his feet dropping three or four rungs at a time. "I don't like the look of the weather, cap'n, not one bit."

"Really?" said Ash doubtfully, glancing up at an expanse of clear sky. "Are you sure?"

Fawl jumped down and looked at his young captain with a touch of amusement. "As sure as we're about to get a pounding from the starboard side," he said.

Suddenly a rogue gust of wind struck the ship from the right, and Sylas lost his balance and had to grab on to the helm to steady himself. The gust passed as quickly as it had come, but Ash was busy for some moments regaining control of the ship.

When the *Windrush* had finally settled, he glanced over at Fawl. "Yes, I see," he said sheepishly. "So we need to be ready for some rough weather?"

Fawl nodded. "And there's the Jaws."

Sylas glanced from Fawl to Ash and back again. "The… Jaws?"

"The only passage into the Kemetian Sea," said Fawl, for some reason taking his cap off as he addressed Sylas, "and so to the Motherland."

"Ah," said Sylas. "But… why the 'Jaws'?"

Fawl formed a C-shape in the air with the weathered finger and thumb of his one hand. "The Jaws is two spurs of mountainous land, one north, one south." He narrowed the distance between his fingertips until barely any light showed between. "So close they nearly touch. If the Dirgh is going to try to stop us reaching the Motherland—"

"As surely he will," interjected Ash.

"As sure as rum is rum," agreed Fawl, turning his gaze back to the tiny gap between his thumb and forefinger, "this, right here, is where he'll do it. Only one run through, mountains all around and nowhere to hide. And this time —" he turned to Sylas — "he'll be prepared for some of your… tricks, Master Sylas, if you don't mind me calling them that."

Another squall suddenly buffeted the sails and made the *Windrush* pitch violently to one side. Sylas and Ash staggered a little, but Fawl simply swayed where he stood, his feet planted firmly on the deck. He was looking out to the starboard side, his leathery brow wrinkled as he peered into the distance. Sylas followed his gaze and saw a dark line on the western horizon where the ocean met the sky and, before it, the white flecks of frothing crests and leaping waves.

"Aye, there's something foul brewing out there," said Fawl. He turned to Ash. "Whatever we need to do to get ready," he said with new urgency, "we'd better get on with it."

For a moment Ash stood silently, pale-faced, staring towards the dark horizon, then he nodded at Fawl. "I'll leave you to prepare the ship," he said briskly. "And you'd better take the helm, Sylas!" Before he had even finished, he had dropped his hands and set out in the direction of the hatchway.

Sylas hurriedly assumed his position in front of the ship's wheel and opened his hands, then he glanced at Ash. "Where are you going?" he called.

"To wake up Naeo!" cried the young captain as he clattered down the steps, cloak crackling like a purple flame behind him.

34

The Glove

*"The glove means more to me every day. It is not just
the magic bound up in its golden thread, it is the sense of
belonging that it provides: the feeling that every time
I slide it over my fingers, I am taking my place among
a unique few — a silent order that spans two worlds
and the course of centuries."*

CORPORAL LUCIEN'S EYES WERE fixed on the screen, staring
disbelievingly at quickfire images of impossibility after
impossibility. The latest was captioned 'Murcia, Spain', and it
showed creatures spilling from a grand circular plaza. He saw
beasts of myth and legend — some of them wolfish, howling and
gnashing, some with the look of devils — accompanied by tribes
of demons; others had the stature of giants, with spider limbs
and saucer eyes.

Lucien shook his head. "It's like a *nightmare*," he breathed.

He reached instinctively into his pocket for another lemon
sherbet and tutted when he found the paper bag empty. He glanced
at Dresch.

"You really should see this," he said.

For a long moment Dresch continued to stare into the

microscope, saying nothing, then she murmured, "What's that?"

His eyes fluttered impatiently. "I said you need to look at this!"

Dresch lifted her head and looked briefly at the screen, then back at her companion. "No," she said, pointing at the microscope, "*you* need to look at *this*. This is... well, *impossible*."

Lucien nodded at the screen. "And this *isn't*?"

She held his gaze. "Yes, well, while everyone *else* is looking at that impossibility, *we* should be looking at this impossibility!" She raised her eyebrows and stepped away from the workbench. "Come on," she said. "Have a look."

Lucien sighed and stepped over to her station, his eyes never leaving the screen.

Just as he leaned into the microscope, there was a sharp knock on the lab door. A young soldier entered and gave a hurried salute.

"What is it?" asked Lucien. He seemed rather pleased to be interrupted.

"Sir, you've been asked to report to Command. I'm here to escort you."

Lucien hesitated, then glanced at Dresch. "Private, I'm not supposed to leave Dr Drescher here unless relieved."

"That's all right, sir," said the soldier. His eyes flicked to Dresch. "Ma'am, you're needed too."

Lucien did not hide his surprise. "They want us *both*?"

"Absolutely, sir," said the private. "Straight from the top, sir."

Lucien regarded Dresch as though seeing her in a new light.

She returned his gaze, then pulled off her gloves with a defiant flourish and began unzipping her biohazard suit. "Well, thank goodness *someone* values what we're doing here," she said tartly. She looked at the private. "Just give me a moment to get changed, please."

Her companions watched in silence as she pulled off the shoulders of her suit, then hopped unselfconsciously from foot to foot as she yanked off her overtrousers. Finally she smoothed down her clothes, wrapped her poppy scarf round her neck and gathered up a folder.

"Ready when you are," she said brightly.

The private hesitated and exchanged a glance with Lucien.

Lucien gave Dresch a level look. "Are you sure you're ready?"

Her face darkened. "Of course I am! This isn't the first time I've been to Command, you know. Even we scientists—"

Lucien raised a hand to silence her and dropped his eyes to her feet. "It's just that you might want to change your shoes."

She looked down at her fluffy slippers topped with pink ears.

She cleared her throat. "Ah yes," she said. She looked at the young private and said pleasantly: "Another moment, please."

A deepening gloom gathered about the camp as the soldier led them quickly across a rutted track to a low concrete building. At its centre were double doors of tarnished steel, guarded by two sentries, who now snapped to attention. One of them examined their identification, then tapped at a keypad and the doors slid back to reveal a small vestibule and a descending concrete staircase lit by a single red lamp. Above, painted in white block lettering, were the words:

BRAVO ONE – COMMAND HEADQUARTERS

Dresch and Lucien walked down the concrete steps and finally emerged into a large grey bunker filled with the cold white glow of strip lighting. Between the concrete pillars scores of people chattered in low voices, apparently waiting for a meeting to begin. Most of them were in formal military uniform or fatigues, but the range of ranks and regiments made it clear that this was no ordinary military briefing. Over the many heads, Dresch and Lucien could see a large, blank television screen on the far wall, next to a podium and a strategic map of the world.

Lucien glanced at Martha. "Not quite the debriefing you were looking for, is it?"

Her eyes were still shifting about the gathering, taking note of who was there. "I'm still going to say my piece," she said firmly. "They need to know."

Lucien grunted. "Well, I don't see how you'll be heard in this mob."

Suddenly a pair of doors flew open at the end of the hall and two soldiers stepped inside and took flanking positions either side. They snapped to attention and silence fell over the assembly. Everyone craned towards the opening.

A tall, thin woman entered, walking briskly despite a limp and a cane. She had a stern, emotionless face and she wore her auburn hair in what looked to be a painfully tight bun on top of her head. She had a natural authority, which was only emphasised by the epaulettes of a three-star general on her narrow shoulders. She stepped on to the low platform below the screen and the map, walked to the podium and leaned into the microphone.

"Thank you all for coming," she said in a Scandinavian accent, scanning the room with her piercing eyes. "We have much to discuss, but first let us get the introductions out of the way."

She reached down to her belt, opened a pouch and drew something out of it. Stepping back from the podium, she raised her hand and pulled on an ornately decorated green glove.

For a moment the room was completely silent, all eyes on the glove. Then a large man near the front fished in his pocket and pulled out his own, slipping it on and holding it aloft. Amid a sea of murmurs, several others around him began rooting in bags and coats, and producing identical green gloves. Soon, to Dresch and Lucien's astonishment, the entire gathering started riffling through their belongings and pulling out green Merisi gloves. Everyone glanced about, seemingly as surprised as each other to see their companions wearing the mark of the Merisi.

Lucien stepped away from Dresch and stared, bemused, as her hand travelled to the pocket of her white lab coat, drew out a green glove and pulled it on. Then he too flipped open a pouch on his belt and pulled out a glove. They eyed each other and smiled.

"I know that for many of you," continued the general, her eyes scanning the room, "the true identity of your companions will come as a surprise. In the interests of security, we have kept your true identities confidential, while keeping a close eye on your whereabouts, and even trying to bring some of you together. Through our efforts, many of the remaining Merisi are here in this room. The rest," she said, turning to the screen behind her, "are here."

The screen blinked into life and revealed a grid of smaller panels, each depicting another gathering like their own. Some looked to be in bunkers, some in municipal halls, some in large tents. Together they showed hundreds of figures gazing into the screen, each of them wearing the green glove of the Merisi.

"They can see us, just as you can see them," said the general, "and, as such, this is the largest gathering of Merisi in the history of the order."

Then, as quickly as the images had appeared, they were gone. The screen went black, blinked twice, flickered, then once again came to life.

At its centre was the sallow face of Franz Jacob Veeglum.

There was a brief murmur round the room, which fell away to an absolute hush.

Veeglum leaned towards the camera, revealing a large Yin Yang symbol carved into the stone wall behind him.

"My friends, I thank you for coming," he said, his voice thin but loud over the loudspeakers. "Let me begin with an apology. I wish, as I am sure you do, that at this critical hour my friend and mentor, Mr Zhi, was here to guide us. But he is not, and I console myself that it is only by his sacrifice that the promise of ze Glimmer Myth may yet come to pass." He lowered his head. "And so he may still save us all. That is his doing. The rest is up to us."

He sat back in his chair. "So welcome, brothers and sisters of the Merisi. It is wonderful to see you assembled as you are in locations around ze world. At last, the entire order of ze Merisi, together! I wish it could be under different circumstances." He gave a slight shrug. "But under what other circumstances could it happen? We are a secret order, never intended for the public eye — even for each other's eyes. This is new for us. This is only meant to happen once. Now. Ze moment for which our order was founded, many centuries ago."

There was a rumble of voices around the hall, which quickly died away. To his surprise, Lucien felt Martha's arm slip through his.

"We had hoped, of course, that it would never reach this point; that all would come to pass without ze need of conflict. But the problem, sisters and brothers, is that, while in our world we could keep the truth a secret, in ze Other we could not. There ze Priests of Souls have long feared Merisu's prophecy, and imagined a different union between the worlds. One zat they control: a union built upon empire, upon masters and slaves. And now, seeing that the Glimmer Myth may soon come about, the last of ze Priests of Souls would turn imagination to reality. Just as Merisu's prophesy seems within our grasp, even as Isia's descendants, Sylas and Naeo, seek an end to their journey, so we are faced with our darkest hour.

"This much you know. We know too, that Thoth plans five

'Undoings', as he calls them, of which we believe we have seen only two: ze Black and ze beasts. But there is something of which you are not aware. It is because of this very important something that I have chosen now to break with centuries of tradition and bring you together. And that I have invited one who is not Merisi to join us now."

At this there was a new hubbub about the room as those gathered shared their surprise. Lucien looked at Dresch.

"A stranger in a meeting of the Merisi?" he said rather wryly. "The world really is coming to an end."

Martha gave a slight smile and pointed to the front. "Look! Something's happening!"

The screen had gone black, but now it blinked and came back to life. There was a murmur of surprise around the hall. The screen was showing the interior of the bunker itself, complete with the platform, the podium and the map of the world.

"Why are they showing us this?" said Martha.

"Because this is what they're showing everyone else," hissed Lucien. "Whoever Veeglum was talking about is here!"

Just then the sentries on the doors snapped to attention again and two figures appeared in the gloomy entrance. The first was tall and gaunt, with thick, round spectacles. His rather unremarkable appearance was improved by a distinctive quilted smoking jacket, once fine but now badly worn. The other man was younger and had a full head of tousled dark hair. He wore a muddy, coarse-woven tunic, filthy trousers and filthy, rather oversized boots.

"*Tasker?*" muttered someone in the crowd. "Is that *Tasker?*"

Then Veeglum's voice suddenly blared from the television screen: "Sisters and brothers," he said, "please welcome Paiscion, Magruman of the Suhl."

35

The Vote

"The vote to appoint the new Bringer is never a straightforward affair, but the year of Veeglum was a particular challenge. It began with a quiet objection and ended with a divisive debate."

PAISCION STEPPED ON TO the platform and looked solemnly round the assembly. He seemed about to speak, but the general ushered him over to the podium and pointed at the microphone. Paiscion eyed it with mistrust, but then leaned into it, bringing his mouth rather too close. As he spoke, the announcement system blared and squealed.

Paiscion jumped back in alarm. Tasker quickly stepped up and whispered something in his ear. The Magruman adjusted his glasses, then began again, this time well away from the microphone.

"Sisters and brothers," he said, his voice loud and sharp in the speakers, "thank you for receiving me. I, and the Suhl, are honoured by your unfailing friendship. As ever, we offer that same friendship in return."

There was a kindly murmur around the hall.

"And as a faithful friend I have come to you at this desperate hour with a rather desperate request." He opened his palms. "Please do not fight."

The chamber erupted with exclamations of surprise, and many turned to their companions to share their disbelief.

Lucien leaned into Dresch. "What's he thinking? He can't really expect us to do nothing?"

"Let's just hear what he has to say," she hissed.

"We do, of course, know all that you face," continued Paiscion, silencing the room. "The evil that spills between the worlds is one the Suhl have been familiar with for generations. Then it was the Undoing, and it took away all that we hold dear. This is not a new war. We know this war and we know that you must not fight it."

A man in a mud-splattered uniform at the front of the hall raised his gloved hand.

"But if I may, Lord Magruman? If you have seen all this for yourself, surely you know why we cannot do nothing! Master Veeglum instructed us to prevent fighting wherever we could and we have tried. We have advised armies to wait, to give ground, to defend. But, all the while, the Black rises in our rivers and lakes, and those beasts pour from the stone circles. Our leaders see what their restraint has brought them and they feel the need to act!"

"You can hardly blame them!" someone in the crowd shouted.

There were grumbles and nods of agreement all around the assembly.

The Magruman peered at the man over his spectacles. "Then you must find another way to make them listen because there is more to this than meets the eye." He lifted his gaze to the rest of the gathering. "Through all of our trials, we have come to dread one evil above all others. It has only become more menacing with the passing of the years, and we are powerless to control it."

"The Black," murmured Martha.

Paiscion's eyes settled back on the man in the muddy uniform. "The Black," he said.

Martha turned to her companion and raised an eyebrow. Lucien pursed his lips.

"We've known the Black for many years," continued Paiscion. "At first it formed in the crucibles of the Three Ways: the Dirghea, the charm schools, the Colleges of Ways. Later, at the Reckoning, it laced the fields of battle, running in streams, pooling in ditches. And, when the battle was done, it ran thick in the river of Gheroth, flowing from Salsimaine out to the sea. Soon we found it deep in the Quintessence mines of the Valley of Outs, seeping from the walls, poisoning the roots of the Living Tree. And it poisoned people too. It ran in the veins of those it touched, tormenting them with pain and fogging their minds."

"So we have to do something about it!" called someone from the heart of the crowd. "Tell us what to do!"

Paiscion shook his head sadly. "With the Black, you will find no swift remedy. It is not so much substance as absence. Void. It is darkness and emptiness, forged in the cauldron of the Three Ways. It hungers and consumes, devouring the things of Nature. And not only the physical but other less tangible things." He tapped the side of his head. "Thoughts and ideas, intellect and reason upon which your science depends."

"You see!" said Dresch to Lucien. "The Black! It's all about the Black!"

Lucien nodded slowly, his eyes fixed on Paiscion. He squeezed Dresch's arm.

"And you think that's why he's sent the Black?" asked someone.

Paiscion sighed. "I don't know the mind of the Dirgh, but he is aware that science is the Fifth Way, the Way that stands as a mirror to Urgolvane, Kimiyya, Druindil and Essenfayle. Science is your strength and, in a war of Ways, your only hope. Its power is undeniable and its reach... well, it extends to the deepest oceans and the furthest stars, so why not to other worlds? I believe *that* is what Thoth fears, almost as much as he fears the Glimmer Myth. He said as much, did he not, when he appeared to us all in the Black? And how better to fight science than with the Black? In a world built upon reason, the Black could do untold harm. If science is knowing, the Black is unknowing. It is blindness and ignorance. It is oblivion."

"So surely," called a woman to Dresch's side, "we HAVE to do something about it! And, if Thoth fears our science, why not *use* it to destroy the Black? Why not—"

"Because that's precisely what he wishes you to do!" exclaimed the Magruman, for a moment losing his composure. "He *wants* you to try to destroy it. You cannot — you *must* not — fight corruption with corruption. You will only feed the contagion!"

There was a long silence and then someone hesitantly raised their hand. "But with respect, Lord Paiscion, what if you're wrong? The Three Ways created the Black, not science. What if science is different?"

Paiscion took a deep breath and nodded. "I had the same thought, but I always come back to the fact that Nature is pure and universal in whichever world. Her destruction is just that, whether by the weapons of science, or by the sorcery of the Three Ways, and we know that it is destruction that the Black thrives upon."

There were some murmurs of agreement, but most of the gathering remained silent. Many were clearly unconvinced.

Then a voice called out from the very back of the bunker: "He's right!"

The gathering turned to see a blonde woman wearing a white lab coat and a colourful scarf embroidered with poppies.

"Dr Martha Drescher," said the woman. "Epidemiologist.

We've been working on the Black for days now. Everything, *everything* we've observed supports the Magruman's view."

The general beckoned to her. "Please come forward, Dr Drescher. Everyone should hear this."

The crowd parted before Dresch, and she made her way to the front of the bunker, trying to keep her head high as she looked left and right at the scores of staring faces. As she walked, she felt her usual boldness begin to fail. She knew the importance of the moment.

Paiscion gave a slight bow as she approached and stood aside for her, sweeping his hand towards the podium and the microphone. "Don't get too close to that thing," he whispered with a wink. "It has a life of its own!"

He chuckled in a way that broke the tension. She smiled and took her place before the gathering and the cameras, and began.

She told the room about her many attempts to identify the Black, all of which had come to nothing. She told them about the patients she had studied, about their reports of fogginess and discomfort. And finally she told them her most recent findings: how the Black had responded to toxins, viruses and corrosive agents. How it had seemed to thrive on them.

When she had finished, there was a horrified silence. Finally Paiscion stepped forward and whispered something in her ear. She stepped to one side to let him speak.

He cleared his throat. "Thank you, Dr Drescher," he began. "I wish with all my heart that I had been wrong, but it is better that we know the whole truth; that everyone knows the whole truth." He looked out at the gathering. "Now we must share it and make sure that the fighting is stopped."

There was a subdued murmur among the crowd.

"They simply won't listen to us!" said a high-ranking officer in the front row. "Not now, not when there's Black in school swimming pools, in rivers, in the water supply! Not when there are beasts pouring from Her Majesty's Treasury, for pity's sake! And don't forget, because the generals certainly haven't, that Thoth now has scientists of his own – weapons scientists, nuclear scientists, microbiologists – we can only imagine what he's planning to do with *them*!"

Paiscion's shoulders sank within his smoking jacket. "Yes, yes, I do see that," he said, grim and expressionless. "But we must try nevertheless. Everything depends upon us trying."

Suddenly the screen behind him blinked and Paiscion's face vanished. In its place, the long, drawn face of Franz Jacob Veeglum appeared. He leaned forward so that his features obscured the room behind him.

"I think there is something we can do," he said. "Something that may stop the fighting and perhaps slow the invasion." His searching green eyes seemed to travel about the room and in that moment, if it was possible, he looked even grimmer and more melancholy than was his custom. "We can put ourselves in ze middle."

He was quiet for a moment, as though to allow his words to settle. An absolute hush fell upon the room.

"We can put ourselves between Thoth's army and the armies of our world," he said. "Ze Merisi do not fight, but we may resist." He sat back, lifted his hand and held his fine embroidered glove to the screen.

For some moments more there was not a murmur, then one woman raised her own gloved hand.

"But, Master Veeglum, with respect, the glove, as – as you know, only *deflects* the Three Ways. We would only be able to contain them for so long, and then... and then, well..."

"We'd be defenceless!" someone called out.

"Which is why I cannot ask any of you to do this," said Veeglum. "You must each decide for yourselves."

Again there was a breathless quiet as the Merisi absorbed what he was saying.

"Isn't this what Thoth wants?" someone called out. "For the Merisi to just... show ourselves? Aren't we just making it easy for him?"

Veeglum's answer was swift. "It hardly matters, not now. If we can stop the fighting, even for a while, it could make all ze difference. Now we need to buy what time we can. That is all we can do."

His pale eyes swept the room so that everyone watching felt his gaze.

Paiscion once again stepped up to the podium. "I think perhaps if you knew what buying that time could mean then your decision might be easier. So let me tell you. I believe each of you has been told about the child Sylas Tate and his significance to the Glimmer Myth?"

There were almost universal nods around the hall.

"And perhaps you know too that not least because of the courage of your brother here, Jeremy Tasker—" he waved a hand towards his youthful companion, who quickly dropped his eyes — "Sylas is now with his Glimmer, Naeo. And so the descendants of Isia — those prophesied by Merisu himself — have been united. But what you do not know is the wonder of their union as I have seen it — as Tasker here has seen it. What you do not know are the miracles they have performed, the astonishing feats of natural power, the deeds that have already vanquished Thoth's forces and freed thousands of Suhl from squalor and slavery. Deeds that confirm them to be the children of our legends and hopes."

Excited whispers rippled through the room, but Paiscion did not pause. Instead he leaned over the microphone, using it now to give his voice depth and volume so that it thrummed through the bunker.

"And what you cannot know is that, when I left Sylas and Naeo, they were beginning a journey aboard a ship forged of Quintessence, borne onwards by Nature's own winds. They are even now flying over hills and plains, across land and sea, to Old Kemet, to the Motherland of Thoth's Empire. There they seek the place that first broke our worlds in two, that rent our souls, and so doing began millennia of doubt and superstition. And perhaps there Sylas and Naeo will find a way to channel their great power and forge a new beginning for us all."

He paused, adjusting his glasses on his nose. "But they need time, brave Merisi. Time to find their way, to find what it is that they are, what it is that they must do. If this world falls to the Black —" he spread his arms wide — "then it will all have been for nothing. Their efforts, our efforts, the Order of the Merisi, the Bringers, the Passing Bell, all of it." Paiscion clenched his fists. "That is what is at stake. That is why they need the time you can give them."

He stepped back from the microphone and lowered his eyes. Still the chamber was hushed, and everyone seemed to be lost in their own thoughts. All at once Paiscion's face disappeared from the screen and it resolved to an image of Franz Veeglum.

"Thank you, Paiscion, for helping us to understand." Once again his eyes searched the room. "So I think it is time for a show of the glove. Ze question is, who will stand?"

The room was silent. Someone cleared their throat, but said nothing. People began glancing about to see if anyone else had raised their hand.

Then Tasker stepped to the front of the podium. "I will," he declared, his gloved hand above his head. He looked round the room. "I *have* seen Sylas and Naeo, and all that they are, but it's not just that. I was in the Winterfern gardens with Mr Zhi when he put himself between Scarpia and Naeo. I saw how he held

Scarpia back for as long as he had to with just this." He opened his gloved hand and turned it about so that the embroidery gleamed in the false light. "And Mr Zhi said something just before he did that. He said, 'Now is a time of sacrifice.' And, whether we like it or not, that's just what it is."

He smiled a slightly wild smile that showed his single golden tooth, and at that moment those who knew him saw that he had changed. It was not just that he had given up on his coiffured hair and fine clothes, it was the fact that now, standing before this great assembly, it was hard to believe that he had ever cared about them. He was, perhaps, much more the man Mr Zhi had hoped him to be.

"Me too," blurted Dresch, raising her gloved hand. "I know we can't fight the Black, and I can't believe that this is all for nothing."

"And me!" came another voice from the back of the room. It was Lucien, his arm held aloft. He grinned at Dresch.

And now gloved hands appeared all round the room, rising in a wave of green velvet, until finally the entire assembly stood together.

The screen blinked and Master Veeglum disappeared to reveal the grid of images. Each of them showed another sea of green gloves held aloft.

"Good then," came Veeglum's voice over the speakers. "We resist, for as long as we are able."

36

Difference

"...so the difference *between our two worlds is perhaps not as profound as we had thought. That must in turn make us wonder about Glimmers and ourselves."*

NAEO KNEW THAT EVERYTHING had changed even before she climbed the ladder. It was not the violent lurching of the ship or the thump of waves against the hull, though they were certainly new. This was inside her.

Something magical had happened that previous night. She had discovered galaxies, and solar systems, and the endless vacuum of space. Sylas had unlocked the universe for her, and she found herself yearning to be with him again, seeing the night sky with that piercing clarity: knowing it as Sylas knew it. She had tried to bring it to mind as she had rushed to get dressed, but somehow it had slipped from her, eclipsed by that all-too-familiar black fog that clouded her thoughts.

The wet winds whipped her hair as she climbed the last two rungs of the ladder and stepped on deck. She looked about her and her eyes went straight to Sylas. It was a surprise because before she had avoided looking at him: he had been half seen, somewhere at the edge of her vision. Now, when she saw him at the helm, it was as she might see anyone else. She saw his high eyebrows, rather like hers; his stubby nose; his broad features, which made him look more kindly, Naeo thought, than her. But there was also a peculiar familiarity about the way he looked and moved that gave her the strangest sense that his body could as easily be hers.

A shock of cold spray stung her cheeks and, with a thrill, she realised that she was not sure if the sensation was hers or his. It was as though she could no longer pinpoint where she ended and he began, and it was only when she felt a pulse of pain through her back that she trusted the sensations as her own.

Naeo took her place next to Sylas and looked out across the ship. The crew were rushing about, lashing ropes, tying down provisions, battening hatches. Triste was sitting alone on a chest not far away, staring at them both intently, a smile playing on his lips. Above, the sky gathered broodingly like a knitted brow, and all about them the slate-grey waters had become wild and angry, sending up foam-topped waves and sheets of icy spray. The *Windrush* had slowed her pace, buffeted by winds and waves.

Sylas's eyes were fixed ahead. "This... isn't... easy," he murmured through gritted teeth.

Then something astonishing happened.

He looked her right in the eye.

Between any other two people it would have been nothing – a simple gesture – but it struck Naeo like a slap. The shock of it faded quickly, but not the effect. The instant Sylas had looked at her, she had been consumed by the winds, the waves and the ship. But not as before. Now, she felt them as Sylas did. She felt his alarm as a wave slewed across their path, his effort as he heaved the ship clear. She felt his care as he caught up those winds that helped and let slip those that did not. She opened her hands and joined his efforts, reaching into the wilderness of the sea and the chaos of the storm.

Sylas sensed her even before she emerged on deck, but not with that sickening feeling of disarray. This was something new, and it took him some moments to realise what it was.

It was relief.

The waves were colossal now, surging and rolling on all sides of the ship, and the winds came from every direction at once, lashing the rigging and ripping at the sails. He had barely been keeping the *Windrush* on course and felt sure that soon he would lose control altogether. But then, with that wash of relief, Naeo was there. She lent herself to his efforts and, at once, the winds turned to fill the sails, lifting the hull, guiding it through the tempest. The *Windrush* banked to one side, then to the other, swerving to avoid two converging waves, sweeping gracefully through the jealous seas.

And her dance drew cries of delight from the crew.

Triste looked on, his Scryer's eyes welling at the beauty of what he saw.

"Incredible," he said to himself. "Incredible."

He turned and looked about him, searching for Simia. He saw her standing by the hatch from which she had just emerged, gazing in wonder at Sylas and Naeo, and at the course of the *Windrush*, until finally her eyes met his.

He smiled in that kindly way he had only now started to show her, and gestured to Sylas and Naeo.

"Well done, Simsi," he mouthed. "Well done."

37

The One from the Waters

"And so, scripture tells us, almost from birth he became
known as 'The One from the Waters'."

FOR ALL HIS AIRS the Duke had always been quite content with
his cardboard home beneath the Hailing Bridge. It was not too
small, certainly not too large, and it had quite splendid river views.
"Snug but well ventilated," was how he liked to describe it. To
the Duke, his cardboard home had always been his castle. In it,
he felt safe, secure and the master of his own universe.

But now all that had changed.

Now, there were sirens on the wind, searchlights in the skies
and sounds in the night that made him wonder if he was in the
grip of a nightmare. Now, the waters of the river were turning
black and the streets of the town were deserted. No one came
along the towpath and, for the first time since he had taken up
residence beneath the Hailing Bridge, the Duke's makeshift walls
felt like the flimsy cardboard that they truly were.

In the beginning, he had heard snippets from passers-by on the
bridge, mutterings about invasions and battles and impossible

things they had seen on television. Then a well-meaning woman had shouted down that he really ought to find a new place to stay, at least for now. But the Duke, of course, had not been up for moving. This was his cardboard castle.

Now, however, he was cursing himself.

It was approaching midnight and there was a chill on the wind, even now in the middle of summer. It carried a scent that he could not quite place – a little like burnt metal perhaps – drifting in from Salisbury Plain.

Something made him creep forward and lift the cardboard flap that served as his window, and peer up at the underside of the Hailing Bridge.

He could see nothing, of course, just the same criss-cross of graffitied girders he had seen a thousand times before. But he heard something. It was like a whisper above the moan of the wind.

He leaned out a little and turned his good ear to the sound.

Suddenly the white flash of an explosion lit up the sky and cast a shadow of the bridge out on to the waters. And there was something else in that shadow – something passing across the bridge. It was a procession of figures striding swiftly along its length: scores, perhaps hundreds of them. But it was not their number that made the Duke shrink into his castle; it was their shape. They walked as men, but each and every one of them had a long, tapering neck, a bristling mane and the protruding snout of a hound.

§

Paiscion sat alone in the bunker, cleaning his glasses with his handkerchief. He lifted them to the light, gave them a final polish, then carefully placed them back on his nose.

"I think Tasker is a good choice, Franz," he said, looking up at the screen. "Perhaps he was rather caught up with himself when we first met him, but much has happened since then. He went through a great deal even before he reached us. You know he was shot during the passing?"

Franz Veeglum gazed down at him from the screen, the pallor of his skin shifting as the connection came and went. "Mr Zhi always had high hopes for him," he said, "but it is good to hear that you too believe he is up to the task. His knowledge of the stones makes him ze obvious choice, but I do hope he is ready. We must defend many places, but none is more important than Stonehenge. It is more than a great gateway between ze worlds, it is a... what do the English say? A..."

"A symbol?" suggested Paiscion. "An icon?"

Veeglum slapped his hand down on his desk. "Zat's it!" he declared. "You understand, of course. For many in this world it is an icon of ze past, of how things have always been. Zat is important now more than ever. And, for ze Suhl and ze Merisi, it has been a symbol of ze bond between our peoples, between our worlds. You might say a symbol of how everything might be."

The Magruman nodded. "You're right. The Circle of Salsimaine was just such a symbol to us once," he said ruefully. "But not any more, of course. Now, it means something quite different to us."

The two men sat in silence then, as they had more than once since the gathering had dispersed. Everyone had hurried away as soon as the vote had been cast to make preparations and begin their many journeys. Only Tasker had lingered a while, to take his leave of Paiscion.

He had offered Paiscion his gloved hand. "It's been an honour."

"The honour is all mine," the Magruman had replied with a smile. Then he had glanced behind at his smoking jacket, which had been hanging over the back of his chair. He had reached for it and held it out. "Take this."

Tasker had stared at it, open-mouthed. "I can't!"

"Of course you can," Paiscion had insisted. "It will be cold out there on Salisbury Plain and... difficult, I think." Tasker had continued to refuse, but then the Magruman had thought for a moment and said: "I told you once that this old jacket gave me comfort. Well, now it would give me comfort if you would take it."

And so finally Tasker had given in. Paiscion had insisted that he put it on and so Tasker had, and then, with a deep bow and a final farewell, he had followed the others. Paiscion had stared after him for some time, remembering himself in that same jacket in times gone by, full of youth, and energy, and confidence. He hoped that it would prove as good a companion to Tasker as it had been to him.

"So what will you do now?" asked Veeglum, breaking their silence. "Will you stay with us? Perhaps go to Stonehenge yourself?"

Paiscion filled his lungs. "I would like nothing more than to return to my brothers and sisters in the valley, but I fear the battle will have been decided long before I can be there to help." He gave Veeglum a small smile. "No, my time is better used here."

Veeglum leaned forward. "Are you sure, old friend? Even though Filimaya is there? You have already sacrificed much to come and warn us about ze Black. We would understand if you wish to return, if only to be with her when... when all this comes to pass."

Paiscion looked away and was quiet for some moments, as though settling an argument with himself. Then he said: "No, for better or worse my place is here. But if you will forgive me, Franz, I believe I must leave you to your battles and seek one of my own."

Veeglum straightened. "Is that so?"

The Magruman nodded. "All the way here I was thinking about Sylas and Naeo, and this journey they are on, to Old Kemet. It

261

makes sense, of course, for them to return to the beginning of it all, and I have started to wonder if it makes just as much sense for me too."

Veeglum blinked slowly and cocked his head. "How so?"

"Because it is the source of the division of the worlds. And Old Kemet, like all things, is itself divided. It has its counterpart in this world, and that place was itself part of the beginning."

Veeglum leaned forward, intrigued. "You are talking about Egypt, yes?"

Paiscion nodded. "We are assuming that, if the division comes to an end, it will happen where it all began. But which side of the divide is that place, Franz? Is it there in Old Kemet, or here in the place you call Egypt?"

Veeglum stared with widening eyes. "You think Sylas and Naeo may be going to the wrong place?"

Paiscion shook his head. "I doubt it. Isia herself sent them there, so Old Kemet must play its part. But I can't help wondering if it *is* only a part. What if it has its mirror here?"

Veeglum ran his gloved fingers through thinning hair. "You are right, of course," he said. "We must at least have someone there."

"Is anyone there now?"

Veeglum shook his head. "The stone circle in Egypt has long been lost beneath ze sands, so zere has been no need."

Paiscion searched Veeglum's face. "Well, I still think I should go. We can leave nothing to chance."

Veeglum grunted. "I will make ze arrangements."

Paiscion bowed his head in thanks. "And you, Franz? What will you do?"

Veeglum shrugged. "There is much to do here in Bagan. When all is said and done, this is the home of ze Merisi. At such a time the Master should be here."

Paiscion put his hands on his knees and pushed himself up. "Good then, Franz," he said. "So, let us get on."

Veeglum nodded. "Travel well, my friend. I will try to speak to you before you arrive."

Paiscion reached for the back of the chair, then chuckled at himself when he remembered that he had given his precious jacket away.

"Paiscion?" Veeglum called from the screen.

The Magruman turned and peered over his spectacles.

"I have been thinking about these 'five Undoings' that Thoth spoke of. Do you think they could have something to do with..." He shook his head and smiled as though what he was suggesting was ridiculous. "That zey just made me think of—"

"The One from the Waters?"

Veeglum stared at him. "As you say," he said.

Paiscion released a long breath, which left him diminished. "I have been thinking the same thing," he said wearily. "Well, we can only hope not, Franz. If this is about him, I dare not think where it will end."

The two men regarded one another for a long moment, seeming to share a dark, unspeakable understanding. Then, without a word, Paiscion turned and left.

Veeglum remained on the screen for some moments, staring solemnly into the empty room, then finally he reached forward and the image died.

38

The Race

*"There is no greater challenge for us now
than the race to understand."*

SIMIA HAD NOT MOVED a muscle since arriving on deck. She simply stared in wonderment. The *Windrush* was now swerving so sharply from side to side that it was all she and the rest of the crew could do to stop themselves from being thrown overboard. But still she stared.

The storm had now reached its fearsome zenith, and the seas roared their complaint, ripping into the passing ship with white-tipped talons. Above, the heavens howled, sending spiralling winds to provoke the seas still further, and overwhelm all that might seek to pass.

But pass the *Windrush* did. Not only that but she flew as though the storm was her element. Waves towered above her, but she swept between them, using them to aid her passage. So deftly did she keep to the furrows that, from a distance, all that could be seen were her gleaming topsails and her bright feather standard fluttering above the spitting surf.

Most of the crew had turned their back to the seas and were staring wide-eyed along the deck to where Sylas and Naeo stood. That was the true spectacle. The two children gestured and worked as one, while all those around them did their bidding: ropes and pulleys, sails and yards, winds and waves. And behind the ship, as though drawn to the effort, a flock of birds — scores of them — trailed the *Windrush*. There were gulls, terns, auks, cormorants, gannets and albatrosses, all of them turning with the ship, weaving in its winds. And at the centre of all this Sylas and Naeo moved together, swaying as the deck pitched and lurched beneath them. They had a shared expression: focused and determined, but also wildly triumphant. There was something about those faces that held the eye, not only an energy but a similarity that was undeniable, one the mirror of the other.

"May I join you?" came a voice at Simia's ear.

She looked up and saw Amelie, her hair dancing in the breeze. Simia smiled and shifted along the chest to make room. They sat together for a while, watching Sylas and Naeo, and the storm, and the waves.

"Triste said their bond had grown stronger," said Amelie at last, "but I must say I wasn't expecting *this*!"

Even over the howling winds, Simia could hear something in Amelie's voice that made her take care over her reply.

"He told me they understand each other better now because of the Glimmertrome," she said.

"They're so... *together*," said Amelie, narrowing her eyes and shaking her head. "They even *look* so alike. I've never seen it so clearly. They could be..." She caught herself and laughed.

"Twins?" suggested Simia, smiling up at her.

Amelie nodded thoughtfully, then slid an arm through Simia's. She drew her close as though against the icy wind, but Simia sensed that it was for the companionship too, and she liked it. They stayed like that for a while, leaning into each other a little.

Finally Amelie said: "Does it sound terribly selfish to say that I don't *like* seeing them together?"

Simia looked up. "Not really. I feel the same sometimes. Quite often actually." She turned back to Sylas and Naeo. "I suppose it's because they're... such a closed book. I mean, I think I've really got to know Sylas, but when he's with Naeo it's like part of him disappears. You know?"

Amelie nodded. "I know exactly what you mean."

"Is that what you argued about? You and Sylas?"

Amelie glanced at her. "He told you?"

"Sort of."

She sighed. "Well, yes, I suppose that is what we argued about, in a roundabout way. I know that the bond between them is supposed to be a good thing for us all, but when I look at Sylas I see only my boy. To me, there isn't anything missing. Not a thing. To me, he's perfect just as he is."

Simia watched Sylas and Naeo swaying gracefully from side to side, lit by the bright halo of the Merisi Band. "Maybe there isn't anything missing, but... don't you think they seem to be *more* when you see them together?"

Amelie smiled and shrugged. "I can see that they can *do* more together. I can see their power. But I can't accept that they *are* more in themselves." She looked at Simia. "I just can't see that my Sylas can be any more than he already is. You know him, Simsi, perhaps better than I do now. Did you really think when you first met him that there was anything missing?"

"No, of course not."

"And that's just it, isn't it?" said Amelie. "We're all in this breathless race to make the Glimmer Myth come true, to bring Sylas and Naeo together, to bring all of us together, but no one's actually asking what that will *mean*. Is it really what we want for each other? For ourselves? I'm not at all sure that I want Sylas to be some blend of himself and Naeo. And neither am I sure that *I* want to be anything other than I am." She squeezed Simia's hand. "And you, Simsi? Aren't you just perfect the way you are?"

Simia flushed a little and laughed. Amelie had a way of making her feel like the child she was — something she hated and loved at the same time.

She thought for a moment and then said: "When Sylas and I were with Isia, when she showed him how we all have a Glimmer, how we're all connected to them in some distant way, I felt... kind of... *hopeful*. Genuinely hopeful. I suppose —" she gave an embarrassed laugh — "I suppose I felt less *alone*." Her eyes shot to Amelie's. "Does that sound sad?"

Amelie shook her head. "No, Simsi. Not at all."

"I mean, I understand what you're saying," said Simia, seeming to gain confidence. "It's beyond strange to think that we might somehow come together with our Glimmer. But with Isia it seemed possible, even kind of... perfect. She made me feel that maybe I'd never been alone all these years and that maybe, all along, I was a whole lot stronger than I'd realised."

Amelie looked surprised. "You don't see how strong you are?"

"No, not really." She glanced at Amelie self-consciously and then blurted: "I mean, do you see how strong *you* are?"

Amelie laughed. "No, but I'm not sure I want to become someone else just to find that strength, do you?"

"Do you really think that's what will happen? That we'll become someone else?"

"I don't know," sighed Amelie. "But no one knows what'll happen and that's the problem."

Again, they both fell quiet. They sat back against the bulwark and watched Sylas and Naeo lost in their wild ballet with the elements. It was still astounding to behold.

After a while Simia said: "I think perhaps you should talk to

Sylas again. He should know why you're so worried, before it's too late."

Amelie nodded. "I will," she said without taking her eyes from her son. "But, Simsi, you're right. It's hard not to believe it's meant to be when you see them like this."

39

The Orbs

"What was surprising to me was that the Suhl
have no concept of the stars and the planets as we
know them. Even the orbs *of the sun and the moon*
are not seen as spheres, or really as physical things,
but rather a mystical presence."

ESPASIAN STOOD ALONE ON Carrion Rock, watching dawn spill
on to the Westercleft Plain below. Long fingers of amber light split
the dewy air, driving back the darkness. And yet the Magruman
was filled with a deepening gloom.

Before him, the great Imperial army rolled against the hills of
the Valley of Outs, seeming just as vast and unstoppable as it had
the previous day. If anything, the dark stain seemed to have leaked
further across the plain. As he squinted towards the Westercleft
Hills, Espasian spied new dark rivers streaking the slopes, flowing
from the peaks to the flats with all the speed of a double-time
march.

He was taken by a sudden weariness and he swayed where he
stood. The pain of the Black surged up his spine and neck, and
that familiar darkness fogged his mind. He planted his feet more
firmly on the rock and gritted his teeth, trying to force it back.

He was still lost in this effort when he felt a presence at his side, and an arm slipped through his.

"What do you see?"

He turned to see Filimaya beside him.

As ever, she looked serene and beautiful: her long silver hair pulled away from her face in a simple braid, her delicate features lit bronze by the dawn. If she shared Espasian's dread, then she concealed it well. He pressed her arm against his side and looked back at the Imperial army.

"They're reinforcing from the west. Eight thousand, perhaps ten."

She nodded, then turned and swept her eyes along the hilltops, taking in the feverish preparations of the Suhl. Armour and weapons, newly foraged from the valley floor, were passed quickly along the lines; warriors clad in gifts of the forest scrambled to their positions and cleared the defences of the detritus of the previous day's battle; children darted bough to bough, carrying messages and provisions back and forth.

"They've found new hope, you know," she said. "You must have heard it last night, in the hills and the Hollow. Everyone is talking of Bayleon and the Spoorrunners. Fathray's calling it 'the Night of the Orbs'. I even heard a song about it this morning, drifting across the lake. It told of the last great run of the Spoorrunners, and Bayleon who ran until the end, and Espasian who opened the valley wide."

She leaned forward, trying to catch his eye, and when Espasian showed no reaction she stepped in front of him. "Bayleon gave us the night, Espasian. Time to recover, to gather the injured, to repair our defences. Without his sacrifice, the valley would have been overrun. Now, at least, we're ready for another day, perhaps another night. And we'll no longer have to face the Ogresh."

Espasian filled his lungs. "Yes," he said, his voice expressionless. "I know."

"Don't blame yourself, Espasian," she implored. "War asks the unthinkable, not only from the fighters but from those who command. You may not be able to make the sacrifice yourself, but you have to ask it of others. Some would say that is even more difficult. Even more courageous."

Her eyes explored his face, looking for a sign that her words were reaching him. "You have kept our hopes alive for a few more hours. And, for each of those few hours, the *Windrush* sails on, and Sylas and Naeo draw a little nearer to the Motherland."

Espasian smiled sadly. "You are right, of course, Filimaya. I just can't help feeling that Bayleon's sacrifice should have counted for more."

For some moments they both watched the great press of men and beasts surging ever forward, gathering in staggering numbers at the bottom of the slope. And then what had seemed chaos moments before became order and discipline. Imperial regiments gathered in tight formations and standard-bearers were ushered forward until they each stood alone before the swelling ranks. Quite suddenly the beat of the battle drums gained in pace and volume to echo thunderously round the hills.

"They're going to charge," said the Magruman under his breath.

He glanced back at the Suhl lines, then walked to the very edge of the rock. He waited until he could be seen and raised his hand high above his head.

At once the Suhl warriors stepped forth, making their way between the shattered defences of roots and earth, formidable in their armour of great plates of bark lashed with vines.

But there were so few. Espasian looked anxiously along their lines as they spread themselves loosely between the banks and roots. There was barely one to each section of the defences. Then he looked down at the great horde before them.

"Too many," he muttered, his eyes darting between the two front lines. "Far too many."

"What are you going to do?" asked Filimaya at his side, her voice taut.

He shook his head. "I'm not sure yet."

"Paiscion shouldn't have gone," said Filimaya, almost to herself. "He should be here to help you."

The sharp report of a horn drew their eyes back to Thoth's army. At once a dozen more Imperial horns sounded all round the valley. The piercing chorus startled birds from the trees, and they squawked and flapped up into the skies, gathering above the hilltops in vast spiralling clouds.

Answering the horns, the Imperial standard-bearers hoisted their ensigns to signal the charge. Without hesitation, the men and beasts of Thoth's army careered up the slope, devouring the hillside in leaps and bounds, yelling and baying lustily as they ran. They were like hunting hounds loosed from the leash, and they had scented their prey.

The two forces met with a violent crash and clatter. The Suhl lost their entire front line of defence in the first impact, their fighters crushed or thrown back by the sheer weight of bodies. Those who were able fell over the wall of roots behind them, gathered themselves and then did their best to stand their ground, fending off two or three adversaries each, thrusting with pikes and spears. Any who knew Essenfayle drew earth, rocks and roots to their aid, desperately trying to make up for their lack of numbers.

But the Imperial army was refreshed and reinforced: more than a match for the thin lines of weary defenders. The Suhl fell by the dozen, lost in the seething press of bodies, and so their numbers were thinned still further. Already there was a breach near the Cleft, and a regiment of Ghor streamed through, howling as they sprinted for the trees.

Espasian lifted his eyes to the sky where the birds chattered and cawed above the valley, lending their voices to the dreadful din of battle.

"Paiscion," he murmured to himself.

He looked back at his failing army and then turned on his heels and scrambled towards the very highest point of Carrion Rock.

"Where are you going?" Filimaya called after him.

He looked over his shoulder. "To do what Paiscion would do!"

In just five more strides, he was there and turning back towards the valley. He looked out across the chaotic scene, then closed his eyes.

For several moments he simply breathed, calming himself, and only when he was completely still did Espasian raise his arms aloft.

As he opened his fingers, the most astonishing thing happened. The entire host of birds fell silent. The flapping and fluttering ceased, and the vast multitude seemed to hang in the air. Thrush and falcon, blackbird and buzzard soared, forming wide, graceful wheels in the sky.

Filimaya was spellbound. "Yes!" she gasped. "*This* is what he would do!"

As she watched, each of the wheels of birds suddenly collapsed inwards. Tens of thousands of feathered bodies tumbled from the skies, plummeting like stones — wings back, necks outstretched — diving towards the canopy of the forest. They fell in complete silence so that few of those caught up in the battle noticed the spectacle above them. And then, as quickly as it had begun, it was over because the birds disappeared into the clouds of leaves.

Filimaya walked slowly to the edge of the rock, staring at the forest.

Nothing stirred.

She glanced uncertainly at Espasian, but his eyes were still closed, his arms still aloft.

Then something caught her attention and she whipped round. It was a rushing sound, like wind raking through leaves, and it was coming from the forest. The entire forest.

Suddenly a flock of tiny birds erupted from the thickets and, further off, some large birds of prey — kites, Filimaya thought — burst from the gloom between the trees, spread their wings wide and then dived towards the battle, beaks and talons outstretched. A scattering of other great birds followed, all along the line, and then the whole forest seemed to give way. Thousands of birds poured forth — thrushes, magpies, falcons, robins, chaffinches and goshawks — and with them came the creatures of the forest floor: lynxes, boar, deer, foxes, rats, stoats and weasels. All of them, birds and beasts, careered down the hillside, soaring, leaping and scurrying straight into the thick of the fight.

The birds stayed in the air only long enough to loft over the battling Suhl, then they fell, squawking and screeching, into the fray. They scratched and clawed, forcing the attacking troops to drop their heads and cover their eyes, flailing wildly, striking their fellow warriors in their confusion. But the attack came from below too. Small teeth tore at hides; sharp claws ripped at legs; tiny feet scuttled through fur and mane, beneath armour and mail, sending soldiers and beasts wild.

Thoth's army at first held its advance, those in front driven on by those in the rear, but it was not long before the harrying, scratching creatures had halted the charge.

From Carrion Rock Filimaya watched a gang of Hamajaks suddenly break from the melee below and run shrieking and gibbering down the hill, pulling tufts of fur from their manes. Scores of Ghorhund turned too, yapping and howling, and soon entire regiments were breaking formation, some of them beginning a full retreat.

A rhythmic beat struck up somewhere along the front — not

the deep, throaty boom of Imperial battle drums, but the sharp report of sticks and clubs thumping against roots, shields and trees.

To Filimaya, the rhythm was unmistakable. It was a Suhl march.

Her eyes sparkled and a smiled flickered on her lips.

She looked excitedly up to the pinnacle of Carrion Rock and saw Espasian, stony-faced, lowering his arms. He staggered where he stood, then fell to his knees, his eyes still fixed and staring.

"Espasian!" she exclaimed, rushing over to him. She knelt beside him and threw an arm round his shoulders to stop him from falling. His body was drenched in cold sweat, his chest heaving, his breaths coming in wheezes. "Are you all right?" she gasped.

For a moment he seemed not to have heard her, but then he nodded.

She held him close, and together they looked down at the hillside, to where the tide of the battle was turning. The Imperial army was now in full retreat, its crazed warriors stumbling and flailing as they were assailed from all sides by the creatures of the Valley of Outs. The Ghor regiment that had breached the lines was charging back out of the forest and now streaked down the hillside, pursued by a flood of creatures large and small. Already the splintered remains of the Suhl defences were clearly visible, and a gap was opening up between the two forces.

Filimaya looked down at Espasian. "There, Espasian," she said softly. "*That* is why Bayleon gave his life."

40

Storms

*"One challenge we face is that we have no idea from
which side of the divide the* storms *will come."*

ASH LAUGHED AND WHOOPED as he staggered along the length
of the ship, beaming at his crewmates. "This is the way to sail,
eh?" he cried, patting a bulkhead. "This is why they call her the
Windrush, no?"

His high spirits were infectious, and he left those under his
command grinning and staring with renewed admiration at Sylas
and Naeo. The pair's feats had become ever more daring and
astonishing. Sometimes the *Windrush* skipped along the face of a
wave at a tilt that would capsize a lesser vessel; sometimes she
rode a foaming ridge so that the seas seemed to have fallen away
altogether, and those afraid of heights cowered, covering their eyes.
Once she rose sharply, pirouetted on a watery peak and then
plunged on in a new direction; and now she bounced from peak
to peak, making her crew cry out in excitement.

The more the *Windrush* danced, the more Ash came to life,
laughing and joking, dancing his own quickstep along the deck.
He paused briefly to speak to Fawl, who barely seemed to notice

him, so rapt was he by the antics of the ship and the gleaming sails.

"Marvellous!" declared the Master of the Ship, gaping in all directions. "These seas are wild enough, but nothing catches them out! Nothin'!" He laughed with abandon. "It's more like they're catching the seas out! In all my years... Just watch her run! Watch her run!"

Ash laughed with him and then made his way towards the bow. There he spied Triste clutching the railing and surveying the seas ahead.

"Best seat in the house!" yelled Ash, slapping his shoulder.

Triste nodded, but did not turn. He stared ahead with an intensity that Ash noticed at once.

"Everything all right, Triste?"

The Scryer glanced at him, but quickly returned his gaze to the waves ahead.

"I'm not sure," he said, his words almost lost in the howling winds and roaring waves.

The smile slowly faded from Ash's face. "Why? What do you see?"

Triste wiped some spray from his brow. "Another storm."

"Another?" repeated Ash, looking back towards the horizon. "How could there be another so close to this?"

"Not a storm like this," said Triste. "This one only a Scryer can see."

All of the light left Ash's face. "What... kind of storm?"

Triste gave him a grim look. "A storm of malice and hate, and every malignity the heart may harbour."

The ship rose on a mighty wave and, as it crested, both men gazed ahead, trying to make out anything of substance on the seas, but all they could see was the indistinct smudge of a faraway headland.

Ash pointed. "That must be the Jaws of Kemet."

The Scryer nodded. "And the storm I see is somewhere just beyond, at its—"

Suddenly the ship lurched awkwardly to one side and both men had to cling on to the rail. The deck slewed violently as the *Windrush* scudded down the side of a wave, banking so steeply that its yards almost touched the neighbouring wave. One of the many chests on deck broke free of its fixing, slid past them and pitched overboard. The keel no longer skipped lightly over the surface, but carved deep into the green-grey waters, threatening to twist about altogether.

Triste and Ash turned to see the deck strewn with luggage and members of the crew. Amelie was clinging on to Simia's hand as they both slid through a sheet of seawater towards the side of the ship. Even Sylas and Naeo were clambering up from a fall, gazing about in confusion and struggling to find one another's hands. They had just taken their place back at the helm when suddenly they looked sharply to starboard and their eyes widened in horror.

A shadow crept across the deck, cast by a mountainous wave, which now towered above the ship. Fawl cried out and signalled desperately at the crew to take hold of something, then charged headlong towards Sylas and Naeo, screaming at them to get down.

But it was too late. With a fateful slowness, the wave arched, its foamy crest teetering above the mainsail. For the briefest moment it seemed to hang there, as though taunting its prey, and then, with a deafening roar, it crashed down upon the deck, sweeping Simia, Amelie and all before it into the sea.

S

The Land Rover stalled for a moment as the driver wrestled with the gears then, with a mechanical growl, it leapt ahead. It lurched violently, forcing Dresch to brace herself against the wall and ceiling, and elbow Lucien in the face. It was the fifth time since they had left camp.

"Sorry!" she said again.

As before, Lucien didn't reply. He was engrossed in the view through the windscreen lit by the leaping beams of the headlights. All he could see was the convoy of two vehicles ahead, and the country road, and looming hedgerows flashing past. But he could not shake the feeling that at any moment something more sinister might appear: a line of dark figures spanning the road, or leaping through the fields alongside them, or perhaps just the gleam of yellow eyes floating in the darkness.

He pulled a paper bag from his pocket and was about to delve in, but then remembered his companions.

"Almond slice?" he asked, holding the bag out to Tasker, Dresch and the driver in turn. "Nabbed them from the canteen before we left."

They each took one, as grateful for the distraction as for the cake.

As they ate, Lucien looked across at Tasker, who was sitting in the passenger seat. His eyes passed over the once-neat hair, now a tangle, and the peculiar smoking jacket, which seemed so out of place on a journey such as this.

"So," said Lucien, finishing a mouthful, "what's the plan?"

Tasker looked at his watch. "We should reach the circle in about ten minutes," he said without turning round, "then the vehicles will separate. They'll drop us on four sides of the henge, and then the twelve of us will continue on foot and make a ring round the stones. The others know the terrain, but you can follow me — we'll be coming in from the south. The army is still there, but it's under orders to fall back when we arrive."

Dresch was about to take a bite of her cake, but when Tasker fell silent she hesitated. "And... then what?" she asked.

Tasker shrugged. "We get as close as we can, and do the best we can, for as long as we can."

Dresch gazed at him for a moment. "And that's it?"

Tasker nodded and took a mouthful of cake.

She lowered her eyes. "Right," she said.

There was a long, heavy silence, filled only by the rumble of the wheels.

Finally Lucien looked up at Tasker. "So you met them?" he asked. "You met Sylas and Naeo?"

Tasker's face brightened and he nodded.

"And you're sure they're the ones we've been waiting for?"

Tasker's golden tooth shone as he smiled. "Oh, I'm sure," he said.

With a sudden lurch, the vehicle left the road and began bouncing down a muddy track, pebbles clattering in the wheel arches.

"Not far now!" called the driver over her shoulder.

They had been off the tarmac for less than a minute when they saw a bright flash somewhere ahead. Shortly afterwards they heard the unmistakable thump of an explosion. They all leaned forward, peering through the windscreen. There was another flash on the horizon, then another, picking out the nearby trees and bushes in a ghastly white. Even by this light, they could see little of the battlefield because it was shrouded in billows of white and grey smoke.

"What should I do?" asked the driver. "Keep going?"

"Yes, as far as you can," said Tasker. "We all have to reach the circle at the same time."

The driver slowed, engaged a low gear and pulled off the track, heading out over open farmland. More explosions lit the night sky as they bounced and fishtailed across the pasture and, by their fierce light, they saw the outline of the stone circle not far away.

Before it, they glimpsed a confusion of dark figures running to and fro, some upright, others on all fours, leaping, sprinting and prowling.

"What the devil...?" murmured Tasker, moving quickly to a side window. He peered out at the open grassland in the flickering light.

"What is it?" asked Lucien, following his eyes.

Then he gaped in horror. The plains around them were no longer rolling pasture but a moonscape of pummelled earth, craters and mire. There were no natural features, no trees or bushes, nothing to show that, until just days before, these had been the verdant expanses of Salisbury Plain.

"It looks..." began Tasker, his face ashen. "It looks just like... the Barrens." He turned back to his companions, his face lit a ghoulish white. "We're making the Barrens all over again here, on this side of the divide."

Another explosion shook the vehicle and this time they felt its heat. The driver shielded her eyes with one hand and heaved at the steering wheel with the other. The vehicle veered, bucking over heaps of upturned roots and banks of earth until finally it came skidding to a halt.

The engine died, and the driver was left panting behind the wheel.

"This'll have to do," she gasped, a wild fear in her eyes. "I can't get any closer without getting bogged down, or — or falling into one of those craters."

Tasker peered through the windscreen, then out of the passenger window, his eyes exploring the terrain. He patted the driver on the shoulder to catch her attention.

"It's OK," he said. "This'll do." He turned to Dresch and Lucien, and looked each of them in the eye. "Well, are you ready?"

Another explosion shook the metal frame of the car and bleached the world about them, making them shield their eyes. When the darkness returned, they heard clods of earth thumping down on the bodywork. They all glanced at one another. Dresch pulled the Merisi glove from her belt. With a frightened smile, she smoothed it over her fingers.

"Let's go," she said.

41

Out of Time

*"We cling to the promise of the Glimmer Myth, as of
course we should. But what if the Dirgh's preparations
are already too advanced? What if we are out of time
before we have truly begun?"*

WHEN NAEO GAVE UP her fight, she sank quickly, sucked down
by powerful currents. For the briefest moment she was relieved by
that watery silence, away from the howling winds and the crashing
waves and bellows and shouts. She looked up and saw a vaulted
ceiling of ethereal blue light, and it appeared almost magical. What
had been savage seas, throwing her this way and that, were now
billowing silver sheets and clouds of sparkling bubbles, and trails
and swirls of foam. And, from here, the dark silhouette of the hull
looked so near that she felt she might reach out and touch it.

But all too soon her lungs began to burn and a new roar filled
her ears: the roar of her blood coursing, her heart hammering.
Instinctively she struck out again with weary limbs, striving for
the *Windrush*, turning everything she had to one last effort. But,
as hard as she struggled, the *Windrush* just drifted further away,
and now the Black pulsed painfully in her shoulders and back, as
though sensing the end.

Her movements slowed and she began to drift.

This is it, she thought. *After everything, this is how it ends. Alone, and quiet, like in that cell in the Dirgheon.*

But then she saw a new silhouette. The shape of a man diving down towards her, his single arm beating the water with such power that already he was almost upon her. And then that arm was about her, drawing her close, heaving her upwards. She felt the man's legs scissoring behind her, driving them towards the surface, and then they exploded into the sound and light of the world above.

Naeo gasped, drawing cold, wet air deep into her aching lungs, panting and coughing as she felt herself heaved upwards again, her shoulder thumping against something hard. She heard frantic voices above as a loop of rope was passed over her head and beneath her arms, and then, all at once, the grey peaks of the sea were below her, and she was being hoisted upwards. Hands grasped at her, pulling at her clothes, hauling her over a railing that raked painfully down her back. But she did not care because above her she saw the glorious golden sails of the *Windrush*.

She saw a procession of frightened faces, including those of Ash, Simia and Amelie, before she was laid down gently on something soft.

And then she was alone again.

For some moments she just lay there on the wet sacking, teeth chattering, staring up at the billowing sails. She was exhausted and her limbs felt leaden and distant as though they belonged to someone else. When finally she managed to lift her head, she saw the rest of the crew crowding at the railing, staring out to sea, and Fawl diving from one of the rope ladders back into the waves.

Naeo wanted to get up and join them, but instead she dropped her head back on to the sacking, and for the first time she allowed herself to think. She had no idea what had gone wrong. It had all felt so perfect, so exciting: Sylas there at her side, feeling as she felt, responding as though they were one. For the first time there had been nothing to separate them. Since that night under the stars, she had understood how Sylas saw the world around him, knew how he felt, saw as he saw. What was Sylas's was truly now hers.

But, in those moments before they had ploughed into the wave, something had happened. It had all unfolded so quickly, and in such confusion, that she struggled to remember.

And then a memory made Naeo stiffen and wince. She reached over her shoulder and felt the raised skin round the scar of Black.

The pain.

It had shot through her just before they had lost control: a sharp, stabbing pain up her spine. Yes, she was sure of it now. That was what had started it: the pain had surged through her, but also through him. Now that they were so close, she knew beyond doubt that Sylas had felt it too.

The shock of the pain had come and gone, but its effect had gripped them. What had been seamless had become a chaos of missed moments, and the more they had done to correct the ship, the more everything had unravelled. It was as though they had suddenly lost their rhythm, each acting independently of the other. She shuddered. And then the wave had come.

A voice brought her back to the moment.

"Naeo!" gasped Simia, her pale face appearing above her. She looked desperate, her red hair plastered across her cheeks, her eyes bloodshot. "Naeo! Can you stand? I know you must be exhausted, but we really need your help! It's – it's just that—" Her voice cracked and her eyes welled up with tears.

Naeo heaved herself upright, wincing from the pain in her back, and saw at once that the entire gathering had turned from the railing and was now looking at her anxiously.

"I'm OK," she said. She tried to push herself up, but failed.

Triste strode over and took her hands to help her to her feet, then he and Simia supported her to the railing. As she approached, the leaping grey waves suddenly loomed before her and her head swam, making her slump in their arms. It was as though her body thought itself back in the maelstrom, being turned over and over by one wave after another.

"Do you need to sit?" asked Ash, stepping through the crowd. He was pale and haggard, his blond locks hanging limply about his face so that he hardly looked himself.

Naeo closed her eyes and breathed, then shook her head. "I'm fine. What's wrong?"

"You don't know?" he said, astonished. "I — I thought you would have felt something."

"Felt... what?" asked Naeo, her stomach tightening. She glanced round at the other faces and almost at once saw Amelie. If the others seemed frightened and anxious, Amelie looked undone. Her eyes were bleary, her white cheeks wet with tears and she was visibly shaking.

She held Naeo's gaze. "It's Sylas," she gasped. "He's still missing!"

Naeo felt sick. The world about her paled and the noise of the storm faded. She felt as though a great weight was pressing down on her chest, making it difficult to breathe.

She turned away from Amelie's desperate face and looked out at the wild seas. The storm showed no sign of abating, the mighty waves still rising well above the deck, their white peaks sending out trails of foam in the wind. The slate-grey waters were peppered with debris from the ship: crates, chests and bundles rolling and bobbing as they were pounded by the surf. Most looked close to sinking.

"He's been out there for so long," Simia said quietly. "I don't know how he could still be…" She trailed off, her lips quivering with emotion.

Naeo knew that Simia was right. Much as she wanted to reassure her — reassure herself — she knew that even the strongest swimmer would have given up long ago in those freezing cold seas.

Just then she saw Fawl break the surface some way from the ship. He turned about, looking in all directions, and then glanced back towards the *Windrush*. With a grim expression, he shook his head.

Amelie gasped and her hands flew to her mouth. She whimpered through her fingers, swaying on her feet. Triste moved quickly to her side and placed an arm round her shoulders to prevent her from collapsing.

With nothing else to do, the crew watched Fawl swimming wearily back to the ship, his body rolling as his single arm powered him along. Simia began shaking her head.

"No!" she moaned through her tears. She turned to Naeo. "Can't you do something? Can't you… I don't know… feel where he is? Take us to him?"

Naeo did her best to quell her own panic. She had no idea how to do as Simia asked. Struck by a thought, she turned to Triste. "Can't you Scry where he is?"

He shook his head sombrely. "Not in water. I've tried. I can't see anything. I'm afraid Simia's right. You're our last chance."

Naeo bit her lip. "OK," she said doubtfully. "I'll do my best."

She took a deep breath and closed her eyes, reaching instinctively for the Merisi Band round her wrist, letting her fingertips trace the smooth surface of the Quintessence. She remembered how it had felt just before everything had gone wrong, holding Sylas's hand, feeling him next to her, knowing his instincts. Then she took herself back to the previous night — how long ago that seemed now — and remembered how it had felt to leave herself behind and see through his eyes. Then she gazed out over the tempest and waited to feel something.

Everyone stared expectantly at her.

They saw her frown with concentration and tighten her grip on the Merisi Band. They saw her close her eyes and mouth something to herself. Moments passed, then a minute, then two, and finally they saw her face crumple and tears cascade down her cheeks.

She gasped, as though she had been holding her breath, then she exclaimed: "I don't see anything!" She turned back to the gathering, avoiding Amelie's eyes. "I just see the waves and the storm!"

The crew of the *Windrush* gazed at her in horrified silence.

"No!" yelled Simia suddenly. "You have to try again!" She took Naeo by the arms and forcibly turned her back towards the seas. "He must be out there! You have to keep trying!"

Naeo opened her mouth to argue, but then saw the anguish and longing written on Simia's face. She hesitated, then gave a brief nod.

She closed her eyes again and took some deep breaths, trying desperately to control her emotions. Once again she thought of Sylas: how it had felt when he was near — how it had been that very morning when she had been below in her cabin, but still somehow with him up on deck. And then she remembered the wave crashing down, and how they had held hands even as they were swept over the railing and let go only as they had somersaulted down into the depths.

Naeo waited. She convinced herself that if she could only sense more keenly, feel more acutely than ever before, she would find him. And this time she would find him alive.

But then she *did* feel something and it was just like before. Again, she wanted to pull away and free herself, but she forced herself to stay. She felt the seas close in above her, and darkness, and silence. She felt as though her limbs were bound and her path to the light was lost. And, worst of all, she could not breathe.

It was like dying.

She gasped in a lungful of air and opened her eyes wide. This time she found the courage to say what she had not before.

"He's gone!" she sobbed. "He's already gone!"

42

Alone

"I know the Glimmer Myth to be true, but O, how I yearn to feel it — to feel that I am not alone*."*

FOR A LONG WHILE everybody simply stared over the side, silent and still. Their eyes no longer scoured the waves as they had before but gazed blankly and hopelessly at the seas that had claimed Sylas Tate. All were lost in their darkest thoughts or could find nothing to say, and so the only sound was the storm, and the mournful whistle of the ropes, and Amelie's quiet sobbing, her head buried in Triste's chest.

When at last someone spoke, it was Fawl. He stood shivering, his dripping shirt open, his hand white-knuckled as it gripped the railing.

"I should've found him," he said, lowering his bloodshot eyes. "It's my fault."

"Come now," said Ash, moving to his side. He placed a hand on the sailor's brawny shoulder. "This is nobody's fault, Fawl, or, if it is, it's as much mine as anyone else's. I shouldn't have pushed them so hard."

Fawl turned and met his eyes. "No, cap'n," he said, his voice hollow, "though it's right good of you to say. I'm a Spoorrunner.

Tracking is in my blood. More than that, I'm Master of the Ship. It would shame me to lose anyone at sea, but to lose Master Tate —" his face rutted in a frown, at once bewildered and anguished — "to lose our one last hope... I just don't know how I—"

He stopped as a hand rested on his. It was soft and warm and delicate — such a contrast to his own — and he stared at it in surprise.

"You did everything you could," said Amelie at his ear, her voice thick with emotion. "Truly."

A single tear rolled down Fawl's cheek and, not wanting to move his hand to wipe it away, he let the tear fall.

"I'm sorry, ma'am," he said, voice cracking. "I'm so sorry."

Beside him, Simia had quietly stepped forward, wrestling with her close-fitting jacket. Before anyone realised what was happening, she had pulled it from her shoulders, tossed it to one side and climbed the railing. Just as she was about to hurl herself into the waves, Triste — who seemed to have understood her intentions before anyone else — lunged forward and grabbed her by the back of the shirt.

"Let me go!" she yelled, trying desperately to free herself.

"Simsi, what are you doing?" asked Ash, taking her by the arm.

"I'm going to keep trying!" she bellowed. "Even if no one else will!"

"You can't, Simsi!" said Ash firmly as he heaved her off the rail. "You have no chance of finding him out there! We'll just lose you too."

Simia turned in his arms and, suddenly full of fury, she pounded his chest with her fists. "Let go of me!" she screamed. "I am not leaving him!" She glared up into Ash's face, teeth bared, eyes streaming. "I AM NOT LEAVING HIM!"

Ash looked down at her calmly, absorbing her blows without

attempting to defend himself. "I'm your friend too, Simsi," he said gently. "I can't let you do this."

Simia struck him several more times, but each blow was less forceful than the last. Slowly the fire seemed to leave her and eventually she sank into his arms. "Not Sylas," she sobbed. "Not Sylas too."

Everyone looked on in mute, horrified hopelessness. No one had any comfort to offer or any idea what was to be done next.

Naeo stood to one side, suddenly and completely alone: not just without Sylas, and her father, but alone in her guilt. It was she and Sylas who had brought it all to this, and now even Sylas was gone. With him went the hopes of Simia, and Amelie, and everyone onboard, and all the people in the Valley of Outs. And her father. And Isia. Everyone.

It had all come to nothing. And it was her fault.

She was consumed by a darkness deeper than anything she had felt in her long years in the Dirgheon. She could not breathe, or see, or think. It was like when she had reached out, looking for Sylas, and found only silence and nothingness.

Perhaps that was why she reached out to him again now: because, beneath the waves, at least she would not be alone. She would be with him.

She grasped the Merisi Band and allowed herself to think of Sylas one last time. In her mind, she was once more plunged into the cold, dark seas – lost in a murky, airless void. But this time she did not recoil because the horrors behind her – seeing the despair of her companions, knowing her own guilt – were so much greater. This time she swam in the darkness, savouring the cold, hoping that there was something of Sylas left to feel.

Her lungs began to ache, whether because she could not breathe, or because she was holding her breath she could not tell, but still she did not pull back. She swam in the darkness and waited.

Then she felt something.

It was a pull. A tug towards something near. A feeling of the familiar. And there it was again: that sense of being held back from the light, of limbs being bound.

But it was *something*. It was *there*, and that meant Sylas was still there!

This time Naeo would not let go. This time she tangled herself in the same bonds and stayed with him, even as her lungs felt as though they would burst and every part of her wanted to escape. If this was the end, she thought, it would be the end of them both.

And then something miraculous happened. Through what she could only imagine were Sylas's eyes, she saw a pool of watery light open above her, bathing her in a blue-grey glow. And by that light she saw that her bonds were not dragging her down to some deathly underworld. They were the tight loops of a braided rope floating beneath the surface. But, even as she began to see them for what they were, they rolled before her, and she was plunged once again into darkness.

Suddenly she was caught up in a struggle — not to breathe or to find Sylas but to get back — back to the *Windrush*. She heaved her mind through the darkness and silence, straining as though her life depended on it, reaching for the Naeo who was still standing at the railing, for the person she had left behind.

Then, with a life-giving gasp, she was there.

"I've found him!" she yelled, staggering and grabbing hold of the railing. "He's alive! Sylas is alive! There!"

She threw out a hand and pointed at a shape rolling on the side of a distant wave. It was a giant bale of rope, a mass of loops and coils that had been swept from the ship.

"He's underneath!" she panted. "It keeps rolling on top of him!" Naeo turned and found her companions staring at her, wide-eyed. "I don't think he can hold on much longer!"

There was a moment's hesitation and then suddenly Fawl leapt on to a rope ladder and started bellowing instructions. The gathering dispersed in a trice: Ash to the helm, the crew to the cleats or up into the rigging, Triste to the bowsprit. Ash spun the wheel and, in no time at all, the ship was coming about, yawing dangerously on the waves.

"We're coming, Sylas!" yelled Amelie into the winds, no longer weeping but resolute. "Hold on!"

With the wind behind her, the *Windrush* suddenly surged, crashing through the waves, ploughing a course towards that distant bundle of rope. She moved as swiftly as any ship might, but still progress seemed far, far too slow.

Alone once again, Naeo leaned over the railing, willing the *Windrush* on, hardly daring to hope.

"Come on!" she breathed. "Come on!"

She became aware of a presence at her side. It was Simia leaning out even further. "Faster!" she shouted, pointing frantically. "There! Just there!"

They were drawing close now, and they could see the dense knot of rope as it topped another wave and slid down on the near side. As it rolled, they could see the dense dark tangle quite clearly, but there was no sign of Sylas. Unconsciously the two girls drew nearer to one another.

"Are you sure?" asked Simia, glancing anxiously at Naeo.

"Yes," said Naeo without hesitation. This was the place. She could feel it.

And then, as another wave tipped the bale of rope, they saw him. Two pale arms, wrapped round a clutch of rope, and above, peeking through a coil, a white face, mouth wide, sucking in another lungful of air.

"There!" yelled Simia, jumping up and down on the spot, jabbing her finger over the side. "He's there! Quickly!"

Even as the words left her lips, something sailed over the railing and, moments later, there was a splash. Naeo and Simia leaned over the side in time to see Fawl burst from the depths and set out at a pace towards Sylas, his powerful arm beating the water so hard that he left a trail of froth in his wake.

43

Again

"The first time I made the passing I was overwhelmed: dazzled by the beauty of it, terrified by the prospect of what was to come. The joy of going again *is that I can savour every moment, burn every second of it into memory."*

SYLAS HAD NEVER BEEN so grateful to hear voices. He was lying limply in the same heap of sacking that had held Naeo just minutes before, shivering so violently that he could not keep any part of him still. Even then, those voices seemed to him wondrous and beautiful because they told him that he was alive. And although, in truth, the deck rolled beneath him as violently as ever it felt to him as steady and safe as any shore.

A succession of anxious faces appeared before him — among them his mother, Ash and Simia — and he heard their soothing words and felt their embraces, but he could give nothing back. He was utterly drained. In those last moments before Fawl had come to him, he had considered giving up his long struggle to survive. To begin with, he had tried to swim back to the ship and call out to his companions, but as the currents had carried him away, and he had taken hold of that bale of rope, he had begun a frantic battle to keep himself from drowning. One moment the rope had been his salvation, keeping him afloat despite the mountainous waves, but in the next it had rolled on top of him, keeping him from the air and the light.

But that was over now, and at last, he was safe. Someone lifted his head and held a mug of hot, sweet Plume to his lips and he gulped it down, feeling its heat flood his chest, warming him to the core. Slowly he felt a little of his strength beginning to return and he raised his head to look about.

His mother and Simia were still at his side, talking in low voices, and several of the crew were nearby, glancing in his direction. Most, however, including Ash, Triste, Fawl and Naeo, were looking in the other direction.

With some effort, and rather in spite of the ministrations of his mother and Simia, Sylas sat up and listened to the conversation.

"Yes, I'm sure of it," said Triste, looking at Ash. "They're waiting for us."

Someone asked a question, which Sylas did not quite catch, but he heard Triste's reply: "A blockade of some kind would be my guess."

"Where exactly?" asked Fawl.

"Hard to be sure, but just beyond the headland, I think, in the Jaws of Kemet."

The Master of the Ship nodded soberly. "Many of them?"

Triste gave a quick nod. There was something about the brevity of that nod that filled Sylas with new dread. For some moments the group fell silent.

"So... what next?" asked one of the crew.

"Well, we're not going round that headland," said Fawl. "Not yet at least."

"Why not?" asked Ash.

Fawl tried to mask his astonishment. "Well, sir, we're hardly in a fit state! We need to recover what we can from the sea and do some repairs. And then..." He turned to Naeo. "Miss, I hope you'll forgive me for saying, but we can't risk running a blockade if what just happened could happen again."

Ash leaned back against the ship's wheel. "We have to go, Fawl, and now. The longer we wait, the more time the enemy has to prepare. If we know they're there, they'll know we're here. And let's not forget what's at stake back in the valley and in the Other. We have to keep on, ready or not."

Fawl was aghast. "But, sir! It could be the end of us!"

"I understand," said Ash. "Really I do. But we have to remember why we're here. The end is probably coming whether we go or not."

Triste cleared his throat. "I'm afraid I agree," he said. "I'm no lover of battle, but it's better to go and give ourselves a fighting chance than to hesitate and find that we've left it too late."

Ash nodded and turned to Naeo. "What do you think, Naeo? Happy to give it a try?"

"I think we have to," said Naeo without hesitation. "We can't wait."

For an instant Naeo's certainty surprised Sylas, but then he realised that he too had no doubt. As the group murmured among themselves, Sylas pushed himself up, ignoring protestations from Simia, then he walked unsteadily towards the group.

"We have to go," he said.

"But we don't even know what went wrong!" argued Simia, catching him up. "It'd be crazy to go before we've worked that out!"

"I agree," said Amelie. "If this can happen in the open sea, how are Sylas and Naeo supposed to take us through a blockade? And with Sylas so weak! They should at least have a rest!"

Ash considered this, his eyes shifting between the two children. Then he said: "So what can you tell us, you two? What went wrong?"

Sylas found himself looking directly at Naeo, and she returned his gaze. Without saying a word, they both knew that he had to speak. When had gone wrong, it had been because of him. He turned to the group and tried his hardest to describe everything he had felt when the storm had overtaken them.

"It was Naeo's pain," he said. "It was like before, and we'd done everything exactly when it needed to be done, but then Naeo felt that pain in her back. But the difference this time was that *I* felt it too. I just wasn't expecting it and, in that split second, I suppose I hesitated. And that was all it took because after that we started to lose... I don't know... rhythm."

"It was like dancing out of time," said Naeo. "As if we couldn't keep in step."

And that was exactly what he had meant. "Yes, dancing out of time," repeated Sylas.

For some moments the gathering was quiet, weighing this new problem.

"Surely we could wait until this afternoon – this evening even?" persisted Amelie. "They need time to work this out, as Simia says. And, as the ship's doctor, I should say that many of the crew need rest. Some are half frozen and—"

"I'm sorry, Amelie," said Triste flatly, "but we can't wait. We mustn't. They have Scryers too, so they know we're here. The longer we dally, the more prepared they will be."

Everyone fell silent, listening to the wind whistling hauntingly through the rigging, the waves still bullying the ship.

"But what if it *does* happen again?" said Fawl, addressing Sylas and Naeo. "What if – through no fault of your own, mind – you get all out of kilter again? Well, then we'd be caught right in the thick of things! And we won't be able to stop and pick up the pieces. We'll be right slap-bang in the middle of an Imperial fleet!"

Some of the crew murmured their agreement.

"If it happens, it happens," said Ash, in a commanding tone. He stepped round the helm and took hold of the wheel. "All we can do now is press on. Those who need dry clothes go below while I get the ship underway. Sylas, Naeo, you go too — get changed and have a quick rest, then come back as quickly as you can. Fawl, you stay here with me, if you please."

The crew hesitated for a moment. but then dispersed quickly, keen to make the most of their last moments of calm. Sylas too went straight to the nearest hatchway and disappeared below, followed closely by Simia and Amelie. Naeo lingered for a moment, peering towards the headland as though weighing what was to come, then she walked with Triste to the bow hatch and headed down to her cabin.

"Fawl, tell me," said Ash when they were finally alone. "Just how do we prepare the *Windrush* for a battle at sea?"

Fawl glanced at him, seeming surprised at the question. "Well, sir, that depends a bit on the type of battle, and how heavy we expect it to be, if you take my meaning."

"The heaviest kind," said Ash.

Fawl nodded and cleared his throat. "Of course." He put his arm on his hip and surveyed the ship. "We need to stow all we can below deck, lash all we can't down, and bring up the stocks of pikes and grappling hooks. We should get some hands up in the rigging ready for some quick work on the sails and to cut away busted canvas and timber. And we need to get all free hands along the railings ready to fight, like when we left the valley. We'll have to lash them to a safety line, mind, to keep them from falling over. Then we—"

"What say I leave you to do all that?" interjected Ash, looking a little flustered. "I'm no seafarer and this is no time for novices. You have my authority now in all things to do with the battle."

"Right you are, sir," said Fawl, but he didn't move. Instead he looked at the headland, stroking his bristled chin.

"It'll be bad, won't it?" said Ash.

Fawl reached out for the ship's wheel and grasped it tightly. "It'll be the worst this old dame has ever seen," he said. "She's up to it, mind. I know she is. But if Master Sylas and Miss Naeo don't do their part..." He trailed off and then glanced at Ash. "Sorry, I might be speaking out of turn."

"Not at all," said Ash. "I asked." He rubbed his hands together and said briskly: "Well, all we can do is make sure we're as prepared as possible. Come on, we'd better get on with it."

44

A Gift from the Gods

"We must waste no more time waiting for a gift from the gods. We must learn from all that has befallen the Suhl and prepare ourselves now."

THE *Mesektet* HAD LEFT land far behind. All about her the waters rose in windswept peaks and heavy swell, but still she gathered speed. She cleaved her way through the Sea of Kemet, her immense keel rolling, her mighty prow plunging and rearing.

But, at her centre, the pool of Black was alive with a tempest of its own. It was filled with the shapes of men and beasts, and it danced with their endless comings and goings. Each of the apparitions turned its face to the dark figure in the gleaming throne, spoke their piece and then fell away as quickly as they had come.

For a long while Thoth sat hunched, regarding his messengers impassively without word or gesture. And then, finally, he raised a bony hand.

The three figures before him dropped into the Black, and instantly the surface became mirror-smooth. It did not stir even when the ship yawed, or when a great gust swept across the deck.

Thoth stared broodingly at the pool. Beside him, Anubikan made a great effort to stay at attention and hold its tongue. It knew that its master preferred silence at moments like these: moments of crisis. But at last it could contain itself no longer and growled an order at the other attendants. They at once bowed and retreated.

It spoke as soon as they were below. "My Lord, these are good tidings," it said in its canine huff. "In their defiance, the Merisi have revealed themselves!"

Thoth said nothing but tilted his hooded head slightly.

Anubikan took this as encouragement. "We know they cannot resist for long. Their powers are but a ghost of yours, great Dirgh!"

It glanced down at its master, looking for some acknowledgement. But, when Thoth did not move, it sensed its error and snapped back to attention.

At last the Dirgh spoke, his many voices swirling with the winds. "As ever, Anubikan, the truth is painfully beyond your grasp."

He rose from his throne, his robes flying up about him. Anubikan shrank away, but its master turned and began pacing round the pool of Black.

"The Merisi are no fools. They know that the glove alone is no match for all that is ranged against them. They know that their best hope is to avoid confrontation."

He reached the far end of the dark pool and knelt, extending his grey-white fingers into the ooze. As they slipped beneath, the surface did not ripple, and it remained perfectly smooth even when he brought his hand back up, cupping a dripping handful of Black.

"For many years I did not appreciate the Black," Thoth said, allowing the oily slick to trail silently between his fingers. "I considered it the necessary cost of breaking Nature's overexacting laws." He lifted his hand so that the Black snaked along his wrist.

"But I was wrong. It is a reward, not a punishment. It is a gift from the gods."

He rose to his feet and turned over his hand so the trail of Black circled his wrist. "Just as it flows from the Three Ways, so it will flow from the Fifth. Now, it has a new world to sustain it. The more they use their weapons of science, the more it will become."

Anubikan's fangs protruded in a grisly smile. "And what will it become, great Dirgh?"

Thoth shook the remaining Black into the pool, then wiped his hand on his lavish robes. "It will become all that they fear the most," he said. "I told them they would suffer as the ancients did and so they shall. But, to succeed, the Black must be allowed to thrive. That is why the Merisi meddle. They seek to silence the weapons of their world, to cut off the Black even as it would thrive."

"But surely the Merisi will last no more than a day, perhaps two?"

"They believe a day or two is all they need," said Thoth, turning to look out to sea, in the direction of the Jaws of Kemet. "They believe in Merisu's myth, in Isia's bloodline, in those cursed children." He fell quiet for a moment, then turned back to the pool. "But they are desperate and they are mistaken. Let them lay themselves before us. Let the children and their friends of the feather sail into the Jaws, just as we expect. Let them all perish, if that is their wish."

Anubikan's eyes glistened, drool dripping from its black lips. "As you say, great Lord!"

"And let us see how the Merisi fare when they face not only the beasts and the Black but another Undoing. A third Undoing."

And, with that, he let out a long, whistling sigh, as though weary. Then he extended his arms over the pool of Black and began.

45

Into the Light

"I wonder how the people of our world will respond
when finally they are brought into the light. Will they
welcome the truth, I ask myself? Or would some
prefer to remain in the dark?"

SALISBURY PLAIN HAD NEVER known a darkness like this. It was an utter pitch-darkness; a darkness that hung heavy in the air and blanketed the flats, that oozed from beneath the ground and swamped ditches and craters, flourishing in the night.

And yet one edge of the plain blazed. All the moonlight had collected in this one spot, forming a bright cascade of silvery rays that filled Stonehenge to the brim, opening the way between the worlds.

Tasker and his companions stood before it, squinting into its light, intent upon the shadows that prowled on the fringes: shapes of hounds and half-castes, apes and demons. Still these abominations spilled across the divide, crowding the circle and straying out on to open ground.

But there the twelve Merisi stood sentinel. Whenever the creatures came too close, the nearest of the twelve would raise their glove and send them yapping and chattering back into the light. Not a single beast had breached the Merisi cordon in more than an hour and, as time had passed, Tasker had grown in confidence. He had begun wielding the glove with ever more assurance, remembering all that Mr Zhi had taught him:

In heart: peace and the pursuit of the whole.

In thought: the tranquil lake beneath the storm.

In body: the stag, the cat and the bear.

And now, as he swept to the side, parrying a trio of Ghorhund, and then pirouetted to deflect a bounding, gibbering Hamajak, part of him wished that Mr Zhi was there to witness this moment.

To see him come of age.

He saw Lucien peering into the liquid light, his gloved hand raised to a pair of snorting Ragers that pounded the mud just a few paces before him. He looked the other way and saw Dresch, her bright scarf trailing behind her in the wind, her hand outstretched towards three hissing, catlike beasts. Beyond her, he could just make out three more Merisi, arms extended, with only the glove between them and the horde.

All of them were standing firm.

And just then, in that brave circle, Tasker felt that perhaps, at last, he was truly worthy of his place among the Merisi. At last Mr Zhi's quiet censure for his petty vanities and selfishness finally made sense to him because only now, after all these years, did he feel truly part of something far, far greater than himself.

Buffeted by a sudden chill wind, he reached up to button his jacket. He felt the velvet of the lapels and the cool brass buttons of Paiscion's smoking jacket and smiled to himself. Now he understood Paiscion's gift. As he buttoned it tight, he felt as though the Magruman too was here; that he was part of this unyielding circle, and that they were not alone. They were not just twelve but many.

They were the Merisi.

"Tasker!" shouted Dresch suddenly. "Look!"

She was pointing to a gathering of beasts. They had formed close ranks, no longer agitated and ill-disciplined but with collective purpose, as though preparing for a new assault. Now, all round the stone circle they were falling into neat lines and columns, readying themselves to march.

Tasker understood at once. The creatures had finally realised that if they came on together their sheer weight of numbers would be overwhelming. It would be a rout.

He tried frantically to imagine what Mr Zhi might do if he was there now, at their side.

Suddenly he stiffened. "Dresch! Lucien!" he yelled. "Do as I do! Tell the others!"

He heard the message called round the circle but, as the faces of the Merisi turned towards him, the low drone of a horn sounded from within the stones. In swift response, the beasts started to advance: Ghor and Ghorhund loping in formation, snouts low; Hamajaks, crazed and frenzied, their leaping figures silhouetted against the light; the Tythish, ranging and spiderlike, towering over the other beasts.

Tasker's heart clamoured, but he stood firm, aware that the other Merisi were watching and following his lead. And then he thought once again of Mr Zhi, who had believed in him, despite his foolishness; the small, gentle Mr Zhi, who had fought like a lion. "*Now is a time for sacrifice,*" he had said.

Tasker's eyes flared. He raised his gloved hand before him and stepped out in the direction of the approaching horde. Even as the beasts drew near, he hastened, striding boldly across the rutted grassland, breaking into a trot. Soon he was running headlong towards the massed ranks of beasts, and he was not for slowing. He glanced across and saw Lucien running fearlessly into the fray. He saw Dresch stumbling forward, her hair wild in the wind, and beyond were more of the Merisi, charging on, drawing the cordon tight.

When Tasker looked ahead, his heart leapt. The approaching droves had slowed. The beasts were glancing one to the other, uncertain what to do and, as he watched, those directly before him came to a complete halt.

Within seconds, the entire front line of Thoth's creatures was hesitating. The rest pressed in behind, leaving those in the lead no means of retreat. In the panic and confusion, some charged, forcing Tasker and his companions to slow down to leap and parry, but the attacks were again wild and uncoordinated, and were quickly rebuffed.

Tasker sensed their chance. "Keep going!" he bellowed. "Drive them back!"

He did not need to look. He knew that his Merisi sisters and brothers were following his lead, running ever faster, drawing the ring ever tighter round the standing stones. And now, at last, the creatures were stumbling backwards, falling over one another in their bid to escape.

"That's it!" yelled Tasker, his golden tooth gleaming in a grin. "Keep going!"

Theirs was the momentum now, and he sensed that they might force the enemy back between the stones, perhaps even close the way between the worlds.

And then his smile faded.

His step slowed.

For a moment even his gloved hand faltered.

He gazed with growing horror into the glare.

In the very centre of the standing stones, the column of light was turning black. The darkness surged upwards like a black fountain, smothering the moonlight, consuming all in its path. It climbed and climbed until it seemed to reach the heavens, and there it flared wide, hanging for a moment in the night sky, snuffing out the stars.

And then it fell.

It plummeted towards the earth at astonishing speed, gathering pace as it went. As it drew ever closer, Tasker saw that it was made up of a million tiny fragments, distinct against what little moonlight still penetrated. And then, with a pulse of revulsion, he realised that they were not falling but flying. Thousands upon thousands of buzzing insects swirled and swarmed, forming dark tentacles that scythed down towards the Merisi: flies and locusts, beetles and bees, mosquitoes and cockroaches. They came as a storm heralded by humming and chattering, hissing and droning.

In desperation, Tasker looked from the beasts to the insects and back to the beasts, realising that if he raised his gloved hand to the skies, the Ghor and Ghorhund would be upon him in a moment and, if he did not, the insects would engulf them all.

He glanced around and saw Lucien staring up into the darkness, arms at his side; he saw Dresch, her face taut and white, her eyes darting between the attacking hordes and the blackened skies.

"No," he murmured.

And then with an overwhelming clarity — a complete certainty as to what must be done — he closed his eyes. "Now is a time of sacrifice," he said to himself.

And, with that, he gathered Paiscion's jacket about him, pulled his glove tightly on to his hand and took one more look at his fellow Merisi.

"Hold back the insects!" he yelled. "Hold for as long as you can, then get back!" He looked steadily at Lucien and Dresch. "Get away, understand?"

And then, before they could reply, he fixed his eyes on the bloom of moonlight between the stones, raised his glove and charged headlong into the marauding beasts. They parted before him, scrambling backwards in surprise, and for a moment — just the briefest moment — it looked as though he might penetrate to the bright core of Stonehenge. But then the creatures seemed to check themselves, realising that theirs was the advantage, that this was but one against many. Suddenly the way closed ahead and, even as Tasker tried his utmost to clear a path, scores of beasts converged behind him. These he could not see nor show the glove, and they closed in upon him, frenzied and wild.

"Get away!" he cried into a storm of noise. "Get yourselves... away!"

And then he was silent.

46
Why?

"Why do we doubt ourselves? Why do we look to
superstitions and scriptures and priests to tell us
what exists in our own mind and body and soul?
That, surely, is the question at the centre of everything."

PAISCION PEERED THROUGH THE plane window, spellbound by
the staggering, implausible beauty of it all. For him this surpassed
the marvels of the Four Ways because it did something that they
could not. It went beyond imagining. Looking down upon the
silver clouds and the penstrokes of rivers sparkling in the moonlight,
he saw a world grander and more astonishing than anything in his
dreams. If there were gods, he thought, this must surely be how
they dreamed.

He smiled inwardly at his foolishness. He had long since given
up on the idea of gods — and how could he think of them now of
all times? It was a whimsical habit, he mused, this talk of gods.
Even more so now, as all that was good in the world was tumbling
down; now, as he winged his way through the heavens in a vessel
conceived and built by humankind.

He felt a cramp in his forearm, and realised that he had been
rigid since the plane took off. He unclenched his hand from the

armrest and rolled his shoulders, feeling the coarse collar of his army-issue coat. How he missed the fit and comfort of his smoking jacket, but how glad he was that it had such a deserving new owner.

He wondered how Tasker was faring at Stonehenge. Another godless task, he thought, and a great burden for one so young. But there was undoubtedly something about him: a boldness and a spirit that no doubt Mr Zhi had seen too. And, if Tasker had to face this fight, Paiscion smiled to himself, at least he was dressed for the job.

A tinny voice sounded from the panel above his head: "Just passing over Winterfern, sir, if you'd like to take a look. Right side of the aircraft."

Paiscion shifted in his seat and peered down. It took him a moment to pinpoint it in the moonlit landscape but, when he did, he knew it at once. He saw the beautiful semicircular atrium built into the side of the hill. It was not as he remembered it, exquisitely crafted with perfect lines and apparently seamless glass. This structure was twisted and broken, but it was still marvellous to behold, particularly like this, from above. He could still see how the delicate network of glass and steel formed a sweeping teardrop exactly like one half of the Yin Yang symbol, while the other half of Winterfern — the part buried beneath the mountainside and marked out by a planting of trees — formed the other half. Two mirrored parts: the atrium, the light; the mountainside, the dark. The sight filled him with renewed admiration for the Merisi, guardians of a balance most could never guess at; keepers of the darkest of secrets and the greatest of truths. Darkness and the light.

He settled back and glanced about the empty cabin, wondering if its thirty or forty seats had once been full of Merisi being ferried here and there across the world, to do their quiet, watchful duty.

Where were they all now? he wondered. And what unimaginable odds must they be facing?

Suddenly the plane lurched sharply, throwing him to one side so that he almost fell into the aisle. The engines began to whine and he heard a rat-a-tat percussion on the exterior of the plane. His eyes shot to the window and he watched in bewilderment as the world was snuffed out by a new deeper blackness. He blinked in astonishment as, moments later, the moonlit world reappeared.

The tinny voice blared out again.

"Please stay in your seat. We seem to be encountering some kind of—"

The voice clicked off. Instantly there was another loud rattle on the metal skin of the plane and again the engines screamed and the plane veered. Once more Paiscion saw a fleeting blackness out of the window, which passed as quickly as the last.

He peered out only to see the same magical scene of silver-puff clouds, gleaming rivers and distant winking lights. At first nothing seemed to have changed, but then he brought his face close to the glass. There was something strange about the clouds. Some of them seemed to cast shadows that sprawled across the landscape, shadows that trailed off into wisps and streaks. And, when Paiscion looked more closely, he realised that these shadows had a sluggish motion of their own. In places, they stretched themselves thin; in others, they spiralled or drew themselves slowly together.

His jaw fell open. These were no shadows. They were palls of blackness, not drifting but moving with a life of their own.

He snapped open his seatbelt, leaned across the empty seats on the other side of the aisle and peered out. Before him, the silver tapestry of clouds was interspersed by a patchwork of yet more dark stains. He watched them for some moments, trying to make sense of what he was seeing, but shook his head in confusion. Just then the wing dipped and he saw one of the dark clouds up close, passing just beneath them. He pressed his face to the window, adjusted his glasses and frowned at the gathering of blackness. It had form and substance, bulging and sprawling like a living thing. At its heart was a churning maelstrom of tiny particles, all of them moving independently.

"Sorry, sir," said the voice from the speaker above his head, "I was saying that there seem to be... well..." There was a pause. "What I'm saying is that there seem to be... *swarms*, sir. We can only think that they're insects. We're going to climb to a higher altitude in the hope that—"

The voice clicked off again as the outside of the plane rattled and the windows went dark. Paiscion threw himself back into his seat just as the engine roared and the plane heaved to an incline, pressing him back into the cushions. For some seconds he was paralysed by the sheer force of the climb, but finally the engines died a little, and the plane levelled off.

He coughed and loosened his collar, then took several steadying breaths. "What have you done?" he murmured, turning back to the window. "What have you done?"

For a long while he gazed languidly out at the chequerboard of white and black clouds, lost in his thoughts, and it was only when musical notes suddenly chirruped from the panel in front of his seat that he came back to himself. He leaned forward, peering at the buttons and the oblong screen at the centre, which now bloomed into life.

A message appeared, reading 'Incoming Call'. Below was a large green lozenge labelled 'Answer'.

Tentatively he touched the lozenge. The screen flared, then an image appeared. It was Franz Veeglum sitting behind a crude wooden desk. The Master's face looked even paler than usual, despite the warm rays of dawn that slanted across the room.

"Hello? Franz?" ventured Paiscion.

"Hello, my friend," said Veeglum, his canned voice sounding dry and weary. "I think you already know why I'm calling?"

Paiscion nodded soberly. "I believe I do."

"They're everywhere," Veeglum said. "They pour from the circles and the Slips — all ze breaches between the worlds. They darken the skies, attack ze crops, pollute ze waters — those that were not already foul with ze Black. People are as terrified of these insects as they are of the beasts. So, ze armies rouse themselves again, as much as we tell them not to." He took a deep breath. "We're defenceless against them. This is far worse than anything we imagined."

The Magruman pursed his lips. "We may not have imagined it, Franz, but in our hearts we knew. He's taking us back. Back to the beginning. To the plagues."

Veeglum hunched forward, resting heavily on his desk. "What was it he said? 'I will make you suffer even as ze ancients suffered'?"

Paiscion nodded.

"So he gives us ze plagues of old," said Veeglum grimly. "And what greater suffering can there be? 'Five times undone,' he said, and so it will be. Not five Undoings, as we thought, but five of the ten plagues of Egypt — our half of them, as he will see it. Our portion of ze misery, or so he doubtless believes."

Paiscion ran his fingers through his thinning hair. "But there is one thing I simply cannot understand. The plagues almost *destroyed* our civilisation. Why risk unleashing them again now?"

"Victory is a powerful motivation, no?" said Veeglum. "But I think there is something else. I have given it a lot of thought in the past hours. I think he vishes to bring ze worlds into balance. His idea of balance."

Paiscion frowned. "In what way?"

"The worlds are different in many respects, but the founding difference is ze plagues. In your world, the plagues of Egypt are a thing of absolute evil. They polluted your rivers, brought disease, pestilence, fire, darkness, death. It was a time of horror zat you try to forget. But here, in our world, it is very different. Here, the time of ze plagues is celebrated. In our teachings, the plagues mark ze beginning of a new and hopeful time, the beginning of a *greater* civilisation. The plagues are a foundation of faith celebrated in festivals and feasts."

Veeglum frowned at his knitted fingers. "And we are different too in how we see ze man who unleashed ze plagues. You will not even speak his name. You call him 'the One from the Waters', and loathe him, and fear his legacy. But the religions of our world rejoice in that name. Here, he is among ze greatest of all ze prophets, the one who spoke to God and led his people from Egypt. To us, he is Moses."

Paiscion recoiled at the name, and looked away as though Veeglum had said something obscene. He was quiet for a moment. "So you think all this is — is Thoth's way of exacting some kind of punishment, because of how your world sees... *him*... the One from the Waters?"

"Punishment perhaps, or maybe this is Thoth's way of teaching us to see ze plagues and Moses in the same way as you. Perhaps he gives them back to us so that we share your horror and outrage at what came before." He opened his palms. "Or perhaps it is just his way of winning."

The Magruman slumped a little in his seat. "No, Franz, you're right," he said. "Think of what the Dirgh said: 'You will know the evils of our world.' He doesn't just want the two worlds to share a future, he wants them to share a past. His version of the past."

Veeglum tapped his desk, and nodded. "So he starts to make the two worlds the same, beginning at ze beginning."

Paiscion closed his eyes. "And so came the first plague, in the rivers," he said, shaking his head. "Not the blood of old, but a pestilence of his own creation: the Black."

"And then the second plague," said Veeglum, staring at the desktop, "the beasts. Just like ze wild beasts of scripture. They didn't come next in the Bible, of course, but they were there."

"And now the third," said Paiscion, opening his eyes. "The insects, just like the lice and locusts of before."

Both men fell silent until finally Veeglum pressed his fingertips together and cocked his head. "You're thinking ze same as me, I imagine?"

Paiscion nodded. "Yes, I'm sure." He cleared his throat. "If this is the third of five plagues," he said gravely, "what comes next?"

47

The Jaws of Kemet

"They seem to see the Jaws of Kemet *as the gateway
from the Motherland. When they are open, they are a portal
to the wider world. When closed, there is no escape."*

THE *Windrush* SAILED ACROSS seas heaving from the recent storm,
the water still heavy with silt and seaweed. Each of her crew was
sombre as they took their posts, some aloft in the golden rigging,
lashed to the yards and stays, the others lining the beams and the
bow. Some grasped hooks and pikes, while those most adept at
Essenfayle stood, empty-handed, fidgeting anxiously.

Simia had positioned herself next to Triste in the foremost part
of the bow, while Sylas and Naeo were back at the helm near Ash,
who directed the ship from the quarterdeck. The only person not
above deck was Amelie, who worked feverishly below in the
doctor's cabin, preparing for what was to come.

No one spoke. All eyes stared ahead, across the dancing seas.
Already the golden ship was rounding the headland, and the
forested slopes were slowly drawing back to reveal the strait
beyond. Soon they would lose their cover and find themselves
between the Jaws.

"Ready!" called Fawl, peering down from his vantage point on one of the rope ladders. He tried to inject his voice with his usual good cheer, but the crew knew him too well and heard only his unease.

Sylas felt a trickle of sweat down the back of his neck. His chill was long gone, but now he felt blood coursing, heart thumping, breath coming short and shallow. He tried to remember the hopefulness he had felt the day before when the *Windrush* had cleaved its way through the Imperial army, scattering men and beasts like so much flotsam and jetsam. He told himself that if she could do that — and over meadows and shale — then anything was possible at sea. But always his thoughts returned to that morning, and the moment he and Naeo had lost control. The moment he had been taken by the icy waves.

"*Surely it's… unnatural to bring two such distinct, different parts together?*" his mother had said. Now, Sylas could not help feeling that she was right. And, whatever the truth, how foolish it had been to argue with her when they might have so little time left.

Ash stepped up beside them. "Are you ready?"

Neither of them replied.

"How's the pain, Naeo?" asked Ash lightly.

"It's all right," said Naeo with as firm a voice as she could muster. "I'm OK."

The pain in her back was indeed better than it had been, but that was not the problem. She could not shake the feeling that it was she who had let everyone down. And the worst part of it was that she had no idea how to stop it happening again. She wished her father was there now, whispering in her ear. "It's all right, Nay-no," he would say. *He* would settle her nerves.

"Just do the best you can, Naeo," said Ash as though hearing her thoughts. "Both of you. Just try to find what you had this morning and keep hold of it. If you can't, don't panic. I'm here. I'll just take over while you two get yourselves together and—"

"Lo! There!"

It was the lookout in the crow's nest. The crew looked up and saw her pointing frantically ahead.

"Ships!" she yelled. "Four score, maybe a hundred! No more than a league away!"

Instantly all eyes searched the Strait of Kemet. It now gaped wide before them, a grey line low on the horizon, flanked on both sides by rolling, parched hills. On the highest peaks — one on either side of the strait — two colossal statues stood sentinel over the span of water. To the left, carved into a sheer face of rock, was the gigantic visage of Thoth, featureless and empty. To the right, the towering effigy of a hunched bird with a cruel, arched beak had been fashioned out of a lonely outcrop of sand-coloured stone. Sylas recognised the bird at once from his time in Salsimaine. It was the ibis, one of Thoth's animal forms and the symbol of his private legion.

Both gigantic statues glowered down at them, making the *Windrush* seem no more than a pine cone bobbing on the waves. But it was not these titans that drew the attention of the crew. Instead everyone now peered ahead to the far end of the strait, where a new nightmare was emerging from the sea haze.

Spanning shore to shore, the looming shadows of at least a hundred vessels stood tall above the waters, their great sails tapering to a point like crooked teeth. With the glistening tongue of the strait beneath, they completed the impression of vast jaws, gaping to swallow the *Windrush* whole.

Already white foam gleamed at the prows of Thoth's vessels as they carved through the heavy seas, charging towards the *Windrush*, converging on the centre of the strait, directly ahead of their quarry.

Sylas and Naeo heard Ash's voice from behind.

"Now, you two," he said, making an obvious effort to calm himself, "this is the moment you've been preparing for. Turn to each other and find the strength you know is there. Don't worry about us. Don't have a thought for the ship. Don't even think about them up ahead. This is all about you now." He put his hands on their shoulders and gazed ahead with bright eyes. "Remember who you are. You're the blood of Isia, two parts of a blessed whole. In you, the Glimmer Myth is fulfilled!"

Sylas and Naeo looked at him in surprise. He sounded more like Paiscion or Espasian than himself. He smiled. "All right," he said with a wink, "so I rehearsed that a little."

But they saw in him then something that stirred them both. It was absolute faith: a complete and certain belief that they would do the impossible.

Sylas's heart swelled. He heard Naeo's breaths coming short and fast — or were they his? He felt her trembling at his shoulder — or was that him? He closed his eyes, clasped her hand and his doubts fell away.

When the winds came, they caught the *Windrush* with such force that those in the rigging had to scramble to hold on. Gleaming ropes snapped taut as the sails filled to overflowing. Joists groaned, decks creaked, railings sang in the gale. The *Windrush* surged forward, her hull heaving through the first wave, bouncing off the second, skipping over the third. Soon she was skimming the surface of the seas, weaving between the peaks of water and keeping to the calm between. All aboard but Sylas and Naeo had to cling to rails and fittings as the shining vessel swept from side to side, careering towards the blockade.

Sylas felt the thrill of togetherness. He sensed Naeo beside him, felt her intuition for the waves, her sense of the wind and the seas. He saw them as she saw them, each part of something greater, each drawing from the other. Like her, he felt his place among them, and with her he wove them into a glorious design of water, air, canvas and timber. They worked in harmony, one calling for the wind, the other steering the ship, one parting the waves ahead, the other lifting the prow. They shifted in their tasks so rapidly and seamlessly that Sylas quickly lost track of which were Naeo's and which were his.

The *Windrush* hurtled now towards the blockade, her feather standard cracking in the gale. Simia shrieked with delight as she clung to the ropes of the bowsprit, her bright hair dancing about her. The rest of the crew squatted, clutching ropes and chains and fittings, doing their best to keep hold of their weapons, while above them all the crazed lookout grinned and whooped, gripping the sides of the crow's nest, straining against the tethers that kept her from being tossed into the sea.

The fleet was near now, and Sylas and Naeo could make out sails of red and black, and Imperial standards, and figures rushing about on dark decks. They could see too how the waters churned and frothed with a swell of pale grey bodies — hundreds, perhaps thousands of Slithen straining at their harnesses as they hauled the heavy warships, reaching impossible, terrifying speeds.

Still Sylas and Naeo did not hesitate, and still the *Windrush* forged on, scything between the waves, heading for the largest gap between the ships. It was hardly an opening at all — barely wide enough to let them pass — but it was the only chink in the vast wall of timber and steel bearing down upon them.

Naeo felt a curious electricity as Sylas squeezed her hand. She knew why he had done it because she could feel it too.

They could do this.

The *Windrush* felt fleet and lithe, taut and responsive, as though she had been made for this moment. And just then Naeo felt as though she had been born for it too. She breathed with the winds, swayed with the decks, and felt her heart leap with every lunge and crash of the prow.

They could do this.

They could do this.

She took a deep breath, filling her lungs, preparing for the final thrilling, terrifying, wonderful, dreadful charge.

And then, somewhere below the nape of her neck, she felt the Black.

It was a niggle at first, a creeping pain. Next it was in her back, rising between her shoulder blades. And then, quite suddenly, it was a piercing pulse of agony sweeping from the small of her back to the base of her skull.

Somehow she kept her focus, and so did Sylas. Thoth's ships were just before them now, an impenetrable forest of red and black, the Slithen leaping dolphin-like to spy their quarry, then diving to rejoin their monstrous shoal. But still the *Windrush* charged.

It was not her pain that caught Naeo off guard, it was the doubt. Quite without warning, an image of that morning forced its way into her mind. She saw the wave, and the *Windrush* rolling beneath it, and Sylas being swept before her into the seas.

It was only a moment, but it was enough.

Sylas had felt a ghost of pain in his own back, but he had resisted it, forced it from his mind. But in its place came the doubt.

It was only a moment, but it was enough.

It was as though his heart had missed a beat, and in that beat the magic with Naeo, the rhythm of give-and-take, had failed. His efforts were suddenly off-time, making him draw the winds an instant too early, turn the keel an instant too late.

And that was all it took. Travelling at such speed, the *Windrush* was upon the next wave in a blink, and this time, instead of glancing off its face, she struck it with shuddering force.

Sylas and Naeo were thrown from their feet. The crew slid, yelling and flailing, some slipping overboard. The bowsprit gave an explosive crack and snapped, striking Simia and sending her sliding on her back down the main deck. The bow bucked, groaned and slewed to one side, sending before it an immense fount of water. And then, amid a shower of brine and splintered wood, the grand old ship settled back on the waves at a dead stop.

The gigantic warships of the Imperial fleet loomed, their great hulls crushing the last few waves that stood between them and their quarry. And across that narrow passage of water, in that sudden, horrifying calm, the crew of the *Windrush* heard the horns and drums of battle, and a thousand delirious cries of triumph.

Epilogue

ESPASIAN STOOD AT THE edge of Carrion Rock, forcing himself to watch.

The birds and beasts of the valley had lost their brave battle, and their sacrifice was everywhere to see. The bodies of foxes and otters, rabbits and rats, badgers and birds of prey littered the hillside. Others limped and whimpered back to the Suhl lines, or into the forest to lick their wounds, while a straggling few fought on: birds swooping down upon the advancing Imperial lines; a pair of bears growling and huffing along the Suhl defences, picking fights where they could; scatterings of smaller creatures charging and retreating, nipping and snapping at the mass of opposing beasts.

But each time fewer returned than had set out, and each time Thoth's troops recovered more ground. A regiment of Ghor had already reached the Suhl defences and were once again in tooth-and-claw combat with the Leaflikes, while just below Espasian a troop of Hamajaks pressed in upon Carrion Rock.

The Magruman scanned the desperate scene, reproaching

himself for calling the animals out of the valley. He had done it because it was the only thing to do, but now it hardly seemed worth it. Now, he felt that same anguish, that crushing sense of responsibility he had felt the previous day when Bayleon had given his life.

He sucked in some icy morning air and looked over at the Suhl lines. They were holding, such as they were, but many brave warriors had fallen in the winding ways between the roots, and those that remained were in their rearmost positions, edging ever backwards, towards the trees. It was a pitiful sight.

He saw the tall man he had come across the previous day, the one with the eyepatch, who had fought valiantly under the gaze of his daughter. What had her name been? An unusual name...

"Faysa," he murmured as he watched the father battling on, clubbing away a lone Ghorhund with a rough-hewn bludgeon.

Then, as the brave defender parried to one side, Espasian saw Faysa herself. It was a heartbreaking sight. She was peering over the defences, jabbing with a hopelessly long pike, doing all she could to inflict some damage without revealing herself. None of the attacking beasts had yet taken an interest in her, but it seemed only a matter of time.

Espasian glanced anxiously at the Imperial forces, which looked as formidable and numerous as ever. A steady train of reinforcements snaked down from the Westercleft Hills, swelling the rear ranks and easily making up the numbers that had fallen in battle. And now something else was happening among the teeming masses. In several places along the battlefront, the Imperial ranks appeared to be moving apart, as if to let something through. Then, not far from Carrion Rock, Espasian saw a solitary figure at the heart of the commotion, marked out by bright, flowing amber robes and a headdress of black. A dreadful chill swept over him. He looked quickly along the front and, wherever there was a disturbance, he glimpsed another figure wearing the same amber robes, striding through the ranks. Already they were drawing close to the front lines.

"No," he breathed. "No!"

He reached into a leather bag slung from his shoulder, brought out a large, engraved horn and put it to his lips. It let out low, haunting moan: the signal to retreat.

Even as it sounded, the robed figures strode out on to open ground. Their gowns were peculiarly bright and elegant compared with the heavy dark armour of the rest of the army.

"Hekas," murmured Espasian contemptuously, recognising their high black headdresses formed of ram's horns wrapped in the coils of a giant cobra. These were the Empire's adepts, those most gifted in the Three Ways. He counted eight of them in all, though he knew that there would be more encircling the valley. He glanced back at his own front line and saw that most of the army had begun a careful retreat back towards the treeline, but some were still fighting. Among them were Faysa and her father, Takk.

Espasian raised the horn once more, but just as he was about to blow it he saw the Hekas raise their arms as one, and in that instant the air was filled with another awful sound. It was a monstrous growl thundering in the depths of the earth. Espasian lowered the horn as he watched trampled meadows far out on the Westercleft Plain buckle and break, yielding up gigantic clods of earth and rock, each the size of a house. They rose steadily into the air, carried upwards by an unseen force, some conjuring of Urgolvane, and there they rolled, showering mud and stone into the gaping craters they left behind. The robed figures threw their arms forward, and at once the colossal clumps of earth soared upwards, arching high into the air.

Even before they reached their zenith, Espasian was at a run, half sprinting and half scrambling down the rear face of Carrion

Rock. As he crashed into the forest, he again raised the horn to his lips, blowing with all his might until its note moaned out over the plain. He pressed on, thrashing through the undergrowth, towards the open hillside.

"Retreat!" he cried before he had even reached the front. "Back into the valley! Back to the—"

And then his voice was lost in an explosion of noise. The ground shook beneath his feet, throwing him to his knees, and then he was struck by a blast of wind. A cloud of earth and debris erupted over the treetops, rolling in over his head. He heaved himself to his feet and staggered on, stumbling over roots and pushing through stems and foliage, until finally he burst from the cover of the trees.

Before him was an apocalyptic scene. Gone were the open slopes, the Suhl defences, the snaking tree roots. Everything was shrouded in a grey-brown cloud: a maelstrom of earth and dust. From this tumult came the Suhl, staggering and blinded, their faces blackened, their arms outstretched as they felt their way towards the trees.

Espasian walked into the filth, grasping hands and shoulders.

"Keep going," he said hoarsely. "Back to the valley now, brave friend."

He stumbled on towards the cries and moans somewhere out there in the gloom, tripping over broken roots and weapons and the fallen, guiding those he could to safety. He could feel the ground dropping away beneath him as he reached what was left of the battlefield, but still he pushed on, clambering over piles of loose earth and rubble, leaving the Suhl lines far behind him. Still he could hear a solitary voice somewhere in the murk. He heard someone crying, and then a groan and a huff, as though they were trying to free themselves. As he mounted a pile of broken earth, he saw not one but two figures: the first bent double, hauling at the limp, lifeless form of the other. What made the sight utterly heart-rending and hopeless was that the figure trying desperately to heave the other to safety was no more than a child. The one she was trying to help was a fully grown man.

As Espasian started towards them, the child fell backwards, sobbing, and as she tried to push herself up she turned to look at him. Her youthful face was smeared with mud and tears, but Espasian knew her at once.

"Faysa!" he exclaimed. And then his eyes fell on the man she was helping. He was harder to recognise. His face was bloodied and covered in mud, his once-powerful body broken. But then Espasian saw the eyepatch.

He ran forward and took Takk beneath the arms. "It's all right, Faysa," he said calmly. "We'll have him in the valley in no time." He began pulling at Takk's body, dragging him over the soft, upturned earth.

Faysa walked at their side, her hands in tight fists, her eyes streaming. Then she said in a quiet voice: "They're coming." She raised a hand and pointed. "They're just there."

Espasian stopped. For the first time he peered beyond where he had found them, further down the hill, and there, silhouetted in the haze, he saw dozens of shapes moving silently and stealthily up the slope towards them. They prowled on all fours, their canine ears and thick, tousled manes clear to see, yellow eyes glaring through the murk.

Espasian did not hesitate. He turned and bellowed up the slope: "Here! We need help here!"

He paused and listened, eyeing the approaching Ghorhund, then he yelled again. "Here, I say!"

A moment later a cry came back. "We're coming, my Lord!"

Espasian's features loosened with relief and he looked down at Faysa. "You'll be fine, brave Faysa," he said, placing his hand gently on her head. "Stay here and look after your father. They'll come for you. Call out if you need to."

Without another word, he turned and strode, directly towards the approaching Ghorhund.

"No!" he yelled, his voice commanding but cracking with rage. "You will not have her!"

Then he broke into a run. He charged down the hill, bounding from bank to bank, cloak billowing as he accelerated towards the bristling regiment of beasts.

The last Faysa saw of Espasian was his lithe figure leaping into the gloom, and all around him the snapping, snarling forms of beasts, teeth bared, claws outstretched. One had sunk its fangs into his shoulder, another had him by the leg and more closed in behind him.

Then the hillside echoed with a chilling howl of triumph.

PART THREE

The Last Night

48

The Blockade

*"The blockade in the Kemetian Sea forced
the Suhl to travel by land, but that soon proved
an even more perilous path."*

NAEO WOKE TO A screaming pain in her back that made her head
swim and threatened to send her back into unconsciousness, but
she fought to stay awake and, with a great effort, she opened her
eyes.

For a moment she struggled to understand what she was seeing:
the criss-cross of ropes, the billow of sails, the glowering face of
the sky. Then she heard Fawl and Ash yelling orders until they
were hoarse.

"Heave her in! Heave, I say!"

"Clear the way there! Make room!"

"For the love of Isia, leave it be! We don't have time!"

"Hup! Send it aloft!"

Naeo gritted her teeth and tried to push herself up, but it was
more than the pain that prevented her: she felt heavy, as though
there was a weight on her chest. She glanced down and, to her
surprise, she saw a mop of brown hair and Sylas's pale, unconscious
face. He was lying over her. She pushed gently at his shoulder and

he rolled away, grunting as he slipped on to the deck, still unconscious.

Naeo leaned on one elbow and looked around. The *Windrush* was in chaos. Crew members ran here and there, scrambling through broken timber and rigging, doing a hundred things at once – heaving, pushing, lashing down, tying off – and, as they worked, their eyes shifted frantically between their task and something up ahead. Only then did Naeo look over the bow of the *Windrush*.

To her horror, she saw that the Imperial ships were no more than four or five lengths away, sailing so closely abreast that there was barely a chink of light between them. They would be upon the hapless *Windrush* in moments.

Naeo's stomach gave a sickening churn and she felt tears well in her eyes. This was all because of her.

"Naeo!" exclaimed Ash, running to her side. His eyes were wild and red-rimmed, his cheeks a ghastly white. "Can you stand? They're almost upon us! We'll have to go back! I've tried to bring her about, but with all the damage—"

Naeo held out her hand. "Help me up?"

He heaved her to her feet, then glanced past her. "Sylas!"

Sylas was sitting up, rubbing his head and looking round. "What... happened?" he asked groggily.

"Worry about that later!" said Ash, pulling him to his feet. "Right now we need to get out of here! If you two can—"

He stopped as they all heard a thump against the hull, somewhere below the waterline. Then another and another.

"Slithen!" exclaimed Ash. He lifted his head and bellowed: "Everyone! Poles and pikes! Watch the sides!" Then he turned and gave Sylas and Naeo a desperate look. "Do something!" he begged. Then he rushed away to grab a weapon.

"Where's Simia?" Sylas yelled after him. "I saw her fall!"

"I'm not sure! Go! Go!"

Sylas looked once more round the decks in the hope of seeing Simia, but instead he saw the first of the Slithen rearing over the side, its pink lips drawn back in a snarl, its long grey fingers snaking over the golden railing. Then a chorus of cries drew his attention back to the bow.

The first of the Imperial ships was careering towards them, just moments from crashing into the hull. Men and beasts leaned eagerly over the railings, brandishing blades and spears, while Hamajaks swung between ropes and yards, chattering with frenzied delight and preparing to leap across to the *Windrush*.

Sylas felt Naeo's hand slip into his and he forced himself to look away. He pushed back his grogginess, and the ache in his head, and threw everything he had into his bond with Naeo.

The first gust struck the *Windrush* head-on, turning her sails inside out and sending her astern, punching through the waves and lofting great sheets of brine high into the air. The second struck her in the side with such force that she leaned over at a perilous angle, tipping wreckage from her decks and dislodging some of the Slithen. Then her bow started to come about.

It was too late. Suddenly, with a gut-wrenching shudder, they were struck by the leading ship of the fleet. A mighty roar of triumph went up as her crew rushed, whooping, to the point of impact, ready to board the *Windrush*.

But their celebration was short-lived. To their dismay, it was their own vessel that had buckled from the blow and, as the *Windrush* slipped away, they saw a deep gash in the mighty hull of their warship stretching from the waterline to the third deck.

With a yell of rage, men and beasts hurled themselves across the void, flailing to reach the golden ropes and rails. But the *Windrush* still had the wind. She reared up fast, opening an ever-increasing gap between the hulls and leaving most of the assailants to tumble into the sea.

Already two more ships had closed in to prevent the *Windrush*'s escape, barring her path to the open sea. Sylas and Naeo summoned everything to their aid. Winds spiralled down from the stormy sky, striking the sails of the *Windrush* so that her masts and yards strained to breaking point, sending her gleaming keel surging forward, driving the Slithen from her path. At Sylas's bidding the waves before her fell away, leaving her path clear, while those behind rose to propel her on.

She struck one vessel with a resounding clap, shearing timbers and fittings from her side. Still she pressed on, Quintessence screeching against wood until she struck the other ship and it rebounded, slewing to one side and twisting from her path. Imperial sailors leapt across the divide from both ships, and this time some of them found the rails. Above, Hamajaks threw themselves from the rigging, landing among the bright ropes and sails.

Now the *Windrush* was out on the open water, building pace, and her golden keel skimmed the surface, already leaving her many pursuers behind. But her crew were in a pitched battle. Hamajaks grunted and screamed as they pounced, Slithen hissed as they swiped and clawed, and the Suhl fought for their lives. Already two lay slain and another had been pitched overboard, still clutching a Hamajak that gnashed and clawed as they fell. Triste was fighting valiantly, his tattooed scalp shining with sweat as he backed towards the bow, fending off a Hamajak with a lump of timber. Fawl was nearby, balancing with astounding skill on a rope ladder while he thrashed at three assailants with a broken yard.

Ash had his back to Sylas and Naeo, beating off any attacker that strayed too close to them with a length of rope and a broken spear.

All fought courageously, but the enemy was greater in number and soon the Suhl were forced back to the quarterdeck, forming a tight huddle.

In the middle of this were Sylas and Naeo, eyes closed, desperate not to lose their concentration.

Ash clambered up on to the helm, peering frantically over the heads of the fighters, trying to see all that was happening onboard. Then he peered back at the pursuing fleet, now some way behind. For long moments he hesitated, then he dropped back into the brawl and thrust his face between Sylas's and Naeo's.

"I need you to make a splash," he panted urgently. "Like before when everything went wrong. Can you do that?"

Naeo's eyes snapped to his. "Are you serious?"

Ash nodded. "But don't actually capsize." And, before she could argue, he turned about. "Just tell me when you're ready!" he shouted over his shoulder.

He began whispering to the crew gathered round him. Each looked at him in surprise, then passed the message on. Ash clambered up on to the ship's wheel, balancing on its wooden spokes, and cast his eyes about his crew, making sure that the message had reached everyone. He looked behind the ship, to check the position of the fleet, and finally he turned expectantly to Sylas and Naeo.

They gave a slight nod.

He jumped down and planted his feet as firmly as he could, then slung an arm round the ship's wheel.

"Now!" he yelled, loud enough to be heard all over the ship. "Hold on!"

All at once each of the Suhl fighters dropped their weapons and looped their arms about their neighbour's, forming an unbroken ring round Sylas and Naeo.

For a dreadful moment the beasts advanced, lunging towards the defenceless Suhl. A Hamajak sank its teeth into the shoulder of a crew member, making her cry out in agony. Another tried to climb over the press of bodies to reach Sylas and Naeo, and seemed

337

about to succeed when the keel suddenly shuddered. The *Windrush* had glanced awkwardly off the side of a wave, setting everything off balance. An instant later there was a terrific boom as the bow plunged deep into the face of another wave. The sheer force of the impact made the rear of the ship lift clear of the waters and rotate in the air, flipping bow to stern before finally coming to a dead stop, sending up a vast sheet of water as high as the topsails.

The collision was so violent that many of the crew cried out in pain, straining to hold on to their neighbours. Sylas and Naeo were thrown backwards, colliding headlong with Ash, who was only able to hold on by wrapping his free arm and a leg round the helm.

But it was worse for the Hamajaks and Slithen. The ship's acrobatics caught them entirely unawares, and they were thrown overboard, squealing and gibbering, splashing through the watery veil and landing far out in the surrounding seas.

In a moment, the entire deck had been cleared but for the terrified crew of the *Windrush*. They stood, gasping, arms still locked tightly together. And pressed tightly between them were Sylas and Naeo.

49

The Gramophone

"I fully understand why the Suhl asked for the gramophone; it is not just a feat of science, engineering and design, but it opens a portal into our world of musical artistry. Nevertheless I do wonder whether it was worth the trials and sacrifices we suffered to bring it."

FOR A LONG WHILE there had been a stunned silence aboard the *Windrush*. Even as Ash sailed the ship on, the crew — perhaps only two-thirds of the number that had sailed into the Jaws of Kemet — stared absently over the stern, watching their assailants struggling in their wake, and thinking of those they had lost. Finally, bewildered and shaken, they had set about tending to the injured and clearing up the ship.

There was no celebration. Everyone knew that, despite the sacrifice of their friends, they had failed. The *Windrush* may have escaped the blockade, but she had not passed the Jaws of Kemet. And so an eerie quiet had descended upon the decks, and all that could be heard was the whip and flutter of winds in the sails, and the occasional groan of the injured being taken to Amelie below, and the sound of the decks being cleared.

But, as the *Windrush* finally passed between the two great

statues and began to slow, there came a new sound. It was a scraping and grumbling, a clunk and clatter issuing from the forward hatch. It became more and more noticeable as the moments passed, and before long many among the crew had stopped to look.

"Will someone *please* help me with this?" came a voice from the hatch.

A flash of red hair appeared above deck, along with the curved edge of something shiny and gold. Simia emerged, flushed and sweating, struggling with something bulky. She gave whatever it was a heave and a large brass horn appeared; another heave and the top of a box came into view.

"Simsi!" called Ash. "Where've you been?" Then he looked at the strange object she was carrying. "What are you *doing*?"

Simia put all her effort into one last push, and her burden finally cleared the hatchway and landed with a clunk on the shining deck. It was Paiscion's gramophone, its horn a little dented, its polished panels glinting in the light.

Ash straightened. "What is *that*?"

Simia heaved herself on to the deck and lay panting, her sweaty hair plastered to her face, a bloody gash across her forehead. She took some moments to catch her breath and then she said: "It's for Sylas and Naeo."

The *Windrush* rolled lazily, waves slapping against her sides, her sails limp in the dying breeze. Tired and disheartened, the crew lounged here and there, resting their limbs. Sylas and Naeo had themselves slumped down on to the deck, their backs propped against the pedestal of the ship's wheel. All eyes were on Simia and the peculiar contraption by her side.

"It's just as well I hadn't quite unstrapped it when we hit that wave," she was saying.

"Yes, but what's it for, Simia?" pressed Ash.

"I was getting to that," she said sharply. She took a breath and continued rather importantly. "I thought of it first this morning, when Sylas and Naeo were talking about how it all went wrong. Something they said made me think of Paiscion and this." She placed her hand on the gramophone's horn, then she looked at Naeo. "You said that when you lost control it was like you were dancing out of time, right?"

Naeo nodded. "It was a bit like that."

"And was it the same just now, at the blockade?"

Naeo frowned, trying to think. "I suppose so. It was the pain that started it, but once I... lost concentration, yes, we did get out of time."

Simia grinned. "Thought so!" She looked at Sylas. "And you said this morning it was like losing rhythm, didn't you?"

"That's right," said Sylas.

"And it was the same just now?"

"In a way, yes."

"So what does that make you think of?" She looked expectantly from one to the other.

"Simia," said Naeo irritably, "what are you getting at?"

"Music!" cried Simia, her smile growing into a grin. "You were saying it was like rhythm and dance — it's like you were talking about music!"

"Simia, really, what's that got to do with *anything*?" snapped Naeo, her frustration getting the better of her. "And, more importantly, how does it get us past that?" She jabbed her finger in the direction of the blockade.

Simia raised her eyebrows and stared hard at Sylas. "Think about it! The *Windrush*... Essenfayle... music..."

But Sylas had already understood. He was thinking back to his first time aboard the *Windrush*, with Paiscion, when he had first come across the gramophone right there on deck. He remembered the rousing music that it had played, and how the fish, birds and clouds had all seemed to respond to the same rhythm.

"You're thinking about the estuary!" he said excitedly. "When Paiscion played—"

"The symphony! Yes!" Simia exclaimed. "It helped you to control everything, didn't it? Make it... come together?"

"That's right!" said Sylas. He remembered Paiscion whispering urgently in his ear. "*Let the music help you!*" he had said. "*Feel its harmony, its song!*"

Naeo leaned in. "So... you think the music might do the same for me and Sylas? Help us keep our rhythm if things go wrong?"

Simia grinned triumphantly. "Exactly! Remember how we were surprised that Paiscion had left his precious gramophone behind? Well, what if he left it here on purpose?"

Ash held up his hands. "Hold on, hold on! Let me get this straight. You think Paiscion left this, *knowing* that it might help you?"

"Why not?" said Sylas, rising to his knees and leaning over the gramophone. "He used it to teach me Essenfayle, and he's always playing it himself. It's hard to believe he left it here by accident."

As the crew began murmuring excitedly among themselves, Sylas started to examine the gramophone carefully. Despite the acrobatics of the ship, it looked in good shape. The arm was still securely in its clasp, and the needle looked intact. He rotated the turntable a little and it moved smoothly. There was a record on it, but not the one Paiscion had played out on the estuary. This one was labelled: *Romeo and Juliet, Sergei Prokofiev*.

"Well, if we're going to try this, we need to try it now," said Ash. He walked to the railing and stared over the side at the Imperial fleet, which had made good time through the narrowest part of the strait and was once again drawing near. Already the shapes of forty or fifty ships were visible, their Imperial standards flickering like flames above the topsails.

"I hate to say this," said one of the crew — a tall, gaunt man who wore his red hair in a ponytail, "but I can't face going at that blockade again. Not after last time. Not if Sylas and Naeo aren't sure they can control the ship this time."

There were murmurs of agreement from others among the crew.

"Perhaps we can find another way?" said someone else. "Over land?"

"No, there's no time," declared Ash firmly. "Think of what's happening in the valley. We *have* to keep on."

There was a long silence.

"But do Sylas and Naeo think this will work?" asked the man with the ponytail.

All eyes shifted to the two children.

"They can't know it will work," protested Ash. "They've never done it before! And even if they had—"

"It'll work."

Everyone, including the young Magruman, turned and stared at Sylas and Naeo in astonishment. They had spoken as one so that it was impossible to tell their voices apart. Later they would wonder how they had taken that decision, but there and then they hardly hesitated.

It was perhaps only Triste who truly understood because he saw the miracle that had passed between them. Confidence in Sylas became conviction in Naeo; conviction in her became certainty in him. It had happened silently and in a trice, but to Triste it had been as bright and bewildering as a lightning flash.

50

Romeo and Juliet

"The gathering was wrapt as I finished the passage from
Hamlet, *and they pressed me for more. I thumbed through*
my dog-eared Shakespeare and read passage after passage
from Macbeth, The Tempest, Romeo and Juliet
and more, all to a spellbound silence."

SIMIA LEANED OVER THE gramophone and carefully unclasped
the tone arm. She drew the needle over the record, then looked
at Fawl.

Fawl glanced at Sylas and Naeo, waited for their nod, then
filled his lungs.

"Let 'er run!" he bellowed.

Instantly Naeo's winds drove hard into the glittering sails, and
the *Windrush* surged ahead, aided by Sylas's waves, which swelled
behind the stern. In moments, the hull was skipping over the
surface, sweeping side to side, keeping to the furrows and, as soon
as they had settled on a pace, Sylas looked across at Simia.

"OK, Simsi," he said.

With trembling fingers, she placed the needle on the record.

The gramophone issued a blaring, screaming, discordant wail.
It was the sound of horns and trumpets, but it was like no music

Sylas had ever heard. It was a jarring, unsettling noise, and he was grateful when, after a few moments, it died away to nothing.

It was such a surprise that both he and Naeo struggled to keep their concentration. The ship swerved a little from its course and struck a stray wave, sending up a plume of spray like a distress signal. Simia panicked and reached over to lift the needle.

"No, Simsi!" cried Sylas. "Let it play!"

Simia took her hand away and waited, glancing anxiously at Ash. Just then the horns and trumpets erupted again, becoming a chilling wail. Kettle drums joined the disharmony and, as they rumbled, the *Windrush* collided awkwardly with a wave and veered away, making Sylas and Naeo stagger. They pressed their eyes shut, struggling to keep their focus on the winds and the ship and, to their relief, she quickly settled back on to an even keel.

"I'm sorry!" Simia cried, reaching again for the arm of the gramophone. "It was a silly idea. I'll take it—"

"No!" interjected Sylas. "No, this *has* to work, Simsi! Leave it!"

Simia glanced at him in surprise, but did as he asked.

The dreadful cacophony soon died away, and this time, to Simia's relief, there was music in its place. But it was a quiet, gentle melody without any rhythm to guide the ship.

Anxiously Sylas looked ahead at the fleet, now terrifyingly close. Some of the ships had slipped behind others to form columns. This gave the impression that there was space to pass through the blockade, but while the *Windrush* might pass the first row of ships she could never slip by them all — her flanks would be too exposed.

"It's a trap!" yelled Fawl. "We can't get through! Bring her about!"

Sylas made the *Windrush* bank so sharply on the side of a wave that her shining keel sent up a curtain of water. She began travelling across the face of the fleet, passing ship after ship, column after column.

Sylas's mind raced. What were they going to do? There seemed to be no way through, and surely there was no way round either. They would be flanked long before they reached the edge of the blockade.

Just then the gramophone issued the deep, threatening note of a tuba and, almost at once, there was an answer from violins and cellos. The tuba responded, beginning a to-and-fro: tuba, followed by strings, tuba, then strings. They paced out a metronomic rhythm, like a march. Now, the violins broke away from the other strings, playing to the same rhythm, but with a new melody: rising and falling, rising and falling, like the swell of the sea, or the swaying motion of the *Windrush*.

Sylas felt a tremor of excitement. In the strings, he heard the dance of winds and waves; in the violins, the *Windrush* sweeping from side to side with a flourish. In that moment, he and Naeo took a decision. They threw themselves into the music and called the winds, waves and the ship to dance to its rhythm.

The gramophone continued to blare, violins and French horns sweeping with the ship back and forth, back and forth, until the *Windrush* had passed far along the front line of the fleet. Perhaps here, Naeo thought, the ships would be less prepared. The roll of a snare drum cut through the music and, an instant later, the *Windrush* was hit in the side by Naeo's winds. The keel turned sharply on a flanking wave, and the ship hurtled towards the blockade.

Sylas and Naeo gripped hands even more tightly. This was it. This was the moment. Naeo had timed the turn perfectly, and now they were sailing directly towards a gap between two columns.

The channel between the first two ships was so narrow that, as they passed, they stared into the faces of the Ghor crews, but they flew past even before their enemy could respond. The tuba was blasting again, urgent and threatening, but still the violins and horns sounded rhythmically above all else, keeping Sylas and Naeo together.

But now, as they had feared, the way before them was narrowing. The Imperial ships were closing the trap.

"Everyone hold on!" yelled Sylas.

With another roll of the snare drum, the *Windrush* took an impossibly sharp turn, passing behind the stern of one ship and clearing the bow of the next by a whisker. She swept quickly between the next column of ships and, as the tuba and the strings resumed their steady march, the *Windrush* began a waltz. Again she turned round the stern of a ship and the bow of the next and, even as she cleared them, she turned again, sweeping past her pursuers as those aboard were still rushing about, wrong-footed by her manoeuvre.

A cry of, "Hurrah!" went up from the *Windrush*, which only further enraged the enemy, now leaping hopelessly into the water.

On the *Windrush* went, carving a snaking path between the ships, passing smoothly between bows and sterns down the length of the column. Most were Ghalak ships, with fortified hulls crusted thick with barnacles and whelks, their crews clad in a light armour of shells. They leapt with great athleticism from their higher deck in a bid to reach the *Windrush* as she scythed past, but such was her pace that all of them missed, or glanced harmlessly away.

Still the music played, and still the *Windrush* waltzed faster and faster. For Sylas everything joined in harmony: wave and keel, wind and sail, himself and Naeo — just like the violins and the cellos, the tuba and the French horns. They passed the Ghalak ships even before their crews had a chance to ready themselves, and suddenly, miraculously, the *Windrush* was careering out into open water. The final ships of the blockade were close, but wrestling with their sails, struggling to come about. There was no chance of them reaching the *Windrush*.

But then Simia shrieked.

Sylas saw her scrambling towards him, pointing frantically off to his side and, before he even had a chance to look, he felt a change in Naeo: a shock, a moment of stillness.

And then she lost the rhythm.

51

Battle

"If the Suhl were as adept in battle *as they are in the natural world, then they may have escaped much of this suffering. But when all is said and done, I know which is the greater gift."*

A FIERCE JOLT OF pain rattled up Sylas's spine, making him want to cry out. But he knew at once that the pain was not his own. It was Naeo's.

The Slithen had come from nowhere, a stowaway from their earlier clash, and now it had found its way to the deck and it had her by the neck, dragging her back towards the railing. It snarled viciously and lashed out with webbed claws as Simia ran at it, but still she came on, charging headlong into its chest and knocking it sideways.

Naeo barely felt the impact because she was still with the waves and the winds and the *Windrush*. She hardly felt the chill of the Slithen's fingers round her neck as it hissed in her ear.

"Come s-s-s-swwim with me!" it whispered.

Even this she did not hear. She had lost the *Windrush* twice before and she would not let it happen again. She did not falter even when she felt the rail against her back, and her body tipping over the side. There was only Sylas, and the swell, and the ship.

Suddenly Ash was beside her, shouting and pulling at her tunic. And then Triste was there too. Naeo was dimly aware of the cold wetness slipping reluctantly from her neck, a weight falling away, the painful scrape of claws on her back. She glimpsed Simia falling to the deck, but she did not look; she could not look: she had to stay with Sylas, and the *Windrush*, and the waves.

Ahead of her two Ghalak ships were closing in, the *Windrush*'s path to the open sea slowly narrowing and then disappearing, lost behind a wall of shell-encrusted timber. There was no way through, and no time to turn. They faced just two ships of an entire fleet and yet there was nothing to be done.

As though to signal the end, the music from the gramophone surged to a sudden, jarring crescendo and, with a rattle of drums, fell silent.

Afterwards she was not sure whether the decision had been hers or Sylas's. Perhaps it had been both. All Naeo knew was that it had been so sudden, so irresistible, that it had seemed to come from somewhere else. It drove back her doubt and overwhelmed her pain and, as she was taken with this new resolve, so the *Windrush* was taken by the winds. Her prow rose, her sails filled and she sped directly towards the Imperial ships.

Somewhere behind she heard Ash's voice: "Everyone away from the sides!" he yelled. "We're going to hit!"

This time the *Windrush* surged on like a battleship. There was no dance just raw, unbridled power, and she punched through the final waves at a charge, throwing up founts of spray. The Imperial ships were far larger and better fortified than the *Windrush*, and now they had pulled one behind the other, forming a wall of double thickness. But as she headed straight for the flank of the first ship it was she who seemed to have the advantage. Ghalak sailors yelled in alarm and scrambled along the decks to move out of her path just as she struck them amidships, her shining keel cleaving through the heavy boards and beams like the head of an axe ripping into the decks beyond. She held firm and true, slicing through cabins, bulwarks and staircases as though they were made of matchwood.

The Suhl stared in bewilderment as they swept through the ship. Ghalak warriors were forced to scramble for something to hold on to as the waves gushed down corridors and swamped the lower decks.

The *Windrush* erupted from the first ship amid a shower of debris and plunged straight into the second. No longer travelling so fast, the impact threatened to bring her shuddering to a halt but, taking a deep gasp of the salty air, Sylas heaved the winds to him. The sails billowed, the ropes snapped taut and the *Windrush* drove onwards, splendid and terrifying, slicing through the crust of shells and piercing the mighty hull beyond.

The Ghalak crew, which had watched the fate of the first ship, mounted a desperate counter-attack, swarming towards the *Windrush*. But, even as they tried to board, the planks beneath their feet buckled and sent them tumbling into the waves. They hurled spears, swords and shards of wood, but almost all of them missed their mark. A determined few jabbed and clawed with boarding hooks, which flailed at the *Windrush* like searching fingers, but all of them missed their target.

All of them but one.

It was the last hopeless sweep of a lone hook clutched by a Ghalak seafarer who hung precariously from a broken companionway. He might have had no more success than the others, but by chance the hook on the head of the pike glanced against a passing yardarm, which threw it a little further across the divide. And that was where it found its mark.

As was his custom, Fawl was standing high on the rope ladder, using his vantage point to call to his shipmates and direct their assault. All the while he used a length of wood to swipe at mangled timbers that might have snagged the *Windrush*'s ropes. Had he not leaned out quite so far, had he not turned at that crucial moment to shout to his crew, it might not have happened.

But he did. The hook caught his leather jacket and yanked him backwards. With no arm to steady himself, he was defenceless. He gasped, flailed and then, with surprising calm, toppled overboard.

For a few dreadful moments Fawl dangled over the waves as his attacker clung to the pike but, as soon as he realised his predicament, he did not hesitate. He seized the shaft with his powerful arm, swung his legs up to brace himself against the passing wreck and kicked back. The unsuspecting sailor was hauled with a yelp from his perch, then both men plunged headfirst into the void.

Cries of alarm went up all around the *Windrush*. Ash and many of the crew scrambled across the deck in a vain attempt to help, and Sylas and Naeo looked on, aghast, as they saw the man who had saved both their lives tumbling between the ships.

At the end Fawl put up no fight, but simply arched his back and fell gracefully towards the frothing seas. It was as though he had always believed that one day he would go to his mother sea and, in that last dreadful moment, he had known that this was the day.

Just before he reached the waves, he broke his silence. "Let her run!" he bellowed and then plunged into the maelstrom.

His cry brought Sylas and Naeo back to themselves. Pummelled by a new surge of wind, the *Windrush* ripped herself free of the last of the wreckage and ploughed on into open waters. Free from clawing timbers, she sliced swiftly through the waves and, as she went, her bright sails filled, her rigging snapped tight and she resumed her dance towards a clear horizon.

For the briefest moment a muted cheer went up from her decks, but it was no celebration. It was a cry of relief. In silence, everyone moved to the stern where they gazed back to where Fawl had disappeared into the waves. For some time they peered into the wreckage and fountains of froth between the ships, searching for any sign of their fallen comrade, but they soon realised that it was hopeless. Both of the gigantic Ghalak ships were foundering, turning the seas about them into a boiling morass of air, water and splinters, and everyone knew in their hearts that any who had fallen into it would be lost. And so instead their eyes turned to the ships themselves, and they watched their demise with a certain grim satisfaction. They saw rigging snap, masts topple, sails drop like shrouds, until finally the shattered husks let out a mournful moan and began their inevitable journey into the waiting depths.

What none of them saw as they watched this spectacle was a small creature scuttling on six legs towards the aft hatchway. It was a hermit crab — a beggar and borrower of shells — and it laboured now beneath a heavy spiralling shell many times its own size. But what made this shell different from the vast numbers that had fallen from the Ghalak hulls was that its surface was as slick and black as oil.

The little crab tottered beneath the weight, sometimes reduced to dragging it slowly but surely to the hatchway. There it paused, turning briefly as though looking back to where Sylas and Naeo stood hand in hand, their wrists glowing bright with Quintessence. At this the creature seemed to hiss — or perhaps it was a whisper — and then it turned, teetered on the brink of the opening and toppled into the darkness below.

52

Insects

*"So it seems they have similar tales of the plagues —
insects, wild beasts, blood in the river and so on — but for
reasons I can't quite fathom, here they seem somehow
more real and to instill more of a sense of dread."*

DRESCH AND LUCIEN TUMBLED over the bank of earth and
lay gasping, muscles burning, hearts raging in their chests.
They were like that for some time, recovering their breath,
gathering their scattered thoughts, until finally they pushed
themselves up and stared, wide-eyed, back towards the stone
circle.

A flare was suddenly lofted above Stonehenge. It cast a stark
light across the plain, bleaching everything a ghastly white.

"Do you think the others made it?" asked Lucien, wiping his
brow with his sleeve.

"Some of them, I think," said Dresch. "But none of us would
have made it if it hadn't been for Tasker." She shook her head,
tears welling in her eyes. "I can't believe he *did* that. He didn't
stand a chance!"

Lucien nodded, gazing thoughtfully at the centre of the stone
circle. "Remember what he said on the way here about a 'time of

sacrifice'? He knew exactly what he was doing. He knew he didn't have a hope, but he did it anyway. He did it for the rest of us."

There was a second flash and they saw another flare arcing through the darkness. It bathed the plain in an unearthly glow, and they saw in the distance several straggling parties of beasts cringing at the bright light and prowling away from the stones, most of them heading east.

Another procession of beasts quickly took their place, but these were quite different: hard-edged and featureless, with plate-steel sides and armoured limbs. They crouched low, huffing and growling as they encircled the stones, forming a new perimeter. In unison, they grunted to a halt, and at once soldiers spilled from their flanks and stalked out into the night. They held weapons to their shoulders, craning their necks to look up into the dark skies.

Dresch and Lucien followed their gaze. By the light of the dying flare, they saw the swarm: a seething, living vortex reaching up from the stone circle and sprawling ever outwards until it passed above the clouds and formed wisps of blackness, just visible against the cosmos. As they watched, they became aware once again of the ceaseless drone reverberating in the air and earth.

Dresch drew her scarf about her. "What do you think they're doing here?"

Lucien rubbed his stubbly cheek, his eyes rising to the highest part of the swarm. "'You will be five times undone,'" he murmured. "That's what Thoth said. The Black was the first, the beasts were the second, the insects must be the third. It's like he's wearing us down."

"Well, it's working," murmured Dresch. "But why insects?"

He narrowed his eyes. "I don't know, but doesn't it—"

A blinding yellow light suddenly streaked upwards from the

perimeter of the stone circle. They heard a fiery roar and crackle and, an instant later, two more ragged tongues of flame jabbed up into the sky towards the swarm.

All at once everything before them became a riotous blaze. The night was banished as fingers of fire criss-crossed the darkness, chasing throngs of insects that whipped and folded above the plain. Thick orange clouds of acrid smoke rolled up towards the heavens, and a noxious chemical scent filled the air.

"Flame-throwers," murmured Lucien, shielding his eyes.

Dresch retreated a little behind the bank. "What do they think they're doing?"

"Fighting back."

"Well, they're making it worse!" she burst out. She pointed at the fringe of the inferno. "Look!"

Lucien peered into the chaos of light and dark, then leaned forward. "What *is* that? Ash?"

Dresch tutted. "It's falling not rising, Lucien! That's no ash!"

He stared more closely at the dark spaces at the edge of the fire, and he saw that it was, indeed, falling as a light, black rain, which swept in curtains away from the flames.

"It can't be," he said breathlessly.

"Just like Paiscion said," breathed Dresch. "'You can't fight corruption with corruption.'"

Lucien's eyes shifted from one tongue of fire to the next, and he saw now that, wherever they sprang up, the flames left behind them a fine mist of blackness. He couldn't see it as it reached the ground, but he could imagine showers of Black drenching the plain and then trickling away into the already brimming ruts and hollows.

"He's not just wearing us down," he murmured.

"What was that?"

Lucien turned to her. "He's not just wearing us down, he's getting us to wear *ourselves* down. It's exactly as Paiscion said: the more we fight, the more we undo ourselves. *That's* why he's sent the insects — to make us fight."

Dresch turned between Lucien and the flames. "Then we have to stop them!"

"What? Tell them to let us take on the fight ourselves? Just the two of us?"

Dresch was quiet for some moments, then she reached out and took his hand. "Come on!"

Lucien pulled against her. "Where?"

"If they won't listen to us here, we have to go back! Talk to the generals, the people in charge!"

"We've tried that before!"

"Then we'll try again!" yelled Dresch. "And, if that doesn't work, then we'll try something else! I'll — I'll get back in my lab. If the Black is at the heart of it all, perhaps it can tell us something after all. Perhaps one of my team has found something. And, if they haven't, I'll — I'll keep looking!"

Lucien was still gazing back at the stone circle.

"Come on!" she shouted. "We can't just sit here, watching — we have to do *something*! Think of Tasker! Think what he did! We have no right to sit here doing nothing!"

He searched her face for some moments. "I'm sorry," he said quietly. "You're right. I just... never thought it would come to this."

"None of us did. How could we?"

Lucien rose to his feet. "Right," he said. "Let's find the truck."

They set off into the shadows but, after only a few paces, Dresch hesitated.

"Lucien?" she said. "Will you do me a favour?"

"Sure, what?"

"It's probably silly, but..." She gave an embarrassed laugh. "Will you... call me Martha? It's just that with everything we've been through, everything that's happening, it feels—"

"Of course," said Lucien, smiling warmly. "And, as you know, I'm James."

§

The Duke lay alone in his cardboard castle, wishing that it was a fortress of stone. The Hailing Bridge had long since fallen silent, the peculiar noises had ceased, and it was at least an hour since he had last seen any of those monstrous canine figures on the far bank of the river. But the Duke had still not slept a wink. Every breath of wind that sang through the lattice of the bridge above, or rustled the cardboard buttresses of his own domain, had him cowering beneath his treasured – if rather holey – Silver Jubilee blanket, as though its royal crests alone might protect him.

But, in truth, nothing made him feel safe. Not now. Everything he had thought of as an Absolute Truth, permanent and unshakable, like his certainty that there were no monsters, that the river would always flow, that nightmares always came to an end, all these seemed as frail as his cardboard castle. And that was before he heard the noise.

It began faintly at first – a distant hiss and hum, which seemed to hang in the air. The Duke's first thought was that it was coming from his old transistor radio. Cursing the modern world, he riffled through his battered wooden trunk, tossing out worn-out shoes, mildewed clothes, stacks of horse-racing pages and cans of anchovies (anchovies were his particular vice), but when he finally found his radio he discovered that not only was it off, but its twenty-year-old batteries were utterly dead.

Meanwhile the hum and hiss had grown louder. Much louder. So loud that he started to wonder if helicopters – military helicopters – were flying down the river towards him to vanquish the monsters, set wrong to right and perhaps restore all that was good in the world. But, as the noise became louder still, the Duke realised that there was no chatter of blades, no thunder of engines and, in fact, the noise sounded more natural than machine.

More animal.

More... *insect*.

He could no longer resist taking a peek and so, with trembling fingers, he lifted the cardboard flap that served as his window.

He saw nothing unusual, just the dark surface of the river, silver beneath the stars and moon and, in the distance, the shifting shadows of trees stretching down the banks of the river.

He frowned. As he watched, the shadows stretched further and further downstream, and they showed no sign of stopping. They were spreading outwards now too — almost bank to bank — covering the entire surface of the river with their darkness. Meanwhile the hum had become clamorous, filling the night air, reverberating round his cardboard walls.

He eyed the spreading shadows carefully. It was coming from them, he was sure of it.

Suddenly the Duke slammed the flap shut and fell on his back, panting.

They were no shadows.

When the swarm reached his cardboard refuge, it struck with such force that the walls almost collapsed. There was a rat-a-tat roar as thousands of winged insects pelted his home, making the whole structure vibrate wildly. The noise was deafening, unbearable and, not knowing what else to do, the Duke threw his Silver Jubilee blanket over his head. With a whimper, he reached out, grabbed his belongings and used them to shore up the walls. Miraculously his flimsy home was holding but, as the assault of insects raged on, it began to slump to one side.

"Leave — Me — Alone!" cried the Duke, pressing his fingers in his ears and closing his eyes tight. He sat like that for a few more moments, then bellowed, "ENOUGH!"

And, with that, he threw away the blanket, hurled himself into the old trunk and slammed the lid.

53

Making Sense

"I have given up on everything making sense*. That is for those who come after. All I can do is understand what I can and give them — and give you — this record."*

SYLAS STUMBLED DOWN THE final two steps of the ladder and made his way wearily towards the Bow Room. Even here, below deck, he could hear the hearty singing of the crew. They had struck up their chorus about an hour after the blockade, filling the heavy silence with a rather forced cheer, which had grown in volume and liveliness ever since. Sylas was glad of it. It had taken his mind away from Fawl and everything that lay ahead, and now it helped him to heave his exhausted body those last few paces towards his mattress.

But, before he reached the Bow Room, he found himself passing the doctor's cabin and he heard his mother's voice from within. To his disappointment, another voice answered her. For a fleeting moment Sylas had thought of opening the door and falling into her arms, putting behind him their hard words of the previous day, and the violence and drama of everything that had happened since.

He sighed and was about to shuffle off when the door sprang open. A large man with a bandage across his shoulder turned to thank Amelie, then nearly leapt out of his skin when he saw Sylas. He murmured a greeting before rushing off down the passage.

Sylas stepped into the cabin. His mother had her back to him and was tidying her treatment table, gathering up bottles of ointment and medicine and slotting them into a rack on the wall.

"Come and see me again tomorrow," she said. "This Salve works miracles, but I'd like to examine you again to be sure."

Sylas was about to say something, but found himself watching his mother arrange her bottles, returning each to its rightful slot in the rack and positioning them so that the labels faced the front. She tapped each one, mouthing their names under her breath, checking they were all where they ought to be.

Sylas was caught off guard by a sudden rush of memories so distant that they barely seemed his, memories of Amelie in her makeshift 'lab' at home, arranging her little jars of chemicals, her rows of seedlings, her papers, her notebooks. It was her ritual, and he had seen her doing it a thousand times. As he continued to watch, another memory came back to him. It was the moment she had given him the box of paints for his kites and pointed to each of the labelled glass bottles, speaking the strange names of the colours under her breath: "*Orivan Red, Grysgar Orange, Girigander Silver, Mislehay Green.*" He remembered her fingers – those beautiful fingers – lifting out each of the colours and then returning them carefully to the box.

"Sylas, my love," she said. "Are you all right?"

He blinked. She had turned and was looking at him in surprise.

"I'm... fine," he said, trying to gather his thoughts. "Sorry, I shouldn't have been staring. I'm just tired."

Amelie laughed. "No need to apologise. Of course you're tired."

She stepped towards him, but he retreated a little. He was quiet for a moment, trying to work out what it was that he wanted to say.

361

"It's good to have you here, Mum," he said finally. "On the *Windrush*. I'm not sure I've said that. I should have."

She smiled the smile that opened him wide. "Come here," she said, reaching out to him.

Sylas walked over and let her fold him to her, losing himself in that safest and warmest of places. In that moment, he wished he could stay there forever. She rocked him from side to side, in silence at first and then she asked him how he was, and how it had been at the blockade, and she told him how proud she was of him, and how afraid for him she had been. Then they fell silent once again, still holding one another tight.

"If anyone should say sorry, Sylas, it's me, not you," she said at last, pulling away a little to look at him. "Sorry for making you think that I don't believe in you and Naeo, and that I don't understand what you're trying to do. I do, better than you can imagine. I know just how important this journey is for you both. For us all."

"Thanks, Mum," said Sylas. "But I do get why you're worried, I do. It's just that... it really *does* feel that we have to do what we're doing. It felt strange to begin with, when I first came here and heard about the Glimmer Myth, and especially when I first met Naeo. Back then, being near Naeo felt like it might tear me apart. But just recently I haven't doubted it at all. Now, being together isn't something we *have* to do, it's what feels right." He searched her face, looking for some sign that she understood.

Amelie smiled, but it was not the smile of moments before. Now she looked troubled. "That's what makes you both so very special," she said.

"But...?"

She dropped her eyes and laughed. "I forget how well you know me." She fidgeted with some bottles still on the treatment table, choosing her next words with great care. "Well, I don't doubt the importance — the *right*ness — of the bond you have with Naeo. How could I? It's there for everyone to see. But what's still hard to grasp is the part of the Glimmer Myth that says that we're all — you, me and everyone else — meant to somehow come together with our Glimmer. That's the part I struggle with. I can't hide it, Sylas, and least of all from you."

Sylas nodded but looked away. He felt that familiar panic rising in him, the feeling that he was alone on this journey, that no one else could truly understand, even his mother, even though she knew him better than anyone in the world. But he remembered their clash the previous day and he tried desperately to control his feelings.

"If I let myself think about it, I'm the same," he said after a while. He leaned up against the treatment table. "I mean, I have no clue what I'm supposed to do when we get to this Academy of Souls. The thought of me and Naeo bringing everyone together with their Glimmer is... well, weird. I can't get my head round it. But I suppose that's the point. You see, Mum, this isn't something I think about. It's something in here." He patted his chest, gazing into her eyes, willing her to understand. "It's something I feel. Does that make any sense?"

Amelie drew in a long breath and nodded. "Of course it does."

"And I suppose the reason I keep going without knowing what comes next, or what might happen if the Glimmer Myth comes true, is that —" he paused and narrowed his eyes, trying to find the right words — "if what happens is anything like when Naeo and I are together then it's going to be OK. More than OK."

Amelie smiled, but still he could see a slight crookedness in her mouth and worry in her eyes.

"What is it, Mum?" he said. "What aren't you saying?"

Amelie folded her arms across her chest, as though she was hugging herself. "The thing is, Sylas," she said, dropping her eyes again, "you're not the only person who's known their Glimmer."

Sylas said nothing. He sensed where this was going and it frightened him.

"But you know that because you remember what it did to me," she said with a weariness that Sylas recalled all too well. "You know how it terrified me, how it took me to my wits' end. Beyond that really. How I couldn't sleep for week after week, how I was afraid of my own shadow. How it finally drove us apart — even you and me, Sylas."

He nodded, trying not to remember the horrifying day when she had been taken away to Winterfern.

She took his hand. "So, my love, you can imagine how all this sounds to me. You describe being with Naeo as something wonderful, but my feelings were just so *different*. Mine were nothing to with being right and natural; mine were about losing myself. Losing you." She squeezed his hand and sucked in a breath. "So, yes, as your mum, I worry deeply about what this will mean for you. And I worry about what it will mean for me and for everyone else."

He felt his hope and resolve leaving him. This time he did not feel the hurt or the defiance of the previous day; this time he understood. He understood because he had seen how it had been for his mum, and now he wondered how he could have been so blind.

"You know, Mum, you've never really told me what it was like. Perhaps you tried to back then but, if you did, I definitely didn't get it."

Amelie took him by the shoulders. "Sylas, of course I didn't tell you about it. I was trying to protect you from it. And do you know what? You don't need to hear about it now. I've already said too much."

"But, Mum, I *want* to hear," said Sylas as firmly as he could, though he was far from sure that he did.

For a moment Amelie seemed in an agony of indecision, then she sighed. "I will tell you because I think you may need to know. If you're sure it's what you want."

He nodded.

"Well," she said, wringing her hands, "I think you know that it started in my dreams — vivid ones — that didn't feel like dreams at all. They were always the same, in a place that felt familiar — though it wasn't anywhere I actually knew. I would be doing things, and saying things, that felt like everyday life, but weren't anything to do with our real lives. They were normal little activities like shopping in a market, or walking by a river, or reading, but they were someone else's. And some of what I experienced was just..." She gave an empty laugh. "Well, to use your word, weird."

She smiled at him hesitantly, seeming to weigh up whether or not to continue. Then she said: "The weirdest dream of all was one I had again and again. And in a way it concerned you, Sylas." She spoke quietly as though uttering a secret. Her eyes held his. "I had a son, Sylas. And he wasn't you."

She paused, and in that moment she looked ashamed. Sylas felt a swelling tide of emotion, but said nothing.

"I think the me that was in those dreams loved him just as I love you. So much so that when I was there, with him, I felt I was losing hold of you." She searched his face. "Does that make any sense?"

Sylas knew exactly what she meant because, once again, he felt he was beginning to lose hold of her. "Yes, I suppose," he said.

"Well, that's where it all started going wrong," continued his mother, wringing her hands. "I began to resent those dreams, hate them even. And they came ever more frequently, and all the time they were more and more vivid. Soon this other life started to be part of me, no matter how much I fought against it." She looked at him apologetically. "I'm sorry, Sylas — this all sounds like madness, doesn't it?"

"No, it doesn't," said Sylas. He remembered when he had eaten the fruit of the Knowing Tree: the terrifying, mystifying feeling of becoming Naeo — not just seeing with her eyes, but *being* her. That was what it must have been like for his mum. Only for him it had, at least, all made some sense. She had encountered a life and a world that wasn't her own, and without any explanation. Worse than that, it had happened night after night.

"It was your Glimmer," he said.

Amelie smiled. "That's right. Though of course I had no idea what a Glimmer was. But the more I realised that this wasn't really me, the more I tried to be myself even while I was dreaming. I tried to have my own thoughts, to find my own mind. It became hard to keep hold of reality. To keep hold of the things..." She trailed off as a tear rolled down her cheek. She wiped it away with her sleeve. "Sorry, Sylas," she blurted. "I didn't mean to get upset. I should stop."

Sylas stepped forward and held on to her. For a while neither of them said a word, but finally Amelie laid her cheek on the top of his head and said: "Now do you understand why I've been so frightened for you? For us all?"

"Of course," said Sylas. And, despite himself, he did. He held her even tighter, and he told himself that it was to comfort her, but in truth it was as much to console himself.

Ever since this strange journey had begun, he had been convinced that it was meant to be. That it was good. That he and Naeo were destined to be together and, through their union, undo a terrible wrong. But now, with the end of their journey almost in sight, he wondered if it made any sense at all.

54

The Academy
of Souls

*"They speak of this Academy of Souls as though it is
the epicentre of all evil: the ultimate source of all their woes."*

SYLAS LAY ON HIS mattress, arms behind his head, hoping that
the sway of the ship or the crew's singing on the deck above might
soon send him off to sleep. He had been close to it several times,
but always his mind crowded with memories of his conversation
with his mother and, in a trice, he was awake again.

He looked over at Simia's mattress, wishing that she was there.
He knew she would help him to clear his thoughts and put
everything in perspective. But she was up on deck, singing heartily
with everyone else, while helping to repair those parts of the rigging
and timberwork that could be salvaged.

Sylas tried to focus on how the conversation with his mother
had ended. *"There's a reason why all this has happened to you,
my love, and not to me,"* she had said. *"Mr Zhi always said that my
bond with my Glimmer was a promise of something greater. That
something is you and Naeo, Sylas."*

But when he pictured her, smiling, he also saw that fleeting shadow pass over her face, and he knew that her doubts had been as real as ever.

And now those doubts were his.

What if they *were* all wrong — Merisu, Isia, Mr Zhi, the Glimmer Myth itself? What if it wasn't the division that was unnatural — at least not any more? What if Nature had already repaired the wrong as best she could, and now the two parts were *meant* to be separate? What if, after all, he and Naeo were the only ones that were meant to find one another, and this quest was just some terrible mistake? Perhaps the gift they shared was better used for something else, something they could be sure was right and good, like defending the valley and their friends, or trying to overcome the Black, or confronting Thoth himself.

These thoughts assailed Sylas again and again until he was muddled and giddy. Eventually he decided to give up on sleep and join the others on deck but, as he pushed himself up, he glimpsed the Samarok half covered by a shirt he had thrown aside. The gems on its cover winked enticingly in the early evening light. He drew it up on to his chest and gazed at it for some moments, absently running his finger down the S-shaped groove in the leather. The Samarok always had answers, he thought. Perhaps he would find some certainty there.

But where to start? He had already read all about Quintessence and the Passing Bell. He thought back to his time with Isia, and to the words that had sent them on this journey. "*Go to the place between the cataracts, to the halls of the Academy of Souls,*" she had said. "*There you will find the truths that go before me, before Merimaat and the Merisi.*"

Then Sylas remembered something else she had said. "*Take the Samarok,*" she had entreated him. "*Learn from it what you can of Merisu and of Merimaat. She came to know more of these truths than any other.*"

He thought of the piece he had read the previous day, the one in Merimaat's own hand, about the Passing Bell. Just as Isia had said, Merimaat was at the centre of it all.

He felt a familiar thrill of excitement as he opened the cover. He flicked through the pages at the beginning, thinking of when he had first read them in the temple, with Isia sitting beside him and a storm gathering outside. He would start right there, he thought, with the passage she had shown him.

He scanned down the first page, allowing the Ravel Runes to reveal themselves. He stopped when he reached the third paragraph, where the Academy of Souls was first mentioned, and he began to read.

In the beginning, there were twelve: one from each of the great Kemetian temples, devout priests, worthy priests, each and all. So they were until one day summoned by their king to a valley between the cataracts, to a secret place not known to common men but hidden deep within the rock. There they bound their minds and souls to a great task: to forge a magic true and absolute – a magic of such power that the emperor king would forever reign supreme.

They laboured for one score years and ten, until each grew old and frail and the world had all but forgotten their academy in the hot rocks of the desert. And then, one day, the greatest of all the priests, the priest of Thoth, sent forth a messenger to the mighty king Ramesses, who was yet upon the throne. It was a message that told of the impossible, a proclamation that shattered the known and the knowable.

The magic had been found.

Only two things would be needed to forge this magic

to end all wars, this so-called Ramesses Shield: first, a circle made entirely of stone – stone taken from the four corners of the Empire; and second a girl, a young, pure girl – a girl in whose veins ran the blood of all of its nations. So proclaimed the priest of Thoth, scribe to the Academy of Souls.

And so commanded Ramesses the Great.

As work began on the stone circle, thousands of clerks and servants and priests began the search for the child – the girl in whose very being was the perfect union of the Empire. This proved the greater task. Long after the stone circle was built and six years after Ramesses' command, a young peasant girl was found. A girl called Isia.

Sylas lifted his eyes from the page and glanced across at Simia's unmade bed, remembering her delight upon discovering that Isia, for all her greatness, was an ordinary daughter of peasants, just like Simia herself.

He looked at the ceiling and listened for a moment to the singing on deck. How he wished this journey would end well for Simia too. She had been at his side from the very beginning, and had asked little or nothing for herself; except, perhaps, that she might know her Glimmer as Sylas knew his. That, at least, was a reason to keep going, he thought.

He dropped his eyes back to the Samarok. The passage moved on quickly, and by the turn of the page it had reached the gathering of the Priests of Souls at the stone circle, and the forging of the Ramesses Shield. He recognised Merisu's account of invocations turning the sky blood-red, and making the ground quake, and the rocks blister, and the sands melt like vapour into the air.

This we saw as we gathered in our shameful circle of magic, as we played with power beyond our imagining. And yet on we chanted, our voices filling with fear: on and on, lost in the devilry of the Ramesses Shield.

When the thunder echoed into silence, we heard Isia's cries, her warnings, her desperate pleas. We saw the child's white-robed figure kneeling at the centre of the circle, imploring each of us in turn to stop, stop before it was too late.

And yet on and on we chanted. On and on.

Sylas paused. He knew where this passage would take him: to the moment when they realised that they had done the unthinkable, the moment when the priests saw Isia herself riven in two. Part of him wanted to read it again, alone and without Isia at his side, but he needed to know more about the Academy of Souls. That was the place where Isia said they would find the truth and an end to their journey.

He turned back to the previous page and searched among the Ravel Runes until he found the words *Academy of Souls*. With his eyes resting on the scrawled letters, he pictured sands and sun-parched rocks, and then tried as best he could to imagine the academy itself: dark, mysterious catacombs deep below the desert.

The Ravel Runes were already in motion, twisting and writhing like hungry snakes, seeking out new passages, new meanings. And then, as quickly as they had begun, they fell still.

The page no longer showed the opening passages of the Samarok but a new entry written in the same unremarkable hand. It was entitled *The Academy of Souls*.

Sylas bit his lip and settled back to read.

The Academy of Souls is first described in early Nubian texts as a place hidden deep in the rocky hills on the eastern bank of the Nile, near Swenett (later Aswan), known to some as the Place That Casts No Shadow. Much of this region was quarried for the stone used in the buildings, pyramids and obelisks of the Empire, but one area was decreed by Ramesses the Great to be a Royal Preserve, and subjects were forbidden to trespass. The hills are famed for their complex of caves and catacombs, and legend has it that these places are home to the shadow that has fled the scorched world above.

Sylas yawned. His exhaustion was finally catching up with him, but he wanted to read on. He screwed up his eyes, then opened them wide and continued.

In this shadow of legend was founded the Academy of Souls, so far from prying eyes that its scholars might spend years forgotten by the very people they served. Little is recorded of the structure of these halls of learning, but Merimaat and Merisu described uncharted miles of passages, chambers and cells. Some were left unused, but the vast majority were claimed by the four faculties of the Academy of Souls: Urgolvane, Druindil, Kimiyya and Essenfayle. Each faculty comprised three Priests of Souls and nine indentured servants known as Magrumen. All lived and worked within their allotted halls, devoted to their task, and none were permitted to stray beyond their own domain.

For a moment Sylas's eyes closed, but as his head began to roll to one side he started, blinked and pressed on.

So they remained for years that became decades, decades that became a lifetime. They worked without the warmth or succour of the world above, confined until they had discovered the prize commanded by their king: the defence for all Kemet that would one day be known as the Ramesses Shield.

In 'Of Souls and Sacrifice', Merisu explains that the only communal space within the Academy of...

Sylas's eyelids drooped but he forced himself to keep going. He read dreamily about a great hall in the academy called the Truth Chamber and Ammut's Pit, the strange catacombs beneath, which the Priests of Souls had used for a peculiar kind of trial. But the deeper the Samarok took him into those mysterious places, the nearer he came to sleep, until finally, his eyes fell shut. As he drifted into dreams filled with desert hills and dark passages, his fingers let the Samarok slip on to the mattress at his side.

§

Naeo stood alone in the stern of the *Windrush*, leaning heavily on the rail, one foot on the lower bar. She gazed out at the first dreamy pinks and oranges of sunset, and she thought of her father. In that moment, she was remembering his sacrifice: the courage it must have taken to allow her to board the *Windrush*, knowing that he might never see her again, knowing the dangers she would endure and the peril he himself faced. Perhaps it had made it easier for him, Naeo mused, to know that she may have been in at least as much danger there in the valley as she was here, aboard the *Windrush*. She hoped that it had.

She drew his threadbare bootlace from her pocket and pulled it absent-mindedly between her fingers, weaving it into shapes while watching the ship's wake tracing a frothing pathway to the sun. How wrong it felt to be sailing still further away from him, especially knowing everything he faced in the Valley of Outs. And yet, she reminded herself, this was what he had wanted. And she knew, deep down, that this was where she needed to be. No matter how painful the sacrifice, this was the journey chosen for her.

With every hour she spent with Sylas onboard the *Windrush*, she was only growing more confident that they were following the right path. Their connection had become something warm and close, something to be trusted, and never more so than earlier that day, with the music blaring and the wind and the waves dancing to its rhythm. Then, as they had broken through the blockade, she had truly understood why her father had been so sure that they were meant to be together.

"Are you all right, Naeo?"

She turned to see Simia standing next to her, fiddling with a lock of her hair, which glowed in the evening light.

"It's just that you've been standing here for a while," continued Simia, looking genuinely concerned. "You didn't join in the singing and you seemed so... sad."

Naeo gazed back at the setting sun. "I'm fine," she said. "Thanks."

"Are you sure? It's just that I—"

"Really, Simia, I'm fine," said Naeo. Then she added: "You wouldn't understand. I was — I was just thinking about my father."

Simia recoiled, looking hurt. Her expression hardened. "Fine, I'll leave you be," she said sharply. She turned to go, but then glanced back over her shoulder. "I had a dad once, you know."

Naeo watched her walk away. She opened her mouth to say something, but she couldn't settle on the right words. She considered going after Simia, but there was no time — the sun had nearly set. How she wished that sometimes, like Sylas, she could find the right words. She sighed and turned back to the setting sun. It was falling ever more quickly now, and as it approached the horizon it spread into an iridescent haze. Naeo's fingers finally came to rest and she freed them from the bootlace and returned it to her pocket. She leaned on the rear railing of the ship, watching closely as the sun finally touched a perfect mirror of itself on the water.

In that precise moment, she closed her eyes. Her mind travelled back to Grail, and the forest, and the treehouse nestled high in the branches of a chestnut tree. And suddenly, leaving her father, and the journey, and the separation felt like no sacrifice at all.

Because there he was.

55

Hope

"I am struck by how the Suhl never seem to lose hope.
Thoth has taken so many things from them,
but he seems quite unable to rob them of that."

FILIMAYA WALKED SOLEMNLY BETWEEN the beds of the Hollow, stopping occasionally to speak to one of the patients, or to consult with the nurses, or just to take in the appalling scene.

The Hollow was no longer a chamber but a vast, seemingly unending space beneath the earth. It had expanded so far to accommodate the growing numbers that the walls now disappeared into the gloom. The hanging clusters of glow-worms above each bed made a Milky Way of lights that winked and twinkled in the furthest reaches of the hospital, giving the only sense of its true scale. They almost lent it the magic of Sylva at night, but here there was no song, no storytelling, no laughter. Here there was nothing to do but wait for morning and try not to think of what was to come.

So Filimaya talked, and smiled, and clasped hands where they were offered. And, wherever her voice was heard or her smile was seen, she raised spirits and checked the despair that threatened to consume all.

She spied the three new patients she wished to check upon and set out towards them, taking care to mask her weariness as she walked, sharing a smile and a word with all she passed. When she drew near, she was disappointed to see that, of the three, only Faysa was conscious, sitting up in the middle bed. Takk and Espasian looked almost as gravely ill as they had when they had first been brought in, their skin pale and clammy, their breathing slow and irregular. Filimaya glanced from one to the other, trying not to let her anxiety show, then she smiled at Faysa.

"They're still resting, I see," she said brightly.

Faysa looked at her with dark-ringed eyes. "They're just the same," she said, her voice hollow. "I thought the Salve would be working by now."

Filimaya sat down on the side of her bed. "The Salve will only work once they are stable. Salve draws upon an inner strength. They first need to rest and regain that strength, then the Salve will begin its work on their wounds. It may take some days before they are well." She glanced anxiously at Espasian. "For Espasian... it could be longer."

Faysa looked over at the Magruman. "I just wish I could do something," she said, holding back her tears. "I wish I could help him like he helped us. We wouldn't be here if it wasn't for him. He saved our lives."

"And you saved his, Faysa. If you and the others hadn't stayed out on the hillside and found him, he would never have made it back to the valley, not in this state. We very nearly lost him."

"But he wouldn't have been hurt at all if it wasn't for me. He ran straight into—"

"He did what he had to do. He is a Magruman, Faysa." Filimaya looked admiringly at his bruised, swollen features. "And a very fine one. What he did wasn't a choice for him — it was what he was born to do. His fate is tied to us all. For him saving you was no different to saving any one of us, or any part of the valley, or even himself." She turned and met Faysa's eyes. "He sees us all as one." She smiled and placed a hand on the girl's arm. "And we are, aren't we? We're all in this together."

Faysa gave a faint smile. "Yes, we are," she said, reaching out to take her father's cold, clammy hand. She placed it in her lap and stroked it thoughtfully. "He has such strong hands. He worked every day of his life, you know, ever since my age. Younger even, I think. He used to buy and sell things all over the place – he was always travelling and having adventures. And, after the Reckoning, he got into smuggling." She had said it with a certain relish, but then added, "Not in a bad way. Just, you know, to get things for our community. And to make ends meet."

Filimaya smiled. "We've all had to do our share of smuggling in recent years."

Faysa nodded and looked back down at her father's hand. "So he's never really stopped, not since I can remember. And I should know – I've travelled with him the past three years. It seems so strange to see him lying here. So quiet. So still." She looked up at Filimaya with glazed eyes. "I really think he'd hate it."

Filimaya placed her hand on top of theirs. "We all need to rest sometimes," she said. "And I'm sure he's very pleased to know that you're here with him, at his side." She stood up and smoothed down her robes. "So, can I trust you to stay with him, and with Espasian, and to let me or one of the nurses know if they need anything? They're two of our most important patients, you know."

Faysa nodded and gave a weak smile as Filimaya turned to leave.

"Filimaya?"

"Yes?"

"Can I ask what's happening?" Faysa glanced at the ceiling. "Up there?"

The light faded a little from Filimaya's face. "I can't lie, Faysa. it's not good. We've lost the defences, but we still have the valley herself. She has her wiles and ways." She glanced up at the labyrinth of roots. "We call her the Valley of Outs for a reason. They made a full assault a while ago, but she had them in a terrible muddle, charging back out as quickly as they came in. It wasn't long before they were fighting among themselves."

At this Faysa gave her first genuine smile. "And are they still attacking us now?"

"No, it's sundown. We probably have until dawn."

Faysa opened her mouth to ask more, but then, to Filimaya's relief, she checked herself, clearly unsure that she wanted to hear the answer.

"So you'll take care of them for me?" asked Filimaya, flicking her eyes to the neighbouring beds.

Faysa nodded.

"Good. I feel better knowing you're here with them."

Filimaya took her leave and continued on her way between the rows of beds, her smile slowly falling from her lips. She stopped more than once along the way to speak to patients and nurses, leaning in with soft words of encouragement and, as she neared the exit, she turned and looked back at Faysa. She had drawn Espasian's hand into her lap too, and was holding both of them tight. At this Filimaya's smile returned.

She took the dirt steps to the tunnel and headed up into the fresh air above. When she stepped out into the forest, the sun had already set and the only light was a glow from between the clouds, which bathed everything in a marine blue. The trees were stark silhouettes and the surface of the lake was lightless and grey. There was no evening chorus — the few birds left were not for singing. The only sound was the breeze through the browning canopy, and the low rumble of battle drums somewhere beyond

379

the hills. Even they were quieter than before, and altogether the Valley of Outs seemed drained and depleted, as though losing her fight for life.

Filimaya leaned against a tree, drew a deep lungful of air and settled back to watch the remaining light gradually fade. Campfires lit up round the lake and on the fringes of the forest, but there was no chatter among the troops, no song or good cheer. Everyone knew as well as Filimaya that without Espasian, and with the Suhl defences breached, the battle was as good as over.

Filimaya's eyes filled with tears and she began singing softly to herself:

"And so we change as change we must,
When standards rot and sabres rust,
When sun is set and night is come,
When all is lost, when naught is won."

"He's thinking of you too," said a voice from behind.

She turned, startled. Bowe was sitting alone on a log just a few paces away, his green eyes glowing in the failing light.

"Paiscion," continued the Scryer. "It *was* him you were thinking of?"

Filimaya quickly wiped her eyes with a handkerchief. "You know perfectly well it was," she said with an embarrassed smile.

Bowe shrugged. "Well, as certainly as I know that, I know he wishes himself here, Filimaya."

She smiled. "I know it too, Bowe." She walked over to the log and sat down next to him. "So, what brings you out here?"

"The sunset," said Bowe, looking up to where the sun had disappeared behind the hills. "I had a promise to keep. To Naeo."

Filimaya looked at him quizzically for a moment, but seemed to think better of asking more. For a while they sat quietly together, watching the darkness spilling down the hills, spreading between the trees, pooling across the lake.

It was Bowe who broke the silence. "I can't help wondering if the valley will see another sunset." He said it matter-of-factly, as though it was of little significance. In truth, it was the only way to hold back a tide of emotion.

Filimaya hooked her arm through his. "I know," she said.

Both fell silent once again, lost in their thoughts, until finally they saw Fathray wandering along the lakeshore, muttering to himself. Filimaya called out to him and the Scribe was so startled that he staggered several steps into the lake. He quickly recovered himself, shook off his feet and came over.

"Lost in my thoughts," he said sheepishly as he sat down next to them.

"My dear Fathray, when are you not?" smiled Filimaya affectionately.

"When I'm paddling in the lake," he grunted.

They all laughed like the old friends that they were.

Bowe looked down at the journal tucked under Fathray's arm. "You've been writing?" he asked.

Fathray glanced at it as though he had forgotten it was there. The smile fell from his face. "Oh... no," he said. "Not tonight. I — I will not be telling this part of the story."

They all exchanged a dark look.

Finally Fathray cleared his throat. "So what is to be done now?"

Filimaya clasped her hands together. "We survive as long as we can." She turned to her companions. "And we hope."

The Scribe nodded. "Any word of Sylas and Naeo?" he asked, voicing what was on all their minds.

She sighed and shook her head. "We know that they made it across the Westercleft Plain, which is a wonder in itself. Nothing more."

Bowe leaned forward, resting his elbows on his knees. "I know something more," he said, gazing at the last blond streak of sunset. "They've made it further than the Westercleft." He looked back at his friends. "Much, much further than that."

56

The Temple
of Merisu

"The Temple of Merisu may be the oldest of the Merisi
stupas, but for me, it remains the most majestic of them all.
Even now, I find myself moved every time I visit."

DRESCH AND LUCIEN STARED intently through the windscreen,
listening to a thin voice crackling over the car radio.

*"...So this seems to be the meaning of these five Undoings. But
remember everything that has brought us to this. Do not think only of
these plagues of Moses. Think of the generations of Merisi who wore
ze glove, the glove that reminds us how all zis began, in ze first stone
circle, with the outstretched hand of Merisu.*

*"Sisters and brothers, for a thousand years and more, ze Merisi
have protected our world from a terrible truth, keeping it a secret
until the moment when ze wrong may itself be undone. Well, zat
moment is now. Somewhere in the other world, two children, ze last
descendants of Isia herself, are nearing the end of their journey.
Now, after all the many years of effort and sacrifice, these children
may need only a few final hours to heal the division of ze worlds.
Today, sisters and brothers, the outstretched hand is not Merisu's,*

but your own. Today we reach out together... so at last we may be one."

There was a long pause and then:

"*Thank you, my friends. This will be my final message. It has been an honour to count myself your brother.*"

There was a silence, a click and then the speakers filled with static.

For some moments they listened to the hiss, as though waiting for more, then Dresch switched the radio off.

She stared out of the windscreen at the dark road ahead, rigid, clutching the steering wheel tightly, jerking it occasionally to stay on the road.

"The plagues of Moses?" she said finally. "Can you believe it? I mean really?"

"Just now I'm not sure what to believe," grunted Lucien.

They both gazed broodingly between the headlights as they passed a service station shrouded in darkness, and then crossed an empty roundabout serving abandoned roads. There was not a soul to be seen.

"What do you remember about them?" asked Dresch, keen to fill the silence. "The plagues of Moses."

Lucien riffled in his pockets, produced a rather unappealing stick of liquorice and bit down on it. "Just what I learned at Sunday school," he said through his mouthful. "That they were meant to show God's power to the pharaoh. Force him to let the Israelites go free."

Dresch nodded. "And they were terrible, weren't they? Unthinkable? Locusts, frogs, disease..."

"Blood in the rivers, beasts," offered Lucien, "hail and fire..." He trailed off.

She bit her lip. "Darkness was one of them. A blanket of darkness across all of Egypt."

Lucien nodded and folded his arms across his chest. "And the last was the worst of all. The death of all the firstborn, in every family in Egypt." He paused and then added: "I hadn't really thought about it before. Just looked at it as a story in the Bible. But it *was* brutal. Horrifying."

There was a long silence. Both listened to the rumble of the tyres on the road, their eyes fixed ahead.

"So, if we've only seen three plagues," said Dresch at last, "and there are going to be five…"

"What comes next?" finished Lucien. He dropped the last of the liquorice into his mouth and chewed anxiously. "Best not to think about it."

Dresch glanced at him and shifted in her seat. "Perhaps you're right," she said. "Until we have to." She rolled her shoulders and pressed herself back into her seat. "How much further to the base?"

"Not far now," murmured Lucien. "Over this hill."

They drove into a deserted town with no sign of life but flickering streetlamps and traffic lights painting the roads red, orange and green. They passed street after empty street, the houses dark and silent, with just the occasional glimmer of light between curtains.

"Do you really think they'll listen?" asked Lucien finally.

Dresch sighed. "We have to try, James," she said. "Like I say, if they keep fighting, they're just going to make it worse. We know that now for sure. We saw what it did to the Black. They *have* to understand."

Lucien grunted. "Maybe," he said. He rummaged absently in his pockets for something else to eat, but found nothing.

They left the town behind them with the last of the streetlamps and plunged back into the darkness of the countryside. Soon they turned off on to a country road and it started to wind up a long, steady slope. The engine of their old Land Rover began to labour and Dresch had to change down a couple of gears, making progress frustratingly slow. They peered between the golden cones of the headlights, lulled by the hum of the engine and the rhythm of the bends, and it was not long before Lucien began to nod off.

Suddenly everything about them flashed. A harsh white light splashed down the road, flooding the verges, the passing trees and the inside of the car. Dresch and Lucien threw up their hands to shield their eyes, but already it was gone. Then another burst of intense blue-white light seared the hillside.

"Pull over!" snapped Lucien.

Dresch slammed her foot on the brake and the vehicle shuddered to a halt.

They glanced at one another, then opened the doors and stepped out. Slowly they walked to the back of the car and turned towards the light.

They gaped at the scene before them.

Salisbury Plain was no longer shrouded in darkness but alive with flecks of brightness that danced and leapt like fireflies. Light erupted from the earth, fanned across the sky, exploded from the clouds. The countryside below was a shifting patchwork of light, like the illuminations of some crazed pinball machine. The night rumbled and boomed, the explosions so frequent that they became a storm of sound raging at the dark.

Instinctively Lucien and Dresch drew near to one another.

"The fourth plague," said Dresch without taking her eyes from the light. "Hail and fire. It has to be."

Lucien walked forward a few steps, his eyes scanning the horizon. Then he turned. "No, this is us," he said, pointing at some streaks of fire in the distance. "Look!"

Dresch peered more closely and felt a creeping chill as she saw, at the leading edge of these penstrokes of flame, a bright white light that appeared just like the blazing tails of missiles. In a panic, she shifted her eyes elsewhere, to streams of light erupting from the earth, and in these she saw the arcing pinpricks of tracer fire. She looked at the blooms of light nearer to hand, and now she recognised the blistering bursts of shells.

"Oh my…" she breathed, raising her hand to her mouth.

"They're attacking the stone circles," said Lucien, shaking his head as he gazed out at the scene. "They must be trying to close the way between the worlds."

Dresch slumped against the vehicle, her face pale in the flashing lights. For a moment she simply stared, her arms limp at her sides, and then quite suddenly she straightened.

"James?" she said, trancelike.

"Yes?"

"This *is* the fourth plague." She looked at him, tears welling in her eyes. "Don't you see? This *is* the storm of hail and fire, just like in the Bible. Only Thoth isn't doing it — it's us. We're doing it to ourselves!"

§

Franz Veeglum heaved at the great stone door and felt a rush of hot, humid air, heavy with the smells of a tropical forest. He stepped on to a well-worn earthen path, which led him off into a jungle thrumming with chirrup and song.

He walked quickly, passing along haphazard avenues of bamboo and teak until at last he stepped into a light so bright that he had to shield his eyes. The fierce sun bleached almost all colour from the scene, but the vision before him was no less grand.

All about him the temples of Bagan soared into the azure sky: their broad stone bases bulging as though under their own weight, then erupting upwards in stunningly crafted spires of silvery gold. These exquisite pinnacles grew ever narrower until finally they became so fine that they seemed to disappear into the shimmering heat. As though to add to the magic, the nearest temple was encased in tens of thousands of tiny bells, none larger than an acorn, which, in the warm breeze, made a sound like the casting of a fairytale spell.

Veeglum strode briskly along the path, his plain green robe fluttering behind him. When he reached the temple, he mounted some crooked stone steps and stopped before the entrance. Above, the lintel was inlaid with intricate golden lettering, which read simply: THE TEMPLE OF MERISU.

He ducked into a cool dark interior and made his way between flaming torches to a staircase, which spiralled up inside the temple. For a large man Veeglum climbed with surprising lightness of foot, and he soon reached the upper levels of the temple, emerging on to a large, round landing.

He paused, looking about him at the circuit of identical wooden doors, then, seeing the one he wanted, he walked over and pushed down on the heavy bronze handle, letting himself inside. The door clunked shut behind him.

He stood in a small, dimly lit chamber, no more than ten paces long and twelve wide. In the middle was a large stone sarcophagus engraved on its end with a beautiful Yin Yang symbol, picked out in gold.

Veeglum stepped up to the great tomb and knelt before it, laying his fingers on the symbol. Just above his fingertips was an engraving, which just said:

MR ZHI
MASTER
So at last we may be one.

Veeglum bowed his head and rested it against the stone.

"I have come to say goodbye, old friend," he said softly. He was silent for a moment, as though hoping for a reply, then he added: "I have done my best, but it was not enough. Now everything rests with ze children."

Again, he paused, his voice ringing from the stone walls until it faded to nothing. Slowly, wearily, he placed both his palms on the centre of the symbol, one on the white, one on the black. He closed his eyes and became so still that he seemed almost to have stopped breathing.

The dust began to settle. Time passed without a whisper.

Then, quite suddenly, he stood and walked quickly from the room.

Moments later he was clattering down the staircase and ducking out into the light and heat. He seemed to deliberate over which path to take, then set off over some rough ground between the temples, loping at an ever-increasing pace, as though with growing resolve. As he went, he reached into his robe, pulled out his green Merisi glove and slid it over his fingers.

Soon Veeglum had passed the last of the temples and plunged back into the jungle. The sound of fairytale bells gave way once again to the overtures of the forest — the whine of cicadas, the song of birds, the hiss of wind through the leaves. He stopped for a moment, closing his eyes as if to savour these sounds, listening intently as though it might be his last time.

Abruptly he set out again, climbing towards a nearby wooded ridge. The higher he went, the quieter the forest became. There were no more cicadas, no more birds, just the hush of the wind. And now, as he neared the top of a rise, there was a new, more ominous sound.

It was the rumble of distant thumps and the booms of explosions.

57
Magrumen
of the Suhl

"It seems to be a lifelong calling, so there have been surprisingly few Magrumen of the Suhl. But it is alarming that recent years have seen so many come and go."

ASH WAS ENJOYING HIMSELF. He threw the ship left and right, conducting the winds and the sails with a flourish. He had long since sent the weary crew below to rest and so tonight, this was his ship. He steered deftly through the surge, banking on the side of waves, rushing along the furrows, leaping from the crests. This was a night for the Ash of old, the Ash that believed in miracles. Ash the Muddlemorph. Ash the prankster. Ash the Magruman of the Suhl.

The prow struck a wave and he laughed triumphantly as he was drenched by the spray. How doubtful he had felt in recent days, how uncertain of his place as captain of the ship. But *now*, now that they had found their way through the Jaws of Kemet and an entire fleet of Imperial ships, that burden was gone. Now he felt that anything was possible. Even making it to the Academy of Souls. Standing there, his crew asleep, alone in the tempest with the gleaming *Windrush* beneath his feet, even that felt possible. Even that.

His eyes were everywhere, searching the waves ahead for the best path, up in the bright rigging, admiring the majesty of the sails, and beyond to bright stars that felt closer than ever. So it was that he did not notice a movement at the hatchway nearby. He did not see the tiny, spindly legs clawing up out of the dark, nor the black coil of a shell passing under the halo of a storm lamp. He did not see the creature's careful, hesitant advance: its scurry and pause, scurry and pause. He was unaware as it reached his boot, and heaved itself up, and climbed swiftly to his shoulder. He did not even notice when it began to speak.

The difficulty was that it did not speak with a single voice. It spoke with hundreds, thousands, perhaps tens of thousands of whispers, familiar and strange, male and female, young and old. They were like a new gale blowing in the night, and Ash could not tell the natural from the conjured – the gale from the heavens and the one that came from the creature. Or, more precisely, from a shell as black as Black itself. Hidden as the whispers were, their words sounded to him like no voice at all, but thoughts.

"You are indeed a master of the waves!" said the voices. "This tempest is nothing before you, prince of the seas! Nothing at all!"

Ash glanced about him, but found that he was still alone. A smile formed at the corners of his mouth.

"Prince of the seas," he mouthed.

"More than that," breathed the voices, "you are king of the tides! And this without a crew, without Merisi Bands, or ancient tomes, or bloodlines, or Glimmers!"

Ash turned sharply and gazed into the dark. Those words did not sound like his. He peered over the stern into the dance of foam and spray. He stared long and hard at the hatchway. He even looked down at himself and stepped to one side, but there was nothing there. He could not see the small black hermit crab clinging high on his shoulder.

And yet, he thought, perhaps there *was* something to those words. Here he was, alone at the helm at night – in a storm, no less – with no help, no magical band of the Merisi, no mystical second self. His mastery of the *Windrush* was just that. And wasn't it something to behold? Ash smiled as he thought of his friends in the Mutable Inn, and his following at the Meander Mill. What would *they* think if they could see him now?

"All this with Essenfayle alone!" came the voices again in his ear. "All this without using any of the other Ways you have learned so well!"

"No one wants my tricks any more," grumbled Ash.

"Because no one wants you to be all you can be!" whispered the voices. "They call you Magruman of the Suhl to make you theirs! But you are more than that! You are more than they will ever let you be!"

Ash frowned. His hold on the winds faltered, and the ship drifted from its path. Something was wrong, but he could not quite grasp what it was. The voices had become hypnotic, intoxicating.

"What if this adventure distracts you from your destiny? Your *own* answer to the division of the worlds?" There was a pause. "What if you are the very first Master of the *Four* Ways?"

Ash almost laughed, but something about those words spoken in voices old and wise, young and adoring, feminine and alluring, found its way to his heart.

He lifted his chin and squared his shoulders. "Master of the Four Ways," he repeated as though trying it on for size.

The *Windrush* sped on into the night. The storm was at its height now, its winds snatching at the sails, its waves lashing at the hull, but Ash stood tall and steady at the helm, directing it all with an ever bolder sweep of his arms and an ever brighter gleam in his eye. And, all the while, the black crab whispered sweet enchantments in his ear.

§

"We're beginning our descent, sir," said the pilot over the intercom. "Check your seatbelt — it could be a bumpy ride."

Paiscion chuckled, grimly amused that the pilot was still worried about a seatbelt when the world was falling down.

He rubbed his eyes and looked out of the window at the rising sun. That, at least, was a blessing. Now, he would no longer see those blooms of white fire pockmarking the blackness below. He had spent the night frustrated, cocooned in the heavens high above the fight and the fire. He had forced himself to watch the sprawling, leaping light of many battles out in the darkness, and tried his best to imagine himself there, in the fray, alongside his sisters and brothers. Because, for the moment, that was all he could do.

He had known the significance of the fire from the very first flash. He had looked down at that first fizzing, flashing crucible of light and he had murmured to himself gravely.

"*The storm of hail and fire*," he had said.

He had known too that this was Thoth's greatest triumph: a plague not even of his making — not the storm of hail and fire of the Bible, and the Qur'an, and the Torah — but a new storm for a new age. A storm for the age of science.

Now, as Paiscion watched the sun dawning over a patchwork of white and black clouds, like some bizarre chessboard in the sky, he reflected on the mastery with which Thoth was playing this game of all games. This game that only its designer could win. For centuries, while the Suhl and the Merisi had waited patiently for the Glimmer Myth to take its course, Thoth had learned, and planned, and prepared, and it had all come to this. A game of strategy that would unite the worlds, not by bringing them together but by conquest. A game chilling and relentless

393

that could only end in victory, just like the plagues of Egypt that had inspired it.

It was unfolding precisely as intended. Now, all that stood between Thoth and his victory were two children aboard a sea-weary ship, travelling to an unknown land to enact a myth of which they knew little.

And, Paiscion thought, what if the great designer had thought of that journey too? What if he had kept some small part of his master plan — one last roll of the dice — for Sylas and Naeo themselves?

"He must have thought of it," said the Magruman under his breath. "Of course he has thought of it."

The plane finally dipped below the clouds and a vista of golden desert opened up below. Most of it was featureless sand, with the exception of two rivers, which carved separate paths across the barren landscape. The greater was a greenish brown, winding like a snake from horizon to horizon. This, Paiscion knew at once, was the Nile: vast and timeless. The river that had poured life into the world.

By comparison the second was a mere trickle. It was no natural river but a winding, sinewy column of thousands upon thousands of tiny figures. From this height he could not make them out, but he knew at once that this was yet another horde of beasts playing its part in the devilish game. They seemed to spring spontaneously from the dusty wastes, from a place where there was a curious circular depression in the sands, and from there they wound their way to an isolated place far out in the desert where they pooled into a wide oblong of darkness: a vast military formation of ranks and columns.

Paiscion looked from there to the settled areas along the banks of the Nile, tapping his fist on his knee as he tried to understand.

"What are they waiting for?" he murmured.

Suddenly the intercom blared back into life. "The airports are closed, sir, because of the insects. They've set up an airstrip in the desert, but it's not meant for jets. It'll be an emergency landing so you'll need to brace yourself."

Paiscion reached tentatively for a blinking green intercom button on the console before him. "This airstrip — is it near the source of the column of beasts?"

There was a hesitation. "Not too close, but a short helicopter ride away," came the reply.

Paiscion looked again at the circular depression in the sands, then he leaned into the console.

"Good," he said. "That is precisely where I need to be."

58

The Glimmer Glass

"Of all the Things in our possession it is only the Glimmer Glass that allows us to glimpse the face that is — and is not — our own. That is why it has been so prized, and more than once, stolen."

SYLAS WOKE WITH A start and sat up, blinking into the darkness. The Bow Room was quiet and still, and in his groggy state it took him a moment to realise what the noise had been. The Samarok had slipped from his chest in his sleep, landing with a thump on the deck at his side. He sighed and sank with relief back on to his mattress.

For a moment his dream flickered at the edge of his mind: glimpses of arid hills and sandstone tunnels, of caverns echoing with the chants of priests and a rumble deep in the belly of the world. But, like all dreams, it was quickly snuffed out. In its place came a memory all too real and close. It spoke to him in a voice — one that he trusted above all others.

"I worry deeply about what this will mean for you... for me... for everyone else."

Sylas groaned and rolled on to his side, his stomach tightening as he remembered more and more of the conversation he had had with his mother. He opened his eyes, hoping to turn his mind to something else. His gaze rested on the darkest corner of the room and the jumble of Paiscion's curious Things. There was a long, thin object that looked like a bunched umbrella, and a toy train and a kettle, and many other items that would have been considered bric-a-brac back home. But among them one Thing stood out from all the rest. It was the grand old chair in which he once had sat, looking into the Glimmer Glass, with Paiscion at his shoulder.

Sylas's eyes drifted inevitably from that to the bright sheen of the mirrors themselves, mounted on opposite walls of the Bow Room.

He frowned and then opened his weary eyes wide.

In the centre of the mirror with the white frame there was a face staring right back at him.

It was Naeo.

She glowed palely in the silver pane, her features set in a quizzical expression, as though she had asked Sylas a question and was waiting for the answer.

He rose on one elbow and glanced about. Almost at once he saw her standing in the shadows. She had her back to him as she gazed into the mirrors. He looked at her face in the white frame and felt a sudden surge of adrenalin.

Somehow he knew why she was there. She had come to speak to him.

He sat up and glanced across at Simia. She was still fast asleep on her back, snoring faintly, her limbs splayed wide. For the first time he and Naeo were truly alone together.

He pushed back the blanket and rose quietly to his feet, taking care not to wake Simia, then he tiptoed across the Bow Room to where Naeo was standing. She seemed to be waiting for him, but she did not turn round. She continued to stare into the Glimmer Glass.

He was surprised by his nerves as he took his place at her shoulder, but there was no discomfort round the Merisi Band, no feeling of his insides slipping out of place. Even so, he did not look into Naeo's face — not directly. Instead he looked into the mirrors.

From here the shimmering panes each showed two images: one of his own face looking straight back, and one of Naeo's looking aside. In this way, each was able to look at the other without their eyes ever meeting. *That* was why she was using the Glimmer Glass, Sylas thought excitedly. In the mirrors, their connection was somehow tamed.

He saw her as he had first seen her in the Glimmer Glass, before they had even found one another. She had a narrower, finer face than his own, with smoother, paler skin. Otherwise she was so much like him.

He was unsure how long they had been staring at each other when Naeo finally spoke.

"You feel... *different*," she said. To his surprise, Sylas knew what she was going to say next even before she said it. "You feel further away."

He found himself answering before she had even finished. "You do too."

"You're not sure any more, are you?" Naeo shot back. "About any of it."

"No."

"Because of your mum."

"Yes."

The exchange of words had happened in an instant, one answering before the other had finished.

Naeo's head tilted inquisitively. "Why?"

"Because she's right. Because we don't know what this will mean. We don't know that we won't do more harm than good."

"We don't know that we *will* either."

"But I saw what knowing her Glimmer did to her day after day."

For some moments Naeo said nothing. She could not see his memories, but she felt how they made him feel.

"Maybe she wasn't *supposed* to know her Glimmer. Not then. Not like that."

"Even if that's right, and it might not be, what about everyone else?" He glanced behind at Simia's sleeping figure. "How can you be sure it'll be all right for Simia? For everyone else on this ship? For everyone in the valley?"

Naeo started to answer before the words had died on his lips, and this time she surprised him.

"Because I'm not frightened."

"*Frightened?*" blurted Sylas.

"Yes, frightened, like you and your mum."

For a moment Sylas simply gaped at her. "Well, let's say I *am* scared," he said, his cheeks reddening. "Why aren't you?"

"Because I'm thinking about the good and not the bad."

"The *good*? What does that mean?"

Naeo answered in a heartbeat. "I'm thinking about the first time Espasian told me about you, how just the thought of you filled me with hope; how, ever since I knew you were there, that hope has always been there too. Even in the darkness, in the Dirgheon. Because I wasn't alone. Because I wasn't beaten. Because there was some other part of me out there, living another life. Someone who knew a whole world I didn't know. Someone who might save me." She glanced across at him, not in the mirrors, but directly into his face. "And you did. You came to the Dirgheon and you were strong when I had nothing left. Remember?"

Sylas's mind raced through his own memories. He remembered how Naeo had visited him in his dreams, and encouraged him, and drawn him on. How he had felt sure of his journey just because she was there. How he had trusted her to go in his place to find his mother. How she had helped him, just as he had helped her.

He turned away from the mirrors and looked at her full in the face. At once any thoughts of arguing died away. Her eyes were full of tears.

"I *believe* in you, Sylas," she said quietly.

And he found himself saying: "I believe in you too, Naeo."

59

Opposites

"It seems to me that all opposites, *when taken together, complete a whole. What is a top without a bottom? A front without a back? What is night without day? Is not any year made up of both summer and winter? So it is with ourselves and our Glimmer. Only together are we truly whole."*

DRESCH STRODE ACROSS HER laboratory to the window and paused with her hand on the blind pull. The sun was blazing outside, but there was a peculiar quality to the light, making the buildings and tents of the military camp look colourless and drab, like in an old photograph. The overhang of clear sky too looked different. It was not the vivid cobalt blue to be expected on a cloudless summer afternoon, but faded and dull.

She heard yet another rally of thumps and booms coming from the south-west, and she saw shrouds of black smoke climbing into the wide spaces, forming dark smears across the horizon. In their midst, a single black swarm warped and contorted itself round the smoke, seemingly untouched by the explosions.

"Fools!" exclaimed Dresch. She let the blind drop with such force that it nearly wrenched itself from the wall.

She turned and crossed her arms, gazing at the pleasing

orderliness of her lab. Almost at once she felt calmer. She found the fluorescent lights oddly comforting after thousands of days in windowless rooms, poring over microscopes, test tubes and notebooks. Nearby she saw another comfort: her trusty slippers nestled under a workbench. She kicked off her boots and, with a sigh of relief, slipped them on. Then she eased herself out of her army jacket and unwound her large muddy poppy scarf before straightening it out and wrapping it round her like a shawl. Another of her rituals.

She rolled a chair on its castors over to the gigantic phial of Black and sat back, staring at the huge glass container. She tilted her head a little to one side, as though pondering a puzzle.

She had been like that for a full twenty minutes when Lucien finally returned. He let the doors swing closed behind him and stood in the shadows at the end of the room. Dresch could see at once that he had failed. His expression was grim and his body language dejected.

"No luck?" she called.

"Same as all the rest," he said, walking towards her. "I was sure my old captain would at least hear me out, but he just said the same thing." He put on a clipped, upper-class accent: " *'You don't expect us to stand by and do nothing, do you, Corporal? You Merisi sorts have had your chance — now leave the fight to us!'* " Lucien tutted in disgust. "They haven't the slightest clue what they're dealing with!"

"I know," said Dresch, turning back to the Black. "Though, of course, neither do we." She wrapped her scarf even more tightly round her. "So that's them all," she said. "It's like you said — none of them will listen."

"Well, we had to try," said Lucien as he drew up a chair and sat down next to her. He followed her eyes to the giant glass column of Black. "What are you doing?"

She leaned forward, her elbows on her knees. "It's all about the Black," she said. "It's more important than anything else, I know it is. But what is it? And why is it here?"

Lucien picked up an apple from a nearby half-eaten packed lunch. "You're the scientist," he said, taking a bite. "But I must admit, right now, I'm still more concerned about things that buzz, bite and bang."

Dresch's eyes flickered with irritation. "But, James, the Black came before everything else. And now..." She trailed off, struggling to organise her thoughts. "Well, hasn't it occurred to you that the other plagues might be *linked* to it somehow?"

"How do you mean?"

She shrugged. "The beasts and the insects are black too, for one thing. Surely *that's* not a coincidence?"

Lucien raised an eyebrow. "Aren't insects normally black?"

She looked at him long and hard. "You idiot! No, they aren't! They're every colour from black to brown to green to bright blazing red! But not these. These are black. All of them. Billions of them. Jet-black, just like the Black itself. And so are the other creatures we've seen — the Ghorhund, the Ghor, those apelike creatures. Black — all of them. If not completely black, then mostly black."

Lucien tossed the apple core into a wastepaper bin. "So you're saying... what? That they're all *made* of the Black?"

Dresch sighed and slumped back in her chair. "Truth is, I don't know what I'm saying." She glared at the cylinder. "I know I don't make any sense, but maybe that's because this stuff doesn't make any sense either! Not *scientific* sense anyway. You saw all the experiments we did." She gestured at the workbenches cluttered with test tubes and Petri dishes. "It's like it's... unknowable. Which itself shouldn't be possible. The foundation of science is that *everything* is knowable."

Lucien sat in silence for some moments, staring at the Black. Then he narrowed his eyes. "Maybe that's the point," he said.

Dresch looked at him, intrigued. "Meaning..."

"What if it *is* unknowable," he said with mounting confidence, "and what if that's why it's here?" He got to his feet and started pacing up and down. "What does science mean, Martha? The word science?"

She opened her hands. "Knowledge."

"Yes! And what's the main difference between the two worlds?"

"As I understand it, they use the Three Ways, four if you include Essenfayle. We use only one — science."

"That's right! Science! Knowledge!" exclaimed Lucien, walking over to the cylinder. "So what if Thoth has sent the Black because it *is* unknowable, because that's exactly what we're least able to defend against? Science is about using reason and — and observation to cast light on things, right?"

She nodded.

"Well, the Black is about the dark! The things we can never know!" He peered through the glass. "If this stuff is made by the Three Ways, then who says it'll *ever* be understood? And what do you get when something can't be understood?"

Dresch thought for a moment. "Ignorance? Doubt?"

"Yes, yes, those things, and also..."

She shook her head, struggling to follow.

He tutted impatiently. "What's worse than doubt?"

Dresch leaned forward. "Fear?"

"Fear!" exclaimed Lucien triumphantly. "And what happens when we're frightened?"

"We run," said Dresch. "And — and if we can't run we fight. And the more we fight..."

"The more we feed the Black!" Lucien's eyes burned with

conviction now. "The Suhl had their Undoing, and this is ours! Do you see? The plagues are just a means to an end!"

Dresch's eyes danced from side to side as she pieced together the puzzle. She lifted her hand to the phial of Black.

"The Undoing of science itself," she said.

The lab was eerily quiet. Lucien leaned against the cylinder of Black while Dresch sat staring vacantly at a dripping tap in the corner. The room was filled with the distant rumble of explosions and a solitary siren. Its thin voice wailed across the camp, piercingly loud, but it seemed to Dresch hopelessly inadequate for the task. *There ought to be a chorus of sirens*, she thought, *a legion of them sounding from every rooftop and hilltop and treetop to the world's end, so that everyone and everything might hear.*

"Of course, if we're right," said Lucien, breaking into her musings, "the real question is where does it all end?"

She drew her eyes to him. "I'm starting to think I don't want to know how it ends."

He nodded. "Unless it ends with Sylas and Naeo."

She gave a weak smile. "Yes. Yes, of course."

Suddenly her gaze shifted from Lucien's face to his gloved hand resting on the glass cylinder. Her eyes grew wide.

Lucien felt a jolt of fear. Slowly he turned and looked at his hand.

There, beneath his fingers, the Black was in turmoil. It rolled back from his glove, creating a churn so violent that it had somehow hollowed out a space within the cylinder: a pocket of nothingness directly beneath his hand. He shifted the velvet glove across the glass and the turbulence moved too, leaving the empty space beneath his palm.

Silently Dresch reached into her pocket and pulled out her green velvet glove. She slipped it over her fingers and, without a word, stepped up beside Lucien, carefully placing her palm on the other side of the cylinder. The Black responded instantly, leaping up the container to find space. They could hear it slap against the glass, gurgling and boiling.

Dresch leaned in, staring at the tumult. "I was thinking as a scientist, not as Merisi," she murmured. "It didn't occur to me to try the glove!"

She frowned at the silver-gold embroidery on the back, then lifted her hand, turned it over and pressed the gleaming threads against the glass.

A great surge of Black rolled up the cylinder, hitting the sides with such force that Lucien had to grasp it with both arms to prevent it from toppling. As his glove touched the glass, the oily swell hurtled up and punched at the steel stopper. To his relief, the seal held.

They exchanged a look of bewilderment.

"It's the threads on the glove!" exclaimed Lucien. "The threads of Quintessence! It's like they're opposites!"

Dresch shook her head. "In Nature, opposites normally *attract*. It's *alike* things that repel." She gazed at the churning Black, fascinated. "It's more like they're two parts of the same thing. The same but different."

Lucien stepped back from the cylinder, looking it up and down. "The same but different," he murmured. "Like a Glimmer."

They exchanged another look.

"Everything in the two worlds has a counterpart," said Dresch. "Why not them?" She thought for a moment, turning the glove so that the Quintessence thread gleamed in the artificial light. She ran a finger over it, at once cool and warm, soft and hard. She looked up at Lucien. "Do you think this might help us?"

He considered this for a moment. "I'm not sure. A few Merisi gloves against all that Black? Against everything?"

Dresch waved her gloved hand before the cylinder and

watched the Black heave in response. "But this is *something*, isn't it?"

He nodded. "It is."

She turned to him. "And really what else do we have? If nobody's going to listen to us, what are we doing here? Shouldn't we be out there?" She lifted her gloved hand. "With these?"

"We've *been* out there, Martha," said Lucien doubtfully. "Honestly I think the only hope we have now is Sylas and Naeo."

She frowned. "Yes, but, James, we're *Merisi*! We can't just wait this out! Hope for the best!"

He said nothing.

Her face fell, then she reached for her coat and pulled it so roughly that her seat almost tipped over. "Fine!" she snapped, her voice quavering. "I'll go alone!"

Lucien grabbed her hand. "Wait, Martha! I just don't want you to get hurt!" He turned her to face him and softened his voice. "Really I don't."

She gazed at him for a moment with red-rimmed eyes and hesitated.

"Especially if it won't make a difference," said Lucien.

She stiffened, a tear streaking down her cheek. "We don't know that it won't! Just like Tasker didn't. Or Mr Zhi. Or — or the others. It's just what we have to do!"

And then, to his astonishment, she threw her arms about him and buried her head in his shoulder. Lucien was taken entirely by surprise, but he pulled her close, first on instinct and then because he wanted to hold her, and be held.

"I know," he said softly. "A time of sacrifice."

She tightened her embrace.

Neither of them was sure how long they stood like that, listening to the explosions and the solitary wail of the siren. For that short while time seemed to leave them be.

Finally Lucien said, "It's quite a thought, isn't it? That somewhere, in another world, there's a part of us that's safe."

Dresch looked up with bleary eyes. "And that tomorrow we'll know who they are," she said with a crooked smile.

They held one another for a few moments more, until there was nothing else to be done. And then together they gathered their things and left.

60

Together, Alone

*"I always felt it, but I feel it even more acutely now
that I know: that sense that even when I am surrounded
by people — even family or the closest friends —
that on some level I am* together, alone *."*

SYLAS FELT THE DARKNESS lean and sway. In the distance, he
heard the rush and thump of waves. He tried to push them away,
to return to the inviting warmth of sleep, but an image fought its
way into his mind.

It was Naeo standing at the Glimmer Glass with tears in her
eyes.

"*I* believe *in you*," she had said.

And then, with a gasp of the cold, briny air, he was awake.

He sat up and looked straight at the Glimmer Glass. Its twin
panes were cold and empty. Naeo was nowhere to be seen. Sylas
saw that the door to the corridor was shut, as he had left it, and
Simia was still spreadeagled on her back, snoring softly. He was
just beginning to wonder if Naeo's visit had been a dream when
he noticed that the Samarok was missing. *Of course*, he thought.
She took it!

He lay back and tried to remember everything about their

409

encounter. He recalled their quickfire exchanges; how he had known what she was asking even as she asked it; and how, in turn, she had seemed to know his mind almost as well as he. But most of all he remembered that last thing she had said. It had taken his breath away.

"I believe in you," he murmured.

Knowing how Naeo felt — knowing how he himself felt, that he was not alone, that he was, and always had been, more — Sylas felt his confidence returning. He knew what they had to do.

Everyone should know their Naeo, he thought, *and they should be known back*.

Everyone should have the chance to know and believe in themselves just like the two of them.

His last memory of the night was in the Bow Room when Naeo had spied the Samarok.

"*Do you think I can read the Ravel Runes?*" she had asked.

"*I know you can*," he had said, picking it up and giving it to her.

He turned over these dreamlike memories until his eyelids once again became heavy. Dimly he noticed the dark blue-grey of early dawn through the porthole. *That's strange*, he thought. His shift should have begun long ago. Ash must be about to wake him. He made a vague effort to fight back his sleepiness, pushing away the blanket, but when he felt the cold he pulled it up again for one last minute of warmth.

Moments later he was asleep.

§

Naeo woke feeling cold and quickly pulled her blanket up round her chin. She lay, empty-headed and groggy for a moment, but then she glanced over at the porthole and saw that the night was no longer black but a dreary, pre-dawn grey.

In a trice, she was awake. Ash should have finished his shift by now. She was about to throw back her blanket and swing out of the hammock when she saw the Samarok next to her, the gems on its cover winking between the folds of the blanket.

She lay back and picked up the ancient book.

Just for a moment, she told herself.

She raised her knees and let the book settle against her thighs. Slowly she pulled back the cover and stared at the handwritten scrawl on the first page. The lettering seemed familiar and she felt sure that it would make some sense, but the more she tried to read, the more confused she became. Just as she started to think she might not be able to decipher it at all, she thought of Sylas.

"*I know you can*," he had said.

Naeo frowned and stared hard at the page. Once again she tried to read the opening passage, and this time she did her best to see now as he would see, to read as he would read. She pictured the stars as she had seen them through his eyes, tried to remember his certainty that he would understand.

She felt a stirring of excitement. Slowly at first the Ravel Runes began to reveal themselves: no longer a confusing scrawl but a succession of exquisite, elegant symbols, their strokes and coils interlocked in a magical weave. She moved her eye along the line, and before long, to her astonishment, she found that she was mouthing words. Words that were not her own.

She pushed herself up in the hammock and leaned over the page. She was trembling with excitement. She was reading the Samarok, a book she had learned about in school and heard whispered of in secret meetings. Now it was there in her lap, ready to reveal its forbidden truths.

Her eyes skipped along, reading quickly now, the mysterious words forming swiftly. The contents of the first page were oddly familiar, as though she had read them before, so she leafed on until she found a passage that was of more interest. She began to read under her breath.

"So they remained for years that became decades, decades that became a lifetime. They worked without the warmth or succour of the world above, confined until they had discovered the prize commanded by their king: the defence for all Kemet that would one day be known as the Ramesses Shield.

"In 'Of Souls and Sacrifice', Merisu explains that the only communal space within the Academy of Souls open to all of the priests and their followers was a central hall known as the Truth Chamber, so called because this was where the fruits of their learning were to be shared and recorded. Since Thoth was the scribe to the gods, all discussions were recorded by Zamon, the Priest of Souls from the Temple of Thoth in Khemenu. So extensive were these writings of Zamon over the years that followed, the Truth Chamber became an extensive library."

Naeo's fingertip traced the name Zamon and then slid across to *the Priest of Souls from the Temple of Thoth.* She lifted her eyes to the pale glow of the porthole.

"Zamon," she whispered, listening to the sound.

So that was Thoth's true name, before he had taken the name of his god. The word formed so easily on her tongue, and yet surely it should have burned on being spoken. The name that came before everything. The man before he became the Dirgh. Thoth himself.

She read on.

"The Truth Chamber housed the entrance to the most feared of the forgotten ways within the network of caves, known as Ammut's Pit. This was the resting

place of the ancient dead: a labyrinth of vaults, cells and catacombs that led deep into the earth, housing the dust and bones of countless generations of Kemetians. The labyrinth was named after the mythical beast of judgement, Ammut, who would devour the souls of the unworthy and allow those of a true heart to pass on into the afterlife.

"The Priests of Souls used the pit to judge their own worthiness. On their first arrival, and every third year thereafter, each of the priests was taken blindfolded deep into Ammut's Pit and there left alone, without light or provision. It is said that only true masters of the elements – earth, air, fire and water – would find their way safely back to the Truth Chamber. Over the years, three of the Priests of Souls were lost..."

A sudden movement at the porthole caught Naeo's eye and she stopped mid-sentence. She set the Samarok aside and drew closer to the glass.

To her astonishment, she saw trees and bushes whisking past, no more than a ship's-length away. So swiftly did they pass that Naeo's eyes had to dance backwards and forwards to glimpse them.

She launched herself from the hammock, pulled on some fresh clothes and ran out of the door, just in time to see Sylas and Simia disappearing up the ladder.

The ship suddenly lurched, throwing her into the wall of the passage, but Naeo ran on until she reached the ladder and then scrambled up towards the light.

61

The Delta

"The limits of the delta mark a boundary between the inhospitable desert and beauty, opulence and plenty."

SYLAS EMERGED BLINKING INTO a cool, fresh morning and was struck at once by the smell. It was nothing like the bracing, sulphury smell of the sea, but rich — almost sweet — and heavy with the scent of greenery. He squinted into the light and turned about, trying to understand what was happening.

To his astonishment, they were no longer at sea at all, but on a river. His first thought was that it must be the Nile, the great river that was to take them southwards to the Academy of Souls. But he quickly saw that this was no grand waterway as he imagined the Nile to be. It was a narrow, overgrown channel bordered by marshes and sprawling mangroves. The ship had to lurch to avoid sandbanks and dense tropical thickets, which lay all about them.

Sylas heard raised voices from the helm, and he turned to see a gathering of the crew badgering their captain with questions. Ash seemed to be ignoring them, apparently far more interested in the workings of the winds and the ship.

"But we won't stand a chance of getting through!" protested the loudest member of the crew, stepping in front of the captain in an attempt to get his attention. He held up a wrinkled parchment. "According to the map, the delta is heaving with villages and towns, to say nothing of the Imperial garrisons!"

"Aye, and these waters are a labyrinth," said an older man gloomily as he pored over another document. "There isn't one of us has been through it before! Fawl might have known a way, but not us! "

Ash turned to him. "We have those charts," he said crisply. "Fathray made sure we had all the maps we need."

"But, Ash — sir," said a small woman at the rear of the group, "shouldn't we at least talk about this? I mean properly, with Sylas and Naeo?"

"For the fourth time," said Ash, his tone unusually irritable, "I didn't have a choice! I saw an Imperial fleet led by the *Mesektet* itself. Do you know what that means? It means Thoth is here personally, with all the forces he brings with him. If we hadn't ducked into this byway, we'd have been captured!"

"But the lookout didn't see anything," said the first crew member.

"And I'll be speaking to her about that later!" snapped the young captain. "But for now kindly return to your posts! I have a ship to sail and you're making it no easier!"

They all hesitated.

"NOW!" yelled Ash.

The group scattered in all directions, glancing back in astonishment at how Ash had spoken. It was not his way, and neither was it the way of the Suhl.

Simia leaned in to Sylas's ear. "What got *his* goat?"

"It might be my fault," said Sylas with a twist of remorse. "I should've taken over at least an hour ago."

They heard a clatter on the steps behind them and then Triste's bald head emerged from the hatchway. He climbed out, his eyes shifting quickly from the passing scenery to the scattering crew, and finally to Ash. He gazed at the young captain for a moment, as if intrigued, then he spied Sylas and Simia and walked over.

"What's going on?" he asked, in a low voice.

Sylas quickly explained what they had heard, adding: "Ash seems really…" He shrugged. "I don't know… just not himself. I feel terrible — Naeo and I were supposed to take over ages ago."

The Scryer pursed his lips thoughtfully, then patted Sylas's arm and walked across to Ash. He stepped in close to the young captain and placed a gentle hand on his shoulder, saying something softly in his ear. Ash nodded and the two had a brief conversation, after which Triste walked swiftly to the hatch and disappeared below.

Sylas and Simia glanced at one another, wondering what was going on.

"Come on," said Simia, setting out for the helm.

To their relief, Ash greeted them with one of his customary grins. "Morning!" he said as though he hadn't a care in the world.

"I'm really sorry, Ash," said Sylas. "This should've been our shift. I didn't sleep so well and I just—"

Ash held up a hand. "It was my decision," he insisted. He winced as he guided the *Windrush* through a particularly narrow stretch of the channel. "Truth is, I enjoyed having the ship to myself for a while. You know, wind in my hair… no one in my ear!"

Sylas had the feeling that something was wrong. Ash seemed oddly cheerful, especially in light of his argument with the crew.

"Is it true?" he asked. "Did you see the fleet?"

Ash nodded. "Right ahead of us and with the *Mesektet* out in front."

"What's the *Mesektet*?" asked Simia.

"Thoth's flagship. The mightiest vessel in the Empire."

"And you think Thoth was onboard?" asked Sylas.

Ash shrugged. "Can't be *sure*, but the *Mesektet* doesn't go far without him."

"So he was *waiting* for us?" said Sylas.

"Waiting for us or following us," said Ash. "That's why I had to go in this way, through the delta. It's the last thing he'd expect."

"Why?" asked Simia.

"Because it's difficult to get through," said Ash matter-of-factly. "A delta is where a river spreads into lots of smaller waterways as it reaches the sea. The channels are shallow and narrow, like this one. But the good thing for us is that they're easy to hide in."

"And... get lost in?" suggested Simia.

Ash's eyelids flickered. He was about to say something when they again heard footsteps on the ladder. Triste climbed back on deck, carrying a large, rolled parchment. He walked over and placed the document down at their feet.

"All right," he said, unfurling it to reveal a large map showing mountains, deserts and waterways. "Here's Fathray's map of the northern part of the Nile." He pointed to a thick blue line that ran up the spine of the map. "This is the Nile, which runs from the south, the bottom of the map, to the north at the top. And here's the delta." He laid his finger at the very top where the Nile fanned out into a maze of tiny, intricate blue lines.

Ash lowered his hands and allowed the winds to die away until the *Windrush* settled down into the green waters. He looked behind and then ahead, to where the channel passed alongside a cliff face, snaking between sandbanks and, seemingly satisfied that nothing was approaching, he squatted down next to Triste and pored over the map. Sylas and Simia leaned in behind them, and Naeo, who until now had been listening at a discreet distance, came over to take a look. Some of the nearby crew also joined the group.

Everyone gazed in dismay at the labyrinth of rivulets. Taken as a whole, the Nile looked like a colossal tree, its giant trunk rising from the bottom of the map until it spanned out into waterways and byways, like the limbs and branches.

"How are we supposed to find our way through *that*?" murmured Simia.

"We could do with Fawl now," muttered someone else.

Sylas pointed to the nearest of the tiny inscriptions. "Are these all villages and towns?" he asked, wondering at the number of them. They were everywhere, not just along the trunk of the Nile, but right through the delta.

"I'm afraid so," said Triste. "It doesn't look like there's any way through without passing at least a score of them — more perhaps." He glanced at Ash. "You're sure this is the only option?"

The young captain shrugged. "Unless we want to sail straight into Thoth's fleet."

Triste lowered his eyes back to the map. "But, if the *Mesektet* is headed down the Nile, her route will be much more direct. She's sure to reach the academy long before we do. Thoth will be ready for us."

There was another gloomy silence.

Simia walked her hands across the map and peered closely at the delta. "Where do you think we are exactly?"

Ash expelled a lungful of air and leaned over. His finger drifted out across the map, circled for a moment and then pointed. "There, I think. We came in on the first of the broader channels."

All eyes settled on one particular blue line, which snaked across the corner of the map.

"Yes, that's it," said a crew member. She pointed. "We've already passed that sharp bend. And that other smaller channel."

Simia placed her fingertips on the map again, spreading them over the surrounding complex of channels. "Look at them," she said thoughtfully. "They're like a maze." She raised her eyes to Sylas. "A bit like the ditches on the Barrens."

Sylas thought back to the network of dusty rifts and dried riverbeds that crazed the Barrens. "I suppose so," he said, frowning. "Why?"

Simia sat back on her haunches. "Well, think about it. We managed to feel our way through those ditches in the dark, right? Just by following our instincts."

Sylas nodded.

"So who says you can't do that here?"

He glanced back down at the map and then gave a half-laugh. "It's hardly the same thing, Simsi."

"So what? I saw what you can do! You didn't have to see your way, Sylas. You knew what was coming, no matter how fast we went, no matter how dark it was! You just felt it!"

Sylas stared at her. "And you really think we could feel our way through *this*?"

"Why not? And, with Naeo's help, you could be fast too!" she said, becoming excited. "So fast that it doesn't matter what we pass along the way – by the time they see us, we'd be gone! We might even be fast enough to beat the *Mesektet*!"

"But, Simsi, you *knew* the Barrens," reasoned Sylas. "You knew the direction we had to take. We don't know *anything* about the Nile."

"We have the map!" she retorted. "And I was thinking, because these are a bit like the ditches in the Barrens, I could be a pretty good navigator! I can point the way, just like Triste did when we were leaving the valley!"

Ash eyed Simia carefully, then looked at Sylas. "So, what do you think?"

Sylas was very far from sure, but he was also very aware of Simia's glare. "It could work, I suppose," he said.

"It will work," came a voice from behind. Everyone turned to see Naeo, chin high, her expression full of resolve. She flicked back her hair. "Well, it has to be worth a go, doesn't it? One thing's for sure: we're lost if we don't do something special and Simia's idea could be it."

"Right!" said Simia, beaming at Naeo.

Ash stood up and sighed. "All right," he said, sounding far from confident. "Let's try it."

62

The Serpent of Wadjet

*"This grand edifice was engraved with a gigantic
snake entwined with papyrus representing the great
Serpent of Wadjet or the so-called 'Lady of Imet',
protector of the Nile delta."*

SYLAS GRIPPED NAEO'S HAND tightly. The banks of the river
were so terrifyingly close that his impulse was to ease the winds
and slow the *Windrush* down, not to fill the sails and hurtle on.
But he forced himself to trust his other instincts. He felt for the
smooth, sluggish waters, and the low forests passing in a blur, and
for Naeo because, if he could not be sure of himself, he could at
least be sure of her.

The grand old ship was skipping lightly over the surface as she
approached the first bend. Naeo closed her hand in Sylas's, her
heart thumping, her breath coming short and sharp. But she did
not stay with those things because, by now, she knew better than
that. Instead she felt outwards, to the roots and sand of the banks,
and the silty currents, and Sylas.

As the ship swept into the turn, Naeo's pulse slowed and she breathed deep and long. All around her the winds rolled, twisting the sails about the masts so that the *Windrush* leaned precariously into the bend. Beneath her, the lines of the keel caught the surface of the river, carving a new seething, frothing path, propelling her in a tight arc.

"Yes!" cried Simia from the bow, wrestling with the map. "Yes, that's it!"

And then the *Windrush* was clear, careering down a stretch of open water. She had barely lost any speed, and thickets and marshes flashed past in a streak of colour. A new bend in the river was already upon them, but here it divided, one larger channel leading away to the left, another narrow one to the right.

Simia jabbed her arm towards the channel on the right.

"Are you sure?" cried Naeo anxiously. "That's so narrow!"

Simia gesticulated to the right so violently that she almost toppled over the bow. "I'm the one with the map, aren't I?" she yelled.

So Sylas and Naeo diverted the winds and turned the sails, and over the ship went, sweeping the surface of the river so that she left a perfect curving penstroke of foam behind her. They heard the scrape of a sandbank, a sharp cry as someone was struck by a branch and then, as suddenly as it had come upon them, the junction was disappearing off the stern.

Sylas squeezed Naeo's hand excitedly.

"Left!" hollered Simia, punching the air.

And so the *Windrush* turned: left then right — right then left. The waters of the Nile washed up the banks behind them, the mangroves and bushes hissing in the breeze, and then they were gone.

They banked and turned, listed and yawed so violently that the crew had to brace themselves against ropes and rails, struggling to hold on. Amelie, who had come up from her cabin, wedged herself in the hatchway and watched everything with marvelling eyes. Ash, meanwhile, stood alone in the stern, seeming oddly unmoved as he fiddled absently with a shiny black shell that he had discovered in his pocket. By contrast, at the other end of the ship, Simia threw her arms about with such abandon that she was kept aboard only by the steadying hand of Triste, who had positioned himself behind her.

"Keep it up, Simsi!" he whispered as Simia's eyes danced between the map and the river ahead.

They continued like this for some minutes, only occasionally cutting a corner too close — or not close enough — and glancing against a bank, a log or a clump of mangroves. But each time the shining hull of the *Windrush* shrugged off the obstacle, corrected her path and flew on.

As they passed between two forested hills, Triste suddenly leaned past Simia and over the railing. He narrowed his eyes, then touched his temple with a finger, muttering something under his breath. Then he wheeled about.

"There's a town ahead!" he yelled down the length of the *Windrush*. "I can see people! Lots of them!"

Sylas and Naeo felt a pulse of panic but, knowing that everything depended on it, they stayed with the winds and each other. Sylas glanced at Ash, wondering if he would tell them to stop, but Ash met his eyes and said nothing.

The crew craned forward over the railing, looking out for some sign of a village or town, but all they could see were more trees, scrub and swamp. Then the lookout bellowed down from the crow's nest.

"Smoke!"

Sure enough, on the starboard side, a grey-brown cloud hung low over a forest of palm trees.

"We should go another way!" cried one of the crew.

Another called out in agreement, but the *Windrush* was whisking along at such speed that some of the smoke was already overhead. They could smell it now, not like the smoke of home but infused with the rich, spicy scents of the tropics.

Sylas glimpsed straight-edged shapes through the palm trees: buildings, scores of them, lining the banks.

"Turn back!" someone yelled.

"No!" Triste shouted down the ship. "There are no Scryers! They don't know we're coming! Go faster if you can!"

Sylas and Naeo leaned a little closer as they lost themselves in the hot wind, and the tepid waters, and the bright sails of the *Windrush*.

Simia lowered herself in the bow, gripping Triste's arm. The crew huddled together, most peering fearfully ahead, but some looking back at Sylas and Naeo. They were a wondrous sight, their joined hands lost in a shining halo, their faces set, their features more alike than ever before. Amelie showed no interest in the town, but watched only her son and Naeo.

Then the *Windrush* was there. So quickly were they upon the settlement that the crew saw everything in fleeting images and snatched sounds. They saw crouching, windowless huts made of mud or clay, and other grander buildings with two floors, latticed windows and whitewashed roofs. They spotted a plaza paved with red clay tiles, surrounded on all sides by what looked like statues of strange creatures, half man, half beast. And, at the centre of the plaza, they spied a flagpole higher than any of the buildings, from which flew an enormous flag. Even at a glimpse, they knew it at once: the red Imperial flag, with Thoth's empty face rippling at its centre.

They heard the sounds of the town too: voices calling out words in the Old Tongue, the hubbub of a market, a bright melody played on pipes the like of which no one aboard had ever heard. But there were no cries of fright, no alarm bells, no drumming to arms. The *Windrush* passed at such speed that those who spotted a blur of gold, or felt a squall of wind, doubted that they had witnessed anything at all.

The only folk of that town disturbed by her passing were those on small fishing vessels made of reeds, which lined the water's edge. They witnessed a sudden, violent gust, a golden flash and then a long fizzing serpent of froth along the centre of the river, extending upstream and down. Seeing this, they fell to their knees and prayed to the great snake goddess Wadjet, convinced that this had been the goddess herself, protector of the delta, called forth by some terrible wrong. They asked her forgiveness — and that of the great Dirgh Thoth — before pulling up their nets and rushing in terror to the nearest bank.

63

With the Dawn

"With the dawn, we sing; with the stag, we leap..."

THE OMINOUS SOUNDS OF hacking and sawing had started long before sunrise, but it was only with the dawn that the meaning of it all became clear. The forests of the Valley of Outs were being felled.

Systematically, one by one, the beeches, birches, firs and oaks that had protected the valley for centuries — and so frustrated the enemy the day before — were being toppled. By the time the sun cleared the hills, the trees that had once crowned their heights were already gone. As the first slants of sunlight reached the lake, the Suhl lined its shore, staring in horror at the destruction. Many wept; others stood mute, barely comprehending what they were seeing.

It was only the first glimpse of a red standard flying high on one of the hills — Thoth's visage clearly visible between its folds — that finally shocked them into action. Cries of dismay echoed round the lake and, moments later, one of the commanders raised his battle horn and blew a sharp call to arms.

At once the meagre army began to gather. Everyone still able to fight bid tearful farewells to their loved ones and assembled as quickly as they could on the two long sides of the lake, seeking out their regimental standards, most of which were replacements scrawled hurriedly on scraps of fabric. Many of the exhausted warriors limped, others wore bandages and splints, but none faltered. They knew they faced impossible odds, and were without a general to lead them, but they also knew the stakes. If they could not slow this final assault, the valley would fall long before the day was done. Women, children, the old and the sick, all would be at the mercy of Thoth's beasts and mercenaries. Whatever awaited them in the forest was a small price to pay.

And so, as the horn sounded the advance, this ragtag army of the weary and the wounded marched without hesitation between the trees and disappeared.

Those left behind watched wordlessly, turning their eyes between the forest and the hilltops. Their enemy could now be seen among the splintered stumps and carcasses of the trees: in the front, the Ghor, wielding great axes with broad blades, in the rear, Ghorhund, Ragers and Hamajaks, heaving away the felled trees with yokes and chains, their bodies steaming in the cold air. Slowly, relentlessly, the front lines were edging ever forward, beginning their descent into the valley.

Filimaya stood where she had watched the sunset the night before, looking at the hundreds of frightened, anguished faces about her. Coming swiftly to a decision, she walked to the shore and turned back to face them.

"Sisters and brothers!" She made sure that everyone was listening before continuing. "Now, more than ever, we must stay strong and together. Our brave warriors are occupied enough without wondering where in the valley we may be, so we must take what provisions we can from our homes and the stores in Sylva, and retreat to the Hollow."

There was a murmur from the gathering, but no one moved,

seemingly reluctant to leave the place where they had bidden their loved ones goodbye. "It is the safest place for us," continued Filimaya, "and it is quite large enough for both the wounded and the well. The valley has made sure of that."

She waited for a moment and, when there was no response, she called: "Come now! Strong and together! Everyone but those on watch at the Retreat follow me!"

She set out up the stony shore towards Sylva. As she passed, she grasped the hand of one old woman who had been gazing absently at the hills and drew her gently but firmly up the slope. A few steps on she took the hand of a teenage girl with blotchy, tear-lined cheeks and led her on. Together the three of them walked forward and only when they were deep in the forest did Filimaya turn to look back. To her relief, the crowds that had been gathered on the shore were following, moving solemnly through the trees.

She let out a sigh. "Well, that's something," she said. She gave her companions a rather forced smile, then led them on, into the avenues of Sylva.

§

Faysa had been awake for almost the entire night. On the few occasions she had begun to fall asleep she had startled herself awake, her mind full of images of her father's limp body on the hillside, or Espasian running headlong into the enemy. Each time she had sat up sharply and turned to her father and to Espasian, checking their breathing, their temperature, their wounds, giving them more Salve, adjusting their blankets. But each time she found them no better than they had been a few hours before, perhaps worse. At one point in the night Espasian's breathing had become so laboured that she had called a nurse to check on him, and after he had been given new dressings and an extra blanket, she had lain, staring at him, for at least an hour as though her watchfulness alone might keep him alive.

428

By dawn, she had given up on sleep altogether. She took her father's hand and held it to her chest, hoping that perhaps her touch or the rhythm of her own breathing might help to revive him. But after another hour there was still no change. Like Espasian, his breathing was shallow, his face slack and pasty, his skin cold to the touch. She could barely believe that the vision before her was her own father: the man who would never sit still, or complain of an illness, or otherwise miss a moment of the life he so loved at his daughter's side.

Faysa could not bear to look any longer at his sallow face, and so instead she turned her eyes to the many bracelets round his wrist — the ones he had collected on his never-ending travels across the Four Lands. Each time he returned he brought with him not only a fantastic tale of his travels, but also a bracelet acquired from some curious place along the way. Such a custom had this become that now his colourful, ornate collection stretched almost to his elbow. He called them his Clinchers, since he only allowed himself to buy one when he had clinched whatever deal he had set out to strike. As Faysa had become old enough to join him on his business travels, they had developed a new custom of finding a matching bracelet for her. ("*Like links of a chain, Fay*," he used to tell her, holding up her Clincher and his, "*clinching us together!*") In this way, over the following years she built a collection of more than a dozen bands of her own.

She laid her father's hand gently at her side, and sat up in bed, pulling her bunch of bracelets over her hand. Then she began arranging them on the bedclothes: the bright blue bracelet they had purchased in Vhoskili, the city of waterfalls; the pewter one they had bartered so hard for in Hamkaris, the adopted home of the Hamajaks; the amethyst band her father had bought her in Sinci as a reward for braving Shame Pass, the perilous pathway through the Grevik Mountains; the spiralling copper snake he had acquired for her with the last silver coin left to her by his mother. For each she found the matching bracelet on her father's wrist, remembering the moment they had found them together, and the place, and the journey that had taken them there. And, as she laid out bracelet after bracelet, tears rolled down Faysa's cheeks. She worked through them until she had laid out every one and remembered every last detail of their story.

As she looked at the entire collection, she became aware that she was having to squint to make out the detail of them and, when she looked up, she saw that the strange glow-worm light that dangled a little way above her head had grown dim. When she glanced about the Hollow, she saw to her alarm that all of the lights had so dimmed, and now she could barely see more than ten beds away. Earlier she had been able to make out the other side of the Hollow quite clearly; now, it was shrouded in an ominous gloom.

Even by this dwindling light, she noticed something else that set her nerves on edge. There were shadows drifting silently down almost every aisle Faysa could see, streaming in through the entrance and passing quickly into the furthest recesses of the Hollow. She saw women and children, the elderly and the sick, all of them carrying bundles of food and clothing. She could make out few of the faces, but those she could looked pale and dazed, as though lost in some terrible dream.

And then she spotted Filimaya walking down the steps into the chamber with the last straggling few. She too was weighed down with packs of food and bedding so that she stooped, walking without her usual grace and ease. But it was not this that frightened Faysa. What struck her to the core were the tears in Filimaya's eyes.

Unconsciously she slipped her hand into her father's and held it tightly.

For some moments she watched Filimaya guiding the last of the newcomers down the central aisle until their shadows faded into the half-light. Then Faysa remembered something else of her trip to Sinci with her father all those years before. As they had made their way between the drab grey bluffs and gaping chasms of Shame Pass, and the misery of that place had started to take its toll, he had taught her a song to keep up her spirits. *"An old Suhl battle song,"* he had called it. *"Perhaps the only one there ever was."*

Faysa pulled her father's hand to her chest and reached out for Espasian's. Then, very softly, she began to sing:

"With the wind, we breathe; with the earth, we sleep,
With the dawn, we sing; with the stag, we leap.
We are the roots of the ancient trees,
We are the hills, we are the seas!
Suhl! we cry. Suhl! Suhl!

"With the hare, we run; with the gull, we cry,
With the wolf, we hunt; with the hawk, we fly..."

64

The Motherland

*"For most, the term 'Motherland' conjures a place
of belonging, sanctuary and unconditional welcome.
For the Suhl, it evokes only revulsion and fear."*

THE WINDS WERE HOT and humid, and Sylas's and Naeo's clothes
clung uncomfortably to their skin, sweat pooling between their
palms. Still they held on tight, anxious not to lose their connection
even for a moment.

The *Windrush* was flying now, skipping over the humming,
pungent waters of the delta, heaving from side to side as she veered
round bends and darted between vessels. Some of these — the
larger ones with square sails — were easy enough to spot in time,
but the smaller ones made with woven reeds kept everyone on
edge, and more than once Simia had to scream a last-minute
warning to Sylas and Naeo to avert calamity. She too was dripping
with sweat as she pointed left and right, pausing only to consult
the map, or to confer briefly with Triste at her shoulder.

Sylas allowed himself a smile at the thought that Simsi had
managed to take command of the *Windrush*. Of course she had.

And it was just as well. The delta was a labyrinth of perilous
twists and dead ends, riddled with vessels of all shapes and sizes.

But Simia and Triste were a formidable partnership. She would read the map and the river while the Scryer saw what she could not: the telltale auras, fogs and trails of people, which for him blazed bright long before anything could be seen by eye.

Already Sylas had lost count of the number of villages and towns they had passed, all of them sweeping by before he even had a chance to turn his head. Normally the first they knew of them were clusters of five or six humble huts sometimes surrounded by a wall. The nearer the centre of the town, the more substantial became the dwellings, until they were villas, painted white, decorated with hieroglyphs or grand murals depicting people and beasts in battle, or sometimes the staring visage of Thoth.

Always, in the middle of every settlement, there was a plaza – sometimes dirt, sometimes tiled, invariably centred round a gigantic flagpole like those Sylas had seen in the slums of Gheroth. And, as in Gheroth, each one was topped by Thoth's standard, his hollow eyes gazing over his homeland, as though reminding everyone that he was everywhere and that he saw all.

The other common feature of these plazas was the perimeter of statues, sometimes carved of wood, sometimes of stone, but always half human, half beast. Sylas heard the crew whispering strange names like Anubis, Wepwawet, Hathor and Ra, the names of the gods the statues represented.

As the *Windrush* darted close to one such gallery of idols, he realised with a chill that many of them looked like Thoth's own creations. There was a jackal-headed beast just like the Ghor or Ghorhund, and a baboon-headed creature that could have been a Hamajak. But the largest of all was a female goddess with the head of a cat, which looked exactly as Ash and Naeo had described Scarpia, in her new transfigured form.

"Bastet," said a senior member of the crew. "The goddess of war."

So that *was how Thoth had chosen Scarpia's new appearance*, thought Sylas.

The *Windrush* sped on, and the further she travelled into the delta, the larger and grander became the towns. The buildings at their centre rose to several storeys, topped with elegant, clay-tiled roofs. Plazas the width of several streets sprawled next to the river, and now the statues were two or three times the height of a person. The Imperial flags were no longer mounted on flagpoles, but streamed out from gigantic tapering pillars of stone topped by a pyramid.

The further they travelled into the delta, the more its sights and sounds had started to bring back the many things Naeo had learned about the Motherland as a young child. She remembered that the boats they had passed were made of acacia and cedar, and that the huts were built of reeds and mud, baked into bricks by the sun. She recalled that the bigger houses were whitewashed to reflect the heat and that their entrance halls served as a shrine to Thoth, or the lion dwarf god, Bes.

They passed through one town so large that it could have been a city, and it was here that they saw the first fortress. It had high stone walls and timber towers that looked out across the town, and what appeared to be military vessels moored at its front, two of them manoeuvring with the disciplined stroke of dozens of oars. Even here, their luck seemed to hold. The *Windrush* threaded her way safely between them and passed without cries of alarm, or the garrison beating to arms. It was only as they sped off into the distance that Naeo thought she heard the piercing note of a horn hanging in the air. Triste too briefly peered back from the ship, his brow furrowed with concentration. But whatever the noise had been it quickly faded, and both of them were soon consumed by the river once again.

As they swept through a vivid green landscape of cultivated

fields, Simia pulled Triste over to show him something on the parchment. They both hunched over it for a moment, speaking quietly to one another, then Simia turned back towards Sylas and Naeo.

"We're nearly there!" she called, breaking into a grin. "Two more turns and we'll be on the Nile!"

65

The End

"We all yearn for the end of this long journey, but do any of us know what the end might look like? And more importantly, do we know how it might feel?"

"It's like the end of the world," breathed Dresch.

"It *is* the end of the world," said Lucien.

Between wafts of thick, acrid smoke, they glimpsed hell itself. Distant palls flashed white, dappling the dark. Flares blazed, fizzing with a sulphurous glare. Searchlights sent up fingers of fire, clawing at the night. Above, a swarm of insects swelled, stretched and spilled, filling what was left of the sky. Below, the broken earth glistened with the Black, reflecting the chaos of the heavens.

Everything shook and growled and huffed like some beast of the underworld raging against its bonds.

On impulse Dresch reached out for Lucien's hand and found that he too was trembling. She looked up into his face, now white and slick with sweat, and she smiled.

"We're not going to get through this, are we?" she said.

Lucien shook his head.

She squeezed his hand. "Then, James, I'm glad I'm with you."

"Me too, Martha," he said.

They held on for a moment, then reluctantly drew their hands apart, pulling out their Merisi gloves and slipping them on.

Dresch found the touch of the silver-gold embroidery peculiarly comforting: cool and solid like metal, but also oddly supple like common thread. At the end, she thought, as her world of reason and science was undone, she had only this. It made no more sense to her than the Black, the insects or the beasts, but at least this ornament of Quintessence was beautiful and good. And for once she did not find its mysteries perplexing or frustrating; they folded about her like the glove itself, warm and close, and made her feel that she could do what needed to be done.

Together they began to walk towards the maelstrom of light and smoke, picking their way round buckled earth and brimming craters. They saw now how the Black retreated from them as it had in the laboratory, its dark surface rolling away in waves, slapping lazily against the sides.

The noise of battle seemed to intensify with every step, becoming an ear-splitting, skull-thrumming clamour, and their entire bodies shook with the convulsions of the earth. Just beyond the halo of the flares, they saw the place where once had been the serene stones of Stonehenge, now a pandemonium of fire.

Dresch felt Lucien take her hand once again, and then he was drawing her close. He held her tight to his chest, and for the briefest time she lost herself, as though there she was safe. Lucien too gave in to her, and closed his eyes, and breathed slow and easy.

After a moment he started to pull away, but she still held him tightly. She looked up at him, her face lit by a blinking white light, her hair a fiery blaze. She was so beautiful to him then. So safe and gentle — all the things that this place was not. Moments passed, he could not tell how long, and then he leaned down and tentatively they kissed. For an exquisite, precious second everything else fell away.

And then darkness became light.

At first Lucien thought it was a trick of the mind, an explosion of some inner fire, but then he felt Dresch stiffen. He realised that the blaze was burning through his eyelids and, when he tried to look, the brightness seared his eyes. He raised his hands against it, and out in the blackness he saw a perfect disc of electric light: a searchlight somewhere across the field of battle, bathing them in its glare.

"Come on!" gasped Dresch, slipping her hand into his.

They walked on together, picking their way over the broken ground, until another searchlight swept down and flooded them with a new blaze of light.

"Let them see the glove!" exclaimed Lucien, suddenly understanding. "They need to know why we're here." Then he added: "But don't let go."

"I won't," said Dresch.

They continued on into the searchlights and the din, with their Merisi gloves held high and their free hands entwined. A third searchlight fell upon them, and then a fourth, so that they could barely see anything but the light, and yet they could tell that something beyond the glare had changed. The last crump of an explosion had echoed into silence, and they could no longer hear the whine of helicopters. Now, the only sound was the low drone of the insects high above.

The searchlights converged upon them like spokes of a wheel, following their every move. But to their surprise there was no signal from the watching army, no loud-hailed command for them to halt. It was as though, at last, the soldiers knew the futility of their fight and were glad to see the Merisi's return.

Then there was a change in the sound of the swarm. For a

moment it waned, as if the insects were moving away, but then it swelled. The droning came on and on, growing in volume and filling the night until the halo of light no longer felt like a bright cocoon keeping the darkness away, but a blindfold. They could hear the insects, but could see nothing.

Dresch pulled Lucien close. "Don't go!" she exclaimed, her voice shaking.

Lucien drew her behind him so that her back was against his. They pressed against each other, wincing into the light, and listened as the drone of the insects grew louder and louder. As one, they raised their gloved hands to the skies and waited for the storm.

66

The Nile

"The mighty waters of the Nile *can truly be said to travel
between worlds: from colossal lakes and parched desert
highlands to the lands of the Pharaohs and lush fertile flats;
from the majestic temples and pyramids of Old Kemet,
to the bustling, polluted cities of our own modern Egypt."*

EVERYTHING SEEMED TO HAPPEN at once.

Sylas caught sight of a brighter passage of water just ahead, through a break in the foliage.

Simia shrieked, gesticulating wildly to one side. "No!" she screamed. "No!"

And, even as Simia's voice rang out, the *Windrush* hurtled down the final stretch of the waterway and launched out into the brightness.

There were boats everywhere: a frenzy of vessels large and small, fast and slow, each picking its way across a great expanse of muddy water so wide that it looked more like a lake than a river. Some fished along the fringes; others sailed at speed down its centre or wove across it, ferrying passengers from one bank to the other.

Into this chaos plunged the *Windrush*, skipping over the surface and careering towards the far bank.

Sylas and Naeo threw the ship into a sharp turn, the keel carving deep into the waters of the Nile. The *Windrush* banked so sharply that some of its rigging almost touched the water on the starboard side, and the crew braced themselves for impact with the opposite bank. To their relief, she cleared it with no more than a few feet to spare, but as soon as she was out of the shallows they found themselves bearing down on a decaying, deserted vessel moored at a jetty. She was much too near to be avoided, and before Sylas and Naeo could even respond the *Windrush* plunged through her flank, sending shards of wood spinning in all directions. The jetty too exploded before the *Windrush*'s gleaming prow, its planks flipping into the golden sails. Such was her pace that before any of the wreckage even had a chance to fall she was long gone, careering upstream, weaving frantically to avoid other craft.

Simia was quickly back at the bow, trying to direct them safely through the mass of vessels. They clipped two more of the larger boats, sheering the oars from one and sending the other into a spin, but somehow they got through with only taps and scrapes.

As the commercial buildings and homesteads along the banks became fewer and further between, Sylas and Naeo stood panting on the deck, breathing properly for the first time since they had entered the Nile. They could see now how truly vast it was: perhaps fifty ship-lengths wide, with banks so distant that they were just two low horizons of greenery and occasional trees. Between them a great expanse of greenish-brown water churned and swirled, sweeping relentlessly towards the sea.

The crew climbed from wherever they had braced themselves and gaped in amazement, moving wordlessly from railing to railing to stare at the surging waters.

Ash placed his hands on Sylas's and Naeo's shoulders and gave them a squeeze.

"Well done," he said. Then he lifted his head to address the crew. "Here's a river worthy of the *Windrush*, eh?"

Many of them nodded and smiled.

"Come on then!" he yelled. "Let's have her looking her best! Glovo, take a couple of others and clear the rigging there! And, Tursc, check the bow — that was some beating she took! Saltan, up the mainmast, if you please, and give the sails a once-over. While you're up there, take a look at the standard. Let's make sure the feather's flying high, eh?"

Pleased to hear their captain sounding more like himself, the crew leapt to work, scurrying in all directions, examining, repairing and fastening.

Sylas and Naeo allowed the *Windrush* to go even faster, making the most of the smooth, wide surface of the river. If she was damaged, the ship showed no sign of it, gathering such speed that her ropes sang and her timbers thrummed.

Simia and Triste left the bow and made their way back along the deck to join Sylas and Naeo. As they reached the helm, Simia nudged Sylas's shoulder.

"You did it!" she said with a grin.

Sylas smiled. "Couldn't have done it without you, Simsi."

"I know you couldn't!" she said with a flash of slightly crooked teeth.

He laughed and turned to gaze out at the great sweep of the river. "I can't quite believe we're here," he said. "Have you ever seen anything like it?"

"Not even remotely," replied Simia. "Dad used to talk about the Nile when I was little — the biggest river in the world, he said, '*the beginning and end of everything*'." She stared into the distance, lost in a memory. "I can see what he meant now."

She glanced at Sylas and seemed to come back to herself. "Have you seen them?" she asked, pointing over the side of the ship.

Sylas had been so taken up with sailing the *Windrush* that he had paid little attention to the banks of the river. He blinked in the direction she was pointing and, at first, saw nothing unusual. "Seen... what?"

Simia jabbed her finger. "Those!"

He peered more closely and saw a broad swathe of green plantations, vineyards and orchards, very similar to those that had lined the river for miles before. But then, looming through the haze, he saw a gathering of immense, ominous shapes. They were identical, perfectly formed pyramids, so vast that together they almost filled the horizon.

Sylas's first thoughts were of the Dirgheon, but he quickly saw that these were different: not dark and jagged-edged but exquisitely smooth and finished in some kind of light-coloured stone, which glowed in the morning sun.

"They're actually... *beautiful*," he murmured.

"Yes, they are," said Triste, who had been listening nearby. "That's what the Dirgheon is meant to look like when it's finished. Thoth stopped work on his Dirghea during the Reckoning, but they say he intends them all to look like these one day."

Naeo pointed to the other side of the river. "They're over there too!"

Everyone looked and saw the faint silhouettes of another group of pyramids, which lined a range of low hills on the opposite bank. Each was slightly different in size, but otherwise they were identical: bright and faultlessly smooth, all of them topped by a shining pinnacle that gleamed alluringly in the sun.

"What are those at the top?" asked Sylas.

"Benben stones," said Triste. "They signify the first piece of land from which all the world was made. They're forged from Quintessence."

Sylas looked at him in surprise. "Quintessence? They have it here?"

The Scryer nodded. "This is where everything began, Sylas. *Everything*, including Quintessence." He looked back at the pyramids. "But it's not just there for show. I read somewhere in Fathray's documents that they use the Benben stones to pass signals up and down the Nile."

For some time everyone gazed at the passing pyramids, noticing more and more as they swept along the Nile. Many were set so far back in the arid hills that their outline could barely be seen, but their pinnacles were still clearly visible, glinting bright in the morning sun.

But it was not just the pyramids that caught their eye as the banks of the Nile whisked past. They saw great buildings unlike any Sylas had seen before, with high outer walls of white or sand-coloured stone. What was peculiar about them was that the walls were not upright but sloping like the base of the pyramids. Many of these buildings had vast frontages adorned with scores of columns and giant, squared-off archways. Some had sweeping staircases and processions of the familiar half-human, half-beast statues of the gods. In places, there were great plinths of stone the length of the *Windrush*, which had been carefully engraved with hundreds of figures, all of them with the unreal look that Sylas remembered from school textbooks about ancient Egypt: head and legs to the side, shoulders to the front.

But there was another disturbing feature of these carvings that he did not remember. All of the faces were missing. As they raced past a colossal wall decorated with a procession of faceless figures, Sylas glimpsed the gouges and slashes where the stone features had been chipped away. They looked just like the defaced statues that had adorned the Temple of Isia.

"That madness began here too," said Triste, following his eyes. "Thoth commanded that all faces should be removed from public carvings and statues."

"*Why?*" asked Sylas.

Triste took out his pipe. "If *he* has to be faceless," he said, striking a flint, "then so must everyone else."

Soon the ship sailed into a town larger and grander than anything they had seen in the delta and they had to weave across the full span of the river to avoid ferries and vessels of trade. In the busiest section of the waterway, they were forced to draw worryingly close to a large, military-looking building with fortified walls. Everyone eyed it fearfully as they passed, but strangely its many watchtowers and battlements seemed almost deserted.

"That's odd," said Ash, staring. "I've counted five, maybe six guards. You'd expect a big garrison for a place like that."

"Makes you wonder where they all are," said Triste ominously.

"Yes," murmured Ash, "it does."

Everyone was still staring at the fortress when there was a cry from the crow's nest.

"A signal!" yelled the lookout, pointing over the stern. "There, on the western tower!"

When they looked, they saw, to their dismay, flames leaping between the castellations of the highest tower. The fire grew taller and brighter even as they watched so that they could still see it even as the fortress began to disappear into the distance.

"They must have seen us!" exclaimed Simia.

"Well, much good it'll do them," said Ash. "By the time they get themselves organised, we'll be long gone."

"Another one!" bellowed the lookout. They saw her gesticulating to a point further along the bank and a second fire flickered into life, this one on the roof of a tall, blockish building some way beyond the green pastures.

Triste dropped his pipe and ran to the nearest rope ladder, clambering up a few rungs and turning his eyes anxiously along the bank. Ash stood on the spokes of the wheel, shielding his eyes against the sun and scanning the terrain.

Everyone fell silent. The crew began to leave their posts to stare over the starboard side so that soon everyone but Naeo, who took it upon herself to keep the *Windrush* at speed, had their eyes trained on the western bank.

Suddenly Sylas lifted his finger. "There!" he exclaimed. "On top of that pyramid. It's getting brighter!"

"That's just the sun," said Ash after a moment.

"No," said Sylas. "Look! It's only that one! The one nearest the signal!"

Sure enough, that particular pyramid pinnacle was glowing far brighter than all the others, despite the fact that it was now far behind them. As they watched, it grew brighter and brighter until quite suddenly it blazed, radiating light in all directions. So searing were the beams that everyone had to shield their eyes and, all about, fields, dunes and hills lit up as though the sun had emerged from behind a cloud.

"Look!" Simia called out, running to the railing. "Now that one's getting brighter!"

The peak of another pyramid a little way behind them was indeed glowing more fiercely and then it too burned with a brilliant light, bathing the surrounding desert in a golden glow.

"And another!" shouted the lookout, pointing to the other side of the river. This time a peak almost level with the *Windrush* began to glow, the capstone of Quintessence seeming to kindle into flame, sending out a burst of light.

"They're sending a signal upriver!" yelled Triste from his vantage point on the rope ladder. "Sylas! Naeo! We need to keep ahead of them, or we'll be lost!"

"Not just upriver! Look!" called Simia from the stern of the ship.

Everyone turned and looked back the way they had come.

Signals burned as far as the eye could see, forming an avenue of lights along the two banks of the river. So bright were they that they could be seen far into the distance, a web of beams clearly visible in the haze, zigzagging between the Benben stones. Already there were at least a dozen signal fires, and another pinprick of light appeared as they watched.

"They're so fast!" gasped Simia.

"And they'll be ahead of us before long!" exclaimed Triste. "Sylas, Naeo, can we go any quicker?"

But Sylas was already back at the helm with Naeo, their hands clasped tightly, their eyes fixed firmly ahead. They reached up into the airy heights above the river, gathering the hot breeze to their will and heaving it down as a single gargantuan blast. The masts groaned and the prow lifted, and the *Windrush* surged, skipping once more along the Nile. Soon she was darting left and right at dizzying speeds, avoiding vessels, piers and pontoons. Sylas and Naeo did their best to lose themselves in their task, focusing on every heave and yaw of the ship, but all the while, off to the side, they were aware of lights blazing into life and racing ever further ahead.

The decks were a blur of crew rushing here and there, hauling on ropes, fastening hatches, scurrying up ladders. Even Triste and Simia busied themselves with the rigging.

Only Ash stood quiet and still, alone at the rear of the ship. He seemed entirely unaware of the commotion among his crew, and instead stared behind the ship at the beams of light, mouthing something under his breath. And, all the while, he held a small black shell in the palm of his hand, rubbing it gently with his thumb.

67

Discovered

"After all these years, and everything we Bringers have discovered *and conveyed this way or that between the worlds, can we say we have fulfilled our purpose? That we have even come close?"*

WORD PASSED QUICKLY FROM the lookouts, conveyed breathlessly from street to street, bathhouse to marketplace, temple to town hall.

"*The* Mesektet *is coming!*"

Street children murmured it in slums and back alleys; servants whispered it in corridors of power; traders called it from stall to stall.

"*The* Mesektet *is coming!*"

In no time at all, fishing boats and ferries had raced for the shore; piers and docks had been cleared; nets, ropes and the bric-a-brac of industry had been bundled into stores.

The womenfolk rushed through the town to find their children and then dragged them home.

"The *Mesektet* is coming!" they hissed as doors were slammed and shutters were bolted. "The Dirgh has returned!"

And, at this, the children trembled and cowered, as though Thoth himself was at the door.

So it was that before the *Mesektet* had even entered the town of Men'at Khufu, the streets were cleared and the waterfront was deserted. The only people to be seen were the city guards and officials, who watched anxiously from the roof terraces and towers of every public building, eyeing the bend in the river round which the *Mesektet* would appear.

They did not wait for long. The first they saw of her was a strange dimming of the light that dulled the surface of the river. Then, just moments later, her massive jet-black form swung into view. Her prow alone was taller than most of the buildings clustered on the shoreline, but above, her colossal sails towered to a staggering height, casting creeping shadows across the town. Despite her size, she moved at an astonishing speed, sweeping round the bend in just moments, propelled not only by the wind but by chains, which fanned out from her bow and dropped into waters churned white by the scaly bodies of a huge shoal of Slithen leaping and diving, leaping and diving.

It was a formidable sight, but what struck a chill into the hearts of all who watched was the blaze of crimson at the bow. They recognised the robes of the Dirgh at once, and already those that were nearest could see the pale glow of his empty visage, and the jutting angles of his wasted limbs.

Everyone held their breath as they watched the *Mesektet* approaching the ceremonial moorings in the centre of the town, quietly praying that she would not slow. Moments later their prayers were answered. She passed the main plaza and sped on to the south, sending out a fan of giant waves in her wake, which splashed over the river walls and spilled across the flagstones beyond.

But just as Men'at Khufu began to breathe again something changed. A bright light slanted through her streets, making the sandstone buildings glow and the Nile sparkle like liquid fire. And, in that very moment, the *Mesektet* slowed. Her sails emptied in a flash and her great prow plunged into the waters, sending out a bloom of waves and froth. The Slithen too pulled up short, as though responding to some silent command.

Right across the town, all eyes turned to the source of the light. They saw a burning light on the pinnacle of the biggest pyramid spraying beams in all directions. Just then the peak of a second pyramid on the opposite bank of the Nile also began to glow. Such a thing had not been seen for many a year, and a frightened clamour filled the streets. But it was quickly drowned out by a horrifying new sound. It was an almighty howl of fury, which thrummed through the town and echoed up into the skies, striking fresh terror into the hearts of all who heard it.

It had come from the *Mesektet*.

When the people of Men'at Khufu turned back to the ship, they saw the crimson-robed figure at her bow swell, finding new form and substance. The Dirgh's arms reached wide, seeming almost to span the ship, his shoulders looming behind his hooded face. The gash of his mouth stretched into a gaping darkness as he bellowed a cry of wild, primal rage.

Suddenly the black sails of the *Mesektet* opened out and up, sprawling and spilling beyond their rightful size. Their surfaces rippled like canvas, but somehow grew like living things, seemingly fed by a blackness at the centre of the ship. Ragged edges spanned out like feathers towards the banks of the river and up into the heavens, and soon they resembled gigantic, upraised wings of darkness plunging all about them into shadow.

All at once the chains at her bow snapped taut, and her wing-like sails filled with a sudden wind. The *Mesektet* surged on, sending out great white waves that swamped the streets at her sides.

And, in moments, she was gone.

§

The crew of the *Windrush* hung from the ladders and peered from the masts and yardarms, watching the procession of signal lights stretching ever further into the unknown. Everyone was on edge, dreading what lay ahead of them now that they had been discovered. Sylas and Naeo scanned the horizon, looking for any sign of Thoth's forces, or another blockade, or a barrier being hauled across their path. They seemed to be passing through a great tract of farmland and open desert, and had not encountered another settlement since the first Benben stone had blazed into life, but anything could lie beyond the next bend. Their only hope was to keep up with the signals as best they could and so the *Windrush* hurtled up the Nile in a blur, gone almost before she had arrived and leaving only a penstroke of foam in her wake.

It was Amelie who at last broke the tension. She appeared above deck laden with refreshments to be passed around: bread, salted meats, biscuits and the last of the fruit, washed down with a purple, berry-flavoured Plume. It was a welcome distraction, and the crew left their posts to gather round her and take their fill. Her kindly smiles also did much to raise spirits. Before long, the decks were filled with chatter, even if eyes rarely strayed from the twists and turns of the river ahead. Amelie and Simia took Sylas and Naeo their share of the meal, and they too managed to talk and relax a little, while keeping one eye firmly on their task.

The only one not to join in was Ash, who made his excuses, saying he was exhausted after his night at the helm and wanted to rest. He ignored the food, but took some of Fathray's papers to peruse and sloped off down the steps, back to his cabin.

The *Windrush* sped on, winding her way down the busy waterway of the Nile and, to their great relief, they still encountered no fortresses or large towns. Everyone aboard settled back into the routines of the ship. Ropes were repaired, sails stitched and decks swabbed. All this served to keep their thoughts from the procession of pyramids, which still punctuated the sands and floodplains, the ominous signal gleaming at their peak.

As they passed a mountain range to the east, the pyramids became much less numerous and, for some happy moments, they began to hope that perhaps they had passed the last of them. But then, as they rounded a long bend, another appeared in the far distance. This was larger than most and, to their dismay, its pinnacle too blazed in the late-morning sun. Worse, a temple sprawled at its base, fronted by a hundred columns the size of old oaks and grand flights of steps, which led all the way down to the Nile. The entrance was a towering, empty arch bordered on both sides by sloping walls, which added to the building's imposing appearance. At least a dozen Imperial banners spilled down the steps, and more had been draped on either side of the doorway so that Thoth's face stared out from every side.

As they drew closer, they saw three giant statues on the flat roof: one of a bird with a cruel, arched beak; another a baboon with a luxuriant mane; and finally Thoth's glaring visage.

Triste, who had been resting against one of the bulwarks, stood and walked quickly to the helm. "This is no place for us," he said to Sylas and Naeo in a low voice. "Hold your speed and keep to the other side of the river." He glanced at a nearby member of the crew. "Go and get Ash," he said.

Simia came and joined them. "Do you know what it is?" she asked.

"They call it Khemenu," said the Scryer gravely. "The Temple of Thoth."

All eyes turned back to the temple. Such was her speed that the *Windrush* was already close to the great edifice, and everyone watched anxiously for movement. They eyed the shadows of the portico and the deeper darkness of the entrance.

"There, look!" shouted one of the crew, pointing into the doorway.

Something glinted in the blackness, then the shadows stirred.

Quite suddenly dozens of figures poured from between the columns, flooding down the steps towards the river. They had the black canine snouts and high ears of the Ghor, but these were opulently dressed, with long, flowing white robes, bright amulets hanging round their necks and golden bands about their forearms. Their cries, however, were chillingly familiar – wild, soulless howls that echoed between the surfaces of stone.

"They were ready for us!" exclaimed Triste, glancing anxiously at Sylas and Naeo. "Can we go any faster?"

Sylas and Naeo did not respond, but the rigging of the *Windrush* strained under a new blast of wind, and she accelerated towards the temple.

All eyes were on the Ghor, which had already reached the shoreline. They may not have been warriors, but they were swift and agile nevertheless, bounding along the riverbank with their customary ease: heads low, their bodies moving in absolute unison.

To everyone's surprise, they were not running towards the *Windrush* but away from her.

"They're heading for the jetty!" yelled Simia. "There! You see?" She pointed ahead to a long pier that projected far out into the river beyond the temple.

The Ghor had a head start and they knew the terrain, leaping in gigantic bounds over ditches and streams, weaving between one another with such precision that they seemed of one mind. Already the first of them had reached the boards of the jetty and now they were charging along the timber walkway.

But the *Windrush* sped on, and in moments she was sweeping past the jetty. Sylas leaned to one side, turning the ship sharply away from the structure and making the keel plough deep into the waters, sending up a great wave of froth and foam. It arched in the air, then thundered down upon the jetty, smashing the most exposed reaches of the structure and swamping its entire length.

The hapless Ghor howled as they were washed into the Nile, left struggling and flailing in the wake of the ship.

As the *Windrush* hurtled on, a great cheer went up from her crew and many threw fists in the air, hollering their defiance. But they would not be heard; such was their speed that already they were rounding the next bend, leaving the temple far behind.

Triste walked to the back railing and gazed thoughtfully along their wake. Simia joined him.

"Triste?" she asked, looking searchingly at his face. "What's wrong?"

He glanced at her. "Nothing," he said. "Just checking we're not being followed."

Simia narrowed her eyes. "No, really," she probed, "what are you thinking?"

Triste smiled. "You really should be a Scryer, Simsi." He turned and leaned against the railing, looking back towards the bow. "I'm thinking about how different it's going to be now they know we're here. And I'm thinking that if that's the reception we get at a temple, what will we face in the next town or fortress?" He glanced over at Sylas and Naeo, his weary eyes shifting between them, seeming to take their measure. "And are they ready for it?"

68

Despair

"If I had faced just a small part of all they have
suffered, I would surely have given in to despair.
But always the Suhl find a way to carry on."

FILIMAYA WAS NOT ONE person, she was many. She was the nurse
darting down the aisles of the Hollow, taking medicine, or bandages,
or refreshments to whoever most needed the dwindling supply. She
was the reluctant commander stopping to talk to the latest wounded
fighter down from the hills, asking them about developments in
the battle, and the positions of the few remaining troops, and the
state of the defences. She was the mother, and grandmother, and
sister, and wife stopping to console the distraught, and the frightened,
and those worried about loved ones. Like Faysa, who still sat
between Takk and Espasian, tending to their every need, willing
them back to health. Filimaya did her best to reassure the diligent
young nurse that she was doing everything that could be done, and
then spent some time persuading her to allow herself a short break
and go up to the forest for some fresh air, promising to take her
place until she returned. Faysa finally relented, but she returned
soon after, perhaps frightened by what she had witnessed above but,
more than anything, anxious to be back at her father's side.

But, if Filimaya was one person more than any other, it was the elder of the Suhl. Her unfailing calm and resilience eased the spirits of everyone massed in the great chamber of the Hollow, and gave them the sense that someone, at least, knew what was to be done and that all would be well.

But now, as she sat alone on the lakeside in a rare moment of escape, Filimaya was none of those people: neither nurse, nor commander, nor mother, nor elder. Now, as she witnessed the devastation of the valley, and watched a procession of exhausted, broken Suhl warriors snaking down from the hills, she was just herself. And she was lost in her own private despair. She gazed disbelievingly at the naked hills, now almost as sparse and lifeless as the Barrens, and she wept. Not so that she might be seen, but quietly: her big eyes welling with tears until they spilled over.

The day was still young, but already Thoth's forces had savaged the valley. In places, trees had been felled almost halfway down the hillsides, leaving vast open spaces littered with broken timber. Nearby she could plainly see the mouth of the secret cave, that magical place where she and Paiscion had met in their youth, now laid bare and open to the skies. Across the lake, she could see the Rift, where Bayleon had given his life, no longer a beautiful green gorge but an exposed gash of crumpled earth, overrun with Hamajaks. And a little further round the valley she could just make out the peak of Carrion Rock, now dominated by a gigantic standard of the Empire, which danced mockingly in the breeze.

It was almost too much to bear, but Filimaya forced herself to take it all in. Without Espasian, who else was there to mark the placements of the enemy, to take note of the threats, to weigh how many troops might still be able to resist? And so she overcame her emotions, wiped the tears from her cheeks, and turned her eyes slowly round the valley, thinking and calculating as she knew Espasian would. *Two hours*, she thought. That was all they had before the enemy would be beating down the entrance to the Hollow. Two hours, maybe less.

Suddenly she heard the sharp crack of a breaking stick, then the sound of someone or something crashing through the foliage. She swung about, instinctively raising her hands before her.

A figure burst from the nearby thicket and stumbled on to the open shoreline. It was a Leaflike dressed from head to toe in the vines, leaves and bark of the forest. She had been at full sprint towards the Hollow, but when she saw Filimaya she slowed and circled back.

"My lady!" she panted. "Sorry to disturb you, but... you're needed..."

"Take a breath," said Filimaya calmly. "Gather yourself, then tell me what this is all about."

The messenger leaned on her knees, the bark plates of her armour grinding as her chest heaved. After three or four deep breaths, she rose.

"I'm from the watch, my lady, at the Retreat. There's something coming. Over the Barrens."

"On foot?" asked Filimaya.

She shook her head. "By air and straight towards the valley. They'll fly right over our defences."

Instinctively Filimaya glanced up at the darkening sky. "Vyrkans?"

"I think so, my lady."

"How many?"

"Hard to tell. More than we can count."

Filimaya nodded and drew a deep breath. "Then lead the way. I should see for myself."

They set out at a pace, running as fast as they could through the deserted avenues of Sylva and, all the while, Filimaya was reworking her calculations: how quickly everyone could be back at the Hollow if they sounded the retreat: how many might be lost before they even got there.

Soon they had reached the Tree of the Feather, and Filimaya called the tree to their aid. They ascended swiftly through the branches, but still the climb seemed to take far too long. When they arrived at the top, they rushed along the last great bough to Merimaat's Retreat and, as they entered, Filimaya saw the watch commander standing in the east window, surrounded by three Leaflikes and Bowe. She nodded to them all in greeting.

"There," said the thickset commander, dispensing with formalities and stepping to one side to let her through. He pointed. "This side of the ruins of Grail. They're already over the Barrens."

Filimaya strained her eyes, peering at a smudge of near blackness at the level of the clouds. There was a chill northerly wind, but she saw at once that this dark smear was heading west, directly towards the Valley of Outs. There was a motion at its heart: a boiling and twisting, as though the murky pall was endlessly remaking itself; and within there was a confusion of things rising and falling, rising and falling, like the beating of wings.

"It has to be Vyrkans," she murmured under her breath, making an effort to sound calm. She turned to the commander. "Can you guess at their speed?"

"Hard to tell, but fast. We've been—"

"They're no Vyrkans," said Bowe, cutting him short.

Filimaya looked at the Scryer in surprise. "Then... what are they?"

He narrowed his eyes. "I'm not sure."

The commander looked at Filimaya. "Shall I raise the alarm, my lady?" he pressed.

"Don't," interjected Bowe. "Not yet."

Filimaya eyed him for a moment, then nodded. "All right, we wait," she said. She looked at the commander. "But be ready."

The commander took a horn from her belt and held it out, her fingers tapping anxiously on its ornate brasswork. Everyone watched and waited.

The approaching blackness was rolling over the fringes of the forest now, but still they could not make out the nature of its quivering, beating heart. It came on swiftly, filling much of the eastern sky, and now they could hear a distant whisper, like wind through a field of corn.

Filimaya stepped forward. "Ah!" she murmured.

Bowe leaned in at her shoulder. "Do you see?"

The commander looked from one to the other. "See *what*? Should I sound the alarm?"

"No," said Filimaya, now sounding certain. "Just watch."

The commander and the other guards peered into the looming veil of blackness. Now they could see the shapes of creatures at its moiling core: a seething knot of bodies twisting and looping, just like a formation of Vyrkans. And yet the nearer they came, the more certain the guards were that it was nothing of the sort. Unlike Vyrkans, these creatures flew with a grace that was natural, a command of the heavens that was mesmerising to behold. They wheeled and soared as though they owned the firmament. And now, as they flew closer still, the watchers could see sleek plumage and hooked beaks; great ruffled crests and wide spans of giant tail feathers.

They were majestic birds of prey, just like the ones that owned the winds above Gheroth; like those that had once flown with Sylas and Naeo as they had escaped the Dirgheon, and that guarded the heights of the Temple of Isia.

They were near now, very near, and moving at such a pace that, in just moments, they were soaring over the Retreat, their mighty wings spread wide, their eyes gleaming silver, a hush of feathers heralding their passing.

As they soared over the Valley of Outs, the flock finally broke its formation. The first dozen birds scattered, gliding swiftly over the barren slopes until they reached the last of the forest beyond, and there they searched out stout trees in which to land. It took some moments because many of the remaining trees looked weak and sickly, almost bare of their leaves, but finally each bird swooped down. The trees bowed low, dropping leaves and creaking under the strain, but then each one held up the proud figure of an eagle, or a buzzard, or an osprey, like a prize.

The main flock still circled high above the lake, waiting until these leaders had landed, and only then did the tight formation become loose, as the remaining birds spiralled down towards the shore.

The commander's eyes were wide. "What are they doing?"

No one answered. All were transfixed.

The birds headed for open ground on the far shore of the lake and, in their final approach, they dispersed, landing silently in a circle. They quickly swept back their wings and hopped about on giant talons until each had their back to the centre of the ring.

Just one gigantic eagle remained aloft, carrying something that looked like a bundle of white cloth gently in its talons. Slowly and with great care, the eagle set it down upon the shore before flapping its mighty wings and swooping away to a nearby vantage point in the trees.

Its burden could now be seen. To the astonishment of the beholders, it was the slender figure of a woman. She was shrouded in white robes, crowned with flowing black locks, and there was something peculiar about her appearance, something that made everyone blink, as though their eyes were playing tricks. As she moved, her figure seemed to become two, the second trailing a little behind the first.

The commander gasped. "Is that...?"

"Yes," said Filimaya with a smile. "That is Isia."

Fathray sat alone on the log, watching in terror as shadows fell soundlessly from the skies, their wings whispering as they came. He glanced about, hoping that others had witnessed what he had seen but, to his dismay, he was quite alone.

He stood and began to creep slowly towards the deeper shadows of the forest.

"Why haven't they sounded the dratted horn?" he murmured to himself. "What's the point of it if we never—"

He stopped. Something huge passed low overhead.

He looked up to see a giant shadow descending towards a dim clearing on the nearby shore. He edged forward and parted some foliage to take a closer look. The shadow was already flapping its mighty wings and taking back to the skies, leaving a lone, shimmering white figure on the shore.

Fathray adjusted his spectacles and stared. He took off his glasses, rubbed them and placed them back on his nose. Then a smile slowly bloomed beneath his whiskers.

"Extraordinary," he murmured.

He pulled the journal from beneath his arm and, with trembling fingers, took the box that contained his quill from his pocket.

"This I will write," he said.

69

The Plague

*"We are hardly blameless, of course. Over the centuries we
have shared so much, both good and bad. Even* the plague,
*it seems, made its way between the worlds, carried by some
unwitting traveller. It is not believed that they were Merisi,
but that is perhaps beside the point."*

THE DOORS OF THE temple at Khemenu were immense and
forbidding, as was only fitting for the great Temple of Thoth. Each
was the height of five people, carved out of the trunks of cedar
trees and covered in hammered brass the thickness of a plate of
armour.

But now these giant doors quivered, clanging against the
doorjambs and the marble floors. Their sturdy hinges quaked and
rattled, as though the earth itself was breaking. And then, quite
suddenly, they sprang open.

Outside, a lone figure made his way up the steps, hunched
forward, his face covered by his crimson hood. He did not pause,
even when the doors slammed against their restraints, sending a
low boom through the halls and hills. He swept inside the temple,
crimson robes flying up round him like tongues of fire, and only
there, on the threshold, did he raise his head.

He gave a low purr of pleasure.

Before him stretched the grandest avenue of statues anywhere in the two worlds. They formed twin orderly lines, right and left, their massive lionlike bodies prone, their two clawed forepaws stretched out in front, their powerful shoulders draped about with a rich, ornamental headdress like a mane. They were sphinxes one and all, with the fearsome body of a lion and the cunning, reasoning head of a human. But Thoth had made them his own. The human nose, chin and cheekbones had been chiselled away, leaving only a blank mask of stone.

The Dirgh walked swiftly down the aisle, his head bowed once again, while his entourage of Ghor priests followed at a safe distance. To their surprise, their master did not take his customary detour to inspect the library of parchments and books that lined the walls behind the statues: works of history, and fiction, and both, all penned by his own hand over the millennia.

But, when he reached the final pair of sphinxes, he did raise his head, if only for a cursory look. These, after all, were the most recent addition to the phalanx of sphinxes, larger and mightier than the others, and with a modification – a borrowing from the Greek sphinxes of the Other: the majestic wings of an eagle flexing high into the air behind them.

Thoth stopped. "Wait," he said in a tumult of voices that boomed through the hall, and his following fell to their knees, pressing their snouts to the floor.

He turned back to the ornamental doors at the end of the hall and breathed three ancient words into the dry air. Three words so old that only he remembered them. Instantly the mechanism whirred and clicked, and the doors swept apart.

Thoth stood for a moment, admiring his inner sanctum. It was a place unsullied by the wearying change of the outside world; a place of fine tapestries, silks, pottery and furnishings – all of them the prizes of conquest — and of small comforts, like his Stradivarius cello, laid on a cushion where he had last left it. In the centre of the chamber, a vast skylight opened to the beautiful blue skies, but it was what lay beneath that drew his attention. He walked on, his eyes fixed on the large, square pool, its surface pitch-black and mirror-smooth. He paused briefly on the surrounding steps and gazed down into oblivion.

"Now you must be all you can be," he murmured.

Then he knelt before the pool and leaned his hooded face out over the mirrored surface. He gave a visible shudder, and recoiled, muttering a curse as ancient as the desert.

He opened his arms wide.

"I am Thoth, three times great, Priest of Souls and scribe to the gods. Soon I will be A'an, Lord of Equilibrium, and I will bring a union of light and hope, or of an endless dark." He put his hands out over the oily surface. And then he said: "So, let it be dark."

As his words died, the pool of Black began to churn, and the chamber was quickly filled with the sound of it slapping and gurgling as it rolled this way and that. Thoth began to breathe incantations, softly at first, but then louder and louder, until soon his mutterings and whispers filled the room. The Black was swirling now, faster and faster, until soon it was a vortex, with a gaping darkness at its centre. The hole grew deeper and wider until the Black was only visible at the edges of the pool.

And then the most peculiar thing happened. The Black disappeared altogether, leaving only darkness: a deep shadow, which pooled within the square of white marble. The surface had no form and reflected no light; it was simply the boundary between light and dark.

As the last of the whispered words disappeared, Thoth's hunched form trembled a little, then sank back on to the steps behind. He wheezed, struggling to recover his breath, then slowly he edged forward and brought his hooded face out over the emptiness.

There was no sign of his ever-changing features. Only the gloom stared back at him. He shifted to one side and then the other, as though admiring his image in a mirror.

"Better," he murmured. And he gave a full-throated laugh: a sudden barking guffaw that filled the chamber and poured out of the skylight, echoing from the surrounding hills. It was a laugh of release, of one suddenly unburdened. A laugh that marked a long-awaited end and a new beginning.

Only when the sound of his triumph had died away did he rise to his feet and climb the steps. At the top he turned and looked up into the cobalt sky, as though listening.

"Now," he murmured, "let us catch ourselves an errant ship."

And then he whistled.

It sounded as though it came from many lips, but it was a perfect single note, low and sustained, clear and haunting. He held it longer than seemed possible with human breath until it spilled out of the chamber and moaned between the hills; until finally it thrummed between rocks and through crevices, and into the dark places beneath the earth.

And that is where it found its answer.

Out through the crevices and rocks and up into the open sky it came, thunderous and terrifying.

A shriek that became a carnivorous roar.

70

A Visitation

*"When I first heard as a youth that we were to be treated
to a visitation from a Magruman of the Suhl I could barely
contain myself. To my embarrassment now, all I could
think about was how to make an impression."*

WORD OF ISIA'S ARRIVAL had spread quickly. The trees beside
the lake were once again teeming with children, and the canopy
danced as they scampered here and there, trying to find the best
view. Several of the great birds were disturbed from their
perches, launching themselves into the air before settling
gracefully in branches nearby. The grassy slopes on the lakeside
too were bustling with Suhl fighters down from the hills, and
Leaflikes from the tunnels, and nurses and patients from the
Hollow.

Everyone but the worst injured, like Takk and Espasian, had
come. After the creeping despair of the previous few hours, hope
was rekindled, and people chattered quietly among themselves.
Even the enemy had paused their assault at the first sight of Isia
and seemed to be watching from their vantage points around the
valley.

Filimaya stood alone on the stony shoreline, resplendent in her finest ceremonial robes, with folds of lavish fabric and glistening embroidery down one arm. When she took her first steps towards the great circle of birds, the gathering quickly fell quiet, watching with great anticipation. Filimaya no longer walked with her customary graceful step, but looked hesitant, as though before Isia her many years had fallen away and she was once again young and uncertain.

As she drew near, the birds turned their great heads and watched impassively with pale, piercing eyes. The nearest of them hopped to one side, opening the way into the circle. Filimaya acknowledged this with a brief bow and, as soon as she was through the gap, the giant buzzard closed the circle once again. Now, only those children perched high in the trees could still see her, and they watched breathlessly as she advanced across the circle.

When she drew close to the lone figure at its centre, Filimaya dropped to her knees, bowing so low that her braid trailed on the ground.

Isia stepped forward, her arms outstretched.

The children gasped. In that brief moment, she was not one figure but two. Trailing behind her was another identical form: a ghostly apparition that matched her every movement. Both figures now stooped, and together they took Filimaya's hands and helped her to her feet.

"Come, Filimaya," she said, in a soft voice that only Filimaya could hear, "there is no need."

She stepped back in a blur of motion, allowing Filimaya to see her properly for the first time: her black eyes, her faultless bronze skin, her youthful, doe-like face.

Filimaya lowered her gaze. "Great Isia. Welcome."

Isia gave a radiant smile. "I am pleased it is you, Filimaya. We can speak as one mother to another."

Filimaya flushed a little. "Mother of our Souls, I would be

honoured, but I am afraid you are mistaken. I have not been blessed with children."

Isia laughed lightly. "You may not have children of your own, Filimaya, but you are the mother of many." She gestured to the faces peering from the trees. "You are the mother of this entire valley!"

Filimaya smiled and flushed a little. "I would be humbled if it were so."

"It is so, Filimaya," said Isia, leaving the matter beyond question. "But now I am afraid that, as mothers, we must speak plainly and quickly. Please, tell me everything that has passed since the battle began."

Filimaya nodded and set about describing all the events of the past days: from Sylas and Naeo's departure aboard the *Windrush*, to the attack of the Ogresh and the sacrifice of the Spoorrunners, and the many assaults and skirmishes that had taken place since then. When she had finished telling of the Hekas and Espasian's injuries, Isia was silent, her arms folded and her head bowed in thought.

Finally she looked up. "You have all proven yourselves worthy guardians of the valley. I only wish that I could have been here sooner, and perhaps helped save Espasian his sacrifice. I came as soon as I knew of the battle, but I needed to break my journey to visit the Kraven."

"The *Kraven*?" said Filimaya, astonished.

Isia nodded. "Yes, the Kraven on the Barrens. I hoped they might perhaps join your cause and fight for the valley."

Filimaya's face brightened. "And will they?"

Isia sighed and shook her head, blurring her features. "I was reminded how little interest the Kraven have in the living, unless it is to hunger for what they have lost. Though they did ask after Sylas. They have encountered him more than once on the Barrens and they have some understanding of his place in things. They sense that if anyone may free them it is he."

"I see," said Filimaya. "But they will not help his friends here in the valley?"

"If Sylas were here, they may well have come, but I am afraid that they cared little for the plight of the Suhl."

"But many of them were once our sisters and brothers!" objected Filimaya.

Isia nodded solemnly. "And yet we must not think of the Kraven as people bound by kinship. They are a wandering loneliness, a trace left because their Glimmer has not died. They are just one of the wrongs caused by the rift between the worlds."

"Of course, I know this," said Filimaya, dropping her eyes. "We are just so desperate for some help that... well, for a moment, I dared to hope." She looked back at Isia. "Without help, we will not last the day."

Isia placed a hand on Filimaya's arm. "That is why I am here. *I* can help you."

Filimaya looked up with new light in her eyes.

Isia gave a beautiful smile, but it quickly faded. "And yet I have been asking myself how, since I am little versed in the ways of war." She gazed at the valley, taking in the barren hilltops and the depleted forest, its trees brown-leafed and drooping. "But perhaps I may be able to help in another way. You say the valley put up a brave defence while her strength lasted?"

"Oh yes," said Filimaya. "We would have been overrun within hours without her help."

Isia nodded. "Of course, there is *another* valley just like this," she said. "Another valley in another world."

"In the Other?"

"You might say this valley's very own Glimmer. A valley not enchanted like this, but nevertheless full of Nature's gifts. If I can

469

call upon that strength and spirit — if *that* place may give to this — then perhaps you may hold a little longer."

Filimaya broke into her first genuine smile since Paiscion had left her. "I had no idea that such a thing was possible!"

"I'm not sure that it is," said Isia cautiously. "I am more familiar with the division of the human soul than that of the natural world. But I will try." She looked out at the pale shimmer of the lake. "Is there a boat that I may use? Just something small, for me alone."

Filimaya looked puzzled. "Of — of course. I will arrange it straight away."

"Thank you. I should get started as soon as I can."

Filimaya bowed and made to leave, but then she hesitated. "Isia," she said, turning back, "might I ask something else of you?"

Isia smiled knowingly. "As one mother to another?"

Filimaya flushed. "As one mother to another. It is just that everyone here has given so much to the fight for the valley. They are exhausted. Frightened. I wonder if you might let them—"

Isia raised her hand. "They will have whatever comfort I can give."

Filimaya bowed. "Thank you," she said and then hurried away.

Isia watched her pass through the cordon of birds that still stood sentinel, and then said something beneath her breath. In that instant, the great eagles, ospreys and buzzards launched themselves up into the darkness, their huge wings making a sudden squall of dust. Each of them flew swiftly and soundlessly towards a different part of the valley so that in just moments Isia stood alone on the shoreline before the gathering of Suhl.

Hundreds of pale faces stared at her in wonder.

"Come," said Isia. She spoke softly, but her voice was heard by all. "Come to me."

470

And, without hesitation, they came. Children clambered down from the treetops, emerging cautiously from the shadows; the wounded made their way on crutches and bandaged limbs; warriors stepped forward, still in their dishevelled armour of bark and vine; men and women, young and old, picked their way over rocks and shingle on to the shore.

Somewhere outside the valley a single battle drum struck up, beating out its menacing rhythm with growing pace and volume, and it was quickly joined by others until, before long, the hills began to rumble.

Isia lifted her arms and, when she spoke, she seemed to breathe into every ear, drowning out the noise. "You are not alone," she whispered. "You have never been alone. Draw close now and listen."

She waited as the congregation of Suhl shuffled forward, leaning closer, then she closed her eyes and dropped her head to her chest.

After some moments those nearest to her began to whisper. In the beginning, they could not be heard over the drums, but soon, as they were joined by more and more of their brothers and sisters, the chorus of hushed voices began to sound like wind in the trees, a wind that soon became a gale.

All the while each of those gathered heard only their own whisper, from their own lips. And yet the words came from somewhere else, across a void. Sometimes they offered solace or gave courage — the kind of words one might murmur to oneself at a moment of doubt or fear. But mostly they spoke of simple things, and idle cares, and the concerns of another life lived far away. These were the words of a thousand Glimmers beyond the rift between the worlds, unconscious of their second selves, and the Suhl, and the siege of the valley, and the gathering on the shoreline. They were something else, a promise of something beyond, of something better.

Sometimes there was fear in those whispers: fear of a different war, of beasts pouring from stone circles, of storms of hail and fire. But even these voices were a comfort because, listening to their second selves, everyone had the answer to a question they had barely asked. They felt a presence, near and true.

In that moment, none of them were alone.

They were — all of them — whole.

71

The Trees

"Were it not for the trees it is unlikely that any of us could have successfully made the passing in those difficult years. Not only did they provide cover, but in the hands of the Magrumen, they were a means of escape."

SYLAS HAD NO IDEA how long he and Naeo had been at the helm. He was exhausted, swaying with every heave of the deck, and now he clung to Naeo more to stay on his feet than to keep their connection. It seemed hours since Ash had left them and gone below, and Sylas yearned for him to return and take a shift at the helm. He found himself struggling to keep his focus on the winds, and the sails, and the busy river ahead.

But at least their worst fear had not come to pass. They continued to sail past pyramids on each side of the river, their pinnacles burning bright with a signal fire, and they could now see more, far ahead of them, disappearing into the distance, but they had not faced an ambush or an impassable blockade across the river. Not yet. But then the settlements they had come across had been small, and the two fortresses utterly deserted. Often they had seen feverish activity on the shoreline — guards rushing here and there, and equipment being dragged from stores — and once something had struck the hull as they had passed a long jetty packed with people, but in each case they were already away before they had really been aware of the threat.

Over time everyone had stopped eyeing the banks of the river quite so closely and settled to their tasks. Simia had abandoned her position in the bow and come to sit in front of Sylas and Naeo on the quarterdeck, spreading two large maps out before her. She studied them closely and occasionally read off a place name as they passed through a village or small town, or pointed out a temple or monument. Neither Sylas nor Naeo replied, being far too occupied with their own task, but she nevertheless kept up a bright, one-sided conversation. Sylas knew what she was doing, of course: she was making sure that she was part of things, and she was helping to keep their focus on what was about them, and not on what was ahead, or what might be behind; and she worked at her new task with all the determination that he had come to admire in her.

The sun was dipping now, bathing the surrounding desert in an orange glow, and in his exhaustion Sylas began to lean dreamily from side to side. It was only Naeo occasionally yanking on his hand that stopped him from falling asleep on his feet. He was just slipping into another reverie, this time thinking about his first visit to the mysterious Shop of Things — how long ago that seemed now! — when suddenly he became aware of Simia standing right before him, looking directly into his face.

"I *said* have you seen those?" She pointed over the bow of the ship. "Whatever they are, they aren't on the maps."

Sylas looked ahead and narrowed his eyes. There were two definite smudges just above the horizon, too low to be clouds, but far too high to be buildings.

He was suddenly wide awake. "I have no idea," he said.

Simia glanced at Naeo, but she too shook her head.

Triste had been sitting on a chest nearby, reading some of Fathray's documents, but when he saw them all staring ahead he took a look for himself. Suddenly he stood, cast the papers aside and walked briskly to the bow.

Simia watched him go for a moment, then glanced back down at the maps and frowned. She knelt and bent low over first one map, then the other. "Unless it's... *those*," she said, bringing her face close to the parchment.

"What, Simsi?" asked Sylas.

She stared at the map, shaking her head. "I'm not sure exactly. Perhaps it's nothing. Just two little drawings either side of the river."

"Drawings of what?"

"I think they're... *trees*," she said with a shrug.

"That's exactly what they are!" called Triste as he made his way back. "But not just any two trees. *The* trees. The ones from the beginning!"

Naeo frowned. "I'm sorry — *what* trees?"

"You *know* them," said Triste, a trace of excitement in his voice. "In a way, you've seen them before. Remember the Arbor Vital, the tree in the Garden of Havens? The one we call the Living Tree?"

The children nodded.

He pointed to the apparition on the western bank of the Nile, which was indeed rapidly taking the shape of a monumental tree, its great limbs open to the sky. "*That* is the *true* Living Tree. The one that has been there since before the Empire was born. It is said that when Merimaat was forced to leave the Motherland she risked her life to take a cutting from it, to help her build a new nation for the Suhl. A nation for Nature and Essenfayle. It was that cutting that she planted in the Garden of Havens, and that breathed life and enchantment into the Valley of Outs."

475

Simia looked at the colossal tree with wide, sparkling eyes, then she turned her gaze to the other bank. "And what about that one?" she asked. She cocked her head to one side, gasped and glanced at Sylas. "Is it... is it something to do with the one we saw in the Temple of Isia? The Knowing Tree?"

"What I know for certain," said the Scryer, "is that this is the Knowing Tree of old so the one in the temple must have been grown from its seed. And, if anyone would want their own Knowing Tree, it is Isia. No one bears the burden of knowing more than her. She alone knows the truth of our broken souls and worlds." Triste looked at the trees admiringly. "I never thought I'd actually see them for myself," he said distractedly. "After all that's happened in the past days I had quite forgotten that we would be passing them."

The two trees were still some way off, but already they towered above the ship. Their vast, sinewy trunks stretched upwards and spread into gigantic boughs and branches, like the fingers of open hands, casting spidery shadows over the land below. But they were similar only in their size. Even at this distance, Sylas could see that the Knowing Tree was speckled with pinks, reds, oranges, yellows and purples – the fruit, perhaps, that he had tasted in the Temple of Isia – while the great limbs of the Living Tree drooped under a heavy burden of gigantic, vibrant green leaves.

Triste had been lost in thought, but suddenly seemed to remember himself. "Simia, get Ash," he said. "He should see this!"

Simia darted off below and Sylas and Naeo slowed the ship a little so that they, and everyone else, could take a proper look at the trees without worrying about the river ahead. Simia returned with Ash surprisingly quickly, and he still held in his hand the clutch of papers he had been studying. Amelie followed closely, apparently keen to see what the commotion was about. When the two of them turned and saw the trees for the first time, they rocked backwards, then stood gaping in astonishment.

After some moments Amelie glanced at Sylas and Naeo, then said something to Ash and walked over to them. She took hold of Sylas's hand and looked back at the trees.

"Just when I think nothing more could surprise me," she said breathlessly. "They're just... beautiful! And — and *impossible*! It's not just the size of them." She pointed at the Living Tree. "The leaves on that one are... well, if they're not giant elm, then they're almost identical to it, but the shape of its crown... well, *that's* more like an oak! And its trunk... its bark... they're all from different trees! Cedar, olive, acacia, tamarisk..."

"They call it the Living Tree," said Sylas.

She glanced at him. "Like the one in the valley?"

He nodded and pointed to the other one. "And that's the Knowing Tree."

Amelie stared in wonder at the great branches of the two trees, which formed an arch over the Nile. "Those names..." she murmured. "They sound like..." She shook her head and laughed as though mocking her own thought. "Well... like the ones in the *Bible*." She looked at Sylas hesitantly. "Don't they? The Tree of Knowledge? The Tree of Life?"

For a moment Sylas's eyes followed a great flock of birds that danced and looped between the boughs. "What if they *are* the ones in the Bible, Mum?" he said. "Triste says the trees have been here since the very beginning, so it stands to reason, doesn't it?"

"Well, I'm not sure that something like that could *ever* stand to reason, Sylas," she mused, narrowing her eyes at the fruit of the Knowing Tree, "and they certainly don't *look* like the ones in the Bible." She frowned and ran a fingertip over her bottom lip. "But then they *would* be several thousand years older by now, and if ever I saw a tree that might be thousands of years old..."

"If lots of our *other* stories came from here," said Sylas, "like magic, and *doppelgängers*, and all the other things, why not that one?"

Amelie gazed at him for a moment. "It's somehow… especially hard to believe," she said, shaking her head. "But… yes, perhaps you're right, Sylas."

Everyone stopped talking as the ship skipped onwards over the slick surface of the river. This stretch was utterly deserted: no fishing skiffs, no ferries, no boats selling goods, not even any farmers working the fields. For those moments it was as though they were entirely alone with the two ancient giants.

But then Simia broke the silence.

"Hey!" she exclaimed. "There's a town! On both sides of the river! Look!"

Everyone peered into the shadows beneath the trees, and sure enough they saw that at their base, where they had heaved up the earth into two broad-topped hills, every inch of ground was crammed with buildings. Some were the size and shape of the villas that they had encountered elsewhere, but most were far too grand to be dwellings, with wide steps, long colonnades and walls covered with engravings.

"I had no idea there was a town here," said Triste. He looked perplexed. "Strange… I didn't sense anyone and… I still can't. Still we're going to have to be careful. The signals are sure to have reached here some time ago so, if there is anyone here, they'll have had plenty of…"

He trailed off.

Like everyone else, he was staring open-mouthed at the buildings.

Even in the shadow of the great trees, every column, wall and tile gleamed with a faultless silvery-gold sheen so that they almost seemed to glow. Wherever stray beams of sunlight struck a wall or rooftop, they set off a blaze so that parts of the great town sparkled. One particular avenue of statues beneath the Living Tree seemed almost alive with light.

"Quintessence!" exclaimed Sylas. "The whole town's made of Quintessence!"

72

Ambushed

"And surely we must do all we can to avoid a repeat of June 21st 1811, that terrible day when not only was our Bringer ambushed and imprisoned, but also thirteen of her Suhl companions."

ASH WALKED SLOWLY TO the railing and stared open-mouthed at the town, shaking his head.

"It's everywhere!" he exclaimed.

As he spoke, the *Windrush* sailed below the first of the giant boughs and they were plunged into its cool shade, which came as a relief after the heat of the desert. Now, they could see the town in all its glory. It was not only the buildings that glistened and gleamed, but the streets themselves, especially those that surrounded the opulent ceremonial buildings at the tops of the hills. Here every flagstone, kerb and gutter shone with a strange, ethereal light.

"It must have something to do with the trees," said Triste thoughtfully. "Perhaps it gathers round the roots, just like in the mines below the Arbor Vital."

Just then Naeo's hand tightened in Sylas's and, at the same moment, he felt a pang of pain in his back, which climbed between his shoulder blades.

"It's not just Quintessence," Naeo murmured, her eyes growing wide.

Triste turned to her. "What was that?"

"I said it's not just Quintessence that the trees draw to them. It's the Black too." She turned to the Knowing Tree and stared. "I can feel it. Lots of it — in the earth and the river, in the roots. Everywhere!"

Sylas followed her eyes and saw at once what she was transfixed by. There, where the massive trunk rose above the gleaming town, its rutted surface was marked by huge dark lines that spiralled upwards within the folds of bark. They might almost have been mistaken for shadows, but when Sylas looked more closely he saw that they were raised from the surface of the trunk, like knotted, rumpled veins, as though the Black had somehow been drawn into the living wood of the tree.

"It's like the tree in the temple!" exclaimed Simia. "*That* was infected with the Black too, remember?"

Sylas met her eyes. "And do you remember what Paiscion said? That wherever there's Quintessence the Black seems to follow?"

"Yes!" exclaimed Simia. "And here there's—"

She was silenced by an almighty explosion of sound.

It had come from the very centre of the deck and, when they looked, they saw a rock the size of a melon bounce high into the air, then clatter across the deck and plunge into the water. For a split second everyone stared after it in shock, but before anyone could say anything there was another calamitous BANG. A second rock shot into the air at the edge of the quarterdeck, then bounced two more times before rolling over the side.

Filled with dread, everyone looked up.

High above, the limbs of the trees were writhing. Hundreds of Hamajaks scampered and leapt along the immense boughs, rushing to keep up with the *Windrush*. The distances between branches were huge, but the Hamajaks were in their element, using hands, limbs and tails to swing from knots in the wood and launch themselves onwards.

With the impact of the first stones, they shrieked and gibbered in triumph, some of them beating their chests, while others reached into heavy leather pouches slung across their bodies and pulled out more huge rocks. These they raised above their heads and tossed directly into the path of the *Windrush*.

Ash stared at the falling rocks in horror. "It's a trap!" he bellowed. "Everyone below!"

The terrified crew threw themselves towards the nearest hatch and scrambled down into the darkness. Ash hesitated. He looked up at the sails, then back at the rocks, and finally straight at Sylas and Naeo. They knew at once what he was thinking. If they went below, the ship would stall, right beneath the Hamajaks, but if they stayed they would surely be crushed.

Ash stepped towards them and then stopped, wearing an agonised expression. "I can't—"

"Go!" they yelled.

He paused a moment longer, still fighting with himself, then he raced to the rear hatch. When he reached it, he found Amelie and Simia frozen in the entrance, staring helplessly at Sylas and Naeo. He threw an arm round each of them and pushed them forcefully down the steps. With a last glance back towards the helm, he thundered down the stairs after them.

Instinctively Sylas and Naeo drew close to one another. They wanted to look up, but they knew it was too late. Instead they pressed their eyes closed and waited.

Almost in the same instant the very air seemed to split in two. A great shock wave of sound erupted from the decks, pounding their ears and making them both cry out. A great wind ripped at their clothes and something heavy glanced against Naeo's hip, then they were deluged with water.

They waited for the inevitable end, but it did not come.

The cacophonous roar became a scattering of isolated bangs and clatters. The cascade fell away, leaving them dripping. The wind subsided.

Slowly they opened their eyes.

Shards of rock and the shattered timbers of chests and casks were strewn about their feet, hanging from the rigging, sprawled across every surface but, to their astonishment, the decks still gleamed solid and true. They looked up and saw that the sails too had somehow remained intact and the ropes that bound them had also held fast.

"The Quintessence!" said Sylas, daring to smile.

But then, high above, they heard the Hamajaks bellow their rage, and moments later they saw another volley of rocks many times larger than the first crashing through the veil of leaves and hurtling down towards the ship.

This time they did not close their eyes. They called the winds and raised the waters of the Nile, hurling the *Windrush* onwards. All the while, they craned their necks, watching the approaching rocks, trying to work out where they would land. Most of them fell harmlessly into the water, but many were right on target. If they veered to one side, slowed or accelerated, they would only lead the ship into another shower of rock. So they pressed on towards the brightness ahead, beyond the shadows of the trees.

As the first few missiles plunged into the waters to starboard, sending up great spouts of froth, Sylas and Naeo leaned into each other again, wincing through the spray.

"One!" murmured Sylas.

"Two!" muttered Naeo.

Then both took a sharp breath.

"Three!" they yelled.

In that instant, they ran forward, their steps precisely in time, as though in a dance they had rehearsed a thousand times. As a dozen rocks crashed down on the deck — one of them in the exact spot where they had been standing — the two children drew to a halt beneath the mainsail. Sylas lifted his hand and the great expanse of golden canvas suddenly ballooned, filled by an enchanted wind, so that the swell of the sail formed a canopy above their heads.

More rocks pummelled the *Windrush*, two of them glancing off the mainsail, another springing off its bulging surface and flying far out into the river. The main barrage hit a moment later, crashing down upon every part of the ship and turning the surrounding waters into a boiling tempest. The *Windrush* rocked perilously from side to side, leaping so violently that it seemed certain she would capsize. Suddenly rocks were bouncing in all directions off the mainsail, threatening to punch the wind right out of it and leave Sylas and Naeo exposed. In desperation, they wrapped themselves tight round the mast, encircling it with their arms and clinging to each other's hands as the deck leapt beneath their feet. All they could do now was close their eyes, press themselves as tightly as they could to the shining timber and wait for the nightmare to end.

They had no idea how long it lasted. They clung to the mast as it quaked and trembled, so deafened by the clamour that they did not notice when it suddenly fell away. Neither did they notice when the last branch of the Living Tree passed overhead, and they left the Hamajaks gibbering and wailing behind them, some of them hurling themselves with abandon into the waters far below. It was only when the *Windrush* passed into the first beam of sunlight, bathing them in its warmth, that they dared to look.

As they opened their eyes, the sails erupted with a fiery radiance, casting a dancing golden light in all directions. With their ears still ringing, they looked about them. There were the shattered remains of rocks everywhere but, to Sylas and Naeo's astonishment, through all the debris the decks still shone, their gleaming surfaces as bright and faultless as ever. Even the wheel, the railings and the ropes of the brave *Windrush* seemed almost entirely unblemished. Meanwhile, ahead of her, the Nile opened wide, and the ship was once again skipping lightly over clear waters.

Breathless and trembling, Sylas looked at Naeo, and she at him. She held out a hand and smiled. Without a word, they clasped each other tight, and their pounding hearts seemed to beat as one.

73

Twilight

"The longer we live through this Undoing the more
I feel that we are living in some kind of twilight,
and that soon, the night will come."

THE VALLEY WAS EERILY quiet. The battle drums had long since ceased their bullying chorus, and Thoth's forces had paused their offensive. Their dreadful work was almost done and they seemed to be resting before the final assault, which would almost certainly come before nightfall. Smoke rose from a thousand campfires all around the valley, and a heavy grey blanket was slowly forming above the lake, mixing with the mists to form a thickening, acrid fog. For now, at least, Isia could still be seen near the centre of the still waters, standing alone in her tiny boat. She seemed almost to be at prayer, with her head raised and her hands upturned at her sides, as though asking a question.

As the sun began to set, the last few hundred Suhl fighters started to emerge from the Hollow and their makeshift shelters beneath rocks and roots. It was clear from the time they took to assemble that none of them relished the task ahead, and yet they had a brightness and confidence that had not been there just a few hours earlier, before they had gathered with Isia — before that strange but familiar voice had whispered at their ear. The strength they had felt then was evident now in the way they talked, and joked, and cajoled. And it was a gift that only grew as they shared it one with the other.

But there was something else that raised their spirits. There was a new freshness in the dewy air: a scent of rising sap, and fertile earth, and sweet, unfurling leaves. Over the past hours the broken, beleaguered valley seemed to have been revived, as though new life and vigour had settled upon her forested slopes. It was nothing that the assembled fighters could see, but they could smell it and feel it, and they knew that it was Isia's doing. It was that same vitality that earlier, on the lakeshore, they had felt coursing through their veins, and now, as they gathered beneath their tattered ensigns, it thrummed in them again.

Filimaya walked the lakeshore, sharing a word here, particularly where spirits seemed to be wavering. She looked quite magnificent dressed in her finest ceremonial robes and with the customary braid in her hair, laced with dazzling new strands of silvery gold. She was no general, but the very sight of her quickened hearts and boosted morale, and Filimaya made sure that every man and woman in that ragged army knew that she was at their side.

As everyone finally joined the assembly and they fell silent, she made her way to a promontory at the edge of the water to address them. But just as she opened her mouth to speak she was surprised to see the entire gathering turning away towards a disturbance in the rear ranks. She followed their gaze to where a formation of Leaflikes was beginning to part, stepping back to leave a way open to the lake. When the last of them moved aside, she saw three figures walking hand in hand.

Filimaya knew the one at the centre at once, though she had never seen Faysa's young face so radiant with a broad, beautiful smile. Then she recognised the tall, lithe figure at Faysa's side. She had only come to know Takk in the Hollow, injured and ailing but, to her astonishment, now he walked upright and proud, and showed little sign of weakness. But it took Filimaya several moments longer to recognise the last of the three companions because his face was shaded by a grand helmet crested with vivid red leaves. But there was something familiar about the way he carried his powerful build, even clad as he was in splendid armour of vines and bark.

Filimaya narrowed her eyes and took a step forward.

"Espasian?" she murmured.

As he drew closer and raised his hand in greeting, there was no doubting it.

"Espasian!" she exclaimed, breaking into a wide smile.

Sure enough, Espasian's familiar white grin spread beneath the shade of his helm.

Hearing Filimaya call his name, the troops looked at this strange figure with new reverence and began to cheer, reaching out to touch his armoured shoulder as he passed.

"Espasian!" they bellowed. "Espasian! Espasian!"

Such was the noise that when the three finally reached Filimaya she had to raise her voice to be heard.

"You're... well?" she said, hardly believing the miracle before her eyes.

The Magruman gave a slight bow by way of answer. "I had a fine nurse," he said, looking down at Faysa, who visibly swelled with pride. "And I think Isia may also have had her part to play. I had... an unusual dream full of places and things I have only ever seen in the Other, and a voice I sometimes thought was my own saying things I could not fathom. It seemed at times that I had escaped myself, and at others... well, that I had only just found myself."

Filimaya smiled. "I believe that had a lot to do with Isia," she said, glancing across the lake.

For a moment Espasian's eyes searched the fog. "Well, what I know is that I woke feeling so strong and well that I wondered why I was in the Hollow until Faysa here explained everything that's happened."

Filimaya looked at Faysa. "You could not have been in better hands. She never left your side." She turned to Takk. "You should be very proud."

Takk grinned. "I know," he said, hoisting Faysa into his arms and holding her close. "I know."

Filimaya embraced Espasian. "You gave me quite a scare!" she said in his ear. Then she added: "I had no idea what I was going to do without you."

Espasian smiled and held her for a moment. "You would have done as you always do, Filimaya," he said, kissing her on the cheek, "and we would all have been the better for it."

He drew away then and cast his eyes across the meagre assembly of troops. His smile faltered for a moment, then he cleared his throat. "Yes, well, we had better get things underway. I'm not sure I quite have the voice for a rousing speech. But perhaps there is something better." He glanced at Faysa, his smile returning. "It wasn't just voices I heard in my sleep. I heard a brave song that I had almost forgotten."

Faysa's eyes widened.

The Magruman winked, then raised his arms to his army, calling for silence. In moments, the troops fell so quiet that the lake could be heard lapping against the shore. Espasian stepped forward, took a deep breath, and then, in a deep baritone, he sang:

"*With the wind, we breathe; with the earth, we sleep.*"

He paused, rocking a little on his heels and letting out a slight wheeze. Filimaya seized his arm excitedly, her eyes bright. "Yes, of course!" she exclaimed.

Then the army sang their reply:

"With the dawn, we sing; with the stag, we leap.
We are the roots of the ancient trees,
We are the hills, we are the seas!
Suhl! we cry. Suhl! Suhl!"

Espasian smiled proudly at his army and at Faysa. Then he pointed to the hills on either side of the valley and instantly cries went up from the captains on the lakeside, giving orders to their regiments. The Suhl army quickly divided in two, each beginning its march to flank the valley.

Again, Espasian filled his lungs and, taking Faysa's hand, they sang together:

"With the hare, we run; with the gull we cry."

And this time, the army was waiting.

"With the wolf, we hunt; with the hawk, we fly!
We are the Nile, deep and wide,
We are the rapids, we are the tide!
Suhl! we cry. Suhl! Suhl"

Espasian gave Faysa's hand to her father and kissed her head. Then he turned and began to march, joining the rear of the nearest column. From here he raised his voice again:

"With the sun, we rise with blaze and wonder."

And watching from her father's side, tears in her eyes, Faysa sang with him.

Then came the army's reply:

"With the storm, we come with fire and thunder!
We are gossamer, light as air,
We are the lion, we are the bear.
Suhl! we cry. Suhl! Suhl!
Suhl! we cry. Suhl! Suhl!"

And, as they sang, they passed into the trees and began their climb towards the crests of the hills. The skies had grown dark, and a red glow over the western reaches of the plain marked the end of day. As if in response to the song, the Imperial battle drums once again began to pound out their dreadful rhythm, rumbling round the valley like a sudden storm.

But out on the lake there was an eerie calm. The mist had begun to thin, and near the very centre of the waters the silhouette of a tiny boat was revealed, captained by a lone, slender figure. As the Suhl continued to sing, Isia raised her arms and, in that very instant, all round the valley giant birds spread their beautiful wings like regal cloaks and launched themselves into the air. They flapped three or four times, then hung on the breeze, drifting in circles over the two armies and calling to one another, as though sharing all they saw. Then, as Isia lowered her arms, the great eagles drew in their wings, stretched out their talons and dived screaming from the sky.

74

Sundown

"As I watched sundown on that hardest of days and all seemed lost, I reminded myself that in another world, right there in that very place, the sun was rising."

SYLAS SAT IN THE bow with his feet dangling over the side, gazing at the waters ahead. The sun was low on the starboard side and had swollen into a deep red orb, which tinged the Nile and everything around it with an ember-like fire. The river was so tranquil that it was hard to believe that just hours before they had passed beneath the giant trees and their journey had almost come to such an abrupt and violent end.

It had taken the crew of the *Windrush* some time to dare to raise their heads above deck, so fearful had they been of another deluge of rock. Triste had emerged first, holding the hatch open just a crack to check that they were clear of the trees but, as soon as he had seen the bright sunshine, he had thrown the cover wide and clattered up the steps, casting his eyes about for Sylas and Naeo. When he had seen them by the mainmast, still holding one another tight, he had let out a great cry of relief and – in a manner quite uncharacteristic of him – rushed over and wrapped them in his long arms, hugging them fiercely. In moments, Amelie and Simia had formed a great huddle, laughing and sobbing together.

For some reason Ash had held himself apart, staring back at the trees, and Sylas had noticed him turning that black, shiny shell between his fingers. But before long he had rejoined the crew and set them to clearing the decks of the shards of rock and broken casks and chests. This was done soon enough, and presently the surfaces shone with such a polish that, excepting a few dents in the railings, it was as though nothing had happened. With the trees now far behind them and no sign of any further pyramids to carry the signal ahead, everyone had begun to relax. The routines of the ship had quickly resumed, and Naeo, who had been complaining of the pains in her shoulders and back that had come on as they had been passing the trees, had taken the opportunity to go below with Amelie. As soon as she had gone, Sylas asked Ash to take over at the helm so that he could rest.

Simia had joined him in the bow, keen to talk about everything that had happened back at the trees, and they had chatted for a while about the strange town made of Quintessence, and the Black, and the Hamajaks. When Sylas had lain back and closed his eyes, keen to try to rest, Simia had unfolded the maps before her and pored over them, making measurements with her fingers and muttering under her breath. Try as he might, Sylas could not sleep, and he gave up all hope of it when Simia suddenly sat bolt upright and declared excitedly that if they kept up this pace they would almost certainly reach the Academy of Souls just after sundown. As Simia rushed off to tell Ash and everyone else, Sylas had leaned his elbows and chin on the railing and gazed ahead of the ship, mulling over everything that had happened and everything to come.

But now, sitting there in the hot breeze, with the sun dipping towards the dusty horizon, he still felt utterly unprepared.

Somewhere out there the Academy of Souls was waiting for them in the half-light, and he still had no idea what they would do when they got there.

"It's beautiful, isn't it?"

His mother had walked up quietly and was standing above him, her lined face bright in the sunset. Sylas nodded and smiled, and she sat beside him, threading her legs beneath the railing. She looked out at the giant sun, and the fields of young flax and barley spread out beneath it.

"If I hadn't seen it myself, I would never have believed it," said Amelie. "The pyramids, the Nile, those trees and now this!" She glanced at Sylas with sparkling eyes and smiled her wide, beautiful smile. "I can't say I'm glad to be here, but this is quite something, isn't it?"

They sat silently for a few moments, listening to the waters of the Nile, watching the sun dipping behind the pyramids, then she turned and looked at him, and put her hand on his.

"I know you must be frightened, Sylas," she said.

Sylas was not sure why, but he pulled his hand away.

"I can only imagine how you must feel," she continued, undeterred. She paused. "You know, when we spoke last night, I didn't say something I should have."

He turned and met her eyes.

"I believe in you," she said, her eyes gleaming in the twilight. "I believe in you with all my heart. You, Sylas, *and* Naeo." She reached out again and pulled his hand on to her lap. "And I'll tell you what I also believe. I believe that you can do things none of us has ever imagined. I've been blind, my love. I understand that now. Blind because I worry about you, but also because I struggle with the fact that there's more to you than I can ever know." She squeezed his hand. "But there *is* more. So much more."

Sylas looked away and was about to mumble a reply when

494

suddenly Amelie gripped his hand tight, and his eyes snapped back to her.

"Now more than ever, Sylas, you need to believe it. Forget what I said last night. Forget my doubts and worries; they came from a good place, but perhaps not the right place." She looked back at the sun, now almost lost behind the distant hills. "One thing's for certain in this strange, broken world. This is where you're meant to be. Here. With Naeo. Doing just this." She looked back at him, her eyes glazed. "Don't you doubt it a moment longer. Just find that strength we all know you have, and do what needs to be done."

§

Naeo lay on her front as Amelie had instructed, waiting for the poultice to take effect. She was glad to rest in her hammock, and in the past hour the pain in her back had indeed started to subside. But even as it had left her, something else had begun to gnaw at her, and this she could not escape. It was a single insistent thought: here they were, drawing ever closer to the Academy of Souls, and she still had no idea what they would do when they got there. And what was worse — what truly terrified her — was that Sylas had no more idea than she did.

Naeo decided that all she could do was read a little more of the Samarok. That, at least, would make her feel that she was preparing for what was to come. She was unsure where to begin so she began where she had left off, with Ammut's Pit — the catacombs below the Academy of Souls — and from there the Ravel Runes naturally took her to another entry about Ammut the beast of judgement, the so-called 'soul-eater'.

She read the ancient legend that those journeying into the afterlife passed first into the 'Hall of Two Truths'. Here the god of the afterlife, the jackal-headed Anubis, would weigh their heart to judge its worthiness. The heart would be placed on one side of a set of scales, and on the other lay a feather, known as the Ma'at feather: the feather of truth. If the heart weighed more than the feather, Ammut would devour it; if it was lighter, the soul would be saved and pass on into paradise.

The mention of the Ma'at feather made Naeo think of the Suhl feather, and when she read that the scales were called the Scales of Ma'at, she became more and more intrigued. She started to read about Ma'at herself, the goddess of truth, justice and harmony. She learned how the ancients believed that she had worn the feather of truth as her emblem, that she had prevented the world descending into chaos, and that it was she who had held the world in balance.

Naeo read entry after entry about Ma'at, and then, by some trick of the Ravel Runes, she was taken to an entry about Merimaat:

...soon she was named in the manner of the Priests of Souls. As a reward for service to the academy, Ramesses had decreed that the priests were to be known as 'Beloved of the Gods', making them greater than any priests of ritual that came before. And so the priest of Su became Meri-Su 'Beloved of Su', the priest of Bes was Meri-Bes, and the priest of Ma'at was named Meri-maat.

But one of the priests did not take up his decreed name. Emboldened by his unrivalled place in the Academy of Souls, Zamon, priest of the Temple of Thoth in Khemenu, began calling himself simply Thoth. Some of the priests considered this a blasphemy, but as scribe to the academy and master of the only official record Zamon could not be challenged. So it was that, as years passed, Zamon, Priest of Thoth became simply Thoth – a new, self-appointed and living god.

Naeo raised her eyes from the page and gazed out of the porthole at the setting sun. So that was how it had all happened – how *he* had happened.

She closed the Samarok and rested her chin in her hands, staring out. Perhaps it was the darkness of her readings about the catacombs and Thoth, but she found herself dreading the close of day. She had the strangest feeling that she did not want the sun to set; that for whatever reason this last glimpse of it was precious. She watched the dipping orb of fire until it started to drop behind some distant hills, slipping slowly into the underworld.

Then, quite suddenly, she pushed herself upright.

How could she have forgotten? Now, of all times!

Her father!

She fixed her eyes on the dying sun and already her mind was ranging back to the forests of Salsimaine, to the treehouse in their favourite tree, to her father and his outstretched hands.

She let out a sigh of relief.

He was there.

Of course he was there.

He smiled back at her, opening his arms. And then, to her surprise, he spoke.

"I believe in you, my Nay-no," he said, pulling her into the treehouse. "I believe in you more than anything else in this world."

In that moment, she felt as though she was there with him, so that when he cupped her chin in his hand and turned her face up to his, she could feel his warmth. See the light in his eyes.

"Now," he said, "do what you must do."

75

The Darkness

*"But after the dazzle and colour
of every sunset comes the darkness."*

"IT CAN'T BE LONG now!" panted Lucien.

"It mustn't... be long!" gasped Dresch.

They might have thought it beautiful if only they could have seen it. That ballet of light and dark. That dance between good and evil. But they could not see it because they were at its mad, tumultuous heart and, if they had stopped even for a moment, they would have been consumed.

As the hours passed, they had begun to act by instinct alone: by the sense of what was there rather than the knowledge of it. They sensed the shadows of the beasts that had not yet taken shape and drove them away. They felt gathering swarms in the heavens and turned them aside before they became an irresistible storm. And, with time, their limbs had remembered long days with the Merisi in their youth, rediscovered that grace for which they had worked so hard. So now they danced, their arms sweeping in wide arcs, their bodies writhing as they slipped past one another in a single motion, stronger together than they could ever be apart.

The machines too were part of the dance. Some circled in the darkness, confusing the creatures that tried to pass. Some rolled together to form an armoured wall, or apart to form a trap. Others still wove through the maze of metal, lights flashing, sirens blaring, sending the beasts into a craze.

But what made the dance complete, what made it all come together as one, were the beams of light. The searchlights that hours before had rested upon Dresch and Lucien as they embraced now swept across the skies, weaving between one another, painting spirals in the clouds. In response, the black swarms writhed and twisted, trying to bathe themselves in the light, and in the process feeding the confusion.

Not a flare was fired, not a shot rang out. The army had learned, at last, to work with the Merisi. It was a dance of science and instinct, and it was a thing of beauty.

"Surely it should be dawn!" yelled Lucien as he darted past Dresch.

"Hold on!" Dresch shouted. "I'll check the time!"

She retreated towards him, her scarf flying up as she pressed herself into his back. She waited, biding her time, choosing a moment between the lunging shadows, and then, in a flash, she raised her watch and turned it to catch a passing beam.

She stared at it disbelievingly.

She stared a moment too long.

Suddenly Lucien was pushing her to the ground, reaching out towards a stampeding figure. Another lurched at them from the side, and another from the rear. In a twisting, leaping motion, he just managed to raise his glove to all three, sending them growling and whimpering back into the dark. But others took their place, sensing a weakness, a misstep in the dance.

Then Dresch was back on her feet, her glove raised. For some minutes the two Merisi separated, going where the dance took them, fighting desperately to regain control. But finally they managed to draw near.

"What happened?" gasped Lucien.

"The time!" panted Dresch. "James, it should've been light more than an hour ago!"

Lucien glanced back at her and caught a glimpse of the terror in her eyes. "Are you sure?"

She nodded.

He looked into the inky sky. "So… what's happening?" When he looked back at her, she was waving her arm in the air, and then pointing out across the battlefield. "Martha, what are you doing?"

But, even as he asked, he understood. One of the searchlights responded to her command and broke the dance, panning slowly across the plain, lighting everything in the direction she had pointed. As it travelled, it revealed column after column of a new blackness. Each of these dark pillars reached up to the sky until they disappeared into the night. They swallowed the light as it passed, and at their heart each of them had an upward motion, as though their deepest shades were rising.

"It… it looks like it's coming from the pools of Black," said Lucien, peering at the sources of the darkness.

"James," said Dresch, staring. "*This* is what it was for."

"What?"

"The Black!" she exclaimed. "Don't you see? *That's* why there's been no dawn!"

"I don't… understand."

"It's changing!" she yelled with tears in her eyes. "The Black is *becoming* the darkness!"

Lucien shook his head. "But… why?"

"Because this is the last plague!" she said with a sob of fear. "The Black was the first plague, and it's going to be the last!"

Lucien turned and gaped at the forest of blackness reaching up into the sky, and finally he understood.

"The everlasting night," he breathed.

Franz Veeglum breathed heavily as he backed his way up the hill. "As Thoth promised," he said. "Ze last night, from which there will be no dawn."

He wiped the sweat from his brow and looked over the lines of beasts now circling the hill, and the swaying palm forests, and the silhouettes of stupas, to the ever-swelling cloud of nothingness.

It was an appalling sight, not for what it was but for what it was not. It lacked all shape, form, substance, meaning. It was not a presence of something but a total, inexplicable absence. Now, early in the tropical afternoon, when the sun ought to have been beating down upon the forests, it was lost behind this hanging fog of darkness, as though night was drawing in.

When Veeglum turned and looked above the great Irrawaddy River, he saw a vast patch of blue sky. But it was an island. The fog of darkness crept towards it from all sides, fed by columns of shadow from the valleys and the mouths of caves. These might have been smoke had they drifted in the wind, but they did not drift. They were nothingness.

"You were right, Paiscion, my friend," murmured Veeglum. "One more plague of Moses, and this too brought upon ourselves." He looked straight up, into a darkness without stars, or moon, or the promise of day. "What better answer to the light of science than ze dark? This will bring us to our knees."

A sudden chorus of howls and gibbering drew his eyes back down to the base of the hill, where he saw an advancing line of beasts: Ghorhund, bodies low and prowling; Ragers, tails lashing the air; Hamajaks, fists beating the earth. He drew a long breath and pulled at the cuff of his Merisi glove, pushing his fingertips tight into the green velvet. Then he raised it and kissed the ornate embroidery that laced the back of his hand.

"Oh, Sylas and Naeo," he whispered, "if you are still alive, this is the time. The time Merisu spoke of centuries before now. Ze time for which you were born." He extended his gloved hand and cleared his parched throat. "This is your time."

Then, as he stepped forward, he began to chant under his breath:

"Reach for the silvered glimmer on ze lake,
Turn to the sun-streaked shadow in your wake,
Now, rise: fear not where none have gone,
For then, at last, we may be one."

§

The Duke woke from a deep, satisfying sleep, his first since that dreadful, thunderous storm — if that was what it was. There had been such booms and thumps of thunder that he had curled up in his old trunk and sung softly to himself — songs he had not sung since his years at the 'Old Place', as he called it — the grim boarding school he had been sent to in his youth. Now, as then, he had wrapped himself in his song like a well-worn blanket and finally sung himself to sleep.

He yawned and tried to stretch, but the creak of wood reminded him that he was still inside the trunk. He opened his eyes and looked about him.

Nothing but thick, impenetrable darkness.

He had the strangest notion that there had been more light when his eyes were closed. The trunk had been the best place to be, but now there were no terrifying noises outside. In fact, there were no sounds at all. He really ought to stretch his limbs and take some refreshment. And, besides, there was an unbearable, noxious stink inside the trunk, an unsavoury blend of damp trousers and old socks.

He pushed gently on the lid and felt it lift. He heard the hinges creak. But, to his surprise, there was no flood of light. Not even a glow. His cardboard home seemed just as dark as the interior of the old chest. He glanced down at his cheap digital watch and pressed the button on the side. A dim golden light flickered into life.

8:50 a.m.

"Nonsense!" he muttered, adding something rather disrespectful about digital watches and the modern world, then he pushed the lid of the trunk open and flopped out on to his back.

For a moment he lay still, enjoying the cleaner, fresher air, but finally he rolled on to his hands and knees and felt his way to the cardboard flap that served as his window.

He pushed it open and blinked in astonishment.

There was no more light *outside* than there was inside. He could see neither the pathway nor the river. He could not even see the night sky. There was only a thick, featureless dark.

He fell back from the window, letting the flap drop into place. Then he drew his knees up to his chest and rocked backwards and forwards.

"Well, this isn't right!" he muttered to himself, his voice loud and jarring.

The longer the Duke sat there, the more he was gripped by panic. It pressed in upon him, closing about his lungs and throat, making his breath come in short, sharp gasps.

When it became too much for him, he reached for the edge of the trunk, pulled himself up and threw himself into it. Then he reached out, fumbled for a moment in the dark and slammed the lid.

He lay in the darkness and pressed his eyes shut.

"It'll be all right in the morning," he said softly to himself.

And then he began to sing.

76
Land

"But the curious thing about this amazing,
surprising, terrifying world, is that every part of it —
every river, lake, ocean and spit of land*, every mountain*
range and desert — is identical to our own."

THE *Windrush* THUMPED GENTLY against the riverbank, straining against her tethers. The crew had tied her off well, but still the waves and eddies of the mighty cataract made her buck and roll.

Sylas walked down the gangplank, relieved to be stepping on to dry land, but nevertheless uneasy at leaving the *Windrush* behind. She had become a trusty friend over the past days, and her timbers and sails had begun to feel like part of him. He turned and took one last look at her towering masts and shining sails gleaming magically even in the dim light of the moon. Above, the feather standard flew proudly from the mainmast.

"Come *on*," cajoled Simia, catching him by the elbow. "We're coming back, you know!"

"I know," said Sylas. He started to turn, but just then he caught sight of his mother standing on the quarterdeck. She raised a hand in farewell, then laid it over her heart. He smiled and waved, trying to look as casual and confident as he could. He thought he saw her smile crumple, but she turned away before he could be certain.

He was glad that they had spent those last couple of hours together, sitting in the bow, sometimes talking, sometimes just being quiet together. He had even managed to fall asleep for a while and, when he had woken, he had found that he was lying with his head in her lap and she had been gently stroking his hair, just like she used to. He had kept his eyes closed for some minutes more, imagining that he was back at their cottage, and that none of this was really happening. But that fiction could not last for long, and all too soon Simia had called from the quarterdeck that they were drawing near to the first cataract. He remembered how his mother's whole body had tensed and then, after a brief pause, she had continued to stroke his hair, perhaps hoping that he would not wake.

"Come on then!" called Ash from the top of the bank. "Are we going or not?"

Sylas stared at his mother for a moment longer, then followed Simia on to the shore. The waiting group set off at once. Ash was in the lead, consulting one of Fathray's documents, which seemed to be showing him the way. Behind him came four of the crew, then Naeo, Simia, Sylas and finally two more sailors who guarded the rear. It had been decided that the rest of the crew — about half its number — would remain behind, including Amelie as ship's doctor, and Triste, who had volunteered to keep watch in the crow's nest.

The expedition climbed steadily, clambering over sand and scrub, enjoying the sensation of firm ground underfoot. The moon was a crescent — no more than a pale, thin arc in the starry sky — but it lent just enough light for the travellers to make out the dark shapes of hills about them, the craggy faces of small cliffs and dried gorges, and the vast stretch of boiling, churning water that they were leaving behind. They could see now that they had been right to moor where they had. The cataract was a formidable sequence of rapids, and its leaping waters were dotted with dangerous, angry-looking rocks.

As they climbed the hill, Ash conjured a dancing bluish green light in the palm of his hand, which he used to light Fathray's parchment.

"Ash," hissed Naeo, "you shouldn't use Kimiyya, especially not here!"

He regarded her coolly. "So what am I supposed to read by?" he scoffed with a harsh, rather unpleasant edge to his voice. "Starlight?"

"I'm sure there's a way with Essenfayle," protested Naeo. "I could..."

But, as she was speaking, Ash abruptly stowed his map and stalked away, snuffing out the light as he went. The crew watched him go in astonishment, then their eyes slowly returned to Naeo.

"He must be tired," she said with a shrug. "Let's keep moving."

Everyone continued up the slope, murmuring among themselves. Simia caught up with Naeo.

"You're right, Naeo," she whispered. "We'll be seen if he keeps doing that!"

Naeo nodded and glanced ahead at Ash. "He just doesn't seem... *himself*," she said. "But arguing with him won't help. Like I say, I think maybe he's just tired. We shouldn't have left him to sail the ship on his own for so long."

Simia grunted, looking unconvinced. "You and Sylas did it for much longer, *and* you had to get past those trees. He didn't have to deal with anything like *that*, did he?"

"Well, there were two of us."

"Oh, were there?" said Simia, quick as a flash. "Really?" She grinned.

Naeo elbowed her in the side and managed a smile.

They continued their climb in silence, sometimes descending for a short while into a dry gully or hollow, but always resuming their ascent on the far side so that soon they were high above the Nile. They occasionally glanced back at the *Windrush*, and always found her still reassuringly visible, glistening in the darkness.

For a while they passed through a rugged, labyrinthine terrain of high, rocky outcrops, and Ash was forced to pause regularly to consult his documents, often — to his companions' exasperation — by the light of the green-blue fire. Their route took them on a winding path that at times seemed to go back on itself, but as they re-emerged on open ground, they saw to their relief that the Nile and the *Windrush* were still behind them — if now a great distance away.

Ash stalked ahead with new confidence, but as he approached a nearby crest he suddenly drew up short. The group behind him also halted, watching closely. He stared ahead, seemingly captivated by something in the desert.

He waved them forward.

Cautiously they all walked up to join him.

They saw what had drawn his attention at once. Before them, on a flat expanse just beyond the folds of hills and canyons, was a perfect circle of flickering torches.

Ash lowered himself to his haunches and signalled to the others to do the same. They all crouched and peered out at the strange lights. After a few moments they saw a movement between the lights. There appeared to be a number of large, beast-like figures patrolling just outside the perimeter of torches. Some of these figures — perhaps eight in all — moved slowly and steadily, seeming to keep watch over the surrounding desert. The black manes, high ears and protruding snouts of Ghor guards were clear to see. Beyond them, forming a perfect circle just inside the torches, were a dozen more massive forms, at least twice the height of the Ghor. These stood perfectly still, looming over a central circular space of open sand.

"It's the stone circle!" exclaimed Simia excitedly, nudging Sylas. "The one Isia told us about!"

Sylas felt his skin prickle as he remembered the entry in the Samarok that Isia had showed them, describing the very first stone circle: the one where the twelve Priests of Souls had gathered and, through their incantations, brought forth the Ramesses Shield.

"This is where it all happened," he murmured, gazing in awe at the twelve colossal stones, one for each of the Priests of Souls, and then at the circular space at the centre, now just rutted sand. "This is where they broke the world in two."

He had said it more to himself than to anyone else, but in the quiet of the desert everyone heard. The significance of it settled upon them like a spectre. They imagined the priests chanting strange incantations, and the sands rumbling, and the skies boiling red. And at the centre of it all they pictured that innocent child, Isia. How alone she must have felt in that moment. How terrifyingly alone.

They all fell quiet as they tried to comprehend what had happened in that place. How this tiny, forgotten fragment of the world had become the beginning of everything: the divided worlds, broken souls, the Glimmer Myth, the Empire, even this very journey, which had at last brought Isia's bloodline back to where it all began.

But Sylas also had that feeling he had experienced so many times since he had first heard the Passing Bell: that this was where he was supposed to be.

It was Naeo who finally broke the silence. "Shouldn't we keep going?" she said, looking at Ash. "The Academy of Souls is close, isn't it?"

He looked down at his map. "I think," he said, tilting it to catch the light of the moon, "that the entrance is in the next valley."

Naeo drew her hand close to the parchment and, in that moment, it was bathed in a brighter celestial light, as though the moonbeams had gathered there, at the tips of her fingers.

Ash glanced at her, then quickly dropped his eyes, trying not to show his surprise. "Yes, I was right. It's hidden in the hills just down... there." He pointed to the south where a stain of shadows gathered in the deepest folds of the landscape.

"Triste won't be able to see us down there," muttered one of the group anxiously.

They all looked back to the river where they could still just make out the faint gleam of the *Windrush*'s prow. They had assured Triste that they would stay within sight so that he could signal them if he saw anything suspicious.

"Well, that's a risk we'll just have to take," said Ash, rising to a stoop and checking about him in all directions. And, with that, he set off along the slope, still in a stoop.

The rest of the group watched him go.

"Well, he's right," said Naeo, getting to her feet. "There's no point staying here."

Warily they set out after him. They snaked along the dry, crumbling slope, following in his footsteps, keeping as close to one another as they could in the failing light. As the way became more treacherous, they started to follow a goat trail, which was narrow but hard-packed and more reliable underfoot than the loose sand and shingle.

The path slowly descended, taking them round boulders and steepening banks of sand and grit. Soon they had dropped far from the reach of the moonlight, and Ash once again kindled the strange fire in his palm so that he could consult Fathray's map. It was recklessly bright, its flickering glare lighting even the far side of the valley, but no one challenged him, sensing that he would not listen.

The further they went, the more the slopes gathered into a close, hugging gully. The darkness was now almost complete so at Simia's suggestion everyone took the shoulder of the person in front, to avoid a misstep.

They were just negotiating an overhanging outcrop of rock when Ash suddenly halted. Everyone drew up sharply behind him. Sylas, who was at the rear, could just make out the Magruman's blond locks turning from side to side.

A blinding light suddenly flared, bathing everything in a fierce blue-white glare. Through squinting eyes, Sylas saw Ash's hand rising above the heads of the group, and with it the bright flame. At first he could see little but the blaze, but then he caught sight of something else flickering in the light. What they had all thought was an overhanging rock was in fact a huge stone lintel, so massive that it was able to support the weight of the hillside above. Beneath it was a gaping blackness: an opening into the very heart of the hill.

Stretching, Ash held his light up even higher. There, etched into the rocky face of the lintel, was a fading inscription made of symbols and hieroglyphs.

When he turned, Sylas saw the white of his teeth.

"This is it!" Ash hissed. "The Academy of Souls!"

77

The Lookout

*"What I wouldn't give to have a secret window
into this world of marvels — some* lookout *that
might mean I never need to leave."*

TRISTE STARED INTO THE inky darkness, his eyes darting about
as though picking out the details of a scene. In that great emptiness,
he saw glints and flashes of colour, momentary streaks and trails
of light. He saw fear and excitement, doubt and wonder, and at
one point, to his surprise, he even saw anger — or had it been
malice? It was muddled and was already fading, as though hidden
behind earth or rock.

"Can you still see them?" asked Amelie.

When Sylas and the others had set off, she had done her best
to busy herself in her cabin below, but there were only a certain
number of times she could arrange and rearrange her store of
medical supplies, and finally her anxieties had got the better of
her, and she had climbed up to the crow's nest to join Triste.

"Only just," said Triste, pointing into the darkness. "They're
over there. They're going underground."

"I'm not sure I really wanted to know that," said Amelie. She
was silent for some moments and then, perhaps to change the

subject, she said: "That's quite a talent you have, Triste. To see as you do."

The Scryer lit his pipe, taking care to hide the flame between his hands. "It can be a curse," he said, lifting the stem to his lips and puffing until the pipe issued a long trail of orange smoke. "But I must say, being with Sylas and Naeo, it's been more wonder than curse."

Amelie leaned back against the railing. "It has?"

He took a drag on his pipe and spoke in puffs of smoke. "The bond between them is extraordinary. But you already know that."

"Not as you know it," Amelie said, intrigued. "Tell me."

"You're aware that we Scryers *see* the connections between people — *see* them rather than feel them? That for us those connections show themselves in colour and form?"

Amelie nodded.

He blew a stream of smoke out into the blackness. "Well, when I look at Sylas and Naeo, there's no colour or form."

She frowned. "So... what *do* you see?"

Triste met her eyes and smiled. "A blaze. It's like looking into the face of the sun."

Amelie's frown deepened. She tilted her head. "And this blaze, is it... a *good* thing?"

"It's the most beautiful thing I've ever seen! It's a constant flow, one to the other: thought... feeling... energy. If one weakens, the other lends their strength; if one questions, the other answers; if one doubts, the other finds hope."

Amelie's eyes began to fill with tears. "With all my heart, I wish I could see it," she said, her voice tight with emotion. She looked out into the night. "Do you think that's what it might be like for us all, if they find what they're looking for? If the Glimmer Myth is true?"

The Scryer raised his eyebrows. "We can only hope."

He seemed about to say more, but suddenly he bowed his head and pressed his eyes shut.

"What is it?" Amelie asked. "Are you all rig—"

Triste raised his hand for silence. He opened his eyes and turned about, peering in all directions.

"What *is it*?" hissed Amelie, frightened now.

"I don't know," he whispered, wide-eyed. "I can't... quite... see."

Suddenly he dropped his pipe to the floor and crushed it underfoot.

Amelie was petrified now, and she stared into the blackness, trying to pick out whatever Triste was seeing.

She leaned into his ear. "Are there... many?" she murmured.

"I can't tell," he said, shaking his head. "Sometimes it looks like one, sometimes two..." His face was clouded with confusion. "Sometimes thousands. *Tens* of thousands. It's as if it—"

He was interrupted by a sound in the heavens. It was barely audible, like a breath of wind over dry grass.

Then it came again, and again.

It was louder each time, until they could hear the unmistakable sound of wings beating the air — giant wings, slow and powerful, thrashing the night air. Whatever it was, it was coming from along the Nile, to the north.

Triste pulled Amelie down into the crow's nest. "Don't make a sound!" he whispered urgently.

She pressed herself as far down as she could and gazed, terrified, into the blackness.

"Shouldn't we signal?" she hissed.

Triste shook his head. "It's too late. They wouldn't see. Not now."

For moments that seemed like hours they listened to the sound drawing nearer and nearer, the great huffs of the wings growing louder and louder. Finally they were so powerful that the crow's nest trembled, and Amelie found herself leaning ever closer to Triste, pressing herself into his shoulder.

All at once the darkness above the *Windrush* roared and opened wide, sending forth a blast of wind that filled the ship's sails and made her tip precariously out into the river. Her moorings strained to breaking point, such that they would have snapped had the gale not died as quickly as it had arisen. Then came another, and another, the unseen wings now beating directly overhead. The crow's nest swayed like a crazed pendulum, and Triste and Amelie had to cling to the sides to keep from being tossed out.

"I can see him!" gasped Triste, turning to Amelie with wide, frightened eyes. "It's Thoth!"

Amelie stared at him. "But how can—"

She was cut short by a voice that boomed out of the night and made their bodies tremble. It was the voice of thousands.

"Give them to me!"

And then somehow the night itself seemed to reach out towards them. Massive talons of shadow raked across the rigging, snapping ropes and tearing the gleaming canvas of the sails. A wing the height of the ship mauled one of the masts, snapping it like driftwood. A dark tail lashed the decks, sweeping two of the crew overboard and crushing the ship's wheel. The shining vessel leaned precariously, her hull striking submerged rocks with a sickening crunch.

In moments, the *Windrush* was devastated, her sails torn to rags, her ropes and yards snapped, her decks littered with broken timber. The terrified crew fled for their lives, leaping into the dark waters or scrambling down the gangplank.

High above, the crow's nest had been toppled. It hung upside down from the mainmast, held in place by no more than a pair of ropes. Somehow Amelie and Triste had managed to cling to the railing and stay inside, pressing themselves back into the basket to keep from being seen. They were buffeted by wind from the wings of the beast, which still hovered above, watching the *Windrush* for any sign of movement. Occasionally it reached out from the darkness and took another swipe, dashing away timbers and ropes, until, at last, it let out a frustrated, feline growl and, in a final act of vandalism, ripped the Suhl standard from its fixing. Triste and Amelie watched as the two halves fluttered down, the feather torn down the middle.

Suddenly Thoth let out a cry of unfettered rage that made the night air quiver, and Amelie and Triste braced themselves, waiting for the end.

But it did not come. Instead the beat of the wings seemed to shift to one side of the ship, and soon they could be heard heading off into the distance.

"He's going!" hissed Amelie.

Triste raised a finger to his lips. He listened, his Scrying eyes peering out into the night, and finally he nodded. "He's gone."

"*Was* it Thoth?" asked Amelie, still terrified.

Triste nodded, his eyes scouring the darkness for signs of movement.

"And what was that... creature?"

"Some monstrous creation of his no doubt. Nothing I've seen before."

Suddenly they heard another bestial shriek out in the night, from the direction Thoth had taken.

"He's going to the academy!" exclaimed Amelie. "We have to warn them!"

Triste fixed his eyes on the silhouettes of the hills. He reached out, took her hand. "It's already too late."

78

The Crucible

*"What monstrosity, what thing of ancient legend will next
emerge from the* crucible *of the birthing chambers?"*

"Surrender thy mind, thy body and thy soul," read Ash, gazing up
at the engraved stone above the entrance. *"Only the devout will
find the Way."*

Simia frowned at the faded hieroglyphs. "You can read *that*?"

"No, I can read *this*," said Ash, holding up one of Fathray's
documents. Just visible in the weak light was a drawing of the
inscription and its translation scrawled beneath.

"This is how the Academy of Souls got its name," said Sylas,
remembering something he had read in the Samarok. "The priests
were supposed to give everything to this place, even their souls."

They all stared at the inscription, weighing its meaning.

"Well, I wouldn't have wanted to be them," said Simia with a
shudder. She touched the rock on one side of the entrance. "I can't
believe Merimaat came here. And Merisu. They were right here,
with Thoth, all those years ago."

Ash cleared his throat. "Well, are we going to do this?"

Without waiting for an answer, he stepped across the threshold
and disappeared into the darkness. Sylas, Naeo and Simia followed,

keeping close to one another for comfort. The others came next, four of them in one group, the last two advancing more slowly, keeping an eye on the path behind.

The passageway was pitch-black and cold, with a breeze blowing up from somewhere far below, where they could see a faint, distant glow — perhaps a doorway at the end of the passage. The loose, gritty floor sloped downwards towards it, and it was so uneven that in places they had to brace themselves against the walls to avoid slipping. They could feel the sharp, deep gashes of the chisels that had hewn their way through the rock thousands of years before.

"They really wanted to hide this place," said Simia quietly.

Something about the passage made her words echo into the darkness and, more alarmingly, come rushing back even louder than before. Everyone froze, eyeing the opening up ahead, expecting to see a movement at any moment.

Nothing stirred.

Ash looked over his shoulder. "Quiet, Simsi!" he murmured angrily.

Simia whispered an apology, but Ash had already turned away and set off down the passage.

As they all continued the descent, even their steps now seemed far, far too loud. They began to move more slowly, almost tiptoeing along. At one point Naeo slipped and the sound of her scuffing heel resonated up and down the passage. Still nothing appeared in the light.

Soon enough, they began to draw near to the opening, and they saw that it resembled the entrance: a high, squared doorway with a massive lintel above. The glow at its centre was cool and silvery, like the moonlight that they had left behind, and they realised to their surprise that they were heading not into some inner chamber but back out into the open air.

As everyone gathered just inside the doorway, Ash crouched and edged forward. When he reached the threshold, he peered out, took some moments to check in all directions and then waved them on.

Sylas, Naeo and Simia crept up behind. Before them was a canyon with almost vertical sides and rockfalls at either end, creating an entirely enclosed space cut off from the outside world. Everyone gazed at the rocky surfaces towering above. Even in the dim moonlight, they could see that there was something very peculiar about them. In places, they looked like normal rock, but in others they seemed to have been charred to a pitch-blackness, or they gleamed as though they were forged of some kind of metal. Strangest of all, there were areas where the rock seemed to have melted, flowing down before solidifying like a frozen waterfall.

Here and there among these disfigured rocks, symbols had been etched into the surface: circles, pentangles, hieroglyphs and others that were so complex that they made little sense to the eye. But at one end of the canyon there was an even more bizarre sight: a pyramidal pile of perfectly spherical rocks, like gigantic cannonballs, smooth and faultless. There were others too, strewn across the canyon floor, but these were chipped and cracked, and many had been shattered by some unimaginable force.

"I've been reading about this place," said Ash. "They called it 'the Crucible'. This is where they first experimented with the Four Ways!" He looked at them with wide, gleaming eyes. "This is where they were born! All of them! Kimiyya, Druindil, Urgolvane, Essenfayle!"

"*Only the devout will find the Way,*" murmured Naeo. "Except they didn't just find one Way, they found four."

Ash turned his eyes about the walls of the canyon. "Just look at how they melted the rock! Twelve Priests of Souls, all acting as one. Their power was devastating. There was nothing they couldn't do!"

"Yes, and look where it got them," said Naeo. "Look where it got us! I don't think—"

Ash put a finger to his lips and gestured upwards. "Listen!" he whispered. "There's something out there."

A pulse of fear ran up Sylas's spine. He held his breath and listened, and after a moment he heard a strange, rhythmical *huff, huff, huff*, coming from somewhere out in the night. It was getting louder, as though whatever was making the noise was drawing ever nearer to the Crucible. Sylas was just about to say that it sounded like gigantic wings when he was stopped short by a terrifying, half-human cry that echoed from the sides of the canyon. A moment later there was a distant crash, like the sound of shattering timbers.

Sylas felt Simia's hand slip into his. "I think it's coming from the *Windrush*!" she hissed.

Ash looked down at the parchment, then his eyes darted quickly about the Crucible, peering into the shadows and crevices. They came to rest on a single spot on the far side. "The entrance is just there!" he exclaimed, pointing. "Straight across! Come with me now!"

With that, he rose to his feet and strode out into the starlight, heading directly towards the opposite side of the canyon. The others hesitated for a moment, looking nervously at the great span of the Crucible floor, then they followed.

They felt horribly exposed. The dark cliffs towered above them, offering a thousand hidden places from which they might be seen. But now they had no choice but to keep on and reach the other side.

Sylas's mind was racing. Had that been a human scream? He was almost certain he had heard words, but he could not make them out. And what was that other sound? Was it the *Windrush*? Surely Simia was right — it had to be. His thoughts flew to his mother and he felt a rising panic. His breath left him and his step faltered.

Then he felt a hand on his back.

It was Naeo.

She had seen him, sensed his panic, and now she was pushing him on — hard — so that he could not resist.

The sounds of splitting timber and the *huff, huff, huff* of mighty wings were clearer now, filling the open sky above. Someone in the darkness panicked and broke into a run, and suddenly they were all running headlong and blind. Already they were halfway across, weaving between the broken spheres of rock, piles of rubble and strange patches of shadow scattered across the sandy floor. These streaks of blackness looked a little like the burn marks on the canyon walls — the residue of some past inferno — but as he ran past them Sylas thought he saw one of them glisten in the moonlight.

Suddenly one of the crew called out from behind, and everyone turned to see him staggering to one side, clutching at his boot, pulling it off his foot. He tossed it clear, and it landed in a blot of darkness. To Sylas's astonishment, the darkness splashed and then swallowed the boot whole.

He looked at the patch closest to him, and then glanced about in all directions, his skin beginning to crawl. Those were no scorch marks; they were silky-smooth mirrors of blackness.

"It's the Black!" he yelled, his voice echoing from the walls of the canyon. "It's everywhere!"

"*Everywhere!*" a voice breathed back.

"*Everywhere!*" came another from behind him, dry and hollow.

He turned and looked full into Simia's face, and he saw the terror in her eyes. She opened her mouth to say something, but the words did not come.

"Keep running!" he yelled, so loudly that his voice rang from every rocky surface. He grabbed Simia's hand, reached for Naeo's and sprinted at full speed into the darkness.

"*Run!*" breathed a voice like a desert wind just behind him.

"*Run!*" came a whisper in his ear.

"*Run!*" came a voice directly ahead of him.

Instinctively Sylas darted to the right to avoid it, but he had only taken two steps when Simia shrieked and pulled so hard on his arm that he skidded to a halt.

He was teetering on the brink of a large pool of Black. Simia yanked him away and they heaved their limbs back into a run. Ash was at their side now, his cloak fluttering behind him like one of the chasing wraiths. Naeo was still next to Sylas and the others were behind, their footsteps wild, their breaths like gasps of terror.

Suddenly there was a startled cry. They heard a murmur, like someone trying to object or raise an alarm, but then the voice became a moan.

Sylas felt a creeping horror. He knew the meaning of that moan. He remembered that awful stomach-wrenching moment out on the Barrens that one of the Kraven had slipped inside him, raking through him like a scourge. He desperately wanted to go back and try to help, but instead he ran. He ran because he knew the Kraven and that there was nothing else to be done. All of them fled with abandon, numb with fear, colliding with rocks, stumbling over the uneven ground, leaping over cracks in the canyon floor. They ran until there was nowhere else to go.

"Stop!" Sylas cried suddenly. He reached out and pulled Simia and Naeo back with all his might, bringing them all skidding to a halt.

They were on the brink of another vast streak of Black directly across their path.

Almost at once the voices returned, closer this time.

"*Where are you running to?*"

"*S-s-s-stay with us-s-s!*"

Then another voice breathed out of the darkness directly ahead. "*S-s-speak with us-s-s a while.*"

Sylas and his companions tried desperately to find a way forward, but everywhere they looked their path was blocked by the Black.

"*These hills-s-s are our home; these s-s-stones are our bones-s-s...*"

"*Now, let them be yours-s-s.*" There was a laugh, dry and wasted. "*And let yours-s-s be ours-s-s.*"

Something brushed against Sylas's arm, and then a ghoulish presence surged, pressing itself into him so that he felt it against his ribs, in his stomach, in his chest. He felt it tugging at his insides, drinking in his warmth, consuming him.

And then Naeo let out a moan of anguish.

In that very instant, the presence in Sylas froze. He felt it shift and then, in a frantic spasm, it heaved itself free.

He staggered backwards, his legs buckling, until he felt Simia's arms close about him.

"It's OK, Sylas," she said in his ear, "I've got you."

He blinked, gasping, trying to regain his senses. The darkness seemed deeper now, the air sharp and bitter on his tongue. He heard Simia's breathing, quick and frightened.

"Naeo!" he heard her call out. And then more urgently: "Ash! Help her!"

At the very same moment as Sylas had fallen, so had Naeo — not because she had herself been attacked, but because she had felt everything Sylas had felt. All at once a squall of breathless whispers swept round them, becoming louder and louder, speaking ancient, forgotten words. The temperature fell so sharply that the crew of the *Windrush* began to shiver, their teeth chattering.

Then, as suddenly as they had begun, the whispers fell silent.

"*You*," hissed a voice in front of Sylas, so close that he felt sure that its owner was almost touching his face. "*You are... they.*" There was a pause. "*You are... Is-s-sia.*"

Sylas was so cold he could barely speak, but some part of him knew that he must. He forced his lips to form the words.

"We are," he said.

The gale of whispers swirled once more and then faded to silence.

"*You are the two,*" said the whisper.

Driven by the same impulse, Sylas and Naeo reached out for one another in the dark, their cold hands clasping tight. As the Merisi Band began to glow, they spoke as one. "We are," they said.

Again, the whispers rushed forth. Sylas and Naeo felt an icy chill draw so close that they could see their own breath.

"*Then you mus-s-st right the wrong,*" said the ghostly voice. "*You mus-s-st right the wrong and s-s-set us-s-s free.*"

Sylas mustered as strong a voice as he could. "We will," he said. "But you must let us go."

There was another surge of whispers. Sylas's lungs were aching now, and he thought he might black out from the cold.

"*The two of Is-s-sia's blood may pass-s-s,*" said the voice finally.

"But what about the others?" he asked.

"*The others-s-s must make their peace with us-s-s.*"

Some of the crew let out a cry of dismay.

"No!" exclaimed Simia, glancing at Sylas.

Instinctively he stood in front of her. "All of us," he insisted, "or none of us!"

The whispers struck up again and, as their fervour increased, he felt himself buffeted angrily by cold, shapeless forms.

"But don't you see?" he shouted. "You won't *need* our friends! You'll be free!"

But the voices showed no sign of abating, and the Kraven began thumping into him, throwing him from side to side and chilling him to the bone.

Suddenly everything around was bathed in a silvery light. The radiance grew brighter and brighter, lighting up the entire huddle of the crew, and as it did so the whispers quickly died away. He could feel the Kraven draw away from him, retreating from the light, and as they left him he became aware of Naeo close by his side, her arms raised towards the heavens, gathering the beams of moonlight.

"WE WILL NOT GO WITHOUT THEM!" she bellowed, turning on the spot, glaring out into the dark.

For some moments there was an absolute hush. The piercing chill subsided as though the Kraven had moved far back into the darkness.

Finally the single voice spoke again. "*Very well. All may pass-s-s,*" it said. "*But, until we are free, none of you will be free.*"

Warily Sylas and Naeo nodded. "All right," they said. Slowly, hesitantly, they and their companions turned to continue their walk across the Crucible.

"*No,*" breathed the voice. "*There!*"

The slick of Black to their side suddenly sprawled, streaming across the floor of the canyon, carried by some unseen force. It stretched into a finger of darkness, as though showing the way. But, to their surprise, it was not pointing in the direction Ash had been leading them, it was guiding them back, to the same side of the canyon as the tunnel. The finger stretched out, longer and longer, thinner and thinner, until finally it came to rest not far from where they had entered.

"*Go!*" came the voice of the Kraven. "*THERE is-s-s the Academy of S-S-Souls.*"

79

Two Stories

"Two stories are being written about this world:
one by the Scribes of the Suhl; the other by the Dirgh himself.
But only one of them will become the truth, and only
one of them will provide the end."

SYLAS AND HIS COMPANIONS followed the trail of Black across the floor of the Crucible. They walked painfully slowly at first, their limbs still numb and heavy after their encounter, but the more distance they placed between them and the Kraven, the more they felt their blood begin to flow, and the warmth returning.

A great promontory of rock cast a dark shadow across the cliff face ahead, and they could see nothing of its features. Ash signalled for them to halt and crept on alone, until he too disappeared into the gloom.

Simia stepped between Sylas and Naeo. "Was it a mistake, do you think?" she murmured, eyeing the place where Ash had vanished.

"That he took us the wrong way?" asked Sylas.

She nodded.

Sylas glanced at her. "I don't know, Simsi... but it's hard to believe that he'd do it deliberately."

"But he's been acting so *strange*," she argued. "So moody and — I don't know... sometimes it's like he doesn't want us to get there!"

"I know what you mean," said Naeo. "I've been thinking the same thing. He's been odd ever since we reached the Nile."

Simia narrowed her eyes. "Well, I'm going to be watching him like a hawk."

They were quiet for a moment, then Sylas lifted his head, staring up at the starry sky. "Have you noticed? The noises have stopped."

Sure enough, there were no more ominous sounds coming from beyond the clifftops. Everything was eerily quiet.

"What do you think's happened?" asked Simia fearfully.

Sylas dropped his eyes. "I'm not sure," he said. "I don't think I want to know."

Just then they saw a movement in the shadows at the foot of the cliff, and the young Magruman strode into the moonlight. He wore a bright, excited expression.

"All clear!" he announced as he jogged up to them. "And just wait until you see this!" With a wink, he turned, waved for them to follow and headed back into the dark.

"It's almost like he's *enjoying* this," grumbled Simia as they all set out after him.

When everyone reached the foot of the rock face, they peered into the shadow and saw not the grand entrance that they were expecting but a crooked cleft rising at an awkward angle to a point high above. Its interior was shrouded in such an impenetrable dark that Sylas wondered what Ash could possibly have seen to excite him.

But their captain was already at the jagged entrance, waiting impatiently. When they drew close, he gestured enthusiastically into the gloom. "Watch!" he said and then stepped across the threshold.

Almost at once they saw a silver gleam far below, deep in the heart of the hillside, like a spark of moonlight. It grew quickly, swelling in the passageway, advancing towards them, then it bloomed into a breathtaking web of beams, passing between mirrors mounted on the walls, floor and ceiling. Everything before them now glowed, lit by a complex web of silvery light.

Simia stared in wonder at the display. "Those mirrors..." she said. "They're just like the ones at the Meander Mill!"

"It's... *beautiful*," said Sylas breathlessly.

"Of course it is!" said Ash, mesmerised. "This is where the Four Ways were born!" And then, as though drawn towards the light, he started down the sloping passageway. "Come on!" he called back. "Let's take a look!"

The others were much more reluctant to enter, and for some moments they hesitated, watching. They saw Ash bathed in the first of the beams, his blond locks gleaming white as he turned on the spot, marvelling at the strange radiance. In that moment, with his eyes bright and his face animated with wonder, he looked like the Ash they knew so well. It crossed Naeo's mind that perhaps it had just been the terrible dark of the Crucible and her own fears that had made her begin to doubt him. And so, when he gestured to them again, she set off down the passage, the others following close behind.

As she passed through the first of the shafts of light and glanced into the mirror from which it emanated, she saw not a single shaft but a dazzling galaxy of pinprick stars and, near to the topmost arc of the mirror, a perfect image of the crescent moon.

"It's the night sky!" she murmured. "They've gathered the starlight!"

She walked on, still gazing into the mirror, and then stumbled into Ash. He was standing stock-still in the centre of the passage, staring at one of the smooth stone walls. When he did not move, Naeo stepped round him to see what he was looking at.

On the left side of the passage, spanning floor to ceiling, was a painting picked out in faded colours. As she took in the details of it, Naeo was filled with a creeping revulsion. She had seen the picture only once, as a young child. It had been shown to her as something forbidden, something to be viewed just once so that its importance might be understood, but then locked away in her memory.

It depicted the sweeping banks of a great river. Between them, the mighty waters were streaked with red, as though the great waterway itself was bleeding. In the foreground, on the nearest bank of the river, stood a lone figure wearing simple peasant's robes and holding a short wooden staff. His hair was shocked with white and his limbs were thin and wasted, but there was something about the way he carried himself that suggested a man of importance and stature.

Naeo raised a hand to her lips and took a step back.

"It's... him!" she murmured.

The others gathered close behind her and peered at the picture.

"The One from the Waters!" exclaimed a crew member in horror.

The others turned sharply and hushed him, as though the words themselves were evil.

Sylas was puzzled. He sensed Naeo's distaste for the picture, but he did not understand why she and the others seemed so appalled.

He glanced at his companions. "What's wrong? Who's the One from the Waters?"

All eyes turned to him and, when he saw Simia glaring, he knew at once that he had said something forbidden. It took him entirely by surprise.

"We don't talk about him," she said with tight lips.

"Why not?"

"Because of what he did!"

"What did he do?"

"We *don't* talk about him!" snapped Naeo.

Sylas stared at her, mystified. He could sense the strength of her feeling — that same horror and revulsion that he had seen in Simia — but he had no idea where it was coming from.

"There's another here!" called Ash, pointing at the opposing wall a little further down the passage. He turned, his face a ghastly shade of grey, and gestured ahead. "And another!"

The group walked towards him and, as they reached the next painting, Simia let out a moan and pressed herself against the other side of the passage.

"It's the second one," said someone else. "The second plague!"

Sylas stared at the picture. It depicted a dusty town on the banks of a river, much like the towns they had passed along the Nile, but here the streets were filled with people fleeing in blind terror. At first he thought they were running away from the river itself but, as he looked more closely, he saw that it was not the waters that had so terrified them, but what was crawling out of them. The banks of the river were teeming with what looked like frogs and reptiles, clambering and slithering over each other. As he took in the entirety of the scene, Sylas noticed the same peasant figure standing in the foreground, dressed in crudely woven robes and holding the short staff.

He felt a growing unease. The picture was appalling, of course, but what affected him more was that it was oddly familiar. Perhaps it was Naeo, he thought. Perhaps *she* knew these pictures and he was seeing them with her eyes.

But, as he walked through another beam of light and the next painting appeared before him, icy fingers climbed his back.

This one showed a desert scene, with a jumble of rocks in the foreground upon which the peasant figure stood, his staff held forth. Nearby there was a town, and leading to it were streaks of darkness, which Sylas thought at first must be rivers of the Black. But, when he looked to the bottom of the picture, to where the darkness drew near, he saw that it was made of legion upon legion of insects scuttling towards the town like some monstrous army.

"I *know* this..." he said under his breath.

He rushed on to join the others at the next picture. This time the peasant figure was further off, standing on a hill and, as before, his staff was outstretched. The town in the foreground seemed to be the same as the one in the last painting, but now the desert wastes around it were crowded with wild beasts. There were wolves and bears, lizards and snakes. There were beasts that crawled — bellies to the dust — and beasts that loped, baring their teeth.

Sylas froze in disbelief as memories rushed back to him. When he had first arrived at Gabblety Row, his uncle had insisted that he attend Sunday school in an old building in the grounds of the Church of the Holy Trinity. It had been a cold, miserable place, and never more so than when they read woeful tales from the Old Testament of the Bible. But nevertheless some of the more affecting stories had stayed with him ever since.

"The plagues!" he blurted, turning to his companions. "The plagues of Egypt! And Moses! The — what did they call him? The *prophet* who..."

He trailed off.

His companions looked stricken. For a moment no one said anything, then one of the crew shouted, "We *never* speak that name!"

His voice echoed eerily down the passage and through the spaces beyond.

Sylas was dumbfounded. When he opened his mouth to

respond, Simia held up her hand. "Sylas, he's right! No one says that name — not *ever*! It's forbidden!"

Sylas looked round the circle of faces, some indignant, some frightened, others looking almost hateful.

"But... why?" he asked.

Simia stared at him in astonishment. "Because of what he did!" she exclaimed, pointing at the picture. "Because of *this*!"

Sylas glanced at it. "But... he was a prophet, wasn't he?" he retorted. "Wasn't he some kind of hero who saved the Israelites from—"

He stopped. As he had said the word 'hero', there had been a collective intake of breath. Everyone was staring at him in horror.

"A *hero*?" repeated Ash, his face twisted with scorn. "You think these horrors were the work of a *hero*?" He took Sylas by the arm and pulled him along the corridor. "Just look at them! Look what he did!"

Sylas stumbled after Ash in a state of shock, trying to make sense of what was happening. They passed painting after painting of Moses with an appalling scene of suffering laid out before him. There were cattle and sheep lying in the dirt, suffering from some kind of disease, their tongues lolling, their eyes rolling. There was another scene of pestilence, but this time in a town, and now those suffering were the people, their skin inflamed and swollen with boils. Next there was a gigantic storm that towered into the sky, the clouds riddled with lightning, while below towns were pelted with what looked like jagged chunks of ice.

This too Sylas remembered from Sunday school. "The storm of hail and fire..." he said to himself.

Ash yanked savagely on his arm, making him cry out. "Come on, we're not finished yet!" he snapped.

"Ash, don't!" called Simia from somewhere behind.

But the young Magruman was already pulling Sylas away, past

more paintings. The next was just as horrifying as those that had gone before: dark clouds hanging above a town, fed by hundreds of trails rising from the dusty earth. They were colossal swarms of locusts swirling about farms and homesteads and towns, stripping them of life. The next was almost as dark as the stone upon which it was painted. Now, the figure of Moses was in silhouette, and the only light came from the lanterns and torches of a town. Everything else was darkness, except in one corner where there was a disappearing glow of sunlight.

"The darkness that can be felt," proclaimed Ash, spitting out the words. Then he pulled Sylas down the passageway to the final picture. "Look!" he insisted, jabbing his finger at it. "*This* is why we never say his name!"

As Sylas looked at the painting, he was aware of Simia and Naeo turning away, as though it was too awful to look at.

The picture showed two adjoining streets in a town, lined with stone and timber dwellings. Outside each of them was a huddle of people gathered about a figure lying in the dusty road.

"The Passover," said Ash. "The death of the firstborn of every household." Then he pointed to one side where the figure of Moses stood, leaning heavily on his staff. "*This* is the work of your hero."

As Sylas's eyes came to rest, he realised that he had stopped breathing. He was looking at a group of people tending to a lifeless figure in the dust. He saw, in their pitiful expressions, grief, bewilderment and unbearable pain. He had seen this image before – or one like it – and it had barely moved him. Then it had been a dusty old tale at Sunday school about a people of which he knew almost nothing. And what he had known – or thought he had known – was that these suffering people, the Egyptians, had dealt out their own suffering upon Moses's tribe: God's chosen people, the Israelites. According to the tale, Moses had brought these plagues as an act of God, to defend his own kind.

Perhaps it was in the vivid way it was painted, but this looked nothing like self-defence. This was brutal and murderous.

Sylas drew his eyes away and, as he did so, he saw one final painting a little further down the passage. Glad to leave the Passover behind, he walked through another sloping shaft of light until the image emerged from the gloom.

It featured the same aged figure of Moses, alone on a mountaintop, surrounded by dark clouds veined with lightning. He was kneeling in the stones and dust, supported by his staff, and before him were two inscribed tablets of stone.

Sylas turned back to his friends, confused, frightened by what all this might mean. He saw them looking at him, and again he had that sickening feeling that, for reasons he could not yet grasp, he was on one side of a divide and they were on the other. Even Naeo was looking at him in a way that made her seem further away than ever.

"Isn't... isn't this when God gave... *him*... the Ten Commandments?"

Yet again his friends stared at him as though he had said something horrendous.

Tears welled in Sylas's eyes. "I don't understand!" he yelled, becoming angry now. "Why do you see all this so differently?"

Suddenly the passageway was filled with noise. It was not Sylas's voice but a thousand voices — ten thousand — hundreds of thousands — all of them speaking at once. They rang from the walls and blared through the empty spaces; they shook the air and thrummed in his bones.

"Because, Sylas Tate, there are two sides to every story," they bellowed. "And this story changed everything!"

80

The Truth Chamber

"They say that the Truth Chamber *was the beating heart of the academy, the centre of all initiation, study, debate and judgement. If there is one place in this world where everything began, where the walls might whisper the answers to all our questions, it must surely be there."*

THE VOICES WERE STILL ringing in their ears as Sylas and his companions tore out of the tunnel and began bounding down the long, rough-hewn staircase that stretched out below them. They were descending into a huge, round hall — part cave, part hewn from the rock — lit by beams of starlight, which fell from a point high in the centre and spidered outwards like the spokes of a wheel, striking mirrors on the walls and then dropping further into the gloom below. A little ahead the staircase came to a gallery that circled the hall, then the steps continued down into the shaded depths.

Sylas thundered on, aware of Simia and the others panting at his ear. When he reached the gallery, he skidded to a halt, wondering whether to follow the staircase or take the gallery. As he glanced about, he saw doorways leading from the circular platform: twelve of them, one for each of the Priests of Souls.

Suddenly the voices boomed out again from somewhere behind.

"This is the Truth Chamber, so hear the truth. You proclaim Moses a prophet, but you are mistaken. In truth, the One from the Waters brought only pestilence and death. You believe that it was the Ramesses Shield that shattered the world, but it was Moses who left it in ruins. Instead he built for himself another world: a world founded on his commandments, fashioned on his idea of God."

Unsure where else to go, Sylas hurried on down the staircase, leaving the gallery behind. He could see more of the lower hall now: walls lined with shelf upon shelf of scrolls — thousands of them, stacked in neat bundles — and on the chamber floor some way below, an arc of tables and an array of bizarre wooden instruments cluttering the floor. There was another section in the rear, beneath a rocky overhang, but it was shrouded in shadow.

"You condemn this Academy of Souls," continued Thoth, "but in truth we simply finished what Moses began. We turned the rift between his world and ours into a defence. We made it so complete, so absolute, that he might never again bring his hateful plagues — his tyranny of fire and disease."

The words clamoured through the hall, but Sylas hardly heard them. He sprang from the bottom of the staircase and looked desperately round the chamber for a way to escape. With a growing, sickening clench of the stomach, he realised that there were no more steps, no passages leading on into the Academy — only the desks, and the scrolls, and the jumble of apparatus. He had led them all into a trap. His eyes came to rest on the shadowy wall of rock and, as that was the furthest point from the staircase, he set out towards it. The others were close behind him.

"You judge this Academy of Souls," continued the chorus of voices, growing louder and more menacing, "but what we did here was the work of the gods. We served our people. We kept them safe. That is why we entombed ourselves in these halls. That is why we gave ourselves to the search for the Ramesses Shield, which you wish to bring to nothing."

As Sylas approached the wall of rock, he could see hieroglyphs etched into the stone above another vivid painting. It depicted a set of scales. From its beam were supported two level pans. In the first, there was a single white feather; in the other was something he did not recognise, something gnarled and knotted. Sylas had a strange sense that he knew the meaning of the image, but he could not quite grasp it.

"I read... about this... in the Samarok!" panted Naeo at his side, her eyes passing quickly over the painting. "These are the scales that... weigh the human heart! Something about... judging whether or not you're worthy to go into the afterlife." Her gaze dropped down the wall of rock. There, half hidden in the shadows, she saw a gaping hole in the stone floor, several paces wide. She pointed. "And that must be Ammut's Pit!"

Even as she said it, Sylas was remembering the passage he had read about the labyrinth of caves named after Ammut, the beast of judgement who devoured the unworthy. Just as he thought that it might offer a way out, a cruel laugh echoed round the Truth Chamber, the voices ringing from the faces of rock.

"You'll find no sanctuary in the pit. It is a trial and a horror. Now, more than ever, for it is flooded with the Black. No, Sylas Tate and Naeo, daughter of Bowe. You have reached your journey's end. Wait now and I will come."

The travellers turned and looked fearfully up the staircase. There, emerging from the passageway, was a lone figure dressed in lavish crimson robes, stooped and angular beneath the folds, limbs jutting grotesquely as he made his way down the steps. He walked slowly, seeming in no rush, and as he neared the gallery he lifted a bony hand as though beckoning to them.

Suddenly, with a yell, one of the crew hurtled into the air and for a moment hung suspended, writhing as though in the clutch of some invisible hand. Just as he managed to turn and look imploringly at his companions, he was again launched upwards. Screaming in terror, he flew towards the gallery and, in a blink, he darted over the railing and through one of the twelve open doorways. With an ear-splitting bang, the door slammed shut behind him.

They were all still taking in what had happened when another of the crew yelped and shot up in the air, arms windmilling, legs kicking. Just before he sailed out of reach, he caught hold of Ash's robe. The young Magruman made a rather belated attempt to grab him, but already their poor shipmate was out of reach, clutching a torn shred of Ash's cloak. With a contemptuous sweep of the finger, Thoth propelled his hollering captive across the chamber and through another of the doorways. It too slammed shut behind him, the bang echoing round the chamber.

"Do something!" Simia yelled at Ash, who was by her side. But, for some reason, the Magruman appeared more preoccupied with the black shell that had fallen from his robe in the scuffle and was now rolling away across the stone floor. He seemed to be wondering what it was and how it had got there.

Meanwhile Sylas and Naeo were looking frantically around for anything they could bring to their aid, but all they saw were books and rock and dust. With an icy chill, they realised that they had unwittingly trapped themselves in a place where Essenfayle was almost useless.

But then Ash seemed to come back to himself. He cast his eyes about, muttering under his breath, then stretched out his hand towards the wooden contraptions on the chamber floor. They responded instantly, leaping up into the air and gathering into a spinning jumble. He braced himself, with arms aloft, seeming to prepare to hurl them, but suddenly Thoth raised his other hand. In that very moment, the wheeling mass of wooden objects froze in the air, then gathered into an ever tighter ball. For a brief moment there was a creak and a squeal, and then, with an almighty boom, the tangle of wood shattered into a million pieces. Splinters fizzed through the air and cracked off the walls, raining down upon Ash and his companions and forcing them to cover their faces.

As all this was happening, the Priest of Souls continued to descend the staircase. He opened his hand and spread his fingers, and immediately two more of the crew flew up into the air. Then another followed them, and another. Suddenly Ash too was lofted into the air, yelling in protest. He struggled against the bonds of Urgolvane that held him, trying to steady himself so that he might use his own powers. But it was hopeless. With a flick of the wrist, Thoth sent him and his companions somersaulting through the void, cartwheeling over the balustrade, and tumbling through separate doorways. Five stout doors slammed shut behind them.

Sylas suddenly felt a clutch at his arm and turned to see Simia's eyes wide with fright, her body rigid. Her feet had been swept from beneath her and already she was sailing into the air.

"Simsi!" he cried, grabbing her arm and pulling at it with all his might.

Naeo took her other arm and heaved just as strongly, but Simia barely slowed. Soon all three of them were hoisted into the air. Sylas felt Simia slipping away and, in desperation, reached one hand across her chest, catching hold of Naeo's coat beyond. In the same instant, Naeo reached behind Simia and caught hold of his sleeve so that the three were in an embrace.

"So you wish your friend to suffer your fate?" bellowed Thoth. "So be it!"

At once all three of them tumbled to the floor, their knees and elbows jarring against the stone. They ignored the pain and scrambled to their feet, backing towards the wall of rock.

Thoth descended a few more steps and then paused, leaning forward and tilting his hooded head, as though peering at them in fascination.

"You puzzle me," he said. "You know the horrors visited upon us in ancient times, the cruelty of the One from the Waters, and yet, even now, you wish to destroy our only defence." He pointed a gnarled finger at Sylas. "I almost understand you, for the religions of your world tell you that Moses was a prophet speaking for the one true god. They have turned the plagues into a morality tale, however warped and barbaric it may be."

His finger jabbed at Naeo. "But *you*, you are of *this* world. You know the truth of the One from the Waters, and yet you would let his descendants once again raise their staff against us. Despite all that we Priests of Souls have done to keep them at bay. All that we have done in your name."

He straightened from his stoop so that they could see some of his pale face in the shadow of his hood.

"Look at how we slaved for you in these halls!" he bellowed, raising an arm towards the thousands of scrolls lining the walls. "See the theses! The formulae! The incantations!"

As he spoke, the bundles of parchments suddenly leapt from their shelves and flew into the middle of the chamber, unfurling as they went to reveal texts, diagrams, patterns and symbols, all of them scrawled in faded ink. They shot at Sylas and Simia and Naeo like a wild flock, so that they had to shield their faces.

"See the dawn of Urgolvane!" boomed Thoth. "And look there! The beginnings of Druindil! Years in the making! Decades in the refinement!"

He swept an arm towards the other side of the hall, and at once more parchments flew from the cabinets, joining the great swarm of papyrus scrolls. "Theories, experiments, essays, arguments! All this in the service of Ramesses and his people, searching for a defence powerful enough to resist the conjurings of the One from the Waters. Look here, the birth of Kimiyya! The greatest of the Four Ways!" A new squadron of parchments soared from their cabinets, swooping down upon the three children and flapping and slapping at them until they cowered. "The Four Ways that would one day build a new and greater Empire, free of its enemies, governed only by those who had shown themselves worthy!"

The chamber now swarmed with parchments, fluttering and rustling as though speaking their secrets. Sylas could no longer see Thoth beyond the press of scrolls, and he only occasionally glimpsed Simia crouching at his side. But Naeo he felt. He sensed in her a swell of feeling so wild that it frightened him.

"And behold! The firstlings of your own beloved Essenfayle right here, in this place you so despise! The first treatises of Merimaat and Merisu recorded here, by my own hand!" More parchments joined the seething cauldron of papers, scrawled with symbols, spells, lists and essays. "All this while forgotten in these halls. All this to keep you safe! All this in your name! In the name of keeping—"

"NOT IN MY NAME!" thundered Naeo.

The squall of parchments suddenly blew itself out. Thousands of papers began fluttering to the floor, like a shower of autumn leaves. As they settled over every surface, Naeo could be seen clearly for the first time, standing before the others, hands clenched at her sides, glaring at Thoth.

He stood on the staircase, his hood thrown back by the gale, revealing his ghastly visage: featureless but alive with a thousand fleeting faces. Again, he inclined his head to one side as if puzzled.

"Not in my name!" repeated Naeo, her voice quavering but defiant. She was full of rage. Rage because of her father; rage because of the Reckoning; rage because of all the cruelty; rage because of everything she had learned and seen in these past days. It was a fury she did not know she could feel. "Not in my name because your shield divided us when it should have brought us together! Because it didn't keep us safe — it made us your slaves! Because you divided us from ourselves and made us less than we were!"

A growl issued from Thoth's throat, and the shadows of his face began to gather. "Delusions!" he thundered. "You blame me for our divided worlds, but everything began with Moses. It was he who incited a war between tribes! He who forced us to defend ourselves. If you are divided, it is because it is part of the shield. It is what had to happen. It is a good not an evil. You are no less. Through the shield you are more!"

"No!" blurted Sylas. It came out so suddenly that he was surprised to hear his own voice echoing about the chamber. He looked across at Naeo and he found her looking back at him. "With Naeo, I've seen things I never knew were in me. With her, I'm — I'm more than I was before! The shield has hidden that from me. Hidden it from everyone!"

The Dirgh regarded him with empty eyes, ancient and fathomless. Then, as the words faded to a distant echo, he began to laugh. "More, he says! And yet they stand here, weak and defenceless, searching for an escape!" The mocking laughter became all-consuming, resonating through the passageways of the Academy of Souls.

Now Simia stepped forward. "STOP!" she bellowed.

Sylas and Naeo looked at her in surprise. Her face was drained of all colour. Her eyes were full of tears. Thoth turned to her, a vague expression of astonishment visible in the shadows of his face.

"You don't get to laugh!" she yelled. "You've broken everything! And the cruel, horrible things you've done to try to keep everything broken... the people you've hurt... the people you've..." Her breaths were coming in sobs now, but she forced herself to continue. "You've made everything worse! Everything less! All of us less!" She glared hatefully at his pallid, shifting features: the face that was at once everyone and no one. "Even yourself! Just — just look at yourself!"

Thoth visibly recoiled. His frail figure stumbled a little on the steps. They could hear his wheezing breaths, quick and shallow.

He seemed to take a moment to gather himself, and then he swelled beneath his robes, a new darkness clouding his face, a bestial growl rasping in his throat.

All of a sudden his white hand shot out towards them and, in the same instant, the three children were gripped so tightly by some invisible force that the breath was squeezed from their lungs. This unseen power heaved them thrashing and kicking into the air, their arms pinned to their sides.

"Let me tell you what I see!" blared the voices of many. "I see Thoth, three times great, Priest of Souls and scribe to the gods. And now, as of this night, I am A'an, Lord of Equilibrium, and emperor of a new union: a union founded upon the one truth, forged in one darkness!"

He pushed his hand forward, and Sylas, Naeo and Simia found themselves sailing helplessly towards the rear wall of the chamber, drawing ever closer to Ammut's Pit. "In this moment, for the first time since the two worlds were born, they share a single night: our night of the stars, and theirs a last night — an interminable night — born of the Black. They will see no dawn until they rejoice in a new union — a union bound by a single Empire."

With Thoth's words raging in his ears, Sylas looked down and saw the gaping chasm of Ammut's Pit directly below, waiting to swallow them whole. He reached out towards the others and found Simia's hand, saw her eyes wide and staring into his.

"Keep hold, Simsi!" he gasped. "Don't let go, not for anything!"

He threw out his other hand towards Naeo, but she was held apart, her arms wheeling as she strained to reach him.

"The Pit of Ammut once weighed the worthiness of the Priests of Souls," boomed the Dirgh. "Now, let it judge your worth! Let us see if your hearts are as true as the Maat feather you hold so dear!"

And, with that, he turned his hand over and opened his fingers wide.

Suddenly the bonds that held the children vanished and they dropped like stones.

"NO!" screamed Sylas, his free hand still reaching towards Naeo.

And then everything went black.

81

The Pit

"But it was on my third passing that I realised why I,
just like the other Bringers, would never make a fourth.
Just as before as the great bell swept above me I was filled
with an overwhelming sense of well-being and joy,
but when I woke, I was sick to the pit of my stomach."

LIMBS FLAILING, SYLAS WATCHED the mouth of the pit shrink
to nothingness, and then the dark became darker still. Darkness
within darkness. Darkness that engulfed him and crept into his
bones and lodged in his heart. Darkness that swamped his mind
and snuffed out his breath. This was a darkness that flowed thick
and oily and cold.

He thought dimly about Naeo and Simia, but already they
seemed somehow far away. If he had not felt Simia's hand in his,
he had the strangest sense that he might forget her altogether.

There was a jarring impact with his shoulder, and then his shin
hit something sharp, which sent a spasm of pain through his leg.
For an instant the shock brought clarity.

I'm in the Black, he thought. *I'm drowning*.

But even this thought was distant, as though it was not his own.

Faces began to appear to him: Espasian, scarred and noble,

smiling as he had when they had parted; Uncle Tobias, leaning too close, sneering as was his way; his mother, a face of contrasts: troubled but warm and inviting, like home. And then came Mr Zhi. He was smiling and saying something in a whisper: "*You can see the world as it is promised to us.*"

As his kindly face faded, another materialised, a face that blurred and shifted. It was Isia — gentle but commanding — her eyes as wise as the ages. She too was speaking, but Sylas could barely make out her words.

"*You have mastered the earth, and the fire...*"

As quickly as her face had come, it drifted away. It was as though these memories were being drawn from him like ink dissolving from a page. But he was not frightened. He felt almost nothing at all. There was only the dark.

Then something shot out of that dark and hit him. An unbearable pain rattled through his skull, setting off a dance of light behind his eyes. Then his back slammed into something hard, and the dark tide pinned him to it, tugging on his limbs and clothes, threatening to wrench Simia's hand from his. He felt her fingernails clawing at his palm.

Again, the pain brought clarity. He was pinioned by the Black against a wall of rock. He could not breathe and soon it would all be over. He must not lose hold of Simia. In the darkness, she was everything.

Lungs burning, Sylas pushed out a heel until he found purchase and, summoning all his strength, he heaved himself towards Simia's hand. Then he flailed with his other foot until it came up hard against an outcrop. He pushed again, and this time he felt Simia's shoulder against his. He slid his other hand across and grabbed her arm and, to his horror, it was limp and lifeless. In a spasm of panic, he threw his arm about her.

S

The pain shot up Naeo's spine and exploded across her shoulders like tongues of flame. But she did not panic because it all seemed strangely distant, like a dream.

Nevertheless the faces were a relief: something to focus on, something other than the darkness and the pain. She saw Filimaya's face, careworn and wise, the brow furrowed with concern. Paiscion came next, his eyes bright behind his glasses, as though he was listening to his music. She saw Mr Zhi looking up at her in the gardens at Winterfern, murmuring: "*Now is a time of sacrifice.*" Then came her father, strong and loving, with those wise eyes, welcoming like home. If she could just hold on to those eyes, it wouldn't matter that the Black had her. It wouldn't matter that she was drowning.

But then her shoulder slammed into a wall of rock and her father's face was ripped away. She was flattened against it and now the Black tore at her, trying to rip her free from that precious hand that had found her in the dark. Simia's hand. She clung on and, to her relief, so did Simia.

But they were losing hold. With all her might, Naeo heaved at the outstretched arm and kicked out at the rock, trying frantically to draw closer. With another kick, another push into the Black, she was there at Simia's side.

And then there was nothing else to be done.

Her lungs screamed, the pain pulsed in her back and she felt herself slipping into the darkness.

This is the end, she thought. *This is what it's like.*

She felt terribly alone then, and so she tried to picture her father's face, but it was lost in the darkness. And so instead she reached round Simia to hold her tight.

Her arm entwined with another.

She knew at once that it was not Simia's because she felt the Merisi Band round the wrist.

A thought suddenly rushed through the darkness.

"Sylas!"

He too was clinging to Simia, but something was pulling him away. The Black about him was surging in a different direction, down another tunnel. Naeo realised that Simia was pinioned just where two tunnels diverged. Sylas had been drifting down one, she another, and somehow Simia had kept them together. She had spread herself wide, grasped their hands tight and refused to let go.

But now Simia's fingers were slack and loose. Her arm had gone limp. They were losing her.

Suddenly Naeo found her fight and she sensed Sylas respond. As one, they summoned all their failing strength and rolled Simia until she was caught by the current. Instantly the Black worked for them, dragging Sylas over the dividing rock, until together the three tumbled into the flow. They twisted and somersaulted in the silent flood, sometimes colliding brutally with jutting rocks. But still they clung tight, closing about Simia to keep her safe. They stretched out their free arms and clawed at the passing rocks, trying desperately to find purchase, but always they were wrenched free.

Precious moments passed, too many moments, and soon their energy failed. Their minds fogged once more and their brief fight was at an end.

At least they were together, Naeo thought. At least she was not alone. She found Sylas's hand and folded her fingers between his.

Sylas's lungs felt like they would explode. He knew he was out of time — that they were all out of time — and, in a final desperate, angry gesture, he swiped at the Black.

His hand slapped hard against a rock.

Instinctively he closed his fingers and they curled about a lump of stone.

He held on.

His arm snapped taut with the force of the Black, and the three swung into the side of the channel. They struck a wall with dreadful force and cried out from the pain.

For a moment they did nothing but hold on, stunned and exhausted. But then they scrambled wildly, hopelessly, knowing that this was their very last chance. Somewhere in the confusion, Sylas's foot caught, his muscles jarred and he launched himself upwards. He felt Simia and Naeo clinging to him as he rose, and then, in an explosion of sound, they all broke the surface.

He and Naeo heaved the cold air into their lungs, hearing the wonderful sound of their own gasps echoing back. They clung to the wall, catching their breath, the Black tugging and gurgling as it passed.

It was still pitch-dark, but Sylas could feel Simia at his side.

"Simsi!" he panted, squeezing her arm. "Simsi, say something!"

But there was nothing. Her head rolled listlessly on to his shoulder.

"Come on, Simsi!" he pleaded. "We're all right now!"

But he knew they were far from all right. A wave of sickness swept over him, almost making him pass out. He was unbearably weak, and he had the feeling that moment by moment the Black was leaching his energy. He felt the beginnings of a chilling pain in his muscles and around his joints, and he knew that that too was the Black.

Naeo knew the Black: it had been with her for longer than she could remember. She pushed on through the pain and the nausea. She explored the darkness with her free hand, feeling the shape of the wall, the low ceiling, the outcrops of rock. And then her hand fell upon an uneven shelf a little way above them.

Hardly daring to hope, she slid her hand along until she found a handhold, then heaved herself up. She managed to get an elbow over the edge and then felt about her with her free hand. The ledge was very near to the ceiling, forming a cavity deep enough for them to crawl inside.

"Hold on, Simsi!" she gasped. "There's something here! Just hold on!"

She heaved herself into the opening, then turned and reached down, pulling at Simia's clothing as Sylas pushed from below. After a few failed attempts they hoisted her on to the edge and then over. Slowly Sylas clambered up and rolled on to his back at her side.

It was a tiny space. Naeo was squeezed painfully into the deepest recess, while on the outside Sylas's shoulder hung over the passing Black. Simia was wedged between them.

With great effort, Sylas wriggled until he was able to prop himself up on his elbow and put his ear to her mouth. Her breaths were weak and halting, and there was a rasping sound, as though the Black had found its way into her throat. He did his best to wipe her face and neck clean of it, then he sank back on to the shelf.

He gazed blindly into the darkness, feeling a great weight on his chest, as though the mass of rock above him was pressing the air from his lungs. He felt a growing urge to close his eyes and sleep.

"Keep... moving..." Naeo murmured weakly. "We have to... stay awake."

Sylas could hear her searching the cavity with her hands, and he reached up and did the same. There was nothing but rock. He fumbled above him and found another impassable wall. Then, painfully slowly, he shuffled down and searched with his feet. More featureless rock. There was no way out, except to roll back into the Black.

His mind was hopelessly muddled now, from exhaustion and from the Black. He was distantly aware that he ought to be terrified, that he should cry out, but he had no energy even for that. He wondered how it had come to this. How it was that he had learned all he had learned, travelled all this way just for it to end like this.

He felt cold to the core, as though the Black had penetrated to his very heart. He reached for Simia's hand, pressing her palm tight between his fingers. He hoped against hope for a flicker of life — a hint of the Simia he knew so well — but there was nothing. She was cold, too cold — smeared with the thick, oily Black.

He felt a swell of despair. How could he have let this happen? How could he have let her do this, to save him? Warm tears seeped from the corners of his eyes and, with sudden anger, he swept them away.

"This can't... be all," he heard Naeo say in the dark, her voice thick and faltering. "This can't be... how it ends."

Sylas stared fiercely into the nothingness, searching his fogged mind for anything that he had missed, anything that might help. He went over what little he could remember of the labyrinth: the tumbling darkness, the cold, the surging torrent. He tried to remember something of the route they had taken. He thought back to Thoth's last words, to the inscriptions on the wall, to the image of the scales. But there was nothing.

He searched further back, to his time on the *Windrush* reading the Samarok, and he tried to remember the entry about Ammut's Pit. He had read it when half asleep and so it came to him in fragments. The priests had been brought to the labyrinth every third year — he remembered that. He recalled that they had faced a test to show that they were worthy to stay in the academy. And there had been something else — something about the test, but in his confusion Sylas could not remember what it was.

In frustration, he hit the ceiling. The heel of his hand caught a sharp piece of rock and pain shot through his wrist. The lump of stone dropped on to his chest, showering him with dust.

And then, suddenly, it came to him.

The Priests of Souls had shown their worthiness here in this labyrinth by mastering the elements.

"Earth, air, fire and water," murmured Sylas, his voice filling the tiny alcove.

With a shiver, he recalled the vision of Isia speaking to him as she had in the Place of Tongues. "You have mastered the earth, and the fire, and the water," he said out loud. "Now master the air."

But he *had* mastered the air. He had done it in the Place of Tongues, with the whirlwind, and many times on the *Windrush*, with Naeo.

Then he felt Naeo's hand slide into his.

"It's not you!" she gasped. "It's me!"

Her eyes were wide as she thought back to Winterfern Hospital and her final moments with Mr Zhi.

"*You must each prove to yourselves that you are able to control the earth, the air, the fire and the water,*" the Merisi Master had said. "*Only then will you be ready to heal the worlds.*"

This had to be what Mr Zhi had meant. This was the place. This was the time.

"I never mastered the earth!" said Naeo.

Trembling, Sylas squeezed her hand. Together they closed their eyes, and reached out into the dark.

82
A Sea of Gold

"Now, twenty years since I came home for the last time,
I would give mountains of silver or a sea of gold
for just one last taste of the Other."

THERE WAS NOTHING IN the rock: nothing of Nature, nothing to embrace. It was solid and immovable. It was unliving and undying. It was blind and deaf and mute.

Try as they might, Sylas and Naeo could find no way in.

But then Sylas remembered something else. In his *Book of Science* — the one given to him by his mother — he had read about rocks: the way they were born, and changed, and died. He had read how they melted, and melded, and became something else. He had read how rocks had lifetimes measured in eons, and how if we could see that kind of time — deep time — we would see mountains rippling like waves: erupting from the earth, reaching for the skies, crumbling to nothing.

And, when he thought of those things, the rock changed. It became something alive, something he could understand and feel. Something that might hear their call.

§

Without knowing why, Naeo became certain that the rock was not cold and empty — that it was thrumming with energy. That it was not blank and featureless as she had thought, but complex. That there were different kinds and ages and colours, all folded and layered, one upon another. That some felt as though they wanted to rise, others to fall, some to push and others to pull. And the more she lost herself in the rock, the more it revealed itself. She saw a thousand points of weakness: rifts, fissures, faults and boundaries between the layers and folds.

Something about them made her think of the cat's cradle, the game she had played since she was little, weaving her father's bootlace between her fingers. She lifted her shivering hands before her in the darkness, and she imagined the twine criss-crossing between her fingertips, like an intricate, three-dimensional map. She held this image before her, and then she reached into the rock.

Now, the bewildering complexity of seams and rifts were the threads of that cat's cradle. Just as Sylas knew instinctively how to read the Ravel Runes, she knew instinctively how to find her way between the threads. She moved her hands and, in her imagination, the faults moved with them. She peered through them as she always had: turning, rolling and twisting them until she saw patterns and pathways. Her hands moved quickly at first, expertly, her imagination exploring the faults, lining them up in different ways; but, as she began to see, she slowed, and became more precise.

Finally she came to a halt, and held her breath.

There was a long silence, punctuated only by the gloop and slurp of the passing Black. But Naeo did not hear. She was lost in the rock now, and Sylas was too. They gathered all of their remaining strength, every thought, and nerve and sinew, and they brought them to bear on the pathway of cracks and fissures that Naeo had found.

They did not hear the first rumble, or feel the tremors that shook the catacombs. They did not see the crack that had appeared in the ceiling of the alcove, showering their legs with dust. They saw nothing until an explosive boom shook them from their trance.

They found themselves in a suffocating cloud of dust, struggling to breathe. But through this thick pall they saw something. Only faint — hardly there — but real.

It was light.

For some time they were too exhausted to do anything but let the dust gradually settle. But, as it fell away, they saw a V-shaped cleft in the rock. It was small, but large enough to crawl into, and somewhere deep within that cleft there was light. They stared at it for some time, drinking in its meagre, life-giving glow. Finally Sylas reached for Simia's hand.

"Come on, Simsi," he said. "We have to go."

But, as soon as he touched her, he froze.

Her fingers had been frighteningly cold before, but now they were deathly. He closed his hand tight round them, hoping for some response, some hint of warmth, but there was nothing. They were limp and lifeless.

"No!" he groaned, pushing himself up on to his elbow.

He leaned over and put his ear to her lips. He controlled his gasps, trying desperately to listen for the tiniest, faintest breath.

Nothing.

He reached up and found her cold, clammy neck, feeling desperately for a pulse. Her head rolled lifelessly to one side.

An uncontrollable moan suddenly burst from somewhere deep in his chest and filled the rocky recess.

"No, Simsi! No!" he groaned. "Don't give up now! There's a way out! We've found a way out!"

His words echoed away down the newly formed tunnel, until

finally they fell silent. All he could hear was the flow of the Black, and Naeo's gentle sobs by their side.

A great empty chasm opened up inside Sylas's chest. He wanted to lie down quietly next to her and fall into that abyss, go with her wherever she had gone. But instead he did the only thing he could still do for her — he reached over and brushed the sodden hair away from her face.

"I'm sorry, Simsi," he said with a sob. "I never should've... I — I should have..."

But the words died. He knew that there was nothing he could have done to stop her from making this sacrifice. She had never allowed him to make any part of this journey alone, or to tell her what she must or must not do. And now she had travelled with him to the very last — and given everything — just to keep him and Naeo together.

He laid his head down on her chest and wrapped his arm round her limp body, as though to keep her warm. He was dimly aware of warm tears rolling across his face, but he made no sound. He just held Simia as tightly as his exhausted body would allow.

He was not sure how long he and Naeo lay there — it could have been minutes, it could have been an hour — but at last he heard Naeo shifting in the darkness, and then her hand slipped into his. The Merisi Band glowed dimly, but not enough to see by.

"We have to go," she said.

Sylas replied almost in the same moment. "We can't leave her."

"It's what she would have wanted. She gave everything to—"

"I'm not leaving her. Not here."

"We have to, Sylas."

"No!" Sylas fired back, the Merisi Band flaring so that briefly, he could see Naeo's pale face. She looked anguished, her cheeks streaked with tears and the Black. "She's spent enough time in the dark on the Barrens!" he protested. "Enough time alone! I'm NOT leaving her!"

Naeo was silent for a moment. "Then we'll have to take it slow," she said quietly.

And so that was what they did. They summoned their weary limbs into motion and, over the following minutes, they shuffled and clawed their way through the cleft. Beyond they found themselves in a barely passable shaft, which zigzagged along the shattered faultiness of the rock, left and right, up and down. They edged forward, pulling themselves on, inch by painstaking inch, then reaching back to haul Simia with them. Their limbs were leaden, not just with exhaustion, but with the terrible numbing, deadening effect of the Black, and so progress was excruciatingly slow. Simia felt far heavier than they knew her to be, and at times she became stuck altogether: some part of her clothing caught on a jagged edge protruding from the wall or floor. They could not bring themselves to heave at her and risk scraping her against the rock, and so each time one of them had to turn in the cramped passage and crawl back to release her. More than once Sylas retched from the exertion as he contorted himself in the tiny space.

After what felt like an hour they had travelled no more than thirty or forty feet. Always the source of the glow was round the next jagged corner, but increasingly it was enough to see by. Nevertheless neither of them dared to look at Simia's face. Instead they focused on the light and, when they turned, they looked only for a fold of fabric to hold on to.

At last the passage broadened a little and became tall enough for them to stand. But, in their weakness, all they could do was claw with fingers and toes, shuffling onwards on their stomachs. By the time the glow brightened into a glare, they no longer lifted their heads. They saved all their energy for their task, heaving themselves slowly on. They became vaguely aware of a noise: a fluid, shapeless sound, vaguely like waves rolling against a distant shore, but they were far from certain that it was not the blood coursing in their ears.

In their dreamlike state, it took them some time to notice that the light was now all around them, and longer still to realise that it had become a beautiful golden radiance. When they did finally see, they stopped, gulping in the air in short, painful breaths.

Sylas thought dimly that perhaps this was enough. Now, at least, Simia was in the light. Now, perhaps, they could let her go. And then he was struck with a strange thought: perhaps they already had. Perhaps this, after all, *was* the afterlife. Perhaps that was where they had been going all along — not just Simia, but all three of them. And now it was all over.

He did his best to master his thoughts, and slowly he heaved his elbows beneath him, and raised his head.

He blinked into the light and knew at once that he was right.

This *was* the afterlife.

Sylas and Naeo sat slumped against the wall of the passage and gazed out at the impossible.

Before them, and spreading into the disappearing distance, was an immense, bright, golden sea, its shimmering surface so beautiful that, despite her despair just moments before, a sob of joy welled in Naeo's chest.

But if this was heaven it was like none she had imagined. This sea was not calm and tranquil as she thought it should be; it was a tempest. While below them it lapped gently against a rocky shore, elsewhere it raged as though at the eye of a storm. The surface bucked, forming gigantic golden waves and in between, silvery spouts erupted, striking the earthen ceiling high above.

That too was strange. This majestic sea was not open to the

night sky, but captive in a cavern of earth and sand. Its walls disappeared right and left, and ahead the roof arched off into the distance. And this peculiar sky boasted no stars, but a galaxy of trailing roots, which dangled down into the shining, convulsing sea below.

Sylas stared at the swells of gold and crests of silver gleaming like the metals of the earth, surging like the waters, leaping like flames, dissolving into air, and he knew what it was. It could be only one thing. Quintessence. That perfect marriage of earth, air, fire and water. A vast ocean of it spread beneath Old Kemet.

And, as he realised what it was, Sylas knew why it was there too. It was gathered to heal Nature's greatest hurt. It was here because this was where the world was broken in two.

This was no afterlife. This was real.

He felt a stirring of warmth in his belly. *This* was why they had travelled to the Academy of Souls. *This* was where the healing had to be done.

If Sylas was left in any doubt, it did not last for long because, as his eyes scanned the shadows at the edges of that immeasurable cavern, he saw that the Quintessence was not alone. The Black was there too. Everywhere. It gushed down the walls and welled up between the rocks; it boiled along the shorelines and dripped from cracks in the ceiling. It surrounded the Quintessence, equal in volume and perhaps even more violent. But, as abundant and tumultuous as it was, it seemed never to touch the Quintessence. The two sparred and parried endlessly, the one pressing the other back, rushing at it, arching over it, surging into it. And yet always, just as they seemed about to collide, they slid away from one another.

Sylas understood this too. It was a primal battle between light and dark, between two mirrored parts of creation. Such was their opposition that they could never meet.

Without thinking, he turned and opened his mouth to share his excitement with Simia, and for the first time he looked her full in the face. His chest ached as he saw how terribly white she was — a blank, empty white that had no place in Simia's face — and how her lips had turned a little blue, and how there was Black trailing from the corner of her mouth down over her chin.

"Oh, Simsi," he murmured, tears welling again. He reached over to caress her cheek and wipe the Black away from her mouth. "If only you could see."

He frowned slightly. He took his hand away from her face and rubbed the thick, oily blackness between his thumb and forefinger. Slowly his eyes turned back to the great sea of Quintessence.

Naeo remembered the drop of Quintessence in the mines of the Valley of Outs: how the Black had gathered about it; how the two had never touched. In some ways, this was the same, but the violence of this tempest could mean only one thing. Here, where it all began, the two were joined in a final battle: Quintessence fighting to heal the world, the Black to pull it apart. And it was a battle that the Black was winning. As great as the sea of Quintessence was, it was hemmed in, assailed on all sides by the Black. Naeo knew the Black: she had lived with its darkness for longer than she could remember. She felt it in her bones and she knew that it would never stop.

There was a sudden movement at her side, and she looked down to see Sylas back on his stomach, heaving at Simia's limp body. He was dragging her on, through the mouth of the passage and out into the cavern. She only had to watch his frantic efforts for a moment before she understood. They had lost Simia to the Black — perhaps, just perhaps, the sea of Quintessence was the place she needed to be.

Naeo slipped down on to her side and kicked out with her heels, pushing herself on. The pain in her back was unbearable now and her head swam with the effort, but with two brave pushes she caught up and grasped Simia's tunic. She began dragging her on, trying her best to match her movements to Sylas's.

It seemed an age before they cleared the opening, but at last they tipped themselves out into the glaring brightness. They were on a steep scree of pebbles and small rocks and, to Naeo's relief, she found that she was able to slide rather than fighting for every inch, and that Simia's body moved more easily over the loose surface. The only obstacles now were the roots trailing down from the ceiling, in which Simia frequently became entangled, forcing them to scramble back up the slope to free her. As she wrestled with the first of these gnarly tendrils, Naeo saw that they were not all alike: some were fine and almost white, others dark brown and thick, as though from a different plant altogether.

Slowly, push by push, they fumbled on towards the golden shore. Naeo became more and more aware of the roar and crash of the seas, but there was something unnerving about those sounds, and it took her some time to realise what it was. There was no wind. She could hear every sound of a raging storm, but there were no winds to feed it.

Sylas could see the Quintessence just ahead, lapping like the waters of a tranquil lake, despite the tempest beyond.

"Nearly there, Simsi," he gasped, but his words were lost in the din.

He felt resistance and turned to see that she was caught against a rock. Taking two deep breaths, he sat up a little, grasped her by the shoulders and, after several attempts, guided her round the obstacle. He sank back, exhausted, and fell heavily against the stones. All at once the loose surface gave way and Sylas found himself caught in a cascade. He did not fight – he could not fight

— he just let himself go, and he drew Simia with him. He heard Naeo cry out as she too was caught in the avalanche of stones.

When they finally slid to a halt, Simia resting against him, Naeo against her, he knew that it was over. They were utterly spent and this was as far as they could go. He gazed up into the swaying roots, and the gold and silver light dancing along their length, and the ethereal spray of droplets sparkling between, and he thought then that this was a kind of heaven. That, if this sea of Quintessence was not truly an afterlife, then it was close to it.

And that was when he felt something cool against his cheek.

Cool but somehow warm.

Soft and at the same time hard.

Wet but also dry.

And then he was doused in a wave of gold.

83

The Answer

"It seems to me that in all our comings and goings,
our careful study and recording in this book, we Bringers
have been asking a question. When, I wonder,
will we receive the answer?"

SYLAS AND NAEO SAT with their knees drawn up, their bare feet in the lapping Quintessence. Gigantic waves advanced and retreated; the cavern boomed and roared; the great battle between light and dark played out before their eyes, sometimes threatening to engulf them. But neither of them flinched. Neither of them moved.

Each held tight to one of Simia's icy hands, even though they knew that she was already lost.

Almost as soon as they felt the touch of Quintessence, their hearts had quickened, their thoughts had sharpened, their energy had begun to return. Before long, they had managed to sit up and, when they removed their shoes and pushed their feet out into the golden fluid, they had begun to feel more revived and refreshed than they could remember. Naeo had not felt this well since before she had been infected with the Black.

As soon as they were strong enough, they had pulled Simia the final few inches into the Quintessence so that she floated high on the surface, rolling on the waves. And, when they had seen black vapour rising from her mouth and nose, and the grime that coated her skin drain away and disappear, they had let themselves believe that the Quintessence might yet bring her back from the dead. Sylas had bent low over her face and whispered to her, implored her to wake up. But her eyes had remained closed and her skin stayed the same deathly white.

Now, sitting on the shore, Sylas clenched his jaw and said: "We took too long. We should have been faster."

"We couldn't go any faster," was Naeo's reply, even as he spoke.

"But we should have," he said flatly. "For Simsi we should have! She deserved to see the end as much as us!"

He gazed at Simia's white face floating in a halo of red hair. She was so peaceful now, so quiet and content. But, to Sylas, that very peace seemed a sacrilege. Simia had never been one to be quiet or content. She had lived with fire in her belly, doing what no one thought she should, or could, battling for what she believed in.

Sylas reached out and pulled a strand of Black-stained hair from Simia's forehead and trailed it out over the Quintessence. The streak of Black dissolved.

"But is this really the end?" said Naeo to herself, or perhaps to Sylas.

Sylas looked at her. "It has to be, doesn't it? I mean, we knew it was all about the Quintessence — Paiscion told us as much — and here it is! A whole ocean of it!" He held his arm out and the Merisi Band glowed to a new piercing brightness. "Just look at what it does to the band! It has to be the answer!"

Feeling a sudden unexpected surge of rage, Sylas struggled to his feet and squared himself to the waves. "Well, are you? Are you the answer?" he bellowed. He kicked at the shallows of Quintessence, sending up a shower of silver and gold, then stepped back, wiping hot, angry tears from his eyes, and ran and kicked again. "ANSWER ME!"

He waited for a moment, staring at the incessant motion of the sea, timeless and powerful, and then fell back on to the stones. "Except you can't, can you?" he blurted. "You can't even help Simsi, who's done more to put everything right than anyone! You can't even do that!"

Naeo, meanwhile, sat quietly, gazing at Sylas and then the tempest. She reached out and scooped up some of the Quintessence so that it gleamed and rippled in her palm, substantial to the touch and yet as light as air, liquid-wet and yet leaving no trace. She peered at it for some time, and then she looked back at the sea and tossed the Quintessence into the shallows.

"We've come," she said to the waves with a weariness in her voice. "We've done everything we were supposed to do. So help us. *Please* help us. Tell us what to do!"

But, if it heard, the sea did not open its face to them. It raged on, consumed by its battle with the Black.

Naeo sank slowly back on to the rocks and covered her face with her arm. There was no pain in her shoulders now. None at all. But she felt no relief, no joy, just an agonising emptiness. The feeling that it had all been for nothing: their companions captured. The valley almost certainly lost. And now Simia gone forever.

"Naeo," murmured Sylas.

His tone was flat, but the very fact that he had spoken her name made her start. She looked across at him, then let out a yell and sprang to her feet.

Something pale and sinewy was snaking between the stones, winding its way so gently and deftly that it did not disturb a single pebble. It slid between where she had been lying and Sylas, who had also leapt to his feet and was staring in horror. It had reached the Quintessence now, and was moving up the side of Simia's leg, slipping beneath her waist. A moment later it appeared on her other side, and looped back over her stomach, then once again wound beneath her, beginning to spiral up her body.

Sylas and Naeo lunged to pull whatever it was from Simia, but they found themselves fixed to the spot. Terrified, they looked down and saw more sinewy tendrils winding up their own legs. But these were not smooth and pale like the ones now entwined about Simia's body: these were dark and rough and gnarled. They tried to kick out at them, twisting wildly to wrestle themselves free, but the tentacles held them in a powerful grip.

Sylas and Naeo looked along the lengths of their restraints, their eyes following the tendrils through the pebbles of the shoreline and then up towards the ceiling high above. There they saw three thick fibres straining and flexing like muscle.

"The roots!" yelled Sylas.

He turned back to Simia to see with horror that she was now completely ensnared by the pale root, and it was lifting her from the golden sea, leaving behind a shower of Quintessence.

"No!" he cried, straining against his bonds. But the roots had coiled so far about his arms that he could barely move and, as he fought against them, they only grew tighter. He and Naeo squirmed and struggled, but all the while the roots crept up and up their legs and their torsos, the fine tips searching and reaching until, at last, they touched the bare skin of their necks.

In that very instant, they both ceased their struggle. A voice sounded loud and clear in their minds.

"*You have nothing to fear.*"

It was no ordinary thought because it came to them with a certainty greater than conviction.

It was knowledge.

Then they too were hoisted into the air.

They rose swiftly, sailing up from the rocky shore and out over the shimmering sea. And, as they were carried aloft, more of their thoughts became certainties, and certainties became knowledge:

> *These are the roots of the Knowing Tree.*
> *The sea is not the end, but it is part of the end.*
> *And now you know how the rest will be made.*
> *It begins with Simia. Simia, who will live again.*

84

Twin Paths

*"It makes one wonder whether we and our Glimmer, as well
as sharing our beginning and end, take* twin paths
*through life, with the same moments of choice, opportunity
and challenge, even if the causes may be very different."*

SYLAS WATCHED NAEO'S LITHE figure walking away, silhouetted
against the stars, her movements looser and more graceful now
that she was free of pain. He wondered why he did not feel
something. He expected a wrench at their parting – a complaint,
perhaps, from the Merisi Band – but there was nothing.

Simia, he thought. *It's because of Simia.*

His eyes followed Naeo until she disappeared behind an outcrop
of rock and then he turned back.

Simia lay where the roots had left her, where the sand and rock
had buckled and opened wide to let them through, and then closed
up, all evidence of the breach quickly lost in the undulating sands.
Now, the only sign of what had happened was a trail where that
last pale root had parted from her and disappeared back into the
cavern below the desert.

She looked so white by the light of the stars and the failing moon — so peaceful and still — that Sylas could barely believe it to be true. He would not have believed it if he had not *known* it.

He took her hand in his. "Simsi?"

There was a magic in the starlit air, and Sylas felt his hairs prickle. He laid his free hand on her forehead and brought his face close to hers.

"Simsi," he said. "Wake up."

A gentle wind played through her hair, and there was a sound like an intake of breath.

She opened her eyes.

Sylas gasped and reared. "Oh my god," he murmured despite himself. And then he brought his hand back to her face. "Simsi!"

For a moment she looked through him, as though focused on something in the far distance. Then she blinked and seemed to see him.

Her face crumpled and tears rolled from her eyes.

Sylas gave her a wide, faltering smile through his own tears, then he pulled her close. "I thought I'd lost you," he said, his voice cracking.

He heard her breath at his ear. Halting. Precious. Miraculous.

She whispered: "You did."

The desert was dark and featureless, but Naeo knew the way. She knew the stars to follow and the stony ridge that she must keep to her left. She knew when she needed to walk in its shadow to keep from being seen and she knew that, when she climbed the approaching crest of sand, she would see the circle of stone ahead.

She knew all this because of the Knowing Tree.

But it was not the knowing that made her walk tall and a little smile play over her lips. It was what she had felt when she had parted from Sylas. It was that peculiar sense that, for all the strength they had found in being together, they were ready to be apart. That after their long journey to see the world as the other saw it, feel as the other felt, they no longer needed to be close.

And there was something else. The more she reflected on the certainties that had flowed from the roots of the Knowing Tree, the more Naeo realised how much she had known already. The very journey she was making now, to the stone circle, was something she had thought about. The journey Sylas was to make too was one that, deep down, she had known had to be made. As soon as she had seen the sea of Quintessence, she had known that it was what they had been looking for. She had even had an idea of how they might use it. The Knowing Tree had simply made it a certainty.

So, as she climbed the dune, there was nowhere else she would have rather been. And, when she thought of her father in the valley, she felt certain that he too would want nothing else for her than to be there, on that sandy crest, walking alone to the stone circle. It was what had to be done.

Her pace was so lively now — without the Black — that she came to the peak more quickly than she had expected. At the right time she lowered herself on to her stomach and crawled forward until she could peer over the edge. At once she saw the ring of flickering torches just ahead and, at their centre, the stone circle.

She looked out for the guards they had seen earlier. She quickly saw two Ghorhund prowling about in the outer shadows, and soon enough she saw three Ghor guards moving at a steady lope between the stones, their eyes and ears alert, searching the night.

For some time she watched the pattern of the patrols, hoping that there might be a way to reach the circle without being seen.

But the guards were too many and too disciplined. Naeo would just have to summon all of her courage and believe.

She collected her thoughts and did her best to steel herself for what she must do. Sylas found his way into her mind. She thought of what she now knew. She thought of her father. But it was when she thought of Sylas that Naeo found the strength she needed.

She raised herself on to one knee and lowered her head, readying herself just as she had in races on the plains of Salsimaine. She pictured herself leaping over the crest and scrambling down the far side, eyes low, looking for the easiest way. She began to breathe quickly and her heart began to race.

Then a sound pierced the silence of the desert.

It was a tortured, screeching animal cry.

In an instant, Naeo was back on her stomach, pressing herself into the sand. For a moment she just listened to the ghastly squeals echoing between the hills. It was a sound she had only heard once: earlier that night, when they had entered the Crucible. And then came another newly familiar sound: a *huff*, *huff*, *huff*, like the beating of wings. And it was growing louder.

Skin tingling, she turned and gazed back the way she had come.

Her stomach tightened to a knot. There was a dark silhouette above the hills, huge and shapeless, snuffing out the stars as it grew larger and larger.

She looked back at the stone circle and saw that the guards too were transfixed. They had gathered on one side of the circle, leaving a large section unguarded.

"Come on, Nay-no!" she muttered to herself. "You can do this!"

And once again she rose on to her haunches. Then she took three short breaths and launched herself over the crest.

§

Sylas held Simia tight round her shoulders — more tightly, in truth, than was necessary — but in that moment she seemed to him a newly rekindled flame, so precious and fragile that just one false step might blow it out. They talked little at first as they picked their way carefully along the rocky riverside. Simia was unsteady and weak, her breath coming in faint gasps, but slowly, as her blood started to flow, she improved and was able to ask Sylas to explain all that had happened.

So he told her about their escape from the pit, and the great cavern, and how he and Naeo had tried to save her by bathing her in the sea of Quintessence. He told her about the roots, and how she had been taken by the Living Tree.

Simia's eyes widened. "How do you know that's what it was?"

"Because the roots that took me and Naeo were the roots of the Knowing Tree," he said.

He explained how the touch of the Knowing Tree had been like eating the fruit in Isia's temple, but also different; that they did not *show* him the truth, it had just come to him, stark and clear. As the root had touched his skin, he had known what it was, and other things too. He had known that the roots were there for the Quintessence, that the trees were infected with the Black and Quintessence was all that kept them alive. He had known that, in their endless retreat from the Black and search for Quintessence, the roots had spread far and wide beneath Old Kemet, particularly here where the Black and the Quintessence had congregated.

He told her that, as he had felt the touch of the Knowing Tree, he had known what they must do. "No, that's not it," he said after a pause. "We knew *what* we should do as soon as we saw the sea of Quintessence. We knew we needed to use it, somehow, to heal the worlds. But the Knowing Tree gave us the *how*."

"And that's why we're going to the *Windrush*?"

"Yes. That's part of the 'how'."

Simia stared at him expectantly. "So, come on, what's the *whole* how?"

"I'll show you when we get to the ship."

Simia was less than impressed, but seemed to have no energy to argue.

Sylas helped her to wade across a stream. "So I still don't understand," she said as she reached the far side. "Why are you and Naeo splitting up? Surely you need each other now more than ever?"

"It's hard to explain."

She tutted. "Try."

He was quiet for a moment, thinking of the right words. "I suppose we don't *need* to be together any more. It's like... I've found the Naeo in me, and she's found the me in her." He laughed. "Does that make any sense?"

Simia looked at him long and hard. "Yes," she said. "I suppose it does."

They continued in silence until finally they walked round a jutting rock and came to a clump of dense scrub shrouding the river ahead. A dry, long-dead cedar tree rose from its heart, leaning precariously over the waters.

"I recognise that tree, Simsi!" Sylas exclaimed. "We're close."

As they took the last few steps, he was filled with a mixture of excitement and dread. He remembered all too vividly the sounds they had heard from the Crucible: the shattering of timber and that freakish animal cry.

They paused before the thicket, glanced nervously at one another and then began pushing their way through. As they emerged from the other side, they stopped and gaped. Simia staggered, so that Sylas had to hold her up.

Before them was the wreck of the *Windrush*.

The top half of the mainmast had toppled on to the shore. The sails were shredded. Frayed ropes hung loosely from shattered yards. Broken timbers lay scattered upon buckled decks. Their beloved *Windrush* — the brave vessel that had saved their lives, and carried them between continents, was in ruins.

And yet what dismayed Sylas more than anything else was the silence. The decks were deserted. There was no sign of the crew or Triste or Sylas's mother.

"Hello?" he ventured, his voice echoing through the broken decks. Then more loudly: "Anyone there?"

There was no reply.

"Thoth," murmured Simia. "It has to have been him."

Sylas was doing his best to contain his panic. "But where *is* everyone?"

"Must have run away," said Simia hurriedly. "I think it's — it's good that there's no one here. It means they escaped, right?"

Sylas peered up at the hills, searching them for movement, but they too were still and empty. He glanced across at the far bank, wondering if they might be hiding there, but the river was far too treacherous to be crossed.

"Maybe," he murmured doubtfully, wishing for one last touch of the Knowing Tree so that he might be sure that his mother was safe.

Simia stared dejectedly at the gleaming wreckage. "Well, we won't be going anywhere on the *Windrush*, that's for sure. What should we do?"

"We should try and find my mum and the crew."

"We can't, Sylas!" she said imploringly. "They could have gone anywhere! It could take us hours. Besides, I can hardly walk the way I am!"

Sylas grunted and bit his lip, thinking.

"I know you're worried," Simia said, "but we have to believe they're all right."

He nodded absently.

"Why don't we go the way Naeo went?" suggested Simia.

"No," said Sylas, his eyes still searching the riverbank. "We have to go our own way, up the Nile."

Simia frowned. "How are we supposed to do that?"

Sylas looked at the shattered hulk. "I'll just have to fix her."

"Fix... that?" gasped Simia, pointing at what was left of the *Windrush*.

He stepped past her and walked along the bank a little closer to the wreck.

"I have to," he said over his shoulder. "And I don't know why, but... I sort of... know I can."

In truth, he was fighting his own doubts but, without waiting for a reply, he raised his hands towards the heap of planks and rigging, and did what he knew he must. He closed his eyes and reached out with his mind, searching for the Quintessence in every part of the ship: coating timbers, layered upon sails, coiled about ropes, covering every door, railing and rivet. When he found it, it felt strangely familiar, as though something about his encounter with it beneath the desert had forged a new connection between them. It was almost as though it was waiting for him.

Simia had been watching him from the riverbank, bemused, wondering what on earth Sylas could have in mind. But, all at once, she had her answer. She gazed in wonderment as the Quintessence began to move and, with it, every part of the wreck. Rope spliced with gleaming rope, timber meshed with shining timber, metal melded with silvered metal. Masts righted as though hoisted by a ghostly crew, buckled decks straightened as if pulled taut by mighty hands, and sails restitched themselves to their resplendent whole. Like a princess dressing in her finery, the *Windrush* slowly roused herself and reclaimed her majesty. Soon enough, the elegant lines of her hull were restored and, within moments, she had righted herself in the waters of the Nile, her sails ready to gather the winds. And, as Simia looked up to the highest reaches of the rigging, she saw the bright feather of the Suhl on the ship's standard dancing against the stars.

For Sylas it was as though the Quintessence was him and he was it. Everything that happened to the *Windrush* that night felt peculiarly natural, almost ordinary, as though he was doing little more than working on one of his kites, setting its wings, pulling its canvas tight, picking out the details with his coloured paints. And so, when he saw Simia beaming at him with that grin that he had come to know so well, her eyes bright, her chest heaving, he was surprised. And when he blinked and looked back at the *Windrush* he was surprised again.

She looked like the ship that had raced down the hills of the Valley of Outs, newly anointed in Quintessence, every timber shining so that the river and the trees about her danced with a golden light.

Sylas grinned at Simia. "Come on," he said. "Let's get going."

She let out a bark of laughter. "OK then!" She staggered over to him. "How did you do that?" she asked as they linked arms and started walking to the gangplank.

"I really don't know."

She drew up short and looked him in the face. "Really?"

Sylas smiled and nodded. "Really." He was about to say more, but then his eyes shifted away from her, back towards the riverbank. He frowned.

"What?" said Simia. "Did you see something?"

"A movement — just there, where the—"

He was interrupted by the snap of a twig somewhere in the undergrowth.

They both tensed and instinctively drew close. Sylas was just beginning to push Simia behind him when a tall figure suddenly stepped from the shadows.

The moonlight revealed long robes, tumbling blond locks and a familiar pale face.

They recognised him in the same instant.

"Ash!" they exclaimed.

85

Flight

"To give an example, who really knows more about flight*?*
We, who have taken to the air ourselves in helicopters
and planes? Or the Suhl, who sense the winds and
feel the flock of starlings carving through the skies?"

NAEO RAN AS SHE had on the plains of Salsimaine. She ran free
from the bite of Black, free from Sylas, free from doubt. She tore
through the darkness, arms pumping, long legs bounding with
ranging, confident strides. Already she could see where she would
enter the circle: between two abandoned torches, their flames
burning low. And beyond she could see the massive stones
themselves slanting into the dark, calling her on.

Yes, that was the place. The ground was level and free from
loose sands that might slow her down, and the guards had loped
away to gaze up into the inky sky.

She was so close. So very close.

"Don't... stop!" she panted. "Don't... look... back!"

But then the dirt beneath her feet quaked and the black sky
roared. Suddenly Naeo could not hear her gasps, or her feet
pounding the dust, or her heart hammering. Everything was

consumed by the sound of beating wings and the blasts of wind that came with every stroke, sending up billows of dust.

She squinted through the murk and saw Ghor guards ahead, but they were cowering low to the ground, staring above her head at whatever was chasing her. Then a new screech filled the night and, all at once, the guards leapt to their feet and fled in terror, streaking out into the darkness.

Naeo had to fight the urge to look. She fixed her eyes between the nearing stones and prepared to make the passing. She dropped her chin, closed her mind to the squalls of dust and turned her thoughts to the moon.

Even at a sprint, she could feel it cool in her belly and chest. She gathered up the moonbeams, weaving them like threads in her cat's cradle, spooling them round the stones. Already she could see the circle brightening before her, shimmering with liquid silver.

Suddenly something massive swept past her, clipping her shoulder and tearing her tunic across the back, but somehow she stayed on her feet. Then a scream of rage split the air, and something colossal tore into the earth between her and the stones. Naeo accelerated towards the gash in the earth, thinking that she might leap across it, but in the next moment her legs were swept from beneath her and then she was tumbling, head over feet. Her shoulder hit one of the stones, wrenching her about so that she was looking back into the open desert.

The darkness shifted before her. By the torchlight, she saw something gargantuan and animal. It reared back on clawed feet and gave another deafening, horrifying shriek, its breath a volcanic storm. In the starlight, Naeo thought she glimpsed a figure sitting astride the beast's mane, long robes flying up in the winds. Then mighty wings swept forward, obscuring everything from view and enveloping the stone circle. The moonlight that had pooled between the stones faltered and began to die.

She struggled to her feet. "No!" she yelled. "You can't stop us!"

She turned and looked desperately round the circle. There, near at hand, a last trace of moonlight flickered beneath an arch of stone. She summoned all her strength and threw herself forward, glancing off one of the stones, tumbling past another, reaching with every sinew for the failing light.

S

Ash pulled the lever to raise the gangplank and waited as it gradually plunged the passageway into darkness. Sylas stood a little behind, watching him closely.

"You still haven't explained," he said. "How did you get away?"

Ash turned, the white of his smile just showing in the gloom. "I should ask you the same thing!"

"But I asked first."

Ash laughed and shrugged. "Nothing much more to tell really. I heard Thoth leave, then managed to prise the doorframe away from the wall." He leaned into Sylas's ear. "I had to use a touch of Urgolvane, but needs must and all that." He patted Sylas on the shoulder. "I know you can keep a secret." Then he walked on down the corridor.

Sylas turned and called after him: "But what about the others? Didn't you get them out too?"

Ash had reached the steps. "I didn't have time," he said. "I wasn't sure when Thoth would be back, and I knew that if you managed to escape you'd need me here, at the *Windrush*. Even then, I nearly missed you, didn't I?" He smiled again before disappearing up the steps.

"But the others need you, Ash!" Sylas shouted after him. "We're OK! You should have stayed to help them!"

Something was wrong. Very wrong. The surly, brooding Ash had been disturbing enough, but this good cheer was even more chilling. He hardly seemed to care about his crew.

Sylas walked over to the steps. "And did you see anyone on your way here?" he called. "My mum? Triste?"

There was no answer. When he reached the deck, he saw Ash by the helm, looking over the stern.

"I said, did you see anyone else on your way here?"

Ash put the shiny black shell back into the pocket of his tunic. "I saw three or four people climbing the hills, but I couldn't make out who they were. They might have been heading for the academy."

Sylas had been staring at the shell, wondering how Ash had recovered it, but now he gaped at him in astonishment. "And you didn't try to stop them?"

A flicker of irritation passed over Ash's face. "No, I didn't because I didn't know it was *worth* stopping them. I didn't know where you were, and my priority was you. It still is, Sylas. You and Naeo. Are you sure she shouldn't be coming with us by the way? I really don't understand why—"

"I've found it!" called Simia, walking towards them from the nearby hatch, clutching a scroll. "It was still in the Bow Room!"

She knelt before them and unrolled it on the shining deck. She looked down with satisfaction.

"The map of the Motherland! Not the one I've been using, but it's good enough. There's the delta," she said, pointing to the tangle of waterways at the top of the map, "and that's the Nile." Her finger traced a line, just visible in the starlight. "And that's where we are now." She tapped a label near the bottom of the map that read *First Cataract*. She looked up at Sylas and put her hands on her hips. "So, come on, now you can tell me the whole how!"

Sylas was quiet for some moments, his eyes travelling across the map. Much of it was unfamiliar — wide reaches of desert and clusters of place names he could not make out. But when he looked to the north-east of the Nile, towards an expanse of water blocked out in blue, he felt a stirring of recognition. He could not understand why but, as his gaze travelled up the eastern coastline of Old Kemet to where the sea entered a narrower channel, the features became more and more familiar. And, when he looked across that channel to a huge V-shaped peninsula, he saw bays, inlets and mountains that he *knew* would be there.

He knelt down next to Simia and pored over the place names and contours. When his eyes fell on one particular feature, he felt a rush of excitement. With the trace of a smile, he extended a finger and placed it on a range of mountains.

"There," he said. "*That's* where we're going."

All three of them leaned over the map. Ash suddenly sat bolt upright and stared at Sylas as though he had lost his senses.

"Mount Sinai?" he said incredulously. "But — but why would you want to go there?"

"For the same reason the One from the Waters did," said Sylas. "Because it's the highest place around." He looked at them both. "It was part of how all this began. Now it'll be part of the end!"

86

The Final Journey

*"And so we must treat each and every passing
as though it might be* the final journey *: our last
chance to witness, to learn, to teach and perhaps,
to shape the destiny of our two worlds."*

NAEO LAY ON THE cold sand, chest heaving, eyes pressed closed, praying with every part of her being that she had made it through. She had felt nothing as she landed — just the impact of the hard, gritty desert sand — but she was sure that there was a change. She didn't know what it was, but there was something. She gathered her courage and opened her eyes.

The shimmering pools of moonlight had disappeared, but even as Naeo watched, a bright bluish light danced across the face of one of the stones of the circle, only to appear an instant later on the next. Now, she saw other lights too, like lances arcing across the moonless sky, and one of these briefly illuminated a yellowish cloud far lower in the sky than it ought to be. And then she became aware of an awful, acrid, metallic stench that reminded her of her visit to the town in the Other.

But it was the noises that convinced her. They were horrifying not in the way of the shrieking cry of the beast — this was no animal sound. This was the sound of the sky splitting and the earth breaking in two.

Fearfully Naeo clambered to her feet and backed towards the nearest stone. There was no sign of the massive winged beast or its master, but other devilish shapes streaked past in the night. Flashes of blue and yellow light showed the head and mane of a Ghorhund, the horns of a Rager, the tusks of a Hamajak. Out in the desert she saw great eruptions of earth, and moments later she was hit by shock waves of sound, which pressed at her skull and rumbled in her ribcage.

It was like a scene from hell itself. She wanted to drop to the ground and cover her head with her arms, but she knew she couldn't. Sylas would be pressing on, Naeo thought, and so must she.

She chose a direction that looked a little less terrifying than the others and headed out into the dark, her eyes scouring the rutted ground ahead of her, using the blinking light of explosions to pick out a way. There were pools of Black everywhere — brimming in ruts and ditches and craters — and it would be all too easy to slip into one.

She kept as low to the ground as she could, praying that she would not be seen, but thankfully any growling machines that roared past seemed to be rushing to battle or base, and the roving packs of beasts were far more interested in the fight than in her.

She clambered over the wreckage of a large gun that seemed to have been torn apart, and struggled across an area of soft, pummelled sand that felt as though it might swallow her whole. The further she went, the more the sounds of battle began to fade, and the more complete the darkness became. It was not like any night she had seen before. There was no faint light from the moon or stars. This was an absolute inky blackness: thick and impenetrable.

That was why she did not see the figure that stepped across her path.

They collided with a thump, and Naeo found herself staggering backwards, teetering on the brink of a crater. She was just falling towards the pool of Black when the figure reached out, caught her by the front of her tunic and pulled her to safety.

Gasping, she gazed up at the man who had saved her. All she could see was his outline, tall and straight-backed. And then she saw the glint of round wire spectacles.

"Naeo?" came a familiar voice. "Naeo! It's me!"

Naeo blinked up into the darkness, hardly daring to believe her ears.

"Paiscion?" she blurted.

"The very same."

She gasped and threw her arms about him, clinging on as tightly as she could. In that terrible place, he seemed to her like an angel, miraculous and safe — but better than an angel because he was from home.

When she drew away, the Magruman knelt and smiled. He put a hand to her cheek. "My child, how wonderful it is to see you safe and well." He regarded her with weary, wise eyes, then he looked behind her. "Are you alone?"

"Yes," she said. "Sylas and Simia stayed behind. But — but how did you know I'd be here?"

The Magruman smiled. "I didn't, but I knew that if I might be able to help, it would here, where it all began."

More distant explosions illuminated his face with blue and orange light. He looked older, Naeo thought, the lines of his face etched more deeply than she remembered.

He glanced at the explosions and then back to her. "I want to hear everything, Naeo — the journey, the academy, everything — but first we need to get somewhere safe. Can you run?"

Naeo opened her mouth to reply, but the words never came.

Her breath rushed from her lungs as though she had been kicked in the chest, and the dark became a blinding white. Paiscion's face bleached into nothingness as a huge shock wave shoved them to one side. She felt the Magruman wrap his arms round her, his body twisting to shield her as they were thrown to the ground. She tried to scream, but it would not come, and then she was drowned in noise: a rending roar that consumed everything, leaving only a haunting, low note.

As she came back to herself, she found her limbs tangled, her cheek pressed into mud. Everything was dark again now, and all that remained of the noise was the loud ringing in her ears.

She felt a hand slip into hers. "Come on, Naeo!" It sounded like a shout, but it was faint in her ear. "Follow me!"

She was heaved painfully to her feet, muscles protesting, and then they were on the move, stumbling across the battlefield. Paiscion pulled her relentlessly on, weaving between Black-brimming craters and ruts of broken earth, yanking her away from pits and furrows even as she was about to fall. The further they went, the more complete became the darkness. It was not just an absence of light: it was thick and substantial, like a mist that she might reach out and touch.

Soon, to her relief, the ground changed beneath her feet, becoming firmer and more level, like flats of sun-dried mud. But Paiscion only quickened his pace. Naeo would have protested had she any breath to cry out.

All of a sudden, he halted so abruptly that she collided with him again.

There were gasps and pants, then she heard him turn.

There were three sudden bangs, like a hand slapping against plate metal, then Naeo leapt back as a blaze of light erupted in the darkness. A strange whine sounded above her head, building in volume, and instinctively she stepped out to run. But Paiscion's grip on her hand tightened and, through the glare, she saw him lean towards her.

"Trust me!" he yelled in her ear.

He guided her through a desert squall and then, to her astonishment, pointed to a half-lit doorway suspended in mid-air. He pushed her forward and she climbed inside.

Naeo found herself in a small, square cabin with a row of seats against one wall and another open door opposite. Paiscion heaved himself in beside her and led her to the seats.

She sat down and looked about her. Everything — the floor, the walls, the ceiling and the many strange fittings — seemed to be made of metal. There was another smaller doorway ahead that looked into a tiny cabin in which she now noticed the back of two seated people, both of them wearing large helmets.

She turned to Paiscion and saw that he was plastered in mud, and one lens of his glasses was smashed. "What *is* this?" she yelled over the din.

"A helicopter!" he bellowed. His face cracked into a smile. "It's quite miraculous, you'll see! It'll take us far from here!"

Naeo stared at him, her mind racing. "A *flying* machine?"

"Yes, but don't worry, they're really very—"

"But can it go far? And fast?"

Paiscion looked at her questioningly, but nodded.

"I know where we need to go!" she exclaimed. She glanced frantically about the cabin. "Do you have a map?"

The Magruman cocked his head to one side, then held up a finger. He went over to the doorway and leaned inside the other cabin. He spoke to the occupants for a moment, then returned to his seat, holding a folded map. He laid it out in front of them.

"Here!" he shouted over the *woop*, *woop*, *woop* of the rotors.

"It shows most of Egypt and the region, but the place names are of this world, Naeo! I'm not sure how helpful it'll be!"

"It doesn't matter!" she yelled, leaning over the map. Her eyes passed quickly up the snaking blue line of the Nile and then across to a wider expanse of blue. When she saw the distinctive V-shaped peninsula in the north, she reached out, her finger hovering over the paper, until carefully she placed it on a printed label written over a mountain range.

Paiscion bent closer and adjusted his broken glasses. Then he leaned closer still. Slowly a smile grew across his face.

"Of course!" he exclaimed, turning to her and gripping her arm. "Of course!" He looked at her then as a father might a daughter, and placed his hand on his heart, then he leapt forward and began shouting instructions into the other cabin.

As he turned back to her, the great flying machine roared, shuddered and launched itself up into the blackness.

87

The Last Night

"Or could we come instead to the last night –
the night that sees no dawn?"

DRESCH AND LUCIEN BACKED slowly towards one another, chests heaving, muscles quivering with the effort. They seemed to have been fighting for hours, but they could not be sure of the time any more. In this endless night, they were not even sure that there was such a thing as time.

But now, at least, the beasts and the insects were quiet. It was hardly a victory, but they were grateful for the respite. Even the army's searchlights had blinked off, perhaps to preserve power, or perhaps because the operators were too exhausted to continue.

The two Merisi leaned against one another to take a little weight off their legs, and scanned the darkness with tired eyes, waiting for the next inevitable assault. But, in truth, their greatest fear was the darkness itself. It was a darkness not meant for this world: a darkness known only in human hearts and nightmares.

"Martha?"

"Yes?"

"I'm not really sure... why we're still fighting."

There was a silence and the darkness poured into it.

"Because it's all we can do," she replied, her voice toneless and hollow.

Lucien rubbed his face, trying to revive himself. "I don't know, maybe it's this darkness, or — or perhaps I'm just exhausted, but... I just can't see the *point* any more." He blinked into the dark. "Not now."

"We have to keep going *because* of the dark," said Dresch. She reached for his hand. "And, when *that* isn't enough any more, we have to keep going for each other. Me for you. You for me."

Lucien closed his numb fingers about hers. "Yes," he said.

And then somewhere in the dark they heard a howl. There was a brief hush, followed by another baying noise. Soon there were howls everywhere, mournful, demented, as though the dark had found its voice.

And then came a rumble in the earth, and a huff in the air, and the charge.

The final battle had raged since twilight, filling the Valley of Outs with the clatter of weapons and the yells of warriors and beasts.

The night had begun well for the defenders of the valley. Inspired by Isia and the return of Espasian, the Leaflikes had led a spirited counter-attack, driving the Imperial army back up the slopes to the north, east and west, and halting their advance to the south. When their assault had faltered, they made use of great mounds of freshly felled trees as makeshift defences, and the valley herself had come to their aid, throwing up roots to foil and confuse, and diverting streams to create morasses and mudslides. In places, the slopes had collapsed altogether, carving deep chasms in the hillside, and stopping the Imperial troops in their tracks.

Even the dark had seemed to fight on the side of the Suhl. When the enemy numbers had at last become too great and the defenders had attempted to retreat, a cloud had passed before the moon, shrouding them in shadow and allowing them to slip away unseen. And yet, when the Imperial forces spied what was happening and charged, they themselves were bathed in moonlight, allowing the Suhl to brace themselves against the attack.

But, throughout those long hours, it was Espasian who had been the valley's most steadfast defender. He had seemed to be everywhere: sometimes striding along the defensive lines, bellowing his support to his fighters; sometimes scrambling over broken defences and throwing himself into battle, parrying and brawling as he went. He had stood shoulder to shoulder with his fellow Suhl, sweeping at Ghorhund and Hamajaks with the bright-edged sword given to him by Merimaat herself — the Maatka Blade as she had called it — and, even with his old injuries, he had proven himself as formidable a sword fighter as any on the battlefield.

And yet, despite his efforts, after almost three hours of brutal fighting the battle had turned decisively against the Suhl. They were simply too few and too exhausted to hold back wave after wave of attack, and finally their lines had been breached not just in one place but in many. Suddenly they had found themselves fighting to the front and to the rear, and the battle had quickly become a rout. Entire regiments of Suhl — as entire as they now were — were cut off or captured, and many were slain. At last Espasian had had no choice but to raise his horn and sound the full retreat, and so the hills of the Valley of Outs had been allowed to fall. Those defenders who were still able tried to make their way back to their loved ones in the Hollow. Some had their secret ways and prevailed, while many more perished as they fled.

So now the hills were lost, and yet still Espasian fought on. He was deliriously tired such that he could barely see what he was fighting. He flailed before him with his sword, swiping at the press of dark bodies and burning eyes, hoping to hold at least some of them at bay. The Maatka Blade was still a fearsome weapon, and its razor edge of Quintessence sliced mercilessly through leather, and steel, and flesh and bone. But the enemy were just so many. They were an endless flood pouring down the hillsides, and between the last of the trees, and over all that remained of glades and thickets. And now they had him surrounded. Now, they sensed the end and came on all the harder.

"Come and get yourselves a Magruman!" Espasian yelled, holding up his bloody blade so that it shone in the moonlight.

And with that he charged yet again, slashing and wounding, sending Hamajaks gibbering and Ragers snorting and Ghorhund whining into the woods. And as he charged he called up the last of the living things – the broken bushes, the saplings, the grasses and weeds – and with them he ensnared legs and claws, so that the beasts stumbled before him, leaving themselves prey to his lightning blade.

He fought like this, wildly and fearlessly, lost in the thrill and the horror of battle, until at last he felt something rip down his back. At first he thought it was his cloak being torn away, perhaps caught upon a stump or rock. But then he heard a rasping snarl at his ear and, to his astonishment, his breastplate suddenly fell before him, and he looked down to see its leather straps bloodied and torn.

Then came the pain. The wound may have been in his back, but the pain was everywhere. It wrung his insides and raged in his head. Then he was falling, his legs buckling beneath him, and somehow the Maatka Blade was no longer in his hands but lying at his side, on the rocky lakeside. He found himself consumed as much by surprise as pain – surprise that after everything it should have come to this, and so quickly, and with so little warning.

As he stared up into the darkness, the dying moon and the pinpricks of stars swimming before him, Espasian saw shadows closing in on all sides; shadows that snarled and huffed and snorted. Shadows with eyes and teeth and tusks.

He drew a long last breath of the valley's winter-fresh air and closed his eyes.

"Leave him!" said a female voice, strong and commanding.

Espasian's eyes opened. The shadows hesitated, looking about for the owner of the voice.

"The Magruman is mine!" she proclaimed, now with twin voices, soft, imperious. "I said leave him!"

One by one the shadows looked out over the lake and then shrank away, ears flattening, heads dropping between shoulders. Espasian managed to turn his head until he could see the silver mists on the lake, and there among them a lone figure standing tall in the prow of a small boat.

As he watched, Isia's arms rose slowly from her sides, leaving a trace of themselves in their wake. The shadows whimpered and whined and jostled, beginning to retreat.

"Do it!" growled a guttural voice close to Espasian's ear. A Ghor commander stepped into view, the great crest of its helm catching the moonlight. It turned to look down at Espasian. "He isn't long for this world anyway."

The horde of beasts started to move away along the shoreline. Their leader stepped out to follow, then hesitated and turned. It crouched down over Espasian, its half-human eyes fixed on his, and it placed a clawed fist on his chest. Espasian waited helplessly for the final blow, holding the commander's gaze. And then, in a tiny gesture, the Ghor's great canine head bowed a little. It was so brief that the troops would probably have missed it, but to Espasian it was unmistakable.

The commander grasped the Maatka Blade and, with a growl of effort, tossed it far out into the lake. It fell into the waters without a splash and quickly disappeared into the depths.

As soon as the commander was gone, Espasian let his head fall, and he saw Isia, still standing in the prow of her boat, watching as the beasts made their way along the shoreline towards Sylva. He had a peculiar sense that she was not there, in the middle of the lake, but by his side. An eerie quiet fell about him and he felt certain that somehow she was leaning over him; that her hand was warm on his forehead.

Then he heard her whisper at his ear: "Rest now, brave Espasian."

Out on the lake he saw her arms fall to her sides. Her slender body swayed precariously and then she slumped down into the boat, leaving a ghost of herself in the mists.

S

Amelie and Triste made their way silently down the final stretch of the passageway and, when they reached the oblong opening at its end, they paused. They gazed out into the Crucible, wondering at its size and strangeness. They looked for any sign of Sylas and Naeo, but saw nothing.

"What *is* this place?" whispered Amelie.

The Scryer shook his head. "I've no idea. I think Fathray's papers said something about it, but Ash took them before I read that far." He looked at her doubtfully. "Are you *sure* you want to do this?"

She gave him a steady look. "For the last time, Triste, we couldn't just wait on the riverside, especially now that the *Windrush* is gone. We have to try and help. And, if that means going into this place... so be it."

Triste looked both ways along the length of the Crucible. "It's just that I don't like this place. There's something about it I – I can't quite *see*."

"Well then, I can't expect you to go on," said Amelie with a sigh, "but I have to. You could wait—"

"No, I'm coming, of course," said Triste. "But, like I say, there's something strange about it. Just — just be ready to run."

Amelie eyed the shadows in the Crucible. "All right."

They stepped into the dim starlight and began making their way out into the centre of the vast open space. Very soon they found several sets of footprints in the dust leading directly across the canyon, and they saw among them those of children. They began to follow, weaving between a patchwork of dark shadows.

They had only walked a short distance when Triste stopped and stiffened. He caught Amelie by the elbow and pulled her to his side.

"What is it?" she whispered.

Triste did not answer. He was peering into all corners of the canyon.

"Triste, you're scaring me," said Amelie.

Then a strange echo came from the darkness: "*You're s-s-s-scaring me.*"

"*S-s-s-scaring me,*" came another, this time from the side.

Triste turned and yanked Amelie's arm so hard that she spun about. "Run!" he yelled. "Back to the tunnel!"

"*To the tunnel!*" echoed a voice.

"*Run!*" breathed another.

"*Run!*"

"*Run!*"

They were not echoes at all but airy voices coming from all sides. When Triste changed direction, they too shifted, so that they were always ahead.

"*Run!*" they whispered.

"*S-s-s-scared,*" they hissed.

Amelie was stiff with fear, and she only managed to run because Triste dragged her, heaving her from side to side to avoid the voices and the black shadows at their feet.

But then, quite suddenly, he skidded to a halt. This seemed to catch the owners of the voices by surprise because they fell quiet.

The Scryer stood, panting and looking about, then he leaned into Amelie's ear. "There's no way back," he murmured. "I'm going to try something."

Amelie looked at him with wide, terrified eyes. "What *are* they?"

"The Kraven," he whispered. "The half-dead. Those who have died before their Glimmer." He glanced about as though he could see them in the darkness. "They came to me once, on the Barrens. Let me try to talk to them again." He drew even closer to her ear. "If I squeeze your hand, just run. I'll try to distract them."

"No, I can't go without you," hissed Amelie. But Triste had already drawn her behind him so that she had her back to his.

"Spirits of the half-life," he called, "I am Triste, Scryer of the Suhl, and this is Amelie Tate, of the bloodline of Isia."

He fell silent, allowing the import of his words to be understood. There was a brief quiet, then a voice sighed: "*Is-s-sia...*"

A chorus of whispers joined the first: "*Is-s-sia...*"

"*Is-s-sia!*"

"*The line of blood!*"

"Amelie is the mother of Sylas Tate," Triste continued, silencing the voices, "the boy who came this way earlier tonight. The boy who travels with his Glimmer."

There was a hesitation, then a voice breathed from the darkness: "*S-S-S-Sylas...*"

"*The boy...*" sighed the others.

"That's right," said Triste. "The boy who, before this night is done, will set you free."

As he said these final words, he slid his hand round Amelie's.

"I won't leave you," she whispered.

Then Triste felt a sudden chill at his ear.

"*We sh-sh-shall s-s-s-see,*" came a whisper.

The presence shifted so that now it was Amelie who felt the cold. "*If by dawn we are not free,*" it said, so close to her that her skin prickled, "*then the mother will give what the s-s-s-son would not.*"

With that, the Crucible was filled with whispers — not the few that they had heard thus far but hundreds, perhaps thousands. And they were everywhere.

"*Give...*" they sighed.

   "*Give...*"

      "*Give...*"

88

Mount Sinai

*"But of all the scripture we have discussed it is the book of
Exodus that causes most consternation. Every one of the tales
of Moses — the plagues, the parting of the seas, Mount
Sinai and the ten commandments — all of them seemed
to fill my listeners with dread and distaste."*

"READY?" CALLED SIMIA FROM the bow.

"Ready!" cried Sylas.

Simia stared ahead of the ship for another few moments, then
turned and waved the open map. "Here!" she yelled. "Turn here!"

At once Sylas turned the winds and tilted the sails, heaving the
Windrush over. She responded beautifully, carving a sparkling arc
in the moonlit waters of the Nile, and then skipping lightly towards
the riverbank.

The sloping sands were upon them in moments, and still the
Windrush did not slow.

"Careful!" shouted Ash, bracing himself against the mainmast.

But Sylas did not flinch. He ploughed on.

The first touch of the bank sent up sheets of sand on either
side of the bow, drawing a shriek of frightened delight from Simia.
She clung tightly to the rail as the prow bucked and then settled,

only to leap again a few moments later as the *Windrush* sliced through the crest of a small dune. She plunged down on the other side, masts creaking, rigging clattering, and briefly steadied before mounting another. She launched herself off its sandy peak and, for a few magical moments, she flew, the only sound the rush of the wind and the song of the ropes. Then she came down with a thump on the face of another ridge, making everyone stagger and reach for something to cling to.

"Sylas, stop this!" yelled Ash. "She'll break up! Let's use the river!"

"No time!" called Sylas. He flashed a smile and pointed. "Anyway, look!"

Ash turned to the sea of sand before the ship and stared, his mouth falling open.

The dunes in their path were moving, rolling, tumbling away like waves. Everywhere before them, peaks of sand surged and leapt with a life of their own, then cascaded away to one side. It was bizarre, and yet strangely beautiful because it seemed as though the dunes were doing something quite within their nature. But, most miraculous of all, in their wake, they left a channel of level sand: a furrow for the *Windrush* to plough.

It was exactly as Sylas had imagined it, but still he gazed in wonderment. Even now, after everything, his part in this world of marvels caught him by surprise.

Simia whooped and punched the air as the ship entered the channel and began gathering pace. "Yes, Sylas!" she cried, laughing into the wind. "That's it!"

And so the *Windrush* sailed on, fleeting across the desert. All around her the sands surged and slumped, like breakers upon a shore, leaving her passage clear. Faster and faster she sailed, carried by the greater winds. Her masts and rigging made their usual complaint, but Sylas knew they could take the strain. He knew with a certainty that surprised him, the same certainty that drove him on now, relentlessly, towards their destination. Towards the mount.

Simia looked out at the starlit landscape, directing Sylas's efforts so that the *Windrush* avoided rocks, ridges and canyons. She steered them round towns and villages, which passed in a blink, leaving the bleary-eyed locals to marvel at such a strange desert squall on a night as still as this.

Ash walked the deck, looking anxiously ahead, and then behind, and then ahead again. Sometimes he sat, turning the black shell between his fingers, lost in his thoughts, and occasionally Sylas thought he heard the young Magruman muttering, as though arguing with himself. Sylas wondered if the black shell had something to do with the strange mood that had fallen upon their friend, but his attention was called away by the sands or the winds. And, when he thought of it again, he consoled himself that soon it would not matter because everything was about to change.

Everything.

They passed towns clinging to the banks of dry riverbeds, followed ridgeways and escarpments, swept between bare-topped hills and, as time passed, the hush of the winds, the hiss of the keel touching the sands and the silver sheen of the moonlight began to make it all seem rather like a dream.

But then, as they traversed a great open expanse of sand and scrub, they heard a distant cry. Sylas was so lost in the winds and his imaginings that he thought it the screech of a passing bird. But then it came again. He turned and saw that Ash had walked to the stern and was gazing back above the sands that closed in their wake.

"What is it?" called Sylas.

There was a long silence. "I think something's following us," replied Ash. "But we're well ahead of whatever it is."

Just then another shriek, nearer than the last, removed any

doubt. It was an almost human cry, but with something about it that was wild and animal. Simia too had turned in the bow.

"It's Thoth," she called anxiously. "It has to be!"

Ash leaned on the rear railing and stared. "Too dark to tell!" he shouted. His gaze settled upon one portion of the sky, and he cocked his head a little to one side. "Too dark," he murmured as a smile curled his lip.

S

Another volley of insects struck the helicopter, making the engine stutter. The rotors missed a beat and Naeo pressed her eyes shut, fearing the worst but, to her relief, an instant later they were back, thumping the air with their precise rhythm.

Paiscion jumped to his feet and kicked out at the new wave of stunned beetles, roaches and locusts that infested the floor of the cabin, and Naeo joined him, bracing herself carefully by the other opening and using the side of her foot to sweep them out into the darkness.

When she dropped back into her seat, her head was reeling with exhaustion. She had been awake for longer than she could remember, and even the flood of adrenalin in her system could not keep her going for a lot longer. And there was something about this darkness too. It looked like night, but it seemed to Naeo more like an impenetrable blanket, palpable and smothering.

She gazed about her at the strange steel cabin as it thrummed and whined, and she marvelled that right now it was hurtling through the darkness at speeds she could barely imagine. There seemed nothing natural about that metal box, imagined and made by humans to do what no human could. It was, quite simply, impossible. But for Naeo the strangest thing about it was that she did not find it frightening. Not at all. Because now she saw it as Sylas would. She saw it for the genius of its invention, and for the natural laws that made it fly.

"How are you doing?" said Paiscion, his voice strangely close now that they were wearing headphones.

"I'm all right," she said. "Tired, but kind of —" she thought for a moment — "ready, if that makes any sense."

He eyed her closely. "So you know what to do when we get there?"

Naeo looked out into the blackness. "It's strange, but I think we *already* knew. The Knowing Tree just made us certain. It kind of... showed us how. Some of it still isn't quite clear to me, but I know it will be when I'm there, with Sylas." She shrugged a shoulder and smiled. "Kind of with him."

Paiscion looked at her quizzically. "I suppose if you were touched by the Knowing Tree, as you say, it stands to reason—"

Suddenly a harsh voice blared through their headphones. "You should buckle up, sir, miss. There's some turbulence ahead."

Paiscion pressed a button on his headphones. "Where are we?" he asked.

"Just approaching the Red Sea, sir," said the pilot. "It's only a short crossing, then we'll be over the Sinai Peninsula."

§

"Look!" yelled Simia excitedly. "Do you see? Between the two hills!"

Sylas started. He had been lulled by the sway of the ship and the murmur of the winds, and in his exhaustion his thoughts had begun to muddle. He peered ahead in the direction Simia was pointing and saw a pencil-thin line of silver surf between two craggy hills.

He shook himself, realising that his mind had been drifting for a while, as though drawn somewhere else. The winds had eased, and the *Windrush* had slowed — not a lot, but enough to set them back. If Sylas was still in any doubt, it did not last. The darkness was suddenly filled with a fearsome cry, and it was terrifyingly close.

He glanced back and saw to his surprise that Ash was not watching over the stern, but resting with his back against the rail, as though it was Sylas he had been watching. The Magruman quickly turned to gaze into the darkness.

"Still nothing to see!" he called.

Sylas eyed him suspiciously and looked up in the direction of the cry. Sure enough, he could see nothing among the stars, but he thought he could hear something beating out a rhythm, like the *huff*, *huff*, *huff* they had heard earlier that night.

He looked around to check the terrain ahead. Already the sea was spread out before them, and he could see boiling surf crashing on a pale shoreline. He yearned to reach that sea. There the *Windrush* would be in her element, and she might outrun her pursuer. He found himself leaning forward, channelling the winds.

The salt air hit him first, flooding his dry nostrils with pungent aromas of the sea. The ship careered down the final reaches of a riverbed, and in a few more moments she was there, plunging through the surf, leaping off one wave, a second, and then settling on an even keel. The prow sent up sparkling clouds of spray, which cascaded down upon them and felt deliciously cool.

Simia turned, laughing wildly. She shouted something, but Sylas did not hear, so consumed was he by the winds and the waves. He lost himself in them as Naeo had lost herself in the stars, and he felt the *Windrush* glide with an ease and grace that was more like flying than sailing. The wind whistled, and the standard cracked, and the ropes sang.

On she flew across the silver-flecked sea, on and on, until their pursuer's cries began to fade once more.

Simia and Ash turned their eyes in wonderment between the blur of passing waves, and the glowing ship, and Sylas, who was glowing now too. The Merisi Band was a searing fire, as though Naeo was still at his side.

Before long, Simia saw something ahead: an uneven scrawl written in silver lines above the horizon. Her skin prickled and she pointed.

"There!" she cried. "Land!"

She snatched up the map and began poring over it, searching frantically for their location among the crude drawings of coastline, hills and mountains.

"Simsi!" called Sylas. "It's all right! I know the way!"

She turned and looked at him in surprise, but his eyes were already fixed ahead, taking in the waters, sands and hills. He checked the position of a headland and then lowered his shoulder. Simia and Ash scrambled to steady themselves as the ship leaned to one side, carving an arc over the shallows, then corrected herself and leapt over a passing coral reef. As Sylas twisted his shoulders, she banked sharply the other way, heading directly for the shore.

In moments, she was there, striking the sand, riding up the beach, bucking over the low banks beyond. She careered across lowlands of desert scrub, bouncing heavily off sunbaked mounds, glancing against jutting rocks. But, as Sylas gained his bearings, the *Windrush* settled to a steadier course, and sailed more smoothly over the dusty terrain, sweeping left and right, avoiding outcrops, cliffs and ditches. Nevertheless progress was far slower than on open water. With so many obstacles to avoid, her path was far from straight, and sometimes her keel dragged in the sand. Soon she began climbing towards the mountains and slowed further still.

Everyone looked warily across the sea for any sign of their pursuer. There was nothing, just an overhang of glimmering stars, and a dying moon, and below a wide expanse of glistening waves.

For a while the *Windrush* crossed open terrain, mountains towering above her on one side, but gradually her path became steeper and more treacherous. At last, as she rounded a hill, a narrow valley opened up on her starboard side.

"Hold on!" cried Sylas, leaning towards the valley.

In a trice, the *Windrush* heaved herself over and skipped across a facing slope, leaving a wake of silver dust. She dropped into the barren valley and began winding her way between bluffs and steep scree slopes. In what seemed moments, the valley divided, and Sylas took her left, letting her climb the facing incline and settle into the higher, craggier valley beyond.

The enchanted ship turned this way and that, her masts and rigging creaking and clattering as they yawed, tilting precariously over drops and ravines. The hull roared as it gouged deep into the dust and grit, and boomed as it hit hidden rocks in its path, but still she surged on. She glanced against hillsides, skipped along ridges, tore down gullies, and the rocks about her no longer seemed obstacles at all. They were just another sea for her to sail on.

"They aren't trying to trip you," Simia murmured to herself, remembering Merimaat's words all those years before, "they're trying to help you."

Sylas was sailing through boulders and bluffs that ought to dash the *Windrush* to splinters, knowing that they would help him, and guide him, and part before him. Simia turned and gazed at him in wonderment, remembering him haring through the ditches on the Barrens, feeling his way as though he had been born to Essenfayle, and she realised that, and everything since, had been just the promise of this.

Suddenly the keel lurched upwards. Simia locked an arm over the railing and clung on for all she was worth as they flew out across a ravine, falling the height of a house before striking the far slope. Astonishingly the ship held together and she swept back across the slope to enter a new mountain pass. Simia was still catching her breath when they reached the heights and a new vista opened before them: a muddle of low hills and scattered rocks rising ever upwards to several rumpled peaks.

She stared for a moment and then lifted the map up, peering at the drawings. Her eyes rose slowly to the mountains, to one rounded summit in the centre. It was distinctive, surrounded by bare folds of rock that looked in the moonlight like a clutch of entwined fingers. Her eyes fell to a drawing of just such a peak.

Simia lowered the map and staggered slowly to her feet.

"Sinai," she murmured. Then she turned and called: "It's Mount Sinai!"

89

The Sphinx

*"Can there be any more splendid and imposing creature
than the Sphinx, with its human head, body of a lion
and sometimes falcon wings. No wonder, perhaps, that
the Dirgh dreams of bringing it to life, and to heel."*

THE HELICOPTER THUNDERED ALONG valleys and mountain
passes, swaying sickeningly one way and then the other. One
moment it lurched upwards, pushing its passengers into their seats,
the next it plummeted down a mountainside, so that their stomachs
seemed to hang in the air. But despite the darkness none of these
gut-wrenching aerobatics took Naeo by surprise. It was as though
she knew these valleys and passes, and as in a Groundrush she
was feeling her way through.

Paiscion, however, sat rigid in his seat, with his eyes shut and
sweat beading his forehead. He was deathly pale in the white light
of the cabin.

"It's all right," said Naeo, holding his arm. "We're nearly there!"

The Magruman opened an eye. "There's nothing 'right' about
this!" he said between his teeth.

Soon the cabin tilted back as the helicopter began to climb.
The engine laboured, the steel frame shuddered and the din of

the rotors grew to a pronounced *thwack*, *thwack*, *thwack*. Naeo's ears popped as the helicopter soared higher and higher. Her heart began to race with anticipation.

"This is it!" she whispered. "This is it!"

She leaned out of the opening at her side and by the single searchlight she made out a strange landscape of desolate, rutted rocks and rounded hillocks. It was only a fragment, but even this she found she knew — almost as though she had been there before.

"Mount Sinai!" she exclaimed excitedly.

The engine screamed as it battled to climb through thinner and thinner air. Fixings rattled, starting to come loose, and lights blinked alarmingly before the pilots.

"Not far now!" murmured Naeo.

She could barely contain her excitement and was about to unbuckle herself to peer through the windscreen of the helicopter when suddenly there was a cry of alarm from one of the pilots. An instant later a familiar roar filled the cabin as they were battered by yet another swarm of insects. The aircraft lurched and twisted, swerving away from the face of the mountain. All at once insects poured through one of the openings, pelting the walls as they swept through to the other" to "swept through to the other doorway.

Naeo and Paiscion cried out and covered their faces.

Even in the chaos, they heard the engine falter. It spluttered, gave a juddering whine and then, to their horror, its growl gave way altogether. Now, all they could hear was the *whip*, *whip*, *whip* of the rotors.

Already the helicopter had ceased its climb, and now it was slewing to one side. A harsh alarm blared in their ears and the cabin was flooded with a blood-red flashing light.

Paiscion took Naeo's hand. "Keep hold!" he cried.

There was an explosion of sparks somewhere outside and, for

an instant, everything was silent. One of the pilots yelled something unintelligible.

Then everything went dark.

§

It would have been eerily silent on the mountaintop were it not for the occasional hiss of sand over ancient rocks, and the flap and flutter of sails.

The *Windrush* stood crookedly on a stony slope, prow high, glowing beneath a slither-thin moon. She gave out a golden glow, and by that light Sylas could see Simia and Ash still standing on the gangway. They were both watching him, Simia a little in front, so keen had she been to go with him. It had felt strange to leave her now, at the end of their journey, but somehow he had known that it was right. He had to do this alone.

Almost alone.

He raised a hand in farewell, and straight away Simia lifted hers in response. She smiled, hesitantly at first, but then she gave him that broad grin he knew so well, full of warmth and courage. He smiled back and set off up the slope.

"Come on, Sylas," he murmured. "You can do this."

The end was finally in sight — just there, where the mountain rounded to a dusty hunch, like a timeworn shoulder carrying all the weight of the world. It was nothing to look at: a barren, featureless hump strewn with rocks and sand and brush. But something about the simple beauty of the place — the pinnacle of a landscape that was barely of this world — made it feel magical and primal. He saw now why Moses had come here, that it was just the place where a god might reach down and touch the lives of humans, or where humans might reach up and touch the face of the universe.

This was the place. It had to be here.

This was the moment it had all been about: his passing between the worlds, his adventures with Simia, his journey to find Naeo and, before any of that, the Merisi, the Bringers, the Samarok, the Glimmer Myth, the Reckoning. All of it had led to this very moment.

Sylas's boots crunched in the grit as he climbed the last steep rise to the summit. His breath came short and sharp.

He was almost there. Now everything, *everything* depended on Naeo.

He had barely had a moment to think of her since they had parted, so consumed had he been by his journey. Now, he allowed himself to think about her impossible task: to pass between the worlds, to find help, to travel all this way. But she *had* to be here. She *had* to be, or it had all been for nothing.

Sylas was no more than twenty paces away now. The wind had dropped altogether, as though Nature herself was holding her breath. His footsteps seemed too loud, his breathing heavy and laboured. He stopped and lifted his head.

Was that a sound?

He walked on a couple of steps, but then stopped again.

Yes, he was sure of it. At first he thought it was another gust of wind whipping up the sand, but the air was still.

Then it became clearer: a definite, familiar

huff...

   huff...

      huff...

Sylas shuddered. It was close, and getting closer.

There might still be time, he thought. There *had* to be time.

He got ready to run, but even as he extended his leg he felt a strange drag on his foot, stopping it from leaving the ground. He tried to throw his weight forward, but his shoulders were wrenched behind, forcing him to take a backward step. The more he strained to go on, the more he felt himself pulled back.

Huff...

   huff...

      huff... came the sound of those mighty wings.

Sylas looked around and saw a movement among the stars. Something huge and dark passing before them, making them blink as it grew closer and closer.

Then came that half-human shriek echoing between the mountains.

As it died away, Sylas heard Simia's raised voice behind him. With all his might, he dragged his heavy limbs about until he could see the *Windrush*.

What he saw was so unexpected that at first he did not understand.

Simia had her back to him and her hands in the air, as though in surrender. When he followed her gaze, his jaw fell open in horror. He saw Ash, his face bloodless, his eyes in a chilling glaze, with one of his arms outstretched towards Sylas, his fist in a tight clench.

"No, Ash!" Simia yelled. "Let him go! You don't want to do this!"

It was only then that Sylas understood. It was Ash who was holding him back. Ash was stopping him from reaching the summit.

Simia glanced over her shoulder, tears streaming down her face, panic in her eyes. Sylas looked out into the night and saw the sprawling shadow closing in on the mountaintop.

Simia walked towards Ash, arms still above her head. Sylas realised now that it was not a gesture of surrender at all. She was trying to put herself between him and Ash.

"Ash!" she shouted. "You're forgetting who you are! Who — who *Sylas* is!"

Without taking his eyes from Sylas, the young Magruman lifted his other hand and swept it towards Simia. Instantly she was hurled to one side, so violently that she only just managed to put her arms out to break her fall. She landed in a crumpled heap.

"No!" screamed Sylas, straining all the harder against his bonds. "Ash, stop this!"

But Ash was impassive, his face set and grim, his arm still outstretched. And now Sylas felt his own arms forced down to his sides, his feet still fixed to the spot. He saw Simia clamber slowly to her feet, pulling the hair away from her face. Without a moment's hesitation, she started to walk towards Ash.

She said something Sylas could not hear. The thrashing of wings was deafening now, but he could not tear his eyes away from Simia. As she drew near to Ash, she was thrown even more brutally across the mountaintop, so that she sprawled on her back fifteen or twenty feet away. This time she lay still.

The anger that had burned in Sylas's chest suddenly roared into rage. "STOP!" he yelled, glaring at Ash.

But Ash seemed entirely unmoved. He simply closed his fingers into a tighter fist, and at the same time Sylas felt the breath being squeezed from his lungs.

He struggled, trying desperately to free himself, but just then his eye was caught by a movement out in the night. The vast shadow in the sky had taken shape. Now, it had two huge, eagle-like wings, but its body was not like that of any bird Sylas had ever seen. It was thickset and powerful, with four muscular legs clawing the air and a great mane gathered about its neck and shoulders. And sitting astride this matted tangle was a hooded figure, leaning forward as though to urge the beast on.

Sylas heard Simia's voice again. He looked back to where she had fallen and was surprised and relieved to see that she was already back on her feet, limping towards Ash. Her clothes were torn, her right hand glistening from a bloody cut, and her arms were stretched out before her, as though she was about to use Essenfayle.

"What are you *doing*?" he muttered.

She was approaching Ash from the side, and he seemed not to have noticed her. Sylas heard Simia's voice again, soft and sobbing, then she stumbled the last two paces towards Ash. He finally became aware of her and took a step back.

"Ash, you're my friend," she was saying. "You're one of us!"

He reached out and in the very same moment Simia was lifted from her feet, twisted in the air and dropped cruelly to the ground, making her cry out in pain. However, in his surprise, Ash did not succeed in throwing her far, and this time Simia was straight back on her feet. She charged at him, covering the open ground in four or five strides. When she reached him, she threw her arms about him.

"You don't mean to do this!" she sobbed. "You have to stop, please, before it's too late!"

Ash reeled and staggered backwards, drawing her with him. For a moment he looked at her blankly, searchingly, as though struggling to remember. Then he seized hold of her shoulders and tried to push her away. But Simia was not for letting go. She buried her head in his chest and slid her arms even further round him.

And then Sylas noticed something. As she fought to hold on, Simia's hands were fumbling, reaching round Ash's body, searching for something. Suddenly she plunged her fingers into the folds of Ash's robes and withdrew a small, black, shiny object.

"The shell!" he hissed. "Yes, Simsi!"

Even as he spoke, Simia wheeled about and hurled the shell far out across the rocks. It bounced once, twice and then disappeared over a bluff.

For a moment everything was still. Simia, Ash and Sylas all stared at the spot where the tiny shell had vanished.

Then the entire mountaintop was smothered in darkness.

90

Myths and Half-truths

"Just how many myths and half-truths *have come to us from the Other may never be known. Perhaps it is enough to understand that we must not trust all that is passed off as truth, even in scripture. And that where we can lay our trust, is in our Glimmer, in ourselves, in our humanity."*

THE DARKNESS THAT HAD settled upon the mountaintop had wings, and talons, and limbs, and teeth. The rock trembled as it settled to a crouch, plunging all below it into shadow and, when it raised its massive head, it split the air with its cry.

For the first time Sylas saw its features picked out in the moonlight. Like so many of Thoth's creations, it was half human and half beast, but this one had no patches of skin and fur; it had only the noble, even beautiful face of a woman. And yet, when she let out that cry, her nose rumpled, her brow gathered and her sharp teeth were bared. She became the most ferocious and feral of all beasts: like the lion that had lent her its claws, her broad, powerful chest and her sinewy tail that lashed the dark.

The mighty Sphinx lowered her head, and her catlike eyes

glowered at Sylas. He felt her breath, hot and dry, and he sensed her ancient, fathomless power. Looking into those pale eyes, he knew that, to her, he was a trifle — a fleeting thing that might be crushed at a whim.

He fought the urge to look away and returned her gaze.

Her eyes narrowed, and for a moment he thought he saw them smile, amused perhaps by the presumption of this tiny human child.

Then he saw a movement beside her. A lone, robed figure walked out from behind her flank: thin and stooped, limbs crooked, head bent. Pale hands went to the brim of the hood and pulled it back to reveal a white, hairless head and the familiar, empty, ever-shifting visage of Thoth.

The Dirgh stared at him now, as if struggling to make sense of something.

"You are *alone* now, after all?" said the voices of many, echoing out into the emptiness.

Sylas met his gaze. "Yes," he said defiantly. "Just me."

Thoth gave a wheezing laugh. "So at last you *are* one," he cackled, glancing up at the Sphinx to share his amusement.

The Sphinx gazed at Sylas like a cat coveting a mouse.

"And *this* was the judgement of Ammut's Pit? To set you on different paths?" Thoth waited for a reply, but when Sylas said nothing he continued. "Surely then you must now see that you were wrong? That you were never meant to be one?"

Sylas shook his head. "No. I'm more sure than ever. We are meant to be together."

Thoth tilted his head. "So you left her and came all the way here... for what purpose? Because the One from the Waters came here? Because you hope that this place might reveal to you some great truth, as you suppose it did to him?"

Sylas glared at the Priest of Souls. He wanted to yell that he was wrong, that he was less alone than he had ever been, that he was here because he knew he had to be, and he and Naeo would still make everything different. But instead he said: "Yes, that's why I'm here."

Just then he felt his bonds give way. His feet shifted beneath him, free to move, and his arms too became loose at his sides. Near the haunches of the Sphinx, he saw Ash and Simia standing in the shadows. Simia was waving frantically and pointing first at the rock beneath her feet and then at Thoth and the beast. She repeated the action, pointing at the rock, then at Thoth, then the Sphinx.

At first Sylas did not understand but, when he looked down at the rocky surface of the mountain, his thoughts flew back to Ammut's Pit and the moment he and Naeo had reached into the rock of the labyrinth and found a way through.

Thoth was laughing, his voices swirling about the mountain. "But you are no prophet!" he mocked, the dark gash of his mouth twisted in derision. "*I* am the bringer of plagues!"

Almost imperceptibly Sylas took a step forward. He summoned all his courage and bellowed: "But still you're not a prophet! A prophet brings the truth, not plagues! You haven't given us the truth — you've ripped it away! You've made everyone — all of us — question the things we should know to be true! You've made us wonder about what we can't do. Wonder about what we don't know." He paused, surprised at how his words came so easily. "Instead you've given us myths and half-truths. You've given us monsters and demons and ghosts. Folklore and legends and superstitions." He walked forward now, his blood coursing. "You haven't made the world better, you've broken it. That's why I've come here. That's why we're both here!"

The Dirgh glanced around. "Both? You are both here after all?"

Sylas swallowed hard. "Yes, we are!"

For a moment Thoth seemed taken aback. He peered round the mountaintop and then became still, seeming to understand. He let out an animal growl and began to swell beneath his robes, the vaguenesses of his face gathering as he grew in stature.

Just then Sylas saw that Ash now had both hands aloft, his head bowed in concentration. Suddenly there was a crump deep within the mountain, followed by a succession of jolts in the rock, growing stronger and getting faster. Then a crack appeared a little way away on the summit, and it quickly zigzagged towards Thoth, sweeping beneath his feet, and then off between the Sphinx's four legs. The Dirgh glanced down in surprise, but the crack was so narrow that he simply stepped away from it. The beast barely seemed to notice it at all.

But, in that moment of distraction, Sylas plunged his every thought and feeling down that narrow crevice. He reached into its depths just as he and Naeo had in Ammut's Pit, seeking out the faults and fissures in the rock. Now, he held them before him in his mind's eye, and he turned them quickly, as once he had turned his kites, checking the joins and alignments, the weaknesses and strengths. When he was sure, he called upon the full weight of the mountain, and heaved it down upon those thousand flaws and fractures.

He waited, expecting to hear something below, the beginning of some devastating collapse. But all he heard was Thoth's cry echoing into silence, and all he felt was the hot wind of the Sphinx's breath.

He opened his eyes and saw Thoth and the Sphinx still there, towering now, the Dirgh's arm stretched towards him, beginning some new sorcery. Then Sylas felt something peculiar in his stomach. A sickening wrench and twist. Suddenly his body began to quiver, his arms to shake uncontrollably, his legs to tangle beneath him. And then, just as he expected to fall, he was lifted from his feet. As he drifted up into the air and began to sail helplessly towards a precipitous drop behind him, he saw the Sphinx's tail lash out in the darkness. It was rapier-fast, and Ash and Simia did not stand a chance. It struck them full in the chest and sent them tumbling down the slope.

"Now, let us see if you are a worthy successor to the One from the Waters," growled the voices of Thoth. "Let us see *your* miracle." He snickered. "Yes, let us see the miracle of flight!"

And with that Sylas began to drift out, over the edge of the cliff, a drop of several hundred feet opening up below him.

"No!" he cried, desperately trying to shift his weight back over the clifftop.

Even as he yelled out, there was a sudden detonation somewhere deep in the mountain: a cannon boom so loud that it might have been thunder. Thoth's gaze shifted, no longer directed at Sylas, but at the dust beneath his feet, which had become like a liquid, boiling and leaping from the vibrations. The Sphinx too was staring at her taloned feet and suddenly she shrieked, rearing on her hind legs and clawing the air as though trying to climb into the sky, her great wings unfurling behind her.

But it was too late. In that instant, the dust and rock beneath her feet simply disappeared, cascading into a dark abyss. And, as the beast reared her head, she began to fall, her half-furled wings suddenly confined within the opening. Thoth let out a yell – the cry of a thousand souls – and before he could lunge to safety he too began to slip away.

But, as he fell, so did Sylas. His limbs suddenly free, Sylas cartwheeled his arms in the air, frantically trying to shift his weight back towards the face of the cliff. He plummeted all too quickly, missing the clifftop and falling five feet, ten.

Suddenly his hand caught hold of an outcrop, wrenching his arm and slamming his body into the cliff. For a moment he was still, panting and numb, battling to come to his senses. Then he looked up.

He could see the top of the cliff clearly, trails of dust pouring from its cracks and crevices. With all his remaining strength, he heaved himself upwards and slid his free hand into a handhold. He scrambled with his feet and found a purchase, then pushed.

It took what felt like an hour to reach the top but, in truth, it could barely have been a minute. When he reached the cliff edge and hauled himself over, spitting out dust, he looked across the expanse of rock and saw Thoth half in and half out of the chasm. He too was struggling to cling on, his pale fingers raking the liquefied dust, trying to find a handhold. Then he spied Sylas. The shock of it can only have lasted an instant, but it was enough. His empty eyes still staring at Sylas, his hands scrabbled, slipped and then reared as he rocked backwards. Then he fell.

Sylas blinked and gasped. He swung his knees beneath him and, extending his hands, lost himself back in the mountain. He drew his hands together and, as they closed, so did the great planes of rock on either side of the chasm, rumbling and grinding towards one another until all that remained was a gash of darkness in the mountaintop, and a hot wind, and a distant echo.

And finally even that fell silent.

91

At Last

"Now rise, fear not where none have gone,
For then, at last, *we may be one."*

SYLAS SANK BACK ON his haunches, chest heaving, his mind still
lost in the dark places of the mountain. Slowly he found his way
back, drawing himself up and up out of the silence of ancient stone,
and suddenly he was there, staring at the gash in the rock, and
the folds of the mountaintop, and nearby Simia and Ash were
drawing themselves slowly to their feet.

Simia wiped blood and dust from her face, shaking visibly, then
she looked across at Sylas. When she saw him, her face widened
into that irrepressible grin.

Sylas grinned back, and then he looked at Ash. The young
Magruman met his gaze, but there was no smile. He looked pale,
and haunted, and full of shame.

"Sorry, Sylas," he mouthed. Slowly he raised his hand to his
heart.

Despite all that had happened – everything that Ash had done
– the sight of him looking so broken was too much for Sylas. He
shook his head.

"It wasn't you," he mouthed. And he smiled.

He turned to look up at the summit. It was such a short distance away — barely twenty paces. He had been so close, and so nearly lost everything. He rose stiffly to his feet and was just resuming his climb when he stopped short. There was a sound, so indistinct that it could have been no more than a mountain breeze. But then it came again, louder, and this time it had shape and form. This time he heard voices. Whispered voices. Thousands of them.

He stopped breathing and turned to the dark gash in the mountain.

"Go!" yelled Ash, waving frantically and striding out towards the chasm.

His heart galloping, Sylas struggled with heavy, unruly limbs up the final stretch of the mountain. His climb felt painfully slow and his legs gave way just before he reached the summit, but still he kept on, hauling himself back to his feet and stumbling the final few paces. At last he stood upon the very pinnacle.

He sucked in a deep draught of air, steadied his stance and closed his eyes.

For a moment he struggled to calm himself — his breathing wild, his thoughts scattered — but, gradually, he came back to himself. He recovered his breath, relaxed his body and waited. Waited to feel what he knew he must.

Naeo.

He shifted nervously, fingers of sweat creeping down his back.

He frowned, but stayed still and quiet, desperate to believe, to hold his concentration.

Then, slowly, he opened his eyes.

She wasn't there.

S

Naeo was lost in the cold and the dark. She felt as though she had fallen into the mountain itself, and its massive bulk was pressing in on her, leaving her no way out. But then she heard a familiar voice calling her name.

"It's all right, Naeo," it said. "I'm here!"

It was Paiscion's voice, and it was close. She pushed back against the dark, heaving herself out of the void.

She blinked, and with bleary eyes she stared at an oblong of pale light. At its centre she saw the silhouette of a head and shoulders, and as it leaned towards her, she saw the familiar glint of Paiscion's spectacles.

"Come on, Naeo, you're going to have to help me," he was saying. "One big push and we'll be there."

She slid her hand into his. There was a strong grasp, a heave and then a spasm of pain through her leg. She cried out, but Paiscion kept pulling, and suddenly Naeo found herself rising through the oblong and into his arms.

He set her down on a dark, rocky surface. It was lit only by one of the helicopter's lights, which blinked and flickered, as though it might soon go out. She felt another stab of pain in her leg and saw that her tunic was torn and bloodied. Instinctively Naeo looked away, not wanting to see any more. Instead she glanced around, trying to understand what had happened. Behind her, she saw the mangled hulk of the helicopter on its side, rotors gone altogether, its tail buckled.

"It's a miracle we got out at all," said the Magruman, shaking his head. "Though I fear that those young pilots..." He trailed off for a moment, then seemed to take hold of himself and pointed. "But look, Naeo."

Her eyes followed his pointing finger along the blinking path cast by the searchlight, and she saw a procession of crude steps made from slabs of stone rising to a peak just a short distance away. There were two humble buildings near the top, one with an apex roof topped by a cross, the other square and blockish.

"A church and a mosque," explained Paiscion. "Religious buildings. They're here because of Moses. Because of what they believe once happened here."

She stared. "This is it? Mount Sinai?"

"The very place."

Ignoring the sharp pain in her leg, Naeo staggered to her feet and began limping away, along the path of light.

"What are you going to do?" called Paiscion.

"I'm going to join him!" she shouted, still walking.

"Join… who?"

She smiled. "Sylas!"

S

Sylas gazed helplessly from the summit as Ash stood by the chasm, his outstretched arms trembling, his face crumpled and glistening with sweat. Despite all his efforts, the chasm was growing, rocks and dust toppling into it as it began to split the mountain. And all the while, the voices from the chasm swirled about the peak.

"*I am Thoth,*" they said, "*three times great, Priest of Souls and scribe to the gods. Now, I am A'an, Lord of Equilibrium, and I will never die!*"

Sylas glanced across at Simia and saw her standing near the edge of the rift, gazing into it in horror, shouting something at Ash. There was a movement within, a little below its jagged edge. Something was climbing up, out of the dark, and with it the shadows themselves spilled out over the rocky surfaces, pooling round Simia's feet. They writhed about her legs, creeping up, taking hold. She tried to retreat, but they moved with her, clinging to her.

She looked up at Sylas.

He could see her terror and confusion, and instinctively he took a step towards her. But before he could take another, she threw up her hand and shook her head.

"No!" she mouthed, a trace of fire in her eyes. "Stay there!"

Sylas was in agony. He was desperate to go to her, but he knew she was right. He could not. He must not. He couldn't help Ash, and he couldn't help her, not now. Their only hope was Naeo.

So he clenched his fists tight, closed his eyes and stepped back.

As he took that single step, he felt as though the mountain, and the desert, and even the rift between the worlds crumbled.

Because there she was.

He felt her more closely and more profoundly than ever before: closer than holding hands, than meeting minds, than sharing dreams, and thoughts, and feelings. Now, they shared all those things and more. Because now theirs was the very same place in the universe.

Now, they were one.

They were one like Isia and her Glimmer were one. But there was a difference too. Isia had been born whole, and divided. Sylas and Naeo had been born apart, and now they were together.

Isia was the beginning. They were the end.

They knew that this was the final step of their journey, and that it must end as they began.

It was time for the Passing Bell to ring again.

Together they turned to the southern sky and made the Glimmer Myth come true.

S

The first the worlds knew of the bell was a rumble in the desert and a quaking among the sands that made them ripple and flow, like liquid. Dunes collapsed, hillsides became cascades and rocks sank slowly down beneath the surface. Among these were the stones of the circle at the Academy of Souls, the circle that had been the beginning of it all. Now, finally, after standing sentinel for more than three thousand years, they slumped, toppled and disappeared into the hungry sands, along with the Ghor that guarded them.

And then the sands offered something in return.

First, a glow appeared upon the surface, a splash of brightness that surged and spread, sweeping out over the dust as though flowing from a spring. Then it arched towards the stars like a vast, metallic rainbow – in places silver, in places gold. Still it rose, towering into the night sky, the arch becoming a half-circle, and then a perfect metal ring, hanging mountainous above the desert.

Sylas was so far away that he could not see it, but he knew that it was there because he imagined it so. This, his last and greatest act of Essenfayle, came easily because the Quintessence was ready and yielding; because Naeo was with him; and because, at the last, they were certain that everyone should know their Glimmer as they knew theirs.

Into their creation, Naeo poured her love for her father because, above all else, she wanted this for him. Sylas filled it with his love for his mother because he wanted her at last to be at peace. And he gave it too his love for Simia, because he wanted her to feel what he felt, and never be alone again.

They could see it in their mind's eye: the graceful, tapering form of the bell growing ever wider as it emerged from the sands, fed by the sea of Quintessence. Its broad lower portions rose from the wastes, so immense that they consumed the Academy of Souls, and vast tracts of the desert, and stretches of the Nile. Up and up it went until the last exquisite curves of the Passing Bell finally cleared the ground. And as it soared higher and higher, the few puffs of cloud in the sky seemed drawn to it, as though jealous of its radiance.

Sylas could hear the clamour of Thoth's voices, feel the mountaintop trembling beneath him, but he did not look. Because now he could see the bell with his own eyes. It was no longer imagined but hanging there in the night sky, bold and bright, like a new moon. It was exquisite, and beautiful, and as natural as anything in the heavens.

It was Nature's own teardrop, shed for all the wrongs done to her world.

Still it climbed, higher and higher. Vast flocks of birds, woken from their slumber, spiralled up and circled at its rim, while clouds still drifted about it, clinging to its sides. Celestial light seemed to gather on its surface, shining bright, reflecting stars and galaxies to the cosmos. It was as though all of Nature had gathered there, yearning to be close.

Knowing what was to come.

92

The Chime

*"The Passing Bell speaks not only to the world,
but to the human soul. Every time I heard the chime
I was filled with an inexpressible joy. I knew
that I had nothing to fear."*

SO DISTANT WAS THE bell that they only realised it had begun its swing when they saw the clouds and the birds left behind, twisting on great eddies of air. It came on quickly, swelling in the night sky, racing over the distant Red Sea. But there was no sound. Now, even Thoth had fallen silent. He stood at the edge of the chasm, robes tattered, just a gentle wheeze coming from his lips. He stared at the approaching bell as though struggling to believe that it was real.

The bell came on, colossal, irresistible, faster than the winds, than the turn of the earth, than thought. It came with the heft of mountains, but it swung with the lightness of air. It filled their vision, towering above the desert, the sea, the mountain range. Its details were already clear: the ornate bands about its top, the perfectly smooth sides below and, round its rim, the sequence of Ravel Runes. It was the inscription given to it by Merimaat: "*So at last we may be one.*"

The bell was over the mountains now, drawing behind it spiralling trails of dust. Ash and Simia stared, their faces glowing in its light, and then they laughed because of the sheer overwhelming beauty of it. And, even surrounded by Thoth's darkness, they knew that everything was as it should be. That this was how it was meant to end.

But Thoth himself seemed to shrink before the bell and, when he turned and gazed up at Sylas, he appeared stricken. Like before, he looked as though he was struggling to comprehend.

"I did it to save us," he said. "I did it for us all."

He looked at Sylas, his face still shifting endlessly between the thousands and millions that he had divided from themselves – and, for a moment, he seemed full of sorrow.

But it was too late. Because now he glowed by the blazing light of the bell and, even as he spoke, it swung overhead, ripping at his robes, blowing away the Black mist, whipping up sand and dust, leaving all in turmoil.

And then, as it cleared the mountain, the Passing Bell chimed.

The sound swelled in the bowl of the bell and then burst upon the mountain, and Sinai, and the sea, and all of the Motherland. It spanned oceans and deserts, flooded the valleys, sang in the cosmos. It rang in the walls of the Temple of Isia, and hummed in the trees of the Valley of Outs. It broke across the worlds, echoed through streets and cities, thrummed in the beams of Gabblety Row, resounded between the stones of Stonehenge. It was heard by every man, woman and child, sleeping or awake.

And this time it rang for them.

Thoth tottered, clasping his ancient hands to his ears. He looked confused, dazed, turning from the bell to Sylas and back to the bell. And then, at last, his shifting features settled. They resolved to a single face: an old, dry, broken face. It lasted only for an instant and then it crumbled to dust, which drifted down into the chasm along with his tattered crimson robes.

§

Espasian was already half departed when it came. He was in the dark and the cold, and his thoughts were sluggish, and his body distant. He was preparing to let go. But then came a tremor in the stony shore of the Valley of Outs: a long, sustained thrum that passed through his body and quickened his faltering heart.

He opened his eyes, expecting to see some last horror of battle, or the end of the valley. But instead he saw moonlit pebbles leaping and dancing along the shore and, out on the lake, the waters rippling, forming strange patterns across the surface.

Then the low moan of the chime surged into him, filling his ears and reverberating in his chest.

He looked up at the night sky and he saw it with another's eyes. He was accustomed to feeling it rather than understanding it. He knew more of the connections between things than of the things themselves. But now he looked at stars, and galaxies, and constellations just as Naeo had through Sylas's eyes, and he understood. He saw now how the universe was made.

But he felt something in the spaces between those pinpricks of light. He felt another part of himself, not far away, but there, just there. The person through whose eyes he now looked, a person inspired by science even as he was by Essenfayle.

His Glimmer, who had shown him the universe.

And he knew then, at the last, that he was not alone, and never had been.

And, knowing that, he closed his eyes and let go.

§

Isia sat alone in her boat, too weak to stand, but not yet ready to leave. She was like a marvelling child, like the child she had been at the beginning when she helped to break the world in two. She gazed about her at the rippling waters, and the dancing stones, and the bright silver light that had fallen upon the valley, and tears of joy rolled down her cheeks. She reached up to wipe them away, and looked in amazement at her hand — at the hand that was no longer two but one. And at that she sobbed and covered her face.

"Thank you, my children," she said. "Thank you."

She felt the chime calling her, the pull of it upon her soul, and she knew that time was short. So she looked about at the shadows of broken trees, and she said something under her breath.

Across the valley, two majestic eagles — the last remaining of those that had come to the valley — lofted themselves into the air and sailed across the lake. They circled above the boat, calling softly to Isia over the sound of the bell, and she spoke quietly in reply.

As a gentle breeze passed through the valley, they tipped their wings and flew away, up and over the hills, and behind them they left a boat floating in the centre of the lake.

Draped across its seat was an empty white robe.

§

Bowe sank to the floor of Merimaat's Retreat and watched the world change forever. First, he saw a distant glow far beyond the horizon, not to the east where the sun should rise, but to the south. And, even as he tried to make sense of this, as he dared to hope that it might have something to do with Naeo, the chime struck the treetop, rattling the woven walls of the retreat.

In that instant, he knew. He knew that this was a dawn unlike any that came before it. A new dawn for a new world. And he knew that it had been kindled by his own daughter.

"My Nay-no," he murmured with a tearful smile. "Not a sunset but a dawn."

And then his Scryer's eyes witnessed a new wonder on the lake of the Valley of Outs. Earlier that night, he had marvelled at the explosion of silver trails that had spread from Isia, connecting two parts of countless souls. And now this flux first glowed to a blinding brightness and then finally broke apart. The many separate trails drifted one from the other, as though they had lost their bond, and, in moments, they swept out over the sides of the valley and dissolved.

He knew he had witnessed the end of Isia, but it filled him with joy. Because this was part of Naeo's new dawn. He felt it in himself: the sense that there was another part of him out there, not distant and remote but there. Right there. And, if before there had been a rift that only Isia could bridge, now it was gone.

Gone for him, gone for Naeo, gone for everyone.

§

As Paiscion watched the bell scything away through the blackness, he staggered. He was giddy, overwhelmed not just by its beauty and power but by the suddenness of it. After all these years, after all the learning and the struggle, after the Reckoning and long winter of the Undoing, it had all come down to a moment. To *this* moment. To the chime of the bell.

With it still ringing in his ears, it took even him some moments to realise that it had changed everything.

It was not just that somewhere out there in the blackness he felt the presence of someone, though that was miraculous enough. It was who that person was, and what she saw, and how she felt.

It was his Glimmer, and she was as real to him as he was to himself. Already he sensed with excitement her grasp of things that had always fascinated but eluded him: things of reason, and record and logic, things of science and technology, born of another world. The Things he had so longed to collect, and study, and understand.

But what most excited him as he watched the bell climbing again into the darkness was her love. It was not the love he had held so long for Filimaya — to that, nothing could compare — but it might have been as strong. And this love was the love of a companion, of a lifetime shared, and not lived apart like his and Filimaya's. This was the love that could have been for them, and perhaps should have been, had they not spent their lives in struggle.

But, feeling it now as his Glimmer felt it, he realised that perhaps it was still there for him to find. That perhaps it was waiting for him back in the Valley of Outs.

S

The Hollow had become a dreadful place, crowded not only with the wounded, but with the hundreds who had sought refuge there. It was no longer a cradle of solace, but one of suffering and despair. The only sounds were moans, and sobs, and quiet prayer, and the battle drums at the door.

Four times the enemy had tried to storm the entrance, and each time the great wooden door had seemed about to yield. It was only the tree roots that crept across it, buttressing its timbers, that had kept those inside from calamity.

But then came the chime. It echoed through the cavernous space of the Hollow, making the walls shake and the earthen ceiling crack, sending down trails of dirt. Some of the more frail and anxious cried out in alarm, and Filimaya was forced to climb the steps and call for calm.

But then something else passed through the great chamber, and everyone became quiet. A kind of daze fell upon them, holding them all in silence even as the chime continued to moan, and earth to fall from the ceiling, and the walls to thrum. And then their expressions changed from those of fear, and exhaustion, and despair to those of childish wonder, and hope, and joy.

The chime took Filimaya too and, as she stood before the assembly, she was forced to turn away to hide her sudden emotion. Because just then, despite all her years and wisdom, she felt the wide-eyed wonder of youth. She had the undeniable sense that all this time there had been more to her than she had known: always there, but beyond reach. And, as she experienced the warmth of this new presence, something else came to her. She felt, for the first time, the fulfilled, fulsome love that had been kept from her, but not from her Glimmer. And, as she felt it, she thought of Paiscion, and wondered if it might yet be hers.

§

In her exhaustion, Dresch thought that the chime was the end: some last violent spasm of the battle that would finally carry them off. Part of her was grateful. She turned to Lucien, who had fallen from the force of it and, before he could stagger to his feet, she knelt and took him in her arms.

They closed their eyes and held each other, waiting for it all to be over, knowing that at least they had given everything and that they would die together. But after a moment or two, as the chime droned on, they realised they were still alive. They opened their eyes and stared out into the blackness, waiting for the next prowling, galloping, leaping horror to rush from the darkness. But nothing came.

And then they both felt it.

A change somewhere deep inside.

A knowing. A certainty.

They knew the answers to questions they had not asked. They felt a presence that was strong despite their weakness, hopeful in the face of their despair.

They pulled away and saw their bewilderment mirrored in each other's faces.

Suddenly a bright light made them wince and look away. When their eyes adjusted, they stared in astonishment as that radiance now spread everywhere about them. This was not the artificial brightness of a searchlight panning across the wastes: it was laced with pink and orange, and it stretched in all directions, illuminating the churned-up battlefield, the scarred stones of Stonehenge, the scattering of wrecked army vehicles.

They lifted their eyes and, to their astonishment, they saw a crack of sunlight sweeping from horizon to horizon, as though the blackness had been torn. Boiling pink and orange clouds rolled back to reveal a widening expanse of clear blue sky. And, from this rip in the heavens, sunbeams poured down upon the world.

Dresch glanced about at the weave of golden rays, and suddenly she convulsed in a sob of relief and joy.

"Look, Martha!" exclaimed Lucien, pointing across the bright battlefield at the broken, rutted earth, the mangled hulks of vehicles, the twisted barbed wire, and at Stonehenge, charred and cracked but not broken. It was the first time she had seen what the beasts had done – what their own weapons had done – and she shook her head in horror.

Lucien looked at her, smiling. "No, Martha, *look*! The beasts! The insects! They're gone!"

She cast her eyes about, blinking in confusion. The creatures that had assailed them all night long were nowhere to be seen. Not on the battlefield. Not between the stones. Not out on the green plains beyond.

And then her eyes darted to one of the craters nearby. Then to another. And another.

The Black was gone too. It had disappeared without a trace, just as it was disappearing now from the skies.

Her legs suddenly gave way and she settled back into the mud. "It's over," she said. "James, I think it's really over!"

He took her hand and said quietly, "Can't you feel it?"

Martha drew a long breath of the chill air and turned her face up to the sun, drinking in its warmth, and in that moment she felt an unexpected certainty. It was that same feeling that others had felt: that she was not alone, that the world was far bigger and more marvellous than she had ever known. In her wonderment, she looked at the parting clouds and the sky above, and saw them afresh: not as things to be discovered and understood, not as vapour and refracted light, but as part of something greater than her. Something she could feel. Something she was a part of.

"I feel it," she said with a growing smile.

S

At the first chime of the Passing Bell Veeglum had stood upon the hill, transfixed, hardly daring to believe. But then he had seen the black sky rip itself open, and the sun pour down, and the hordes of beasts dissolve into the light as if they had been nothing but shadow. Then he had believed. By the second chime, everything had been brightness, and the gash in the sky had become a gaping hole, and his pale green eyes had shone with tears. He had dropped to his knees, and spoken quietly to his old friend and master.

"They did it, my friend," he had said, his voice thick with emotion. "Sylas and Naeo, zey did it all. Everything as Merisu told us." He turned then to the east, back towards the temples of old Bagan. "So now, let us see."

The third chime came and, as it had died away, the darkness had retreated still further, so that the skies had looked almost as they should at twilight. Then came the fourth chime, just as powerful as the first. Still Veeglum had watched the east, his eyes fixed on the treeline and the pointed pinnacles of the temples. He had watched flocks of birds knitting in the sky, weaving a path towards the temples, circling over Bagan as though they too had expected something to happen.

As the chime had started to die, a smile had curled the corner of Veeglum's mouth.

The shining peaks of the temples had begun to rise into the air, surging upwards as though heaved aloft by some herculean force. As they had risen, their exquisitely crafted, tapering sides had been revealed, sweeping ever outwards until they formed the arcs of a broad bowl below. Soon eight, nine and then ten gigantic, teardrop-shaped temples had hung high above the forests of Bagan, their open bowls dropping clods of earth into the gaping foundations below.

"There zey are," Veeglum had murmured, the words choking him. "There zey are."

Now came the fifth chime. As it resonated in the skies and the earth, the ten colossal teardrops began to swing down across the forests — not in one direction, but each in their own, so that they radiated outwards from a central point. And, as they swung away, each of them rang out, temples becoming bells, each speaking a higher note than the last. They climbed a harmonious scale, peal upon peal, until together they made an exquisite chorus.

And so the chime of the Passing Bell shared the sky and the earth with the full-throated answer of the Merisi, a song of joy and celebration.

A song of farewell. Because their work was done.

§

"Let them," said Triste between blue lips and gritted teeth. "They mean you no harm."

As the first chime had thumped into his chest, he had seen it sweep through the assembly of Kraven like wind through a field of barley. They had swayed from the force of it and, although he had heard nothing but the chime, he had sensed them cry out — not in pain or dismay but in surprise. After drifting numbly through endless time they had felt this as keenly as any sensation of their past lives. He had seen it in the vivid colours that blazed about them: the oranges and greens, blues, purples and yellows — all the colours his Scryer's eyes might see in a jostling crowd of the living.

But he had also seen something new — silver and gold — picking out their thin, translucent forms in an ethereal light.

With the second chime, some of them had taken flight, like leaves blown up in a great wind. For a moment they had hung there in the darkness, now little more than faint wisps of silvery gold, and then they had simply dissolved. And so it had been with each successive chime: more and more of the ghostly forms flying up like flocks of startled birds, and then fading into the night, as though released at last from their mortal bonds.

By the fifth chime, only the last few remained — those gathered about Triste and Amelie. These seemed the strongest and the most reluctant to go, and so when they were finally lofted into the air they reached out with icy, fading fingers and touched. The sensation took Triste straight back to the Barrens, when the Kraven had almost robbed him of his life. But now he did not shrink away. He remembered how they had let him live — not once now but twice — and when he saw their yearning, he sensed their long, sorrowful plight more keenly than ever. So he spread his arms wide and gave them one last touch of life before they went.

"Let them," he said. "They mean you no harm."

But Amelie was not alarmed. She barely even felt the perishing cold of their touch. She was lost in the world about her: the world she had thought she knew, but had only half known. She was seeing it with different eyes, eyes that, by some accident, she had seen with before, in nightmares. The eyes of her Glimmer. But now they were wide, and they were her own.

She gazed up at the night sky and saw the same cosmos she had studied and come to understand, but now she saw it as never before. She could sense the cold of its void, the heat of its fire, its endless motion. She knew its vastness, but now it felt near, almost as though it was part of her. She felt the connection between the stars, the planets and the moons, their pull and their push, their spin and vibration. She felt how all this was connected to the turn of the earth, the winds and tides, even her beloved trees and plants. It was all related in ways that her science would always struggle to understand. And for her the heart of this vast web of connections was her Glimmer: not a ghostly presence that might tear her away from herself, but a companion. Her Glimmer was the instinct to her reason, the answer to questions her science had never thought to ask.

This, she realised, was what Sylas had felt with Naeo. This was why he had made his journey, why he had resisted her. And now he had shared his gift with everyone and, perhaps most importantly, with her. Because now nothing could keep them apart.

The Kraven touched her hands until her skin gleamed with crystals of ice, but Amelie felt a burgeoning warmth. Because, for her, each chime of the Passing Bell told her that Sylas had reached the end of his journey. That he was safe. And that soon he would be home.

§

The tenth and final chime of the Passing Bell found Simia sitting on a rock near the peak of Mount Sinai. As each chime had struck, she had felt the same wonder as everyone else, the same presence of someone near, the same sense that her world was so much more than she had ever known. That *she* was so much more.

Now, as she gazed after the bell, watching its last sweep back over the Red Sea towards the Nile, something made her look up at Sylas.

He was standing on the peak, his tattered clothes ruffled by the raking wind of the bell, and he was smiling at her.

Seeing him then, she felt an overwhelming, heart-bursting joy. She grinned, and his smile widened and he laughed, and turned back to gaze out at the bell.

As they watched it together, shrinking into the east, something came to Simia that had not been clear all this time. Sylas's journey had been her own. She had been part of it from the beginning. She had faced its perils, seen its wonders and, even as it was now ending for him, it was drawing to a close for her too. Because, at last, she would never be alone again.

Epilogue

NAEO STOOD BEFORE THE grand open doorway of the Temple of Isia, and stared in awe at the soaring white walls and, above, the exquisitely carved circular platform that jutted out above their heads. She knew this place — of course she did — because Sylas had been here. But nothing could prepare her for its scale and beauty and, to her surprise, she felt a little nervous to enter. Perhaps it was because Isia felt so close here, almost as though she was gazing down from the platform, or perhaps waiting just beyond the doorway.

Unconsciously Naeo slipped her hand into her father's, and she was grateful when his large fingers enfolded hers.

"Tell me why we're here again?" she murmured.

"Because you should see it, Nay-no," he said. "Isia would have wanted it, and it's part of your story. Now more than ever."

She looked up at him. "Why now more than ever?"

"You'll see," Bowe said with a smile.

They walked through the entrance and into the towering hall beyond, centred round the gnarled boughs of the Knowing Tree.

Scores of priestesses lined the hall, waiting expectantly and, to Naeo's embarrassment, they all gave a low bow when she entered.

She and her father returned the courtesy. At once the priestesses parted, whispering excitedly among themselves and, as they did so, they revealed the beginning of two spiralling staircases, which wound up the inside walls of the temple. Soon Naeo and Bowe were making their way up one of these, climbing through the boughs of the Knowing Tree. Naeo had the sense that the branches had changed since Sylas's visit, and she noticed then that they were free from the veins of Black that had so troubled them before, and now they were even heavier with the colourful fruit.

Of course they are, she thought.

"I knew we weren't done climbing trees, Nay-no," her father said, squeezing her hand.

She laughed in that free, easy way she could with him, and only him.

He grinned and nodded upwards. "But what a treehouse this is, eh?"

She looked, and gasped at the grace and majesty of the circular tower above them, with its breathtaking double helix of spiralling staircases, and its walls lined with thousands upon thousands of paintings, and its twisting light beams, which fell from a disc of brightness high above.

She grinned back at him and they continued to climb, circling round and round the tower, passing countless paintings that traced the history of the world. To begin with, Naeo was fascinated, and she wondered at the range and intricacy of the paintings. But her mood quickly grew sombre as they reached the beginnings of the Undoing. She continued wordlessly through the plight of the Suhl, and the last days of Salsimaine, and the Reckoning.

Before long, they came to the image of the Passing Bell calling

640

Sylas to begin his journey between the worlds and, at this, Naeo paused. For her this was personal, and it felt strange — not wrong but unnerving — to see it depicted here, among all these images of the greatest moments of history.

"Come on," said her father softly. "There's more."

He led her up, climbing towards the brightness of the chamber above and, as they rose, she saw more pictures of Sylas at the Meander Mill, on the Barrens, aboard the *Windrush* with Paiscion and in the Dirgheon. There were paintings of Naeo too, in the Valley of Outs and at the Circle of Salsimaine, but she tried not to look too closely at those.

Still they climbed, and Naeo saw depictions of the battle for the Valley of Outs, including one heroic image of Espasian on Carrion Rock. There were pictures of Sylas and Naeo's journey too. They began with an exquisite painting of the *Windrush* shining bright with Quintessence, picked out in silvery-gold paint. And they ended with the Academy of Souls, and their confrontation with Thoth, and the sea of Quintessence.

Surprised, Naeo asked: "When was all this done?"

"In the past few days," said Bowe. "The priestesses felt the tower should be completed as soon as possible. It's what Isia would have wanted: to have it all recorded here so that it will always be known." He glanced up at the images on the very rim of the tower, just where it met the cavernous chamber above. "And, of course, the very last moment is the most important of all."

Naeo followed his eyes and saw an exquisitely beautiful image. It showed Sylas on Mount Sinai and above him the Passing Bell depicted in gleaming gold and silver, sweeping over the mountaintop. But the painting did not stop there. As Naeo looked round the rim of the tower, she saw more and more shimmering paintings of the bell until, on the far side, she came to another image of Mount Sinai, topped by another figure, and with a tingle in her spine she realised that it was her: the other half of the story, in another world. Still the paintings went on, sweeping back to the other side of the tower with more images of the bell. She counted ten in all.

"One for each chime," said Bowe, putting his arm round her shoulder. "Ten chimes that finally brought the worlds together." He smiled at her. "And us, of course."

Naeo looked back at the beautiful images of the bell. They were the perfect way to finish the tower and to mark the end of everything that came before: not a circle of stones but a circle of Quintessence, showing the ten peals of the Passing Bell.

Bowe took her hand. "Come on," he said. "There's one last thing I want to show you."

He led her up, into the brightness of Isia's great chamber, and across the polished white floor, beneath the many thousands of painted faces that gazed down from the walls and the ceiling. He guided her through one of the many arches and out into the winds of the great stone platform, where all of Gheroth was laid before them. They walked to the very spot where Sylas and Simia had once stood with Isia herself, to the very edge of the platform where the winds whipped and buffeted, making them draw closer together. And there they stood, holding one another, staring out at a world transformed.

"You did this, my Nay-no," said Bowe. "You did this."

They saw people milling about in the streets, noisy and cheerful, busy with the work of building a new city. They saw the slums of the Suhl being dismantled, buildings being erected, shops being opened. At the very heart of the city they saw the Dirgheon, its pinnacle missing, its terraced sides crawling with people taking away blocks of stone to be used elsewhere in the city.

There was a new vision for the world, and everywhere people were striving to make it real.

Above all this, from every rooftop and tower, a new standard flew. No longer Thoth's empty face, but a purple flag emblazoned with a lone white feather. The feather of truth.

But Naeo quickly realised that this was not all that her father had brought her to see. Because her eyes were drawn far beyond this hubbub, out past the last of the buildings and shacks, to the beginnings of the Barrens. And there she saw no cracked earth, no gloom, no lifeless grey.

She saw green. The green of wide rolling pastures, bright beneath shafts of sunlight.

The green of the plains of Salsimaine.

§

Sylas settled himself carefully on the roof of Gabblety Row, one leg either side of the ridgeline. He was relieved to find that his old kite-flying perch still felt just the same. The fire had added more twists to the terrace's old joints, and now the ridgeline meandered along its length, but even that added to the curiosity of the old building, Sylas thought. And what was very pleasing – if not truly miraculous – was that the fire had never spread beyond the rooms Sylas and his uncle had shared.

Sam Clump, the locksmith, had told Sylas how the residents of Gabblety Row had worked together to fight the freakish fire that had erupted that night. Of course, in light of everything that had happened since, the blaze now hardly seemed strange at all. But, at the time, the fire and Tobias Tate's sudden death had shaken the old terrace right to its rickety foundations.

Sylas had been shocked to hear of his uncle's death, and even more so when he heard that the ill-tempered old accountant had become rather lost when his nephew had disappeared. He realised then that they had been companions of a sort and, just as his uncle had missed him, some part of him would miss his uncle.

But, in truth, Sylas much preferred his new companions in the adjacent apartment of Gabblety Row. His mother had made herself at home at once, and every room, including his garret room, was quickly freshened and brightened. Already they were heaving with every indoor plant she could find in this world or that, and all of them thrived under her care. She seemed so happy and contented, and she was sleeping too. Sleeping like she had not slept for years.

But still some nights she would knock on the trapdoor of his room, and climb with him on to the roof, and they would lie on their backs like they used to on the hill behind their cottage, and hold hands, and stare up at the stars. Only now they didn't just name the stars, they felt them too, and everything else in the night sky.

That feeling for the world had not gone away. None of it had gone away. Change was in the air and everyone was talking about it.

That very day, he and his mother had been walking up to the Hailing Bridge and, just before they crossed it, that old homeless person, the Duke, had rushed up to Sylas and shaken his hand until Sylas feared it might come off. He had become accustomed to such attention, of course, in the past weeks and months, and he was gracious as the Duke told him all the wonders and the horrors he had seen, and how it had all been worth it because now — and here he had sniffed the air as though he could smell the change — now he was finally going to leave his unconventional cardboard home, and try his luck at being a magician, and travel, and become a man of the world. Both worlds perhaps.

As ever when Sylas heard that people were embarking upon such great change, he had felt rather anxious.

"Are you sure?" he had asked.

"Oh yes!" the Duke had replied, rather surprised. "Why?"

The Duke had thought for a moment, thumbing the lapels of his filthy jacket. Then he had said simply: "Because I know I can."

And, at that, he had given Sylas a broad smile and trotted away to finish his preparations.

Sylas took a deep lungful of evening air and looked happily around him at the town. Change was written there too. Some buildings were being reconstructed, but not as before: now they were not angular and harsh, made of concrete and steel and glass; they were built of logs and timber and things that had been used before, in a way that reminded Sylas of the insides of the Meander Mill. And there were gardens upon the roofs, and in places glass windows harvesting the sun, channelling its life-giving light into the rooms within.

And that was not all. Just behind him the ruins of the Church of the Holy Trinity now sported a billboard that read: OPENING SOON! THE TWO WORLDS EDUCATION CENTRE & WATER GARDENS. Already the grounds of the old church were being transformed with beautiful plants and flowers from both worlds, and silver streams were flowing brightly between the stems and leaves, just like in the Valley of Outs. And Sylas could hear them too, because for reasons he could only guess at the two angry, unruly roads that met at the corner of Gabblety Row were quieter and better behaved than before.

Further afield, the large factory that huddled at the base of the forested hills had changed too. The chimneys no longer belched black and white smoke into the sky, and works were afoot to dismantle and replace and install. Word had it that the factory would never be quite the same again.

"You weren't going to start without me, were you?"

Sylas looked down the sloping roof to his garret-room window. A flash of red hair blazed in the morning sun as Simia clambered out on to the parapet and started up the tiled roof.

"No, I just wanted to sit here for a bit first," he said. "I love it up here."

Simia heaved her leg over the ridge of the roof and plonked herself down to face him.

She looked about her and grinned. "Me too," she said. Her eyes travelled to what he was holding. "So this is it, the big moment! You're finally going to show me your bird of paper and string!"

Sylas looked down at the newly made canvas kite in his hand. It was one of the finest he had ever built, as good as any he had lost in the fire, except perhaps the very last. Its entire body was bright with colours and rich with intricate designs and Ravel Runes, which looked — to the untrained eye — just like feathers shimmering in the sunlight.

"Well, it's about time, isn't it?" he said with a smile.

And then he lifted it high, turned its eagle's head towards the hills and, as the first gust of wind caught its wings, he gave it a gentle push.

It needed nothing more. It soared, tugging loop after loop of twine out of Sylas's hands, climbing swiftly into the wide blue sky.

Simia let out a yelp and grabbed his knee in excitement, and he looked down to see her as happy as he had ever seen her: cheeks flushed, hair ablaze, eyes shining bright with tears. He gazed at her for some moments until she noticed. Her smile faltered for a second, but she quickly looked away.

"Look, Simsi," he said. "Watch this!"

He paid out the line swiftly now from both hands, and up the kite soared, catching the stronger winds, climbing higher and higher. And then he pulled on one string and the kite performed a perfect turn in the sky. Then he pulled the other and it swooped the other way.

"Like this," Sylas said, repeating the action, "and this." And all the while the kite tipped and turned and wheeled.

Finally, with his eyes still on the kite, he held out the loops of twine. "Take them," he said. "You try."

But Simia did not move. He looked down and saw her gazing out across the town, towards the hills.

"Look, Sylas," she said breathlessly, and pointed.

He looked out at the old factory and saw something hanging in the sky above the town. Then he realised it was not one thing but many: a flock of huge birds riding on the winds, heading directly towards Gabblety Row. Even as he watched, he picked out the shapes of hawks and ospreys, buzzards and eagles, and then he heard them calling over the new peace that had fallen upon the town.

"They're coming, Sylas!" whispered Simia, shaking his knee. "They're coming here!"

And so they were. Soon they were above the terrace and spiralling down, plummeting from their great height until they flew in a tight circle about the kite, tighter and tighter until the strings of the kite could no longer be seen and the canvas bird was one among them, looping, banking, twisting, playing like the birds of a mobile Sylas had seen a lifetime ago.

Passers-by stopped to stare. The drivers of cars got out, gazing in wonderment at the beautiful display. Simia held her hands to her mouth, grinning through her fingers. And Sylas clutched the strings between sweaty fingertips and laughed, and stared with wide, wet eyes. Because before him was everything he had imagined. Before him were his dreams.

Acknowledgements

THE WRITING AND PUBLICATION of this book has been an epic journey in itself, with more than its fair share of delays — both those of my making and those out of my hands — and so I must begin by thanking you, patient reader, for waiting so long for this last instalment of the story and for seeing it through to the end. I hope that by some measure it has been worth the wait, or at the very least, that you enjoyed it. It has often been the thought of waiting readers that has sustained me, and some readers have gone one step further to encourage me along the way — a special thank you to them.

This project has also, of course, tested the commitment of those directly involved, particularly those who were there from the beginning, and most notably Ben Illis, my unfailingly supportive agent; and Nick Lake, who has steered the publishing from the very first drafts of *The Bell Between Worlds*. Thanks to them both for joining me on the twists, turns and byways of this great adventure, for keeping faith and for sharing the vision. Thanks, too, to the brilliant publishing professionals who have added their magic to this instalment: Sam Stewart, Laure Gysemans, Francesca Lecchini-Lee, Elorine Grant, Hannah Marshall and Geraldine Stroud at HarperCollins *Children's Books*; Jane Tait the copyeditor; Mary O'Riordan the proofreader and Matt Kelly for the stunning cover. A book is a solitary effort in the writing but a team effort in the making.

I was lucky enough to have some brilliant early readers — Ben Truesdale, Jem Paris-Johnstone, Ethan Ward, Florence Gundle, David Williamson, Adrian, Heather, Melinda, Mike and my mum. Thanks to them all for their insights and encouragement. And although she hasn't read a word, thank you to my lovely daughter, Ella, because the thought of her reading these books one day has helped to make them happen.

Last but by no means least, where would I be without my collaborator-in-chief, my executive editor, my confidant, fellow adventurer and wife, Emily? Thank you, Em, for sharing every moment of this long but wonderful expedition to the ends of my imagination. If I have a Glimmer, I hope they might be a bit like you.